Mickey Spillane

FIVE COMPLETE
MIKE HAMMER NOVELS

About the Author

Frank Morrison (Mickey) Spillane was born in Brooklyn in 1918 and later attended Kansas State College. He is one of the best-known writers of hard-boiled detective fiction, and his private eye, Mike Hammer, has been called the epitome of the breed.

Spillane has written more than twenty mystery-suspense novels, many of which have been made into movies, including *I, The Jury; My Gun Is Quick;* and *Kiss Me, Deadly,* all included in this volume. He has also been involved with two successful television series based on his popular detective, Mike Hammer.

Mickey Spillane

FIVE COMPLETE MIKE HAMMER NOVELS

I, The Jury

Vengeance Is Mine

The Big Kill

My Gun Is Quick

Kiss Me, Deadly

AVENEL BOOKS · NEW YORK

This omnibus edition was originally published in separate volumes
under the titles: *I, The Jury*, copyright 1947 by E. P. Dutton
& Company, Inc. Copyright © renewed 1975 by Mickey Spillane;
Vengeance Is Mine, copyright 1950 by E. P. Dutton & Company,
Inc. Copyright © renewed 1978 by Mickey Spillane; *The Big Kill*,
copyright © 1951 by E. P. Dutton & Company, Inc.; *My Gun Is
Quick*, copyright 1951 by Mickey Spillane; *Kiss Me, Deadly*,
copyright 1952 by E. P. Dutton & Company, Inc. Copyright ©
1987 by Mickey Spillane

This 1987 edition is published by Avenel Books, distributed by
Crown Publishers, Inc., 225 Park Avenue South, New York, New
York 10003, by arrangement with E. P. Dutton, a division of New
American Library.

Printed and Bound in the United States of America

Library of Congress Cataloging-in-Publication Data
Spillane, Mickey, 1918–
    Mickey Spillane: five complete Mike Hammer.
    Contents: I, the jury—Vengeance is mine—The big kill—[etc.]
    1. Hammer, Mike (Fictitious character)—Fiction. 2. Detective
and mystery stories, American. I. Title. II. Title: Five complete
Mike Hammer novels.
PS3537.P652A6 1987   813′.54   86-25907
ISBN 0-517-62950-X
h g f e d c b

Book Design by June Marie Bennett

contents

I, The Jury

DEDICATED TO MY WIFE

chapter one ▬▬▬▬▬▬▬▬▬▬▬▬

I SHOOK THE rain from my hat and walked into the room. Nobody said a word. They stepped back politely and I could feel their eyes on me. Pat Chambers was standing by the door to the bedroom trying to steady Myrna. The girl's body was racking with dry sobs. I walked over and put my arms around her.

"Take it easy, kid," I told her. "Come on over here and lie down." I led her to a studio couch that was against the far wall and sat her down. She was in pretty bad shape. One of the uniformed cops put a pillow down for her and she stretched out.

Pat motioned me over to him and pointed to the bedroom. "In there, Mike," he said.

In there. The words hit me hard. In there was my best friend lying on the floor dead. The body. Now I could call it that. Yesterday it was Jack Williams, the guy that shared the same mud bed with me through two years of warfare in the stinking slime of the jungle. Jack, the guy who said he'd give his right arm for a friend and did when he stopped a bastard of a Jap from slitting me in two. He caught the bayonet in the biceps and they amputated his arm.

Pat didn't say a word. He let me uncover the body and feel the cold face. For the first time in my life I felt like crying. "Where did he get it, Pat?"

"In the stomach. Better not look at it. The killer carved the nose off a forty-five and gave it to him low."

I threw back the sheet anyway and a curse caught in my throat. Jack was in shorts, his one hand still clutching his belly in agony. The bullet went in clean, but where it came out left a hole big enough to cram a fist into.

Very gently I pulled the sheet back and stood up. It wasn't a complicated setup. A trail of blood led from the table beside the bed to where Jack's artificial arm lay. Under him the throw rug was ruffled and twisted. He had tried to drag himself along with his one arm, but never reached what he was after.

His police positive, still in the holster, was looped over the back of the chair. That was what he wanted. With a slug in his gut he never gave up.

I pointed to the rocker, overbalanced under the weight of the .38. "Did you move the chair, Pat?"

"No, why?"

"It doesn't belong there. Don't you see?"

Pat looked puzzled. "What are you getting at?"

"That chair was over there by the bed. I've been here often enough to remember that much. After the killer shot Jack, he pulled himself toward the chair. But the killer didn't leave after the shooting. He stood here and watched him grovel on the floor in agony. Jack was after that gun, but he never reached it. He could have if the killer didn't move it. The trigger-happy bastard must have stood by the door laughing while Jack tried to make his last play. He kept pulling the chair back, inch by inch, until Jack gave up. Tormenting a guy who's been through all sorts of hell. Laughing. This was no ordinary murder, Pat. It's as cold-blooded and as deliberate as I ever saw one. I'm going to get the one that did this."

"You dealing yourself in, Mike?"

"I'm in. What did you expect?"

"You're going to have to go easy."

"Uh-uh. Fast, Pat. From now on it's a race. I want the killer for myself. We'll work together as usual, but in the homestretch, I'm going to pull the trigger."

"No, Mike, it can't be that way. You know it."

"Okay, Pat," I told him. "You have a job to do, but so have I. Jack was about the best friend I ever had. We lived together and fought together. And by Christ, I'm not letting the killer go through the tedious process of the law. You know what happens, damn it. They get the best lawyer there is and screw up the whole thing and wind up a hero! The dead can't speak for themselves.

They can't tell what happened. How could Jack tell a jury what it was like to have his insides ripped out by a dumdum? Nobody in the box would know how it felt to be dying or have your own killer laugh in your face. One arm. Hell, what does that mean? So he has the Purple Heart. But did they ever try dragging themselves across a floor to a gun with that one arm, their insides filling up with blood, so goddamn mad to be shot they'd do anything to reach the killer. No, damn it. A jury is cold and impartial like they're supposed to be, while some snotty lawyer makes them pour tears as he tells how his client was insane at the moment or had to shoot in self-defense. Swell. The law is fine. But this time I'm the law and I'm not going to be cold and impartial. I'm going to remember all those things."

I reached out and grabbed the lapels of his coat. "And something more, Pat. I want you to hear every word I say. I want you to tell it to everyone you know. And when you tell it, tell it strong, because I mean every word of it. There are ten thousand mugs that hate me and you know it. They hate me because if they mess with me I shoot their damn heads off. I've done it and I'll do it again."

There was so much hate welled up inside me I was ready to blow up, but I turned and looked down at what was once Jack. Right then I felt like saying a prayer, but I was too mad.

"Jack, you're dead now. You can't hear me any more. Maybe you can. I hope so. I want you to hear what I'm about to say. You've known me a long time, Jack. My word is good just as long as I live. I'm going to get the louse that killed you. He won't sit in the chair. He won't hang. He will die exactly as you died, with a .45 slug in the gut, just a little below the belly button. No matter who it is, Jack, I'll get the one. Remember, no matter who it is, I promise."

When I looked up, Pat was staring at me strangely. He shook his head. I knew what he was thinking. "Mike, lay off. For God's sake don't go off half-cocked about this. I know you too well. You'll start shooting up anyone connected with this and get in a jam you'll never get out of."

"I'm over it now, Pat. Don't get excited. From now on I'm after one thing, the killer. You're a cop, Pat. You're tied down by rules and regulations. There's someone over you. I'm alone. I can slap someone in the puss and they can't do a damn thing. No one can kick me out of my job. Maybe there's nobody to put up a huge fuss if I get gunned down, but then I still have a private cop's license with the privilege to pack a rod, and they're afraid of me. I hate hard, Pat. When I latch on to the one behind this they're going to wish they hadn't started it. Some day, before long, I'm going to have my rod in my mitt and the killer in front of me. I'm going to watch the killer's face. I'm going to plunk one right in his gut, and when he's dying on the floor I may kick his teeth out.

"You couldn't do that. You have to follow the book because you're a Captain of Homicide. Maybe the killer will wind up in the chair. You'd be satisfied, but I wouldn't. It's too easy. That killer is going down like Jack did."

There was nothing more to say. I could see by the set of Pat's jaw that he wasn't going to try to talk me out of it. All he could do was to try to beat me to him and take it from there. We walked out of the room together. The coroner's men had arrived and were ready to carry the body away.

I didn't want Myrna to see that. I sat down on the couch beside her and let her sob on my shoulder. That way I managed to shield her from the sight of her fiancé being carted off in a wicker basket. She was a good kid. Four years ago, when Jack was on the force, he had grabbed her as she was about to do a Dutch over the Brooklyn Bridge. She was a wreck then. Dope had eaten her nerve ends raw. But he had taken her to his house and paid for a full treatment until she was normal. For the both of them it had been a love that blossomed into a beautiful thing. If it weren't for the war they would have been married long ago.

When Jack came back with one arm it had made no difference. He no longer was a cop, but his heart was with the force. She had loved him before and she still loved him. Jack wanted her to give up her job, but Myrna persuaded him to let her hold it until he really got settled. It was tough for a man with one arm to find employment, but he had many friends.

Before long he was part of the investigating staff of an insurance company. It had to be police work. For Jack there was nothing else. Then they were happy. Then they were going to be married. Now this.

Pat tapped me on the shoulder. "There's a car waiting downstairs to take her home."

I rose and took her by the hand. "Come on, kid. There's no more you can do. Let's go."

She didn't say a word, but stood up silently and let a cop steer her out the door. I turned to Pat. "Where do we start?" I asked him.

"Well, I'll give you as much as I know. See what you can add to it. You and Jack were great buddies. It might be that you can add something that will make some sense."

Inwardly I wondered. Jack was such a straight guy that he never made an enemy. Even while on the force. Since he'd gotten back, his work with the insurance company was pretty routine. But maybe an angle there, though.

"Jack threw a party last night," Pat went on. "Not much of an affair."

"I know," I cut in, "he called me and asked me over, but I was pretty well knocked out. I hit the sack early. Just a group of old friends he knew before the army."

"Yeah. We got their names from Myrna. The boys are checking on them now."

"Who found the body?" I asked.

"Myrna did. She and Jack were driving out to the country today to pick a building site for their cottage. She got here at eight A.M. or a little after. When Jack didn't answer, she got worried. His arm had been giving him trouble lately and she thought it might have been that. She called the super. He knew her and let her in. When she screamed the super came running back and called us. Right after I got the story about the party from her, she broke down completely. Then I called you."

"What time did the shooting occur?"

"The coroner places it about five hours before I got here. That would make it about three fifteen. When I get an autopsy report we may be able to narrow it down even further."

"Anyone hear a shot?"

"Nope. It probably was a silenced gun."

"Even with a muffler, a .45 makes a good-sized noise."

"I know, but there was a party going on down the hall. Not loud enough to cause complaints, but enough to cover up any racket that might have been made here."

"What about those that were here?" Pat reached in his pocket and pulled out a pad. He ripped a leaf loose and handed it to me.

"Here's a list Myrna gave me. She was the first to arrive. Got here at eight thirty last night. She acted as hostess, meeting the others at the door. The last one came about eleven. They spent the evening doing some light drinking and dancing, then left as a group about one."

I looked at the names Pat gave me. A few of them I knew well enough, while a couple of the others were people of whom Jack had spoken, but I had never met.

"Where did they go after the party, Pat?"

"They took two cars. The one Myrna went in belonged to Hal Kines. They drove straight up to Westchester, dropping Myrna off on the way. I haven't heard from any of the others yet."

Both of us were silent for a moment, then Pat asked, "What about a motive, Mike?"

I shook my head. "I don't see any yet. But I will. He wasn't killed for nothing. I'll bet this much, whatever it was, was big. There's a lot here that's screwy. You got anything?"

"Nothing more than I gave you, Mike. I was hoping you could supply some answers."

I grinned at him, but I wasn't trying to be funny. "Not yet. Not yet. They'll come though. And I'll relay them on to you, but by that time I'll be working on the next step."

"The cops aren't exactly dumb, you know. We can get our own answers."

"Not like I can. That's why you buzzed me so fast. You can figure things out as quickly as I can, but you haven't got the ways and means of doing the dirty work. That's where I come in. You'll be right behind me every inch of the way, but when the pinch comes I'll get shoved aside and you slap the cuffs on. That is, if you can shove me aside. I don't think you can."

"Okay, Mike, call it your own way. I want you in all right. But I want the killer, too. Don't forget that. I'll be trying to beat you to him. We have every scientific facility at our disposal and a lot of men to do the leg work. We're not short in brains, either," he reminded me.

"Don't worry, I don't underrate the cops. But cops can't break a guy's arm to make him talk, and they can't shove his teeth in with the muzzle of a .45 to remind him that you aren't fooling. I do my own leg work, and there are a lot of guys who will tell me what I want to know because they know what I'll do to them if they don't. My staff is strictly ex officio, but very practical."

That ended the conversation. We walked out into the hall where Pat put a patrolman on the door to make sure things stayed as they were. We took the self-operated elevator down four flights to the lobby and I waited while Pat gave a brief report to some reporters.

My car stood at the curb behind the squad car. I shook hands with Pat and climbed into my jalopy and headed for the Hackard Building, where I held down a two-room suite to use for operation.

chapter two ▬▬▬▬▬▬▬▬▬▬▬▬▬▬

THE OFFICE WAS locked when I got there. I kicked on the door a few times and Velda clicked the lock back. When she saw who it was she said, "Oh, it's you."

"What do you mean—'Oh, it's you'! Surely you remember me, Mike Hammer, your boss."

"Poo! You haven't been here in so long I can't tell you from another bill collector." I closed the door and followed her into my sanctum sanctorum. She had million-dollar legs, that girl, and she didn't mind showing them off. For a secretary she was an awful distraction. She kept her coal-black hair long in a page-boy cut and wore tight-fitting dresses that made me think of the curves in the Pennsylvania Highway every time I looked at her. Don't get the idea that she was easy, though. I've seen her give a few punks the brush off the hard way. When it came to quick action she could whip off a shoe and crack a skull before you could bat an eye.

Not only that, but she had a private cop's ticket and on occasions when she went out with me on a case, packed a flat .32 automatic—and she wasn't afraid to use it. In the three years she worked for me I never made a pass at her. Not that I didn't want to, but it would be striking too close to home.

Velda picked up her pad and sat down. I plunked myself in the old swivel chair, then swung around facing the window. Velda threw a thick packet on my desk.

"Here's all the information I could get on those that were at the party last night." I looked at her sharply.

"How did you know about Jack? Pat only called my home." Velda wrinkled that pretty face of hers up into a cute grin.

"You forget that I have an in with a few reporters. Tom Dugan from the *Chronicle* remembered that you and Jack had been good friends. He called here to see what he could get and wound up by giving me all the info he had—and I didn't have to sex him, either." She put that in as an afterthought. "Most of the gang at the party were listed in your files. Nothing sensational. I got a little data from Tom who had more personal dealings with a few of them. Mostly character studies and some society reports. Evidently they were people whom Jack had met in the past and liked. You've even spoken about several yourself."

I tore open the package and glanced at a sheaf of photos. "Who are these?" Velda looked over my shoulder and pointed them out.

"Top one is Hal Kines, a med student from a university upstate. He's about twenty-three, tall and looks like a crew man. At least that's the way he cuts his hair." She flipped the page over. "These two are the Bellemy twins. Age, twenty-nine, unmarried. In the market for husbands. Live off the fatta the land with dough their father left them. A half interest in some textile mills someplace down South."

"Yeah," I cut in, "I know them. Good lookers, but not very bright. I met them at Jack's place once and again at a dinner party."

She pointed to the next one. A newspaper shot of a middle-aged guy with a broken nose. George Kalecki. I knew him pretty well. In the roaring twenties he was a bootlegger. He came out of the crash with a million dollars, paid up his income tax, and went society. He fooled a lot of people but he didn't fool me. He still had his finger in a lot of games just to keep in practice. Nothing you could pin on him though. He kept a staff of lawyers on their toes to keep him clean and they were doing a good job. "What about him?" I asked her.

"You know more than I do. Hal Kines is staying with him. They live about a mile above Myrna in Westchester." I nodded. I remembered Jack talking about him. He had met George through Hal. The kid had been a friend of George ever since the older man had met him through some mutual acquaintance. George was the guy that was putting him through college, but why, I wasn't sure.

The next shot was one of Myrna with a complete history of her that Jack had given me. Included was a medical record from the hospital when he had made her go cold turkey, which is dope-addict talk for an all-out cure. They cut them off from the stuff completely. It either kills them or cures them. In Myrna's case, she made it. But she made Jack promise that he would never try to get any information from her about where she got the stuff. The way he fell for the girl, he was ready to do anything she asked, and so far as he was concerned, the matter was completely dropped.

I flipped through the medical record. Name, Myrna Devlin. Attempted suicide while under the influence of heroin. Brought to emergency ward of General Hospital by Detective Jack Williams. Admitted 3-15-40. Treatment complete 9-21-40. No information available on patient's source of narcotics. Released into custody of Detective Jack Williams 9-30-40. Following this was a page of medical details which I skipped.

"Here's one you'll like, chum," Velda grinned at me. She pulled out a full-length photo of a gorgeous blonde. My heart jumped when I saw it. The picture was taken at a beach, and she stood there tall and languid-looking in a white bathing suit. Long solid legs. A little heavier than the movie experts consider good form, but the kind that make you drool to look at. Under the suit I could see the muscles of her stomach. Incredibly wide shoulders for a woman, framing breasts that jutted out, seeking freedom from the restraining fabric of the suit. Her hair looked white in the picture, but I could tell that it was a natural blonde. Lovely, lovely yellow hair. But her face was what got me. I thought Velda was a good looker, but this one was even lovelier. I felt like whistling.

"Who is she?"

"Maybe I shouldn't tell you. That leer on your face could get you into trouble, but it's all there. Name's Charlotte Manning. She's a female psychiatrist with offices on Park Avenue, and very successful. I understand she caters to a pretty ritzy clientele."

I glanced at the number and made up my mind that right here was something that made this business a pleasurable one. I didn't say that to Velda. Maybe I'm being conceited, but I've always had the impression that she had designs on me. Of course she never mentioned it, but whenever I showed up late in the office with lipstick on my shirt collar, I couldn't get two words out of her for a week.

I stacked the sheaf back on my desk and swung around in the chair. Velda was leaning forward ready to take notes. "Want to add anything, Mike?"

"Don't think so. At least not now. There's too much to think about first. Nothing seems to make sense."

"Well, what about motive? Could Jack have had any enemies that caught up with him?"

"Nope. None I know of. He was square. He always gave a guy a break if he deserved it. Then, too, he never was wrapped up in anything big."

"Did he own anything of any importance?"

"Not a thing. The place was completely untouched. He had a few hundred dollars in his wallet that was lying on the dresser. The killing was done by a sadist. He tried to reach his gun, but the killer pulled the chair it hung on back slowly, making him crawl after it with a slug in his gut, trying to keep his insides from falling out with his hand."

"Mike, please."

I said no more. I just sat there and glowered at the wall. Someday I'd trigger the bastard that shot Jack. In my time I've done it plenty of times. No sentiment. That went out with the first. After the war I've been almost anxious to get to some of the rats that make up the section of humanity that prey on people. People. How incredibly stupid they could be sometimes. A trial by law for a killer. A loophole in the phrasing that lets a killer crawl out. But in the end the people have their justice. They get it through guys like me once in a while. They crack down on society and I crack down on them. I shoot them like the mad dogs they are and society drags me to court to explain the whys and wherefores of the extermination. They investigate my past, check my fingerprints and throw a million questions my way. The papers make me look like a kill-crazy shamus, but they don't bear down too hard because Pat Chambers keeps them off my neck. Besides, I do my best to help the boys out and they know it. And I'm usually good for a story when I wind up a case.

Velda came back into the office with the afternoon edition of the sheets. The kill was spread all over the front page, followed by a four-column layout of what details were available. Velda was reading over my shoulder and I heard her gasp.

"Did you come in for a blasting! Look." She was pointing to the last paragraph. There was my tie-up with the case, but what she was referring to was the word-for-word statement that I had made to Jack. My promise. My word to a dead friend that I would kill this murderer as he had killed him. I rolled the paper into a ball and threw it viciously at the wall.

"The louse! I'll break his filthy neck for printing that. I meant what I said when I made that promise. It's sacred to me, and they make a joke out of it. Pat did that. And I thought he was a friend. Give me the phone."

Velda grabbed my arm. "Take it easy. Suppose he did. After all, Pat's still a cop. Maybe he saw a chance of throwing the killer your way. If the punk knows you're after him for keeps he's liable not to take it standing still and make a play for you. Then you'll have him."

"Thanks, kid," I told her, "but your mind's too clean. I think you got the first part right, but your guess on the last part smells. Pat doesn't want me to have any part of him because he knows the case is ended right there. If he can get the killer to me you can bet your grandmother's uplift bra that he'll have a tail on me all the way with someone ready to step in when the shooting starts."

"I don't know about that, Mike. Pat knows you're too smart not to recognize when you're being tailed. I wouldn't think he'd do that."

"Oh, no? He isn't dumb by any means. I'll bet you a sandwich against a marriage license he's got a flatfoot downstairs covering every exit in the place ready to pick me up when I leave. Sure, I'll shake them, but it won't stop there. A couple of experts will take up where they leave off."

Velda's eyes were glowing like a couple of hot brands. "Are you serious about that? About the bet, I mean?"

I nodded. "Dead serious. Want to go downstairs with me and take a look?" She grinned and grabbed her coat. I pulled on my battered felt and we left the office, but not before I had taken a second glance at the office address of Charlotte Manning.

Pete, the elevator operator, gave me a toothy grin when we stepped into the car. "Evening, Mr. Hammer," he said.

I gave him an easy jab in the short ribs and said, "What's new with you?"

"Nothing much, 'cepting I don't get to sit down much on the job anymore." I had to grin. Velda had lost the bet already. That little piece of simple repartee between Pete and myself was a code system we had rigged up years ago. His answer meant that I was going to have company when I left the building. It cost me a fin a week but it was worth it. Pete could spot a flatfoot faster than I can. He should. He had been a pickpocket until a long stretch up the river gave him a turn of mind.

For a change I decided to use the front entrance. I looked around for my tail but there was none to be seen. For a split second my heart leaped into my throat. I was afraid Pete had gotten his signals crossed. Velda was a spotter, too, and the smile she was wearing as we crossed the empty lobby was a thing to see. She clamped onto my arm ready to march me to the nearest justice of the peace.

But when I went through the revolving doors her grin passed as fast as mine appeared. Our tail was walking in front of us. Velda said a word that nice girls don't usually use, and you see scratched in the cement by some evil-minded guttersnipe.

This one was smart. We never saw where he came from. He walked a lot faster than we did, swinging a newspaper from his hand against his leg. Probably, he spotted us through the windows behind the palm, then seeing what exit we were going to use, walked around the corner and came past us as we left. If we had gone the other way, undoubtedly there was another ready to pick us up.

But this one had forgotten to take his gun off his hip and stow it under his shoulder, and guns make a bump look the size of a pumpkin when you're used to looking for them.

When I reached the garage he was nowhere to be seen. There were a lot of doors he could have ducked behind. I didn't waste time looking for him. I backed the car out and Velda crawled in beside me. "Where to now?" she asked.

"The automat, where you're going to buy me a sandwich."

chapter three ∎∎∎∎∎∎∎∎∎∎∎∎∎∎∎∎∎

I DUMPED VELDA at her hairdresser's after we ate, then headed north to Westchester. I hadn't planned to call on George Kalecki until the following day, but a call to Charlotte's office dealt that one out. She had left for home, and the wench in the reception room had been instructed not to give her address. I told her I'd call later and left a message that I wanted to see her as soon as possible. I couldn't get that woman off my mind. Those legs.

Twenty minutes later I was pulling the bell outside a house that must have cost a cool quarter million. A very formal butler clicked the lock and admitted me. "Mr. Kalecki," I said.

"Who shall I say is calling, sir?"

"Mike Hammer. I'm a private detective." I flashed my tin on him but he wasn't impressed.

"I'm rather afraid Mr. Kalecki is indisposed at the moment, sir," he told me. I recognized a pat standoff when I saw one, but I wasn't bothered.

"Well, you tell him to un-dispose himself right away and get his tail down here or I'll go get him. And I'm not kidding, either."

The butler looked me over carefully and must have decided that I meant what I said. He nodded and took my hat. "Right this way, Mr. Hammer." He led me to an oversize library and I plunked myself in an armchair and waited for George Kalecki.

He wasn't long coming. The door banged open and a grey-haired guy a little stouter than his picture revealed came in. He didn't waste words. "Why did you come in after my man informed you that I was not to be disturbed?"

I lit a butt and blew the smoke at him. "Don't give me that stuff, chum. You know why I'm here."

"No doubt. I read the papers. But I'm afraid that I can't help you. I was home in bed when the murder occurred and I can prove it."

"Hal Kines came in with you?"

"Yes."

"Did your servant let you in?"

"No, I used my own key."

"Did anyone else beside Hal see you come in?"

"I don't think so, but his word is good enough."

I sneered into his face. "Not when the both of you are possible murder suspects, it isn't."

Kalecki turned pale when I said that. His mouth worked a little and he looked ready to kill me. "How dare you say that," he snarled at me. "The police have not made an attempt to connect me with that killing. Jack Williams died hours after I left."

I took a step forward and gathered a handful of his shirt front in my fist. "Listen to me, you ugly little crook," I spat in his face, "I'm talking language you can understand. I'm not worried about the cops. If you're under suspicion it's to me. I'm the one that counts, because when I find the one that did it, he dies. Even if I can't prove it, he dies anyway. In fact, I don't even have to be convinced too strongly. Maybe just a few things will point your way, and when they do I'm going after you. Before I'm done I may shoot up a lot of snotty punks like you, but you can bet that one of them will have been the one I was after, and as for the rest, tough luck. They got their noses a little too dirty."

Nobody had talked to him like that the past twenty years. He floundered for words but they didn't come. If he had opened his mouth right then, I would have slammed his teeth down his throat.

Disgusted with the sight of him, I shoved him back toward an end table in time to push myself aside far enough to keep from getting brained. A crockery vase smashed on my shoulder and shattered into a hundred fragments.

I ducked and whirled at the same time. A fist came flying over my head and I blocked it with my left. I didn't wait. I let fly a wicked punch that landed low then came up with the top of my skull and I rammed the point of a jaw with a shattering impact. Hal Kines hit the floor and lay there motionless.

"Wise guy. A fresh kid that tries to bust me from behind. You're certainly not training him right, George. Time was when you stood behind a chopper yourself, now you let a college kid do your blasting, and in a houseful of mirrors he tries to sneak up behind me." He didn't say anything. He found a chair and slid into it, his eyes narrow slits of hate. If he had a rod right then he would have let me have it. He would have died, too. I've had an awful lot of practice sneaking that .45 out from under my arm.

The Kines kid was beginning to stir. I prodded him in the ribs with my toe until he sat up. He was still pretty green around the gills, but not green enough to sneer at me. "You lousy bastard," he said. "Have to fight dirty, don't you."

I reached down and grabbed him under the arm and yanked him to his feet. His eyes bugged. Maybe he thought he was dealing with somebody soft. "Listen, pimple face. Just for the fun of it I ought to slap your fuzzy chin all around this room, but I got things to do. Don't go playing man when you're only a boy. You're pretty big, but I'm three sizes bigger and a hell of a lot tougher and I'll beat the living daylights out of you if you try anything funny again. Now sit down over there."

Kines hit the sofa and stayed there. George must have gotten his second wind because he piped up. "Just a moment, Mr. Hammer. This has gone far enough. I am not without influence at city hall. . . ."

"I know," I cut in. "You'll have me arrested for assault and battery and have my license revoked. Only when you do that, keep a picture in your mind of what your face will look like when I reach you. Someone already worked over your nose, but it's nothing compared to what you'll look like when I get done with it. Now keep your big mouth shut and give me some answers. First, what time did you leave the party?"

"About one or a little after," George said sullenly. That checked with Myrna's version.

"Where did you go after you left?"

"We went downstairs to Hal's car and drove straight home."

"Who's we?"

"Hal, Myrna and myself. We dropped her off at her apartment and came here after putting the car in the garage. Ask Hal, he'll verify it."

Hal looked at me. It was easy to see that he was worried. Evidently this was the first time he had been mixed up in anything so deep. Murders don't appeal to anyone.

I continued with my questioning. "Then what?"

"Oh, for Pete's sake, we had a highball and went to bed. What else do you think we did?" Hal said.

"I don't know. Maybe you sleep together." Hal stood up in front of me, his face a red mask of fury. I put my mitt in his face and shoved him back on the sofa. "Or maybe," I went on, "you don't sleep together. Which means that either one of you had plenty of time to take the car back out and make the run to town to knock off Jack and get back here without anyone noticing it. If you do sleep together you both could have done it. See what I mean?

"If either of you think you're clean you'd better think again. I'm not the only one that has a mind that can figure out angles. Right now Pat Chambers has it all figured out on paper. He'll be around soon, so you'd better be expecting him. And if either of you are tapped for the hot seat, you'd do a lot better by letting Pat pick you up. At least that way you'll live through a trial."

"Someone calling me?" a voice said from the doorway. I spun around. Pat Chambers was framed in the hardwood paneling wearing his ever-present grin.

I waved him over. "Yeah. You're the main topic of conversation around here at this moment." George Kalecki got up from the overstuffed cushions and walked to Pat. His old bluster was back.

"Officer, I demand the arrest of this man at once," he fairly shouted. "He broke into my home and insulted me and my guest. Look at the bruise on his jaw. Tell him what happened, Hal."

Hal saw me watching him. He saw Pat standing ten feet away from me with his hands in his pockets and apparently no desire to stop what might happen. It suddenly hit him that Jack had been a cop and Pat was a cop and Jack had been killed. And you don't kill a cop and get away with it. "Nothing happened," he said.

"You stinking little liar!" Kalecki turned on him. "Tell the truth! Tell how he threatened us. What are you afraid of, this dirty two-bit shamus?"

"No, George," I said quietly, "he's afraid of this." I swung on him with all of my hundred and ninety pounds. My fist went in up to the wrist in his stomach. He flopped to the floor vomiting his lungs out, his face gradually turning purple. Hal just looked. For a second I could have sworn I saw a satisfied leer cross his swollen face.

I took Pat by the arm. "Coming?" I asked him.

"Yeah, nothing more to do here."

Outside Pat's car was drawn up under the covered portico. We climbed in and he started it up and drove around the house to the graveled driveway to the highway and turned south toward the city. Neither of us had spoken until I asked him, "Get an earful back there?"

He gave me a glance and nodded. "Yeah, I was outside the door while you were going through your spiel. Guess you laid it out the same way I did."

"By the way," I added, "don't get the idea I'm slipping. I was onto the tail you put on me. What did he do, call from the front gate or the filling station where I left my heap?"

"From the station," he answered. "He couldn't catch on to why the hike and called for instructions. By the way. Why did you walk a mile and half to his house?"

"That ought to be easy, Pat. Kalecki probably left instructions not to admit me after he read that piece in the papers. I came in over the wall. Here's the station. Pull up."

Pat slid the car off the road to the cindered drive. My car was still alongside the stucco house. I pointed to the grey-suited man sitting inside asleep. "Your tail. Better wake him up."

Pat got out and shook the guy. He came to with a silly grin. Pat motioned in my direction. "He was on to you, chum. Maybe you had better change your technique."

The guy looked puzzled. "On to me? Hell, he never gave me a tumble."

"Nuts," I said. "Your rod sticks out of your back pocket like a sore thumb. I've been in this game awhile myself, you know."

I climbed into my buggy and turned it over. Pat stuck his head in the window and asked, "You still going ahead on your own, Mike?"

The best I could do was nod. "Natch. What else?"

"Then you'd better follow me in to town. I have something that might interest you."

He got in the squad car and slid out of the cinders to the highway. My tail pulled out behind Pat and I followed him. Pat was playing it square so far. He was using me for bait, but I didn't mind. It was like using a trout for bait to catch flies as far as I was concerned. But he was sticking too close to me to make the game any fun. Whether he was keeping me from being blasted or just making sure I didn't knock off any prominent Joes whom I suspected I couldn't say.

The article in the paper didn't have enough time to work. The killer wouldn't be flushed as quickly as that. Whoever pulled the trigger was a smart apple. Too damned smart. He must have

considered me if he was in his right mind at all. He had to
consider the cops even if it was an ordinary job. But this was a
cop killing which made it worse. I was sure of one thing though,
I'd be on the kill list for sure, especially after I made the rounds
of everyone connected with it.

So far, I couldn't find anything on Kalecki or Kines. No motive
yet. That would come later. They both had the chance to knock
off Jack. George Kalecki wasn't what people thought him to be.
His finger was still in the rackets. Possibilities there. Where Hal
came in was something else again. He was tied up in some way.
Maybe not. Maybe so. I'd find out.

My thoughts wandered around the general aspects of the case
without reaching any conclusions. Pat went through the city sans
benefit of a siren, unlike a lot of coppers, and we finally pulled
up to the curb in front of his precinct station.

Upstairs he pulled open the bottom drawer of his desk and
drew out a pint of bourbon from a lunch box. He handed me a
man-sized slug of the stuff and set up one for himself. I poured
mine down in one gulp.

"Want another?"

"Nope. Want some information. What were you going to tell
me?" He went over to a filing cabinet and drew out a folder. I
noticed the label. It read, "Myrna Devlin."

Pat sat down and shook out the contents. The dossier was
complete. It had everything on her that I had and more. "What's
the angle, Pat?" I knew he was getting at something. "Are you
connecting Myrna with this? If you are you're barking up the
wrong tree."

"Perhaps. You see, Mike, when Jack first found Myrna trying
to go over the railing of the bridge, he treated her like any other
narcotic case. He took her to the emergency ward of the hospital."
Pat rose and shoved his hands in his pockets. His mouth talked,
but I could see that his mind was deep in thought. "It was through
constant contact with her that he fell in love. It was real enough
for him. He saw all the bad side of her before he saw the good.
If he could love her then he could love her anytime."

"I don't follow, Pat. I know Myrna as well as Jack did. If you
smear her all over the papers as a number-one candidate for the
hot squat you and me are going to have it out."

"Don't fly off the handle, Mike. There's more to it than that.
After she was released, she made Jack promise not to follow it
up any further. He agreed."

"I know," I cut in, "I was there that night."

"Well, Jack held up his end to her all right, but that didn't take in the whole department. Narcotics comes under a separate bureau. The case was turned over to them. Myrna didn't know anything about it, but while she was out, she talked. We had a steno taking down every word she said and she said plenty. Narcotics was able to snare a ring that was operating around the city, but when they made the raid there was some shooting, and during it the one guy that would have been able to spill the beans caught one in the head and the cycle stopped there."

"That's news to me, Pat."

"Yeah, you were in the army then. It took awhile to track the outfit down, nearly a year. It didn't stop even then. The outfit was working interstate and the feds were in on it. They laid off Myrna when they went into her history. She was a small-town girl here in the city to break into show business. Unfortunately, she got mixed up with the wrong outfit and got put on the stuff by one of her roommates. Their contact was a guy who was paying for protection as a bookie, but who used the cover to peddle dope. His guardian angel was a politician who now occupies a cozy cell in Ossining on the Hudson.

"The head of the outfit was a shrewd operator. No one knew or saw him. Transactions were made by mail. Dope was sent in to post-office boxes, very skillfully disguised. In each box was a number to send the cash to. That turned out to be a box somewhere, too."

That I couldn't figure. Pat turned and sat down again before he went on, but I beat him to it with a question.

"Something screwy, Pat. The whole thing's backwards. The stuff is usually paid for in advance, with the peddlers hoping they come through with enough decks to make money on it."

Pat lit a butt and nodded vigorously. "Exactly. That's one reason why we had trouble. Undoubtedly there's stuff sitting in post-office boxes right now loaded to the brims with the junk. It isn't an amateur's touch, either. The stuff came in too regularly. The source was plentiful. We managed to dig up a few old containers that hadn't been destroyed by the receiver and there were no two postmarks alike."

"That wouldn't be hard to work if it was a big outfit."

"Apparently they had no trouble. But we had operatives in the towns the stuff was sent from and they went over the places with a fine-tooth comb. Nothing was turned up. They checked the transient angle since it was the only way it could have been done. Busses and trains went through these towns, and it's possible that the packages could have been dropped off by a person posing as a traveler. Each place was used once. So there was no way of telling where the next one was coming from."

"I get the picture, Pat. Since the last outfit was pulled, have they found any other sources?"

"Some. But nothing they could connect with the last. Most of it was petty stuff with some hospital attendant sneaking it out of stock and peddling it on the outside."

"So far you haven't told me where Myrna comes into this. I appreciate the information, but we're not getting anyplace. What you've given me is strictly police stuff."

Pat gave me a long, searching glance. His eyes were screwed up tight like he was thinking. I knew that look well. "Tell me," he said, "hasn't it occurred to you that Jack, being a cop, could have welshed on his promise to Myrna? He hated crooks and sneaks, but most of all he hated the dirty rats that used people like Myrna to line their own pockets."

"So what?" I asked.

"So this. He was in on things in the beginning. He might have been holding back something on us. Or he might have gotten something from Myrna we didn't know about. Either he spoke up at the wrong moment or he didn't. But somebody was afraid of what he knew and bumped him." I yawned. I hated to disillusion Pat but he was wrong. "Fellow, you are really mixed up. Let me show you where. First, classify all murders. There are only a few. War, Passion, Self-Protection, Insanity, Profit and Mercy Killings. There are some others, but these are enough. To me it looks like Jack was killed either for profit or self-protection. I don't doubt but what he had something on someone. It must have been something he had known all along, and suddenly realized its importance, or it was something he recently found out. You know how active he was in police work even though he was disabled and attached to the job with the insurance company.

"Whatever it was, he apparently wanted to make a choice. That's why you heard nothing about it. The killer had to have something he had, and killed to get it. But you searched the place, didn't you?" Pat agreed with a movement of the eyes. "And there was nothing removed, was there?" He shook his head. "Then," I went on, "unless it was something Jack had outside, which I doubt, it wasn't a killing for profit. The killer knew that Jack had some poop which would mean exposure or worse. To protect himself, the killer knocked Jack off. Self-protection."

I picked up my battered hat from the desk and stretched. "Got to blow, pal. Since I'm not on an expense account or a salary, this is one job I can't afford to lose time on. Thanks for the try, anyway. If I turn anything up I'll let you know."

"How long after?" Pat said with a smile.

"Just long enough to keep the jump on you," I shot back at him. I fished for a smoke and pulled a wreck of a butt from my pocket, waved so long to Pat and walked out. My tail was waiting for me, trying to look inconspicuous in a crowd of cigar-smoking detectives in the anteroom. As I stepped outside I flattened myself into a niche in the brick wall. The guy came out, stopped and looked frantically both ways up and down the street. I stepped out and tapped him on the shoulder.

"Got a light?" I asked, flipping the ancient butt between my lips. He turned beet-red and lit me. "Instead of playing cops and robbers," I told him, "why not just walk along with me?"

He didn't quite know what to say, but got out an "Okay." It sounded more like a growl. The two of us ambled over to my car. He got in and I slid under the wheel. There was no use trying to talk to the guy. I couldn't get a word out of him. When I hit the main stem, I went down a side street past a little hotel. After I pulled up in front of it, I got out with my tail right behind me, went through the revolving door, kept right on going until I was outside where I went in. That left my tail still in the door. I bent down and stuck a rubber wedge I had taken from my car window under the door and walked back to the car. Inside the door, the cop was pounding on the glass and calling me dirty names. If he wanted me, he had to go out the back door and around the street. I saw the clerk grinning. That wasn't the first time I had used his hotel for that gag. All the way downtown my window shook like it would fall out, which reminded me that I had better get some more wedges in case I was tailed again.

THE ANTEROOM WAS ultramodern, but well appointed. Chairs that looked angular were really very comfortable. Whoever decorated the interior had a patient's mental comfort well in mind. The walls were an indescribable shade of olive, cleverly matched with a dull-finished set of drapes. The windows admitted no light, instead, the soft glow came from hidden bulbs installed directly into the wall. On the floor an ankle-thick carpet muffled any sound of footsteps. From somewhere came the muted tones of a string quartet. I could have fallen asleep right there if the secretary who had given me the telephone brushoff didn't motion me over to the desk. From her tone it was evident that she knew that I was no patient. With a full day's growth of beard and the wrinkled ruin of a suit I had on, I was lower than the janitor in her estimation.

She inclined her head toward the door behind her and said, "Miss Manning will see you now. Please go in." With special emphasis on the please. When I went past her she drew back slightly.

"Don't worry, honey," I told her out of the corner of my mouth, "I won't bite. This is just a disguise." I yanked open the door and went in.

She was better than her picture. She was delicious. There was a lot about her that couldn't be put into words. Charlotte Manning was sitting at her desk, hands folded in front of her as if she were listening for something. Beautiful was a poor description. She was what you would expect to find in a painting if each of the world's greatest artists added their own special technique to produce a masterpiece.

Her hair was almost white as I thought. It fell in such soft curls you wanted to bury your face in it. Each of her features were modeled exquisitely. A smooth forehead melted into alive, hazel eyes, framed in the symmetrical curves of naturally brown eyebrows, studded with long, moist lashes.

The dress she wore was not at all revealing, being a long-sleeved black business garb, but what it attempted to conceal was pure loveliness. Her breasts fought the dress as valiantly as they had the bathing suit. I could only imagine how the rest of her looked since the desk blocked my vision.

All this I saw in the three seconds it took to walk across the room. I doubt if she saw any change in my expression, but she could have sued me if she knew what went on in my mind.

"Good morning, Mr. Hammer. Please sit down." Her voice was like liquid. I wondered what she could do if she put a little passion in it. Plenty, I bet. It wasn't hard to see why she was a successful psychiatrist. Here was a woman anyone could tell their troubles to.

I sat down in the chair beside her and she swung around to meet my eyes with a steady, direct gaze. "I presume you are here on police business?"

"Not exactly. I'm a private detective."

"Oh." When she said that her voice held none of the usual contempt or curiosity I find when I tell that to someone. Instead, it was as if I had given her a pertinent piece of information.

"Is it about the death of Mr. Williams?" she asked.

"Uh-huh. He was a close buddy of mine. I'm conducting a sort of personal investigation of my own."

She looked at me quizzically at first, then, "Oh, yes. I read your statement in the papers. As a matter of fact, I attempted to analyze your reasoning. I've always been interested in things of that sort."

"And what conclusion did you reach?"

Charlotte surprised me. "I'm afraid I justify you, although several of my former professors would condemn me if I made that statement public." I saw what she meant. There's a school of thought that believes anyone who kills is the victim of a moment's insanity, no matter what the reason for the killing.

"How can I help you?" she went on.

"By answering a few questions. First, what time did you get to the party that night?"

"Roughly, about eleven. I was held up by a visit to a patient."

"What time did you leave?"

"Around one. We left together."

"Then where did you go?"

"I had my car downstairs. Esther and Mary Bellemy drove with me. We went to the Chicken Bar and had a sandwich. We left there at one forty-five. I remember the time because we were the only ones there and they were getting ready to close at two. I dropped the twins off at their hotel, then went straight to my apartment. I reached there about a quarter after two. I remember the time there, too, since I had to reset my alarm clock."

"Anybody see you come into the apartment?"

Charlotte gave me the cutest little laugh. "Yes, Mr. District Attorney. My maid. She even tucked me into bed as usual. She would have heard me go out, too, for the only door to my apartment has a chime on it that rings whenever the door opens, and Kathy is a very light sleeper."

I couldn't help but grin at that. "Has Pat Chambers been here to see you already?"

"This morning, but much earlier." She laughed again. Shivers went through me when she did that. She radiated sex in every manner and gesture. "What is more," she continued, "he came, he saw, and he suspected. By now he must be checking my story."

"Pat's not letting any grass grow under his feet," I mused. "Did he mention me at all?"

"Not a word. A very thorough man. He represents efficiency. I like him."

"One thing more. When did you make the acquaintance of Jack Williams?"

"I'm afraid I'm not at liberty to reveal that."

I shook my head. "If it was in reference to Myrna, you needn't be. I was on the ground floor there."

She seemed surprised at that. But I knew Jack had kept the entire affair of Myrna's past as close to his vest as possible. "Well," she said, "that was it. He called me in under advice from a doctor to attend Myrna. She had suffered a severe shock. I doubt if you can comprehend what it means to one addicted to narcotics to go 'cold turkey' as they call it. It means an immediate and complete removal from the source of the drug. The mental strain is terrific. They have violent convulsions, their bodies endure the most racking pain there is. Nerve ends eaten raw are exposed to unbelievable torture, and you can give them no relief. Quite often they destroy themselves in fits of madness.

"The cure is far from an easy one. Having made the decision, they are separated from outside contact in padded cells. During the earlier stages of it, they change their minds and beg to be given the drug. Later the pain and tension mount to such dizzy heights that they are completely unrational. All the while, their body fights the effects of the drug, and it emerges finally either cured or unfit to continue life. In Myrna's case, she lived through it. Jack was worried what this would do to her mentally and called me. I treated her while she was undergoing the cure, and afterwards. Since she was released I have never visited her in a professional capacity."

"Well, I guess that's all then. I do have some other things I would like to discuss with you about the case. But I want to do a little checking first."

She gave me another of those smiles. Any more of them and she'd find out what it was like to be kissed from under a set of whiskers. "If it's about the time element of my story—or should I say alibi?—then I suggest you hurry over to my apartment before my maid goes on her weekly shopping spree."

The woman knew all the answers. I tried to keep my face straight, but it was too much work. I broke out my lopsided grin and picked up my hat. "That's partly it. Guess I don't trust anybody."

Charlotte rose and gave me the look at her legs I'd been waiting for. "I understand," she remarked. "To a man friendship is a much greater thing than to a woman."

"Especially when that friend gave an arm to save my life," I said.

A puzzled frown creased her forehead. "So you're the one." It was almost a gasp. "I didn't know, but I'm glad I do now. I have heard so much about you from Jack, but they were stories in the third person. He never mentioned a thing about his arm, although Myrna later told me why he lost it."

"Jack didn't want to embarrass me. But that's only part of the reason why I'm going to get his murderer. He was my friend even before that."

"I hope you get him," she said sincerely. "I truly hope you do."

"I will," I said.

We stood there a moment just looking at each other, then I caught myself. "I have to leave now. I'll see you soon."

Her breath seemed to catch in her throat a moment before she said softly, "Very soon, I trust." I was hoping that light in her eyes meant what I thought it did when she said it.

I parked a few feet away from the blue canopy of the apartment house. The doorman, for once conservatively dressed, opened the door of my car without wrinkling his mouth in disgust. I gave him a nod and went into the outer foyer.

The name over the bell was stamped in aluminum. "Manning Charlotte," it read, without a series of degrees following it like the doctor's below. That guy must have had a letter complex. I rang the bell and walked in when the buzzer sounded.

She lived on the fourth floor, in a suite facing the street. A coal-black maid in a white uniform answered the door. "Mistah Hammah?" she asked me.

"Yeah, how didja know?"

"De police gennimuns in de front room was 'specting you.

Come in, please." Sure enough, there was Pat sprawled in a chair by the window.

"Hi, Mike," he called. I threw my hat on an end table and sat down on a hassock beside him.

"What did you find, Pat?"

"Her story checks. A neighbor saw her come in at the proper time; her maid confirmed it." For once I was relieved. "I knew you'd be along, so I just parked the carcass until you showed up. By the way, I wish you'd be a little easier on the men I detail to keep track of you."

"Easier, hell. Keep 'em off my neck. Either that or get an expert."

"Just for your own protection, Mike."

"Nuts. You know me better than that. I can take care of myself." Pat let his head fall back and closed his eyes. I looked around the room. Like her office, Charlotte Manning's apartment was furnished in excellent taste. It had a casual air that made it look lived in, yet everything was in order. It wasn't large; then too it had no reason to be. Living alone with one maid, a few rooms was all that was necessary. Several good paintings adorned the walls, hanging above shelves that were well stocked with books of all kinds. I noticed one bookcase that held nothing but volumes on psychology. At one end of the room a framed diploma was the only ornament. A wide hallway opened off the living room and led to a bedroom and the kitchen, with a bathroom opposite. Beside the foyer was the maid's room. Here the color scheme was not conducive to mental peace, but designed to add color and gaiety to its already beautiful occupant. Directly opposite the hassock I was parked on was a sofa, a full six feet long. It gave me ideas, which I quickly ignored. It was no time to play wolf. Yet.

I nudged Pat with my foot. "Don't let's be going to sleep, chum. You're on taxpayers' time."

He came out of his reverie with a start. "Only giving you time to size things up, junior. Let's roll."

Kathy, the maid, came scurrying in when she heard us making sounds of leaving. She opened the door for us and I heard the sound of the chimes Charlotte had spoken of. "Does the gong go off when the bell rings too?" I asked her.

"Yassuh, or when de do' opens, too."

"Why?"

"Well, suh, when I'se not to home, Miss Charlotte has to answer de do'. Sometimes when she's busy in de blackroom de bell rings and she just opens de lock. Den when de visitors come up she knows when dey comes in. She can't leave in de middle of her work in de blackroom to answer both de bell and de do."

I looked at Pat and he looked at me. "What's the blackroom?" I practically demanded.

Kathy jumped like she was shot. "Why, where she makes pitchers from de fillums," she answered. Pat and I left feeling a little foolish. So Charlotte made a hobby of photography. I reminded myself to brush up on details so we'd have something to speak about the next time we met. Besides that, I mean.

chapter five ▆▆▆▆▆▆▆▆▆▆▆▆▆

DOWNSTAIRS, PAT AND I went across the street to a tiny delicatessen and sat in a booth with two bottles of beer. He asked me if I had gotten anywhere yet and I had to give him a negative answer.

"What about motive?" I put to him. "I'm up the creek on that angle, mainly because I haven't looked into it. When I get all the case histories down I'll begin on the motive. But did you dig up anything yet?"

"Not yet," Pat answered. "Ballistics checked on the slug and it came from an unidentified .45. According to the experts, the barrel was nearly new. We followed that up by inquiring into the sale of all guns, but got nowhere. Only two had been sold, both to store owners who were recently robbed. We took some samples of the slugs, but they didn't match."

"For that matter it might have been a gun sold some time ago, but unfired until recently," I said.

"We thought of that, too. Records still don't account for it. None of those at the party have ever owned a gun to our knowledge."

"Officially," I added.

"Yes, that's a possibility. It isn't hard to come in possession of a gun."

"What about the silencer? The killer was no novice about firearms. A silencer plus a dumdum. He wanted to make sure

Jack died—not too fast. Just definitely died."

"No trace of that, either. Where it may have come from is a rifle. There are a few makes of rifle silencers that can be adjusted to a .45."

We sipped the beer slowly, each of us thinking hard. It was a full two minutes before Pat remembered something and said, "Oh, yeah, almost forgot. Kalecki and the Kines kid moved into an apartment in town this morning."

That was news. "What for?"

"Someone took a shot at him through his window late last night. Missed by a hair. It was a .45 slug, too. We checked it with the one that killed Jack. It was the same gun."

I almost choked on my beer. "You almost forgot," I said with a smirk.

"Oh, and one other thing."

"What?"

"He thinks you did it."

I banged my glass down on the table so hard Pat jumped. "Why, that dirty snivelling louse! That does it. This time I'll smash his face all over the place!"

"There you go, racing your motor again, Mike. Sit down and pipe down. As he said, he wasn't without a little influence at city hall, and they made us look into you. But don't forget, you've knocked off a few undesirable citizens before and the slugs from your gun were photographed. We keep all the prints and tried in the worst way to match 'em, but they don't match. Besides, we knew where you were last night. They raided the joint ten minutes after you left."

I got kind of red in the face and sat down. "You got one hell of a way of breaking things to me, Pat. Now let's quit the joking and tell me where Kalecki and company moved to."

Pat grinned. "They live right around the corner in the same apartment hotel the Bellemy twins occupy, but on the second floor. The Midworth Arms."

"Have you been there yet?"

"Not to see the twins. I saw George and Hal, though. Had quite a time telling him that it would do no good to place a charge against you for assault and battery after the other night. Didn't take much talking, either. Evidently he's heard a lot about the way you operate, but just likes to keep his own courage up with a lot of talk."

Both of us poured down the remainder of the beer and got up to leave. I outfumbled Pat and got stuck for the check. Next time he'd buy. Cop or no cop. We parted outside the door, and as soon as he took off I started around the corner for the Midworth Arms. I wanted to get the lowdown when anyone accused me of murder—attempted or successful. The real reason why Pat was sure it wasn't me was because the killer missed. I wouldn't have.

I knew Kalecki probably had tipped the doorman and the super off not to admit me, so I didn't bother messing with them. Instead I walked in like a regular resident and took the elevator to the second floor. The operator was a skinny runt in his late twenties who wore a built-in leer. I was the only one in the car, and when we stopped I pulled a bill from my pocket and showed him the color of it.

"Kalecki. George Kalecki. He's new in this dump. What apartment and the green is yours," I said.

He gave me a careful going over, that one. Finally put his tongue in his cheek and said, "You must be that Hammer mug. He gimme a ten not to spot him for you."

I opened my coat and pulled my .45 from its holster. The kid's eyes popped when he saw it. "I *am* that Hammer mug, junior," I told him, "and if you don't spot him for me *I'm* giving you this." I motioned toward his teeth with the gun barrel.

"Front 206," he said hastily. My bill was a five. I rolled it up in a ball and poked it in his wide-opened mouth, then shoved the rod back.

"The next time remember me. And in the meantime, act like a clam or I'll open you up like one."

"Y-yes, sir." He practically leaped back in the car and slammed the door shut.

206 was down the hall, the apartment facing on the street. I knocked, but there was no answer. Hardly breathing, I put my ear against the wood paneling of the door and kept it there. That way the wood acts as a sounding board, and any noise made inside is magnified a hundred times. That is, except this time. Nobody was home. Just to be sure, I slid a note under the door, then walked away and took the stairs down to the first landing. There I took off my shoes and tiptoed back up. The note was still sticking out exactly as I had placed it.

Instead of fooling around I brought out a set of skeleton keys. The third one did it. I snapped the deadlock on the door behind me—just in case.

The apartment was furnished. None of Kalecki's personal stuff was in the front room except a picture of himself on the mantel when he was younger. I walked into the bedroom. It was a spacious place, with two chests of drawers and a table. But there was only one bed. So they did sleep together. I had to laugh even if I did mention it to get a rise out of them before.

A suitcase was under the bed. I opened that first. On top of six white shirts a .45 was lying with two spare clips beside it. Man, oh man, that caliber gun is strictly for professionals, and they were turning up all over the place. I sniffed the barrel, but it was clean. As far as I could tell, it hadn't been fired for a month. I wiped my prints off and put the gun back.

There wasn't much in the chest of drawers, either. Hal Kines had a photo album that showed him engaging in nearly every college sport there is. A lot of the shots were of women, and some of them weren't half bad, that is if you like them tall and on the thin side. Me, I like 'em husky. Toward the end of the book were several showing Kalecki and Hal together. In one they were fishing. Another was taken alongside a car in camping clothes. It was the third one that interested me.

Both Hal and Kalecki were standing outside a store. In this one Hal wasn't dressed like a college kid at all. In fact, he looked quite the businessman. But that wasn't the point—yet. In the window behind him was one of those news releases they plant in stores facing the street that are made up of a big photo with a caption below it. There were two. One was indiscernible, but the other was the burning of the *Morro Castle*. And the *Morro Castle* went up in flames eight years ago. Yet here was Hal Kines looking older than he looked now.

I didn't get any more time to look around. I heard the elevator doors slam and I walked into the front room. When I got there someone was fiddling at the lock. There was a steady stream of curses before I clicked up the deadlock and opened the door. "Come in, George," I said.

He looked more scared than amazed. Apparently he really believed that it was me who took the shot at him. Hal was behind him ready to run as soon as I made one move. George recovered first.

"Where do you get off breaking into my apartment. This time . . ."

"Oh, shut up and come in. It's just as monotonous for me. If you'd stay home awhile, you'd be better off." The two of them stamped into the bedroom. When he came out he was red as a beet. I didn't give him a chance to accuse me of anything.

"Why all the artillery?" I asked him.

"For guys like you," he snarled, "for guys that try potting me through a window. Besides, I have a permit to carry it."

"Okay, you got a permit. Just be sure you know who you use that rod on."

"Don't worry, I'll give you a warning first. Now, if you don't mind, will you tell me what you are doing here?"

"Sure, sonny. I want the low-down on the bang, bang. Since I was the one accused of it, I'd like to know just what I was supposed to have done."

George slid a cigar from its wrapper and inserted it in a holder. He took his time lighting it up before he spoke.

"You seem to have police connections," he said finally. "Why don't you ask them?"

"Because I don't like second-hand information. And if you're smart you'll talk. That gun was the killer's gun, and I want the killer. You know that. But that isn't all. The killer made one try and missed, so you can bet your boots there'll be another."

Kalecki took the cigar out of his mouth. Little lines of fear were racing around his eyes. The guy was scared. He tried to hide it, but he didn't do very well. A nervous tic tugged at the corner of his mouth.

"I still see nothing I can tell you that would help. I was sitting in the big chair by the window. The first thing I knew the glass shattered beside me and the bullet hit the back of the chair. I dropped to the floor and crawled to the wall to be out of sight of whoever fired the shot."

"Why?" I said slowly.

"Why? To save myself, of course. You don't think I was just going to sit there and get shot at, do you?" Kalecki gave me a look of contempt but I ignored it.

"You don't get the point, George," I told him. "Why were you shot at to begin with?"

Little beads of sweat were popping out on his forehead. He wiped his brow nervously. "How should I know? I've made enemies in my time."

"This was a very particular enemy, George. This one killed Jack, too, and he's coming back after you. He may not miss the next time. Why are you on his list?"

He was really jumpy now. "I—I don't know. Honest I don't." He was almost apologetic the way he spoke now. "I tried to think it out but I don't get anywhere. That's why I moved to the city. Where I was, anyone could get to me. At least here there are other people around."

I leaned forward. "You didn't think enough. You and Jack had

something in common. What was it? What did you know that
Jack did? What did you have on somebody that Jack might have
tumbled to? When you answer that question you'll have your
killer. Now do I bang your head on the floor to help you remember
or do you do it yourself?"

He stood up straight and paced across the room. The thought
of being on a kill list had him half bugs. He just wasn't as young
as he used to be. This sort of thing got him down.

"I can't say. If there's anything, it's a mistake. I didn't know
Jack long. Hal knew him. He met him through Miss Manning.
If you can figure out a tie-up in there I'll be glad to tell you what
I know. Do you think I want to get knocked off?"

That was an angle I had forgotten about. Hal Kines was still
sitting in the armchair beside the mantelpiece dragging heavily on
a cigarette. For an athlete he wasn't holding to training rules at
all. I still couldn't get the picture of Hal out of my mind. The
one taken eight years ago. He was only a young punk, but that
shot made him look like an old man. I don't know. Maybe it
was an abandoned store that had the picture in it for years.

"Okay, Hal, let's hear what you know." The kid turned his
head toward me, giving me an excellent view of his Greek-god
profile.

"George mentioned everything."

"How do you know Miss Manning?" I asked him. "When did
you meet her? After all, a babe like that plays ball in a bigger
league than you can pay admission to see."

"Oh, she came to school last year and gave a lecture on practical
psychology. That's what I'm majoring in. She had several students
visit her clinic in New York to see her methods. I was one of
them. She became interested in me and assisted me no end. That's
all."

It wasn't hard to see why she'd become interested in him. It
made me mad to think of it, but he could have been right. Maybe
it was purely professional interest. After all, a woman like that
could have just about any male she wanted, including me.

I went on. "And what about Jack? When did you meet him?"

"Shortly afterwards. Miss Manning took me to his apartment
for supper with him and Myrna. I got involved in a drunken
brawl right after a football game. It was the last one of the season
and all training rules were off. I guess we all went a bit too far,
but we wrecked a joint. Jack knew the proprietor and instead of
turning us in, made us pay for the place. The following week I
was studying the case history of a homicidal maniac in the city

wards when I met him again. He was glad to see me and we had dinner together. We became rather good friends in a short time. I was glad to know him, because he helped me immensely. The type of work I was doing involved visits to places where I ordinarily would not have access to, but with his help I managed to get to them all."

For the life of me I couldn't make anything out of it. Jack never spoke too much about anyone. Our association had started by having an interest in police work and our friendship had developed over firing ranges, ballistics tables and fingerprint indexes. Even in the army we had thought about it. Life on the side was only incidental. He had mentioned his friends. That's about all. Myrna I knew very well. Kalecki from his underworld contacts. The Bellemy twins from the newspapers mostly, and the short time I had seen them before.

There was nothing more to be gained by hanging around here. I slapped my hat back on and walked toward the door. Neither of them thought to say so long, so I stepped out and slammed the door as hard as I could. Outside I wondered when George had gotten hold of the .45. Pat had said none of those at the party had ever owned a gun. Yet George had one and a permit to carry it. Or at least he said so. Well, if anything cropped up where a .45 was involved, I'd know where to look first.

The Bellemy twins lived on the fifth floor. Their apartment was in the same position as Kalecki's. The only difference was that they answered the bell. The door had a chain lock on the inside and a plain, but vaguely pretty face was meeting mine through the six-inch opening.

"Yes?"

I couldn't tell which of the twins I was speaking to, so I said, "Miss Bellemy?" She nodded. "I'm Mr. Hammer, private investigator. I'm working on the Williams case. Could you . . ."

"Why, of course." The door closed and the chain removed from the lock. When the door opened again, I was facing a woman that had athlete written all over her. Her skin was brown from the sun except for the wrinkle spots beside her eyes, and her arms and shoulders were as smooth-muscled as a statue's. This one certainly didn't have justice done her by her photos. For a moment it struck me why they were having any trouble finding husbands. As far as I could see, there wasn't anything wrong with this particular twin that the money she had couldn't cover. Plenty of guys would take her without any cash settlement at all.

"Won't you come in?"

"Thank you." I stepped inside and surveyed the place. Not much different from Kalecki's, but it had a light perfume smell instead of a cigar odor. She led me to a pair of divans separated by a coffee table and waved toward one. I sat down and she took the other.

"Now what is it you wish to see me about?"

"Perhaps you'd better tell me which Miss Bellemy I'm speaking to so I won't get my twins crossed."

"Oh, I'm Mary," she laughed. "Esther has gone shopping, which means she's gone for the day."

"Well, I guess you can tell me all I need to know. Has Mr. Chambers been to see you yet?"

"Yes. And he told me to expect you, too."

"I won't have much to ask. You knew Jack before the war, didn't you?" She acknowledged with a nod. "Did you notice anything particular the night of the party?" I continued.

"No, nothing. Light drinking and a little dancing. I saw Jack talking rather earnestly to Myrna a few times, and once he and Mr. Kines went out in the kitchen for about fifteen minutes, but they came back laughing as though they had been telling jokes."

"Did any of the others team up at all?"

"Umm, no, not to speak of. Myrna and Charlotte had a conference for a while, but the boys broke it up when the dancing started. I think they were talking about Myrna's wedding plans."

"What about afterwards?"

"We had a bite to eat, then came home. Both of us had forgotten our keys as usual and had to wake the super up to let us in. Both of us went right to bed. I knew nothing about the murder until a reporter awakened us with a phone call to get a statement. We expected a visit from the police at once and stayed at home to receive them, but no one came until today."

She stopped short and cocked her head a little. "Oh," she said, "you must excuse me. I left the water running in the tub." She ran to the narrow hallway and disappeared into the bathroom. Maybe I was getting old. I didn't hear any water running.

A couple of magazines were lying in a rack beside the divan. I picked one up and thumbed through it, but it was one of those pattern and fashion jobs without any pictures and I dropped it. Two new copies of *Confessions* were on the bottom of the pile. These were better than the rest, but still the same old story. One was a humdinger about a gal that meets a detective in a big city. He does her dirt and she tries to throw herself in front of a subway train. Some nice young jerk grabs her in time and makes a respectable woman of her.

I had just gotten to where he was leading her to the justice of the peace when Mary Bellemy came back. Only this time she made my head swim. Instead of the grey suit she had on before, she wore a sheer pink negligee that was designed with simplicity as the motif. Her hair was down out of the roll and her face looked clean and strong.

Whether or not she planned it I don't know, but she passed momentarily in front of the light streaming in from the window and I could see through everything she had on. And it wasn't much. Just the negligee. She smiled and sat down beside me. I moved over to make some room.

"I'm sorry I had to leave you, but the water wouldn't stay hot very long."

"That's all right, most women take all day at that."

She laughed again. "Not me. I was too anxious to hear more about this case you're working on." She crossed her legs and leaned forward to pick a cigarette from the box on the table. I had to turn my head. At this stage of the game I couldn't afford to get wrapped up with a love life. Besides, I wanted to see Charlotte later.

"Smoke?" she offered.

"No thanks." She leaned back against the divan and blew a ring at the ceiling.

"What else can I tell you? I can speak both for my sister and myself since we were together until the next evening." The sight of her in that carelessly draped sheer fabric kept my mind from what she was saying. "Of course, you can check with my sister later," she added, "exactly as Mr. Chambers did."

"No, that won't be necessary. Those details are minor. What I'm after now are the seemingly unimportant ones. Personality conflicts. Things you might have noticed about Jack the past few days. Any remark that might have been passed or something you overheard."

"I'm afraid I can't help you there. I'm not very good at eavesdropping and I don't collect gossip. My sister and I have remained fairly isolated in our home, that is, until we came to town. Our circle of friendship reaches out to our neighbors who like isolation as much as we do. Rarely do we entertain guests from the city."

Mary drew her legs up under her on the divan and turned on her side to face me. During the process the negligee fell open, but she took her time to draw it shut. Deliberately, she let my eyes feast on her lovely bosom. What I could see of her stomach was smooth parallel rows of light muscles, almost like a man's. I licked my lips and said, "How long do you expect to remain in town?"

She smiled. "Just long enough so Esther can get her shopping spree over with. Her main joy in living is wearing pretty clothes, regardless of whether or not she's seen in them."

"And yours?"

"My main joy in living is living." Two weeks ago I couldn't picture her saying that, but I could now. Here was a woman to whom time and place didn't mean a damn thing.

"Tell me," I started, "how can you tell the difference between you and your sister?"

"One of us has a small strawberry birthmark on the right hip."

"Which one?"

"Why don't you find out?" Brother, this girl was asking for trouble.

"Not today. I have work to do." I stood up and stretched.

"Don't be a sissy," she said.

Her eyes were blazing into mine. They were violet eyes, a wild blazing violet. Her mouth looked soft and wet, and provocative. She was making no attempt to keep the negligee on. One shoulder had slipped down and her brown skin formed an interesting contrast with the pink. I wondered how she got her tan. There were no strap marks anywhere. She uncrossed her legs deliberately and squirmed like an overgrown cat, letting the light play with the ripply muscles in her naked thighs.

I was only human. I bent over her, taking her mouth on mine. She was straining in the divan to reach me, her arms tight around my neck. Her body was a hot flame; the tip of her tongue searched for mine. She quivered under my hands wherever I touched her. Now I knew why she hadn't married. One man could never satisfy her. My hand fastened on the hem of the negligee and with one motion flipped it open, leaving her body lean and bare. She let my eyes search every inch of her brown figure.

I grabbed my hat and jammed it on my head. "It must be your sister who has the birthmark," I told her as a I rose. "See you later."

I half expected to hear a barrage of nasty words when I went through the door and was disappointed. Instead, I heard a faint, faraway chuckle. I would love to have known how Pat reacted to that act. It had dawned on me all of a sudden that she was left in my path as a sort of booby trap while Pat went on his own way. Huh, I'd wrap that guy up for this little trick. There was a neat tomato down on Third Avenue who loved to play tricks herself, especially against the police. Later, perhaps. . . .

chapter six ▊▊▊▊▊▊▊▊▊▊▊▊▊▊

VELDA WAS STILL at the office when I got there. When I saw the light on I stopped in front of a mirrored door and gave myself a thorough inspection for lipstick marks. I managed to wipe my mouth clean, but getting it off my white color was something else again. I could never figure out why the stuff came off women so easy and off the men so hard. Before I fooled around Mary Bellemy again I'd be sure she used Kleenex first.

I went in whistling. Velda took one look at me and her mouth tightened up. "Now what's the matter?" I could see something was wrong.

"You didn't get it off your ear," she said.

Uh-oh. This gal could be murder when she wanted to. I didn't bother to say anything more, but walked into my office. Velda had laid out a clean shirt for me, and an unwrinkled tie. Sometimes I thought she was a mind reader. I kept a few things handy for emergencies, and she generally knew when that would be.

At a washbowl in the corner I cleaned up a bit, then got into my shirt. Ties always were a problem. Usually Velda was on hand to help me out, but when I heard the door slam I knew I'd have to go it alone.

Downstairs I stopped in at the bar and had a few quick ones. The clock on the wall said it was early, so I picked out an empty booth and parked to spend a few hours. The waiter came over and I told him to bring me a rye and soda every fifteen minutes. This was an old custom and the waiter was used to it.

I dragged a list from my pocket and jotted down a few notes concerning Mary Bellemy. So far, the list was mainly character studies, but things like that can give a good insight into a crime. Actually, I hadn't accomplished much. I had made the rounds of the immediate suspects and had given them a good reason to sweat.

The police were doing things in their own methodical way, no doubt. They certainly weren't the saps a lot of newshawks try to make them. A solution to murder takes time. But this murder meant a race. Pat wasn't going to get the jump on me if I could help it. He'd been to the same places I had, but I bet he didn't know any more.

What we were both searching for was motive. There had to be one—and a good one. Murder doesn't just happen. Murder is planned. Sometimes in haste, but planned nevertheless.

As for the time element, George Kalecki had time to kill Jack. So did Hal Kines. I hated to think of it, but Charlotte Manning did too. Then there was Myrna. She too could have circled back to do it, leaving time to get home unnoticed. That left the Bellemy twins. Perhaps it was accidental, but they established their arrival time by letting the super open the door for them. Nice thinking if it was deliberate. I didn't bother to ask whether they left again or not. I knew the answer would be negative. Twins were peculiar; they were supposed to be uncannily inseparable. I've noticed it before in other sets, so these two wouldn't be any different. If it came to it they would lie, cheat or steal for each other.

I couldn't quite picture Mary Bellemy as being a nymphomaniac though. From all I've read of the two, they were sweet and demure, not young, not old. They kept strictly to themselves, or at least that's what the papers said. What a woman will do when she's alone with a man in her room is another thing. I was looking forward to seeing Esther Bellemy. That strawberry birthmark ought to prove sort of interesting.

Then there was the potshot at Kalecki. That stumped me. The best thing to do was to take a run up town and check up on his contacts. I signaled the waiter over and asked for a check. The guy frowned at me. I guess he wasn't used to me leaving after so few.

I got in my car and drove to the Hi-Ho Club. It used to be a bootleg spot during prohibition, but changed into a dingy joint over the years. It was a very unhealthy spot for strangers after dark, but I knew the Negro that ran the joint. Four years ago he had backed me up in a little gunplay with a drunken hood and I paid him back a month later by knocking off a punk that tried to set him for a rub-out when he refused to pay off for protection. My name goes pretty strong up that way and since then they let him strictly alone to run his business anyway he pleased. In this racket it's nice to have connections in places like that.

Big Sam was behind the bar. He saw me come in and waved

to me with a wet rag over a toothy grin. I shook hands with the guy and ordered a brew. The high yellow and the tall coal black next to me were giving me nasty looks until they heard Big Sam say "Howday, Mistah Hammah. Glad to see yuh. Long time since yuh done been in dis part of town."

When they heard my name mentioned they both moved their drinks six feet down the bar. Sam knew I was here for more than a beer. He moved to the end of the bar and I followed him.

"What's up, Mista Hammah? Somethin' I can do fuh yuh?"

"Yeah. You got the numbers running in here?"

Sam gave a quick look around before he answered. "Yeah. De Boys take 'em down same's they do the othah places. Why?"

"Is George Kalecki still the big boy?"

He licked his thick lips. Sam was nervous. He didn't want to be a squealer, yet he wanted to help me. "It's murder, Sam," I told him. "It's better you help me than have the bulls drag you to the station. You know how they are."

I could see he was giving it thought. The black skin of his forehead furrowed up. "Okay, Mistah Hammah. Guess it's all right. Kalecki is still head man, but he don't come around hisself. De runners do all the work."

"Is Bobo Hopper doing the running yet? He was with Kalecki some time. Hangs out here all the time, doesn't he?"

"Yassuh. He's head now, but he don' do no mo' running. He done had a good job the last few months. Keeps bees, too."

This was new. Bobo Hopper was only half human, an example of what environment can do to a man. His mental age was about twelve, with a build that went with it. Underfed all his life, he developed into a skinny caricature of a person. I knew him well. A nice Joe that had a heart of gold. No matter how badly you treated him, you were still his friend. Everything was his friend. Birds, animals, insects. Why, once I saw him cry because some kids had stepped on an anthill and crushed a dozen of its occupants. Now he had a "good" job and was keeping bees.

"Where is he, Sam? Back room?"

"Yassuh. You know where. Last I seed him he was looking at a pitcher book of bees."

I polished the beer off in one swallow, hoping the guys that had used it before me didn't have anything contagious. When I passed the high yellow and his friend, I saw their eyes follow me right through the doors of the back room.

Bobo Hopper was sitting at a table in the far corner of the

room. The place used to be fixed up with a dice table and a couple of wheels, but now the stuff was stacked in a corner. High up on the wall a single barred window was trying hard to keep out what light seeped down the air shaft, leaving all the work to the solitary bulb dangling on the wire strand from the ceiling. Rubbish was piled high along one side, held back by a few frail pieces of beer poster cardboards.

On the walls a few dirty pictures still hung from thumbtacks, the scenes half wiped out by finger smudges and dust. Someone had tried to copy the stuff in pencil on the wallpaper, but it was a poor try. The door to the bar was the only exit. I fished for the bolt lock, but there was nothing to slide it into so I let it be.

Bobo didn't hear me come in, he was so absorbed in his book. For a few seconds I looked at the pictures over his shoulders, watching his mouth work as he tried to spell out the words. I slammed him on the back.

"Hey, there, don't you say hello to an old friend?"

He half leaped from his chair, then saw that it was me and broke into a big smile. "Gee, Mike Hammer! Golly, I'm glad to see you." He stuck out a skinny paw at me and I took it. "Whatcha doin' down here, Mike? Come down just to see me, huh? Here, lemme get you a chair." He rolled an empty quarter keg that had seen better days over to the table and I parked on it.

"Hear you're keeping bees now, Bobo. That right?"

"Gee, yeah, an' I'm learning all about it from this book here. It's lotsa fun. They even know me, Mike. When I put my hand near the hive they don't bite me at all. They walk on me. You should see them."

"I'll bet it's a lot of fun," I told him. "But bees are expensive to keep, aren't they?"

"Naw. I made the hive from an egg box. And painted it, too. They like their hive. They don't fly away like the other guys' do. I got 'em on my roof where the landlady lets me keep 'em. She don't like bees, but I brought her a tiny bit of honey and she liked that. I'm good to my bees."

He was such a nice kid. He bubbled over with enthusiasm. Unlike so many others who were bitter. No family, no home, but now he had a landlady who let him keep bees. Bobo was a funny kid. I couldn't quiz him or he'd clam up, but when you got him talking about something he liked he'd spiel on all day for you.

"I hear you've got a new job, Bobo. How are you making out?"

"Oh, swell, Mike. I like it. They call me the errand manager." They probably meant "erring," but I didn't tell him that.

"What kind of work is it?" I asked. "Very hard?"

"Uh-uh. I run errands and deliver things and sweep and everything. Sometimes Mr. Didson lets me ride his bicycle when I deliver things for his store. I have lots of fun. Meet nice people, too."

"Do you make much money?"

"Sure. I get most a quarter or a half buck every time I do something. Them Park Avenue swells like me. Last week I made nearly fifteen bucks." Fifteen bucks. That was a lot of dough to him. He lived simply enough; now he was proud of himself. So was I.

"Sounds pretty good, Bobo. How did you ever manage to run down such a good job?"

"Well, you remember old Humpy?" I nodded. Humpy was a hunchback in his late forties who shined shoes in Park Avenue offices. I used him for an eye several times. He'd do anything to make a buck.

"Old Humpy got T.B.," Bobo continued. "He went up in the mountains to shine shoes there and I took his place. Only I wasn't so good at it like him. Then folks asked me to do little things for them and I did. Now I go down there every day early in the morning and they give me things to do like running errands. I got a day off today on account of I gotta see a guy about buying a queen bee. He's got two. Do you think five bucks is too much to pay for a queen bee, Mike?"

"Oh, I don't think so." I didn't know a queen bee from a king cobra, but queens usually run high in any species. "What did Mr. Kalecki say when you quit running numbers for him?"

Bobo didn't clam up like I expected. "Gee, he was swell. Gimme ten bucks 'cause I was with him so long and told me I could have my old job back whenever I wanted it." No wonder. Bobo was as honest as the day was long. Generally a runner made plenty for himself, taking a chance that the dough he clipped wasn't on the number that pulled in the shekels. But Bobo was too simple to be dishonest.

"That was pretty nice of Mr. Kalecki," I grinned, "but you do better when you're in business for yourself."

"Yeah. Some day I'm just gonna raise bees. You can make a lot of money from bees. Even own a bee farm, maybe."

Bobo smiled happily at the thought of it. But his smile passed into a puzzled frown. His eyes were fastened on something behind me. I had my back to the door, but when I saw Bobo's face, I knew that we weren't alone in the back room any longer.

The knife went under my chin very slowly. It was held loosely enough, but the slim fingers that held it were ready to tighten up the second I moved. Along the blade were the marks of a whetstone, so I knew it had been sharpened recently. The forefinger was laid on the top of the four-inch blade in proper cutting position. Here was a lug that knew what it was all about.

Bobo's eyes were wide open with terror. His mouth worked, but no sound came from it. The poor kid began to sweat, little beads that ran in rivulets down his sallow cheeks. A brown-sleeved arm came over my other shoulder and slid nicely under my coat lapel, the hand reaching for my rod.

I clamped down and kicked back. The table went sailing as my feet caught it. I got the knife hand and pulled down hard, and the high yellow landed in a heap on top of me. Just in time I saw the foot coming and pulled my head aside. The coal black missed by inches. I didn't. I let go the knife hand and grabbed the leg. The next moment I was fighting for my life under two sweating Negroes.

But not for long. The knife came out again and this time I got the hand in a wristlock and twisted. The tendons stretched, and the bones snapped sickeningly. The high yellow let out a scream and dropped the knife. I was on my feet in a flash. The big black buck was up and came charging into me, his head down.

There was no sense to busting my hand on his skull, so I lashed out with my foot and the toe of my shoe caught the guy right in the face. He toppled over sideways, still running, and collapsed against the wall. His lower teeth were protruding through his lip. Two of his incisors were lying beside his nose, plastered there with blood.

The high yellow was holding his broken wrist in one hand, trying to get to his feet. I helped him. My hand hooked in his collar and dragged him up. I took the side of my free hand and smashed it across his nose. The bone shattered and blood poured out. That guy probably was a lady killer in Harlem, but them days were gone forever. He let out a little moan and slumped to the floor. I let him drop.

Just for the hell of it, I went through his pockets. Not much there. A cheap wallet held a few photos of girls, one of them white, eleven dollars and a flock of number stubs. The coal black covered his ruined face when I went near him, rolling his eyes like a cow. I found a safety-razor blade in his pocket with a matchstick through it. Nice trick. They palm the blade, letting it protrude a bit through the fingers, and slap you cross the face.

The matchstick keeps it from sliding through their fingers. That blade can cut a face to pieces.

The Negro tried to pull away, so I smashed him again. The pad of my fist landing on that busted jaw was too much for him. He went out too. Bobo was still in his chair, only now he was grinning again. "Gee, Mike, you're pretty tough. Wish I was like that."

I pulled a five spot from my pocket and slipped it in his shirt pocket. "Here's something to buy a king for that queen bee, kid," I said to him. "See you later." I grabbed the two jigs by their collars and yanked them out of the door. Big Sam saw me coming with them. So did a dozen others in the place. Those at the door looked like they expected something more.

"What's the idea, Sam? Why let these monkeys make a try for me? You know better than that."

Big Sam just grinned broader than ever. "It's been a long time since we had some excitements in here, Mistah Hammah." He turned to the guys at the bar and held out a thick palm. "Pay me," he laughed at them. I dropped the high yellow and his friend in a heap on the floor as the guys paid Sam off. The next time they wouldn't bet against me.

As I was waving so long to Sam, Bobo came running out of the back room waving the five. "Hey, Mike," he yelled. "Queens don't need no kings. I can't buy a king bee."

"Sure they do, Bobo," I called over my shoulder. "All queens have to have kings. Ask Sam there, he'll tell you." Bobo was trying to find out why from Sam when I left. He'd probably spend the rest of his life getting the answer.

The drive home took longer than I had expected. Traffic was heavy and it was nearly six when I got there. After I parked the car I took the stairs to my apartment and started to undress. My clean shirt was a mess. Blood was spattered all over the front of it and my tie was halfway around my neck. The pocket of my jacket was ripped down the seam. When I saw that I wished I'd killed that bogie. In these days decent suits were too hard to get.

A hot and cold shower made me feel fine. I got rid of my beard in short order, brushed my teeth and climbed into some fresh clothes. For a moment I wondered whether it would be decent to wear a gun when calling on a lady, but habit got the better of me. I slipped the holster on over my shirt, shot a few drops of oil in the slide mechanism of my .45 and checked my clip. Everything in order, I wiped the gun and shoved it under my arm. Anyway, I thought, my suit wouldn't fit unless old

ironsides was inside it. This was a custom-made job that had space
built into it for some artillery.

I checked myself in the mirror to be sure I hadn't forgotten
anything. Without Velda to give me a once-over before I went
anywhere, I couldn't tell whether I was dolled up for a circus or
a night club. Now I wished I had been more careful with the
Bellemy mouse. Velda was too good a woman to lose. Guess I
could expect the silent treatment for a week. Someday I'd have
to try treating her a little better. She was kind of hard on a guy
though, never approved of my morals.

The jalopy needed gas so I ran it into a garage. Henry, the
mechanic, and an old friend of mine, lifted the hood to check
the oil. He liked that car. He was the one who installed an
oversized engine in it and pigged down the frame. From the
outside it looked like any beat-up wreck that ought to be retired,
but the rubber was good and the engine better. It was souped up
to the ears. I've had it on the road doing over a hundred and the
pedal was only half down. Henry pulled the motor from a limousine that had the rear end knocked in and sold it to me for a
song. Whenever a mech saw the power that was under the hood,
he let out a long low whistle. In its own way it was a masterpiece.

I pulled out of the garage and turned down a one-way street
to beat the lights to Charlotte's apartment. I couldn't forget the
way she looked through me the last time we met. What a dish.

The road in front of her house was lined with cars, so I turned
around the block and slid in between a black sedan and a club
coupé. Walking back to her place I kept hoping she didn't have
a dinner date or any company. That would be just my luck. What
we would talk about was something else again. In the back of my
mind was the idea that as a psychiatrist, she would have been
more observant than any of the others. In her line it was details
that counted, too.

I rang the downstairs bell. A moment later the buzzer clicked
and I walked in. The maid was at the door to greet me, but this
time she had on her hat and coat.

"Come right in, Mistah Hammah," she said. "Miss Charlotte's
expecting ya'll." At that I really raised my eyebrows. I threw my
hat down on a table beside the door and walked in. The maid
stayed long enough to call into the bedroom, "He's heah, Miss
Charlotte."

That cool voice called back. "Thank you. You can go ahead
to the movies now." I nodded to the maid as she left and sat on
the couch.

"Hello." I jumped to my feet and took the warm hand she offered me.

"Hello yourself," I smiled. "What's this about expecting me?"

"I'm just vain, I guess. I was hoping so hard that you'd call tonight. I got ready for you. Like my dress?" She swirled in front of me, and glanced over her shoulder at my face. Gone was the psychiatrist. Here was Charlotte Manning, the woman, looking delightfully young and beautiful. Her dress was a tight-fitting blue silk jersey that clung to her like she was wet, concealing everything, yet revealing everything. Her hair hung long and yellow to her neck, little tight curls that sparkled. Even her eyes had cupids in them.

She strode provocatively across the room and back toward me. Under the dress her body was superb unlike what I imagined the first time. She was slimmer, really, her waist thin, but her shoulders broad. Her breasts were laughing things that were firmly in place, although I could see no strap marks of a restraining bra. Her legs were encased in sheer nylons and set in high heels, making her almost as tall as I was. Beautiful legs. They were strong looking, shapely. . . .

"Well, do you like it?" she asked again.

"Lovely. And you know it." I grinned at her. "You remind me of something."

"What?"

"A way of torturing a guy."

"Oh, please, I can't be that bad. Do I affect you like that? Torture you, I mean?"

"No, not quite. But if you take a guy that hasn't seen a woman in five years, let's say, and chain him to a wall and let you walk past him the way you did just now—well, that would be torture. See what I'm getting at?"

Her laugh was low and throaty. She threw back her head a little and I wanted to grab her and kiss the beauty of her throat. Charlotte took my arm and led me to the kitchen. The table was laid out for two. On the table was a big pile of fried chicken and another equally large basket of French fries.

"Just for us. Now sit down and eat. I've already held supper an hour waiting for you."

I was dumbfounded. Either she kept a complete file of my likes and dislikes or she was clairvoyant. Chicken was my specialty.

As I pulled out a chair and sat down, I said, "Charlotte, if there was an angle to this, I'd think the chow was poisoned. But even if it is, I'm going to eat it anyway."

She was putting a red-bordered apron on. When she finished she poured the coffee. "There is an angle," she said casually.

"Let's have it," I said through a mouthful of chicken.

"When you came in to see me I saw a man that I liked for the first time in a long time." She sat down and continued. "I have hundreds of patients, and surprisingly enough, most of them are men. But they are such little men. Either they have no character to begin with or what they had is gone. Their minds are frail, their conception limited. So many have repressions or obsessions, and they come to me with their pitiful stories; well, when you constantly see men with their masculinity gone, and find the same sort among those whom you call your friends, you get so you actually search for the real man."

"Thanks," I put in.

"No, I mean it," Charlotte went on. "I diagnosed you the moment you set foot in my office. I saw a man who was used to living and could make life obey the rules he set down. Your body is huge, your mind is the same. No repressions."

I wiped my mouth. "I got an obsession though."

"You have? I can't imagine what it is."

"I want a killer. I want to shoot a killer." I watched her over a drumstick, chewing a mile a minute on the succulent dark meat. She tossed her hair and nodded.

"Yes, but it's a worthwhile obsession. Now eat up."

I went through the pile of chicken in nothing flat. My plate was heaped high with bones. Charlotte did all right, too, but I did most of the damage. After a piece of pie and a second cup of coffee I leaned back in my chair, contented as a cow.

"That's a wonderful cook you've got there," I remarked.

"Cook, hell," she laughed. "I did all that myself. I haven't always been wealthy."

"Well, when the time comes for you to get married, you're not going to have to go out of your way to get a husband."

"Oh, I have a system," she said. "You're getting part of it right now. I lure men to my apartment, cook for them, and before they go home I have my proposal."

"Don't look now," I told her, "but it's been tried on me before."

"But not by an expert." We both laughed at that. I suggested we do the dishes and she handed me an apron. Very politely, I laid it on the back of a chair. It just wouldn't go well with my mug. If anyone I knew happened to breeze in and catch me in a rig like that I'd spend the rest of my life living it down.

After we finished the dishes we went into the living room. Charlotte curled up in the armchair and I half fell on the sofa. We lit cigarettes, then she smiled at me and said, "All right, you can tell me why you came up to see me. More questions?"

I shook my head. "I confess. Don't beat me with that whip. I started out with two things in mind. The first one was to see you with your hair down. It turned out better than I expected."

"And the other?"

"To see if you, as a practicing psychiatrist, could throw some light on the murder of my good friend, Jack Williams."

"I see. Perhaps if you'll tell me more explicitly what you want, I'll be able to help you."

"Good enough. I want details. The murder isn't old enough to get well into it yet, but I will. It's entirely reasonable that someone at the party knocked off Jack. It's just as reasonable that it was someone completely outside. I've made some character studies, and what I've found I don't like. However, that may not be a good reason for murder. What I want from you is an opinion, not one based on fact or logic, but an opinion, purely professional, on how you think those I mentioned may tie into this thing and whom you'd line up for the killer."

Charlotte took a deep drag on her cigarette, then crushed it out in an ashtray. Her mind was working hard, it was reflected in her expression. A minute passed before she spoke. "You are asking me to do a difficult thing, pass judgment on a person. Usually it takes twelve men and a judge, after hours of deliberation, to do the same thing. Mike, after I met you, I made it my job to look into your character. I wanted to know what a man like you was made of. It wasn't hard to find out. The papers have been full of your episodes, editorials were even written about you, and not very favorable ones, either. Yet I found people who knew you and liked you. Little people and big people. I like you. But if I were to tell you what I thought I'm afraid I'd be passing a sentence of death on a person. No, I won't tell you that, you'd be too quick to kill. That I don't want. There's so much about you that could be nice if only your mind wasn't trained to hate too fiercely.

"What I will do is give you that which I have observed. It takes time to think back, and I've taken the whole afternoon to do just that. Little things I thought I had forgotten are clear now and they may make sense to you. I'm used to personal conflict, the struggle that goes on within one's mind, not with differences between two or more people. I can notice things, put them in their proper places, but I can't do more than file them away. If a person hates, then I can find the reason for his hatred and possibly help him to rationalize more clearly, but if that hatred has consumed him to the point of murder, then I can but say I might have expected it. The discovery of murderers and motives belongs to more astute minds than mine."

I was listening intently to every word, and I could see her point. "Fair enough," I said, "then tell me what you have observed."

"It isn't too much. Jack had been in a state of nervous tension for a week before the party. I saw him twice and neither time had he seemed any better. I remarked about it, but he laughed and told me he was still trying to rehabilitate himself to civilian life. At the time it seemed reasonable to me. A man who has lost a limb would naturally find life awkward for some time.

"The night of the party he was still as tense as ever. Somehow, it radiated to Myrna. She worried about him anyway, and I could see that she was nearly as upset as he was. Nothing visible, however, just those little things. A tendency to anger at the dropping of a glass or a sudden sound. Both Jack and she covered it up nicely, so I imagine that I was the only one who noticed anything.

"Mr. Kalecki came to the party in a grouch. Perhaps anger would be a better word, but I couldn't figure out with whom he was angry. He snapped at Harold Kines several times and was completely uncivil to Mary Bellemy."

"How?" I asked.

"They were dancing and she said something or other. I didn't hear what it was, but he scowled and said, 'The hell with that stuff, sister.' Right after that he took her back to the group and walked away."

I laughed. She didn't know what was so funny until I told her. "Mary Bellemy probably propositioned George right on the floor. Guess he's getting old. She's a nymphomaniac."

"Oh, yes? How did you find out?" The way she said it was with icebergs.

"Don't get ideas," I said. "She tried it on me but I wasn't in the market."

"Right then?"

"No, never. I like to do some of the work myself, not have it handed to me on a platter."

"I'll have to remember that. I did suspect that Mary was like that, but I never gave it much thought. We were only casual friends. Anyway, when we were leaving, Jack stopped me by the door and asked me to stop back to see him sometime during the week. Before he could say anything further, the gang called me and I had to leave. I never saw him again."

"I see." I tried to mull it over in my mind, but it didn't work out. So Jack had something bothering him, and so did Myrna. It might have been that they were worried about the same thing. Maybe not. And George. He was upset about something, too.

"What do you make of it?" Charlotte asked.

"Nothing, but I'll think it over." Charlotte got up from the chair and came over to the sofa and sat down. She laid her hand on mine and our eyes met.

"Mike, do me a favor. I'm not asking you to stay out of this and let the police handle it, all I want is for you to be careful. Please don't get hurt."

When she spoke like that I felt as if I had known her a lifetime. Her hand was warm and pulsing lightly. I felt myself going fast— and I had seen her only twice.

"I'll be careful," I told her. "Why are you worrying?"

"Here's why." She leaned forward, her lips parted, and kissed me on the mouth. I squeezed her arms so hard my hands hurt, but she never moved. When she drew away her eyes were soft and shining. Inside me a volcano was blazing. Charlotte looked at the marks on her arms where I held her and smiled.

"You love hard, too, don't you, Mike?"

This time I didn't hurt her. I stood up and drew her toward me. I pressed her to me, closely, so she could feel the fire I had in me. This kiss lasted longer. It was a kiss I'll never forget. Then I kissed her eyes, and that spot on her throat that looked so delicious. It was better than I expected.

I turned her around and we faced the windows overlooking the street. She rubbed her head against mine, holding my arms around her waist tightly. "I'm going now," I said to her. "If I don't, I'll never leave. The next time I'll stay longer. I don't want to do this wrong. I will if you keep me here."

She tilted her head up and I kissed her nose. "I understand," she said softly. "But whenever you want me, I'll be here. Just come and get me."

I kissed her again, lightly this time, then went to the door. She handed me my hat and pushed my hair back for me. "Good-bye, Mike."

I winked at her. "So long, Charlotte. It was a wonderful supper with a wonderful girl."

It was a wonder I got downstairs at all. I hardly remember getting to my car. All I could think of was her face and that lovely body. The way she kissed and the intensity in her eyes. I stopped on Broadway and dropped into a bar for a drink to clear my head. It didn't help so I went home and hit the sack earlier than usual.

chapter seven ▬▬▬▬▬▬▬▬▬▬

I WOKE UP before the alarm went off, which is pretty unusual. After a quick shower and shave, I whipped up some scrambled eggs and shoveled them into me. When I was on my second cup of coffee the boy from the tailor shop came in with my suit nicely cleaned and pressed. The pocket was sewed up so that you could never have told it was torn. I dressed leisurely and called the office.

"Hammer Investigating Agency, good morning."

"Good morning yourself, Velda, this is your boss."

"Oh."

"Aw, come on, honey, " I pleaded, "quit being sore at me. That lipstick came under the line of business. How can I work when you've got me by the neck?"

"You seem to do all right," her reply came back. "What can I do for you, *Mister* Hammer?"

"Any calls?"

"Nope."

"Any mail?"

"Nope."

"Anybody been in?"

"Nope."

"Will you marry me?"

"Nope."

"Well, so long then."

"Marry? Hey . . . wait a minute, Mike. MIKE! Hello . . . hello. . . ."

I hung up very gently, laughing to myself. That would fix her. The next time she'd do more than say "nope." I'd better start watching that stuff. Can't afford to trip myself up; though with Velda maybe it wouldn't be so bad at that.

The police had taken their watchdog away from Jack's apartment. The door was still sealed pending further investigation and I didn't want to get in dutch with the D.A.'s office by breaking it, so I looked around a bit.

I had just about given up when I remembered that the bathroom window bordered on an air shaft, and directly opposite it was another window. I walked around the hall and knocked on a door. A small, middle-aged gent poked his head out and I flashed my badge on him. "Police," was all I had to say.

He didn't bother looking the badge over, but opened the door in haste. A good respectable citizen that believed in law and order. He stood in front of me, clutching a worn smoking jacket around his pot belly and trying to look innocent. Right then he was probably thinking of some red light he ran a month ago, and picturing himself in the line-up.

"Er . . . yes, officer, what can I do for you?"

"I'm investigating possible entries into the apartment of Mr. Williams. I understand you have a window that faces his. Is that right?"

His jaw dropped. "Wh-why, yes, but nobody could have gone through our window without us seeing him."

"That isn't the point," I explained to him. "Somebody could have come down from the roof on a rope. What I want to do is see if that window can be opened from the outside. And I don't want to shinny down a rope to do it."

The guy sighed with relief. "Oh, I see. Well, of course, just come this way." A mousey-type woman stuck her head from the bedroom door and asked, "John, what is it?"

"Police," he told her importantly. "They want me to help them." He led me to the bathroom and I pushed up the window. It was some job. Those modest folks, fearing somebody might peek, must never have had it open. When it went up, a shower of paint splinters fluttered to the floor.

There was Jack's bathroom window, all right. A space of three feet separated the two walls. I worked myself to the outside sill while the little guy held my belt to steady me. Then I let myself fall forward. The guy let out a shriek and his wife came tearing in. But all I did was stick my hands out and lean against the opposite wall. He thought I was a goner.

The bathroom window went up easily. I pulled myself across the space, thanked the guy and his wife, and slithered inside. Nothing had been moved around much. The fingerprint crew had left powder tracings on most of the objects that could have been handled, and where Jack's body had lain were the chalk marks outlining the position. His artificial arm was still on the bed where he had put it. The only thing that was gone was his gun, and stuck in the empty holster was a note. I pulled it out and read it. "Mike," it said, "don't get excited over the gun. I have it at headquarters." It was signed, "Pat."

How do you like that? He thought I'd find a way to get in. I put the note back with an addition at the bottom. "Thanks, chum," I wrote, "I won't." I scrawled my name underneath it.

It was easy to see that the police had been over everything in the place. They had gone at it neatly, but completely. Everything was replaced much the same as it had been. There were just a few things not quite in order that made it possible to tell that it had been searched.

I started in the living room. After I pushed the chairs to the middle of the floor and examined them, I went around the edges of the carpet. Nothing there but a little dirt. I found three cents under the cushions of the couch, but that was all. The insides of the radio hadn't been touched for months, as evidenced by the dust that had settled there. What books were around had nothing in them, no envelopes, no bookmarks or paper of any sort. If they had, the police got them.

When I finished, I replaced everything and tried the bathroom but, except for the usual array of bottles and shaving things in the cabinet, it was empty.

The bedroom was next. I lifted the mattress and felt along the seams for any possible opening or place where it may have been stitched up. I could have cursed my luck. I stood in the middle of the floor stroking my chin, thinking back. Jack had kept a diary, but he kept it on his dresser. It wasn't there now. The police again. I even tried the window shades, thinking that a paper might have been rolled up in one of them.

What got me was that I knew Jack had kept a little pad of notes and addresses ever since he was on the force. If I could find that, it might contain something useful. I tried the dresser. I took every shirt, sock and set of underwear out of the drawers and went through them, but I might as well not have taken the time. Nothing.

As I emptied the bottom drawer a tie caught and slipped over the back. I pulled the drawer all the way out and picked up the tie from the plywood bottom. I also picked up something else. I picked up Jack's little book.

I didn't want to go through it right then. It was nearly ten o'clock and there was a chance that either the police might walk in on me or the little guy get suspicious enough of my being away so long he'd call a copper. As quickly as I could, I put the stuff back in the drawers and replaced them in the dresser. The book I stuck in my hip pocket.

The little guy was waiting for me in his own bathroom. I squeezed out Jack's window and made a pretense of looking for rope marks along the upper sill. His eyes followed me carefully. "Find anything, officer?" he asked me.

"Afraid not. No marks around here at all. I checked the other windows and they haven't even been opened." I tried to look up to the roof, but I couldn't get back far enough until I stepped across to his side, then I wormed my way into the bathroom and poked my head out and craned my head to make it look like I was really trying.

"Well, I guess that's all. Might as well go out through your door as climb back inside there, okay?"

"Certainly, officer, right this way." He steered me to the front room like a seeing-eye dog and opened up for me. "Any time we can be of service, officer," he called to me as I left, "let us know. Glad to help."

I drove back to the office in short order and walked into the reception room, pulling the book from my pocket. Velda stopped typing. "Mike."

I turned around. I knew what was coming.

"What is it, honey?"

"Please don't fool with me like that."

I gave her a big grin. "I wasn't fooling," I said. "If you were on your toes I'd be an engaged man right now. Come on inside a minute." She trailed in after me and sat down. I swung my feet up on the battered desk and riffled through the book. Velda was interested.

"What is it?" she asked curiously, leaning over to get a better look.

"A notebook of Jack's. I swiped it from his room before the police could get it."

"Anything in it?"

"Maybe. I haven't looked yet." Starting at the front was a list of names, all crossed out. Each page was dated, the earliest starting three years ago. Occasionally there were references to departmental cases with possible suspects and the action to take. These, too, were crossed out as having been completed.

About the middle of the book notes began to appear that

apparently were still active or pending, for no black X's marked them. I jotted these down on a list and Velda checked them against news clippings in my files. When she finished she laid down my notes with the word "solved" after each. Evidently the cases had been cleared up while Jack was still in the army.

I wasn't getting much at all from this. Jack had inserted a single page with one word across it. "WHOOPIE!" It was dated the day of his discharge. The next page had a recipe for veal paprika, and at the bottom was a notation to put more salt in than the recipe called for.

There were two more pages of figures, an itemized account of what he had spent for clothes balanced against what he had in a bank account somewhere. Then came a brief remark: "Eileen Vickers. Family still in Poughkeepsie."

She must have been a girl from home. Jack was born in Poughkeepsie and lived there until he went to college. The next few pages had some instructions from the insurance company. Then Eileen Vickers' name cropped up again. This time it read: "Saw E. V. again. Call family." The date was exactly two weeks before Jack had been killed.

She turned up again five pages further on. In heavy pencil Jack had: "R. H. Vickers, c/o Halper. Pough. 221. Call after 6." Then below it: "E. V. al. Mary Wright. No address. Get it later."

I tried to puzzle out what it meant. To me it looked like Jack had met a girl from home and had talked to her. She had told him that her family was still in Poughkeepsie. Evidently he tried to call them and found that they were staying with Halper, and in order to get them, called at supper time. Then the next part. E. V., Eileen Vickers, all right, but she was traveling under an alias of Mary Wright and gave no address.

I thumbed through the pages quickly, and there she was again. "E. V. Call family. Bad shape. Trace and raid 36904 the 29th." And today was the 29th. There was one page left. It was an afterthought, a memo to himself: "Ask C. M. what she can do."

. . .

C. M., Charlotte Manning. He had reference to what Charlotte told me about. He wanted her to stop back during the week, but never got the chance to see her.

I reached for the phone and dialed operator. When she cut in I asked for the Poughkeepsie number. There were some clicks as the connection was completed, then a timid voice answered.

"Hello," I said. "Is this Mr. Vickers?"

"No," the voice replied, "this is Mr. Halper. Mr. Vickers is still at work. Can you leave a message?"

"Well, I wanted to find out if he had a daughter in the city. Do you know . . ."

The voice interrupted me. "I'm sorry, but it would be better if you didn't mention that to Mr. Vickers. Who is calling, please?"

"This is Michael Hammer, investigator. I'm working with the police on a murder and I'm trying to run down what might be a lead. Now, can you tell me what the story is here?"

Halper hesitated a moment, then said, "Very well. Mr. Vickers hasn't seen his daughter since she went to college. She became enmeshed in a sinful life with a young man. Mr. Vickers is a very stern gentleman, and as far as he is concerned, she might as well be dead. He'll have nothing to do with her."

"I see, thank you." I hung up and turned to Velda. She was staring at the number I had jotted down. 36904.

"Mike."

"What?"

"Do you know what this is?" I looked at the number. It could have been a reference to a police file, but when I glanced at it a third time, I felt as though I had seen it before.

"Uh-uh. I should know it, I think. Something vaguely familiar about it."

Velda took a pencil from her pocket and swung the pad around. "Suppose you write it this way," she said. She put the numbers down to read: XX3–6904.

"Well, I'll be damned! A phone number."

"Roger, pal. Now fill in the first two letters of an exchange for the X's and you'll have it."

I jumped to my feet and went to the files. Now I remembered where I had seen that number before. It was on the back of a card I had taken from a pimp. The little runt had tried to sell me a deal and I slapped him silly for it. I came back with a folder of note paper, cards, and numbers, scratched on the back of menus.

I picked one out of the file. "LEARN TO DANCE," it read, "TWENTY BEAUTIFUL GIRLS." On the back of it was a number. I compared it to the one from Jack's book. The same. Only this one had an exchange, LO, for Loellen. That was the number, all right, LO3–6904. Velda took it from my hand and read it.

"What is it, Mike?"

"It's the telephone number of a call house. If I'm not mistaken, that's where I'm going to find the Vickers girl." I reached for the phone, but Velda put her hand out to stop me.

"You're not actually going there, are you?"

"Why not?"

"Mike!" Her voice was indignant, hurt.

"For Pete's sake, honey, do I look like a dope? I'm not going to buy anything. After all those pictures the army showed me of what happens to good little boys who go out with bad little girls, I'm even afraid to kiss my own mother."

"Okay, go ahead, but watch your step, by damn, or you're going to have to get a new secretary." I ran my fingers through her hair and dialed the number.

The voice I got this time had a little life in it. Behind the "hello" I could see a frowsy blonde about fifty in a gaudy dress dangling a butt from her lips.

"Hello," I said, "you booked for the night?"

"Who is this?"

"Pete Sterling. Got your number from a little guy downtown."

"All right. Come up before nine or you won't make the beginning of the entertainment. Want to stay all night?"

"Maybe. I'll know better then. Book me for the night anyway. Guess I can get away from home." I winked at Velda when I said it, but she didn't wink back.

"You're down. Bring cash. Ring three longs and a short when you come."

"I got it." I cradled the phone.

There were tears in Velda's eyes. She was trying to remain grim, but she couldn't hold them back.

I put my arms around her and hugged her gently. "Aw, look, honey," I whispered, "I have to take a realistic approach to this case. Otherwise, how the hell am I going to get anywhere?"

"You don't have to go that far," she sniffled.

"But I told you I wouldn't. For crying out loud, I'm not that bad off that I have to patronize those places. There's lots of dames I could park with if I felt like it."

She put her hands against my chest and shoved. "And don't I know it," she practically yelled. "I wouldn't trust you to . . . oh, gee, Mike, I'm sorry. I only work here. Forget it."

I pinched her nose and smiled. "Work here, hell. I wouldn't know what to do without you. Now behave yourself and stick near your phone either here or at home. I may need you to pick up a few angles for me."

Velda gave a little laugh. "Okay, Mike. I'll watch the angles, you watch out for the curves. Huba huba."

She was cleaning off my desk when I left.

chapter eight ▐████████████████████

MY FIRST CALL was to Pat. He wanted to know how I was making out but I didn't give him much. Later he could know about the Vickers girl, but first I wanted to get in my two bits. I picked a few numbers from the phone book and included the call-house number among them. I held on while Pat checked the addresses for me and passed on the information. After I thanked him, I checked with the phone book to make sure he had given me straight stuff. They checked. Pat was playing it square enough.

In case he fished around with the numbers I gave him, it would be some time before he got to the one I was working on.

This time I left my heap halfway down the block. 501 was the number I wanted, and it turned out to be an old brownstone apartment three stories high. I cased it from a spot across the street, but no one came or went. On the top floor a room was lit up faintly with no signs of life in it. Evidently I was early. The house was flanked on each side by another equally as drab and with as little color to it as the streets of a ghost town.

This was no regular red-light district. Just a good spot for what went on. An old, quiet neighborhood patrolled several times nightly by a friendly cop, a few struggling businesses in the basement apartments. No kids—the street was too dull for them. No drunks lounging in doorways either. I pulled on my cigarette for the last time, then crushed it under my heel and started across the street.

I pushed the button three longs and a short. Very faintly I heard the ring, then the door opened. It wasn't the frowsy blonde I had expected. This woman was about fifty, all right, but her dress was conservative and neat. She had her hair done up in a roll with only the slightest suggestion of make-up. She looked like somebody's mother.

"Pete Sterling," I said.

"Oh, yes, won't you come in?" She closed the door behind me

while I waited, then motioned toward the sitting room off the hall. I went in. The transformation was startling. Unlike the dull exterior, this room was exciting, alive. The furniture was modern, yet comfortable. The walls were paneled in rich mahogany to blend with the redecorated mantel and the graceful staircase that curved down into the far end of the room. I could see why no light shone through the windows. They were completely blocked off with black velvet curtains.

"May I take your hat?" I snapped out of it long enough to hand over my lid. Upstairs a radio was playing, but there was no other sound. The woman came back after a moment and sat down, motioning me to be seated opposite her.

"Nice place you have here," I remarked.

"Yes, we're very secluded here." I was waiting for her to ask the questions, but she seemed in no hurry. "You told me on the phone that you had met one of our agents and he sent you here. Which one was it?"

"A little ratty guy. He didn't make it sound as good as this. I slapped him around some."

She gave me a tight smile. "Yes, I remember, Mr. Hammer. He had to take the week off." If she thought she'd catch me jumping she was crazy.

"How did you spot me?"

"Please don't be so modest. You've made too many headlines to be entirely unknown. Now tell me something, why did you choose to come here?"

"Guess," I said.

She smiled again. "I imagine it can even happen to you, too. All right, Mr. . . . er . . . Sterling, would you like to go upstairs?"

"Yeah. Who's up there?"

"An assortment you'll find interesting. You'll see. But first, twenty-five dollars, please." I fished out the dough and handed it over.

She led me as far as the stairs. There was a push button mounted on the side of the newel post and she pushed it. Upstairs a chime rang and a door opened, flooding the stairs with light. A dark-haired girl wrapped in a transparent robe stood in the doorway.

"Come on up," she said.

I took the stairs two at a time. She wasn't pretty, I could see that, but the make-up enhanced what she had. A beautiful body, though. I walked in. Another sitting room, but this one was well occupied. The madam had meant what she said when she told me there was an assortment. The girls were sitting there reading or smoking; blondes, brunettes and a pair of redheads. None of them had much on.

Things like this were supposed to make your heart beat faster, only I didn't react that way. I thought of Velda and Jack. Something was here that I wanted and I didn't know how I was going to take it. Eileen Vickers was the one, but I never saw her. The alias—Mary Wright. It seemed feasible that she would not use her right name working here and not to evade income taxes either.

Nobody gave me a tumble, so I supposed I was to make the selection. The girl who led me in kept watching me expectantly. "Want someone special?" she asked.

"Mary Wright," I told her.

"She's in her room. Wait here, I'll get her." The girl disappeared through the door and was back a moment later. "Right down the hall, next to last door."

I nodded and went through the door and found myself in a long hallway. On either side the wall was peppered with doors, newly built. Each one had a knob, but no key hole. The next to last door was the same as the others. I knocked and a voice called out for me to come in. I turned the knob and pushed.

Mary Wright was seated in front of a dressing table, combing her hair. All she was wearing was a brassiere and a pair of step-ins. That and house slippers. She eyed me through the mirror.

She might have been pretty once, but she wasn't any longer. There were lines under her eyes that weren't put there by age. She had a faint twitch in her cheek that she tried to conceal, but it came through anyway. I guessed her age somewhat in the late twenties. She looked a lot older, but I accounted for that.

Here was a girl that had seen plenty of life, all raw. Her body was just a shade too thin, well fed, but emotionally starved. Empty, like a dead snail. Her profession and her past were etched into her eyes. She was a girl you could beat without getting a whimper out of her. Maybe her expression would change, but another beating more or less would mean nothing. Like the others, she wasn't too made-up. Far from being plain, but not at all gaudy.

Her hair was a chestnut brown like the irises of her eyes. She must have had some sun lately or spent time under a lamp, for there was a faint tinge of tan covering what I could see of her skin. There was nothing startling about her shape. Average. Not very heavy in the breasts, but her legs were nice. I felt sorry for the girl.

"Hello." Her voice was pleasant enough. She sat there as though she was getting ready to go out and I was a husband casually looking for a cuff link. "Early, aren't you?"

"Sort of, but I was getting tired of hanging around a bar." I got in a quick look around the room, then went to an end table and ran through a set of books. My fingers felt under the table edge before I inspected the walls. I was looking for wires. These places have been rigged for sound more than once and I didn't want to get snared in a trap. The bed was next. I got down on my hands and knees and looked under it. No wires.

Mary had been watching me curiously. "If it's a dictaphone you're searching for, we haven't any," she said. "And the walls are soundproofed besides." She stood up in front of me. "Want a drink first?"

"No."

"Afterwards, then."

"No."

"Why?"

"Because I didn't come here for that."

"Well, for goodness' sake, what did you come for, to make small talk?"

"You hit it, Eileen." I thought she'd pass out. At first she got deathly white, then her eyes hardened and her lips tightened. I could see that this wasn't going to be so easy.

"What's the gag, mister? Who are you?"

"The monicker is Mike Hammer, kid. I'm a private eye."

She knew who I was all right. She tightened up all over when she heard my name. A traceless fear crept into her body. "So you're a shamus. What does that have to do with me? If my father sent you . . ."

I cut her short. "Your father didn't send me. Nobody did. A pal of mine got killed a short time ago. His name was Jack Williams." Her hand flew to her mouth. For a second I thought she'd scream. But she didn't. She sat down on the edge of the bed, and a tear trickled down her cheek leaving a streak in the make-up.

"No. I—I didn't know."

"Don't you read the papers?" She shook her head. "Among his things I found your name. He'd seen you just before, hadn't he?"

"Yes. Please, am I under arrest?"

"No. I don't want to arrest anybody. I just want to shoot somebody. The killer." The tears were coming freely now. She tried to wipe them away but they came too fast.

It was hard to understand. Here was a dame I had tagged as

being as hard as they come, yet she thought enough of Jack to cry when I told her he was dead. And she hated her father, apparently. Well, that was a woman. There was still that much left in her.

"Not Jack. He was so nice. I—I really tried to keep this from him, but he found out. He even got me a job before, but I couldn't keep it." Mary rolled over on her face and buried her head in the pillow. She was sobbing hard now.

I sat down next to her. "Crying won't help. What I want are a few answers. Come on, sit up and listen." I raised her by the shoulders. "Jack wanted to have this place raided tonight, but the message never reached the police. He was killed before he could do anything about it. What's going on tonight?"

Mary straightened up. Her tears were gone now and she was thinking. I had to let her take her time. "I don't know," she said finally. "Jack had no cause to do anything. Places like this flourish in the city and they don't have to pay off to anyone."

"Maybe there's more to it than you think," I added. "Just who is expected tonight?"

She continued, "The show. Lots of people come to see it. You know the kind. Usually there's a convention in town and prospective buyers are brought here for a little fun. I never see any important people. The kind that are in the public eye, I mean. Just fairly prosperous people."

I knew the kind. Fat greasy people from out of town. Slick city boys who played the angles and were willing to shell out the dough. Rich jokers of both sexes who liked smut and filth and didn't care where they got it. A pack of queers who enjoyed exotic, sadistic sex. Nasty people. Clerks who scraped their nickels to go and then bragged on the street corners.

I tried a different approach. "How did you get in this, Mary?"

"Nuts. It's a long story, but I wouldn't tell you."

"Listen. I'm not trying to pry into your life. I want you to talk about this, the whole thing. Something you say may have no meaning to you, but may throw some light on the whole affair. I'm convinced that whatever you are connected with has a contributing factor to Jack's death. I could do it differently. I could slap it out of you. I could wreck this whole setup if I felt like it. But I'm not going to; it would take too long. It's up to you."

"All right. If you think it would help. I wouldn't do it if it weren't for him. In all my life he was one of the very few square guys I ever met. He gave me plenty of breaks, trying to help me, but I failed him, every time. Generally I start bawling when I tell this, but too much water has gone under the bridge to make it upset me any more."

I sat back and dragged out a cigarette and offered her one. She took it and we lit up. I leaned back on the bed and waited.

"It started in college. I went to the Midwest to become a teacher. It was a co-ed school, and in due time I met a fellow. His name was John Hanson. Tall and good-looking. We intended to get married. One night we parked after a football game and you know what happened. Three months later I had to leave school. John didn't want to get married yet, so he took me to a doctor. When the operation was over I was shaky and nervous. We set up an apartment, John and I, and for a while lived as man and wife without benefit of clergy.

"How my folks got wind of it, I don't know. Those things happen. I got a letter from my father completely disowning me. That same night John didn't come home. I waited and waited, then called the school. He had dropped from the curriculum. Disappeared. My month was nearly up in the apartment and I didn't know what to do.

"Now the unpleasant part. I started to receive visitors. Male visitors. What they offered was the only way I could make any money. That kept on for a few weeks before the landlord found out and kicked me out of the place. No, I didn't walk the streets. A car came and got me and I was driven to a rooming house.

"It wasn't like this. It was dirty and dingy. The madam was an old hag with a mean temper and liked to throw things at us. The first thing she did was to tell me that she had a record of my activities that she would hand over to the police if I didn't cooperate. What could I do?

"Then one night I had a talk with my roommate. She was a character. Tough as an apple and she knew how to sell herself. I told her all that had happened to me and she laughed like a fiend. The same damned thing had happened to her. But here's the hitch. I described John. He was the guy that put her in the spot, too. She flew off the handle when she heard that. Both of us looked all over for him, but that was the last time I saw him.

"I was part of a big outfit. We were shipped around wherever we were needed. I wound up here quite awhile ago and that's that. Any questions?"

The same old story. I felt sorry for her even if she didn't feel sorry for herself. "How long ago were you in college?" I asked.

"That was twelve years ago."

"Umm." As far as I could see there wasn't a thing to be gained.

I reached in my wallet and pulled out a five spot and a card. "Here's where you can locate me if you dig up anything else. And here's a fin for yourself. I have some heavy thinking to do so I'm going to blow."

She looked at me amazed. "You mean . . . you don't want anything else?"

"No. But thanks anyway. Keep your eyes open."

"I will."

I found a different way out and hit the downstairs hall from a rickety flight of steps that was half hidden behind a flowered set of drapes. The woman in charge was sitting in the waiting room reading. She put down the book long enough to say, "Leaving already? I thought you wanted to spend the night."

As I picked up my hat, I said, "I did, but I guess I'm not as young as I used to be." She didn't bother to get up to let me out.

Back in the car I started up and ran it closer to the house. I wanted to see who might be coming. Jack had a good reason for wanting that place raided or he wouldn't have mentioned it in his book. A show. A show with convenient chambers for the indiscreet later on. A place that quack doctors like to see well packed so they could work their own racket on suckers that got caught up with V. D. Inwardly, I said a silent thanks to Uncle Sam for showing me those posters and films.

I sat back against the cushions and waited for something to happen. Just what, I couldn't say. So far there was no rhyme or reason to anything. It was too jumpy. Jack's death. The people he was connected with. His book of notes and this. The only thing there was in common was an undertone. The deep tone that spelled hate and violence, a current of fear that seemed to fit in wherever I looked. I could feel it, yet see nothing.

Take Eileen: A prostitute. Taking a quick trip to the grave because she got messed up with a rat who knocked her up, played with her awhile, then took off. That kind of guy ought to be hunted down and strung up by the thumbs. I'd like to do it personally. And her roommate. Another dame in the same profession who got there the same way. It must have made Eileen feel pretty low when she found out the same guy put her in the fix, too. John Hanson, never heard of him. She might have been a decent kid, too. Those guys get it in the neck in the long run. But that was over twelve years ago. That would make Eileen about . . . let's see, entered college around eighteen . . . maybe she met him when she was nineteen, and twelve would put her at thirty-one. Hell, she looked a lot older. If her father had been the least bit sensible he could have prevented all this. A kind word when kindness was important, a home to go to, and she never would have been trapped. Just the same, it seemed pretty damned funny that the old man could get wind of what went on in a Midwest college when he was living a thousand miles away in Poughkeepsie, New York. That kind of news travels fast anywhere, though. Probably a jealous schoolgirl with a dirty mind and a poison pen. Maybe another of Hanson's babes. I'll bet he had plenty of them. Going from bad to worse. Not financially—Eileen was making plenty of cash even if she only got a ten-percent cut. The joint she worked in had money written all over it. A syndicated outfit with lots of the long green. For instance, this show tonight. It meant a rake-off in the thousands. And . . .

I was letting my mind ramble on so fast I hardly noticed the taxi that pulled up in front of the stoop. A young punk in a double-breasted suit stepped out and gave a hand to the fat boy with him. A greasy slob, coming in for the show or some fun, maybe both. I thought I recognized the kid from a bookie's uptown, but I wasn't sure. The fat guy I had never seen before. There were no questions at the door, so I supposed they were well known there.

Five minutes later another car drove up and a pair of dillies climbed out. The man, if you could call him that, was done up in a camel's-hair coat, his skinny neck protruding above a flaming-red ascot. He had a marcel that was brand-new. His companion was a woman. The only way you could tell was by the skirt. The rest of her was strictly male. She walked with a swagger and he minced his way to the sidewalk holding on to her arm. Fruit.

She did the bell ringing and pushed him in ahead of her. Fine people. There's everything in this world. It's too bad they were hiding behind the door when sexes were handed out. They got what was left over and not enough of it at that.

I sat there a whole hour watching a cross section of humanity that came from every walk of life. If I had an infrared camera I could have made a fortune. Eileen probably wasn't well read enough to identify persons as being important, but I was. There were four politicians from my own ward there. Plus a few who hardly skipped a week without having their pictures in the papers for something or other. Everyone was going in, no one coming out. That meant the show was on. Generally a half hour was enough time to transact their kind of business.

Twenty minutes went by and no more cars. If Jack had expected to snag somebody in there it wasn't anyone at the party or someone whom he had connections with that I knew about. I didn't get it.

Then I did. Or at least I thought I did.

I started the motor and pulled away from the curb, then made a U turn in the middle of the block. I tried to beat out the red lights, but the traffic got away from me. Even the short cuts didn't help, so I cut back to the main thoroughfare and took it straight up to Jack's apartment.

This time I went in the front door. I broke the seal and the flimsy padlock with my gun butt and opened the lock with one of my skeleton keys. Before I did anything else I went for the phone hoping that it hadn't been disconnected. It hadn't. I dialed my number and waited. Then, "Police Headquarters."

"Hello, give me Captain Chambers, Homicide. Shake it." Pat was on in an instant.

"Captain Chambers speaking."

"Pat, this is Mike Hammer, I'm at Jack's apartment. Listen, get a couple of men and whip up here, and if you took any books from here bring them along. One other thing. Better tell the riot squad to stand by for an emergency call."

Pat grew excited. "What's up, Mike, got anything?"

"I may have," I answered, "but if you don't snap it up I may lose it." I hung up before he could ask any more questions. I turned on the lamp in the living room and pulled out what books were lying between cast bronze ends and stacked in the bookcase. I found what I was looking for. Three of them were college yearbooks, and they were dated from the past fifteen years. I remembered having seen them when I was in the apartment the last time. They didn't mean much then, but they did now.

While I was waiting for Pat I scanned through them. They were student publications, all from Midwestern schools. What I was looking for was a picture of John Hanson.

It might be that simple. Jack saw Eileen after a long time and knew what she was doing. A cop wouldn't have much trouble checking those things. He knew what happened to her and he knew the guy. On the flyleaf of each book was the name and address of a secondhand bookstore near Times Square, and the tab it was typed on was clean, so they had been recently bought. If Jack had tracked the guy down and approached him he set himself up for murder. Maybe the guy had a business or a family, but what he had could easily be wrecked by having that kind of information passed on to the wrong people.

I went through them fast, then again very carefully, but there was no picture labeled with the name Hanson. I was cursing softly to myself when Pat came in. Under his arm he had three more of the same kind of books.

"Here you are, Mike," he said, dumping the books on the sofa beside me. "Now give." In as few words as possible I told him where I stood. He watched me gravely and made me repeat a few things to keep track of things in his mind.

"So you think this Eileen Vickers may be the key, huh?"

I signified with a nod of my head. "Possibly. You go through these books and look for the guy. She said he was tall and good-looking, but dames in love all think their men are good-looking. By the way, why did you pick up these books?"

"Because these three were in the living room, open. He was reading them just before he was killed. It seemed funny to me that he should be going through old college yearbooks and I took them along to match the pics with some of our samples."

"And . . .?"

"And I found two women who had been committed for bigamy, one guy that later hung for murder, and a friend of mine who runs a hardware store downtown and I see every day. Nothing else."

The both of us sat down and read those damn books from cover to cover. When we were done we traded and read them again to make sure we didn't skip anything. John Hanson was nowhere to be found.

"Looks like a wild-goose chase, Mike." Pat was frowning at the pile. He stuck a cigarette in his mouth and lit it. "Are you sure that was what Jack was looking for?"

"Hell, yes, why not? The dates on these things tie in. They're twelve years old." I dragged the black book out of my hip pocket and tossed it to him. "Take a look," I said, "and don't tell me I was withholding evidence."

As Pat glanced through it he said, "I won't. I was up here the day after you. Found it under the bottom drawer of his dresser, didn't you?"

"Yeah, how did you know?"

"At home I happened to drop something over the back of a drawer like that myself. When I thought it over, I knew it was one place we hadn't looked. Incidentally, I found your note."

He finished with the pad and stuck it under his coat. I didn't need it anymore. "I think you may be right, Mike. Where to now?"

"The bookstore. Jack may have had other books. I should have asked Eileen what school she went to, damn it, but I didn't catch on until later."

Pat went to the phone book and thumbed through it until he found the number of the bookstore. The place was closed, but the owner was still there. Pat told him who he was and to stay put until we arrived. I turned out the lights and we left after Pat posted one of his men at the door.

I didn't bother with the jalopy. We piled into the squad car and headed for Times Square with the siren wailing. Traffic pulled off to one side to let us pass and we made record time. The driver turned off on Sixth and stopped across the street from the bookstore.

The blinds were drawn, but a light still glowed from within. Pat knocked and the weazened little proprietor fussed with the lock and let us in. He was nervous as a hen with a yardful of chicks and kept pulling at the bottom of his vest. Pat got to the point after he flashed his badge.

"You had a customer come in here a few days ago and buy several college yearbooks." The little guy shook all over. "Do you keep a record of the sales?"

"Yes and no. We record the sales tax, yes, but the books we don't keep. This is old stock as you can see."

"Never mind," Pat said. "Do you remember what ones he took out with him?"

The guy hesitated a second. "N-no. Maybe I can find out, yes?"

With the little guy leading the way, we went to the rear of the store and he climbed a rickety ladder to the top shelf. "We don't have many calls for these. I remember we had about two dozen. Ah, yes. There are perhaps ten gone."

Ten. Three were in Jack's apartment, and Pat had three. That left four unaccounted for. "Hey," I called up to him, "can you remember what schools they were from?"

He shrugged his skinny shoulders. "I don't know. They have been here a long time. I didn't even take them down. I remember I was busy and showed him where they were and he climbed up and got them."

This wasn't getting us anyplace. I shook the ladder and he grabbed the wall for support. "Take 'em all down," I told him. "Just toss them to me. Come on, we haven't got all night."

He pulled the books from the shelves and let them tumble to the floor. I caught a few, but the rest spilled all over. Pat helped me carry them to the wrapping table, then the little guy came over to join us. "Now," I said to him, "get out your invoices. These must have been signed for when you bought 'em and I want to see the receipts."

"But that was so long ago, I . . ."

"Damn it, shake your tail before I boot it all over the store. Don't be piddling around with me!" He shot off like a scared rabbit.

Pat laid his hand on my arm. "Slack off, Mike. Remember, I work for the city and this guy is a taxpayer."

"So am I Pat. We just haven't got time to fool around, that's all."

He was back in a minute with an armful of dusty ledgers. "Some place in here I have the items marked. You want to look for them now?" I could see he was hoping we'd take them along, otherwise it would mean an all-night job. Pat knew that, too, but he used his head. He called headquarters and asked for a dozen men. Ten minutes later they were there. He told them what to look for and passed the ledgers out.

The guy was a hell of a bookkeeper. His handwriting was hardly legible. How he arrived at his balances I didn't know, but I wasn't after that. I threw down the ledger I had after a half hour and picked up another. I was in the middle of the second when a patrolman called Pat over.

He pointed to a list of items. "This what you're looking for, sir?"

Pat squinted at it. "Mike. Come here."

There it was, the whole list, bought at one time from an auctioneer who had sold the estate of a deceased Ronald Murphy, a book collector.

"That's it," I said. We took the list to the table and compared it with the books there while Pat was dismissing the men. I found the four that were missing. One was from the Midwest, the others were from schools in the East. Now all we had to do was to get a copy of the yearbooks from somewhere.

I handed the list to Pat. "Now locate them. I haven't got an idea where we'll do it."

"I have," Pat said.

"Where?" I asked hopefully.

"Public library."

"At this time of night?"

He gave me a grin. "Cops do have some privileges," he told me. Once again he got on the telephone and made a few calls. When he was done he called the bookman over and pointed to the mess we had made of his wrapping desk. "Want us to help you with that?"

The guy shook his head vigorously. "No, no. In the morning is plenty of time. Very glad to help the police. Come again if you want." The city was full of self-respecting citizens. He'll probably want a ticket fixed sometime and come knocking on Pat's door—as if that could help him in this town.

Pat's calls were very effective. They were waiting for us when we got to the library. An elderly gentleman, looking extremely nervous, and two male secretaries. We passed through the turnstile and a guard locked the door behind us.

The place was worse than a morgue. Its high, vaulted ceilings were never reached by the feeble light that struggled to get out of the bulbs. Our footsteps echoed hollowly through the corridors and came back to us in dull booming sounds. The statues seemed to come alive as our shadows crossed them. The place was a bad spot to be in at night if you had the jitters.

Pat had told him what we were looking for and we wasted no time. The elderly librarian sent his two men somewhere into the bowels of the building and they returned in ten minutes with the four yearbooks.

We sat down there under the light of a table lamp in a reading room and took two books apiece. Four books. Jack had had them and somebody had taken them. He had ten altogether, but the others hadn't been of any use to the one that stole the rest.

The librarian peered at us intently over our shoulders. We flipped page after page. I was about to turn the last leaf of the sophomore section over when I stopped. I found John Hanson. I couldn't speak, I just stared. Now I had the whole picture.

Pat reached out and tapped my hand and pointed to a picture. He had found John Hanson, too. I think Pat caught on as quickly as I did. We both reached for another book and went through them, and we both found John Hanson again. I threw the books on the table and yanked Pat to his feet.

"Come on," I said.

He raced after me, stopping long enough in the main lobby to put through another call for a squad. Then we shot past a startled guard and dashed to the curb and into the police car. Pat really let the siren go full blast and we threaded our way through traffic. Ahead of us we saw the blinking red light of the police truck and pulled up on it. Another car came out of a side street and joined us.

The same cars were still there. The police blocked the street off at either end and fell in behind Pat and me as we went up the stoop. This time there were no three longs and a short. A fire ax crashed against the lock and the splintered door swung inward.

Somebody screamed and others picked it up. The place was a bedlam, but the cops had it under control in a minute. Pat and I didn't stick around downstairs. He let me lead the way through the modern waiting room, up the stairs and into the room on the landing. It was empty. We took the door off the small foyer into the hall of doors and ran to the next to last one on the left.

The door opened under my touch and a blast of cordite fumes stung my nostrils. Eileen Vickers was dead. Her body was completely nude as she lay there on the bed, eyes staring vacantly at the wall. A bullet hole was directly over the heart, a bullet hole that was made by a .45.

We found John Hanson, all right. He lay at the foot of the bed with his head in a puddle of his own blood and brains, and with a hole squarely between the eyes. On the wall was more of his goo, with the plaster cracked from where the bullet entered.

He was a mess, this John Hanson. At least that's what he called himself. I called him Hal Kines.

chapter nine ■■■■■■■■■■■■■■■

WE LEFT THE place exactly as it was. Pat whistled for a patrolman and had him stand guard inside the door. All exits to the house had been blocked off, and the crowd milled within the ring of cops on the main floor. Two other captains and an inspector joined us. I threw them a nod and ran for the back of the house.

Those shootings had taken place not two minutes before we came in. If the killer wasn't in the crowd he was just around the corner. I found the back door in a hurry. It led into an undersized yard that was completely surrounded by an eight-foot-high fence. Someone had taken the trouble to keep the grass cut and the place cleaned out. Even the fence had been white-washed.

I went around that place looking for prints, but the grass hadn't been trampled in a week. If anyone had gone over that fence he certainly would have left some sort of a mark. There was none.

The cellar opened into the place, but the door was locked from the outside with a padlock; so was the door that led between the building and the one next door. The killer never took the back way.

I jumped the steps into the small kitchen and went through the hall to the showroom. Quite a place. All the restraining partitions had been torn down and a stage set up at one end. The cops had the audience back in the cushioned movie-type seats and the girls of the show herded into a compact group on the stage.

Pat came at me from across the room. "What about the back?" he asked breathlessly.

"Nothing doing. He didn't go that way."

"Then the killer is in here. I couldn't find a place even a mouse could get out. The streets are blocked and I got some men behind the houses."

"Let's go over the gang here," I said.

The both of us went down the rows of seats looking over the faces that didn't want to be seen. There was going to be a lot of fixing done tomorrow if some of these jokers didn't want to lose their happy homes. We searched every face. We were looking for George Kalecki, but he either got out in time or never was there.

Neither was the madam.

The homicide boys arrived and we went to Eileen's room. They found what I expected them to find. Nothing. Downstairs I could hear the anguished wails of the girls and the louder voices of some of the men yapping in pretty determined tones. How the commissioner was going to get around this was beyond me. When the pics were taken Pat and I took a good look at what was left of Hal Kines. With a pencil I traced a few very faint lines along his jaw line.

"Very neat, isn't it?"

Pat shot a quick look at me. "Neat enough, but tell me about it. I know who, but not why."

I had difficulty keeping my voice under control as I spoke. "Hal isn't a college kid. I caught that when I saw a shot of him and George against the background of the *Morro Castle,* but I never fitted it in. This bastard was a procurer. I told you George had his finger in the rackets. I thought it was the numbers, but it turned out to be more than that. He was part of a syndicate that ran houses of prostitution. Hal did the snatch jobs, oh, very subtly, then turned them over to George. It wouldn't surprise me if Hal had been the big cheese."

Pat looked more closely at the lines on his face and pointed out a few more just under his hairline. They were hard to see because the blood had matted the hair into a soggy mass.

"Don't you see, Pat," I went on. "Hal was one of these guys who looked eternally young. He helped nature a bit with a few plastic-surgery operations. Look at those yearbooks we found, every one from a different college. That's where he got his women, small-town girls going to an out-of-state school. Knocks them up, puts the squeeze on them and here they are. God knows how many he got from each place. I bet he never spent more than one semester in a place. Probably worked out a scheme for falsifying his high-school records to gain admittance, then got busy with his dirty work. Once he had the dames, they couldn't get out of it any more than a mobster can break away from the gang."

"Very cute," Pat said, "very cute."

"Not too," I told him. "This wrecks my theory. I had him slated for the first kill, but I know now he didn't do it. Jack got on to him somehow, and either Hal saw the books in his apartment and caught wise or the other one did. This was why Jack wanted the place raided tonight, before this could happen. He knew Hal would be here and he wanted him caught with his pants down. If I had taken his advice Eileen might have been alive."

Pat walked over to the wall and dug the slug out of the plaster with a penknife. The one in Eileen hadn't gone all the way through; the coroner was busy dislodging it. When he had it out he handed it to Pat. Under the light Pat examined them carefully before he spoke. Then, "They're both .45's, Mike. And dumdums."

He didn't have to tell me that. "Somebody sure likes to make sure they stay dead," I said through tight lips. "The killer again. There's only one. The same lousy bastard that shot Jack. Those slugs will match up sure as hell. Damn," I spat out, "he's kill crazy! Dumdums in the gut, head and heart. Pat, I'm going to enjoy putting a bullet in that crazy son of a bitch more than I enjoy eating. I'd sooner work him over with a knife first."

"You're not going to do anything of the sort," Pat remarked softly.

The coroner's men got the bodies out of there in a hurry. We went downstairs again and checked with the cops who were taking down the names and addresses of the people. The patrol wagon was outside and the girls were loading into it. An officer came up to Pat and saluted him.

"No one got through the line, sir."

"Okay. Have some men hold and the rest search the alleyways

and adjacent buildings. Make everyone identify himself satisfactorily or arrest them. I don't care who they are, understand?"

"Yes, sir." The cop saluted and hurried away.

Pat turned to me. "This madam, would you recognize her again?"

"Hell, yes. Why?"

"I have a folder of persons convicted or suspected of running call houses at the office. I want you to look them over. We got her name from the girls, or at least the only name they knew her by. She was called Miss June. None of the guests here knew her at all. Half the time one of the girls answered the door. She always came herself if the proper signal wasn't given."

I held Pat back a moment. "But what about George Kalecki. He's the guy I want."

Pat grinned. "I have the dragnet out for him. Right now a thousand men are looking for the guy. Think you stand a better chance?"

I let that one ride. Before I went looking for George Kalecki I wanted to do a few other things first. Even if he was the killer, there were others behind the racket that had to be nailed and I wanted them all, not just the trigger puller. It was like a turkey dinner. The whole outfit would be the meal, the killer the dessert. I wish I knew how Jack had gotten the lead on Hal. Now I would never know.

But Jack had connections. Maybe he had run across Hal before, or knew Kalecki's end of it and suspected the rest, and when he met up with Eileen, put two and two together. A guy that operated as long as Hal had couldn't cover himself completely. There had to be a break in the trail somewhere. Whatever Jack did, he did it fast. He knew right where to look to find John Hanson, and he found him the way we did and maybe plenty more times—in the yearbooks of the colleges.

Even if Hal killed Jack, how did his own murderer get the gun? That weapon was as hot as the killer and not a toy to be passed around. No, I didn't think Hal killed Jack. He might have spotted the books and told someone else. That would be the killer. That was what the killer was after. Or was it? Maybe it was just incidental. Maybe the killer only had a remote tie-up with Hal. If that was it Jack was killed for another reason, and the killer, knowing there still was the bare possibility of being traced through that tie-up, didn't take the chance and swiped the books to keep Hal clean.

And where the hell did that leave me? Right up the creek again.

I couldn't sit back and wait for something to happen again and work from there. Right now I had to start thinking. Little things were beginning to show their heads. Not much, but enough to show that behind it all was a motive. I didn't see it yet, but I would. I wasn't after a killer now. I was after a motive.

I told Pat that I was going home to bed and he wrote me a pass to get through the police lines. I walked down the street and gave the note to a red-faced cop and went on. A cruising cab came by and I grabbed it to Jack's apartment. My buggy was still outside, and after I paid off the cabby I got in my own heap. There was a lot of work to do tomorrow and I needed some sleep.

Twenty minutes later I was home in bed smoking a cigarette before I went to sleep, still thinking. I couldn't get anywhere, so I crushed out the butt and turned over.

My first stop after breakfast was Kalecki's apartment. As I expected, Pat had been there before me. I asked the cop on duty at the entrance if there was any message for me and he handed over a sealed envelope. I ripped the flap open and pulled out a sheet of paper. Pat had scrawled. "Mike . . . nothing here. He pulled out without bothering to pack a bag." He signed it with a large "P." I tore the note up and dumped the pieces in a trash basket outside the apartment house.

It was a fine day. The sun was warm and the streets full of kids making a racket like a pack of squirrels. I drove to the corner and stopped in a cigar store where I put in a call to Charlotte's office. She wasn't there, but her secretary had been told to tell me that if I called, I could find her in Central Park on the Fifth Avenue side near 68th Street.

I drove in from the cutoff on Central Park West and drove all around the place, circling toward Fifth. When I came out I parked on 67th and walked back to the park. She wasn't on any of the benches, so I hopped the fence and cut across the grass to the inside walk. The day had brought out a million strollers, it seemed like. Private nurses in tricky rigs went by with a toddler at their heels, and more than once I got the eye.

A peanut vendor had just finished giving me change when I saw Charlotte. She was pushing a baby carriage toward me, waving her hand frantically to catch my attention. I hurried up to her.

"Hello, kitten," I said. It made my mouth water to look at her. This time she had on a tight green suit. Her hair resembled a waterfall cascading over her collar. Her smile was brighter than the day.

"Hello, Mike. I've been waiting for you." She held out her hand

and I took it. A firm grip, not at all like a woman's. Without letting go I hooked her hand under my arm and fell behind the carriage. "We must look like the happiest newlyweds in the world," she laughed.

"Not so new," I said, motioning toward the carriage. Her face flushed a little and she rubbed her head against mine, "How come you're not working?" I asked her.

"On a day like this? Besides, I don't have an appointment until two, and a friend asked me if I would mind her child while she attended to some business."

"Like kids?"

"I love them. Someday I'm going to have six of my own."

I whistled. "Wait up, take it easy. Maybe I won't make that much money. Six mouths are a lot to feed."

"So what, I'm a working girl, and, er, is that a proposal, Mr. Hammer?"

"Could be," I grinned. "I haven't been pinned down yet, but when I look at you I'm ready to be."

If the conversation had gone any further there's no telling where it would have wound up. But I got back to the case again. "By the way, Charlotte, have you seen the morning papers?"

"No, why?" she glanced at me curiously.

"Hal Kines is dead."

Her jaw dropped and wrinkles of amazement appeared in her forehead. "No," she breathed heavily. I took a tabloid out of my back pocket and showed her the headlines. I could see that she was taken aback. "Oh, Mike, that is terrible! What happened?"

I pointed toward an empty bench. "Can we sit down a few minutes?"

Charlotte consulted her watch and shook her head. "No," she told me, "I have to meet Betty in a few minutes. Tell you what, walk me to the gate, then we can drive back to my office for a few drinks after I meet her. You can tell me on the way."

I went through the entire previous evening without omitting a detail. Charlotte listened carefully without once asking a question. Her mind was trying for the psychological aspect of it. I had to stop near the end. Betty was waiting for her. After the introduction, we had a few minutes' chat and said good-bye to Betty, who walked off with the baby.

We went in the other direction, following the stone wall of the fence to 67th. I don't think we had gone more than ten feet, when a car pulled abreast of us. No time to think. I saw the ugly snout of the gun sticking out the window and landed in a heap on Charlotte. The bullet smashed against the wall waist high, throwing rock splinters in our faces. George Kalecki didn't have time for a second shot. He threw the car into gear and went tearing down Fifth Avenue. If it had worked it would have been perfect. No other cars around to give chase. For the first time, not even a taxi.

I picked Charlotte up and dusted her off. Her face was white and shaken, but her voice was steady enough. Two strollers came hurrying up, thinking we had fallen. Before they reached us, I got the slug from the dirt under the wall where it had dropped. It was a .45. I thanked the two who tried to help us, explaining that we had tripped, and we went on.

Charlotte waited a moment, then said: "You're getting close, Mike. Somebody wants you out of the way."

"I know it. And I know who that was—our friend, Kalecki." I gave a short laugh. "He's scared. It won't be long now. That skunk is ready to break any minute. If he weren't he wouldn't make a play for me in broad daylight."

"But, Mike, please don't laugh about it. It wasn't that funny."

I stopped and put my arms around her shoulders. I could feel her trembling a little. "I'm sorry, darling. I'm used to being shot at. You might have gotten hit, too. Let me take you home, you'll have to change your clothes. That spill didn't do you much good."

Charlotte didn't speak much riding home. She started to, but stopped. Finally I said, "What is it, Charlotte?"

She frowned a little. "Do you think it was because of the rash promise you made to Jack after he was killed that Kalecki wants you out of the way?"

"Maybe. That's the best reason I know of. Why?"

"Could it be that you know more than anyone else concerning this whole affair?"

I thought that over a moment before I said, "I don't think so. The police have every bit of information I have except, perhaps, the incentive and the personal insight I picked up."

We drove on in silence after that. It was nearly ten o'clock when we got to the apartment. We went up the stairs instead of waiting for the elevator and rang the bell. No one came to the door and Charlotte fumbled for her key. "Damn," she said. "I forgot this is the maid's day off." We went inside and the bell rang again when we opened the door.

"Make a drink while I shower, Mike." Charlotte laid a bottle of bourbon on the coffee table and went into the kitchen for some ice and ginger ale.

"Okay. Do you mind if I use your phone first?"

"Not at all. Go right ahead," she called back.

I dialed Pat's number and had to wait for the operator to go through a half-dozen extensions before he finally located him. "Pat?"

"Yeah, Mike, go ahead."

"Get this. Kalecki didn't take a powder, he's still in the city."

"How do you know?"

"He tried to dust me off a little while ago." Pat listened intently as I gave him the details. When I got through, he asked:

"Did you get the number of the car?"

"Uh-uh. It was a late model Caddy, about a '41. Dark blue with lots of chrome. He passed me going toward the city."

"Swell, Mike, I'll put it on the air. Have you got the bullet with you?"

"Hell, yes. And it's a .45, too. Better get ballistics to check it. This one wasn't a dumdum, though. Just a nice normal slug. Suppose I drive down to see you this afternoon."

"Do that," Pat answered. "I'll be here the rest of the day unless something breaks.

"And one other thing, Mike," he added.

"Yeah?"

"We checked the slugs that killed Kines and the Vickers woman."

"They came from the same gun? The one that . . ."

"Right, Mike. The killer again."

"Damn," I said.

I hung up and took the slug from my pocket. Maybe it would match, maybe not. I was thinking of the rod Kalecki had in his luggage under his bed. And he had a permit for it too, he said. I wished now that I had taken that gun along to compare it in a ballistics box instead of leaving it to my sense of smell and sight to determine whether or not it had been fired recently.

I wrapped the hunk of metal in a wad of paper and stuck it in my pocket, then whipped up a pair of highballs. I called out to Charlotte to come and get it, but she yelled for me to bring it in to her.

Maybe I should have waited a second, or knocked. I did neither. Charlotte was standing beside the bed completely naked. When I saw her beautiful body that way my blood boiled inside me and the drink shook in my hand. She was more beautiful than I imagined. So damned smooth. She was more startled than I. She made a grab for the robe on the bed and held it in front of her, but not before I saw a blush suffuse her entire body.

She was having as hard a time getting her breath as I was. "Mike," she said. Her voice trembled slightly when she spoke, and her eyes never left mine. I turned my back while she slipped into the robe, then turned back and handed her the drink.

Both of us finished them in one draught. It added nothing to the fire that was running through me. I felt like reaching out and squeezing her to pieces. We put the glasses down on the dresser top. We were awfully close then. One of those moments.

She came into my arms with a rush, burying her face in my neck. I tilted her head back and kissed her eyes. Her mouth opened for me and I kissed her, hard. I knew I was hurting her, but she didn't pull away. She returned that kiss with her lips, her arms and her body. She was on fire too, trying desperately to get close to me through space that wasn't there any more.

I had my arm around her shoulders and my hands fastened in her hair, crushing her to me. Never before had I felt like this, but then, never before had I been in love. She took her mouth away from mine and lay in my arms, limp, breathing heavily, her eyes closed.

"Mike," she whispered, "I want you."

"No," I said.

"Yes. You must."

"No."

"But, Mike, why? Why?"

"No, darling, it's too beautiful to spoil. Not now. Our time will come, but it must be right."

I put my arm under her and carried her out of the room. If I stayed in that bedroom any longer I couldn't have held on to my sanity. I kissed her again as she lay in my arms, then put her down outside the bathroom door and mussed her hair. "Go take your shower," I said in her ear.

She smiled at me through sleepy eyes and entered, then closed the door softly. I picked up the glasses, and for a brief second eyed the bed, longingly. Maybe I was a damned fool, I don't know. I went on into the living room.

I waited until I heard the shower running before I picked up the phone. Charlotte's secretary answered promptly with the usual hello.

"This is Mike Hammer again," I said. "I'm expecting a friend and I told him to call your office, so when he does tell him where I went, will you?"

"Oh, that won't be necessary," she replied. "He already has. I told him you'd be in the park. Did you miss him?"

"No, he'll be along," I lied.

So, somebody is on my tail, I told myself as I hung up. Good old George. Followed me, lost me, but figured I'd see Charlotte, very clever.

I made another drink, then stretched out on the sofa. He must have tailed me and I never got wise. I couldn't figure how he knew I'd see Charlotte unless it was written all over me. They say love is like that. But what a way to get put on the spot. He picked the time and place nicely. If I hadn't ducked, Kalecki would have scored a bull's-eye. He did his shooting at point-blank range. What the hell, Kalecki knew the score. If the cops picked him up in the dragnet it would be a miracle. I'll bet he had plenty of places he could hole up in if the time came. George was a smart apple. I wasn't worried about the police flushing him any more. Mr. Kalecki was reserved—for me. Pat was going to be awfully sore.

Charlotte was out and dressed in record time. Neither of us spoke about what had happened, but each knew that it was foremost in the other's mind. She made herself a drink, then sat down beside me. "How did you know I was coming today?"

She gave me a bright smile. "Mike, darling, I've been expecting you ever since I saw you. Or am I doing it wrong?"

"Not as far as I'm concerned."

"But you told me that you like to do the chasing."

"Not with you. Time is too damned important."

When she settled in my arms I told her about the call to her office. She didn't like it a bit. "You're not trying to be very careful, Mike. If it is Kalecki, he is smart. Please, Mike, watch yourself. If anything happens to you, I'll . . ."

"You'll what?"

"Oh, Mike, can't you see that I love you?"

I stroked her golden hair and blew in her ear. "Yes, silly, I can see it. It must be sticking out all over me the same way."

"Yes," she said, "it is." We both grinned at each other. I felt like a school kid. "Now, let's get back to business before I rush off to the office," she went on. "You came to see me for something besides just being nice. What was it?"

It was my turn to be amazed. "Now, how the hell did you know that?" I demanded.

Charlotte patted my hand. "How many times do I have to remind you that I am a practicing psychiatrist? It doesn't mean that I can read minds, but I can study people, observe their behavior and determine what lies underneath. Especially," here she gave a coy smile, "when you really take an interest in a person."

"You win." I blew a couple of smoke rings and continued. "What I want is everything you know about Hal Kines."

She came back to earth abruptly at the mention of his name. "That's what I thought after you spoke about what happened. Well, you know that he was in a medical school. Pre-med to be exact. From what you said, he was there ostensibly to procure women for this vice syndicate. Isn't that an unusual way of doing it?"

"No. Not when you know people," I said. "In order to have a good hold on the girls they have to break them away from their homes, then get them trapped in the mill. I imagine they have some sort of evidence concerning their activities that they hold over their heads. So what can the girls do? They've been betrayed, kicked out of their homes, no one to turn to, but the door is open to the old profession. At least they can eat and have a roof over their heads—and make plenty of cash. Then once they're in they can't get out even if they wanted to. It takes time, but it's big business and pays off. Using a method like this, Hal could get the girl he wanted without running too much of a personal risk."

"I see." She mulled over what I had said a moment, then gave me the rest. "Anyway, I gave a lecture at the school by invitation of the board and, after examining the records and work of the student body specializing in psychiatry, chose several students to study my clinical methods. Hal Kines was one of them. He was an excellent worker, knew what he was doing every minute. He was far in advance of the others.

"At first I credited it to natural ability and a medical home background, but now I can see that it was simply the result of so much training in the field. After sixteen years of being exposed to teaching you are bound to pick up something."

"I guess so," I cut in. "How about his outside contacts?"

"He lived at an apartment hotel three blocks from me while he was here. During the time he was at school he lived in a dorm, I suppose. On weekends he would visit the clinic and stay with Mr. Kalecki. Hal never spoke much about outside matters, he was so wrapped up in his work. He was in a scrape one day and Jack Williams helped him out."

I nodded. "Yeah, I know all about that from Hal himself. What about his personal side? Did he ever make a pass at you?"

"No. Never attempted one. Do you think he might have been, er, after me to join his syndicate?"

"Why, that dirty . . ." I stopped there when I saw her laughing silently at me. "I doubt that. You were too smart to get caught in that kind of web. I think he was with you either to have an excuse to stay in the city, or really study psychiatry to help him in his work."

"Did it ever occur to you that he might have been here to kill Jack?"

That idea wasn't a new one to me. I'd been playing with it all day. "Could have been. I thought it over. Maybe he was here because Jack had already caught on and was making him stay. Jack was soft-hearted, but not when it came to a thing like that. Not being in the department any longer, he couldn't put the screws on him officially, but held something over his head to make him stay."

"Then who killed Jack—Hal?"

"That," I said, "is something I'd give both legs and one arm to know. Just so long as I had one arm to shoot with. And that's something I'm going to find out before long."

"And what about Hal and this girl, Eileen?"

"The killer got them both. The way I see it, Hal Kines went there to kill the girl, but before he got the chance the killer knocked them both off."

"But if that was the case, how would Jack have known he would be there to kill her?"

"You've got something there, Charlotte. Maybe Jack knew he'd be there for some reason. Think so?"

"Perhaps. Either that or he knew the killer would be there, too. But until then the killer hadn't killed, so he had another purpose in the visit. Sounds sort of scrambled, doesn't it?"

"You're not kidding," I laughed. "But as the plot thickens it thins out, too. Whatever the motive, it takes in a lot of people. Three of them are dead, one is running around the city taking potshots at me, and the killer is someplace sitting back quietly giving all of us the horse laugh. What the hell, let him laugh. He won't be doing it much longer. There's too many people working on this case and they'll uncover something. Murder is a hard thing to hide. Pat is setting a fast pace in this race. He wants the trigger-happy son as badly as I do, but I'll be damned if he's going to get him. From now on I'm going to get out in front of Pat and stay there. Let him stick close to my heels; when the time comes for me to put a bullet in the killer's gut I'm going to be alone.

Just me, the rat and a single bullet. It'll go in neat, right in the soft part of the belly. One steel-jacketed slug that will be as effective as ten dumdums."

Charlotte was listening intently, her eyes wide. She was making a typical study of me as though she were hearing the story of a confessed murderer and trying to analyze the workings of the mind. I cut in short and gave her a friendly push. "Now you think I'm off my nut, I bet."

"No, Mike, not at all. Have you been like that just since the war? So hard, I mean."

"I've always been like that," I said, "as long as I could remember. I hate rats that kill for the fun of it. The war only taught me a few tricks I hadn't learned before. Maybe that's why I lived through it."

I checked my watch; it was getting late. "If you want to keep your appointment, you'd better hurry."

Charlotte nodded. "Drive me back to the office?"

"Sure. Get your coat."

We drove back slowly, timing it so that we'd have as much time together as possible. We made small talk, mentioning neither the case nor the near affair in the apartment. When we reached Park Avenue, and turned off to stop, Charlotte said, "When will I see you again, Mike?"

"Soon," I answered. "If the joker that called today to see where I went tries it again, have your secretary tell him that I'm meeting you on this corner. Then try to get hold of me and maybe we can ambush the lug. It was Kalecki, all right; your secretary will probably recognize his voice when she hears it again."

"Okay, Mike. What if Mr. Chambers calls on me?"

"In that case, verify the story of the shooting, but forget about the phone call. If we can trap him, I want it to be my own party."

She leaned in and kissed me again before she left. As she walked away I watched the flashing sleekness of her legs disappear around the corner. She was a wonderful woman. And all mine. I felt like I should let out a loud whoop and do a jig.

A car honked behind me, so I threw the car into gear and pulled away from the curb. I was stopped for a red light two blocks away when I heard my name yelled from across the street. The cars alongside me obscured the person, but I could see a brown-suited figure dancing between them trying to get to my jalopy. I opened the door and he got in. "Hello, Bobo," I said. "What are you doing up this way?"

Bobo was all excited over meeting me. "Golly, Mike. Sure is

nice seeing you. I work up here. No place special, just all the places." Words bubbled out of him like out of a water faucet. "Where are you going?"

"Well, I was going downtown, but maybe I can drive you someplace. Where are you going?"

Bobo scratched his head. "Lessee. Guess I can go downtown first. Gotta deliver a letter around Canal Street."

"Swell, I'll drop you off there."

The light turned and I swung on to Broadway and turned left. Bobo would wave at the girls on the street, but I knew how he felt. "Hear anything more about Kalecki?" I asked.

He shook his head. "Naw. Something's happened to him. I saw one of the guys today and he ain't working for him no more."

"How about Big Sam's place? No news from there?"

"Nope. Anyway, since you beat up the two jigs nobody will talk to me. They're scared I might get you after 'em." Bobo let out a gleeful chuckle. "They think I'm a tough guy, too. My landlady heard about it and told me to stay away from you. Isn't that funny, Mike?"

I had about as many friends as a porcupine up that way. "Yeah," I said. "How's the bee situation?"

"Oh, good, good, good. Got me a queen bee. Hey. That wasn't true what you said. A queen bee don't need a king bee. It said so in the book."

"Then how are you going to get more bees?" That puzzled him.

"Guess they lay eggs, or something," he muttered.

Canal Street lay straight ahead, so I let Bobo out when I stopped for the red light. He gave me a breezy "so long" and took off down the street at a half trot. He was a good kid. Another harmless character. Nice though.

chapter ten ■■■■■■■■■■■■■■■■■■■

PAT WAS WAITING for me on the firing range. A uniformed patrolman took me to the basement and pointed him out. Pat was cursing over a bad score when I tapped him on the shoulder.

"Having trouble, bub?" I grinned at him.

"Nuts. I think I need a new barrel in this gun." He took another shot at the moving target, a figure of a man, and got it high up on the shoulder.

"What's the matter with that, Pat?"

"Hell, that would just knock him over." Pat was a perfectionist. He caught me laughing at him and handed me the gun. "Here, you try it."

"Not with that." I pulled the .45 out and kicked the slide back. The target popped up and moved across the range. The gun bucked in my hand. I let three go one after the other. Pat stopped the target and looked at the three holes in the figure's head.

"Not bad." I felt like pasting him.

"Why don't you tell me I'm an expert?" I said. "That's shooting where it counts."

"Phooey. You've just been working at it." I shoved the rod under my coat and Pat pocketed his. He pointed toward the elevator.

"Let's go up. I want to check that slug. Got it with you?" I took the .45 out and unwrapped it, then handed it over. Pat studied it in the elevator, but markings weren't defined clearly enough to be certain of anything. A bullet hitting a stone wall has a lot less shape left than one that has passed through a body.

The ballistics room was empty save for ourselves. Pat mounted the slug inside a complicated slide gadget and I turned the lights out. There was a screen in front of us, and on it was focused an image of two bullets. One was from the killer's gun, the other was the slug Kalecki fired at me. My souvenir still had some lines from the bore of the gun that came out under magnification.

Pat turned the bullet around on its mount, trying to find markings that would match with the other. He thought he did once, but when he transposed the images one on top of the other there was quite a difference. After he had revolved the slug several times he flicked the machine off and turned on the lights. "No good, Mike. It isn't the same gun. If Kalecki did the other shooting, he used another gun."

"That isn't likely. If he kept it after the first killing he'd hang on to it."

Pat agreed and rang for one of his men. He handed the bullet over to him and told him to photograph it and place it in the files. We sat down together and I gave him the full details of the shooting and my views on the Kines kill. He didn't say much. Pat is one of those cops who keep facts in their heads. He stores them away without forgetting an item, letting them fume until they come to the surface by themselves.

It constantly amazed me that there were men like him on the force. But then, when you get past the uniforms and into the inner workings of the organization you find the real thinkers. They have all the equipment in the world to work with and plenty of inside contacts. The papers rag the cops too much, I thought, but in the pinch they called the game. Not much went on that they didn't know about. There was vice. As much as in any outfit, but there were still men like Pat that no money could buy. I would have been one myself if there weren't so damn many rules and regulations to tie a guy down.

When I finished, Pat stretched and said, "Nothing I can add to it for you. Wish I could. You've been a great help, Mike. Now tell me one thing. You gave me facts, this time give me an opinion. Who do you think did it?"

"That, chum, is the sixty-four-dollar question," I countered. "If I had any definite idea, you'd have a justified homicide on your hands. I'm beginning to think of someone outside of those we know. Hell, man, look at the corpses we have floating around. And Kalecki on the loose with a rod. Maybe he did it. He has reason to. Maybe it's the guy behind him again. It could fit in with this syndicate that runs the houses of prostitution. Or the numbers racket George worked. Jack could have found out about that, too. Maybe it was a revenge kill. Hal fouled up enough women in his life. Suppose one of them found out how he did it and made a play for him. When she saw that Jack was going to arrest him she killed Jack, then killed Hal, shooting Eileen to keep her from spouting off what she had seen."

"Maybe it wasn't a girl like that. Could be the brother or father of one. Or a boy friend for that matter. There's lots of angles."

"I thought of that, Mike. For my money, it's the most plausible idea I've had." Pat stood up. "I want you to come upstairs with me. We have a friend of yours there that you might like to see."

A friend? I couldn't begin to guess whom he was talking about. When I queried him about it he smiled and told me to be patient. He led me into a small room. Two detectives were there with a woman. Both of them fired questions at her, but received no answers. She sat with her back to the door and I didn't recognize her until I stood in front of her.

Friend, hell. She was the madam that ran out the night Hal and Eileen were killed.

"Where did you pick her up, Pat?"

"Not far from here. She was wandering on the streets at four A.M. and the patrolman picked her up on suspicion."

I turned to the madam. Her eyes were vacant from the long hours of questioning. She held her arms across her ample breasts in a defiant attitude, though I could see that she was near the breaking point. "Remember me?" I asked her.

She stared at me through sleep-filled eyes a moment, then said dejectedly, "Yes, I remember."

"How did you get out of that house when it was raided?"

"Go to hell."

Pat drew up a chair in front of her and sat backwards on it. He saw what I was driving at right away. "If you refuse to tell us," Pat said quietly, "you're liable to find yourself facing a charge for murder. And we can make it stick."

She dropped her arms at that one and licked her lips. This time she was scared. Then her fear passed and she sneered. "You go to hell, too. I didn't kill them."

"Perhaps not," Pat answered, "but the real killer left the same way you did. How do we know you didn't show him the way? That makes you an accessory and you might just as well have pulled the trigger."

"You're crazy!" Gone was the composure she had the first time I met her. She didn't look respectable any more. By now her hair had a scraggly appearance and the texture of her skin showed through in the light. White, porous skin. She bared her teeth and swallowed. "I—I was alone."

"The charge will still stick."

Her hands fell into her lap and shook noticeably. "No. I was alone. I was at the door when the police came up. I knew what it was. I ran for the exit and left."

"Where is the exit?" I cut in.

"Under the stairs. A button that works the panel is built into the woodwork."

I thought back fast. "All right, so you saw the cops coming. If you ran for the stairs the killer would have been coming down as you ran out. Who was it?"

"I didn't see anybody, I tell you! Oh, why don't you let me alone!" Her nerve broke and she sank into the chair with her face buried in her hands.

"Take her out," Pat directed the two detectives. He looked at me. "What do you make of it?"

"Reasonable enough," I told him. "She saw us coming and beat it. But the killer had a little luck. We broke in about two minutes after the shooting. The rooms are soundproofed and no one heard the shots. The killer probably figured on mixing with the crowd and leaving when the show was over or before, if there was nobody at the door. He was coming down the stairs and heard us.

"However, when the madam made a run for it those plans had to be tossed overboard. He ducked back long enough so the old hag didn't see him and followed her through the secret panel. When we examine it I'll bet we find that it doesn't close very fast. We ran upstairs, you remember, and the others took care of the guests. The way we set the road block, the killer had time to get away before the policemen could take their places. We were in a hurry and didn't have a chance to plan this thing."

I proved to be right. We went back to the house and looked for the panel. It was right where she said it was. The thing wasn't too cleverly contrived. The button was built into the heart of a carved flower. It activated a one sixteenth horsepower motor connected to the electric circuit with a cutoff and a reverse. Pat and I entered the passage. Light seeping through the cracks in the wall was all we needed. When the place was redecorated this was built in. It ran back ten feet, took a sharp left turn and steps led down to the basement. There we were between walls. A door led into the basement of the house next door. When it was closed it looked like a part of the wall.

It was a safe bet that the people in the house didn't know that it was there themselves. The rest was easy. Out the basement door to an open yard that led to the street. The time consumed was less than a minute. We went through the passageway with a searchlight, not skipping an inch, but there wasn't a clue to be found. Generally when someone was in haste he could be counted on to lose something or mark a trail. But no such luck. We went back to the waiting room and pulled out a smoke.

"Well?"

"Well what, Pat?"

"Well, I guess you were right about the timing," he laughed.

"Looks that way. What did you get on Kines' past, if anything?"

"Reports from twenty-seven schools so far. He never spent more than a semester anywhere except at this last place. More often a month was enough. When he left there were several girls who'd dropped from the school too. Add it up and you get a nice tally. We've had a dozen men on the phone all day and they're not half finished yet."

I thought that over and cursed Hal before I said, "What did he have in his pockets when the boys went over him?"

"Nothing much. Fifty some in bills, a little loose change, a driver's license and an owner's certificate for his car. There were some club cards, too, but of the school. He went around clean. We found his car. It was empty except for a pair of silk panties in the glove compartment. By the way, how did he get in here if you had your eyes open?"

I dragged on the butt, thinking over those that came in here. "Got me. He never came alone, that's a sure thing. The only way he could have done it was to impersonate someone by stuffing pillows or something under his jacket, or . . ." I snapped my fingers. "Now I remember. A crowd of six or more came in and they blocked out a few others that were behind them. They all mingled at the foot of the steps and came in together to get off the street as fast as they could."

"Was he alone?" Pat waited anxiously for my answer.

I had to shake my head. "I can't say, Pat. It does seem funny that he would come in here deliberately with the murderer, knowing that he was going to get knocked off."

The afternoon was running into evening and we decided to call it a day. Pat and I separated outside and I drove home to clean up. The case was beginning to get on my nerves. It was like trying to get through a locked door with a bulldog tearing at you.

So far I had investigated a lot of angles; now I had one more to go. I wanted to find out about that strawberry mark on a certain twin's hip.

I had my dinner sent up from a place down at the corner and polished off a quart of beer with it. It was nearly nine when I put in a call to the Bellemy apartment. A soft voice answered.

"Miss Bellemy?"

"Yes."

"This is Mike Hammer."

"Oh," she hesitated a second, then. "Yes?"

"Is this Mary or Esther?"

"Esther Bellemy. What can I do for you, Mr. Hammer?"

"Can I see you this evening?" I asked. "I have some questions I'd like to ask you."

"Can't they be asked over the phone?"

"Hardly. It would take too long. May I come up?"

"All right. I'll be waiting."

I thanked her and said good-bye, then climbed into my coat and went downstairs to my car.

Esther was the replica of her sister. If there was a difference, I couldn't see it. I hadn't taken time to look for any the first time

I met them. Probably all in the personality. Mary was strictly a nymphomaniac, now let's see how this sister was.

She greeted me cordially enough. She was wearing a dinner dress that was a simple thing, cunningly revealing the lovely lines of her body. Like Mary, she too had a tan and the appearance of having led an athletic life. Her hair was different. Esther had hers rolled up into a fashionable upsweep. That was the only thing I objected to. With me, a girl in upswept hair looks like she needs a pail and mop, ready to swab down the kitchen floor. But the way she was otherwise built more than made up for that objection.

I took a seat on the divan I had before. Esther went to a cabinet and took out glasses and a bottle of Scotch. When she came back with the ice and had the drinks poured she said, "What is it you wanted me to tell you, Mr. Hammer?"

"Call me Mike," I said politely. "I'm not used to formalities."

"Very well, Mike." We settled back with the drinks.

"How well did you know Jack?"

"Casually. It was a friendship that comes with constantly meeting after an introduction, but not an intimate one."

"And George Kalecki? How well did you know him?"

"Not well at all. I didn't like him."

"Your sister gave me the same impression. Did he ever make a pass at you?"

"Don't be silly." She thought a moment before continuing. "He was grouchy about something the night of the party. Hardly sociable, I'd say. He didn't strike me as being a gentleman. There was something about his manner that was repulsive."

"That isn't unusual. He was a former racketeer. Still active in some circles, too."

When she crossed her legs I couldn't think of anything more to ask her. Why don't women learn to keep their skirts low enough to keep men from thinking the wrong things? Guess that's why they wear them short.

Esther saw my eyes following the outlines of her legs and made the same old instinctive motion of covering up. It didn't do a bit of good. "On with the game," she told me.

"What do you do for a living, if you don't mind?" I knew the answer already, but asked it just to have something to say.

Her eyes glittered impishly. "We have a private income from stock dividends. Father left us his share in some mills down South. Why, are you looking for a rich wife?"

I raised my eyebrows. "No. But if I were I'd be up here more often. What about your home? You have quite an estate, haven't you?"

"About thirty acres in lawn and ten in second-growth woods. A twenty-two-room house sits right in the middle surrounded by a swimming pool, several tennis courts and generally a round dozen ardent swains who never tire of telling me how lovely I am just to get their paws on half of it."

I whistled. "Hell, someone told me you occupied a modest residence." Esther laughed gaily, the sound coming from deep in her throat. With her head tilted back like that she gave me the full view of her breasts. They were as alive as she was.

"Would you like to visit me sometime, Mike?"

I didn't have to think that over. "Sure. When?"

"This Saturday. I'm having quite a few up there to see a tennis match under lights at night. Myrna Devlin is coming. Poor girl, it's the least I can do for her. She's been so broken up since Jack died."

"That's an idea. I'll drive her up. Anybody else coming that I know?"

"Charlotte Manning. No doubt you've met her."

"No doubt," I grinned.

She saw what I meant and wiggled a finger at me. "Don't get any ideas like that, Mike."

I tried to suppress a smile. "How am I going to have any fun in a twenty-two-room house if I don't get ideas?" I teased her.

The laugh in her eyes died out and was replaced by something else. "Why do you think I'm asking you up as *my* guest?" she said.

I put my drink down on the coffee table, then circled it and sat down beside her. "I don't know, why?"

She put her arms around my neck and pulled my mouth down close to hers. "Why don't you find out?"

Her mouth met mine, her arms getting tighter behind me. I leaned on her heavily, letting my body caress hers. She rubbed her face against mine, breathing hotly on my neck. Whenever I touched her she trembled. She worked a hand free and I heard snaps on her dress opening. I kissed her shoulders, the tremble turned into a shudder. Once she bit me, her teeth sinking into my neck. I held her tighter and her breathing turned into a gasp. She was squirming against me, trying to release the passion that was inside her.

My hand found the pull cord on the lamp beside the divan and the place was in darkness. Just the two of us. Little sounds.

No words. There wasn't need for any. A groan once or twice. The rustle of the cushions and the rasping sound of fingernails on broadcloth. The rattle of a belt buckle and the thump of a shoe kicked to the floor. Just the breathing, the wetness of a kiss. Then silence.

After a bit I turned the light back on. I let my eyes rove. "What a little liar you are," I laughed.

She pouted. "Why do you say that?"

"No strawberry mark—Mary."

She gave another chuckle and pulled my hair down in my face. "I thought you'd be interested enough to go looking for it."

"I ought to swat you."

"Where?"

"Forget it. You'd probably like it."

I got up from the divan and poured a drink while Mary readjusted herself. She took the drink from me and polished it off in one gulp. I reached for my hat as I rose to leave. "Does that date still hold for Saturday?" I asked.

"Damn well told," she smirked, "and don't be late."

I sat up late that night with a case of beer. We were coming around the turn into the home stretch now. With a spare pack of butts and the beer handy, I parked in the overstuffed rocker by the open windows and thought the thing out. Three murders so far. The killer still on the loose.

Mentally, I tried to list the things that were still needed to clean up the case. First, what did Jack have that caused his death? Was it the books, or something else? Why did Hal die? Did he go to that house to kill her, to threaten her, to warn her? If the killer was someone I knew how did he follow him in without me seeing him? Plenty to go over here. Lots of probable answers. Which was right?

And George Kalecki. Why was he on the loose? If he had no part in it there was no reason for him to lam. Why did he shoot at me—just because he knew I was after the killer? Possible, and very probable. He had every reason to be the one.

There wasn't a single person at the party who didn't have the opportunity to kill Jack. But motive was another thing. Who had that? Myrna?—I'd say no. Purely sentimental reasons.

Charlotte? Hell, no. More sentimental reasons. Besides, her profession didn't go with crime. She was a doctor. Only a casual friend of Jack's through Myrna's sickness. No motive there.

The twins, how about them? One a nymphomaniac, the other I never studied. Plenty of money, no troubles that I knew about.

Where did they fit? Did Esther have a motive? Have to find out more about her. And the strawberry mark. Could Mary have been snubbed by Jack? Possible. The way she was, her passions could get the better of her. Could she have made a play for Jack, been rebuffed, then taken it out in murder? If so, why take the books?

Hal Kines. He's dead.

Eileen Vickers. Dead. Too late to do anything about it now.

Could there be two murderers? Could Hal have killed Jack, then killed Eileen, and been in turn killed with his own gun there in the room? A great possibility, except that there was no sign of a struggle. Eileen's nude body. Was she professionally prepared to receive a visitor and surprised when her old lover walked in! Why? Why? Why?

Where was the secret to all this hidden? Who did it? It wasn't in Kalecki's apartment; not in Jack's, unless I couldn't read signs any more.

Was there an outsider?

Hell. I finished another bottle of beer and set the empty down at my feet. I was slowing up. Couldn't think any more. I wish I knew just where George Kalecki came in. That tie-up would prove important. To me, it looked as if the next step would be to find him. If Hal were alive . . .

I cut my thoughts short and slapped my leg. Damn, how could I be so simple. Hal hadn't operated out of the city. He had been going to school. If he had any record of his operations they were there. And that might be exactly what I needed.

As quickly as I could, I dressed. When I had my coat on I shoved an extra clip of cartridges in my pocket and phoned the garage to bring my car around.

It was almost midnight, and a sleepy attendant drove up as soon as I got downstairs. I stuffed a dollar bill into his hand, hopped in and pulled away. Luckily, there was no traffic to worry about this time of night. I beat out a few lights and turned on the West Side Express Highway and headed north. Pat had told me the town the college was in. Ordinarily it was a good three hours' drive from the city, but I didn't intend to take that long.

Twice the highway patrol came out of a cutoff after me, but they didn't stay with my overpowered load very long. I was a little afraid that they might radio ahead to try to throw up a road block to stop me, but nothing happened.

The signs told me when to turn and I got on an unkept country road that had so many ruts I had to slow down, but when the counties changed, so did the road. It changed into a smooth macadam, and I made the rest of the trip going full out.

Packsdale was five miles ahead. The chamber of commerce sign said it was a town of thirty thousand and the county seat. Huba huba. The college wasn't hard to find. It sat on a hill a mile north of town. Here and there some lights were lit, probably those in the corridors. I slammed on the brakes in time to swing into a gravel drive and roll up to an impressive-looking two-story house squatting a hundred feet back on the campus. The guy must have been in the army. Along the drive he had a yellow and black sign that read: "Mr. Russell Hilbar, Dean of Men."

The house was completely blacked-out, but that didn't stop me. I put my finger on the bell and never took it off until the lights blazed up in the place and I could hear footsteps hurrying to the door. The butler stood there with his mouth open. He had thrown on his working jacket on top of a nightshirt. Most ridiculous sight I ever saw. Instead of waiting to be admitted and announced, I pushed into the room and nearly knocked over a tall distinguished guy in a maroon dressing robe.

"What is this, sir? Who are you?"

I flashed my badge and he squinted at it. "Mike Hammer, Investigator from New York."

"Aren't you out of your territory?" he stormed. "What do you want?"

"You had a student here named Harold Kines, didn't you? I want to see his room."

"I'm afraid that's impossible. Our county police are handling the affair. I'm sure they are capable. Now if you'll please . . . "

I didn't let him go any further. "Listen, buddy," I pounded on his chest with a stiffened forefinger, "it's quite possible that right now there's a murderer loose on this campus. If he isn't a murderer he's liable to be one if you don't use your knob and tell me where I can find the room. And if you don't," I added, "I'll smack you so hard you'll spill your insides all over the joint!"

Russell Hilbar backed up and grabbed the edge of a chair for support. His face had gone pasty white and he looked ready to faint. "I—I never thought . . . " he stammered, " . . . Mr. Kines' room is on the lower floor in the east wing. The room number is 107, right on the southeast corner. But the county police have closed it pending a further investigation and I have no key."

"The hell with the county police. I'll get in. Turn these lights off and don't move out of the house. And stay away from the phone."

"But the students—will they . . . ?"

"I'll take care of them," I said as I closed the door.

Outside I had to orientate myself to find the east wing. I picked a low rectangular building out to be the dorms and I wasn't wrong. The grass muffled any sounds I made, and I crept up on the corner of the wing. I prayed silently that my hunch wasn't wrong and that I wasn't too late. As much as possible, I stayed in the shadows, working my way behind the bushes set against the wall.

The window was shoulder high, and down all the way. I took off my hat and put my ear close to the pane, but I couldn't detect any sound from inside. I took the chance. My fingers went under the sash and I pushed the window up. It slid without a creak. I jumped, and pulled myself into the room, then slid off the sill and landed on my face.

That fall saved my life. Two shots blasted from the corner of the room. The slugs smashed into the window sill behind me and threw splinters in my face. For a brief moment the room was lit up with the weird red glow of the gunflash.

My hand darted under my coat and came out with my rod. Our shots came almost together. I let three go as fast as my finger could pull the trigger. Something tugged at my jacket and I felt my ribs burn. There was another shot from across the room, but it wasn't directed at me. It went off into the floor of the room and the guy that fired it followed it down.

This time I didn't take a chance. I jumped the gap between us and landed on a body. I kicked for the gun and heard it skid across the floor. Only then did I switch on the lights.

George Kalecki was dead. My three shots had all caught him in the same place, right in the chest around the heart. But he had time to do what he came to do. In one corner, and still warm, was a pile of ashes in a green metal box.

chapter eleven ▰▰▰▰▰▰▰▰▰▰▰

THE NEXT SECOND there was a furious pounding on the door and voices raising cain outside. "Get away from that door and shut up," I yelled.

"Who's in there?" a voice demanded.

"Your uncle Charlie," I shot back. "Now can that chatter and get the dean up here fast as you can and tell him to call the police."

"Watch the window, fellows," the voice hollered. "The door is still sealed and he must have gone in that way. That's it, Duke, take the rifle. No telling who it is."

These crazy college kids. If one of them got jumpy with that rifle I'd be a dead duck. I stuck my head out the window as four of them came tearing around the corner at top speed. When they saw me they stopped in a flurry of dust. I waved to the big tow-headed kid carrying a .22 repeater. "Come here, you."

He marched up to the window with the gun out in front of him like he was going to bayonet somebody. He was scared stiff. I palmed my tin and shoved it under his nose. "See this badge?" I said. "I'm a cop, New York. Now keep your noses out of here. If you want to do something, post a guard around the campus until the cops get here and don't let anyone out. Understand?"

The kid bobbed his head eagerly. He was glad to get away from there. The next second he was shouting orders all over the place. Good ROTC material. The dean came running up blowing like a sick horse. "What happened?" His voice nearly broke when he spoke.

"I just shot a guy. Call the cops and be sure the kids stay out of here." He took off like a herd of turtles and I was left alone save for the curious voices outside the door. What I had to do had to be done before a lot of hayseed county cops took over.

I let George lay where he had fallen, taking time only to notice the gun. It was a .45, same as mine, and the one he had in his room when I searched it. I recognized a scratch on the butt.

The green box was my next step. I sifted the ashes carefully, trying to determine what they had been. The blackened cover of a note pad lay on the bottom, but it dissolved into dust at my touch. These ashes had been one or more books. I would have given a million dollars to know what they had had in them.

Not a word was visible, so thoroughly had George burned them. I looked around the spot on the floor where the box was originally. A few ashes were there, too. One was larger than the rest and not as well burned through. It had a string of numbers on it. I wondered how he concealed the fire. From outside it would have lit the room up as much as the overhead light would have.

I found out in a moment. A throw rug lay on the floor. When I turned it over the underside was blackened. Stuck to the mesh of the weave was a half-page leaf of the paper. It would have gone well at a murder trial. George was named as the trigger man in a murder, and where the proof could be found was also revealed—in a safe-deposit box in an uptown bank. It even gave the number and the code word. The key was in trust with the bank officer.

So George was a murderer. I had always thought he went that far back in the old days. Well, here was something to prove it. At least it more than justified my self defense act in gunning him down. I tucked the charred bit into a small envelope I carry for things like this, addressed it to myself and put a stamp on it. This time I used the door. I broke the seal with my shoulder and nearly bowled over a half-dozen kids. When I shooed them away I looked around for a post box and found one at the end of the corridor. I dropped it in and went back to wait for the arrival of the cops.

It was coming out now. Heretofore I thought Kalecki was the big wheel behind the syndicate, but now I could see that he was only a small part of it. Hal Kines had been the big shot. His methods were as subtle as those he used in obtaining his women. He went to enough trouble, but it was worth it. First he picked on guys with a dubious past, and ones against whom he wouldn't run into much trouble obtaining evidence. When he compiled it, he presented the stuff, or a photostat, and made the guy work with him. If I could have gotten the information that was burned we could have broken the filthiest racket in the world. Too late now, but at least I had a start. Maybe there were duplicates in the strong box, but I doubted that. Hal probably kept his evidence in different boxes for different people. That way, if he had to put the pressure on the group, he could send a note to the cops to investigate such and such a box without having any of his others disturbed. Nice thinking. Very farsighted.

I felt sort of good over having nailed Kalecki, but he still wasn't the one I wanted. If this kept up there wouldn't be anyone left at all. There was an outsider in this case. There had to be. One that nobody knew about, except, perhaps, those that were dead.

The county police arrived with all the pomp and ceremony of a presidential inaugural address. The chief, a big florid-faced farmer, pranced into the room with his hand on the butt of a revolver and promptly placed me under arrest for murder. Two minutes later, after a demonstration of arm waving, shouting and bulldozing of which I did not think myself capable, he retreated hastily and just as promptly unarrested me. However, to soothe his ruffled feelings I let him inspect my private operator's licence, my gun permit and a few other items of identification.

I let him listen to me put in the call to Pat. These county cops have no respect for authority outside their own limits, but when he got on the phone, Pat threatened him with calling the governor unless he cooperated with me. I gave him what details were necessary to keep him busy awhile, then took off for New York.

Going back I took it easier. It was early morning when I stopped outside of Pat's office and my eyes wouldn't stay open. He was waiting for me nevertheless. As quickly as I could I gave him the details of the shooting. He dispatched a car upstate to get photographs and see if there was anything to be learned from the ashes of the burned notebooks.

I didn't feel like going home, so I called Charlotte. She was up and dressed for an early appointment.

"Can you stay put until I get there?" I queried.

"Certainly, Mike. Hurry up. I want to hear what happened."

"Be there in fifteen minutes," I said, then hung up.

It took thirty, traffic was pretty heavy. Charlotte was in the door while Kathy was dusting. She took my coat and hat and I headed for the sofa. I relaxed with a sigh, and she bent down and kissed me. I hardly had enough energy to kiss her back. With her there beside me I told the whole story. Charlotte was a good listener. When I finished she stroked my forehead and my face.

"Is there anything I can do to help?" she asked.

"Yeah. Tell me what makes a nymphomaniac."

"So? You've been to see her again!" Her answer was indignant.

"Business, darling." I wondered when I'd be able to stop using that line.

Charlotte laughed. "That's all right. I understand. As for your question, a nymphomaniac can be either a case of gradual development through environment or born into a person. Some people are oversexed, a glandular difficulty. Others can be repressed in childhood, and when they find themselves in an adult world, no longer the victim of senseless restrictions, they go hog wild. Why?"

I evaded the why and asked, "Can the ones with emotional difficulty go bad?"

"You mean, will they kill as a result of their emotional overload? I'd say offhand, no. They find an easier out for their emotions."

"For instance," I parried.

"Well, if a nymphomaniac showers a great deal of emotion on a person, then is rebuffed, instead of killing the one who spurned her, she simply finds another with whom to become emotionally entangled. It's quicker, besides being more effective. If she suffers a loss of prowess from the rebuff, this new person renews her. See?"

I got what she was driving at, but there was still something else. "Would it be likely for both the twins to be nymphomaniacs?"

Charlotte gave me that delightful laugh. "Possible, but it doesn't happen to be so. You see, I know them rather well. Not too well, but enough to determine their characters. Mary is beyond help. She likes to be the way she is. I daresay she has more fun than her sister, but Esther has seen so many of her escapades and helped her out of trouble, that she has a tendency to turn away from love affairs herself. Esther is a charming enough person, all right. Just about everything her sister has without the craze for men. When a man does drop into Esther's life, she'll take it naturally."

"I'll have to meet her," I said, sleepily. "By the way, are you going to their place this weekend?"

"Why yes, Mary invited me. I'll be late getting there, but I won't miss the game. However, I have to come back right after it. Are you going?"

"Uh-huh. I'm going to drive Myrna up. That is, I still have to call her so she'll know about it."

"Swell," she said. That was the last word I heard. I fell into a sleep as deep as the ocean.

When I awoke I glanced at my watch. It was nearly four in the afternoon. Kathy heard me stir and came into the room with a tray of bacon and eggs and coffee.

"Heah's yo' breakfast, Mistah Hammah. Miss Charlotte tell me to take good care of ya'll till she comes home." Kathy gave me a toothy white smile and waddled out after setting the tray down.

I gulped the eggs hungrily and polished off three cups of coffee. Then I called Myrna and she told me that it was okay to pick her up at ten A.M. Saturday. I hung up and poked around the bookshelves for something to read while I waited. Most of the fiction I had read, so I passed on to some of Charlotte's textbooks. One was a honey called *Hypnosis as a Treatment for Mental Disorders.* I skimmed through it. Too wordy. It gave the procedure for putting a patient into a state of relaxation, inducing hypnosis, and suggesting treatment. That way, the patient later went about effecting his own cure automatically.

That would have been a nice stunt for me to learn if I could do it. I pictured myself putting the eye on a beautiful doll and— hell, that was nasty. Besides, I wasn't that bad off. I chose one that had a lot of pictures. This one was titled, *Psychology of*

Marriage. Brother, it was a dilly. If it weren't for the big words I would have enjoyed it. I wished they would write stuff like that in language for the layman.

Charlotte came in when I was on the last chapter. She took the book out of my hand and saw what I was reading. "Thinking of anything special?" she asked.

I gave her a silly grin. "Better get the low-down now while I'm able to. Can't say how long I'm going to have the strength to hold off." She kissed me and whipped me up a Scotch and soda. When I downed it I told Kathy to get my hat and coat. Charlotte looked disappointed.

"Have to leave so soon? I thought you'd stay to dinner at least."

"Not tonight, honey. I have a job for my tailor and I want to get cleaned up. I don't suppose *you'd* have a razor handy." I pointed to the bullet hole in my coat. Charlotte got a little white when she saw how close it had come.

"Are . . . are you hurt, Mike?"

"Hell, no. Got a bullet burn across the ribs but it never broke the skin." I pulled up my shirt to confirm it, then got dressed. The phone rang just then and she took it.

She frowned once or twice, said, "Are you sure? All right, I'll look into it." When she hung up I asked her what the matter was. "A client. Responded to treatment, then lapsed into his former state. I think I'll prescribe a sedative and see him in the morning." She went to her desk.

"I'll run along then. Maybe I'll see you later. Right now I want to get a haircut before I do anything else."

"Okay, darling." She came over and put her arms around me. "There's a place on the corner."

"That'll do as well as any," I told her between kisses.

"Hurry back, Mike."

"You bet, darling."

Luckily, the place was empty. A guy was just getting out of the chair when I went in. I hung my coat on a hook and plunked into the seat. "Trim," I told the barber. After he ogled my rod a bit, he draped me with the sheet and the clippers buzzed. Fifteen minutes later he dusted me off and I walked out of there slicked down like an uptown sharpie. I got the boiler rolling and turned across town to get on Broadway.

I heard the sirens wailing, but I didn't know it was Pat until the squad car shot past me and I saw him leaning out of the side window. He was too busy to notice me, but cut across the intersection while the cop on the corner held traffic back. Further down the avenue another siren was blasting a path northward.

It was more a hunch than anything else, the same kind of a hunch that put me on the trail of George Kalecki. And this one paid off, too, but in a way I didn't recognize at first. As soon as the cop on the corner waved us on, I followed the howl of police cars and turned left on Lexington Avenue. Up ahead I saw the white top of Pat's car weaving in and out of the lanes. It slowed down momentarily and turned into a side street.

This time I had to park a block away. Two police cars had the street barred to traffic at either end. I flashed my badge and my card to the patrolman on the corner. He let me pass and I hurried down to the little knot of people gathered outside a drugstore. Pat was there with what looked like the whole homicide bureau. I pushed my way through the crowd and nodded to Pat. I followed his eyes down to the crumpled figure on the sidewalk. Blood had spilled out of the single hole in the back, staining the shabby coat a deep maroon. Pat told me to go ahead and I turned the face around to see who it was.

I whistled. Bobo Hopper would keep bees no longer.

Pat indicated the body. "Know him?"

I nodded. "Yeah. Know him well. His name is Hopper, Bobo Hopper. A hell of a nice guy even if he was a moron. Never hurt anything in his life. He used to be one of Kalecki's runners."

"He was shot with a .45, Mike."

"What!" I exploded.

"There's something else now. Dope. Come over here." Pat took me inside the drugstore. The fat little clerk was facing a battery of detectives led by a heavy-set guy in a blue serge suit. I knew him all too well. He never liked me much since I blew a case wide open under his very nose. He was Inspector Daly of the narcotics squad.

Daly turned to me. "What are you doing here?" he demanded.

"Same thing you are, I think."

"Well, you can start walking as of now. I don't want any private noses snooping around. Go on, beat it."

"One moment, Inspector." When Pat talked in that tone of voice he could command attention. Daly respected Pat. They were different kinds of cops. Daly had come up the hard way, with more time between promotions, while Pat had achieved his position through the scientific approach to crime. Even though they didn't see eye to eye in their methods, Daly was man enough to give Pat credit where credit was due and listen to him.

"Mike has an unusual interest in this case," he continued. "It was through him we got as far as we have. If you don't mind, I would like him to keep in close touch with this."

Daly glared at me and shrugged his beefy shoulders. "Okay. Let him stay. Only be sure you don't withhold any evidence," he spat at me.

The last time I was involved in a case he was working on I had to play my cards close to my vest, but hanging on to the evidence I had led me to a big-time drug dealer we never would have nailed otherwise. Daly never forgot that.

The head of the narcotics bureau was blasting away at the druggist and I picked up every word. "Once more now. Give me the whole thing and see what else you can remember."

Harried to the breaking point, the druggist wrung his pudgy hands and looked at the sea of faces glaring at him. Pat must have had the most sympathetic expression, so he spoke to him.

"I was doing nothing. Sweeping out under the counter, maybe. That is all. This man, he walks in and says fill a prescription. Very worried he was. He hands me a broken box that has nothing written on the cover. He says to me he will lose his job and nobody will trust him if I can't do it. He drops the box he was delivering and somebody steps on it and his prescription is all over the sidewalk.

"This powder was coming out of the sides. I take it in the back and taste it yet, then test it. Pretty sure I was that I knew what was in it, and when I test it I was positive. Heroin. This should not be, so like a good citizen I phone the police and tell them what I have. They tell me to keep him here, but how do I know that he is not a gangster and will shoot me?" Here the little guy stopped and shuddered.

"I have a family yet. I take my time, but he tells me to hurry up and puts his hand in a pocket. Maybe he has a gun. What can I do? I fill another box with boric acid, charge him a dollar and he walks out. I leave my counter to go see where he goes, but before I get to the door he falls to the sidewalk. He is shot. All the way dead. I call police again, then you come."

"See anyone running off?" Pat asked.

He shook his head. "Nobody. At this time it is slow. Nobody on the street."

"Did you hear a shot?"

"No. That I could not understand. I was too scared. I see the blood from the hole and I run back inside."

Pat stroked his chin. "How about a car. Did any go by at that time?"

The little guy squinted his eyes and thought back. Once he started to speak, stopped, then reassured, said, "Y-yes. Now that you remind me, I think one goes by just before. Yes. I am sure of it. Very slow it goes and it was turning." He continued hurriedly from here. "Like it was coming from the curb maybe. It goes past, then when I am outside it is gone. I don't even look for it after that, so scared I am."

Daly had one of his men taking the whole thing down in shorthand. Pat and I had heard enough. We went outside to the body and checked the bullet angle. From the position of where it lay, the killer had been going toward Lexington when the shot was fired. The packet of boric acid, now a blood red, lay underneath Bobo's hand. We patted the pockets. Empty. His wallet held eight dollars and a library card. Inside the coat was a booklet on the raising of bees.

"Silencer," Pat said. "I'll give ten to one it's the same gun."

"I wouldn't take that bet," I agreed.

"What do you make of it, Mike?"

"I don't know. If Kalecki were alive it would involve him even deeper. First prostitution, now dope. That is, if Bobo was still working for Kalecki. He said not, and I believed him. I thought Bobo was too simple to try to deceive anybody. I'm not so sure now."

We both stared at the body a bit, then walked down the street a way by ourselves. I happened to think of something.

"Pat."

"Uh-huh."

"Remember when Kalecki was shot at in his home? When he tried to put the finger on me?"

"Yeah. What of it?"

"It was the killer's gun. The killer we want fired that shot. Why? Can you make anything out of it? Even then Kalecki was on the spot for something and he moved to town for his own protection. That's what we want, the answer to the question of why he was shot at."

"That's going to take some doing, Mike. The only ones that can tell us are dead."

I gave him a grin. "No. There's still someone. The killer. He knows why. Have you anything to do right now?"

"Nothing I can't put off. This case will be in Daly's hands for a while. Why?"

I took his arm and walked him around the block to my car. We got in and headed toward my apartment.

The mailman was just coming out when we got there. I opened my box and drew out the envelope I addressed to myself at the college and ripped it open. I explained to Pat I had to get the piece of charred evidence out of the hands of those hick cops while I could and he agreed that I did it right.

Pat knew the ropes. He put in three phone calls and when we reached the bank a guard ushered us into the office of the president. By that time he had already received the court order by phone to permit us to inspect the box listed on the slip.

It was there, all of it. Evidence enough to hang George Kalecki a dozen times over. I was really grateful now that I had put a slug into him. The guy was a rat, all right. He had his fingers in more than I had suspected. There were photostats of checks, letters, a few original documents, and plenty of material to indict George Kalecki for every vice charge there was, including a few new ones. But nothing else. Where George had gone there was no need for a court. Hal Kines had tied him up in a knot with both ends leading to the hot squat if he had tried to make a break.

Pat ran over the stuff twice, then scooped them all into a large envelope, signed for it and left. Outside I asked, "What are you going to do with the junk?"

"Go over it carefully. Maybe I can trace these checks even though they are made out to cash and don't show the signature on the reverse side. How about you?"

"Might as well go home like I planned. Why, got something else?"

Pat laughed. "We'll see. I had the idea you might be holding out on me, so I wasn't going to tell you this, but since you're still playing it square I'll let you in on something."

He took a pad from his pocket and flipped it open. "Here's some names. See if you know anything about them."

Pat cleared his throat.

"Henry Strebhouse, Carmen Silby, Thelma B. Duval, Virginia R. Reims, Conrad Stevens." Pat stopped and waited, looking at me expectantly.

"Strebhouse and Stevens spent a stretch in the big house," I said. "I don't know the others. Think I saw the Duval girl's name in the society columns once."

"You did. Well, you're not much help, so I'll tell you. Each one of these people is in city or private sanitariums. Dope fiends."

"That's nice," I mused. "How did it get out?"

"Vice squad reported it."

"Yeah. I know they've been on something like that, but it's

funny it didn't reach the papers. Oh, I get it. They haven't found the source yet, huh? What is it?"

Pat gave me a wry grin. "That's what Daly would like to know. None of them will reveal it. Not even under threat of imprisonment. Unfortunately for us, some of them have connections too high up for us to try to extract information the hard way. We did get this, though, the stuff was delivered to them via a half-witted little guy who didn't know from nothing."

I let my breath go out hard. "Bobo!"

"Exactly. They'll be able to identify him—if they will. Maybe his death will make them clam up even tighter."

"Damn," I said softly, "and while they're under treatment we can't push them. Our hands are tied very neatly. There's a tie-up, Pat, there has to be. Look how closely all this is connected. At first glance it seems to be loose as hell, but it's not. Bobo and Kalecki . . . Hal and Kalecki . . . Hal and Eileen . . . Eileen and Jack. Either we've run into an outfit that had a lot of irons in the fire or else it was a chain reaction. Jack started it going and the killer knocked him off, but the killer had to cover up something else. From then on it was a vicious circle. Brother, have we run into something!"

"You're not kidding. And we're standing right in the bottom of the well. Now what?"

"Beats me, Pat. I see a little light now, a few things are falling into place."

"What?"

"I'd rather not say. Just little things. They don't point in any direction except to tell me that the killer has a damn good motive for all this."

"Still racing me, Mike?"

"You can bet your pretty white tail on that! I think we're in the home stretch, but the track is muddy now and bogging us down. We'll have to plod through it to firmer ground before we can start whipping it up." I grinned at him. "You won't beat me out, Pat."

"What do you bet?"

"A steak dinner."

"Taken."

I left him then. He grabbed a cab back to the office and I went up to my apartment. When I took off my pants I felt for my wallet. It was gone. That was nice. Had two hundred berries in my billfold and I couldn't afford to lose it. I put my pants back on and went down to the car. Not there, either. I thought. I might have dropped it in the barber shop, but I paid that bill with change I had in my side pocket. Damn.

I climbed back in the car and turned it over, then headed south to Charlotte's apartment. The lobby door was open and I walked up. I rang the bell twice, but no one answered. Someone was inside, though, and I could hear a voice singing *Swanee River*. I pounded on the door and Kathy opened it up.

"What's the matter," I asked her, "doesn't the bell ring anymore?"

"Sho'nuff, Mistah Hammah. Ah think so. Come in. Come in."

When I walked in the door Charlotte came running out to meet me. She had on a stained smock and a pair of rubber gloves. "Hey, honey," she smiled at me. "You sure made that trip fast. Goody, goody, goody." She threw her arms around me and tilted her head for a kiss. Kathy stood there watching, her teeth flashing whitely in her mouth.

"Go 'way," I grinned. Kathy turned her back so I could kiss her boss. Charlotte sighed and laid her head against my chest.

"Going to stay now?"

"Nope."

"Oh . . . why? You just got here."

"I came to get my wallet." I walked over to the sofa with her and ran my hand down behind the cushions. I found it. The darn thing had slipped out of my hip pocket while I was asleep and stuck there.

"Now I suppose you're going to accuse me of stealing all your money," Charlotte pouted.

"Idiot." I kissed the top of her blonde head.

"What are you doing in this outfit?" I fingered the smock.

"Developing pictures. Want to see them?" She led me to her darkroom and turned out the lights. As she did so, a red glow came from the shield over the sink. Charlotte put some films in the developer, and in a few moments printed up a pic of a guy sitting in a chair, hands glued to the metal arms, and a strained expression on his face. She flicked the overhead on and looked over the photo.

"Who's this?"

"A clinical patient. As a matter of fact, that is one that Hal Kines had released from the charity ward of the city hospital to undergo treatment in our clinic."

"What's the matter with him? The guy looks scared to death."

"He's in a state of what is commonly known as hypnosis. Actually there's nothing more to it than inducing in the patient a sense of relaxation and confidence. In this case, the patient was a confirmed kleptomaniac. It wasn't found out until he was admitted to the city ward after being found nearly dead of starvation on the streets.

"When we got to the bottom of his mental status, we found that in childhood he had been deprived of everything and had to steal to get what he wanted. Through a friend, I got him a job and explained why he had been like that. Once understanding his condition, he was able to overcome it. Now he's doing quite well."

I put the pic back in a rack and looked the place over. She had certainly spent enough fixing up the darkroom. I saw where I was going to have to earn more than I did to support a wife who had such a lavish hobby.

Charlotte must have read my mind. "After we're married," she smiled, "I'll give all this up and have my pictures developed at the corner drugstore."

"Naw, we'll do all right." She grabbed me and hung on. I kissed her so hard I hurt my mouth this time. It was a wonder she could breathe, I held her so tightly.

We walked to the door arm in arm. "What about tonight, Mike? Where will we go?"

"I don't know. To the movies, maybe."

"Swell, I'd like that." I opened the door. When I did I pointed to the chime behind it. "How come it doesn't ring anymore?"

"Oh, phooey." Charlotte poked under the rug with her toe. "Kathy has been using the vacuum in here again. She always knocks out the plug." I bent down and stuck it back in the socket.

"See you about eight, kitten," I said as I left. She waited until I was nearly out of sight down the stairs, then blew me a kiss and shut the door.

chapter twelve ▪▪▪▪▪▪▪▪▪▪

MY TAILOR HAD a fit when he saw the bullet hole in my coat. I guess he was afraid he was coming close to losing a good customer. He pleaded with me to be careful, then told me he'd have the cloth rewoven by next week. I picked up my other suit and went home.

The phone was ringing when I opened the door. I dropped the suit over the back of a chair and grabbed the receiver. It was Pat.

"I just got a report on the bullet that killed Bobo Hopper, Mike."

"Go on." I was all excited now.

"Same one."

"That does it, Pat. Anything else?"

"Yeah, I have Kalecki's gun here, too. The bullet doesn't fit except with the ones he let loose at you. We traced the serial number and it was sold down South. It went through two more hands and wound up in a pawnshop on Third Avenue where it went to a guy named Goerge K. Masters."

So that was how George got the gun. No wonder there was no record of it before. Kalecki was his middle, and probably a family, name. I thanked Pat and hung up. Now why the hell would Kalecki be using that name? Not unless he was liable to be traced through his real one for a crime committed some time ago. At any rate, the question would have to remain unanswered unless Pat could make some sense out of the evidence we found in the safe-deposit box. You can't prosecute a corpse.

After I ate, I showered and was getting dressed when the phone went off again. This time it was Myrna. She wanted me to pick her up earlier, if I could, tomorrow morning. That was all right with me and I told her so. She still sounded pretty bad and I was glad to do what I could to help her out. Maybe the ride into the country would do her good. Poor kid, she needed something to cheer her up. The only thing that had me worried was that she might try going back on the junk again to get Jack's death out of her mind. She was a smart girl. There were other ways. Some day she would settle down with a nice fellow and Jack would be but a memory. That's the way nature made us. Maybe it's best.

Charlotte met me in front of the apartment house. When she saw me coming she tapped her foot impatiently as though she had been waiting an hour. "Mike," she said fiercely, "you're late. A whole five minutes. Explain."

"Don't beat me with that whip," I laughed. "I got held up in traffic."

"A likely excuse. I bet you were trying to see what makes a nymphomaniac tick again." She was a little devil.

"Shut up and climb in. We'll never get a seat in the show otherwise."

"Where are we going?"

"I'm in the mood for a good 'who-dun-it' if you are. Maybe I can pick up something new in detecting techniques."

"Swell. Let's go, Macduff."

We finally found a small theater along the stem that didn't have a line outside a mile long, and we sat through two and a half hours of a fantastic murder mystery that had more holes in it than a piece of swiss cheese, and a Western that moved as slowly as the Long Island Rail Road during a snowstorm.

When we got out I thought I had blisters on my butt. Charlotte suggested having a sandwich, so we stopped in a dog wagon for poached eggs on toast, then moved on down to a bar for a drink. I ordered beer, and when Charlotte did the same I raised my eyebrows.

"Go ahead, get what you want. I got dough."

She giggled. "Silly, I like beer. Always have."

"Well, glad to hear it. I can't make you out. An expensive hobby, but you drink beer. Maybe you aren't going to be so hard to keep after all.'

"Oh, if it comes to a pinch, I can always go back to work."

"Nothing doing. No wife of mine is going to work. I want her at home where I know where she is."

Charlotte laid her beer down and looked at me wickedly. "Has it ever occurred to you that you've never even proposed to me? How do you know I'll have you?"

"Okay, minx," I said. I took her hand in mine and raised it to my lips. "Will you marry me?"

She started to laugh, but tears came into her eyes and she pushed her face against my shoulder. "Oh, Mike, yes. Yes. I love you so much."

"I love you, too, kitten. Now drink your drink. Tomorrow night at the twins' place we'll duck the crowd and make some plans."

"Kiss me."

A couple of wise guys were watching me leeringly. I didn't care. I kissed her easy like.

"When do I get my ring?" she wanted to know.

"Soon. I have a few checks coming in this week or next and we can go down to Tiffany's and pick one up. How's that?"

"Wonderful, Mike, wonderful. I'm so happy."

We finished the beer, had another, then started out. The pair of wise guys threw me a "hey, hey" as I passed. I dropped Charlotte's arm for a second, then put my hands on each side of their heads and brought them together with a clunk like a couple of gourds. Both the guys were sitting upright on their stools. In the mirror I could see their eyes. They looked like four agate marbles. The bartender was watching me, his mouth open. I waved to him and took Charlotte out. Behind me the two guys fell off their stools and hit the deck like wet rags.

"My protector." She squeezed my arm.

"Aw shadup," I grinned. I felt pretty good right then.

Kathy was sleeping, so we tiptoed in. Charlotte put her hand over the chime to stop its reverberations, but even then we heard the maid stop snoring. She must have gone over on her back again because the snoring resumed.

She took off her coat, then asked, "Want a drink?"

"Nope."

"What then?"

"You." The next second she was in my arms, kissing me. Her breasts were pulsating with passion. I held her as closely as I could.

"Tell me, Mike."

"I love you." She kissed me again. I pushed her away and picked up my hat.

"Enough, darling," I said. "After all, I'm only a man. One more kiss like that and I won't be able to wait until after we're married." She grinned and threw herself at me for that kiss, but I held her off.

"Please, Mike?"

"No."

"Then let's get married right away. Tomorrow."

I had to smile. She was so damn adorable. "Not tomorrow, but very soon, honey, I can't hold out much longer."

She held the chime while I opened the door. I kissed her lightly and slipped out. I could see where I wouldn't get much sleep that night. When Velda heard about this she'd throw the roof at me. I hated to tell her.

My alarm went off at six. I slapped the button down to stop the racket, then sat up and stretched. When I looked out the window the sun was shining—a beautiful day. A half-empty bottle of beer was on the night table and I took a swallow. It was as flat as a table-top mesa.

After a shower I threw a robe around me and dug in the pantry for something to eat. The only box of cereal had teeth marks in it where a mouse had beaten me to it, so I opened a sack of potatoes and onions and stripped them into a pan of grease and let the whole mess cook while I made coffee.

I burned the potatoes, but they tasted good just the same. Even my coffee was agreeable. This time next month I'd be eating across the table from a gorgeous blonde. What a wife she was going to make!

Myrna was up when I called her. She said she'd be ready at eight and reminded me not to be late. I promised her I wouldn't, then buzzed Charlotte.

"Hello, lazy," I yawned.

"You don't sound so bright yourself this time of the morning."

"Well, I am. What are you doing?"

"Trying to get some sleep. After the state you left me in last night I didn't close my eyes for three hours. I lay in bed wide awake."

That made me feel good. "I know what you mean. What time will you be at the Bellemy place?"

"Still early in the evening unless I can break away sooner. At least I'll be there for the game. Who is it that's playing?"

"I forget. A couple of fancy hot shots that Mary and Esther imported. I'll be waiting for you to show up, so make it snappy."

"Okay, darling." She kissed me over the phone and I gave her one back before I hung up.

Velda wouldn't be in the office yet, so I called her at home. When she answered I could hear a background of bacon sizzling on the fire. "Hello, Velda, Mike."

"Hey, what are you doing up so early?"

"I have an important date."

"Anything to do with the case?"

"Er . . . it may have, but I'm not sure. I can't afford to miss it. If Pat calls, tell him I can be reached at the home of the Misses Bellemy. He has their number."

Velda didn't answer at first. I knew she was trying to figure out what I was up to. "All right," she said finally. "Just watch what you're doing. Anything I can take care of while you're gone?"

"No, guess not."

"By the way, how long are you going to be gone this time?"

"Maybe until Monday, maybe not."

"Very well, see you, Mike. So long."

I threw her a quick so long and put the phone on its chocks. Oh, how I hated to tell Velda about Charlotte! If only she wouldn't cry. What the hell, that's life. Velda just missed. If Charlotte hadn't come along I would have tied up with her. I used to feel like I wanted to, but never had time. Oh, well.

Myrna was dressed and ready when I arrived. She had packed

a bag and I took it down to the car. She didn't look too good. There were still dark spots under her eyes and her cheekbones were a little too prominent. She had bought a new dress for the occasion, a nice flowered print, and under the light blue of the wool coat it made her face look lovely, that is, unless you looked too closely.

I didn't want to mention Jack at all, so we talked about the day and anything trivial that came up. I knew she had seen the front-page headlines about me knocking off Kalecki, but she avoided the subject.

It was a nice day. Out of the city the roads were fairly empty and we rolled along at a conservative fifty. That way I didn't have to bother about the highway patrol. We passed a few open lots where the kids were getting in an early ball game. I saw tears come into Myrna's eyes when we passed some small cottages. I winced. She was taking it hard.

Gradually I led the conversation around to the tennis match that night and got her mind off what she was thinking. It wasn't long afterward that we pulled into the private drive of the Bellemy estate. I thought we were early, but there were two dozen others there before us. A row of cars ran along the side of the mansion and one of the twins came out to meet us. I didn't know which one it was until she said, "Hello, sissy."

"Hello, Mary," I said through a smile. She had on a halter and a pair of shorts that left nothing to the imagination. Both pieces were so tight every line of her body showed through and she knew it. I couldn't get my eyes off her legs, and walking up to the house she kept brushing against me.

That had to cease. I shifted Myrna's grip over to keep a barrier between us and Mary broke out into a giggle. At the house she turned Myrna over to a maid, then turned to me. "Didn't you bring some sport clothes along?"

"Yup. But all the sports I intend to indulge in will be done at the bar."

"Nuts. Go get in a pair of slacks. There's a golf game to be held behind the house and a lot of the kids are looking for partners for a tennis game."

"For Pete's sake, I'm no athlete."

Mary stood off a few feet and looked me over from top to bottom. "You look like an athlete if I ever saw one."

"What kind?" I joked.

"A bed athlete." Her eyes said that she wasn't joking.

She walked back to the car with me to get my clothes. When

we got in the house she showed me to a room, an oversized thing with a huge four-poster smack in the middle of it.

Mary couldn't wait until I closed the door. She flung herself at me and opened her mouth. Hell, couldn't disappoint the hostess, so I kissed her.

"Now scram while I get dressed," I told her.

Her mouth went into a pout. "Why?"

"Look," I tried to be convincing, "I don't get undressed in front of women."

"Since when?" she asked impishly.

"It was dark then," I told her. "Besides, it's too early for that."

I got another one of those sexy smiles. Her eyes were begging me to undress her. "Okay . . . sissy." She closed the door behind her and I heard that deep-throated laugh.

The gang outside was making a racket and I poked my head out the window to see what was up. Directly beneath me two underweight males were having a hair-pulling match while four others egged them on. What a place. The two boys hit the dirt together and followed by a slap or two. I grinned. A couple of pansies trying to decide who would be Queen of the May. I drew a pitcher of water from the sink and let it go on their blonde heads.

That ended the fight. They both let out a falsetto scream and got up running. The gang saw me and howled. It was a good gag.

Mary met me downstairs. She was lounging against the porch railing smoking a cigarette. I came out in slacks and a sweat shirt and tossed her a hello. Myrna joined us at the same time swinging a tennis racket against her legs. I could see that Mary was disappointed at not getting me alone. The three of us walked across the lawn to the courts with Mary hanging on to my arm. Before we quite reached there another edition of her stepped out of a group of players and waved to us. Esther Bellemy.

She was another to make your mouth drool. She recognized me immediately and offered a firm handshake. Her manner was cool and reserved. I saw what Charlotte meant when she said Esther wasn't like her sister. However, there seemed to be no resentment or jealousy. Esther had her admirers, too. We were introduced all around to a lot of people whose names I forgot as soon as I met them, and Mary carted me off to a vacant court for a game of singles.

Tennis wasn't in my line, she found out. After a hectic ten minutes I had batted the balls over the fence and we gathered them up and put them in a box and laid the rackets down. Mary sat on a bench beside me with her brown legs stuck out in front of her while I cooled off.

"Why are we wasting time out here, Mike? Your room is so much nicer."

Some dame. "You rush things, Mary. Why aren't you more like your sister?"

She gave me a short laugh. "Maybe I am."

"How do you mean?"

"Oh, nothing, I guess. But Esther keeps her eyes open, too. She's no virgin."

"How do you know?"

Mary giggled and folded her knees under her hands. "She keeps a diary."

"I bet yours is a lot thicker," I said.

"Uh-huh, lots."

I took her hand and pulled her from the bench. "Come on, show me where the bar is."

We took a flagstone path back to the house and entered through a pair of French windows. The bar was built off a trophy room that was well packed with cups and medals, decorated with live-oak paneling and blown-up photographs of the Bellemy sisters winning everything from a golf game to a ski jump. They certainly were an active pair. The curious thing about it was that they didn't like publicity. I wondered where the rumor started that they were looking for husbands. Husbands that would satisfy, maybe.

I guess Mary gave me up as hopeless for a while. She left me with a bartender who sat at the end of the thirty-foot bar reading a stack of comic magazines, getting up only long enough to pour me a fresh drink every time I emptied my glass.

Several times I had company, but not for long. Myrna came in once, then left after a few pleasant words. Some other tootsies tried their hand at making a strange face but were dragged off by their boy friends who chased them into the bar. One of the pansies I doused did his bit, too, and all it took to get him out was a strong hand on the seat of his shorts and another around his neck. The whole deal was getting very monotonous. I wished Charlotte would get here. I thought I'd have a nice time with Mary, but compared to Charlotte she was a flop. Mary only had sex. Charlotte had that—plus a lot more.

I managed to sneak out without the bartender seeing me and found my room. There I changed back to my street clothes, patted old junior under my arm and lay down on the bed. Now I felt normal.

The drinks did more to me than I thought. I didn't pass out, I simply fell asleep, but quick. The next thing I knew someone was shaking me and I looked up into the prettiest face in the world. Before my eyes were all the way open, Charlotte kissed me, then mussed my hair.

"Is this the way you greet me? I thought you'd be at the gate waiting for me with open arms."

"Hello, beautiful." I said.

I pulled her down on the bed and kissed her. "What time is it?" She looked at her watch.

"Seven-thirty."

"Holy cow! I slept the whole day out practically!"

"I'll say you have. Now get dressed and come downstairs for dinner. I want to see Myrna."

We got up and I saw her to the door, then washed my face and tried to smooth the wrinkles out of my coat. When I thought I was presentable enough I went downstairs. Mary saw me and waved me over. "You're sitting by me tonight," she told me.

The crowd was beginning to file in and I found the place card with my name on it. Charlotte was sitting directly opposite me at any rate. I felt much better at that. The two of them ought to be fun unless Mary started playing kneesy under the table.

Charlotte sat down with a smile and Myrna was next to her. Through the appetizer they spoke to each other earnestly, laughing occasionally over some private joke.

I glanced down the table to see if there was anyone I knew. One face seemed fairly familiar, although I couldn't place it. He was a short, skinny guy, dressed in a dark grey flannel. His only conversation was with the heavy-set woman opposite him. There was so much chatter at the table I couldn't get a line on what they were talking about, but I saw him sneak a few side glances my way.

He happened to turn his full face toward me for a moment, then I recognized him. He was one of the men I had seen going into Madam June's call house the night of the raid.

I nudged Mary and she quit talking to the guy on her other side long enough to look my way. "Who's the squirt down at the end?" I asked, motioning with my fork.

Mary picked him out and said, "Why, that's Harmon Wilder, our attorney. He's the one who invests our money for us. Why?"

"Just curious. I thought I recognized him."

"You should. He used to be one of the best criminal lawyers in the country before he gave it up for a private practice in something less sensational."

I said, "Oh," then returned to my food. Charlotte had found my foot under the table and tapped it with her toe. Behind the table the lawn was moon-lit—a perfect night. I'd be glad when supper was over.

Mary tried me out in conversation all too suggestive. I saw Charlotte give her a glance that was full of fire, winked, then cut Mary off pretty sharply. She sort of got the idea that something was up between me and Charlotte and whispered into my ear. "I'll get you tonight, big stuff—after she's gone."

She yelped when I stuck my elbow in her ribs.

Dinner ended when one of the fruits fell out of his chair at the table's end. Right after that there was a lot of noise and the two tennis players who were to be featured in the game that night stood up and toasted success to each other with glasses of milk.

I managed to get through to Charlotte and took Myrna and her out to the courts together. A lot of cars were driving up, probably some neighbors invited just for the game. The floodlights had been turned on over the sunbaked clay, and bleacher seats had been erected sometime during the latter part of the afternoon while I was asleep.

There was a general scramble for seats and we missed. Charlotte and Myrna spread their handkerchiefs down on the grass along the border of the playing field and we waited while the crowd got six deep behind us. I had never seen a real tennis game, but from what I had seen, I didn't think there were that many people who liked the game.

There were announcements over a portable loud-speaker and the players took their places. Then they went into action. I had more fun watching the spectators' heads going back and forth like a bunch of monkeys on sticks than I did the game itself.

These boys were pretty good. They worked up a terrific sweat but they kept after that ball, running themselves ragged. Occasionally there would be a spectacular play and the crowd would let out a cheer. On a high bench, the referee announced the score.

Myrna kept pressing her hand to her head, then between sets she excused herself to Charlotte and me saying that she wanted to go to the cloakroom and get an aspirin.

No sooner had she left when Mary plunked herself down in the same spot beside me and started her routine. I waited for

Charlotte to start something, but she merely smiled grimly and let me fight it out myself.

Mary tapped her on the shoulder. "Can I borrow your man a few minutes? I want him to meet some people."

"Sure, go ahead." Charlotte winked gaily at me and made believe she was pouting, but she knew she had me. From now on Charlotte had nothing to worry about. Just the same I felt like throttling Mary. Just sitting there had been nice.

We wormed out through the gang who had moved up to take new places and stretch themselves between sets. Mary took me around to the other side, then started walking toward the woods.

"Where're the people you wanted me to meet?" I asked.

Her hand groped for mine in the darkness. "Don't be silly," she answered. "I just want you to myself for a while."

"Look, Mary," I explained, "it's no good. The other night was a mistake. Charlotte and I are engaged. I can't be fooling around with you. It isn't fair to either of you."

She tucked her arm under mine. "Oh, but you don't have to marry me. I don't want that. It takes all the fun out of it."

What was I going to do with a woman like that? "Listen," I told her, "you're a nice kid and I like you a lot, but you are a serious complication to me."

She let my arm go. We were under a tree now, and it was pitch black. I could barely see the outline of her face. The moon which not so long ago had been out in full brilliance had disappeared behind a cloud. I kept talking to her, trying to dissuade her from putting a line on me, but she didn't answer. She hummed snatches from a tune I heard her breathing in the darkness, but that was all.

When I had about exhausted myself, she said, "Will you kiss me just once more if I promise to let you alone?"

I breathed a little easier. "Sure, honey. Just one more kiss."

Then I stretched out my arms to hold her to kiss, and I got the shock of my life. The little devil had taken off all her clothes in the darkness.

That kiss was like molten lava. I couldn't push her away, nor did I want to now. She clung to me like a shadow, squirming and pulling at me. The sound of the crowd cheering the game a hundred yards away dimmed to nothingness and all I could hear was the roaring in my ears.

The game was almost over when we got back. I scrubbed the lipstick away from my mouth and dusted off my clothes. Mary saw her sister and was gracious enough to let me alone for a

while, so while I still had the chance I skirted the crowd and tried
to find Charlotte. She was where I had left her, only she had
gotten tired of sitting down. She and a tall youngster were splitting
a coke together. That made me mad.

Hell, I was a fine one to be pulling a jealousy stunt after what
I just did. I called to her and she came back to me.

"Where have you been?"

"Fighting," I lied, "fighting for my honor."

"You look it. How did you make out? Or shouldn't I ask?"

"I did it all right. It took time though. You been here all the
time?"

"Yep. Just like a good little wife, I sit home while my husband
is out with other women," she laughed.

The shout that ended the tennis game came simultaneously with
the scream from the house. That scream stifled any cheer that
might have been given. It rang out in the night again and again,
then dwindled off to a low moan.

I dropped Charlotte's hand and ran for the house. The bartender
was standing in the doorway as white as a sheet. He could hardly
talk. He pointed up the stairs and I took them two at a time.

The first floor opened on the cloakroom, an affair as big as a
small ballroom. The maid was huddled on the floor, out like a
light. Beyond her was Myrna, a bullet hole clean through her
chest. She still had her hands clutched futilely against her breasts
as though to protect herself.

I felt her pulse. She was dead.

Downstairs the crowd was pounding across the lawn. I shouted
to the bartender to shut the doors, then grabbed the phone and
got the gatekeeper. I told him to close the gates and not let anyone
out, hung up, and dashed downstairs. I picked out three men in
overalls whom I had taken for gardeners and asked them who
they were.

"Gardener," one said. The other was a handyman on the estate
and the third was his helper.

"Got any guns around here?" They nodded. "Six shot guns and
a 30.30 in the library," the handyman said.

"Then get 'em," I ordered. "There's been a murder upstairs
and the killer is someplace on the grounds. Patrol the estate and
shoot anybody you see trying to get away. Understand?"

The gardener started to argue, but when I pulled my badge on
him, he and the others took off for the library, got the guns,
returned a minute later and shot out the door.

The crowd was gathered in front. I stepped outside and held

up my hand for silence. When I told them what had happened there were a few screams, a lot of nervous talk, and everyone in general had the jitters.

I held up my hand again. "For your own benefit you had better not try to leave. There are men posted with orders to shoot if anyone tries to run for it. If you are wise, you'll find someone who was standing near by you during the game and have an alibi ready. Only don't try to dummy one because it won't work. Stay here on the porch where you can be reached at a moment's notice."

Charlotte came in the door, her face white, and asked, "Who was it, Mike?"

"Myrna. The kid has nothing to worry about any more. She's dead. And I have the killer right under my nose someplace."

"Can I do something, Mike?"

"Yeah. Get the Bellemy sisters and bring them to me."

When she went for them I called for the bartender. Shaking like a leaf he came over to me. "Who came in here?"

"I don' see nobody, boss. I see one girl come in. I never see her come out 'cause she's daid upstairs."

"Were you here all the time?"

"Yassuh. All de time. I watch for the folks to come in heah for a drink. Then I goes to the bar."

"What about the back door?"

"It's locked, boss. Only way is in through heah. Don' nobody come in 'cept de girl. She's daid."

"Quit saying that over and over," I stormed. "Just answer my questions. Did you leave here for a second?"

"Nosuh, boss, not hardly a second."

"What's not hardly?"

The kid looked scared. He was afraid to commit himself one way or another. "Come on, speak up."

"I got me a drink once, boss. Just beer, that's all. Don't tell Miss Bellemy."

"Damn," I said. That minute was time enough to let a murderer in here.

"How quickly did you come back? Wait a minute. Go in there and get beer. Let me see how long it took you." The bartender shuffled off while I timed him. Fifteen seconds later he was back with a bottle in his hand.

"Did you do it that fast before? Think now. Did you drink it here or in there?"

"Here, boss," he said simply, pointing to an empty bottle on the floor. I yelled to him not to move, then ran for the back of the house. The place was built in two sections, this part an addition to the other. The only way in was through the French windows to the bar and the back door, or the one connecting door to the other section. The windows were bolted. So was the back door. The twin doors between the two sections of the building were firmly in place and locked. I looked for other possible entries, but there were none. If that were so I could still have the killer trapped somewhere inside.

Quickly, I raced up the stairs. The maid was recovering and I helped her to her feet. She was pasty-faced and breathing hard, so I sat her down on the top step as Charlotte came in with the twins.

The maid was in no condition to answer questions. I shouted down to Charlotte to call Pat Chambers as fast as she could and get him up here. He could call the local cops later. Mary and Esther came up and took the maid out of my hands and half carried her downstairs to a chair.

I went into the murder room and closed the door after me. I didn't worry about fingerprints. My killer never left any.

Myrna had on her blue coat, though I couldn't see why. The night was far too warm for it. She lay in front of a full-length mirror, doubled up. I looked closely at the wound. Another .45. The killer's gun. I was bent down on my knees looking for the bullet when I noticed the stuff on the rug. A white powder. Around it the nap of the carpet had been ruffled as though someone had tried to scoop it up. I took an envelope from my pocket and got some of the grains inside. I felt the body. It was still warm. But then, at this temperature, *rigor mortis* wouldn't set in until late.

Myrna's hands were clenched together so tightly I had difficulty working my fingers under hers. She had clawed at her coat trying to hold the wound, and fibers of wool were caught under her fingernails. She had died hard, but fast. Death was merciful.

I felt under the coat, and there in the folds of the cloth was the bullet, a .45. I had my killer here. All I had to do was find him. Why he should kill Myrna was beyond me. She was as far out of the case as I was. The motive. The motive. What the hell kind of a motive was it that ate into so many people? The people the killer reached out and touched had nothing to give. They were all so different.

Jack, yes. I could see where he'd got mixed up in murder, but Myrna, no. Look at Bobo. Nothing could make me believe he was part of the picture. Where was motive there? Dope, he had been delivering it. But the connection. He never lived long enough to tell where he got the package or to whom it was going.

I shut the door softly behind me out of respect for the dead. Esther Bellemy had the maid in a chair at the foot of the stairs trying to comfort her. Mary was pouring herself a stiff whiskey, her hands trembling. This hit her hard, whereas Esther was well composed. Charlotte came in with a cold compress and held it against the maid's head.

"Can she talk yet?" I asked Charlotte.

"Yes, I think so. Just be easy with her."

I knelt in front of the maid and patted her hand. "Feel better?" She nodded. "Good, I just want to ask you a few questions, then you can lie down. Did you see anyone come or go?"

"No. I—I was in the back of the house cleaning up."

"Did you hear a shot?"

Another negative.

I called over to the black man. "What about you, hear anything?"

"Nosuh, I don' heah nuthin'."

If neither had heard the shot, then the silencer must still be on the .45. And if the killer had it around, we'd find it. That kind of a rig is too big to hide.

I went back to the maid. "Why did you go upstairs?"

"To straighten out the clothes. The women had left them all over the bed. That's when I saw the b-body." She buried her face in her hands and sobbed quietly.

"Now, one more thing, did you touch anything?"

"No, I fainted."

"Put her to bed, Charlotte; see if you can find something to make her sleep. She's pretty upset."

Between Charlotte and Esther they half dragged the maid to bed. Mary Bellemy was pouring one drink after another in her. She wouldn't be standing up much longer. I took the bartender aside. "I'm going upstairs. Don't let anyone in or out unless I say so, you hear? You do and you'll wind up in jail yourself." I didn't have to say anything else. He stammered out a reply that I didn't get, then locked and bolted the front door.

My killer had to be somewhere around. He had to leave through the front door unless he went out an upstairs window. Everything else was locked up tightly. But except for the little bit of time the bartender was away from the door, someone was there. That time had been enough to let the killer in, but not enough to let him back out again. Not without being seen by the bartender, that is. If he had seen someone and had been told to keep his mouth shut, I would have known it. I could swear that he was telling the truth. Besides, my killer would have knocked him off as well, and as easily, rather than take the risk of exposure.

From the top of the stairs, the hall crossed like a T. Doors opened off the one side, and each proved to be a guest room. I tried the windows. Locked. I went up and down both ends of the T trying to find where the exit was. Each room I inspected and searched with my rod in my fist, waiting, hoping.

The murder room was the last room I tried. And that's where the killer got out. The window slid up easily, and I looked down fifteen feet to a flagstone walk below. If he had jumped he wouldn't be walking now. The drop was enough to break a leg, especially on those stones. Around the building and directly under the window ran a narrow ledge. It projected out about eight inches from the wall and was clean of dust or dirt on both sides of the window. I lit a match and looked for heel marks in the concrete of the ledge, but there were none. Not a mark. This was enough to drive me nuts.

Even the eight inches wasn't enough to walk across on barefaced brick. I tried it. I got out on the ledge and tried first to walk along with my face to the wall, then with my back to it. In both cases I almost took a spill. It would take a real athlete to cross that. Someone who was part cat.

Inside the room, I pulled the window down and went back to the hall. At either end a window overlooked the grounds. I didn't see it at first, but when I stuck my head out there was a fire-escape ladder built into the wall adjacent to the window. Oh, how pretty if it could be done. The killer strikes, then out the window to the ledge, and around to the fire escape. Now I had an acrobat on my hands. Swell, more headaches.

I went downstairs and took the bottle away from Mary in time to salvage a drink from the wreckage and ease her into a chair. She was dead drunk.

A half hour later I had still gotten nowhere when I heard the pounding of feet outside and told the bartender to open up.

Pat and his staff walked in escorted by some county police. How that guy could get around the red tape of city limitations and restrictions was beyond me. He went upstairs at once, listening as I gave him the details.

I finished as he was bent over the body. The county coroner bustled in, declared the girl officially dead and made out a report. "How long since she died?" Pat asked.

The coroner hemmed and hawed, then said, "Roughly, about

two hours. This warm weather makes it difficult to place the time exactly. Tell better after an autopsy."

Two hours was close enough. It had happened while I was out in the bushes with Mary Bellemy.

Pat asked me, "Everyone here?"

"Guess so. Better get a guest list from Esther and check up. I posted guards around the wall and at the gate."

"Okay, come on downstairs."

Pat herded the entire group of them into the main room in the other section of the building. He had them packed in like sardines. Esther gave him a guest list and he read off names. As each one heard his name called, he sat on the floor. The detectives watched closely to be sure none of them moved until they were supposed to. Half the group was seated when Pat called out "Harmon Wilder."

No answer. He tried again, "Harmon Wilder." Still no answer. My little friend had vanished. Pat nodded to a detective who moved to a phone. The manhunt was on.

Six names later Pat sang out, "Charles Sherman." He called it three more times and no one answered. That was a name I hadn't heard before. I walked over to Esther.

"Who is this Sherman?"

"Mr. Wilder's assistant. He was here during the game. I saw him."

"Well, he's not here now."

I relayed the information to Pat and another name went out to call cars and police stations. Pat read down the list; when he was done there were still twenty standees. Gate crashers. You find them everywhere. The total number crammed into that house was over two hundred and fifty persons.

Pat assigned a certain number to each detective and some to me. Because I had been on the scene he let me take all the servants, the twins, Charlotte, and ten others from the party. Pat took the gate crashers for himself. As soon as he gave out the list, he quieted the assembly and cleared his throat.

"Everyone present here is under suspicion for murder," he said. "Naturally, I know that you all couldn't have done it. You are to report to each of my men as your name is called. They will speak to you separately. What we want is your alibi, whom you were with at the game, or wherever you were"—he checked his watch—"two hours and fifty minutes ago. If you can vouch for someone standing near you, do it. By doing so you are only insuring your own alibi. I want the truth. Nothing else. We will catch you if you try falsifying your statements. That is all."

I collected my group and took them out on the porch. The household help I disposed of first. They had all been together and spoke for one another. The ten new faces assured me that they had been with certain parties and I took their statements. Mary had been with me, so she was out. Esther had been beside the referee's stand most of the time and this was corroborated by the rest. I shooed them away, Esther leading her still half-out sister. I saved Charlotte until last so we could have the porch together.

"Now you, kitten," I said. "Where were you?"

"You have a nerve," she said laughingly. "Right where you left me."

"Aw, don't get sore, baby, I was trapped."

I kissed her and she said, "After that all is forgiven. Now I'll tell you where I was. Part of the time I was sipping a coke with a nice young gentleman named Fields, and part of the time exchanging witticisms with a rather elderly wolf. I don't know his name, but he was one of those that weren't on the list. He has a spade beard."

I remembered him. I put down "spade beard," no name. Charlotte stayed close to me as we walked back into the room. Pat was picking up the list as his men finished and cross-checking them to see if the stories held water. A couple had the names confused, but they were soon adjusted. When all were in we compared them.

Not a single one was without an alibi. And it didn't seem sensible that Wilder and Sherman should have run off—they had been accounted for, too. Pat and I let out a steady stream of curses without stopping. When we got our breaths Pat instructed his men to get names and addresses of everyone present and told them to inform the guests that they had better stay within reaching distance or else.

He was right. It was practically an impossibility to hold that many people there at once. It looked like we were still following a hopeless trail.

Most of the cars left at once. Pat had a cop handing out the coats since he didn't want anyone messing up the murder room. I went up with Charlotte to get hers. The cop pulled out her blue job with the white wolf collar and I helped her into it.

Mary was still out so I didn't say good-bye to her. Esther was at the door downstairs, as calm as ever, seeing the guests out, even being nice to the ones that didn't belong there.

I shook hands with her and told her I'd see her soon and

Charlotte and I left. Instead of driving up, she had taken the train, so we both got into my car and started back.

Neither one of us spoke much. As the miles passed under my wheels I got madder and madder. The circle. It started with Jack and had ended with him. The killer finally got around to Myrna. It was crazy. The whole pattern was bugs. Now my motive was completely shot to hell. Myrna fitted in nowhere. I heard a sob beside me and caught Charlotte wiping tears from her eyes. That was easy to see. She had taken a liking to Myrna.

I put my arm around her and squeezed. This must seem like a nightmare to her. I was used to death sitting on my doorstep, she wasn't. Maybe when the dragnet brought in Wilder and Sherman there would be an answer to something. People just don't run away for nothing. The outsider. The answer to the question. Could either of them have been the outsider that belonged in the plot? Very possible. It seemed more possible now than ever. Manhunt. The things the cops were best at. Go get them. Don't miss. If they try to run, kill the bastards. I don't care if I don't get them myself, so long as someone does. No glory. Justice.

When I stopped in front of Charlotte's place I had to stop thinking. I looked at my watch. Well after midnight. I opened the door for her.

"Want to come up?"

"Not tonight, darling," I said. "I want to go home and think."

"I understand. Kiss me good night." She held out her face and I kissed her. How I loved that girl. I'd be glad when this was over with and we could get married.

"Will I see you tomorrow?"

I shook my head. "I doubt it. If I can find time I'll call you."

"Please, Mike," she begged, "try to make it. Otherwise I can't see you until Tuesday."

"What's the matter with Monday?" I asked her.

"Esther and Mary are coming back to the city and I promised to have supper with them. Esther is more upset than you realize. Mary will get over it fast enough, but her sister isn't like that. You know how women are when they get in a spot."

"Okay, baby. If I don't see you tomorrow, I'll give you a call Monday and see you Tuesday. Maybe then we can go get that ring."

This time I gave her a long kiss and watched her disappear into the building. I had some tall thinking to do. Too many had died. I was afraid to let it go further. It had to be now or not at all.

I tooled the jalopy back to the garage, parked it and went upstairs to bed.

chapter thirteen ▬▬▬▬▬▬▬▬▬▬

SUNDAY WAS A FLOP. It opened with the rain splattering against the windows and the alarm shattering my eardrums. I brought my fist down on the clock, swearing at myself because I set it automatically when I didn't have to get up at all.

This was one day when I didn't have to shower or shave. I burned my breakfast as usual and ate it while I was in my underwear. When I was stacking the dishes, I glanced at myself in the mirror, and a dirty, unkempt face glared back at me. On days like this I look my ugliest.

Fortunately, the refrigerator was well stocked with beer. I pulled out two quarts, got a glass from the cabinet, a spare pack of butts, and laid them beside my chair. Then I opened the front door and the papers fell to the floor. Very carefully, I separated the funnies from the pile, threw the news section in the waste basket and began the day.

I tried the radio after that. I tried pacing the floor. Every ashtray was filled to overflowing. Nothing seemed to help. Occasionally I would flop in the chair and put my head in my hands and try to think. But whatever I did, I invariably came up with the same answer. Stymied. Nuts.

Something was trying to get out. I knew it. I could feel it. Way back in the recesses of my mind a little detail was gnawing its way through, screaming to be heard, but the more it gnawed, the greater were the defences erected to prevent its escaping.

Not a hunch. A fact. Some small, trivial fact. What was it? Could it be the answer? Something was bothering me terrifically. I tried some more beer. No. No. No . . . no . . . no . . . no . . . no. The answer wouldn't come. How must our minds be made? So complicated that a detail gets lost in the maze of knowledge. Why? That damn ever-present WHY. There's a why to everything. It was there, but how to bring it out? I tried thinking around the issue, I tried to think through it. I even tried to forget it, but the greater the effort, the more intense the failure.

I never noticed the passage of time. I drank, I ate, it was dark out and I turned the lights on and drank some more. Hours and minutes and seconds. I fought, but lost. So I fought again. One detail. What was it? What was it?

The refrigerator was empty all of a sudden and I fell into bed exhausted. It never broke through. That night I dreamed the killer was laughing at me. A killer whose face I couldn't see. I dreamed that the killer had Jack and Myrna and the rest of them hanging in chains, while I tried in vain to beat my way through a thin partition of glass with a pair of .45's to get to them. The killer was unarmed, laughing fiendishly, as I raved and cursed, but the glass wouldn't break. I never got through.

I awoke with a bad taste in my mouth. I brushed my teeth, but that didn't get rid of the taste. I looked out the window. Monday was no better than the day before. The rain was coming down in buckets. I couldn't stand to be holed up any longer, so I shaved and got dressed, then donned a raincoat and went out to eat. It was twelve then; when I finished it was one. I dropped in a bar and ordered one highball after another. The next time I looked at the clock it was nearly six.

That was when I reached in my pocket for another pack of cigarettes. My hand brushed an envelope. Damn, I could have kicked myself. I asked the bartender where the nearest drugstore was and he directed me around the corner.

The place was about to close, but I made it. I took the envelope out and asked him if he could test an unknown substance for me. The guy agreed reluctantly. Together we shook the stuff on to a piece of paper and he took it into the back. It didn't take long. I was fixing my tie in front of a mirror when he came back. He handed me the envelope with a suspicious glance. On it he had written one word.

Heroin.

I looked in the mirror again. What I saw turned the blood in my veins to liquid ice. I saw my eyes dilate. The mirror. The mirror and that one word. I shoved the envelope into my pocket viciously and handed the druggist a fin.

I couldn't talk. There was a crazy job bubbling inside me that made me go alternately hot and cold. If my throat hadn't been so tight I could have screamed. All this time. Not time wasted, because it had to be this way. Happy, happy. How could I be so happy? I had the WHY, but how could I be so happy? It wasn't right. I beat Pat to it after all. He didn't have the WHY. Only I did.

Now I knew who the killer was.

And I was happy. I walked back to the bar.

I took a last drag on the cigarette and flipped it spinning into the gutter, then turned and walked into the apartment house. Someone made it easy for me by not closing the lobby door tightly. No use taking the elevator, there was still plenty of time. I walked up the stairs wondering what the finale would be like.

The door was locked but I expected that. The second pick I used opened it. Inside, the place was filled with that curious stillness evident in an empty house. There was no need to turn on the lights, I knew the layout well enough. Several pieces of furniture were fixed in my mind. I sat down in a heavy chair set catercorner against the two walls. The leaves of a rubber plant on a table behind the chair brushed against my neck. I pushed them away and slid down into the lushness of the cushions to make myself comfortable, then pulled the .45 from its holster and snapped the safety off.

I waited for the killer.

Yes, Jack, this is it, the end. It took a long time to get around to it, but I did. I know who did it now. Funny, the way things worked out, wasn't it? All the symptoms were backwards. I had the wrong ones figured for it until the slip came. They all make that one slip. That's what the matter is with these cold-blooded killers; they plan, oh, so well. But they have to work all the angles themselves, while we have many heads working the problem out. Yeah, we miss plenty, but eventually someone stumbles on the logical solution. Only this one wasn't logical. It was luck. Remember what I promised you? I'd shoot the killer, Jack, right in the gut where you got it. Right where everyone could see what he had for dinner. Deadly, but he wouldn't die fast. It would take a few minutes. No matter who it turned out to be, Jack, I'd get the killer. No chair, no rope, just the one slug in the gut that would take the breath from the lungs and the life from the body. Not much blood, but I would be able to look at the killer dying at my feet and be glad that I kept my promise to you. A killer should die that way. Hard, nasty. No fanfare except the blast of an unsilenced .45 going off in a small, closed room. Yeah, Jack, no matter whom it turned out to be, that's the way death would come. Just like you got it. I know who did it. In a few minutes the killer will walk in here and see me sitting in this chair. Maybe the killer will try to talk me out of it, maybe even kill again, but

I don't kill easy. I know all the angles. Besides, I got a rod in my fist, waiting. Waiting. Before I do it I'll make the killer sweat— and tell me how it happened, to see if I hit it right. Maybe I'll even give the rat a chance to get me. More likely not. I hate too hard and shoot too fast. That's why people say the things about me that they do. That's why the killer would have had to try for me soon. Yes, Jack, it's almost finished. I'm waiting. I'm waiting.

The door opened. The lights flicked on. I was slumped too low in the chair for Charlotte to see me. She took her hat off in front of the wall mirror. Then she saw my legs sticking out. Even under the make-up I could see the color drain out of her face.

Yes, Jack, Charlotte. Charlotte the beautiful. Charlotte the lovely. Charlotte who loved dogs and walked people's babies in the park. Charlotte whom you wanted to crush in your arms and feel the wetness of her lips. Charlotte of the body that was fire and life and soft velvet and responsiveness. Charlotte the killer.

She smiled at me. It was hard to tell that it wasn't forced, but I knew it. *She knew I knew it.* And she knew why I was here. The .45 was levelled straight at her stomach.

Her mouth smiled at me, her eyes smiled at me, and she looked pleased, so glad to see me, just as she had always been. She was almost radiant when she spoke. "Mike, darling. Oh, baby, I'm so glad to see you. You didn't call like you promised and I've been worried. How did you get in? Oh, but Kathy is always leaving the door open. She's off tonight." Charlotte started to walk toward me. "And please, Mike, don't clean that awful gun here. It scares me."

"It should," I said.

She stopped a few feet away from me, her face fixed on mine. Her brows creased in a frown. Even her eyes were puzzled. If it were anyone but me they'd never have known she was acting. Christ, she was good! There was no one like her. The play was perfect, and she wrote, directed and acted all the parts. The timing was exact, the strength and character she put into every moment, every expression, every word was a crazy impossibility of perfection. Even now she could make me guess, almost build a doubt in my mind, but I shook my head slowly.

"No good, Charlotte, I know."

Her eyes opened wider. Inside me I smiled to myself. Her mind must have been racing with fear. *She* remembered my promise to Jack. She couldn't forget it. Nobody could, because I'm me and I always keep a promise. And this promise was to get the killer, and she was the killer. And I had promised to shoot the killer in the stomach.

She walked to an end table and picked a cigarette from a box, then lit it with a steady hand. That's when I knew, too, that she had figured an out. I didn't want to tell her that it was a useless out. The gun never left her a second.

"But . . ."

"No," I said, "let me tell you, Charlotte. I was a little slow in catching on, but I got it finally. Yesterday I would have dreaded this, but not now. I'm glad. Happier than I've been in a long time. It was the last kill. They were so different. So damn cold-blooded that I had it figured for a kill-crazy hood or an outsider. You were lucky. Nothing seemed to tie up, there were so many complications. It jumped around from one thing to another, yet every one of those things was part of the same basic motive.

"Jack was a cop. Someone always hates cops. Especially a cop that is getting close to him. But Jack didn't know just who he was getting close to until you held a rod on him and pumped one into his intestines. That was it, wasn't it?"

She looked so pathetic, standing there. Twin tears welled up and rolled down her cheeks. So pathetic and so helpless. As though she wanted to stop me, to tell me I was wrong—to show me *how* wrong I was. Her eyes were pools of supplication, begging, pleading. But I went on.

"It was you and Hal at first. No, just you alone. Your profession started it. Oh, you made money enough, but not enough. You are a woman who wanted wealth and power. Not to use it extravagantly, but just to have it. How many times have you gone into the frailty of men and seen their weaknesses? It made you afraid. You no longer had the social instinct of a woman—that of being dependent upon a man. You were afraid, so you found a way to increase your bank account and charge it to business. A way in which you'd never be caught, but a dirty way. The dirtiest way there is—almost."

The sorrow drifted from her eyes, and there was something else in its stead. It was coming now. I couldn't tell what it was, but it was coming. She stood tall and straight as a martyr, exuding beauty and trust and belief. Her head turned slightly and I saw a sob catch in her throat. Like a soldier. Her stomach was so flat against the belt of her skirt. She let her arms drop simply at her sides, her hands asking to be held, and her lips wanting to silence mine with a kiss. It was coming, but I dared not stop now. I couldn't let her speak or I would never be able to keep my promise.

"Your clientele. It was wealthy, proud. With your ability and appearance and your constant studies, you were able to draw such a group to you. Yes, you treated them, eased their mental discomfitures—but with drugs. Heroin. You prescribed, and they took your prescription—to become addicts, and you were their only source for the stuff and they had to pay through the nose to get it. Very neat. So awfully neat. Being a doctor, and through your clinic, you could get all the stuff you needed. I don't know how your delivery system worked, but that will come later.

"Then you met Hal Kines. An innocent meeting, but isn't that the way all things start? That's why I had trouble with the answer, it was all so casual. You never suspected him of his true activities, did you? But one day you used him as a subject for an experiment in hypnosis, didn't you? He was a fool to do it, but he had no choice if he wanted to play his role. And while he was under hypnosis you inadvertently brought to light every dirty phase of his life.

"You thought you had him then. You told him what you had discovered and were going to fit him into your plans. But you were fooled. Hal was not a college kid. He was an adult. An adult with a mature, scheming mind, who could figure things out for himself—and he had already caught wise to what you were doing and was going to hold it over *your* head. All you got out of that was a stalemate. Remember the book on your shelf—*Hypnosis as a Treatment for Mental Disorders?* It was well thumbed. I knew you were well versed in that angle, but I never caught on until yesterday."

She was standing in front of me now. I felt a hot glow go over me as I saw what she was about to do. Her hands came up along her sides pressing her clothes tightly against her skin, then slowly ran under her breasts, cupping them. Her fingers fumbled with the buttons of the blouse, but not for long. They came open—one by one.

"You and Hal held on tightly, each waiting for the other to make a break, but there was too much of a risk to take to start anything. That's where Jack came in. He was a shrewd one. That guy had a brain. Sure, he helped Hal out of a small jam, but in doing so something aroused his suspicions, and all the while he pretended to be helping Hal with his work he was really investigating him. Jack found out what Hal was up to, and when by accident he met Eileen, she confirmed it. Jack knew about the show through her, and since Hal was the brains of the outfit, knew, too, that he would be there.

"But let's jump back a little bit. Jack wanted to see you about something during the week. You yourself told me that. No, Jack didn't suspect you, but he thought that since you were connected with him through the school and the clinic, you might be able to keep a tab on him.

"But the night of the party you saw the yearbooks Jack had collected and knew why he had them. And you were afraid that if he exposed Hal, the guy would think you had something to do with it and turn you in, too. So you came back. When your maid went back to sleep you simply detached the chime behind the door and left, being careful not to be seen. What did you do, swipe Jack's key to the place before you left? I don't doubt it. Then you got him in the bedroom. You shot him and watched him die. And while he tried to pull himself toward his gun you made a psychological study of a man facing death, telling the story, and drawing the chair back inch by inch until his body gave up. Then you went home. That was it, wasn't it? No, you don't have to answer me because there could be no other way."

Now there were no more buttons. Slowly, ever so slowly, she pulled the blouse out of her skirt. It rustled faintly as silk does against wool. Then the cuff snaps—and she shrugged the blouse from her shoulders and let it fall to the floor. She wore no bra. Lovely shoulders. Soft curves of hidden muscles running across her body. Little ripples of excitement traversing the beautiful line of her neck. Breasts that were firm and inviting. Soft, yet so strong. She was so pretty. Young and delicious and exciting. She shook her head until her hair swirled in blonde shimmering waves down her back.

"But in the yearbooks you took from Jack's apartment were notations about Eileen. Her picture was in one, too, with Hal's. You knew that murder didn't stop there and saw how to cover one killing by committing another. You told Hal what you found, and sent him to threaten Eileen, and followed him in. Then, while the show went on, you killed them both, thinking that the murders would have to be hushed and the bodies disposed of by the others in the syndicate if they wanted to continue operation of the call house. You were right there. Somebody would have taken care of the matter if we hadn't come along so fast. When we crashed the joint you saw the madam run for it and followed her, and she never knew it, did she? How damn lucky you were. Coincidence and Lady Fortune were with you all the way. Neither Pat nor I thought to query *you* on an alibi for that night, but I bet you had a honey prepared.

"Let's not leave out George Kalecki. He found out about you. Hal must have gotten drunk and spilled the works. That's why he was surly the night of the party. He was worried and sore at Hal. Hal told you that George knew and you tried to pot him and missed. The only time you did miss. So he moved to town to get closer to the protection of the police. He couldn't tell them why, though, could he? You were still safe. He tried to implicate me to get me on the ball and run the killer down before the killer got to him.

"And after Hal's death, when we were walking along the park and George tried his hand with a gun, he wasn't shooting at me as I thought. It was you whom he wanted. He tailed me figuring I'd lead him to you. He knew he would be next on your list unless he got you first. George wanted out, but before he could blow he had to try to get the evidence Hal compiled or else take a chance on being sent to the chair if the stuff was ever found. Tough. I got him first. If he hadn't shot at me I wouldn't have killed him and he would have talked. I would have loved to make him yell his lungs out. Once more you were lucky."

Her fingers were sliding the zipper of her skirt. The zipper and a button. Then the skirt fell in a heap around her legs. Before she stepped out of it she pushed the half slip down. Slowly, so I could get the entire exotic effect. Then together, she pushed them away with a toe. Long, graceful, tanned legs. Gorgeous legs. Legs that were all curves and strength and made me see pictures that I shouldn't see any more. Legs of a golden color that needed no stockings to enhance. Lovely legs that started from a flat stomach and rounded themselves into thighs that belonged more in the imagination than reality. Beautiful calves. Heavier than those you see in the movies. Passionate legs. All that was left were the transparent panties. And she was a real blonde.

"Then Bobo Hopper. You didn't plan his death. It was an accident. Coincidence again that he had a former connection with George Kalecki. He had a job that he was proud of. He worked in your neighborhood running errands, delivering messages and sweeping floors. Only a simple moron who worked for nickels, but a happy egg. A guy that wouldn't step on ants and kept a beehive for a hobby. But one day he dropped a package he was delivering for you—a prescription, you told him. He was afraid he'd lose his job, so he tried to get the prescription refilled at a druggist, and it turned out to be heroin that you were sending to a client. But meanwhile the client called you and said the messenger hadn't shown up. I was there in your apartment that day, remember? And when I went for a haircut, you hurried out in your car, followed the route Bobo would have taken and saw him go in the drugstore, waited, and shot him when he came out.

"No, your alibi is shot. Kathy was home and never saw or heard you leave. You pretended to be in your darkroom, and no one ever disturbs a person in a darkroom. You detached the chimes and left, and came back without Kathy being any the wiser. But in your hurry you forgot to reconnect the chimes. I did it. Remember that, too? I came back for my wallet and there you were, a perfect alibi.

"Even then I didn't get it. But I started narrowing it down. I knew there was a motive that tied the thing up. Pat has a list of narcotic addicts. Someday, when they are cured, we'll get something from them that will lay it at your feet.

"Myrna was next. Her death was another accident. You didn't plan this one, either, but it had to be. And when I left you at the tennis game it gave you the chance. When did the possibilities of the consequence of her leaving occur to you? Immediately, I bet, like Bobo. You have an incredible mind. Somehow you think of everything at once. You knew how Bobo's mind would work and what might have happened, and you knew the woman, too. That comes as a result of being a psychiatrist. I was asleep when you arrived at the Bellemy place. You had a coat the same color as Myrna's, but with a fur collar. And you knew, too, that women have a bad habit of trying on each other's clothes in private. You couldn't afford that chance because you had a deck of heroin in your coat pocket, or possibly traces of the stuff. And you were delivering it to Harmon Wilder and Charles Sherman—that's why they ran, because they had some of the junk on them.

"Yes, you were a little too late. Myrna found the stuff in your pocket. She knew what it was. She should. Until Jack came along she lived on the stuff. You found her with it in her hand and shot her. Then you took off your coat, threw it on the bed with the others, and put Myrna's on her while she lay there on the floor. As for powder burns, simple. Pull the nose out of a slug and fire the gun at her body as a blank. You even dropped the slug that went through her in the folds of the coat. Have you burned your coat yet? I bet—since it had powder burns on it. But some of the blue fibers were still under her fingernails, from a coat the same color as yours. That and the mirror was the final clue. That and the heroin you missed. A girl stands in front of a mirror for just one thing, especially in a room full of clothes.

"I don't know where you get your luck, Charlotte. You came in while the bartender went for a drink, but you couldn't afford to be seen going out. Not after you committed a murder. So you took the ledge around the building to the fire escape like a human fly. I was too broad to make it, but you weren't. You took your shoes off, didn't you? That's why there were no scratches in the cement. During the excitement of the game no one noticed you leave or return. Some kind of mass psychology, right?

"No, Charlotte, no jury would ever convict you on that, would they? Much too circumstantial. Your alibis were too perfect. You can't break an alibi that an innocent person believes is true. Like Kathy, for instance.

"But I would, Charlotte. And later we can take our time to worm out the truth without the interference of a court trial. We won't have to worry about a smart lawyer cracking our chains of circumstance and making them look foolish to a jury. We will know the answer as we do the problem, but the solution will take time. A trial wouldn't give us that time.

"No, Charlotte, I'm the jury now, and the judge, and I have a promise to keep. Beautiful as you are, as much as I almost loved you, I sentence you to death."

Her thumbs hooked in the fragile silk of the panties and pulled them down. She stepped out of them as delicately as one coming from a bathtub. She was completely naked now. A suntanned goddess giving herself to her lover. With arms outstretched she walked toward me. Lightly, her tongue ran over her lips, making them glisten with passion. The smell of her was like an exhilarating perfume. Slowly, a sigh escaped her, making the hemispheres of her breasts quiver. She leaned forward to kiss me, her arms going out to encircle my neck.

The roar of the .45 shook the room. Charlotte staggered back a step. Her eyes were a symphony of incredulity, an unbelieving witness to truth. Slowly, she looked down at the ugly swelling in her naked belly where the bullet went in. A thin trickle of blood welled out.

I stood up in front of her and shoved the gun into my pocket. I turned and looked at the rubber plant behind me. There on the table was the gun, with the safety catch off and the silencer still attached. Those loving arms would have reached it nicely. A face that was waiting to be kissed was really waiting to be splattered with blood when she blew my head off. My blood. When I heard her fall I turned around. Her eyes had pain in them now, the pain preceding death. Pain and unbelief.

"How c-could you?" she gasped.

I only had a moment before talking to a corpse, but I got it in.

"It was easy," I said.

Vengeance Is Mine

TO
JOE AND GEORGE
WHO ARE ALWAYS READY FOR
A NEW ADVENTURE
AND TO
WARD . . .
WHO USED TO BE

chapter one ■■■■■■■■■■■■■■■■

THE GUY WAS dead as hell. He lay on the floor in his pajamas with his brains scattered all over the rug and my gun was in his hand. I kept rubbing my face to wipe out the fuzz that clouded my mind but the cops wouldn't let me. One would pull my hand away and shout a question at me that made my head ache even worse and another would slap me with a wet rag until I felt like I had been split wide open.

I said, "Goddamn it, stop!"

Then one of them laughed and shoved me back on the bed.

I couldn't think. I couldn't remember. I was wound up like a spring and ready to bust. All I could see was the dead guy in the middle of the room and my gun. My gun! Somebody grabbed at my arm and hauled me upright and the questions started again. That was as much as I could take. I gave a hell of a kick and a fat face in a fedora pulled back out of focus and started to groan, all doubled up. Maybe I laughed, I don't know. Something made a coarse, cackling sound.

Somebody said, "I'll fix the bastard for that!" but before he could the door opened and the feet coming in stopped all the chatter except the groan and I knew Pat was there.

My mouth opened and my voice said, "Good old Pat, always to the rescue."

He didn't sound friendly. "Of all the damn fool times to be

drunk. Did anyone touch this man!" Nobody answered. The fat face in the fedora was slumped in a chair and groaned again.

"He kicked me. The son of a bitch kicked me . . . right here."

Another voice said, "That's right, Captain. Marshall was questioning him and he kicked him."

Pat grunted an answer and bent over me. "All right, Mike, get up. Come on, get up." His hand wrapped around my wrist and levered me into a right angle on the edge of the bed.

"Cripes, I feel lousy," I said.

"I'm afraid you're going to feel a lot worse." He took the wet rag and handed it to me. "Wipe your face off. You look like hell."

I held the cloth in my hands and dropped my face into it. Some of the clouds broke up and disappeared. When the shaking stopped I was propped up and half pushed into the bathroom. The shower was a cold lash that bit into my skin, but it woke me up to the fact that I was a human being and not a soul floating in space. I took all I could stand and turned off the faucet myself, then stepped out. By that time Pat had a container of steaming coffee in my hand and practically poured it down my throat. I tried to grin at him over the top of it, only there was no humor in the grin and there was less in Pat's tone.

His words came out of a disgusted snarl. "Cut the funny stuff, Mike. This time you're in a jam and a good one. What the devil has gotten into you? Good God, do you have to go off the deep end every time you get tangled with a dame?"

"She wasn't a dame, Pat."

"Okay, she was a good kid and I know it. There's still no excuse."

I said something nasty. My tongue was still thick and uncoordinated, but he knew what I meant. I said it twice until he was sure to get it.

"Shut up," he told me. "You're not the first one it happened to. What do I have to do, smack you in the teeth with the fact that you were in love with a woman that got killed until you finally catch on that there's nothing more you can do about it?"

"Nuts. There were two of them."

"All right, forget it. Do you know what's outside there?"

"Sure, a corpse."

"That's right, a corpse. Just like that. Both of you in the same hotel room and one of you dead. He's got your gun and you're drunk. What about it?"

"I shot him. I was walking in my sleep and I shot him."

This time Pat said the nasty word. "Quit lousing me up, Mike. I want to find out what happened."

I waved my thumb toward the other room. "Where'd the goons come from?"

"They're policemen, Mike. They're policemen just like me and they want to know the same things I do. At three o'clock the couple next door heard what they thought was a shot. They attributed it to a street noise until the maid walked in this morning and saw the guy on the floor and passed out in the doorway. Somebody called the cops and there it was. Now, what happened?"

"I'll be damned if I know," I said.

"You'll be damned if you don't."

I looked at Pat, my pal, my buddy. Captain Patrick Chambers, Homicide Department of New York's finest. He didn't look happy.

I felt a little sick and got the lid of the bowl up just in time. Pat let me finish and wash my mouth out with water, then he handed me my clothes. "Get dressed." His mouth crinkled up and he shook his head disgustedly.

My hands were shaking so hard I started to curse the buttons on my shirt. I got my tie under my collar but I couldn't knot it, so I let the damn thing hang. Pat held my coat and I slid into it, thankful that a guy can still be a friend even when he's teed off at you.

Fat Face in the fedora was still in the chair when I came out of the bathroom, only this time he was in focus and not groaning so much. If Pat hadn't been there he would have laid me out with the working end of a billy and laughed while he did it. Not by himself, though.

The two uniformed patrolmen were from a police car and the other two were plain-clothes men from the local precinct. I didn't know any of them and none of them knew me, so we were even. The two plain-clothes men and one cop watched Pat with a knowledge behind their eyes that said, "So it's one of those things, eh?"

Pat put them straight pretty fast. He shoved a chair under me and took one himself. "Start from the beginning," he said. "I want all of it, Mike, every single detail."

I leaned back and looked at the body on the floor. Someone had had the decency to cover it with a sheet. "His name is Chester Wheeler. He owns a department store in Columbus, Ohio. The store's been in his family a long time. He's got a wife and two kids. He was in New York on a buying tour for his business." I looked at Pat and waited.

"Go on Mike."

"I met him in 1945, just after I got back from overseas. We were in Cincinnati during the time when hotel rooms were scarce. I had a room with twin beds and he was sleeping in the lobby. I invited him up to share a bed and he took me up on it. Then he was a captain in the Air Force, some kind of a purchasing agent, working out of Washington. We got drunk together in the morning, split up in the afternoon, and I didn't see him again until last night. I ran into him in a bar where he was brooding into a beer feeling sorry for himself and we had a great reunion. I remember we changed bars about half a dozen times, then he suggested we park here for the night and we did. I bought a bottle and we finished it after we got up here. I think he began to get maudlin before we hit the sack but I can't remember all the details. The next thing I knew somebody was beating my head trying to get me up."

"Is that all?"

"Every bit of it, Pat."

He stood up and looked around the room. One of the plain-clothes men anticipated his question and remarked, "Everything is untouched, sir."

Pat nodded and knelt over to look at the body. I would like to have taken a look myself, but my stomach wouldn't stand it. Pat didn't speak to anyone in particular when he said, "Wound self-inflicted. No doubt about it." His head jerked up in my direction. "You know, you're going to lose your license over this, Mike."

"I don't know why. I didn't shoot him," I said sourly.

Fat Face sneered, "How do you know you didn't, wise guy?"

"I never shoot people when I'm drunk," I snarled, "unless they push me around and make like they're tough."

"Wise guy."

"Yeah, real wise."

"Cut it out, the both of you," Pat snapped. Fat Face shut up and let me alone with my hangover. I slouched across the room to a chair in the corner and slid down into it. Pat was having a conference over by the door that wound up with everyone but Fat Face leaving. The door hadn't closed shut before the coroner came in, complete with wicker basket and pallbearers.

The little men in my head started up with their hammers and chisels, so I closed my eyes and let my ears do the work. The medical examiner and the cops reached the same conclusion. It was my gun that shot him. A big round .45 fired at very close range. The fingerprint boys picked my prints off the rod and the other guy's too. His were on top.

A call came in for Pat right then and while he was on the phone I heard Fat Face suggest something to the M.E. that brought me straight up in the chair.

Fat Face said, ". . . Murder just as easy. They were drunk and had an argument. Bright eyes plugged him and put the gun in his hand to make it look like suicide. Then he soused himself up with liquor to make it look good."

The M.E. bobbed his head. "Reasonable enough."

"You dirty fat slob, you!" I came out of the chair like a shot and spun him around on his heels. Cop or no cop, I would have caved his nose in for him if Pat hadn't dropped the phone and stepped in between us. This time he took my arm and didn't let go until he finished his phone call. When the body had been hoisted into the basket and carted off Pat unbuttoned his coat and motioned for me to sit on the bed.

I sat.

He had his hands in his pockets and he spoke as much to the plain-clothes man as to me. His words didn't come easy, but he didn't stumble over them exactly. "I've been waiting for this, Mike. You and that damn gun of yours were bound to get in trouble."

"Stow it, Pat. You know I didn't shoot the guy."

"Do I?"

"Hell, you ought to . . .?"

"Do you know you didn't?"

"It was a closed room and I was so far gone I didn't even hear the gun go off. You'll get a paraffin test on the body that will prove it anyway. I'll go for one myself and that will settle that. What are we jawing about?"

"About you and that rod, that's what! If the guy was a suicide you'll be up the creek without a license. They don't like for people to be carrying firearms and a load of liquor too."

He had me cold on that one. His eyes swept the room, seeing the clothes on the backs of the chairs, the empty whisky bottle on the windowsill, the stubs of cigarettes scattered all over the floor. My gun was on the desk along with a spent casing, with the white powder clotting in the oil, still showing the prints.

Pat closed his eyes and grimaced. "Let's go, Mike," he said.

I put on my coat over the empty holster and squeezed between the two of them for the ride down to headquarters. There was a parking-lot ticket in my pocket, so I didn't worry about my heap.

Fat Face had that look in his eyes that said he was hoping I'd make a break for it so he could bounce me one. It was rough having to disappoint the guy.

For once I was glad to have a friend in the department. Pat ran the tests off on me himself and had me stick around downstairs until the report was finished. I had the ash tray half filled before he came back down. "What did it show?" I asked him.

"You're clean enough. The corpse carried the powder burns all right."

"That's a relief."

His eyebrows went up. "Is it? The D.A. wants to have a little talk with you. It seems that you managed to find an awfully fussy hotel to play around in. The manager raised a stink and carried it all the way upstairs. Ready?"

I got up and followed him to the elevators, cursing my luck for running into an old buddy. What the hell got into the guy anyway? It would have been just as easy for him to jump out the damn window. The elevator stopped and we got out. It would have been better if there was an organ playing a dirge. I was right in the spirit for it.

The D.A. was a guy who had his charming moments, only this time there weren't any photographers around. His face wore a tailor-made look of sarcasm and there was ice in his words. He told me to sit down then perched himself on the edge of the desk. While Pat was running through the details he never took his eyes off me nor let his expression change one bit. If he thought he was getting under my skin with his professional leer he had another think coming. I was just about to tell him he looked like a frog when he beat me to it.

"You're done in this town, Mr. Hammer, I suppose you know that."

What the hell could I say? He held all the cards.

He slid off the desk and stood at parade rest so I could admire his physique, I guess. "There were times when you proved yourself quite useful . . . and quite trying. You let yourself get out of hand once too often. I'm sorry it happened this way, but it's my opinion that the city is better off without you or your services." The D.A. was getting a big whang out of this.

Pat shot him a dirty look, but kept his mouth shut. I wasn't a clam. "Then I'm just another citizen again?"

"That's right, with no license and no gun. Nor will you ever have one again."

"Are you booking me for anything?"

"I can't very well. I wish I could."

He must have read what was coming in the lopsided grin I gave him because he got red from his collar up. "For a D.A. you're a pain in the behind," I said. "If it wasn't for me the papers would have run you in the comic section long ago."

"That will be enough, Mr. Hammer!"

"Shut up your yap or arrest me, otherwise I'll exercise my rights as a citizen, and one of 'em happens to be objecting to the actions of any public official. You've been after my hide ever since you walked into this office because I had sense enough to know where to look for a few killers. It made nice copy for the press and you didn't even get an honorable mention. All I have to say is this . . . it's a damn good thing the police are civil service. They have to have a little bit of common sense to get where they are. Maybe you were a good lawyer . . . you should have kept at it and quit trying to be king of the cops."

"Get out of here!" His voice was a short fuse ready to explode any second. I stood up and jammed on my hat. Pat was holding the door open. The D.A. said, "The very first time you so much as speed down Broadway, I'm going to see to it personally that you're slapped with every charge in the book. That will make good press copy too."

I stopped with my hand on the knob and sneered at him, then Pat jerked my sleeve and I closed the door. In the hallway he kept his peace until we reached the stairs; it was as long as he could hold it. "You're a fool, Mike."

"Nuts, Pat. It was his game all the way."

"You could keep your trap closed, couldn't you?"

"No!" I licked the dryness from my lips and stuck a cigarette in my mouth. "He's been ready for me too long now. The jerk was happy to give me the shaft."

"So you're out of business."

"Yeah. I'll open up a grocery store."

"It isn't that funny, Mike. You're a private investigator and a good cop when you have to be. There were times when I was glad to have you around. It's over now. Come on in my office . . . we might as well have a drink on it." He ushered me into his sanctum sanctorum and waved me into a chair. The bottom drawer of his desk had a special niche for a pint bottle and a few glasses, carefully concealed under a welter of blank forms. Pat drew two and handed one over to me. We toasted each other in silence, then spilled them down.

"It was a pretty good show while it lasted," Pat said.

"Sure was," I agreed, "sure was. What happens now?"

He put the bottle and glasses away and dropped into the swivel chair behind his desk. "You'll be called in if there's an inquest. The D.A. is liable to make it hard on you out of meanness. Meanwhile, you're clear to do what you please. I vouched for you. Besides, you're too well known to the boys to try to drop out of sight."

"Buy your bread and butter from me, will you?"

Pat let out a laugh. "I wish you wouldn't take it so lightly. You're in the little black book right now on the special S-list."

I pulled out my wallet and slid my license out of the card case and threw it on his desk. "I won't be needing that any more."

He picked it up and examined it sourly. A large envelope on the filing cabinet held my gun and the report sheet. He clipped the card to the form and started to put it back. On second thought he slid the magazine out of the rod and swore. "That's nice. They put it in here with a full load." He used his thumb to jack the shells out of the clip, spilling them on the desk.

"Want to kiss old betsy good-by, Mike?"

When I didn't answer he said, "What are you thinking of?"

My eyes were squinted almost shut and I started to grin again. "Nothing," I said, "nothing at all."

He frowned at me while he dumped the stuff back in the envelope and closed it. My grin spread and he started to get mad. "All right, damn it, what's so funny? I know that look . . . I've seen it often enough. What's going through that feeble mind of yours?"

"Just thoughts, Pat. Don't be so hard on a poor unemployed pal, will you?"

"Let's hear those thoughts."

I picked a cigarette out of the container on his desk, then put it back after reading the label. "I was just thinking of a way to get that ticket back, that's all."

That seemed to relieve him. He sat down and tugged at his tie. "It'll ge a good trick if you can work it. I can't see how you can."

I thumbed a match and lit up a smoke. "It won't be hard."

"No? You think the D.A. will mail it back to you with his apologies?"

"I wouldn't be a bit surprised."

Pat kicked the swivel chair all the way around and glared at me. "You haven't got your gun any more, you can't hold him up."

"No," I laughed, "but I can make a deal with him. Either he *does* mail it back with his apologies or I'll make a sap out of him."

His palms cracked the desk and he was all cop again. This much wasn't a game. "Do you know anything, Mike?"

"No more than you. Everything I told you was the truth. It'll be easy to check and your laboratory backs up my statements. The guy was a suicide. I agree with you. He shot himself to pieces and I don't know why or when. All I know is where and that doesn't help. Now, have you heard enough?"

"No, you bastard, I haven't." This time he was grinning back at me. I shoved my hat on and left him there still grinning. When I closed the door I heard him kick the desk and swear to himself.

I walked out into the glaring brightness of midday, whistling through my teeth, though by rights I should have been in a blue funk. I hopped in a cab at the corner and gave him my office address. All the way uptown I kept thinking about Chester Wheeler, or what was left of him on the rug. An out-and-out suicide and my gun in his mitt, they said. Private citizen Michael Hammer, that's me. No ticket, no gun and no business, even my hangover was gone. The driver let me out in front of my building and I paid him off, walked in and pushed the bell for the elevator.

Velda was curled up in my big leather chair, her head buried in the paper. When I walked in she dropped it and looked at me. There were streaks across her face from wiping away the tears and her eyes were red. She tried to say something, sobbed and bit her lip.

"Take it easy, honey." I threw my coat on the rack and pulled her to her feet.

"Oh, Mike, what happened?" It had been a long time since I'd seen Velda playing woman like this. My great big beautiful secretary was human after all. She was better this way.

I put my arms around her, running my fingers through the sleek midnight of her hair. I squeezed her gently and she put her head against my cheek. "Cut it, sugar, nothing is that bad. They took away my ticket and made me a Joe Doe. The D.A. finally got me where he wanted me."

She shook her hair back and gave me a light tap in the ribs. "That insipid little squirt! I hope you clobbered him good!"

I grinned at her G.I. talk. "I called him a name, that's what I did."

"You should have clobbered him!" Her head went down on

my shoulder and sniffed. "I'm sorry, Mike. I feel like a jerk for crying."

She blew her nose on my fancy pocket handkerchief and I steered her over to the desk. "Get the sherry, Velda. Pat and I had a drink to the dissolution of the Mike Hammer enterprise. Now we'll drink to the new business. The S.P.C.D., Society for the Prevention of Cruelty to Detectives."

Velda brought out the makings and poured two short ones. "It isn't that funny, Mike."

"I've been hearing that all morning. The funny part is that it's *very* funny."

The sherry went down and we had another. I lit a pair of smokes and stuck one between her lips. "Tell me about it," she said. The tears were gone now. Curiosity and a little anger were in her eyes, making them snap. For the second time today I rehashed what I know of it, bringing the story right through the set-up in the D.A.'s office.

When I finished she said some very unladylike curses and threw her cigarette at the waste basket. "Damn these public officials and their petty grievances, Mike. They'll climb over anybody to get to the top. I wish I could do something instead of sitting here answering your mail. I'd like to turn that pretty boy inside out!" She threw herself into the leather chair and drew her legs up under her.

I reached out a toe and flipped her skirt down. On some people legs are just to reach the ground. On Velda they were a hell of a distraction. "Your days of answering the mail are over, kid."

Her eyes got wet again, but she tried to smile it off. "I know. I can always get a job in a department store. What will you do?"

"Where's your native ingenuity? You used to be full of ideas." I poured another glass of sherry and sipped it, watching her. For a minute she chewed on her fingernail, then raised her head to give me a puzzled frown.

"What are you getting at, Mike?"

Her bag, green leather shoulder-strap affair, was lying on the desk. I raised it and let it fall. It hit the polished wood with a dull clunk. "You have a gun and a license to carry it, haven't you? And you have a private operator's ticket yourself, haven't you? Okay, from now on the business is yours. I'll do the legwork."

A twitch pulled her mouth into a peculiar grin as she realized what I meant. "You'll like that, too, won't you?"

"What?"

"The legwork."

I slid off the edge of the desk and stood in front of her. With Velda I didn't take chances. I reached out a toe again and flipped her dress up to the top of her sheer nylons. She would have made a beautiful calendar. "If I went for any I'd go for yours, but I'm afraid of that rod you use for ballast in your handbag."

Her smile was a funny thing that crept up into her eyes and laughed at me from there. I just looked at her, a secretary with a built-in stand-off that had more on the ball than any of the devil's helpers I had ever seen and could hold me over the barrel without saying a word.

"You're the boss now," I said. "We'll forget about the mail and concentrate on a very special detail . . . getting my license and my gun back where it belongs. The D.A. made me out a joker and put the screws on good. If he doesn't send 'em back with a nice, sweet note, the newspapers are going to wheel out the chopping block for the guy.

"I won't even tell you how to operate. You can call the signals and carry the ball yourself if you want to. I'll only stick my nose in during the practice sessions. But if you're smart, you'll concentrate on the body of Chester Wheeler. When he was alive he was a pretty nice guy, a regular family man. All the grisly details are in the paper there and you can start from that. Meanwhile, I'll be around breaking ground for you and you'll spot my tracks here and there. You'll find some signed blank checks in the drawer for your expense account."

I filled the sherry glass up again and drained it in one gulp. It was a beautiful day, a real dilly. My face cracked into a smile that was followed by a short rumble of pleasure.

Once more Velda said, "It *isn't* funny, Mike."

I lit another cigarette and pushed my hat back on my head. "You'll never know how real funny it actually is, kid. You see, only one bullet killed Chester Wheeler. I always carry six in the clip and when Pat emptied it out there were only four of them."

Velda was watching me with the tip of her tongue clenched between her teeth. There wasn't any kitten-softness about her now. She was big and she was lovely, with the kind of curves that made you want to turn around and have another look. The lush fullness of her lips had tightened into the faintest kind of snarl and her eyes were the carnivorous eyes you could expect to see in the jungle watching you from behind a clump of bushes.

I said it slowly. "If you had that gun in your hand pointed at somebody's belly, could you pull the trigger and stand ready to pull it again if you had to?"

She pulled her tongue back and let her teeth close together. "I wouldn't have to pull it twice. Not now I wouldn't."

She was watching me as I walked across the office. I looked over my shoulder and waved so-long, then closed the door fast. She still hadn't bothered to pull her dress back down, and like I said, I wasn't taking any chances.

Someday she wasn't going to get so smart with me.

Or maybe she would.

chapter two ████████████████████

THE PAPERS WERE full of it that night. The tabloids had me splashed all over the front pages and part of the middle section. The same guys that hung on my tail when they had wanted a story took me apart at the seams in their columns. Only one bothered to be sentimental about it. He wrote me an epitaph. In rhyme. The D.A. was probably laughing his head off.

In another hour he'd be crying in his beer, the jerk.

I finished off an early supper and stacked the dishes in the sink. They could wait. For fifteen minutes I steamed under a shower until my skin turned pink, then suffered under a cold spray for a few seconds before I stepped out and let a puddle spread around my feet. When I finished shaving I climbed into a freshly pressed suit and transferred a few hundred bucks from the top drawer to my wallet.

I took a look in the mirror and snorted. I could have been a man of distinction except for my face and the loose space in my jacket that was supposed to fit around a rod. That at least I could fix. I strapped on a mighty empty holster to fill out the space under my arm and felt better about it. I looked in the mirror again and grimaced. It was a hell of a shame that I wasn't handsome.

Last night was a vague shadow with only a few bright spots, but before I started to backtrack there was something I wanted to do. It was just past seven o'clock when I found a parking place near the hotel that had caused all the trouble. It was one of those old-fashioned places that catered to even older-fashioned people and no fooling around. Single girls couldn't even register there unless they were over eighty. Before I went in I snapped the back off my watch, pushed out the works and dropped it in my shirt pocket.

The desk clerk wasn't glad to see me. His hand started for the telephone, stopped, then descended on the desk bell three times, loud and clear. When a burly-shouldered individual who kept the lobby free of loiterers appeared the clerk looked a little better. At least his shaking stopped.

There wasn't any need to identify myself. "I lost the works out of my watch last night. I want 'em back."

"But . . . the room hasn't been cleaned yet," he blurted.

"I want 'em now," I repeated. I held out a thick, hairy wrist and tapped the empty case. The burly guy peered over my shoulder interestedly.

"But . . . "

"Now."

The house dick said, "I'll go up with 'im and we can look for it, George."

Evidently the clerk was glad to have his decisions made for him, because he handed over the keys and seemed happy at last.

"This way." The dick nudged me with his elbow and I followed him. In the elevator he stood with his hands behind his back and glared at the ceiling. He came out of it at the fourth floor to usher me down the hall where he put the key in the lock of number 402.

Nothing had changed. The blood was still on the floor, the beds unmade and the white powder sprinkled liberally around. The dick stood at the door with his arms crossed and kept his eyes on me while I poked around under the furniture.

I went through the room from top to bottom, taking my time about it. The dick got impatient and began tapping his fingernails against the wall. When there was no place left to look the dick said, "It ain't here. Come on."

"Who's been here since the cops left?"

"Nobody, feller, not even the cleaning girls. Let's get going. You probably lost that watch in a bar somewhere."

I didn't answer him. I had flipped back the covers of the bed I slept in and saw the hole right in the edge of the mattress. The slug had entered the stuffing right near the top and another inch higher and I would have been singing tenor and forgetting about shaving.

Mattress filling can stop a slug like a steel plate and it couldn't have gone in very far, but when I probed the hole with my forefinger all I felt was horsehair and coil springs. The bullet was gone. Someone had beaten me to it. Beaten me to a couple of things . . . the empty shell case was gone too.

I put on a real bright act when I made like I found my watch works under the covers. I held it up for the guy to see then shoved it back in the case. He grunted. "All right, all right. Let's get moving." I gave him what was supposed to be a smile of gratitude and walked out. He stuck with me all the way down and was even standing in the doorway to see me go down the street to my car.

Before long he was going to catch all kinds of hell.

So would the desk clerk when the cops got wise to the fact that Chester Wheeler was no more of a suicide than I was. My late friend of the night before had been very neatly murdered.

And I was due for a little bit of hell myself.

I found a saloon with an empty parking place right out in front and threw a buck on the bar. When my beer came I took a nickel from the change and squeezed into a phone booth down the end. It was late, but Pat wasn't a guy to leave his office until things were cleaned up and I was lucky this time.

I said, "Michael Q. Citizen, speaking."

He laughed into the receiver. "How's the grocery business?"

"Booming, Pat, really booming. I have a large order for some freshly murdered meat."

"What's that?"

"Just a figure of speech."

Oh."

"By the way, how clear am I on the Wheeler death?"

I could almost see the puzzled frown on his face . . . "As far as I can see you can't be held for anything. Why?"

"Just curious. Look, the boys in blue were in that room a long time before I came back to the land of the living. Did they poke around much?"

"No, I don't think so. It was pretty obvious what happened."

"They take anything out with them?"

"The body," he said, "your gun, a shell casing, and Wheeler's personal belongings."

"That was all?"

"Uh-huh."

I paused a moment, then; "Don't suicides generally leave a note, Pat?"

"Generally, yes. That happens when they're sober and there

isn't a witness. If they've thought about it awhile they usually try to explain. In a fit of passion they rarely waste the time."

"Wheeler wasn't a passionate man, I don't think," I told him. "From all appearances he was an upright businessman."

"I thought of that. It *was* peculiar, wasn't it? Did he look like the suicide type to you?"

"Nope."

"And he didn't mention anything along that line beforehand. Hmmm."

I let a few seconds go by. "Pat . . . how many slugs were left in my rod?"

"Four, weren't there?"

"Correct. And I hadn't shot it since I was on the target range with you last week."

"So . . . ?" His voice had an uneasy tinge to it.

Real softly I said, "That gun never has less than six in it, chum."

If he had been a woman he would have screamed. Instead he bellowed into the phone and I wouldn't answer him. I heard him shouting, "Mike, goddamn it, answer me . . . *Mike!*"

I laughed just once to let him know I was still there and hung up.

All he needed was five minutes. By that time he'd have the D.A. cornered in his office like a scared rabbit. Sure, the D.A. was big stuff, but Pat was no slouch either. He'd tell that guy off with a mouthful of words that would make his hair stand on end and the fair-haired boy of the courts wouldn't dare do a thing.

It was getting funnier all the time. I went back to the bar and drank my beer.

The after-supper crowd began drifting in and taking places at the bar. At eight-thirty I called Velda but she wasn't home. I tried again an hour later and she still wasn't there. She wasn't at the office, either. Maybe she was out hiring a sign-painter to change the name on the door.

When I finally shifted into the corner up against the cigarette machine I started to think. It didn't come easy because there hadn't been any reason to remember then and we had let the booze flow free. Last night.

Famous last words.

Last night the both of us had thrown five years to the wind and brought the war back to the present. We were buddies again. We weren't the kind of buddies you get to be when you eat and sleep and fight with a guy, but we were buddies. We were two-strong and fighting the war by ourselves. We were two guys who had met as comrades-in-arms, happy to be on the right side and giving all we had. For one night way back there we had been drinking buddies until we shook hands to go finish the war. Was that the way it was supposed to be? Did some odd quirk of fate throw us together purposely so that later we'd meet again?

Last night I had met him and drunk with him. We talked, we drank some more. Was he happy? He was after we ran into each other. Before that he had been curled over a drink at the bar. He could have been brooding. He could have been thinking. But he was happy as hell to see me again! Whatever it was he had been thinking about was kicked aside along with those five years and we had ourselves one hell of a drinking bout. Sure, we fought the war again. We did the same thing anybody else did when they caught up with someone they knew from those days. We talked it and we fought it and we were buddies again decked out in the same uniform ready to give everything for the other guy on our side whether we knew him or not. But the war had to give out sometime. The peace always has to come when people get too tired of fighting. And yet, it was the end of our talk that brought the cloud back to his eyes. He hadn't wanted it to stop or be diverted into other channels. He told me he had been in town a week and was getting set to go home. The whole deal was a business trip to do some buying for his store.

Yeah, we were buddies. We weren't long, but we were buddies good. If we had both been in the jungle and some slimy Jap had picked him off I would have rammed the butt of a rifle down the brown bastard's throat for it. He would have done the same for me, too. But we weren't in any damn jungle. We were right here in New York City where murder wasn't supposed to happen and did all the time. A guy I liked comes into my own city and a week later he's dead as hell.

One week. What did he do? What happened? Who was he with? Where was the excuse for murder, here or in Columbus, Ohio? A whole damn week. I slapped my hat on the stool to reserve it and took another few nickels from my change and wormed into the phone booth again. There was one other question, what was I going to do about it? My face started to go tight again and I knew the answer.

I dialed two numbers. The second got my man. He was a private investigator the same as I used to be except that he was essentially honest and hard-working. His name was Joe Gill and he owed me a favor that he and his staff could begin repaying as of now.

I said, "This is Mike, Joe. Remember me?"

"Hell," he laughed, "with all your publicity how could I forget you? I hope you aren't after a job."

"Not exactly. Look, you tied up right now?"

"Well . . . no. Something on your mind?"

"Plenty, friend. You still doing insurance work?"

Joe grunted an assent. "That's *all* I'm doing. You can keep your guns and your tough guys. I'll track down missing beneficiaries."

"Care to do me a favor, Joe?"

He only hesitated a second. "Glad to, Mike. You've steered me straight plenty of times. Just name it."

"Swell. This guy that died in the hotel room with me, Chester Wheeler—I want some information on him. Not a history . . . I just want him backtracked over the past week. He's been in town doing some buying for his store in Columbus, Ohio, and I want a record of what he'd done since he hit town. Think it can be done?"

I could hear his pencil rasping on paper. "Give me a few hours. I'll start it myself and put the chain gang out on the details. Where can I reach you?"

I thought for a moment, then told him, "Try the Greenwood Hotel. It's a little dump on a side street up in the Eighties. They don't ask questions there."

"Right. See you later."

I cradled the receiver and picked my way back through the crowd to the bar. My hat was hanging over a pin-up lamp on the wall and my seat was occupied and the guy was spending my money for beer.

I didn't get mad, though. The guy was Pat.

The bartender put down another beer and took some more of my change. I said, "How's tricks, kid?"

Pat turned around slowly and looked at me for the first time. His eyes were clouded and his mouth had a grim twist to it. He looked tired and worried. "There's a back room, Mike. Let's go sit down. I want to talk to you."

I gulped my beer down and carried a full one back to the booth. When I slid my deck of Luckies across the table to him he shook his head and waited until I lit up. I asked, "How did you find me?"

He didn't answer. Instead he popped one of his own, very softly, very forcefully. He wasn't kidding around. "What's it all about, Mike?"

"What's what?"

"You know." He leaned forward on his arms, never taking his eyes off my face. "Mike, I'm not going to get excited this time. I'm not going to let you talk me into losing a lot of sleep any more. I'm a police officer, or at least I'm supposed to be. Right now I'm treating this like it might be something important and like you know more about it than I do. I'm asking questions that are going to be answered. What's going on?"

Smoke drifted into my eyes and I squinted them almost shut. "Supposing I told you Chester Wheeler was murdered, Pat."

"I'd ask how, then who."

"I don't know how and I don't know who."

"Then why, Mike? Why is it murder?"

"Two shots were fired from my gun, that's why."

He gave the table a rap with his knuckles. "Damn you, Mike, come out with it! We're friends, but I'm tired of being hamstrung. You're forever smelling murder where murder isn't and making it come out right. Play it square!"

"Dont I always?"

"With reservations!"

I gave a sour laugh. "Two shots out of that rod. Isn't that enough?"

"Not for me it isn't. Is that all you have?"

I nodded and dragged in on the butt.

Pat's face seemed to soften and he let the air out of his lungs slowly. He even smiled a little. "I guess that's that, Mike. I'm glad I didn't get sweated up about it."

I snubbed the cigarette out on the table top. "Now you've got me going. What are you working up to?"

"Precedent, Mike. I'm speaking of past suicides."

"What about 'em?"

"Every so often we find a suicide with a bullet in his head. The room has been liberally peppered with bullets, to quote a cliché. In other words, they'll actually take the gun away from the target but pull the trigger anyway. They keep doing it until they finally have nerve enough to keep it there. Most guys can't handle an automatic anyway and they fire a shot to make sure they know how it operates."

"And that makes Wheeler a bona fide suicide, right?"

He grinned at the sneer on my face. "Not altogether. When you pulled your little razzmatazz about the slugs in your gun I went up in the air and had a handful of experts dig up Wheeler's itinerary and we located a business friend he had been with the day before he died. He said Wheeler was unusually depressed and talked of suicide several times. Apparently his business was on the downgrade."

"Who was the guy, Pat?"

"A handbag manufacturer, Emil Perry. Well, if you have any complaints, come see me, but no more scares, Mike. Okay?"

"Yeah," I hissed. "You still didn't say how you found me."

"I traced your call, friend citizen. It came from a bar and I knew you'd stay there awhile. I took my time at the hotel checking your story. And, er . . . yes, I did find the bullet hole in the mattress."

"I suppose you found the bullet too?"

"Why yes, we did. The shell case too." I sat there rigid, waiting. "It was right out there in the hall where you dropped it, Mike. I wish you'd quit trying to give this an element of mystery just to get me in on it."

"You chump!"

"Can it, Mike. The house dick set me straight."

I was standing up facing him and I could feel the mad running right down into my shoes. "I thought you were smart, Pat. You chump!"

This time he winked. "No more games, huh, Mike?" He grinned at me a second and left me standing there watching his back. Now I was playing games. Hot dog!

I thought I was swearing under my breath until a couple of mugs heard their tomatoes complain and started to give me hell. When they saw my face they told their dames to mind their business and went on drinking.

Well, I asked for it. I played it cute and Pat played it cuter. Maybe I was the chump. Maybe Wheeler did kill himself. Maybe he came back from the morgue and tried to slip out with the slug and the shell too.

I sure as a four letter word didn't. I picked up my pack of butts and went out on the street for a smell of fresh air that wasn't jammed with problems. After a few deep breaths I felt better.

Down on the corner a drugstore was getting rid of its counter customers and I walked in past the tables of novelties and cosmetics to a row of phone booths in the back. I pulled the Manhattan directory out of the rack and began thumbing through it. When I finished I did the same thing with the Brooklyn book. I didn't learn anything there so I pulled up the Bronx listing and found an Emil Perry who lived in one of the better residential sections of the community.

At ten minutes after eleven I parked outside a red brick one-family house and killed the motor. The car in front of me was a new Cadillac sedan with all the trimmings and the side door bore two gold initials in Old English script, E.P.

There was a brass knocker on the door of the house, embossed with the same initials, but I didn't use it. I had the thing raised when I happened to glance in the window. If the guy was Emil Perry, he was big and fat with a fortune in jewels stuck in his tie and flashing on his fingers. He was talking to somebody out of sight and licking his lips between every word.

You should have seen his face. He was scared silly.

I let the knocker down easy and eased back into the shadows. When I looked at my watch ten minutes had gone by and nothing happened. I could see the window through the shrubs and the top of the fat man's head. He still hadn't moved. I kept on waiting and a few minutes later the door opened just far enough to let a guy out. There was no light behind him so I didn't see his face until he was opposite me. Then I grinned a nasty little grin and let my mind give Pat a very soft horse-laugh.

The guy that came out only had one name. Rainey. He was a tough punk with a record as long as your arm and he used to be available for any kind of job that needed a strong arm.

I waited until Rainey walked down the street and got in a car. When it pulled away with a muffled roar I climbed into my own heap and turned the motor over.

I didn't have to see Mr. Perry after all. Anyway, not tonight. He wasn't going anywhere. I made a U-turn at the end of the street and got back on the main drag that led to Manhattan. When I reached the Greenwood Hotel a little after midnight the night clerk shoved the register at me, took cash in advance and handed me the keys to the room. Fate with a twisted sense of humor was riding my tail again. The room was 402.

If there was a dead man in it tomorrow it'd have to be me.

I dreamt I was in a foxhole with a shelter half dragged over me to keep out the rain. The guy in the next foxhole kept calling to me until my eyes opened and my hand automatically reached for my rifle. There was no rifle, but the voice was real. It came from the hall. I threw back the covers and hopped up, trotting for the door.

Joe slid in and closed it behind him. "Cripes," he grunted, "I thought you were dead."

"Don't say that word, I'm alone tonight. You get it?"

He flipped his hat to the chair and sat on it. "Yeah, I got it. Most of it anyway. They weren't very co-operative at the hotel seeing as how the cops had just been there. What did you do to 'em?"

"Put a bug up his behind. Now the honorable Captain of Homicide, my pal, my buddy who ought to know better, thinks I'm pulling fast ones on him as a joke. He even suspects me of having tampered with some trivial evidence."

"Did you?"

"It's possible. Of course, how would I know what's evidence and what's not. After all, what does it matter if it *was* a suicide?"

Joe gave a polite burp. "Yeah," he said.

I watched him while he felt around in his pocket for a fistful of notes. He tapped them with a forefinger. "If I charged you for this you'd of shelled out a pair of C's. Six men lost their sleep, three lost their dates and one caught hell from his wife. She wants him to quit me. And for what?"

"And for what?" I repeated.

He went on: "This Wheeler fellow seemed pretty respectable. By some very abstract questioning here and there we managed to backtrack his movements. Just remember, we had to do it in a matter of hours, so it isn't a minute-by-minute account.

"He checked in at the hotel immediately upon arriving eight days ago. His mornings were spent visiting merchandising houses here in the city where he placed some regular orders for items for his store. None of these visits were of unusual importance. Here are some that may be. He wired home to Columbus, Ohio, to a man named Ted Lee asking for five thousand bucks by return wire. He received it an hour later. I presume it was to make a special purchase of some sort.

"We dug up a rather sketchy account of where he spent his evenings. A few times he returned to the hotel slightly under the influence. One night he attended a fashion show that featured a presentation of next year's styles. The show was followed by cocktails and he may have been one of the men who helped one of a few models who had a couple too many down the elevator and into a cab."

I started to grin. "Models?"

He shook his head. "Forget it," he told me, "it wasn't a smoker with a dirty floor show for dessert."

"Okay, go on."

"From then on he was in and out of the hotel periodically and each time he had a little more of a jag on. He checked in with you and was dead before morning. The hotel was very put out. That's it."

He waited a second and repeated, "That's it, I said."

"I heard you."

"Well?"

"Joe, you're a lousy detective."

He shot me an impatient glance tainted with amazement. "*I'm* a lousy detective? You without a license and *I'm* the lousy detective? That's a hell of a way of thanking me for all my trouble! Why I've found more missing persons than you have hairs on that low forehead of yours and . . . "

"Ever shoot anybody, Joe?"

His face went white and his fingers had trouble taking the cigarette out of his mouth. "Once . . . I did."

"Like it?"

"No." He licked his lips. "Look, Mike . . . this guy Wheeler . . . you were there. He *was* a suicide, wasn't he?"

"Uh-uh. Somebody gave him the business."

I could hear him swallow clear across the room. "Uh . . . you won't need me again, will you?"

"Nope. Thanks a lot, Joe. Leave the notes on the bed."

The sheaf of papers fell on the bed and I heard the door close softly. I sat on the arm of the chair and let my mind weave the angles in and out. One of them had murder in it.

Someplace there was a reason for murder big enough to make the killer try to hide the fact under a cloak of suicide. But the reason has to be big to kill. It has to be even bigger to try to hide it. It was still funny the way it came out. I was the only one who could tag it as murder and make it stick. Someplace a killer thought he was being real clever. Clever as hell. Maybe he thought the lack of one lousy shell in the clip wouldn't be noticed.

I kept thinking about it and I got sore. It made me sore twice. The first time I burned up was because the killer took me for a sap. Who the hell did he think I was, a cheap uptown punk who carried a rod for effect? Did he think I was some goon with loose brains and stupid enough to take it lying down?

Then I got mad again because it was my friend that died. My friend, not somebody else's. A guy who was glad to see me even after five years. A guy who was on the same side with me and gave the best he could give to save some bastard's neck so that bastard could kill him five years later.

The army was one thing I should have reminded Pat of. I should have prodded his memory with the fact that the army meant guns and no matter who you were an indoctrination course in most of the phases of handling lethal weapons hit you at one time or another. Maybe Chester Wheeler *did* try to shoot himself. More likely he tried to fire it at someone or someone fired it at him. One thing I knew damn well, Chet had known all about automatics and if he did figure to knock himself off he wasn't going to fire any test shot just to see if the gun worked.

I rolled into bed and yanked the covers up. I'd sleep on it.

chapter three ▪▪▪▪▪▪▪▪▪▪▪▪

I STOOD ON the corner of Thirty-third Street and checked the address from Joe's notes. The number I wanted was halfway down the block, an old place recently remodeled and refitted with all the trimmings a flashy clientele could expect. While I stared at the directory a covey of trim young things clutching hatboxes passed behind me to the elevator and I followed them in. They were models, but their minds weren't on jobs. All they talked about was food. I didn't blame them a bit. In the downstairs department they were shipshape from plenty of walking, but upstairs it was hard to tell whether they were coming or going unless they were wearing falsies. They were pretty to look at, but I wouldn't give any of them bed room.

The elevator slid to a stop at the eighth floor and the dames got out. They walked down the corridor to a pair of full-length frosted plate-glass doors etched with ANTON LIPSEK AGENCY and pushed in. The last one saw me coming and held the door open for me.

It was a streamlined joint if ever there was one. The walls were a light pastel tint with a star-sprinkled ceiling of pale blue. Framed original photos of models in everything from nylon step-ins to low slung convertibles marched around the walls in a double column. Three doors marked PRIVATE branched off the ante-room, while a receptionist flanked by a host of busy stenos pounding typewriters guarded the entrance to the main office. I dumped my cigarette into an ash tray and grinned at the receptionist. Her voice had a forced politeness but her eyes were snooty. "Yes?"

"The Calway Merchandising Company had a dinner meeting the other night. Several models from this agency were present for the fashion show that came later. I'm interested in seeing them . . . one of them, at least. How can I go about it?"

She tapped her pencil on the desk. Three irritable little taps. Evidently this was an old story to her. "Is this a business or . . . personal inquiry, sir?"

I leaned on the edge of the desk and gave her my real nasty smile. "It could be both, kid, but one thing it's not and that's *your* business."

"Oh . . . oh," she said. "Anton—Mr. Lipsek, I mean—he handles the assignments. I'll . . . call him."

Her hands flew over the intercom box, fumbling with the keys. Maybe she thought I'd bite, because she wouldn't take her eyes off my face. When the box rattled at her she shut it off and said I could go right in. This time I gave her my nice smile, the one without the teeth. "I was only kidding, sugar."

She said "Oh" again and didn't believe me.

Anton Lipsek had his name on the door in gold letters and under it the word MANAGER. Evidently he took his position seriously. His desk was a roll-top affair shoved in a corner, bulging with discarded photographs and sketches. The rest of the room was given over to easels, display mounts and half-finished sketches. He was very busy managing, too.

He was managing to get a whole lot of woman dressed in very little nothing in place amid a bunch of props so the camera would pick up most of the nothing she was wearing and none of the most she was showing. At least that's what it looked like to me.

I whistled softly. "Ve-ry nice."

"Too much skin," he said. He didn't even turn around.

The model tried to peer past the glare of the lamps he had trained on her. "Who's that?"

Anton shushed her, his hands on her nice bare flesh giving a cold professional twist to her torso. When she was set just right he stepped back behind the camera, muttered a cue and the girl threw her bosoms toward the lens and let a ghost of a smile play with her mouth. There was a barely audible click and the model turned human again, stretching her arms so far over her head that her bra filled up and began overflowing.

They could make me a manager any day.

Anton snapped off the lights and swiveled his head around.

"Ah, yes. Now, sir, what can I do for you?"

He was a tall, lanky guy with eyebrows that met above his nose and a scrimy little goatee that waggled when he talked and made his chin come to a point. "I'm interested in finding a certain model. She works here."

The eyebrows went up like a window shade. "That, sir, is a request we get quite often. Yes, quite often."

I said very bluntly, "I don't like models. Too flatchested."

Anton was beginning to look amazed when she came out from behind the props, this time with shoes on too. "Tain't me you're talkin' about, podner." An unlit cigarette was dangling from her mouth. "Got a light?"

I held a match under her nose, watching her mouth purse around the cigarette when she drew in the flame. "No, you're exceptional," I said.

This time she grinned and blew the smoke in my face.

Anton coughed politely. "This, er, model you mentioned. Do you know her?"

"Nope. All I know is that she was at the Calway Merchandising affair the other night."

"I see. There were several of our young ladies present on that assignment, I believe. Miss Reeves booked that herself. Would you care to see her?"

"Yeah, I would."

The girl blew another mouthful of smoke at me and her eyelashes waved hello again. "Don't you ever wear clothes?" I asked her.

"Not if I can help it. Sometimes they make me."

"That's what I'd like to do."

"What?"

"Make you."

Anton choked and clucked, giving her a push. "That will be enough. If you don't mind, sir, this way." His hand was inviting me to a door in the side of the room. "These young ladies are getting out of hand. Sometimes I could . . ."

"Yeah, so could I." He choked again and opened the door.

I heard him announce my name but I didn't catch what he said because my mind couldn't get off the woman behind the desk. Some women are beautiful, some have bodies that make you forget beauty; here was a woman who had both. Her face had a supernatural loveliness as if some master artist had improved on nature itself. She had her hair cut short in the latest fashion, light tawny hair that glistened like a halo. Even her skin had a creamy texture, flowing down the smooth line of her neck into firm, wide shoulders. She had the breasts of youth—high, exciting, pushing against the high neckline of the white jersey blouse, revolting at the need for restraint. She stood up and held her hand out to me, letting it slip into mine with a warm, pleasant grip. Her voice had a rich vibrant quality when she introduced herself, but I was too busy cursing the longer hemlines to get it. When she sat down again with her legs crossed I stopped my silent protests of long dresses when I saw how tantalizingly nice they could mold themselves to the roundness of thighs that were more inviting when covered. Only then did I see the nameplate on the desk that read JUNO REEVES.

Juno, queen of the lesser gods and goddesses. She was well named.

She offered me a drink from a decanter in a bar set and I took it, something sweet and perfumy in a long-stemmed glass.

We talked. My voice would get a nasty intonation then it would get polite. It didn't seem to come out of me at all. We could have talked about nothing for an hour, maybe it was just minutes. But we talked and she did things with her body deliberately as if I were a supreme test of her abilities as a woman and she laughed, knowing too well that I was hardly conscious of what I was saying or how I was reacting.

She sipped her drink and laid the glass down on the desk, the dark polish of her nails in sharp contrast against the gleaming crystal. Her voice eased me back to the present.

"This young lady, Mr. Hammer . . . you say she left with your friend?"

"I said she *may* have. That's what I want to find out."

"Well, perhaps I can show you their photographs and you can identify her."

"No, that won't do it. I never saw her myself either."

"Then why . . ."

"I want to find out what happened last night, Miss Reeves."

"Juno, please."

I grinned at her.

"Do you suppose they did . . ." she smiled obliquely, "anything wrong?"

"I don't give a damn what they did. I'm just interested in knowing. You see, this pal of mine . . . he's dead."

Her eyes went soft. "Oh, I'm awfully sorry. What happened?"

"Suicide, the cops said."

Juno folded her lower lip between her teeth, puzzled. "In that case, Mr. Hammer . . ."

"Mike," I said.

"In that case, Mike, why bring the girl into it? After all . . ."

"The guy had a family," I cut in. "If a nosy reporter decides to work out an angle and finds a juicy scandal lying around, the family will suffer. If there's anything like that I want to squelch it."

She nodded slowly, complete understanding written in her face. "You *are* right, Mike. I'll see the girls as they come in for assignments and try to find out who it was. Will you stop by tomorrow sometime?"

I stood up, my hat in my hand. "That'll be fine, Juno. Tomorrow then."

"Please." Her voice dropped into a lower register as she stood up and held her hand out to me again. Every motion she made was like liquid being poured and there was a flame in her eyes that waited to be breathed into life. I wrapped my hand around hers just long enough to feel her tighten it in subtle invitation.

I walked to the door and turned around to say good-by again. Juno let her eyes sweep over me, up and down, and she smiled. I couldn't get the words out. Something about her made me too warm under my clothes. She was beautiful and she was built like a goddess should be built and her eyes said that she was good when she was bad.

They said something else, too, something I should know and couldn't remember.

When I got to the elevators I found I had company. This company was waiting for me at the far end of the hall, comfortably braced against the radiator smoking a cigarette.

This time she had more clothes on. When she saw me coming she ground the butt under her heel and walked up to me with such deliberate purpose that my eyes began to undress her all over again.

"Make me," she said.

"I need an introduction first."

"Like hell you do." The light over the elevator turned red and I heard the car rattling in the well. "Okay, you're made." She turned her grin on me as the car slowed up behind the steel doors. "Right here?"

"Yup."

"Look out, bub, I'm not the coy type. I may take you up on it."

"Right here?" I asked.

"Yup."

I let out a short laugh as the doors opened and shoved her in. It could be that she wasn't kidding and I hated audiences. When we hit the ground floor she linked her arm in mine and let me lead her out to the street. We reached Broadway before she said, "If you *really* need an introduction, my name is Connie Wales. Who're you?"

"Mr. Michael Hammer, chick. I used to be a private investigator. I was in the papers recently."

Her mouth was drawn up in a partial smile. "Wow, am *I* in company."

We reached Broadway and turned north. Connie didn't ask where we were going, but when we passed three bars in a row without stopping I got an elbow in the ribs until I got the hint. The place I did turn into was a long, narrow affair with tables for ladies in the rear. So we took a table for ladies as far down as we could get with a waiter mumbling under his breath behind us.

Both of us ordered beer and I said, "You're not very expensive to keep, are you?"

"Your change'll last longer this way," she laughed. "You aren't rich, or are you?"

"I got dough," I said, "but you won't get it out of me, girlie," I tacked on.

Her laugh made pretty music and it was real. "Most men want to buy me everything I look at. Wouldn't you?" She sipped her brew, watching me over the rim of the glass with eyes as shiny as new dimes.

"Maybe a beer, that's all. A kid I knew once told me I'd never have to pay for another damn thing. Not a thing at all."

She looked at me soberly. "She was right."

"Yeah," I agreed.

The waiter came back with his tray and four more beers. He sat two in front of each of us, picked up the cash and shuffled away. As he left Connie stared at me for a full minute. "What were you doing in the studio?"

I told her the same thing I told Juno.

She shook her head. "I don't believe you."

"Why?"

"I don't know. It just doesn't sound right. Why would any

reporter try to make something out of a suicide?"

She had a point there, but I had an answer. "Because he didn't leave a farewell note. Because his home life was happy. Because he had a lot of dough and no apparent worries."

"It sounds better now," she said.

I told her about the party and what I thought might have happened. When I sketched it in I asked, "Do you know any of the girls that were there that night?"

Her laugh was a little deeper this time. "Golly, no, at least not to talk to. You see, the agency is divided into two factions, more or less . . . the clotheshorses and the no-clotheshorses. I'm one of the sugar pies who fill out panties and nighties for the nylon trade. The clotheshorses couldn't fill out a paper sack by themselves so they're jealous and treat us lesser paid kids like dirt."

"Nuts," I said. "I saw a few and they can't let their breaths out all the way without losing their falsies."

She almost choked on her drink. "Very cute, Mike, very cute. I'll have to remember all your acid witticisms. They'll put me over big with the gang."

I finished the last of the beer and shoved the empties to the edge of the table. "Come on, kid. I'll take you wherever you want to go then I'll try to get something done."

"I want to go back to my apartment and you can get something done there."

"You'll get a slap in the ear if you don't shut up. Come on."

Connie threw her head back and laughed at me again. "Boy oh boy, what ten other guys wouldn't give to hear me say that?"

"Do you say that to ten other guys?"

"No, Mike." Her voice was a whisper of invitation.

There wasn't an empty cab in sight so we walked along Broadway until we found a hack stand with a driver grabbing a nap behind the wheel. Connie slid in and gave him an address on Sixty-second Street then crowded me into the corner and reached for my hand.

She said, "Is all this very important, Mike? Finding the girl and all, I mean."

I patted her hand. "It means plenty to me, baby. More than you'd expect."

"Can I . . . help you some way? I want to, Mike. Honest."

She had a hell of a cute face. I turned my head and looked down into it and the seriousness in her expression made me nod before I could help myself. "I need a lot of help, Connie. I'm not sure my friend went out with this girl; I'm not sure she'll admit it if she did and I can't blame her; I'm not sure about anything any more."

"What did Juno tell you?"

"Come back tomorrow. She'll try to find her in the meantime."

"Juno's quite a . . . she's quite a . . ."

"Quite," I finished.

"She makes that impression on everybody. A working girl doesn't stand a chance around that woman." Connie faked a pout and squeezed my arm. "Say it ain't so, Mike."

"It ain't so."

"You're lying again," she laughed. "Anyway, I was thinking. Suppose this girl *did* go out with your friend. Was he the type to try for a fast affair?"

I shoved my hat back on my head and tried to picture Chester Wheeler. To me he was too much of a family man to make a decent wolf. I told her no, but doubtfully. It's hard to tell what a guy will or won't do when he's in town without an overseer or a hardworking conscience.

"In that case," Connie continued, "I was thinking that if this girl played games like a lot of them do, she'd drag him around the hot spots with him footing the bill. It's a lot of fun, they tell me."

She was getting at something. She shook her head and let her hair swirl around her shoulders. "Lately the clotheshorses have been beating a path to a few remote spots that cater to the model-and-buyer crowd. I haven't been there myself, but it's a lead."

I reached over and tipped her chin up with my forefinger. "I like the way you think, girl." Her lips were full and red. She ran her tongue over them until they glistened wetly, separated just a little to coax me closer. I could have been coaxed, only the cab jolted to a stop against the curb and Connie stuck out her tongue at the driver. She made a wry face and held on to my hand just to be sure I got out with her. I handed the driver a bill and told him to keep the change.

"It's the cocktail hour, Mike. You will come up, won't you?"

"For a while."

"Damn you," she said, "I never tried so hard to make a guy who won't be made. Don't I have wiles, Mike?"

"Two beauties."

"Well, that's a start, anyway. Leave us leave."

The place was a small-sized apartment house that made no pretense at glamour. It had a work-it-yourself elevator that wasn't working and we hoofed it up the stairs to the third floor where

Connie fumbled in her pocket until she found her key. I snapped on the light like I lived there permanently and threw my hat on a chair in the living room and sat down.

Connie said, "What'll it be, coffee or cocktails?"

"Coffee first," I told her. "I didn't eat lunch. If you got some eggs put them on too." I reached over the arm of the chair into a magazine rack and came up with a handful of girlie mags that were better than the post cards you get in Mexico. I found Connie in half of them and decided that she was all right. Very all right.

The smell of the coffee brought me into the kitchen just as she was sliding the eggs onto a plate and we didn't bother with small talk until there was nothing left but some congealed egg yolk. When I finally leaned back and pulled out my deck of Luckies she said, "Good?"

"Uh-huh."

"Will I make somebody a good wife?"

"Somebody."

"Bastard." She was laughing again. I grinned back at her and faked a smack at her fanny. Instead of pulling away she stuck it out at me so I laid one on that made her yowl.

We had the cocktails in the living room. The hands on my watch went around once, then twice. Every so often the shaker would be refilled and the ice would make sharp sounds against the metal surface. I sat there with a glass in my hand and my head back, dreaming my way through the haze. I ran out of matches and whenever I put a cigarette in my mouth Connie would come across the room with a light for me.

A nice guy who was dead.

Two shots gone.

One bullet and one shell case found in the hall.

Suicide.

Hell.

I opened my eyes and looked at Connie. She was curled up on a studio couch watching me. "What's the program, kid?"

"It's almost seven," she said. "I'll get dressed and you can take me out. If we're lucky maybe we can find out where your friend went."

I was too tired to be nice. My eyes were heavy from looking into the smoke that hung in the air and my belly felt warm from the drinks. "A man is dead," I said slowly. "The papers said what the cops said, he died a suicide. I know better. The guy was murdered."

She stiffened, and the cigarette bent in her fingers. "I wanted to find out why so I started tracing and I found he might have been with a babe one night. I find where the babe works and start asking quesions. A very pretty model with a very pretty body starts tossing me a line and is going to help me look. I start getting ideas. I start wondering why all the concern from a dame who can have ten other guys yet makes a pass at a guy who hasn't even got a job and won't buy her more than beer and takes her eggs and coffee and her cocktails."

Her breath made a soft hissing noise between her teeth. I saw the cigarette crumple up in her hand and if she felt any pain it wasn't reflected in her face. I never moved while she pushed herself up. My hands were folded behind my head for a cushion and stayed there even while she stood spraddled-legged in front of me.

Connie swung so fast I didn't close my eyes for it. Not a flat palm, but a small, solid fist sliced into my cheek and cracked against my jaw. I started to taste the blood inside my mouth and when I grinned a little of it ran down my chin.

"I have five brothers," she said. Her voice had a snarl in it. "They're big and nasty but they're all men. I have ten other guys who wouldn't make one man put together. Then you came along. I'd like to beat your stupid head off. You have eyes and you can't see. All right, Mike, I'll give you something to look at and you'll know why all the concern."

Her hand grabbed her blouse at the neckline and ripped it down. Buttons rolled away at my feet. The other thing she wore pulled apart with a harsh tearing sound and she stood there proudly, her hands on her hips, flaunting her breasts in my face. A tremour of excitement made the muscles under the taught flesh of her stomach undulate, and she let me look at her like that as long as it pleased me.

I had to put my hands down and squeeze the arms of the chair. My collar was too tight all of a sudden, and something was crawling up my spine.

Her teeth were clamped together. Her eyes were vicious.

"Make me," she said.

Another trickle of blood ran down my chin, reminding me what had happened. I reached up and smacked her across the mouth as hard as I could. Her head rocked, but she still stood there, and now her eyes were more vicious than ever. "Still want me to make you?"

"Make me," she said.

chapter four ████████████████

WE ATE SUPPER in a Chinese joint on Times Square. The place was crowded but nobody had eyes for the meal; they were all focused on Connie including mine and I couldn't blame them any. If low-cut gowns were daring, then she took the dare and threw it back at them.

I sat across the table wondering if skin could really be that soft and smooth, wondering how much less could be worn before a woman would be stark naked. Not much less.

The meal went that way without words. We looked, we smiled, we ate. For the first time I saw her objectively, seeing a woman I had and not just one I wanted. It was easy to say she was beautiful, but not easy to say why.

But I knew why. She was honest and direct. She wanted something and she let you know it. She had spent a lifetime with five men who treated her as another brother and expected her to like it. She did. To Connie, modeling was just a job. If there was glamour attached to it she took it without making the most of it.

It was nearly nine o'clock when we left, straggling out with full bellies and a pleasant sensation of everything being almost all right. I said, "Going to tell me the schedule?"

Her hand found mine and tucked it up under her arm. "Ever been slumming, Mike?"

"Some people think I'm always slumming."

"Well, that's what we're going to do. The kids all have a new craze on an old section of town. They call it the Bowery. Sound familiar?"

I looked at her curiously. "The Bowery?"

"You ain't been around recently, bub. The Bowery's changed. Not all of it, but a spot here and there. Not too long ago a wise guy spotted himself a fortune and turned a junk joint into a tourist trap. You know, lousy with characters off the street to give the place atmosphere all the while catering to a slightly upper crust who want to see how the other half lives."

"How the hell did they ever find that?"

A cab saw me wave and pulled to the curb. We got in and I told him where to go and his hand hit the flag. Connie said, "Some people get tired of the same old thing. They hunt up these new deals. The Bowery is one of them."

"Who runs the place?"

Connie shrugged, her shoulders rubbing against mine. "I don't know, Mike. I've had everything second hand. Besides, it isn't only one place now. I think there're at least a dozen. Like I said, they're model-and-buyer hangouts and nothing is cheap, either."

The cab wound through traffic, but over to a less busy street and made the running lights that put us at the nether end of Manhattan without a stop. I handed the driver a couple of bills and helped Connie out of the door.

The Bowery, a street of people without faces. Pleading voices from the shadows and the shuffle of feet behind you. An occasional tug at your sleeve and more pleading that had professional despair in the tone. An occasional woman with clothes too tight giving you a long, steady stare that said she was available cheap. Saloon doors swung open so frequently they seemed like blinking lights. They were crowded, too. The bars were lined with the left-overs of humanity keeping warm over a drink or nursing a steaming bowl of soup.

It had been a long time since I had made the rounds down here. A cab swung into the curb and a guy in a tux with a redhead on his arm got out laughing. There was a scramble in his direction and the redhead handed out a mess of quarters then threw them all over the sidewalk to laugh all the louder when the dive came.

The guy thought it was funny too. He did the same thing with a fin, letting it blow out of his hand down the street. Connie said, "See what I mean?"

I felt like kicking the bastard. "Yeah, I see."

We followed the pair with about five feet between us. The guy had a Midwestern drawl and the dame was trying to cover up a Brooklyn accent. She kept squeezing the guy's arm and giving him the benefit of slow, sidewise glances he seemed to like. Tonight he was playing king, all right.

They turned into a bar that was the crummiest of the lot on the street. You could smell the stink from outside and hear the mixture of shrill and raucous voices a block away. A sign over the doorway said NEIL'S JOINT.

The characters were there in force. They had black eyes and missing teeth. They had twitches and fleas and their language was out of the gutter. Two old hags were having a hair-pull over a joker who could hardly hold on to the bar.

What got me was the characters who watched them. They were even worse. They thought it was a howl. Tourists. Lousy, money-heavy tourists who thought it was a lot of fun to kick somebody else around. I was so damn mad I could hardly speak. A waiter mumbled something and led us to a table in the back room that was packed with more characters. Both kinds.

Everybody was having a swell time reading the dirty writing on the walls and swapping stories with the other half. The pay off was easy to see. The crowd who lived there were drinking cheap whisky on the house to keep them there while the tourists shelled out through the nose for the same cheap whisky and thought it was worth it.

It sure was fun. Nuts.

Connie smiled at a couple of girls she knew and one came over. I didn't bother to get up when she introduced us. The girl's name was Kate and she was with a crowd from upstate. She said, "First time you've been here, isn't it, Connie?"

"First . . . and last," she told her. "It smells."

Kate's laugh sounded like a broken cowbell. "Oh, we're not going to stay here long. The fellows want to spend some money, so we're going over to the Inn. Feel like coming along?"

Connie looked at me. I moved my head just enough so she'd know it was okay by me. "We'll go, Kate."

"Swell, come on over and meet the gang. We're meeting the rest later on. They wanted to see all the sights including . . ." she giggled, "those houses where . . . you know." She giggled again.

Connie made a mouth and I grunted.

So we got up and met the gang. If it weren't that I had Connie with me they would have treated me like another character too. Just for a minute, maybe, then a few fat guts would have been bounced off the walls. There was Joseph, Andrew, Homer, Martin and Raymond and not a nickname in the pack. They all had soft hands, big diamonds, loud laughs, fat wallets and lovely women. That is, all except Homer. He had his secretary along who wasn't as pretty as she was ready, willing and able. She was his mistress and made no bones about it.

I liked her best. So did Connie.

When I squeezed their hands until they hurt we sat down and had a few drinks and dirty jokes then Andrew got loud about bigger and better times elsewhere. The rest threw in with him and we picked up our marbles and left. Martin gave the waiter a ten-spot he didn't deserve and he showed us to the door.

Connie didn't know the way so we just followed. The girls did all the steering. Twice we had to step around drunks and once we moved into the gutter to get out of the way of a street brawl. They should have stayed in the gutter where they belonged. I was so hopping mad I could hardly speak and Connie rubbed her cheek against my shoulder in sympathy.

The Bowery Inn was off the main line. It was a squalid place with half-boarded-up windows, fly-specked beer signs and an outward appearance of something long ago gone to seed.

That was from the outside. The first thing you noticed when you went in was the smell. It wasn't. It smelled like a bar should smell. The tables and the bar were as deliberately aged with worm holes and cigarette burns as the characters were phony. Maybe the others couldn't see it, but I could.

Connie grimaced. "So this is The Inn I've heard so much about."

I could hardly hear her over the racket. Everybody was running forward to greet everybody else and the dames sounded like a bunch of pigs at a trough. The fat bellies stood back and beamed. When the racket eased off to a steady clamor everybody checked their coats and hats with a one-eyed bag behind a booth who had a spittoon on the counter to collect the tips.

While Connie was helloing a couple of gaunt things from her office I sidled over to the bar for a shot and a beer. I needed it bad. Besides, it gave me a chance to look around. Down at the back of the room was a narrow single door that hung from one hinge and had a calendar tacked to it that flapped every time it opened.

It flapped pretty often because there was an unending stream of traffic coming and going through that door and the only characters inside there had on evening gowns and tuxes with all the spangles.

Connie looked around for me, saw me spilling down the chaser and walked over. "This is only the front, Mike. Let's go in where the fun is. That's what they say, anyway."

"Roger, baby. I need fun pretty bad."

I took her arm and joined the tail end of the procession that was heading for the door on one hinge and the calendar.

We had quite a surprise. Quite a surprise. The calendar door was only the first. It led into a room with warped walls and had to close before the other door would open. The one hinge was only a phony. There were two on the inside frame nicely concealed. The room was a soundproof connection between the back room and the bar and it was some joint, believe me.

Plenty of thousands went into the making of the place and there were plenty of thousands in the wallets that sat at the fancy chrome-trimmed bar or in the plush-lined seats along the wall. The lights were down low and a spot was centered on a completely naked woman doing a strip tease in reverse. It was nothing when she was bare, but it was something to watch her get dressed. When she finished she stepped out of the spot and sat down next to a skinny bald-headed gent who was in one hell of a dither having a dame alongside him he had just seen in the raw. The guy called for champagne.

Everybody whooped it up.

Now I saw why the place was a popular hangout. The walls were solid blocks of photographs, models by the hundreds in every stage of dress and undress. Some were originals, some were cut from magazines. All were signed with some kind of love to a guy named Clyde.

Connie and I tipped our glasses together and I let my eyes drift to the pictures. "You up there?"

"Could be. Want to look around?"

"No. I like you better sitting where I can see you personally."

A band came out and took their places behind the stand. Homer excused himself and came around the table to Connie and asked her to dance. That left me playing kneeses with his mistress until she looked at the floor anxiously and practically asked me to take her out there.

I'm not much for dancing, but she made up for it. She danced close enough to almost get behind me and had a hell of an annoying habit of sticking her tongue out to touch the tip of my ear. Homer did all right for himself.

It took an hour for the party to get going good. At eleven-thirty the place was jammed to the rafters and a guy couldn't hear himself think. Andrew started talking about spending money again and one of the girls squalled that there was plenty of it to throw away if the boys wanted some sporting propositions. One of them got up and consulted with a waiter who came back in a minute and mumbled a few words and nodded toward a curtained alcove to one side.

I said, "Here we go, kid."

Connie screwed up her face. "I don't get it, Mike."

"Hell, it's the same old fix. They got gambling tables in the back room. They give you the old peephole routine to make it look good."

"Really?"

"You'll see."

Everybody got up and started off in the direction of the curtain. The pitch was coming in fast now. I began to think of Chester Wheeler again, wondering if he made this same trip. He had needed five grand. Why? To play or to pay off? A guy could run up some heavy sugar in debts on a wheel. Suicide? Why kill yourself for five grand? Why pay off at all? A word to the right cop and they'd tear this place down and you could forget the debts.

One of the girls happened to look over her shoulder and screamed, "Oh, there's Clyde. Hello, Clyde! Clyde . . . hello!"

The lean guy in the tux turned his cold smile on her and waved back, then finished making his rounds of the tables. I felt my mouth pulling into a nasty grin and I told Connie to go ahead.

I walked over to Clyde.

"If it ain't my old pal Dinky," I said.

Clyde was bent over a table and the stiffness ran through his back, but he didn't stop talking until he was damned good and ready. I stuck a Lucky between my lips and fired it just as the lights went down and the spot lit up another lewd nude prancing on the stage.

Then Clyde swung his fish eyes on me. "What are you doing here, shamus?"

"I was thinking the same thing about you."

"You've been here too long already. Get out." The stiffness was still in his back. He threaded through the tables, a quick smile for someone here and there. When he reached the bar a bottle was set up in front of him and he poured himself a quick shot.

I blew a stream of smoke in his face. "Nice layout."

His eyes were glassy with hate now. "Maybe you didn't hear me right."

"I hear you, only I'm not one of your boys to jump when you speak, Dink."

"What do you want?"

I blew some more smoke at him and he pulled out of the way. "I want to satisfy my curiosity, Dink. Yeah, that's what I want to do. The last time I saw you was in a courtroom taking the oath from a wheel chair. You had a bullet in your leg. I put it there, remember? You swore that you weren't the guy who drove a getaway car for a killer, but the bullet in your leg made you out a liar. You did a stretch for that. Remember now?"

He didn't answer me.

"You sure came a long way, kid. No more wheel spots for you. Maybe now you do the killing?"

His upper lip curled over his teeth. "The papers say you don't carry a gun anymore, Hammer. That's not so good for you. Keep out of my way."

He went to raise his drink to his mouth, but I swatted his elbow and the stuff splattered into his face. His face went livid. "Take it easy, Dink. Don't let the cops spot you. I'll take a look around before I go."

My old friend Dinky Williams who called himself Clyde was reaching for the house phone on the end of the bar when I left.

To cross the room I had to walk around behind the spot and it took me a minute to find the curtain in the semidarkness. There was another door behind the curtain. It was locked. I rapped on the panel and the inevitable peephole opened that showed a pair of eyes over a nose that had a scar down the center.

At first I thought I wasn't going to get in, then the lock clicked and the door swung in just a little.

Sometimes you get just enough warning. Some reflex action shoves you out of the way before you can get your head split open. My hand went up in time to form a cushion for my skull and something smashed down on my knuckles that brought a bubbling yell up out of my throat.

I kept going, dove and rolled so that I was on my back with my feet up and staring at the ugly face of an oversize pug who had a billy raised ready to use. He didn't go for the feet, but he didn't think fast enough to catch me while I was down.

I'm no cat, but I got my shoes under me in a hurry. The billy swung at my head while I was still off balance. The guy was too eager. He missed me. I didn't miss. I was big, he was bigger. I had one bad hand and I didn't want to spoil the other. I leaned back against the wall and kicked out and up with a slashing toe that nearly tore him in half. He tried to scream. All I heard was a bubbling sound. The billy hit the floor and he doubled over, hands clawing at his groin. This time I measured it right. I took a short half step and kicked that son of a bitch so hard in the face that his teeth came out in my shoe.

I looked at the billy, picked it up and weighed it. The thing was made for murder. It was too bulky in my pocket so I dropped it in the empty shoulder holster under my arm and grunted at the guy on the floor who was squirming unconsciously in his own blood.

The room was another of those rooms between rooms. A chair was tilted back against the wall beside the door, the edge of it biting into the soundproofing. Just for kicks I dragged the stupe over to the chair, propped him in it and tilted it back against the wall again. His head was down and you could hardly see the blood. A lot could go on before he'd know about it, I thought.

When I was satisfied with the arrangement I snapped the lock off the door to accommodate the customers and tried the other door into the back room. This one was open.

The lights hit me so hard after the semidarkness of the hall that I didn't see Connie come over. She said, "Where've you been, Mike?"

Her hand hooked in my arm and I gave it an easy squeeze. "I got friends here too."

"Who?"

"Oh, some people you don't know."

She saw the blood on the back of my hand then, the skin of the knuckles peeled back. Her face went a little white. "Mike . . . what did you do?"

I grinned at her. "Caught it on something."

She asked another question, one I didn't hear. I was too busy taking in the layout of the place. It was a gold mine. Over the babble you could hear the click and whir of the roulette wheels, the excited shrieks when they stopped. There were tables for dice, faro spreads, bird cages and all the games and gadgets that could make a guy want to rip a bill off his roll and try his luck.

The place was done up like an old-fashioned Western gambling hall, with gaudy murals on every wall. The overhead lights were fashioned from cartwheels and oxen yokes, the hanging brass lanterns almost invisible in the glare of the bright lights inside them. Along one wall was a fifty-foot bar of solid mahogany complete with brass rail, never-used cuspidors and plate-glass mirrors with real bullet holes.

If ever I had a desire to be surrounded by beauty, I would have found it there. Beauty was commonplace. It was professional. Beauty was there under a lot of make-up and too much skin showing. Beauty was there in models who showed off what they liked to advertise best. It was like looking into the dressing room of the Follies. There was so much of it you tried to see it all once and lost out with your hurry.

It was incredible as hell.

I shook my head. Connie smiled, "Hard to believe, isn't it?"

That was an understatement. "What's the pitch?"

"I told you, Mike. It's a fad. It caught on and spread like the pox. Pretty soon it'll get around, the place will be jammed and jumpin', then the whole deal will get boring."

"So they'll move on to something else."

"Exactly. Right now it's almost a club. They're fawned over and fought over. They make a big splash. Wait till it all catches up with them."

"And all this in the Bowery. Right in the middle of the Bowery! Pat would give his right arm for a peep at this. Maybe I'll let him give me a left arm too."

I stopped and peered around again. Beauty. It was starting to get flat now. There were too many big bellies and bald heads in the way. They spoiled the picture. I spotted Homer and Andrew in the crowd having a big time at the crap table. Evidently Homer was winning because his babe was stuffing the chips he handed her into a bag that wouldn't take too many. The ones she had left over got tied up in her handkerchief.

We made a complete tour of the place before picking out a leather-covered corner spot to watch the shindig and drink at the same time. A waiter in a cowboy outfit brought us highballs and crackers and said it was on the house. As soon as he left Connie asked, "What do you think, Mike?"

"I don't know, sugar. I'm wondering if my pal would have gone for this."

"Wasn't he like the rest?"

"You mean, was he a man?"

"Sort of."

"Hell, he probably would. What guy wouldn't take in a hot spot with a babe. He's alone in the city, no chaperon and bored stiff. His work is done for the day and he needs a little relaxation. We'll leave it at that. If he did get persuaded to come it didn't take much persuasion."

I lit a cigarette and picked up my drink. I had a long swallow and was following it with a drag on the butt when the crowd split apart for a second to let a waiter through and I had a clear view of the bar.

Juno was sitting there laughing at something Anton Lipsek just said.

The ice started to rattle against my glass and I had that feeling up my spine again. I said to Connie, "Get lost for a little while, will you?"

"She's truly beautiful, isn't she, Mike?"

I blushed for the first time since I wore long pants. "She's different. She makes most of them look sick."

"Me too?"

"I haven't seen her with her clothes off. Until then you're the best."

"Don't lie, Mike." Her eyes were laughing at me.

I stood up and grinned back at her. "Just in case you really want to know, she's the best-looking thing I ever saw. I get steamed up watching her from fifty feet away. Whatever a dame's supposed to have on the ball, she's got it. My tongue feels an inch thick when I talk to her and if she asked me to jump I'd say, 'How high?' and if she asked me to poop I'd say, 'How much?'. But here's something you can tuck away if it means anything to you. I don't like her and I don't know why I don't."

Connie reached over and took a cigarette from my pack. When it was lit she said, "It means plenty to me. I'll get lost, Mike. But just for a little while."

I patted her hand and walked over to where the queen of the gods and goddesses was holding court. When she saw me her smile made sunshine and the funny feeling started around my stomach.

She held out her hand and I took it. "Mike, what are you doing here?"

Juno guided me to a stool on Olympus, letting go my hand almost reluctantly. More eyes than Anton Lipsek's watched me enviously. "I was sidetracked into a flirtation when I left your office."

Anton wiggled his beard with an "Ah hah!" He caught on fast.

"I guess it pays to be physical," Juno smiled. Her eyes drifted over the crowd. "There aren't too many men here who are. You're rather an attraction."

So was she. You might say she was over-clothed by comparison, but not overdressed. The front of the black gown came up to her neck and the sleeves came down to meet her gloves. The width of her shoulders, the regal taper of her waist was sheathed in a shimmering silk that reflected the lights and clung tenaciously to her body. Her breasts rose full and high under the gown, moving gently with her breathing.

"Drink?"

I nodded. The music of her voice brought the bartender to life and he put a highball in front of me. Anton joined us in a toast, then excused himself and walked over to the roulette wheel. I deliberately swung around on the stool, hoping she'd follow me so I could have her to myself.

She did, smiling at me in the mirrors that had bullet holes.

"I have news for you, Mike. Perhaps I should let it keep so I could see you again tomorrow."

My hand started to tighten around the glass. One of the bullet holes was in the way so I turned my head to look at her. "The girl . . ."

"Yes. I found her."

Ever have your insides squeeze up into a knot so hard you thought you'd turn inside out? I did. "Go on," I said.

"Her name is Marion Lester. I presume you'll want to see her yourself of course. Her address is the Chadwick Hotel. She was the third one I spoke to this afternoon and she readily admitted what had happened, although she seemed a little frightened when I told her the full story."

"All right, all right, what did she say?" I took a quick drink and pushed the glass across the bar.

"Actually . . . nothing. Your friend *did* help her into a cab and he saw her home. In fact, he carried her upstairs and tucked her into bed with her clothes on, shoes and all. It seems as if he was quite a gentleman."

"Damn," I said, "damn it all to hell anyway!"

Juno's fingers found mine on the bar rail and her smile was replaced by intense concern. "Mike, please! It can't be that bad. Aren't you glad it was that way?"

I cursed under my breath, something nice and nasty I had to get out. "I guess so. It's just that it leaves me climbing a tree again. Thanks anyway, Juno."

She leaned toward me and my head filled with the fragrance of a perfume that made me dizzy. She had gray eyes. Deep gray eyes. Deep and compassionate. Eyes that could talk by themselves. "Will you come up tomorrow anyway?"

I couldn't have said no. I didn't want to. I nodded and my lip worked into a snarl I couldn't control. Even my hands tightened into fists until the broken skin over my knuckles began to sting. "I'll be there," I said. I got that funny feeling again. I couldn't figure it, damn it, I didn't know what it was.

A finger tapped my shoulder and Connie said, "I'm losted, Mike. Hello, Juno."

Olympus smiled another dawn.

Connie said, "Can we go home now?"

I slid off the stool and looked at the goddess. This time we didn't shake hands. Just meeting her eyes was enough. "Good night, Juno."

"Good night, Mike."

Anton Lipsek came back and nodded to the both of us. I took Connie's arm and steered her toward the door. Joseph, Andrew, Martin, Homer and Raymond all yelled for us to join the party then shut up when they saw the look on my face. One of them muttered, "Sour sort of fellow, isn't he?"

The joker with the bashed-in face wasn't in his chair where I had left him. Two other guys were holding the fort and I knew what they were doing there. They were waiting for me. The tall skinny one was a goon I knew and who knew me and licked his lips. The other one was brand, spanking new. About twenty-two maybe.

They looked at Connie, wondering how to get her out of there so she wouldn't be a witness to what came next. The goon I knew licked his lips again and rubbed his hands together. "We been waiting for you, Hammer."

The kid put on more of an act. He screwed up his pimply face to make a sneer, pushing himself away from the wall trying to make shoulders under his dinner jacket. "So you're Mike Hammer, are ya? Ya don't look so tough to me, guy."

I let my hand fool with the buttons on my coat. The billy in the empty holster pushed against the fabric under my arm and looked real as hell. "There's always one way you can find out, sonny," I said.

When the kid licked his lips a little spit ran down his chin. Connie walked ahead of me and opened the door. I walked past the two of them and they never moved. In a little while they'd be out of a job.

Not an empty table showed in this first back room. The show was over and the tiny dance floor was packed to the limit. The late tourist crowd was having itself a fling and making no bones about it. I scanned the sea of heads looking for Clyde. It was a hell of a change from Dinky Williams. But he wasn't around. We picked up our stuff from the hag at the checkroom and I tossed a dime in the spittoon. She swore and I swore back at her.

The words we used weren't unusual for the front section of the Bowery Inn, and no heads turned except two at the bar. One was Clyde. I waved my thumb toward the back. "Lousy help you hire, Dink." His face was livid again.

I didn't even look at the babe. It was Velda.

chapter five

I WAS SITTING in the big leather chair in the office when Velda put her key in the lock. She had on a tailored suit that made her look like a million dollars. Her long black page-boy hair threw back the light of the morning sunshine that streamed through the window and it struck me that of all the beauty in the world I had the best of it right under my nose.

She saw me then and said, "I thought you'd be here." There was frost in her voice. She tossed her handbag on the desk and sat in my old chair. Hell, it was her joint now anyway.

"You move pretty fast, Velda."

"So do you."

"Referring to my company of last night, I take it."

"Exactly. Your legwork. They were very nice, just your type."

I grinned at her. "I wish I could say something decent about your escort."

The frost melted and her voice turned soft. "I'm the jealous type, Mike."

I didn't have to lean far to reach her. The chair was on casters that moved easily. I wound my fingers in her hair, started to say something and stopped. Instead, I kissed the tip of her nose. Her fingers tightened around my wrist. She had her eyes half closed and didn't see me push her handbag out of reach. It tipped with the weight of the gun in it and landed on the floor.

This time I kissed her mouth. It was a soft, warm mouth. It was a light kiss, but I'll never forget it. It left me wanting to wrap my arms around her and squeeze until she couldn't move. No, I didn't do that. I slid back into my chair and Velda said, "It was never like that before, Mike. Don't treat me like the others."

My hand was shaking when I tried to light another cigarette. "I didn't expect to find you down the Bowery last night, kid."

"You told me to get to work, Mike."

"Finish it. Let's hear it all."

Velda leaned back in the chair, her eyes on mine. "You said to concentrate on Wheeler. I did. The papers carried most of the details and there was nothing to be learned here. I hopped the first plane to Columbus, visited with his family and business associates and got the next plane back again."

She picked her handbag off the floor and extracted a small black loose-leaf pad, flipping the cover back to the first page. "Here is the essence of what I learned. Everyone agreed that Chester Wheeler was an energetic, conscientious husband, father and businessman. There has never been any family trouble. Whenever he was away he wrote or called home frequently. This time they had two picture post cards from him, a letter and one phone call. He phoned as soon as he arrived in New York to tell them he'd had a successful trip. He sent one card to his son, a plain penny post card. The next card was postmarked from the Bowery and he mentioned going to a place called the Bowery Inn. Then he wrote a letter to his wife that was quite commonplace. A postscript to his twenty-two-year-old daughter mentioned the fact that he had met an old high school friend of hers working in the city. That was the last they heard until they were notified of his death.

"When I dug up his business friends I got nowhere. His business was fine, he was making a lot of money, and he had no worries at all."

I clamped my teeth together. "Like hell you got nowhere," I said softly. My mind drifted back over that little conversation with Pat. A little talk about how a guy named Emil Perry said Wheeler had been depressed because business was rotten. "You're sure about his business?"

"Yes. I checked his credit rating."

"Nice going. Continue."

"Well . . . the only lead I saw was this place called the Bowery Inn. I did some fast quizzing when I got home and found out what it was all about. The man who runs the place you seemed to know. I put on an act and he fell for it. Hard. He didn't seem to like you much, Mike."

"I can't blame him. I shot him once."

"After you left he couldn't talk for five minutes. He excused himself and went into the back room. When he returned he seemed satisfied about something. There was blood on his hands."

That would be Dinky, all right. He liked to use his hands when he had a couple of rods backing him up. "That all?"

"Practically. He wants to see me again."

I felt the cords in my neck pull tight. "The bastard! I'll beat the pants off him for that!"

Velda shook her head and laughed. "Don't you get to be the jealous type too, Mike. You don't wear it so well. Is it important that I see him again?"

I agreed reluctantly. "It's important."

"Is it still murder?"

"More than ever, sugar. I bet it's a big murder, too. A great big beautiful murder with all the trimmings."

"Then what do you suggest I do next?"

I gave it a thought first, then looked at her a moment. "Play this Clyde. Keep your eyes open and see what happens. If I were you I'd hide that P.I. ticket and leave the gun home. We don't want him putting two and two together and getting a bee in his bonnet.

"If you follow me on this you'll see the connection. First we have Wheeler. We have the fact that he *might* have taken a model out that night and he *might* have gone to the Inn where he *might* have run into something that meant murder. If Clyde didn't enter into this I'd skip the whole premise, but he makes it too interesting to pass up.

"There's only one hitch. Juno found the girl he left with the night of the party. She didn't go out with him!"

"But, Mike, then . . ."

"Then I'm supposing he *might* have gone with somebody else some other time. Hell of a lot of mights in this. Too many. At least it's something to work on, and if you stick around this Clyde character long enough something will turn up one way or another."

Velda rose, her legs spread apart, throwing out her arms in a stretch that made her jacket and skirt fill up almost to bursting. I had to bend my head down into a match to get my eyes off her. Clyde was going to get a hell of a deal for his money. I slapped my hat on and opened the door for her.

When we reached the street I put her in a taxi and watched until she was around the corner. It was just nine-thirty, so I headed for the nearest phone booth, dropped a nickel in the slot and dialed police headquarters. Pat had checked in, but he couldn't be located at present. I told the switchboard operator to have him meet me in a spaghetti joint around the corner from headquarters in a half-hour and the guy said he'd pass the message on. I found my heap and climbed in. It was going to be a busy day.

Pat was waiting for me over a half-finished cup of coffee. When he saw me come in he signaled for another coffee and some pastry. I threw my leg over the chair and sat down. "Morning, officer. How's every little thing in the department?"

"Going smoothly, Mike."

"Oh, too bad."

He set his coffee cup down again. His face was absolutely blank. "Don't start anything, Mike."

I acted indignant. "Who, me? What could I start that's not already started?"

The waiter brought my coffee and some Danish and I dunked

and ate two of them before either of us spoke again. Curiosity got the best of Pat. He said, "Let's hear it, Mike."

"Are you going to be stupid about it, Pat?"

His face was still frozen. "Let's hear it, Mike."

I didn't make any bones about trying to keep it out of my eyes or the set of my jaw. My voice came up from my chest with a nasty rumble and I could feel my lip working into a snarl that pulled the corners of my mouth down.

"You're a smart cop, Pat. Everybody knows it but most of all I know it and you know it yourself. You know something else besides. I'm just as smart. I said Wheeler was murdered and you patted me on the head and told me to behave.

"I'm saying it again, Pat. Wheeler was murdered. You can get in this thing or I can do it alone. I told you I wanted that ticket back and I'm going to get it. If I do a lot of reputations are going to fall by the wayside including yours and I don't want that to happen.

"You know me and you know I don't kid around. I'm beginning to get ideas, Pat. They think good. I've seen some things that look good. Things that put more taste in the flavor of murder. I'm going to have me another killer before long and a certain D.A. is going to get his nose blown for him."

I don't know what I expected Pat to do. Maybe I expected him to blow his top or start writing me off as a has-been in the brain department. I certainly didn't expect to see his face go cold and hear him say, "I gave you the benefit of the doubt a long time ago, Mike. I think Wheeler was murdered too."

He grinned a little at my expression and went on. "There's a catch. Word reached the D.A. and he looked into it and passed his professional opinion in conjunction with the Medical Examiner. Wheeler was, beyond doubt, a suicide. I have been told to concentrate my efforts on more recent developments in the wide field of crime."

"Our boy doesn't like you either now, eh?"

"Ha."

"So?"

"What do you know, Mike?"

"Just a little, pal. I'll know more before long and I'll drop it in your lap when there's enough of it to get your teeth in. I don't suppose your prestige suffered from the D.A.'s tirade."

"It went up if anything."

"Good. Tonight I'll buzz you with all the details. Meanwhile you can look up the whereabouts of one former torpedo called Rainey."

"I know him."

"Yeah?"

"We had him on an assault and battery charge a while back. The complainant failed to complain and he was dismissed. He called himself a fight promoter."

"Street brawls," I said sourly.

"Probably. He was loaded with jack but he had a room in the Bowery."

"*Where,* Pat?" My eyes lit up and Pat went grim.

"The Bowery. Why?"

"Interesting word. I've been hearing a lot about it these days. See if you can get a line on him, will you?"

Pat tapped a cigarette on the table. "This is all on the table, isn't it?"

"Every bit of it, chum. I won't hold back. I'm curious about one thing, though. What changed your mind from suicide to murder?"

Pat grinned through his teeth. "You. I didn't think you'd chase shadows. I said I wouldn't get excited this time but I couldn't help myself. By the time I reached the office I was shaking like a punk on his first holdup and I went down to take a look at the body. I called in a couple of experts and though there were few marks on the body it was the general opinion that our lad Wheeler had been through some sort of a scuffle prior to taking a bullet in the head."

"It couldn't have been much of a fuss. He was pretty damn drunk."

"It wasn't," he said. "Just enough to leave indications. By the way, Mike . . . about that slug and shell we found in the hall. Was that your work?"

I let out a short, sour laugh. "I told you that once. No. Somebody had a hole in his pocket."

He nodded thoughtfully. "I'll check the hotel again. It had to be either a resident or a visitor then. It's too bad you didn't lock the door."

"A lock won't stop a killer," I said. "He had all the time in the world and could make as much noise as he wanted. Most of the guests were either half deaf or dead to the world when the gun went off. It's an old building with thick walls that do a nice job of muffling sound."

Pat picked up the check and laid a dollar on top of it. "You'll contact me tonight then?"

"You bet. See you later and tell the D.A. I was asking for him."

It took fifteen minutes to get to the Chadwick Hotel. It was another side-street affair with an essence of dignity that stopped as soon as you entered the lobby. The desk clerk was the Mom type until she spoke then what came out made you think of other things. I told her I wanted to see a certain Marion Lester and she didn't bother to question or announce me. She said, "Room 312 and go up the stairs easy. They squeak."

I went up the stairs easy and they squeaked anyway. I knocked on the door of 312, waited and knocked again. The third time I heard feet shuffling across the floor and the door opened just far enough to show wide blue eyes, hair curlers and a satin negligee clutched tightly at the throat. I jumped the gun before she could ask questions with "Hello, Marion, Juno told me to see you."

The wide eyes got wider and the door opened the rest of the way. I closed it behind me and made like a gentleman by sweeping off my hat. Marion licked her lips and cleared her throat. "I . . . just got up."

"So I see. Rough night?"

". . . No."

She took me through the miniature hall into a more miniature living room and waved for me to sit down. I sat. She said, "It's so early . . . if you don't mind, I'll get dressed."

I told her I didn't mind and she shuffled into the bedroom and began pulling drawers out and opening closets. She wasn't like the other girls I knew. She was back in five minutes. This time she had a suit on and the curlers were out of her hair. A little make-up and her eyes didn't look so wide either.

She sat down gracefully in a straight-backed chair and reached for a cigarette in a silver box. "Now, what did you want to see me about, Mr. . . ."

"Mike Hammer. Just plain Mike." I snapped a match on my thumbnail and held it out to her. "Did Juno tell you about me?"

Marion nodded, twin streams of smoke sifting out through her nostrils. Her voice had a tremor in it and she licked her lips again. "Yes. You . . . were with Mr. Wheeler when he . . . he died."

"That's right. It happened under my nose and I was too drunk to know it."

"I'm afraid there's little I can . . . tell you, Mike."

"Tell me about that night. That's enough."

"Didn't Juno tell you?"

"Yeah, but I want to hear you say it."

She took a deep drag on the butt and squashed it in a tray. "He took me home. I had a few too many drinks, and . . . well, I was feeling a little giddy. I think he rode around in a cab with me for a while. Really, I can't remember everything exactly . . ."

"Go on."

"I must have passed out, because the next thing I knew I woke up in my bed fully clothed and with an awful hangover. Later I learned that he had committed suicide, and frankly, I was very much upset."

"And that's all?"

"That's all."

It's too bad, I thought. She's the type to show a guy a time if she wanted to. It was just too damn bad. She waited to see what I'd say next, and since it was still early I asked, "Tell me about it from the beginning. The show and all, I mean."

Marion smoothed out her hair with the flat of her hand and looked up at the ceiling. "The Calway Merchandising Company made the booking through Miss Reeves . . . Juno. She . . ."

"Does Juno always handle those details?"

"No, not always. Sometimes they go through Anton. You see, Juno is really the important one. She makes all the contacts and is persuasive enough to throw quite a few accounts to the agency."

"I can see why," I admitted with a grin.

She smiled back. "Our agency is perhaps the most exclusive in town. The models get paid more, are more in demand than any others, and all through Miss Reeves. A call from her is equal to a call from the biggest movie studio. In fact, she's managed to promote several of the agency models right into pictures."

"But to get back to the show . . ." I prompted.

"Yes . . . the call came in and Juno notified us at once. We had to report to Calway Merchandising to pick up the dresses we had to show and be fitted. That took better than two hours. One of the managers took us to the dinner where we sat through the speeches and what have you, and about an hour beforehand we left to get dressed. The show lasted for fifteen minutes or so, we changed back to our street clothes and joined the crowd. By that time drinks were being served and I managed to have a couple too many."

"About meeting Wheeler, how'd you manage that?"

"I think it was when I left. I couldn't make the elevator any too well. We got on together and he helped me down and into a cab. I told you the rest."

There it was again. Nothing.

I pushed myself out of the chair and fiddled with my hat. "Thanks, kid. That cooks it for me, but thanks anyway. You can go back to bed now."

"I'm sorry I couldn't help you."

"Oh, it helps a little. At least I know what not to look for. Maybe I'll be seeing you around."

She walked ahead of me to the door and held it open. "Perhaps," she said. "I hope the next time is under more pleasant circumstances." We shook hands briefly and her forehead wrinkled. "Incidentally, Juno mentioned reporters. I hope . . ."

"They can't make anything out of it as long as things stand that way. You can practically forget about it."

"I feel better now. Good-by, Mr. Hammer."

"So long, kid. See ya."

I crouched behind the wheel of my car and made faces at the traffic coming against me. It was a mess to start with and got messier all the time. Murder doesn't just happen. Not the kind of murder that gets tucked away so nicely not a single loose end stuck out.

Damn it anyway, where *was* a loose end? There had to be one! Was it money? Revenge? Passion? Why in hell did a nice guy like Wheeler have to die? Stinking little rats like Clyde ran around and did what they damn well pleased and a nice guy had to die!

I was still tossing it around in my mind when I parked along that residential street in the Bronx. The big sedan was in the driveway and I could make out the E.P. in gold Old English script on the door. I pulled the key out of the ignition and walked up the flagstone path that wound through the bushes.

This time I lifted the embossed knocker and let it drop.

A maid in a black and white uniform opened the door and stood with her hand on the knob. "Good morning. Can I help you?"

"I want to see Mr. Perry," I said.

"Mr. Perry left orders that he is not to be disturbed. I'm sorry, sir."

"You go tell Mr. Perry that he's gonna get disturbed right now. You tell him Mike Hammer is here and whatever a guy named Rainey can do I can do better." I grabbed the handle and pushed the door and she didn't try to stop me at all when she saw my face. "You go tell him that."

I didn't have long to wait. She came back, said, "Mr. Perry will see you in his study, sir," waved her hand toward the far end of the hall and stood there wondering what it was all about as I walked past.

Mr. Perry was the scared fat man. Now he was really scared. He didn't sit—he occupied a huge leather chair behind a desk and quivered from his jowls down. He must have been at peace with himself a minute before because an opened book lay facedown and a cigar burned in an ash tray.

I threw my hat on the desk, cleared away some of the fancy junk that littered it and sat on the edge. "You're a liar, Perry," I said.

The fat man's mouth dropped open and the first chin under it started to tremble. His pudgy little fingers squeezed the arms of his chair trying to get juice out of it. He didn't have much voice left when he said, "How dare you to . . . in my own home! How dare you . . ."

I shook a butt out of the pack and jammed it in the corner of my mouth. I didn't have a match so I lit it from his cigar. "What did Rainey promise you, Perry, a beating?" I glanced at him through the smoke. "A slug in the back maybe?"

His eyes went from the window to the door. "What are you . . ."

I finished it for him. "I'm talking about a hood named Rainey. What did he promise you?"

Perry's voice faded altogether and he looked slightly sick. I said, "I'll tell you once then I want an answer. I told you whatever Rainey can do I can do better. I can beat the hell out of you worse. I can put a slug where it'll hurt more and I'll get a large charge out of it besides.

"I'm talking about a guy you said you knew. His name was Wheeler, Chester Wheeler. He was found dead in a hotel room and the verdict was suicide. You informed the police that he was despondent . . . about business you said."

Emil Perry gave a pathetic little nod and flicked his tongue over his lips. I leaned forward so I could spit the words in his face. "You're a damned liar, Perry. There was nothing the matter with Wheeler's business. It was a stall, wasn't it?"

The fear crept into his eyes and he tried to shake his head.

"Do you know what happened to Wheeler?" I spoke the words only inches away from him. "Wheeler was murdered. And you know something else . . . you're going to be in line for the same thing when the killer knows I'm on your tail. He won't trust your not talking and you, my fat friend, will get a nice nasty slug inbedded somewhere in your intestines."

Emil Perry's eyes were like coals in a snowbank. He held his breath until his chin quivered, his cheeks went blue and he passed out. I sat back on the edge of the desk and finished my cigarette, waiting for him to come around.

It took a good five minutes and he resembled a lump of clay someone had piled in the chair. A lump of clay in a business suit.

When his eyes opened he made a pass at a perspiring decanter on the desk. I poured out a glass of ice water and handed it to him. He made loud gulping sounds getting it down.

I let my voice go flat. "You didn't even know Wheeler, did you?"

His expression gave me the answer to that one.

"Want to talk about it?"

Perry managed a fast negative movement of his head. I got up and put my hat on and walked to the door. Before I opened it. I looked back over my shoulder. "You're supposed to be a solid citizen, fat boy. The cops take your word for things. You know what I'm going to do? I'm going out and find what it is that Rainey promised you and really lay it on."

His face turned blue and he passed out before I closed the door. The hell with him. He could get his own water this time.

chapter six ▬▬▬▬▬▬▬▬▬▬▬▬▬

THE SKY HAD clouded over putting a bite in the air. Here and there a car coming in from out of town was wearing a top hat of snow. I pulled in to a corner restaurant and had two cups of coffee to get the chill out of my bones, then climbed back in the car and cut across town to my apartment where I picked up my topcoat and gloves. By the time I reached the street there were gray feathers of snow in the air slanting down through the sheer walls of the building to the street.

It was twelve-fifteen before I found a parking lot with room to rent. As soon as I checked my keys in the shack I grabbed a cab and gave the driver the address of the Anton Lipsek Agency on Thirty-third Street. Maybe something could be salvaged from the day after all.

This time the sweet-looking receptionist with the sour smile didn't ask questions. I told her, "Miss Reeves, please," and she spoke into the intercom box. The voice that came back was low and vibrant, tinged with an overtone of pleasure. I didn't have to be told that she was waiting for me.

The gods on Olympus could well be proud of their queen. She was a vision of perfection in a long-sleeved dress striding across the room to meet me. The damn clothes she wore. They covered everything up and let your imagination fill in the blanks. The sample she offered was her hands and face but the sample was enough because it made you want to undress her with your eyes and feel the warm flesh of a goddess. There was a lilt to her walk and a devil in her eyes as we shook hands, a brief touch that sent my skin crawling up my spine again.

"I'm so glad you came, Mike."

"I told you I would." The dress buttoned up snug at the neck and she wore but one piece of jewelry, a pendant. I flipped it into the light and it threw back a shimmering green glow. I let out a whistle. The thing was an emerald that must have cost a fortune.

"Like it?"

"Some rock."

"I love beautiful things," she said.

"So do I." Juno turned her head and a pleased smile flashed at me for a second and disappeared. The devils in her eyes laughed their pleasure too and she walked to her desk.

That was when the gray light from the window seeped into the softness of her hair and turned it a gold that made my heart beat against my chest until I thought it would come loose.

There was a bad taste in my mouth.

My guts were all knotted up in a ball and that damnable music began in my head. Now I knew what that creepy feeling was that left my spine tingling. Now I knew what it was about Juno that made me want to reach out and grab her.

She reminded me of another girl.

A girl that happened a long time ago.

A girl I thought I had put out of my mind and forgotten completely in a wild hatred that could never be equaled. She was a blonde, a very yellow, golden blonde. She was dead and I made her that way. I killed her because I wanted to and she wouldn't stay dead.

I looked down at my hands and they were shaking violently, the fingers stiffened into talons that showed every vein and tendon.

"Mike . . .?" The voice was different. It was Juno and now that I knew what it was I could stop shaking. The gold was out of her hair.

She brought her coat over to me to hold while she slipped into it. There was a little piece of mink fur on her hat that matched the coat. "We *are* going to lunch, aren't we?"

"I'm not here on business."

She laughed again and leaned against me as she worked the gloves over her fingers. "What were you thinking of a minute ago, Mike?"

I didn't let her see my face. "Nothing."

"You aren't telling the truth."

"I know it."

Juno looked at me over her shoulder. There was a pleading in her eyes. "It wasn't me . . . something I did?"

I forced a lopsided smile. "Nothing you did, Juno. I just happened to think of something I shouldn't have."

"I'm glad, Mike. You were hating something then and I wouldn't want you to hate me." She reached for my hand almost girlishly and pulled me to the door at the side of the room. "I don't want to share you with the whole office force, Mike."

We came out around the corner of the corridor and I punched the bell for the elevator. While we waited she squeezed my arm under hers, knowing that I couldn't help watching her. Juno, a goddess in a fur coat. She was an improvement on the original.

And in that brief second I looked at her the light filtered through her hair again and reflected the sheen of gold. My whole head rocked with the fire and pain in my chest and I felt Charlotte's name trying to force itself past my lips. Good God! Is this what it's like to think back? Is this what happened when you remember a woman you loved then blasted into hell? I ripped my eyes away and slammed my finger against the buzzer on the wall, holding it there, staring at it until I heard metal scraping behind the doors.

The elevator stopped and the operator gave her a princely nod and a subdued murmur of greeting. The two other men in the car looked at Juno, then back to me jealously. She seemed to affect everyone the same way.

The street had taken on a slippery carpet of white that rippled under the wind. I turned up my coat collar against it and peered down the road for a cab. Juno said, "No cab, Mike. My car's around the corner." She fished in her pocket and brought out a gold chain that ran through two keys. "Here, you drive."

We ducked our heads and went around the block with the wind whipping at our legs. The car she pointed out was a new Caddy convertible with all the trimmings that I thought only existed in show windows. I held the door open while she got in, slammed it shut and ran around the other side. Stuff like this was really living.

The engine was a cat's purr under the hood wanting to pull away from the curb in a roar of power. "Call it, Juno. Where to?"

"There's a little place downtown that I discovered a few months ago. They have the best steaks in the world if you can keep your mind on them. The most curious people in the world seem to eat there . . . almost fascinating people."

"Fascinating?"

Her laugh was low, alive with humor. "That isn't a good word. They're . . . well, they're most unusual. Really, I've never seen anything like it. But the food is good. Oh, you'll see. Drive down Broadway and I'll show you how to go."

I nodded and headed toward the Stem with the windshield wipers going like metronomes. The snow was a pain, but it thinned out traffic somewhat and it was only a matter of minutes before we were downtown. Juno leaned forward in the seat, peering ahead at the street corners. I slowed down so she could see where we were and she tipped her finger against the glass.

"Next block, Mike. It's a little place right off the corner."

I grinned at her. "What are we doing . . . slumming? Or is it one of those Village hangouts that have gone uptown?"

"Definitely not uptown. The food is superb." Her eyes flashed just once as we pulled into the curb. I grinned back and she said, "You act all-knowing, Mike. Have you been here before?"

"Once. It used to be a fag joint and the food was good then too. No wonder you saw so many fascinating people."

"Mike!"

"You ought to get around a little more, woman. You've been living too high in the clouds too long. If anybody sees me going in this joint I'm going to get whistled at. That is . . . if they let me in."

She passed me a puzzled frown at that. "They tossed me out one time," I explained. "At least they started to toss me out. The reinforcements called for reinforcements and it wound up with me walking out on my own anyway. I had my hair pulled. Nice people."

Juno bit her lip trying to hold back a laugh. "And here I've been telling all my friends where to go to find wonderful steaks! Come to think of it a couple of them were rather put out when I mentioned it to them a second time."

"Hell, they probably enjoyed themselves. Come on, let's see how the third side lives."

She shook the snow out of her hair and let me open the door for her. We had to go through the bar to the hat-check booth and I had a quick look at the gang lined up on the stools. Maybe ten eyes met mine in the mirror and tried to hang on but I wasn't having any. There was a pansy down at the end of the bar trying to make a guy who was too drunk to notice and was about to give it up as a bad job. I got a smile from the guy and he came close to getting knocked on his neck. The bartender was one of them too, and he looked put out because I came in with a dame.

The girl at the hat-check booth looked like she was trying hard to grow a mustache and wasn't having much luck at it. She gave me a frosty glare but smiled at Juno and took her time about looking her over. When the babe went to hang up the coats Juno looked back at me with a little red showing in her face and I laughed at her.

"Now you know, huh?" I said.

Her hand covered the laugh. "Oh, Mike, I feel so very foolish! And I thought they were just being friendly."

"Oh, very friendly. To you, that is. I hope you noticed the cold treatment I got and I usually get along with any kind of dame."

The dining room was a long, narrow room with booths along the sides and a few tables running down the middle. Nobody was at the tables, but over half the booths were filled if you can call two people of the same sex sitting along the same side filled. A waiter with a lisp and hair that curled around his neck came over and curtsied then led us to the last booth back.

I ordered a round of cocktails to come in front of the steaks and the waiter gave me another curtsy that damn near had a kiss in it. Juno opened a jeweled cigarette case and lifted out a king size. "I think he likes you, Mike," she said. "Smoke?"

I shook my head and worked the next to last one out of my

crumpled pack. Outside at the bar somebody stuck a nickel in the jukebox and managed to hit a record that didn't try to take your ears off. It was something sweet and low-down with a throaty sax carrying the melody, the kind of music that made you want to listen instead of talk. When the cocktails came we picked them up together. "Propose a toast, Mike."

Her eyes shone at me over the glass. "To beauty," I said, "To Olympus. To a goddess that walks with the mortals."

"With very . . . wonderful mortals," Juno added.

We drained the glasses.

There were other cocktails and other toasts after that. The steaks came and were the best in the world like she said. There was that period when you feel full and contented and can sit back with a cigarette curling sweet smoke and look at the world and be glad you're part of it.

"Thinking, Mike?"

"Yeah, thinking how nice it is to be alive. You shouldn't have taken me here, pretty lady. It's getting my mind off my work."

Her face knitted in a frown. "Are you *still* looking for a reason for your friend's death?"

"Uh-huh. I checked on that Marion babe, by the way. She was the one. Everything was so darned aboveboard it knocked the props out from under me. I was afraid it would happen like that. Still trying, though, still in there trying."

"Trying?"

'Hell yes. I don't want to wind up a grocery clerk." She didn't get what I meant. My grin split into a smile and that into a laugh. I had no right to feel so happy, but way back in my head I knew that the sun would come up one day and show me the answer.

"What brought that on? Or are you laughing at me?"

"Not you, Juno. I couldn't laugh at you." She stuck out her tongue at me. "I was laughing at the way life works out. It gets pretty complicated sometimes, then all of a sudden it's as simple as hell, if hell can be simple. Like the potbellies with all the bare-backed babes in the Bowery. You know something . . . I didn't think I'd find you there."

She shrugged her shoulders gracefully. "Why not? A great many of your 'potbellies' are wonderful business contacts."

"I understand you're tops in the line."

I could see that pleased her. She nodded thoughtfully. "Not without reason, Mike. It has meant a good deal of exacting work both in and out of the office. We only handle work for the better houses and use the best in the selection of models. Anton, you know, is comparatively unknown as a person, simply because he refuses to take credit for his photography, but his work is far above any of the others. I think you've seen the interest he takes in his job."

"I would too," I said.

Her tongue came out again. "You would, too. I bet nothing would get photographed."

"I bet a lot would get accomplished."

"In that case you'd be running headlong into our code of ethics."

"Nuts. Pity the poor photographer. He does all the work and the potbellies have all the fun." I dragged on my cigarette and squinted my eyes. "You know, Clyde has a pretty business for himself."

My casual reference to the guy brought her eyebrows up. "Do you know him?"

"Sure, from way back. Ask him to tell you about me someday."

"I don't know him that well, myself. But if I ever get the chance I will. He's the perfect underworld type, don't you think?"

"Right out of the movies. When did he start running that place?"

Juno tapped her cheek with a delicate forefinger. "Oh . . . about six months ago, I think. I remember him stopping in the office to buy photographs in wholesale lots. He had the girls sign all the pictures and invited them to his opening. It was all very secret of course. I didn't get to go myself until I heard the girls raving about the place. He did the same thing with most of the agencies in town."

"He's got a brain, that boy," I drawled. "It's nice to have your picture on the wall. He played the girls for slobs and they never knew it. He knew damn well that a lot of them traveled with the moneybags and would pull them into his joint. When word got around that there was open gambling to boot, business got better and better. Now he gets the tourists too. They think it's all very smart and exciting . . . the kind who go around hoping for a raid so they can cut their pictures out of the papers and send them home to the folks for laughs."

She stared at me, frowning.

"I wonder who he pays off?" I mused.

"Who?"

"Clyde. Somebody is taking the long green to keep the place going. Clyde's shelling out plenty to somebody with a lot of influence, otherwise he would have had the cops down his throat on opening night."

Juno said impatiently, "Oh, Mike, those tactics went out with the Prohibition era . . ." then her voice got curious. "Or didn't they?"

I looked across the table at this woman who wore her beauty so proudly and arrogantly. "You've only seen the best side of things so far, kid. Plenty goes on you wouldn't want to look at."

She tossed her head. "It seems incredible that those things still happen, Mike."

I started to slap my fist against my palm gently. "Incredible, but it's happening," I said. "I wonder what would happen if I shafted my old buddy Dinky Williams?" My mouth twisted into a grin. "Maybe it's an angle. Maybe . . ." I let my sentence trail off and stared at the wall.

Juno signaled the waiter and he came back with another round of cocktails. I checked my watch and found myself in the middle of the afternoon. "We'll make these our last, ok?"

She leaned her chin on her hands, smiling. "I hate to have you leave me."

"It's not a cinch for me, either." She was still smiling and I said, "I asked another beautiful girl who could have had ten other guys why she picked me to hold hands with. She gave me a good answer. What's yours, Juno?"

Her eyes were a fathomless depth that tried to draw me down into them. Her mouth was still curved in a smile that went softer and softer until only a trace of it was left. Full, lovely lips that barely had to move to form the words. "I detest people who pamper me. I detest people who insist upon putting me on a pedestal. I think I like to be treated rough and you're the only one who has tried it."

"I haven't tried anything."

"No. But you've been thinking of it. Sometimes you don't even speak politely."

She was a mind reader like all good goddesses should be and she was right. Quite right. I didn't know what the hell was going on in my head, but sometimes when I looked at her I wanted to reach across the table and smack her right in the teeth. Even when I thought of it I could feel the tendons in the back of my hand start twitching. Maybe a goddess was just too damn much for me. Maybe I'd been used to my own particular kind of guttersnipe too long. I kicked the idea out of my mind and unlocked the stare we were holding on each other.

"Let's go home," I said. "There's still some day and a long night ahead of me."

She was wanting me to ask her to continue this day and not break it off now, but I didn't let myself think it. Juno pushed back her chair and stood up. "The nose. First I must powder the nose, Mike." I watched her walk away from me, watched the swing of her hips and the delicate way she seemed to balance on her toes. I wasn't the only one watching, either. A kid who had artist written all over her in splotches of paint was leaning against the partition of the booth behind me. Her eyes were hard and hot and followed Juno every step of the way. She was another one of those mannish things that breed in the half-light of the so-called aesthetical world. I got a look that told me I was in for competition and she took off after Juno. She came back in a minute and her face was pulled tight in a scowl and I gave her a nasty laugh. Some women, yes. Others, nix.

My nose got powdered first and I waited by the door for her after throwing a good week's pay to the cashier.

The snow that had slacked off started again in earnest. A steady stream of early traffic poured out of the business section, heading home before the stuff got too deep. Juno had snow tires on the heap so I wasn't worried about getting caught, but it took us twice the time to get back uptown as it did to come down.

Juno decided against going back to the office and told me to go along Riverside Drive. At the most fashionable of the cross streets I turned off and went as far as the middle of the block. She indicated a new gray stone building that stood shoulder-to-shoulder with the others, boasting a doorman in a maroon uniform and topcoat. She leaned back and sighed, "We're home."

"Leave the car here?"

"Won't you need it to get where you're going?"

"I couldn't afford to put gas in this buggy. No, I'll take a cab."

I got out and opened the door. The maroon uniform walked over and tipped his hat. Juno said, "Have the car taken to the garage for me please?"

He took the keys. "Certainly, Miss Reeves."

She turned to me with a grin. The snow swirling around her clung to the fur of her collar and hat, framing her face with a sprinkling of white. "Come up for a drink?" I hesitated, "Just one, Mike, then I'll let you go."

"Okay, baby, just one and don't try to make it any more."

Juno didn't have a penthouse, but it was far enough up to make a good Olympus. There was no garishness about the place, big as it was. The furnishings and the fixtures were matched in the best of taste, designed for complete, comfortable living.

I kept my coat and hat on while she whipped up a cocktail, my eyes watching the lithe grace of her movements. There was an unusual symmetry to her body that made me want to touch and feel. Our eyes met in the mirror over the sofa and there was the same thing in hers as there must have been in mine.

She spun around with an eloquent gesture and held out the glasses. Her voice was low and husky again. "I'm just a breeze past thirty, Mike. I've known many men. I've had many men too, but none that I really wanted. One day soon I'm going to want you."

My spine chilled up suddenly and the crazy music let loose in my head because she had the light in her hair again. The stem of the glass broke off in my fingers, tearing into my palm. The back of my neck got hot and I felt the sweat pop out on my forehead.

I moved so the light would be out of her hair and the gold would be gone from it, covering up the insane hatred of memory by lifting my hand to drink from the bowl of the broken glass.

It spoiled the picture for me, a picture that should be beautiful and desirable, scarred by something that should be finished but kept coming back.

I put the pieces of the glass down on the window sill and she said, "You looked at me that way again, Mike."

This time I forced the memory out of my mind. I slipped my hand over hers and ran my fingers through her hair, sifting its short silky loveliness. "I'll make it up to you sometime, Juno. I I can't help thinking and it hasn't got anything to do with you."

"Make it up to me now."

I gave her ear a little pull. "No."

"Why?"

"Because."

She pouted and her eyes tried to convince me.

I couldn't tell her that it was because there was a time and place for everything, and though this was the time and place she wasn't the person. I was only a mortal. A mortal doesn't undress a goddess and let his eyes feast and his hands feel and his body seek fulfillment.

Then too maybe that wasn't the reason at all. Maybe she reminded me of something else I could never have.

Never.

She said it slowly. "Who was she, Mike? Was she lovely?"

I couldn't keep the words back. I tried, but they were there.

"She was lovely. She was the most gorgeous thing that ever lived and I was in love with her. But she did something and I played God; I was the judge and I the jury and the sentence was death. I shot her right in the gut and when she died I died too."

Juno never said a word. Only her eyes moved. They softened, offered themselves to me, trying to convince me that I wasn't dead . . . not to her.

I lit a cigarette and stuck it in my mouth, then got the hell out of there before her eyes became too convincing. I felt her eyes burning in my back because we both knew I'd be back.

Juno, goddess of marriage and births, queen of the lesser gods and goddesses. Why wasn't she Venus, goddess of beauty and love? Juno was a queen and she didn't want to be. She wanted to be a woman.

Darkness had come prematurely, but the reflected lights on the whiteness of the snow made the city brighter than ever. Each office building discharged a constant stream of people clutching their collars tight at the throat. I joined the traffic that pressed against the sides of the buildings trying to get away from the stinging blast of air, watching them escape into the mouths of the kiosks.

I grabbed a cab, stayed in it until I reached Times Square, then got out and ducked into a bar for a quick beer. When I came out there were no empty cabs around so I started walking down Broadway toward Thirty-third. Every inch it was a fight against the snow and the crowd. My feet were soaked and the crease was out of my pants. Halfway there the light changed suddenly and the cars coming around the corner forced the pedestrians back on the curb.

Somebody must have slipped because there was a tinkle of glass then a splintering crash as the front came out of a store showcase on the corner. Those who jumped out of the way were crammed in by others who wanted to see what happened. A cop wormed in through the melee and stood in front of the window and I got out through the path he left behind him.

When I reached Thirty-third I turned east hoping to find a taxi to get over to the parking lot and decided to give it up as a bad job and walk the rest of the way after one more look.

I stepped out on the curb to look down the street when the plate glass in a window behind me twanged and split into a spider web of cracks. Nobody had touched it this time, either. A car engine roared and all I saw was the top half of a face looking out from the back window of a blue sedan and it was looking straight at me for a long second before it pulled out of sight.

My eyes felt tight and my lips were pulled back over my teeth. My voice cut into the air and faces turned my way. "Twice the same day," I said, "right on Broadway, too. The crazy bastard, the crazy son-of-a-bitch!"

I didn't remember getting to the car lot or driving out through traffic. I must have been muttering to myself because the drivers of cars that stopped alongside me at red lights would look over and shake their heads like I was nuts or something. Maybe I was. It scares me to be set up as a target right off the busiest street in the world.

That first window. I thought it was an accident. The second one had a bullet hole in the middle of it just before it came apart and splashed all over the sidewalk.

The building where I held down an office had a parking space in the basement. It was empty. I drove in and rolled to a corner and locked up. The night man took my keys and let me sign the register before letting me take the service elevator up to my floor.

When I got out I walked down the corridor, looking at the darkened glass of the empty offices. Only one had a light behind it and that one was mine. When I rattled the knob the latch snapped back and the door opened.

Velda said, "Mike! What are you doing here?"

I brushed right past her and went to the filing cabinet where I yanked at the last drawer down. I had to reach all the way in the back behind the rows of well-stuffed envelopes to get what I wanted.

"What happened, Mike?" She was standing right beside me, her lip caught between her teeth. Her eyes were on the little .25 automatic I was shoving in my pocket.

"No bastard is going to shoot at me," I told her. My throat felt dry and hoarse.

"When?"

"Just now. Not ten minutes ago. The bastard did it right out in the open. You know what that means?"

That animal snarl crossed her face and was gone in a second. "Yes. It means that you're important all of a sudden."

"That's right, important enough to kill."

She said it slowly, hoping I had the answer. "Did you . . . see who it was?"

"I saw a face. Half of it. Not enough to tell who it was except that it was a man. That face will try again and when it does I'll blow the hell out of it."

"Be careful, Mike. You don't have a license anymore. The D.A. would love to run you in on a Sullivan charge."

I got up out of my crouch and gave her a short laugh. "The law is supposed to protect the people. If the D.A. wants to jug me I'll make a good time out of it. I'll throw the Constitution in his face. I think one of the first things it says is that the people are allowed to bear arms. Maybe they'll even have to revoke the Sullivan Law and then we'll really have us a time."

"Yeah, a great whizbang, bang-up affair."

For the first time since I came in I took notice of her. I don't know how the hell I waited so long. Velda was wearing a sweeping black evening gown that seemed to start halfway down her waist, leaving the top naked as sin. Her hair, falling around her shoulders, looked like onyx and I got a faint whiff of a deep, sensual aroma.

There was no fullness to the dress. It clung. There was no other word for it. It just clung, and under it there wasn't the slightest indication of anything else. "Is that all you got on?"

"Yes."

"It's cold outside, baby." I know I was frowning but I couldn't help it. "Where you going?"

"To see your friend Clyde. He's invited me out to supper."

My hand tightened into a fist before I could stop it. Clyde, the bastard! I forced a grin through the frown. It didn't come out so well. "If I knew you would look like that I'd have asked you out myself."

There was a time when she would have gotten red and slammed me across the jaw. There was a time when she would have broken any kind of a date to put away a hamburger in a diner with me. Those times had flown.

She pulled on a pair of elbow-length gloves and let me stand there with my mouth watering, knowing damn well she had me where it hurt. "Business, Mike, business before pleasure always." Her face was blank.

I let my tone get sharp. "What were you doing here before I came in?"

"There's a note on your desk explaining everything. I visited the Calway Merchandising Company and rounded up some photographs they took of the girls that night. You might want to see them. You take to pretty girls, don't you?"

"Shut up."

She glanced at me quickly so I wouldn't see the tears that made her eyes shine. When she walked to the desk to get her coat I started swearing under my breath at Clyde again because the bastard was getting the best when I had never seen it. That's what happens when something like Velda is right under your nose.

I said it again. This time there was no sharpness in my voice. "I wish I had seen you like that before, Velda."

She took a minute to put on her coat and it was so quiet in that room I could hear her breathing. She turned around, the tears were still there. "Mike . . . I don't have to tell you that you can see me any way you like . . . anytime."

I had her in my arms, pressing her against me, feeling every warm, vibrant contour of her body. Her mouth reached for mine and I tasted the wet sweetness of her lips, felt her shudder as my hands couldn't keep off the whiteness of her skin. My fingers dug into her shoulders leaving livid red marks. She tore her mouth away with a sob and spun around so I couldn't see her face, and with one fast motion that happened too quickly she put her hands over mine and slid them over the flesh and onto the dress that clung and down her body that was so warmly alive, then pulled away and ran to the door.

I put a cigarette in my mouth and forgot to light it. I could still hear her heels clicking down the hall. Absently, I reached for the phone and dialed Pat's number out of habit. He said hello three times before I answered him and told him to meet me in my office.

I looked at my hands and the palms were damp with sweat. I lit my cigarette and sat there, thinking of Velda again.

chapter seven ▰▰▰▰▰▰▰▰▰▰

IT TOOK PAT thirty minutes to get there. He came in stamping the snow off his shoes and blowing like a bull moose. When he shed his coat and hat he threw a briefcase on the desk and drew up a chair.

"What are you looking so rosy about, Mike?"

"The snow. It always gets me. How'd you make out today?"

"Fine," Pat said, "just fine and dandy. The D.A. made a point of telling me to keep my nose clean again. If he ever gets boosted out of office I'm going to smack him right in the sneezer." He must have read the surprise on my face. "Okay, okay, it doesn't sound like me. Go ahead and say it. I'm getting tired of being snarled up in red tape. You had it easy before you threw away your ticket and you didn't know it."

"I'll get it back."

"Perhaps. We have to make murder out of suicide first."

"You almost had another on your hands today, chum."

He stopped in the middle of a sentence and said, "Who now?"

"Me."

"You!"

"Little me. On a crowded street, too. Somebody tried to pop me with a silenced gun. All they got was two windows."

"I'll be damned! We got a call on one of those windows, the one on Thirty-third. If the slug didn't poke a hole through all the scenery and land where it could be found it would have passed for an accident. Where was the other one?"

I told him and he said he would be damned again. He reached for the phone and buzzed headquarters to have them go through the window for the slug. When he hung up I said, "What's the D.A. going to do when he hears about this?"

"Quit kidding. He isn't hearing anything. You know the rep you have . . . the bright boy'll claim it's one of your old friends sending a greeting card for the holidays."

"It's too early for that."

"Then he'll grab you on some trumped-up charge and get himself a big play in the papers. The hell with him."

"You aren't talking like a good cop now, feller."

Pat's face darkened and he leaned out of his chair with his teeth bared to the gums. "There's a time when being a good cop won't catch a killer. Right now I'm teed off, Mike. We're both on a hot spot that may get hotter and I don't like it. It might be that I'm getting smart. A little favorable publicity never hurts anybody and if the D.A. tries to trim my corns I'll have a better talking point if I have something I can toss at him."

I laughed. Cripes, how I laughed! For ten years I had sung that song to him and now he was beginning to learn the words.

It was funnier now than it was in the beginning.

I said, "What about Rainey? You find him?"

"We found him."

"Yeah?"

"Yeah what. He was engaged in the so-called legitimate profession of promoting fights. Some arena on the island. We couldn't tap him for a thing. What about him?"

There was a bottle of booze in the desk and I poured out two shots. "He's in this, Pat. I don't know just how he fits, but he's there." I offered a silent toast and we threw them down. It burned a path to my stomach and lay there like a hot coal. I put down the glass and sat on the window sill. "I went out to see Emil Perry. Rainey was there and had the guy scared silly. Even I couldn't scare him worse. Perry said Wheeler had spoken of suicide because business was bad, but a check showed his outfit to be making coin hand over fist. Riddle me that one."

Pat whistled slowly.

I waited for him to collect his thoughts. "Remember Dinky Williams, Pat?"

Pat let his head move up and down. "Go on." His face was getting that cop look on it.

I tried to make it sound casual. "What's he doing now? You know?"

"No."

"If I were to tell you that he was running a wide-open gambling joint right here in the city, what would you do?"

"I'd say you were crazy, it's impossible, then put the vice squad on it."

"In that case I won't tell you about it."

He brought his hand down on the desk so hard my cigarettes jumped. "The hell you won't! You'll tell me about it right now! Who am I supposed to be, a rookie cop for you to play around with?"

It was nice to see him get mad again. I eased down off the window sill and slumped in my chair. His face was red as a beet. "Look, Pat. You're still a cop. You believe in the integrity and loyalty of the force. You may not want to, but you'll be duty-bound to do just what you said. If you do a killer gets away."

He went to talk but I stopped him with a wave of my hand. "Keep still and listen. I've been thinking that there's more to this than you or I have pictured. Dink's in it, Rainey's in it, guys like Emil Perry are in it too. Maybe lots more we don't know about . . . yet. Dinky Williams is cleaning up a pretty penny right this minute running wheels and bars without a license. Because I told you that don't go broadcasting it around. It may hurt you to be reminded of the fact, but just the same it has to be . . . if Dinky Williams runs a joint, then somebody is getting paid off. Somebody big. Somebody important. Either that or a whole lot of small somebodies who are mighty important when you lump them all together. Do you want to fight that setup?"

"You're damned well told I do!"

"You want to keep your badge? You think you can buck it?" His voice was a hoarse whisper. "I'll do it."

"You have another think coming and you know it. You'd just *like* to do it. Now listen to me. I have an inside track on this thing. We can play it together or not, but we're doing it my way or you can stick your nose in the dirt and root up the facts yourself. It won't be easy. If Dinky *is* paying off we can get the whole crowd at once, not just Dinky. Now call it."

I think if I had had a license it would have been gone right there, friend or no friend. All I had was a name on the door that didn't mean anything now. Pat looked at me with disgust and said, "What a great Captain of Homicide *I* am. The D.A. would give his arm for a recording of this little conversation. Okay, Inspector, I'm waiting for my orders."

I gave him a two-fingered salute. "First, we want a killer. To get him we need to know why Wheeler was killed. If you were to mention the fact that a certain guy named Clyde was heading for trouble you might get results. They won't be pretty results, but they might show us where to look."

"Who's Clyde?" There was an ominous tone in his voice.

"Clyde is Dinky's new monicker. He got fancy."

Pat was grinning now. "The name is trouble, Mike. I've heard it mentioned before." He stood up and pulled a cigarette from my deck of Luckies. I sat there and waited. "We're getting into ward politics now."

"So?"

"So you're a pretty smart bastard. I still say you should've been a cop. You'd be Commissioner by now or dead. One or the other. You might still be dead."

"I almost was this afternoon."

"Sure, I can see why. This Clyde guy has all the local monkeys by their tails. He gets everything fixed, everything from a parking ticket to a murder rap. All you have to do is mention the name and somebody starts bowing and scraping. Our old friend Dinky has really come up in the world."

"Nuts. He's a small-time heel."

"Is he? If it's the same guy we're talking about he's able to pull a lot of strings."

Pat was too calm. I didn't like it. There were things I wanted to ask him and I was afraid of the answers. I said, "How about the hotel? You checked there, didn't you?"

"I did. Nobody registered the day of the killing, but there were quite a few guests admitted to other rooms that same night. They all had plausible alibis."

That time I let out a string of dirty words. Pat listened and grinned again. "Will I see you tomorrow, Mike?"

"Yeah. Tomorrow."

"Stay away from store windows."

He put on his hat and slammed the door. I went back to looking at the pictures Velda had left on my desk. The girl named Marion Lester was laughing into the camera from the folds of a huge fur-collared coat. She looked happy. She didn't look like she'd be drunk in another couple of hours and have to be put to bed by a friend of mine who died not long after.

I slid all the photos in the folder and stuffed them in the desk drawer. The bottle was still half full and the glass empty. I cured that in a hurry. Pretty soon it was the other way around, then there was nothing in either of them and I felt better. I pulled the phone over by the cord and dialed a number that I had written on the inside of a matchbook cover.

A voice answered and I said, "Hello, Connie . . . Mike."

"My ugly lover! I thought you'd forgotten me."

"Never, child. What are you doing?"

"Waiting for you."

"Can you wait another half-hour?"

"I'll get undressed for you."

"You get dressed for me because we may go out."

"It's snowing." She sounded pained. "I don't have galoshes."

"I'll carry you." She was still protesting when I stuck the receiver on its arms.

There was a handful of .25 shells in the drawer that I shoveled into my pocket, little bits of insurance that might come in handy. Just before I left I pulled out the drawer and hauled out the envelope of photographs. The last thing I did was type a note for Velda telling her to let me know how she made out.

The guy in the parking lot had very thoughtfully put the skid chains on my buggy and earned himself a couple of bucks. I backed out and joined the line of cabs and cars that pulled their way through the storm.

Connie met me at the door with a highball in her hand and shoved it at me before I could take off my hat. "My hero," she said, "my big, brave hero coming through the raging blizzard to rescue poor me."

It was a wonderful highball. I gave her back the empty and kissed her cheek. Her laugh was little bells that tinkled in my ear. She closed the door and took my coat while I went inside and sat down. When she joined me she sat on the sofa with her legs crossed under her and reached for a smoke. "About tonight . . . we are going where?"

"Looking for a killer."

The flame of the match she held trembled just a little. "You . . . know?"

I shook my head. "I suspect."

There was real interest in her face. Her voice was soft. "Who?"

"I suspect a half-dozen people. Only one of them is a killer. The rest contributed to the crime somehow." I played with the cord on the floor lamp and watched the assorted expressions that flickered across her face.

Finally she said, "Mike . . . is there some way I can help? I mean, is it possible that something I know might have a meaning?"

"Possibly."

"Is that . . . the only reason you came here tonight?"

I turned the light off and on a few times. Connie was staring at me hard, her eyes questioning. "You don't have much faith in yourself, kid," I grinned. "Why don't you look in the mirror sometime? You got a face that belongs in the movies and a body that should be a crime to cover. You have an agile mind too. I'm only another guy. I go for all that.

"The answer is yes, that's all I came here for tonight. If you were anybody else I still would have come, but because you're you it makes it all the nicer and I look forward to coming. Can you understand that?"

Her legs swung down and she came over and kissed my nose, then went back to the couch. "I understand, Mike. Now I'm happy. Tell me what you want."

"I don't know, Connie. I'm up a tree. I don't know what to ask for."

"Just ask anything you want."

I shrugged. "Okay, do you like your work?"

"Wonderful."

"Make a lot of jack?"

"Oodles."

"Like your boss?"

"Which one?"

"Juno."

Connie spread her hands out in a noncommittal gesture. "Juno never interferes with me. She had seen my work and was impressed with it. When I had a call from her I was thrilled to the bones because I hit the top. Now all she does is select those ads that fit me best and Anton takes care of the rest."

"Juno must make a pile," I said observingly.

"I guess she does! Besides drawing a big salary she's forever on the receiving end of gifts from overgenerous clients. I'd almost feel sorry for Anton if he had the sense to care."

"What about him?"

"Oh, he's the arty type. Doesn't give a hoot for money as long as he has his work. He won't let a subordinate handle the photography, either. Maybe that's why the agency is so successful."

"He married? A wife would cure that."

"Anton married? That's a laugh. After all the women he handles, and I do mean handles, what mere woman would attract that guy. He's positively frigid. For a Frenchman that's disgraceful."

"French?"

Connie nodded and dragged on her smoke. "I overheard a little secret being discussed between Anton and Juno. It seems that Juno met him in France and brought him over here, just in time for him to escape some nasty business with the French court. During the war he was supposed to have been a collaborator of a sort . . . taking propaganda photos of all the bigwig Nazis and their families. As I said, Anton doesn't give a hoot about money or politics as long as he has his work."

"That's interesting but not very helpful. Tell me something about Clyde."

"I don't know anything about Clyde except that looking like a movie gangster he is a powerful attraction for a lot of jerks from both sexes."

"Do the girls from the studio ever give him a play?"

She shrugged again. "I've heard rumors. You know the kind. He hands out expensive presents to everybody during the holidays and is forever treating someone to a lavish birthday party under the guise of friendship when it's really nothing but good business practice. I know for a fact that the crowd has stuck to the Bowery longer than they ever have to another fad. I'm wondering what's going to happen when Clyde gets ordinary people."

"So am I," I said. "Look, do something for me. Start inquiring around and see who forms his clientele. Important people. The kind of people who have a voice in the city. It'll mean getting yourself invited to the Inn but that ought to be fun."

"Why don't you take me?"

"I'm afraid that Clyde wouldn't like that. You shouldn't have any trouble getting an escort. How about one of those ten other guys?"

"It can be managed. It would be more fun with you though."

"Maybe some other time. Has one of those ten guys got dough?"

"They all have."

"Then take the one with the most. Let him spend it. Be a little discreet if you start to ask questions and don't get too pointed with them. I don't want Clyde to get sore at you too. He can think of some nasty games to play." I had the group of photos behind my back and I pulled them out. Connie came over to look at them. "Know all these girls?"

She nodded as she went through them. "Clotheshorses, every one. Why?"

I picked out the one of Marion Lester and held it out. "Know her well?"

She made a nasty sound with her mouth. "One of Juno's pets," she said. "Came over from the Stanton Studio last year when Juno offered her more money. She's one of the best, but she's a pain."

"Why?"

"Oh, she thinks she's pretty hot stuff. She's been playing around a lot besides. One of these days Juno will can her. She's got a tramp complex that will lose the agency some clients one of these days." She riffled through some of the others and took out two, one a shot of a debutante-type in a formal evening gown that was almost transparent. "This is Rita Loring. You wouldn't think it, but she saw thirty-five plenty of years ago. One of the men at the show that night hired her at a fabulous sum to model exclusively for him."

The other photo was a girl in a sports outfit of slacks, vest and blouse, touched with fancy gimcracks that women like. She was photographed against a background that was supposed to represent a girls' dormitory. "Little Jean Trotter, our choice teen-age type. She eloped the day before yesterday. She sent Juno a letter and we all chipped in to buy her a television set. Anton was quite perturbed since she left in the middle of a series. Juno had to pat his hand to calm him down. I never saw him get so mad."

She handed the pictures back to me and I put them away. The evening was early so I told her to get busy on the phone and arrange herself a date. She didn't like it, but she did it so I'd get jealous. She did the damndest job of seduction over a telephone I'd ever heard. I sat there and grinned until she got mad and took it out on the guy on the other end. She said she'd meet him in a hotel lobby downtown to save time and hung up.

"You're a stinker, Mike," she said.

I agreed with her. She threw my coat at me and climbed into her own. When we reached the street entrance I did like I said and carried her out to the car. She didn't get her feet wet, but the snow blew up her dress and that was just as bad. We had supper in a sea-food place, took time for a drink and some small talk, then I dumped her in front of the hotel where she was to meet her date. I kissed her so-long and she stopped being mad.

Now I had to keep me a couple of promises. One was a promise to outdo a character named Rainey. I followed a plow up Broadway for a few blocks, dragging along at a walk. To give it time to get ahead of me I pulled to the curb on a side street and walked back to a corner bar. This time I went right to the phone and shoved in a nickel.

I had to wait through that nickel and another one before Joe Gill finally pulled himself out of the tub and came to the phone. He barked a sharp hello and I told him it was me.

"Mike," he started, "if you don't mind, I'd rather not . . ."

"What kind of a pal are you, chum? Look, you're not getting into anything. All I want is another little favor."

I heard him sigh. "All right. What is it now?"

"Information. The guy is Emil Perry, a manufacturer. He has a residence in the Bronx. I want to know all about him, socially and financially."

"Now you're asking a toughie. I can put some men on his social life, but I can't go into his financial status too deeply. There're laws, you know."

"Sure, and there're ways to get around them. I want to know about his bank accounts even if you have to break into his house to get them."

"Now, Mike."

"You don't *have* to do it, you know."

"What the hell's the use of arguing with you. I'll do what I can, but this time we're even on all past favors, understand? And don't do me any more I'll have to repay."

I laughed at him. "Quit being a worrier. If you get in trouble I'll see my pal the D.A. and everything will be okeydoke."

"That's what I'm afraid of. Keep in touch with me and I'll see what I can do."

"Roger, 'Night, Joe."

He grunted a good-by and the phone clicked in my ear. I laughed again and opened the door of the booth. Soon I ought to know what Rainey had on the ball to scare the hell out of a big shot like Perry. Meanwhile I'd find out if I could be scared a little myself.

The *Globe* presses were grinding out a late edition with a racket that vibrated throughout the entire building. I went in through the employees' entrance and took the elevator up to the rewrite room where the stutter of typewriters sounded like machine guns. I asked one of the copy boys where I could find Ed Cooper and he pointed to a glass-enclosed room that was making a little racket all its own.

Ed was the sports editor on the *Globe* with a particular passion for exposing the crumbs that made money the easy way, and what he didn't know about his business wasn't worth knowing. I opened the door and walked into a full-scale barrage that was pouring out of a mill as old as he was.

He looked up without stopping, said, "Be right with you, Mike."

I sat down until he finished his paragraph and played with the .25 in my jacket pocket.

My boy must have liked what he wrote because he had a satisfied leer on his face that was going to burn somebody up. "Spill it, Mike. Tickets or information?"

"Information. A former hood named Rainey is a fight promoter. Where and who does he promote?"

Ed took it right in stride. "Know where the Glenwood Housing project is out on the island?"

I said I did. It was one of those cities-within-a-city affairs that catered to ex-G.I.'s within an hour's drive from New York.

"Rainey's in with a few other guys and they built this arena to get the trade from Glenwood. They put on fights and wrestling bouts, all of it stinko. Just the same, they pack 'em in. Lately there's been some talk of the fight boys going in the tank so's a local betting ring can clean up. I got that place on my list if it's any news to you."

"Fine, Ed. There's a good chance that Rainey will be making the news soon. If I'm around when it happens I'll give you a buzz."

"You going out there tonight?"

"That's right."

Ed looked at his watch. "They got a show on. If you step on it you might catch the first bout."

"Yeah," I said, "It oughta be real interesting. I'll tell you about it when I get back to the city." I put on my hat and opened the door. Ed stopped me before I got out.

"Those guys I was telling you about—Rainey's partners—they're supposed to be plenty tough. Be careful."

"I'll be very careful, Ed. Thanks for the warning."

I went out through the clatter and pounding beat of the presses and found my car. Already the snow had piled up on the hood, pulling a white blind over the windows. I wiped it off and climbed in.

One thing about the city; it was mechanized to the point of perfection. The snow had been coming down for hours now, yet the roads were passable and getting better every minute. What the plows hadn't packed down the cars did, with big black eyes of manhole covers steaming malevolently on every block.

By the time I reached the arena outside the Glenwood area I could hear the howling and screaming of the mob. The parking space was jammed and overflowed out onto the street. I found an open spot a few hundred yards down the street that was partially protected by a huge oak and rolled in.

I had missed the first bout, but judging from the stumble-bums that were in there now I didn't miss much. It cost me a buck for a wall seat so far back I could hardly see through the smoke to the ring. Moisture dripped from the cinder-block walls and the seats were nothing more than benches roughed out of used lumber. But the business they did there was terrific.

It was a usual crowd of plain people hungry for entertainment and willing to pay for it. They could do better watching television if they stayed home. I sat near the door and let my eyes become accustomed to the semidarkness. The last few rows were comparatively empty, giving me a fairly full view of what went on in the aisles.

There was a shout from the crowd and one of the pugs in the ring was counted out. A few minutes later he was carted up the aisle and out into the dressing room. Some other gladiators took their places.

By the end of the fourth bout everybody who was going to be there was there. The two welters who had waltzed through the six rounds went past me into the hall behind the wall trailing their managers and seconds. I got up and joined the procession. It led to a large, damp room lined with cheap metal lockers and wooden plank benches with a shower room spilling water all over the floor. The whole place reeked of liniment and sweat. Two heavies with bandaged hands were playing cards on the bench keeping score with spit marks on the floor.

I walked over to one of the cigar-smoking gents in a brown striped suit and nudged him with a thumb. "Where's Rainey?"

He shifted the cigar to the other side of his mouth and said, "Inna office, I guess. You gotta boy here tonight?"

"Naw," I told him. "My boy's in bed wita cold."

"Tough. Can't maka dime that way."

"Naw."

He shifted the cigar back bringing an end to that. I went looking for the office that Rainey was inna. I found it down at the end of the hall. A radio was playing inside, tuned to a fight that was going on in the Garden. There must have been another door leading to the office because it slammed and there was a mumble of voices. One started to swear loudly until another told him to shut up. The swearing stopped. The voices mumbled again, the door slammed, then all I heard was the radio blaring.

I stood there a good five minutes and heard the end of the fight. The winner was telling his story of the battle over the air when the radio was switched off. I opened the door and walked in.

Rainey was sitting at a table counting the receipts for the night, stacking the bills in untidy piles and keeping the tally in a small red book. I had my hand on the knob and shut the door as noiselessly as I could. There was a barrel bolt below the knob and I slid it into the hasp.

If Rainey hadn't been counting out loud he would have heard me come in. As it was, I heard him go into the five thousand mark before I said, "Good crowd, huh?"

Rainey said, "Shut up," and went on counting.

I said, "Rainey."

His fingers paused over a stack of fives. His head turned in slow motion until he was looking at me over his shoulder. The padding in his coat obscured the lower half of his face and I tried to picture it through the back window of a sedan racing up Thirty-third Street. It didn't match, but I didn't care so much either.

Rainey was a guy you could dislike easily. He had one of those faces that looked painted on, a perpetual mixture of hate, fear and toughness blended by a sneer that was a habit. His eyes were cold, merciless marbles hardly visible under thick, fleshy lids.

Rainey was a tough guy.

I leaned against the door jamb with a cigarette hanging from my lips, one hand in my pocket around the grip of the little .25.

Maybe he didn't think I had a gun there. His lip rolled up into a snarl and he reached under the table.

I rapped the gun against the door jamb and even through the cloth of the coat you could tell that it was just what it was. Rainey started to lose that tough look. "Remember me, Rainey?"

He didn't say anything.

I took a long shot in the dark. "Sure, you remember me, Rainey. You saw me on Broadway today. I was standing in front of a plate-glass window. You missed."

His lower lip fell away from his teeth and I could see more of the marbles that he had for eyes. I kept my hand in my pocket while I reached under the table and pulled out a short-nosed .32 that hung there in a clip.

Rainey finally found his voice. "Mike Hammer," he said, "What the hell got into you?"

I sat on the edge of the table and flipped all the bills to the floor. "Guess." Rainey looked at the dough then back to me.

The toughness came back in a hurry. "Get out of here before you get tossed out, copper." He came halfway out of his seat.

I palmed that short-nosed .32 and laid it across his cheek with a crack that split the flesh open. He rocked back into his chair with his mouth hanging, drooling blood and saliva over his chin. I sat there smiling, but nothing was funny.

I said, "Rainey, you've forgotten something. You've forgotten that I'm not a guy that takes any crap. Not from anybody. You've forgotten that I've been in business because I stayed alive longer than some guys who didn't want me that way. You've forgotten that I've had some punks tougher than you'll ever be on the end of a gun and I pulled the trigger just to watch their expressions change."

He was scared, but he tried to bluff it out anyway. He said, "Why don'tcha try it now, Hammer? Maybe it's different when ya don't have a license to use a rod. Go ahead, why dont'cha try it?"

He started to laugh at me when I pulled the trigger of the .32 and shot him in the thigh. He said, "My God!" under his breath and grabbed his leg. I raised the muzzle of the gun until he was looking right into the little round hole that was his ticket to hell.

"Dare me some more, Rainey."

He made some blubbering noises and leaned over the chair to puke on the money that was scattered around his feet. I threw the little gun on the table. "There's a man named Emil Perry. If you go near him again I'll put the next slug right where your shirt meets your pants."

I shouldn't have been so damn interested in the sound of my own voice. I should have had the sense to lock the other door. I should've done a lot of things and there wouldn't have been anybody standing behind me saying, "Hold it, brother, just hold it right there."

A tall skinny guy came around the table and took a long look at Rainey who sat there too sick to speak. The other one held a gun in my back. The skinny one said, "He's shot! You bastard, you'll catch it for this." He straightened up and backhanded me across the mouth nearly knocking me off the table. "You a heist artist? Answer me, damn you!" The hand lashed out into my mouth again and this time I did go off the table.

The guy with the gun brought it down across the back of my neck throwing a spasm of pain shooting through my head and shoulders. He stood in front of me this time, a short pasty-faced guy with the urge to kill written all over him. "I'll handle this, Artie. These big boys are the kind of meat I like."

Rainey retched and moaned again. I picked myself up slowly and Rainey said, "Gimme the gun. Lemme do it. God-damn it, gimme that gun!" The skinny guy put his arms around his waist and lifted him to his feet so he could hobble over to the wall where I was.

The guy with the automatic in his hand grinned and took a step nearer. It was close enough. I rammed my hand against the slide and shoved it back while his finger was trying like hell to squeeze the trigger. It didn't take much effort to rip it right out of his hand while I threw my knee between his legs into his groin. He hit the floor like a bag of wet sand and lay there gasping for breath.

Someday the people who make guns will make one that can't be jammed so easily. The skinny guy holding Rainey let go and made a dive for the .32 on the table.

I shot him in the leg too.

That was all Rainey needed. The toughness went out of him and he forgot about the hole in his thigh long enough to stagger to his chair and hold his hands up in front of him, trying to keep me away. I threw the automatic on the table with the .32.

"Somebody told me you boys were pretty rough," I said. "I'm a little disappointed. Don't forget what I told you about Emil Perry."

The other guy with the hole in his leg sobbed for me to call a doctor. I told him to do it himself. I stepped on a pack of ten-dollar bills and they tore under my shoe. The little guy was still vomiting. I opened the door and looked back at the three tough guys and laughed. "A doctor'll have to report those gunshot wounds," I reminded them. "It would be a good idea to tell him you were cleaning a war souvenir and it went off."

Rainey groaned again and clawed for the telephone on the table. I was whistling when I shut the door and started back toward my car. All that time gone to waste, I thought. I had been playing it soft when I should have played it hard.

There had been enough words. Now the fun ought to start.

chapter eight

I WAS IN bed when Joe called. The alarm had been set for eleven-thirty and was five minutes short of going off. I drawled a sleepy hello and Joe told me to wake up and listen.

"I'm awake," I said. "Let's hear it."

"Don't ask me how I got this stuff. I had to do some tall conniving but I got it. Emil Perry has several business accounts, a checking account for his wife and a large personal savings account. All of them except his own personal account were pretty much in order. Six months ago he made a cash withdrawal of five thousand bucks. That was the first. It's happened every other month since then, and yesterday he withdrew all but a few hundred. The total he took out in cash was an even twenty thousand dollars."

"Wow," I said. "Where did it go?"

"Getting a line on his personal affairs wasn't as easy as I thought. Item one, he has a wife and family he loves almost as much as his standing in the community. Item two, he likes to play around with the ladies. Item three, put item one and two together and what do you have?"

"Blackmail," I said. "All the setup for blackmail. Is that all?"

"As much as I had time for. Now, if there's nothing else on your mind and I hope there isn't, I'll be seeing you never again."

"You're a real pal, Joe. Thanks a million."

"Don't do me any more favors, Mike, hear?"

"Yeah, I hear. Thanks again."

There was too much going on in my head to stay in bed. I crawled under the shower and let it bite into my skin. When I dried off I shaved, brushed my teeth and went out and had breakfast. Fat little Emil scared to death of Rainey. Fat little Emil making regular and large withdrawals from the bank. A good combination. Rainey had to get dough enough to throw in the kitty to build that arena someway.

I looked out the window at the gray sky that still had a lot of snow in it, thinking that it was only the beginning. If what I had in mind worked out there ought to be a lot more to come.

The little .25 was still in the pocket of my jacket and it slapped against my side as I walked out to the elevator. The streets were clear and I told the boy to take off the chains and toss them in the trunk. He made himself another couple of bucks. When I backed out of the garage I drove across to Broadway and turned north pointing for the Bronx.

This time the big sedan with the gold initials was gone. I drove around the block twice just to be sure of it. All the blinds on the upper floor were drawn and there was a look of desertion about the place. I parked on the corner and walked back, turning in at the entrance.

Three times I lifted the heavy bronze knocker, and when that didn't work I gave the door a boot with my foot. A kid on a bicycle saw me and shouted, "They ain't home, mister. I seen 'em leave last night."

I came down off the stoop and walked over to the kid. "Who left?"

"The whole family, I guess. They was packing all kinds of stuff in the car. This morning the maid and the girl that does the cleaning left too. They gimme a quarter to take some empty bottles back to the store. I kept the deposit too."

I fished in my pocket for another quarter and flipped it to him. "Thanks, son. It pays to keep your eyes open."

The kid pocketed the coin and took off down the street, the siren on the bike screaming. I walked back up the path to the house. A line of shrubs encircled the building and I worked my way behind them, getting my shoes full of snow and mud. Twice I stopped and had a look around to be sure there weren't any nosy neighbors ready to yell cop. The bushes did a good job. I felt all the windows, trying them to see if they were locked. They were.

I said the hell with it and wrenched a stone out of the mud and tapped the glass a good one. It made a racket but nobody came around to investigate. When I had all the pieces picked out of the frame I grabbed the sill and hoisted myself into the room.

If sheet-covered chairs and closed doors meant what it looked like, Emil Perry had flown the coop. I tried the lamp and it didn't work. Neither did the phone. The room I was in seemed to be a small study, something where a woman would spend a lot of time. There was a sewing machine in the corner and a loom with a half-finished rug stretched out over nails in the framework.

The room led into a hallway of doors, all closed. I tried each one, peering into the yellow light that came through the blinds. Nothing was out of place, everything had been recently cleaned, and I backed out a little bit madder each time.

The hallway ran into a foyer that opened to the breezeway beside the house. On one side I could see the kitchen through a small window in the wall. On the other side a heavily carpeted flight of stairs led to the next floor.

It was the same thing all over again. Everything neat as a pin. Two bedrooms, a bathroom, another bedroom and a study. The last door faced the front of the house and it was locked.

It was locked in two places, above and below the knob.

It took me a whole hour to get those damn things open.

No light at all penetrated this room. I flicked a match on my thumbnail and saw why. A blackout shade had been drawn over the other shade on each of the two windows. It didn't hurt to lift them up because nobody could see in through the outermost shade.

I was in Emil Perry's own private cubicle. There were faded pictures on the wall and some juicy calendar pinups scattered around on the tables and chairs. A day bed that had seen too many years sagged against one wall. Under one window was a desk and a typewriter, and alongside it a low, two-drawer filing cabinet. I wrenched it open and pawed through the contents. Most of it was business mail. The rest were deeds, insurance papers and some personal junk. I slammed the drawers shut and started taking the place apart slowly.

I didn't find a damn thing.

What I did find was in the tiny fireplace and burned to a crisp. Papers, completely burned papers that fell to dust as I touched them. Whatever they were, he had done a good job of burning them. Not one corner or bit showed that was anything but black.

I swore to myself and went back to the filing cabinet where I slid out an insurance policy on Perry's wife. I used the policy as a pusher to get all the bits into the envelope, then sealed the flap and put the policy back in the drawer.

Before I went out I tried to make sure everything was just like he had left it. When I gave a few things an extra adjustment I closed the door and let the two locks click into place.

I went out the same way I came in, making a rough attempt at wiping out the tracks I had left in the snow and mud behind the bushes. When I climbed in behind the wheel of my car I wasn't feeling too bad. Things were making a little more sense. I turned on the key, let the engine warm up and switched back to Manhattan.

At Fifty-ninth Street I pulled over and went into a drugstore and called the Calway Merchandising outfit. They gave me Perry's business address and I put in a call to them too. When I asked for Mr. Perry the switchboard operator told me to wait a moment and put through a connection.

A voice said, "Mr. Perry's office."

"I'd like to speak to Mr. Perry, please."

"I'm sorry," the voice said, "Mr. Perry has left town. We don't know when he'll be back. Can I help you?"

"Well . . . I don't know. Mr. Perry ordered a set of golf clubs and wanted them delivered today. He wasn't at home."

"Oh . . . I see. His trip was rather sudden and he didn't leave word here where he could be reached. Can you hold the parcel?"

"Yeah, we'll do that," I lied.

Emil Perry had very definitely departed for parts unknown. I wondered how long he'd be away.

When I got back in my car I didn't stop until I had reached my office building. I had another package waiting for me. If I hadn't gone in through the basement it would have been a surprise package. The elevator operator gave a sudden start when I stepped in the car and looked at me nervously.

I said, "What's the matter with you?"

He clicked his tongue against the roof of his mouth. "Maybe I shouldn't tell you this, Mr. Hammer, but some policemen went up to your office a little while ago. Real big guys they were. Two of 'em are watching the lobby besides."

I stepped out of that car fast. "Anybody in my office now?"

"Uh-huh. That pretty girl who works for you. Is there any trouble, Mr. Hammer?"

"Plenty, I think. Look, forget you saw me. I'll make it up to you later."

"Oh, that's all right, Mr. Hammer. Glad to help."

He closed the door and brought the elevator upstairs. I walked over to the phone on the wall and dropped in a nickel, then dialed my own number. I heard the two clicks as both Velda's phone and the extension were lifted at the same time.

Velda sounded nervous when she said good morning. I held my handkerchief over the mouthpiece and said, "Mr. Hammer, please."

"I'm sorry, but he hasn't come in yet. Can I take a message?"

I grunted and made like I was thinking, then, "Yes, if you please. He is to meet me at the Cashmore Bar in Brooklyn in an hour from now. I'll be a few minutes late, so if he calls in, remind him."

"Very well," Velda replied. Her voice had a snicker in it now, "I'll tell him."

I stood there by the phone and let ten minutes go by slowly, then I put in another nickel and did the same thing over again. Velda said, "You can come up now, Mike. They're gone. Brooklyn is a long way off."

She had her feet up on the desk paring her nails with a file when I walked in. She said, "Just like you used to do, Mike."

"I don't wear dresses you can see up, though."

Her feet came down with a bang and she got red. "How'd you find out . . ." her head nodded toward the door, "about them?"

"The elevator operator put me wise. He goes on our bonus list. What did they want?"

"You."

"What for?"

"They seemed to think you shot somebody."

"That sniveling little bastard had the nerve to do it!" I threw my hat at the chair and ripped out a string of curses. I swung around, mad as hell. "Who were they?"

"They let me know they were from the D.A.'s office." A little worried frown drew lines across her forehead. "Mike . . . is it bad?"

"It's getting worse. Get me Pat on the phone, will you?"

While she was dialing I went to the closet and got out the other bottle of sherry. Velda handed me the phone as I finished pouring two glasses.

I tried to make my voice bright but there was too much mad in it. I said, "It's me, Pat. Some of the D.A.'s boys just paid me a visit."

He sounded amazed. "What are you doing there, then?"

"I wasn't here to receive them. A dirty dog sent them on a wild-goose chase to Brooklyn. What goes on?"

"You're in deep, Mike. This morning the D.A. sent out orders to pick you up. There was a shooting out on the island last night. Two guys caught a slug and one of them was a fellow named Rainey."

"Sounds familiar. Was I identified?"

"No, but you were seen in the vicinity and overheard threatening this Rainey fellow just a short time before."

"Did Rainey say all this himself?"

"He couldn't very well. Rainey is dead."

"What!" My voice sounded like an explosion.

"Mike . . ."

My mouth couldn't form an answer.

Pat said it again. "Mike . . . did you kill him?"

"No," I got out. "I'll be in the bar up the street. Meet me there, will you? I have things to talk about."

"Give me an hour. By the way, where were you last night?"

I paused. "Home. Home in bed sound asleep."

"Can you prove it?"

"No."

"Okay, I'll see you in a little while."

Velda had drained both glasses while I was talking and was filling them up again. She looked like she needed them. "Rainey's dead," I told her. "I didn't kill him but I wish I had."

Velda bit her lip. "I figured as much. The D.A. is tagging you for it, isn't he?"

"Right on the nose. What happened last night?"

She handed me a glass and we lifted them together. Hers went down first. "I won some money. Clyde got me slightly drunk and propositioned me. I didn't say no; I said later. He's still interested. I met a lot of people. That's what happened."

"A waste of time."

"Not entirely. We joined a party of visiting firemen and some very pretty young ladies. The life of the party was Anton Lipsek and he was quite drunk. He suggested they go up to his apartment in the Village and some of them did. I wanted to go but Clyde made a poor excuse of not being able to break away from his business. One other couple refused too, mainly because the boy friend was ahead on the roulette wheel and wanted to go back to it. The girl with him was the same one you had that night."

"Connie?"

"Is that her name?" she asked coldly.

I grinned and said it was.

Velda rocked back in her seat and sipped the sherry. "Two of the girls that went along with Anton worked with Connie. I heard them talking shop a few minutes before your girl friend made some catty remarks that brought the conversation to a halt."

She waited until I had finished my drink. "Where were *you* last night?"

"Out to see a guy named Rainey."

Her face went white. "But . . . but you told Pat . . ."

"I know. I said I didn't kill him. All I did was shoot him in the leg a little bit."

"Good heavens!" Then *you* did . . ."

I rocked my head from side to side until she got the idea. "He wasn't hurt bad. The killer did me one better and plugged him after I left. That's the way it had to be. I'll find out the details later." I stuck a cigarette in my mouth and let my eyes find hers while I lit it. "What time did you meet Clyde last night?"

Her eyes dropped and her lips went into a pout. "He made me wait until twelve o'clock. He said he was tied up with some work. I got halfway stood up, Mike, and right after you were telling me how nice I looked."

The match burned down to my fingers before I put it out. "That gave him a chance to get out to Rainey, kill him, and get back. That just about does it!" Velda's eyes popped wide-open and she swallowed hard. "Oh, no, Mike . . . no I—I was with him right after . . ."

"On Dinky it wouldn't show if he just killed a guy. Not on Dinky. He's got too many of 'em under his belt."

I picked up my hat from the chair where I had tossed it and straightened out the wrinkles in the crown. "If the police call again stall 'em off. Don't mention Pat. If the D.A. is there call him a dirty name for me. I'll be back later."

When I stepped out the door I knew I wasn't going to be anywhere later. A big burly character in high-top shoes got up off the top step where he was sitting and said, "Lucky the boys left a couple of us here after all. They're gonna be mad when they get back from Brooklyn." Another character just as big came from the other end of the hall and joined in on the other side.

I said, "Let's see your warrant."

They showed it to me. The first guy said, "Let's go, Hammer, and no tricks unless you want a fist in your face." I shrugged and marched over to the elevator with them.

The operator caught wise right off and shook his head sadly. I could see he was thinking that I should've known better. I squeezed over behind him as some others got on and by the time we hit the lobby I felt a little better. When the operator changed his uniform tonight he was going to be wondering where that .25 automatic came from. Maybe he'd even turn it in to the cops like a good citizen. They'd have a swell time running down that toy.

There was a squad car right outside and I got in with a cop on either side of me. Nobody said a word and when I pulled out a pack of butts one of the cops slapped them out of my hands. He had three cigars stuffed in the breast pocket of his overcoat and when I faked a stretch my elbow turned them into mush. I got a dirty look for that. He got a better one back.

The D.A. had his office all ready for me. A uniformed cop stood by the door and the two detectives ushered me to a straight-backed chair and took their places behind it. The D.A. was looking very happy indeed.

"Am I under arrest?"

"It looks that way, doesn't it?"

"Yes or no?" I gave him the best sarcasm I could muster. His teeth grated together.

"You're under arrest," he said. "For murder."

"I want to use the telephone."

He started smiling again. "Certainly. Go right ahead. I'll be glad to speak to you through a lawyer. I want to hear him try to tell me you were home in bed last night. When he does I'll drag in the super of your apartment, the doorman and the people who live on both sides of you who have already sworn that they heard nothing going on in your place last night."

I picked up the phone and asked for outside. I gave the number of the bar where I was supposed to meet Pat and watched the D.A. jot it down on a pad. Flynn, the Irish bartender, answered and I said, "This is Mike Hammer, Flynn. There's a party there who can vouch for my whereabouts last night. Tell him to come up to the D.A.'s office, will you?"

He was starting to shout the message down the bar when I hung up. The D.A. had his legs crossed and kept rocking one knee up and down. "I'll be expecting my license back some time this week. With it I want a note of apology or you might not win the next election."

One of the cops smacked me across the back of my head.

"What's the story?" I asked.

The D.A. couldn't keep still any longer. His lips went thin and he got a lot of pleasure out of his words. "I'll tell you, Mr. Hammer. Correct me if I'm wrong. You were out to the Glenwood Arena last night. You argued with this Rainey. Two men described you and identified you from your picture. Later they were all in the office when you opened the door and started shooting. One was hit in the leg, Rainey was hit in the leg and head. Is that right?"

"Where's the gun?"

"I give you credit enough to have gotten rid of it."

"What happens when you put those witnesses on the stand?"

He frowned and grated his teeth again.

"It sounds to me," I told him, "that they might make pretty crummy witnesses. They must be sterling characters."

"They'll do," he said. "I'm waiting to hear who it is that can alibi you."

I didn't have to answer that. Pat walked in the office, his face gray around the mouth, but when his eyes lit on the smirking puss of the D.A. it disappeared. Bright boy gave him an ugly stare. Pat tried for a little respect and didn't make it. I've heard him talk to guys in the line-up the same way he did to the D.A. "*I* was with him last night. If you had let the proper department handle this you would have known it sooner. I went up to his apartment about nine and was there until four A.M. playing cards."

The D.A.'s face was livid. I could see every vein in his hand as he gripped the end of the desk. "How'd you get in?"

Pat looked unconcerned. "Through the back way. We parked around the block and walked through the buildings. Why?"

"What was so interesting at this man's apartment that made you go there?"

Pat said, "Not that it's any of your business, but we played cards. And talked about you. Mike here said some very uncomplimentary things about you. Shall I repeat them for the record?"

Another minute of it and the guy would have had apoplexy. "Never mind," he gasped, "never mind."

"That's what I mean about having witnesses with sterling characters, mister," I chipped in. "I take it the charges are dropped?"

His voice barely had enough strength to carry across the room. "Get out of here. You, too, Captain Chambers." He let his eyes linger on Pat. "I'll see about this later."

I stood up and fished my other deck of Luckies. The cop with the smashed cigars still sticking out of his pockets watched me with a sneer. "Got a light?" He almost gave me one at that until he realized what he was doing. I smiled at the D.A., a pretty smile that showed a lot of teeth. "Remember about my license. I'll give you until the end of the week."

The guy flopped back in his chair and stayed there.

I followed Pat downstairs and out to his car. We got in and drove around for ten minutes going nowhere. Finally Pat muttered, "I don't know how the hell you do it."

"Do what?"

"Get in so much trouble." That reminded me of something. I told him to stop and have a drink, and from the way he swung around traffic until we found a bar I could see that he needed it.

I left him at the bar to go back to the phone booth where I dialed the *Globe* office and asked for the sports editor. When Ed came on I said, "This is Mike, Ed. I have a little favor to ask. Rainey was knocked off last night."

He broke in with, "Yeah, I thought you were going to tell me if anything happened. I've been waiting all day for you to call."

"Forget it, Ed, things aren't what you're thinking. I didn't bump the bastard. I didn't know he was going to get bumped."

"No?" His tone called me a liar.

"No," I repeated. "Now listen . . . what happened to Rainey is nothing. You can do one of two things. You can call the D.A. and say I practically forecasted what was going to happen last night or you can keep quiet and get yourself a scoop when the big boom goes off. What'll it be?"

He laughed, a typical soured reporter's laugh. "I'll wait, Mike. I can always call the D.A., but I'll wait. By the way, do you know who Rainey's two partners were?"

"Tell me."

"Petey Cassandro and George Hamilton. In Detroit they have quite a rep, all bad. They've both served stretches and they're as tough as they come."

"They're not so tough."

"No . . . you wouldn't think so now, would you? Well, Mike, I'll be waiting to see what gives. It's been a long time since I had a scoop on the police beat."

Pat wanted to know what I did and I told him I called the office. I straddled the stool and started to work on the highball. Pat had his almost finished. He was thinking. He was worried. I slapped him on the back. "Cheer up, will you? For Pete's sake, all you did was make the D.A. eat his words. That ought to make you feel great."

Pat didn't see it that way. "Maybe I'm too much cop, Mike. I don't like to lie. If it wasn't that I smelt a frame I would have let you squirm out of it yourself. The D.A. wants your hide nailed to his door and he's trying hard to get it."

"He came too damn close to getting it to suit me. I'm glad you got the drift of the situation and knew your way around my diggings well enough to make it sound good."

"Hell, it *had* to sound good. How the devil would you be able to prove you were home in bed all night? That kind of alibi always looks mighty foolish on a witness stand."

"I'd never be able to prove it in a million years, chum," I said. The drink almost fell out of his hand when it hit him. He grabbed my coat and spun me around on the stool. "You *were* home in bed like you said, weren't you?"

"Nope. I was out seeing a guy named Rainey. In fact, I shot him."

Pat's fingers loosened and his face went dead-white. "God!"

I picked up my glass. "I shot him, but it wasn't in the head. Somebody else did that. I hate like hell to put you on the spot, but if we're going to tie into a killer the both of us'll do better than just one."

Pat rubbed his face. It still didn't have its normal color back. I thought he was going to get sick until he gulped down his drink and signaled for another. His hands shook so bad he could hardly manage it without the ice chattering against the glass.

"You shouldn't've done it, Mike," he said. "Now I'll have to take you in myself. You shouldn't've done it."

"Sure, take me in and have the D.A. eat your tail out. Have him get you booted off the force so some incompetent jerk can take your place. Take me in so the D.A. can get his publicity at the expense of the people. Let a killer go around laughing his head off at us. That's what he wants.

"Hell, can't you see how the whole thing smells? It reeks from here to there and back again." Pat stared into his glass, his head shaking in outrage. "I went to see Emil Perry. Rainey was there. Perry tied up with Wheeler because he gave an excuse for Wheeler's suicide when actually he didn't even know the guy except to say hello to at business affairs. Perry ties in with Wheeler and Rainey ties in with Perry.

"Every month Perry had been pulling five grand out of his bank. Smell it now. Smells like blackmail, doesn't it? Go on, admit it. If you won't here's something that will *make* you admit it. Yesterday Perry withdrew twenty grand and left town. That wasn't traveling expenses. That was to buy up his blackmail evidence. I went out to his house and found what was left of it in his fireplace."

I reached inside my coat for the envelope and threw it down in front of him. He reached for it absently. "Now I'll tell you what started the Rainey business. When I first saw Perry I told him I was going to find out what it was that Rainey had on him and lay the whole thing in the open. It scared him so much he passed out. Right away he calls Rainey. He wants to buy it back and Rainey agrees. But meanwhile Rainey has to do something about it. He took a shot at me right on Broadway and if I had caught a slug there wouldn't have been a single witness, that's the way people are.

"When I went out to see him I put it to him straight, and just to impress him I ploughed a hole in his leg. I did the same thing to one of his partners."

I didn't think Pat had been listening, but he was. He turned his head and looked at me with eyes that had cooled down to a sizzle. "Then how did Rainey stop that other bullet?"

"Let me finish. Rainey wasn't in this alone by a long shot. He wasn't that smart. He was taking orders and somewhere along the line he tried to take off on his own. The big boy knew what was cooking and went out to take care of Rainey himself. In the meantime he saw me, figured I'd do it for him, and when I didn't he stepped in and took over by himself."

Pat was picturing the thing in his mind, trying to visualize every vivid detail. "You've got somebody lined up, Mike. Who?"

"Who else but Clyde? We haven't tied Rainey to him yet, but we will. Rainey isn't hanging out in the Bowery because he likes it. I'll bet ten to one he's on tap for Clyde like a dozen other hard cases he keeps handy."

Pat nodded. "Could be. The bullet in Rainey's leg and head were fired from the same gun."

"The other guy was different. I used his pal's automatic on him."

"I don't know about that. The bullet went right through and wasn't found."

"Well, I know about it. I shot him. I shot them both and left the guns right there on the table."

The bartender came down and filled up our glasses again. He shoved a bowl of peanuts between us and I dipped into them. Pat popped them into his mouth one at a time. "I'll tell you what happened down there, Mike. The one guy who wasn't shot dragged his partner outside and yelled for help. He said nobody came so he left Rainey where he was figuring him to be dead and pulled his buddy into a car and drove to a doctor over in the Glenwood development. He called the cops from there. He described you, picked out your picture and there it was."

"There it was is right. Right there you have a pay-off again. The killer came in after I left and either threatened those two guys or paid 'em off to put the bee on me and keep still as to what actually did happen. They both have records in Detroit and one carried a gun. It wouldn't do either one of 'em any good to get picked up on a Sullivan charge."

"The D.A. has their affidavits."

"You're a better witness for me, kid. What good is an affidavit from a pair of hoods when one of the finest sticks up for you?"

"It would be different under oath, Mike."

"Nuts. As long as you came in when you did it never gets that far. The D.A. knew when he was licked. In one way I'm glad it happened."

Pat told me to speak for myself and went back to his thinking. I let him chase ideas around for a while before I asked him what he was going to do. He said, "I'm going to have those two picked up. I'm going to find out what really happened."

I looked at him with surprise and laughed. "Are you kidding, Pat? Do you really think either one of those babies will be sticking around after that?"

"One has a bullet hole in his leg," he pointed out.

"So what?" I said. "That's nothing compared to one in the head. Those guys are only so tough . . . they stop being tough when they meet somebody who's just a little bit tougher."

"Nevertheless, I'm getting out a tracer on them."

"Good. Thats going to help *if* you find them." I doubt it. By the way, did you check on the bullets that somebody aimed at me?"

Pat came alive fast. "I've been meaning to speak to you about that. They were both .38 specials, but they were fired from different guns. There's more than one person who wants you out of the way."

Maybe he thought I'd be amazed just to be polite, at least. He was disappointed. "I figured as much, Pat. It still works down to Rainey and Clyde. Like I said, when I left Perry, he must've called Rainey. It was just before lunch-time and maybe he figured I'd eat at home. Anyway, he went there and when I stopped to pick up my coat and gloves he started tailing me. I wasn't thinking of a tail so I didn't give it a thought. He must have stuck with me all day until I was alone and a good target."

"That doesn't bring Clyde into it."

"Get smart, Pat. If Rainey was taking orders from Clyde then maybe Clyde followed *him* around too, just to be sure he didn't miss."

"So Clyde took the second shot at you himself. You sure made a nice package of it. All you need is a photograph of the crime."

"I didn't see enough of his face to be sure it was him, but it was a man in that car, and if he shot at me once he'll shoot at me again. That'll be the last time he'll shoot anyone."

I finished my drink and pushed it across the bar for more. We both ordered sandwiches and ate our way through them without benefit of conversation. There was another highball to wash them down. I offered Pat a Lucky and we lit up, blowing the smoke at the mirror behind the bar.

I looked at him through the silvered glass. "Who put the pressure on the D.A., Pat?"

"I've been wondering when you were going to ask that," he said.

"Well . . ."

"It came from some odd quarters. People complaining about killers running loose and demanding something be done about it. Some pretty influential people live out in Glenwood. Some were there when the questioning was done."

"Who."

"One's on the Board of Transportation, another is head of a political club in Flatbush. One ran for state senator a while back and lost by a hair. Two are big businessmen and I do mean big. They both are active in civic affairs."

"Clyde has some fancy friends."

"He can go higher than that if he wants to, Mike. He can go lower where the tougher ones are too if it's necessary. I've been poking around since I last saw you. I got interested in old Dinky Williams and began asking questions. There weren't too many answers. He goes high and he goes low. I can't figure it, but he's not a small-timer anymore."

I studied the ice in the glass a minute. "I think, pal, that I can make him go so low he'll shake hands with the devil. Yeah, I think it's about time I had a talk with Clyde."

chapter nine

I DIDN'T GET to do what I wanted to do that night because when I went back for my car I checked into the office long enough to find Velda gone and a note on my desk to call Connie. The note was signed with a dagger dripping blood. Velda was being too damn prophetic.

Dagger or no dagger, I lifted the phone and dialed her number. Her voice didn't have a lilt in it today. "Oh, Mike," she said, "I've been so worried."

"About me?"

"Who else? Mike . . . what happened last night? I was at the club and I heard talk . . . about Rainey . . . and you."

"Wait a minute, kitten, who did all this talking?"

"Some men came in from the fights on the island and they mentioned what happened. They were sitting right behind me talking about it."

"What time was that?"

"It must have been pretty late. Oh, I don't know, Mike. I was so worried I had Ralph take me home. I . . . I couldn't stand it. Oh, Mike . . ." Her voice broke and she sobbed into the phone.

I said, "Stay there. I'll be up in a little while and you can tell me about it."

"All right . . . but please hurry."

I hurried. I passed red lights and full-stop intersections and heard whistles blowing behind me twice, but I got up there in fifteen minutes. The work-it-yourself elevator still wasn't working so I ran up the stairs and rapped on the door.

Connie's eyes were red from crying and she threw herself into my arms and let me squeeze the breath out of her. A lingering perfume in her hair took the cold out of my lungs and replaced it with a more pleasant sensation. "Lovely, lovely," I said. I laughed at her for crying and held her at arm's length so I could look at her. She threw her head back and smiled.

"I feel so much better now," she said. "I had to see you, Mike. I don't know why I was so worried but I was and couldn't help it."

"Maybe that's because I remind you of your brothers."

"Maybe but that's not it." Her lips were soft and red. I kissed them gently and her mouth asked for more.

"Not in the doorway, girl. People will talk." She reached around behind me and slammed it shut. Then I gave her more. Her body writhed under my hands and I had to push her away to walk into the living room.

She came in behind me and sat down at my feet. She looked more like a kid who hated to grow up than a woman. She was happy and she rubbed her cheek against my knees. "I had a lousy time last night, Mike. I wish I could have gone with you."

"Tell me about it."

"We drank and danced and gambled. Ralph won over a thousand dollars then he lost it all back. Anton was there and if we had gone with him he wouldn't have lost it."

"Was Anton alone again?"

"He was while he stayed sober. When he got a load on he began pinching all the girls and one slapped his face. I didn't blame her a bit. She didn't have anything on under the dress. Later he singled out Lillian Corbett—she works through the agency—and began making a pass at her in French. Oh, the things he was saying!"

"Did she slap him too?"

"She would have if she understood French. As it was the dawn began to break and she gave him the heave-ho. Anton thought it was all very funny so he switched back to English and started playing more games with Marion Lester. She didn't have any objections, the old bag."

I reached down and ran my fingers through her hair. "So Marion was there too?"

"You should have seen her switching her hips on the dance floor. She got Anton pretty well worked up and he isn't a man to work up easily. A guy about a half a head shorter than she was moved in on Anton and outplayed him by getting him soused even worse. Then he took Marion over and Anton invited everyone up to his place. What a time they must have had."

"I bet. What did you do then?"

"Oh, some more gambling. I wasn't having much fun. Ralph would rather gamble than dance or drink any day. I sat and talked to the bartender until Ralph lost the money had had won, then we went back to a table and had a couple of champagne cocktails."

Her head jerked up and that look came back on her face. "That was when those men came in. They talked about the shooting and about Rainey and you. One said he read about you in the papers not so long ago and how you were just the type to do something like that and then they started betting that the cops would have you before morning."

"Who lost the bet?"

"I don't know. I didn't turn around to look. It was bad enough sitting there hearing them talk about it. I . . . I started to get sick and I guess I cried a little. Ralph thought it was something he did to me and began pawing me to make up for it. I made him take me home. Mike . . . why didn't you call me?"

"I was busy, Sugar. I had to explain all that to the cops."

"You didn't shoot him, did you?"

"Only a little bit. Not enough to kill him. Somebody else did that."

"Mike!"

I rocked her head and laughed at her. "You got there early, didn't you?" Connie nodded yes. "Did you see Clyde at all during that time?"

"No . . . come to think of it, he didn't show up until after midnight."

"How'd he look?"

Connie frowned and bit her thumb. Her eyes looked up into mine after a while and she grimaced. "He seemed . . . strange. Nervous, sort of."

Yes, he would seem nervous. Killing people leaves you like that sometimes. "Did anyone else seem interested in the conversation? Like Clyde?"

"I don't think he heard about it. There was just those men."

"Who else was there, Connie? Anybody that looked important?"

"Quit kidding. Everybody is important. You don't just walk into the Bowery Inn. Either you're pretty important or you're with somebody who is."

I said, "I got in and I'm a misfit."

"Any beautiful model is better than the password," she grinned.

"Don't tell me they have a password."

"Clyde used to . . . to the back rooms. A password for each room. It's gotten so you don't need it now. That's what those little rooms are for between the larger rooms. They're soundproof and they're lined with sheet steel."

I tightened my fingers in her hair and pulled her head back so I could look into her face. "You found out a lot in a hurry. The first time you were there was with me."

"You told me I had brains too, Mike. Have you forgotten already? While I sat on my fanny at the bar while Ralph gambled the bartender and I had a very nice discussion. He told me all about the layout including the alarm and escape system. There are doors in the wall that go off with the alarm in case of a raid

and the customers can beat it out the back. Isn't that nice of
Clyde?"

"Very thoughtful."

I gave the hassock she was sitting on a push with my foot.
"Gotta go, Sugar, gotta go."

"Oh, Mike, not yet, please."

"Look, I have things to do much as I'd like to sit here. Someplace
in this wild, wild city, there's a guy with a gun who's going to
use it again. I want to be around when he tries."

She tossed her hair like an angry cat and said, "You're mean.
I had something to show you, too."

"Yeah?"

"Will you stay long enough to see it?"

"I guess I can."

Connie stood up, kissed me lightly on the cheek and shoved
me back in the chair. "We're doing a series for a manufacturing
house. Their newest number that they're going to advertise arrived
today and I'm modeling it for a full-page, four-color spread in
the slick mags. When the job is done I get to keep it."

She walked out of the room with long-legged strides and into
the bedroom. She fussed around in there long enough for me to
finish a cigarette. I had just squashed it out when she called out,
"Mike . . . come here."

I pushed open the door of the bedroom and stood there feeling
my skin go hot and cold then hot again. She was wearing a floor-
length nightgown of the sheerest, most transparent white fabric I
had ever seen. It wasn't the way the ad would be taken. Then
the lights would be in front of her. The one in the room was
behind her and she didn't have anything on under it.

When she turned the fabric floated out in a billowy cloud and
she smiled into my eyes with a look that meant more than words.

The front of it was wide open.

"Like me, Mike?"

My forefinger moved, telling her to come closer. She floated
across the room and stood in front of me, challenging me with
her body. I said, "Take it off."

All she did was shrug her shoulders. The gown dropped to the
floor.

I looked at her, storing up a picture in my mind that I could
never forget. She could have been a statue standing there, a statue
molded of creamy white flesh that breathed with an irregular
rhythm. A statue with dark, blazing eyes and jaunty breasts that
spoke of the passion that lay within. A statue that stood in a

daring pose that made you want to reach out to touch and pull so close the fire would engulf you too.

The statue had a voice that was low and desiring. "I could love you so easily, Mike."

"Don't," I said.

Her lips parted, her tongue wet them. "Why?"

My voice had a rough edge to it. "I can't take the time."

The coals in her eyes jumped into flame that burned me. I grabbed her by the shoulders and pulled her against my chest, bruising her lips against mine. Her tongue was a little spear that flicked out, stabbing me, trying to wound me enough so I wouldn't be able to walk away.

I didn't let it stab me deep enough. I shoved her back, tried to talk and found that my voice wasn't there anymore.

So I walked away. I walked away and left her standing there in the doorway, standing on a white cloud stark naked, the imprints of my fingers still etched in red on her shoulders.

"You'll get the person you're after, Mike. Nothing can stop you. Nothing." Her voice was still husky, but there was a laugh behind it, and a little bit of pride, too. I was closing the door when I heard her whisper, "I love you, Mike. Really and truly, I do."

Outside, the snow had started again. There was no wind, so it drifted down lazily, sneaking up on the city to catch it by surprise. What few stragglers were left on the street stuck close to the curb and looked back over their shoulders for taxis.

I got in the car and started the wipers going, watching them kick angrily through the snow that had piled up on the windshield. At least the snow made all cars look alike. If anybody with a gun was waiting for me he'd have a fine time picking out my head from the others.

Thinking about it made me mad. One gun was in an exhibit folder at police headquarters and the other was probably hanging in a locker if it hadn't been thrown away. It gave me an empty, uneasy feeling to be traveling without a rod slung under my arm. Sullivan Law? Hell, let me get picked up. It was all right for some harmless citizen to forget there were kill-crazy bastards loose, but one of them was looking for me.

There was a .30-caliber Luger sitting home in the bottom drawer of my dresser with a full clip of shells. It was just about the same size as a .45 too, just the right size to fit in my holster.

A plow was going by in front of my apartment house when I

got there, so I figured it would be another hour at least before it would be around again and safe enough to park there.

I took the stairs instead of waiting for the elevator and didn't bother to shuck my coat when I opened the door. I felt for the light switch, batted it up, but no light came on. I cursed the fuse system and groped for a lamp.

What is it that makes you know you're not alone? What vague radiation emanates from the human body just strongly enough to give you one brief, minute premonition of danger that makes you act with animal reflexes? I had my hand around the base of the lamp when I felt it and I couldn't suppress the half-scream half-snarl that came out of my throat.

I threw that lamp as hard as I could across the wall, letting the cord rip loose from the socket as it smashed into a thousand pieces against the wall. There were two muffled snorts and a lance of flame bit into the darkness, bracketing me.

I didn't let it happen again. I dove toward the origin of the snorts and crashed into a pair of legs that buckled with a hoarse curse and the next moment a fist was smashing against my jaw driving my head against the floor. Somehow I got out of the way of that fist and slugged out with my forearm trying to drive him off me.

My feet got tangled in the table and kicked it over. The two vases and the bar set splintered all over the room with a hellish racket and somebody in the next apartment shouted to somebody else. I got one arm under me then and grabbed a handful of coat. The guy was strong as a bull and I couldn't hold it. That fist came back and worked on my face some more with maniacal fury I couldn't beat off. I was tangled in my coat and there were lights in the room now that didn't come from the lamps.

All I knew was that I had to get up . . . had to get my feet under me and heave to get that thing off my back. Had to get up so I could use my hands on any part of him I could grab. I did it without knowing it and heard him ram into a chair and knock it on its side.

My teeth must have been bared to the gums and I screamed when I went in for the kill because I had him cold.

Then my legs got tangled in the lamp cord and I went flat on my face. My head hit something with a sharp crack that was all noise and no pain because there's a point at which pain stops and unconsciousness takes over, and in that second between I knew the killer was deciding between killing me or making a break for it. Doors started to slam and he decided to run and I let my eyes close and drew in the darkness like a blanket around me and slept an unnatural sleep that was full of soft golden hair and billowy white nightgowns I could see through and Velda in a dress she was more out of than in.

The man bending over me had a serious round face with an oval-shaped mouth that worked itself into funny shapes. I began to laugh and the serious face got more serious and the mouth worked more furiously than before. I laughed at that funny little mouth going through all those grotesque distortions for quite a while before I realized he was talking.

He kept asking me my name and what day it was. At last I had sense enough to stop laughing and tell him my name and what day it was. The face lost its seriousness and smiled a little bit. "You'll be all right," it said. "Had me a bit worried for a minute." The head turned and spoke to somebody else. "A slight concussion, that's all."

The other voice said it was too bad it wasn't a fracture. I recognized the voice. In another minute or two the face came into focus. It was the D.A. He had his hands in his coat pockets trying to look superior like a D.A. should look because there were people around.

I wormed into a sitting position that sent knives darting through my brain. The crowd was leaving now. The little man with the funny mouth carrying his black bag, the two women with their hair in curlers, the super, the man and woman who seemed to be slightly sick. The others stayed. One had a navy blue uniform with bright buttons, two wore cigars as part of their disguise. The D.A., of course. Then Pat. My pal. He was there too almost out of sight in the only chair still standing on its own legs.

The D.A. held out his palm and let me look at the two smashed pellets he was holding. Bullets. "They were in the wall, Mr. Hammer. I want an explanation. Now."

One of the cigars helped me up on my feet and I could see better. They all had faces with noses now. Before they had been just a blur. I didn't know I was grinning until the D.A. said, "What's so funny? I don't see anything funny."

"You wouldn't."

It was too much for the bright boy. He reached out and grabbed me by the lapels of my coat and pushed his face into mine. Any other time I would have kicked his pants off for that. Right now I couldn't lift my hands.

"What's so funny, Hammer? How'd you like . . ."

I turned my head and spit. "You got bad breath. Go 'way."

He half threw me against the wall. I was still grinning. There was white around his nostrils and his mouth was a fine red line of hate. "Talk!"

"Where's your warrant?" I demanded easily. "Show me your warrant to come in my house and do that, then I'll talk, you yellow-bellied little bastard. I'm going to meet you in the street not long from now and carve that sissified pasty face of yours into ribbons. Get out of here and kiss yourself some fat behinds like you're used to doing. I'll be all right in a few minutes and you better be gone by then and your stooges with you. They're not cops. They're like you . . . political behind-kissers with the guts of a bug and that's not a lot of guts. Go on, get out, you crummy turd."

The two detectives had to stop him from kicking me in the face. His legs, his knees, his whole body shook with coarse tremors. I'd never seen a guy as mad as he was. I hoped it'd be permanent. They took him out of there and with their rush they never noticed that Pat stayed on, still comfortably sunk in the chair.

"I guess that's telling him," I said. "A man's home is his castle."

"You'll never learn," Pat said sadly.

I fumbled for a butt and pushed it between my lips. The smoke bit into my lungs and didn't want to let go. I got a chair upright and eased into it so my head wouldn't spin. Pat let me finish the butt. He sat back with his hands folded in his lap and waited until I was completely relaxed. "Will you talk to me, Mike?"

I looked at my hands. The knuckles were skinned all to hell and one nail was torn loose. A piece of fabric was caught in it. "He was here when I came in. He took two shots at me and missed. We made such a racket he ran for it after I fell. If I hadn't fallen the D.A. would have had me on a murder. I would have killed the son-of-a-bitch. Who called him in?"

"The neighbors called the precinct station," Pat told me. "Your name was up and when it was mentioned the desk man called the D.A. He rushed right over."

I grunted and kneaded my knuckles into my palm. "Did you see the slugs he had?"

"Uh-huh. I dug 'em out myself." Pat stood up and stretched. "They were the same as the ones in the windows on Broadway. That's twice you've been missed. They say the third time you aren't so lucky."

"They'll be matching the bullets from one of those rods."

"Yeah, I expect they will. According to your theory, if they match the one from the Broadway window, the guy who attacked you was Rainey. If they fit the one from the Thirty-third Street incident it's Clyde."

I rubbed my jaw, wincing at the lump and the scraped flesh. "It couldn't be Rainey."

"We'll see."

"See hell! What are you waiting for? Let's go down and grab that louse right now!"

Pat smiled sorrowfully. "Talk sense, Mike. Remember that word *proof?* Where is it? Do you think the D.A. will support your pet theory . . . now? I told you Clyde could pull strings. Even if it was Clyde he didn't leave any traces around. No more traces than the guy who shot Rainey and the other punk at the arena. He wore gloves too."

"I guess you're right, kiddo. He could even work himself up a few good alibis if he had to."

"That's still not the answer," Pat said. "If we were working on a murder case unhampered it would be different. On the books Wheeler is still a suicide and we'd be bucking a lot of opposition to make it look different."

I was looking at my hand where my thumb and forefinger pinched together. I was still holding a tiny piece of fabric. I held it out to him. "Whoever he was left a hunk of his coat on my fingernail. You're a specialist. Let the scientists of your lab work that over."

Pat took it from my fingers and examined it closely. When he finished he pulled an envelope from his pocket and dropped it in. I said, "He was a strong guy if ever I met one. He had a coat on and I couldn't tell if he was just wiry-strong or muscle-strong, but one thing for sure, he was a powerhouse.

"Remember what you said, Pat . . . about Wheeler having been in a scuffle before he died? I've been thinking about it. Suppose this guy was tailing Wheeler and walked into the room. He figured Wheeler would be in bed but instead he was up going to the bathroom or something. He figured to kill Wheeler with his hands and let it look like we had a drunken brawl. Because Wheeler was up it changed his plans. Wheeler saw what was going to happen and made a grab for my gun that was hanging on the chair.

"Picture it, Pat. Wheeler with the gun . . . the guy knocks it aside as he fires and the slug hits the bed. Then the guy forces the gun against Wheeler's head and it goes off. A scrap like that would make the same kind of marks on his body, wouldn't it?"

Pat didn't say anything. His head was slanted a little and he was going back again, putting all the pieces in their places. When they set just right he nodded. "Yes, it would at that." His eyes narrowed. "Then the killer picked up one empty shell and dug the slug out of the mattress. A hole as small as it left wouldn't have been noticed anyway. It would have been clean as a whistle if you didn't know how many slugs were left in the rod. It would have been so pretty that even you would have been convinced."

"Verily," I said.

"It's smooth, Mike. Lord, but it's smooth. It put you on the spot because you were the only one looking for a murderer. Everyone else was satisfied with a suicide verdict." He paused and frowned, staring at the window. "If only that damn hotel had some system about it . . . even a chambermaid with sense enough to keep on her toes, but no. The killer walks out in the hall and drops his slug and shell that we find hours later."

"He was wearing an old suit."

"What?"

"It must have been old if it had a hole in the pockets."

Pat looked at me and the frown deepened. His hand fished for his notebook and he pulled out several slips of paper stapled together. He looked through them, glanced up at me, then read the last page again. He put the book back in his pocket very slowly. "The day before Wheeler died there were only two registered guests," he said. "One was a very old man. The other was a comparatively young fellow in a shabby suit who paid in advance. He left the day *after* Wheeler was shot *before* we were looking for anyone in the hotel, and long enough afterward to dispel any suspicions on the part of the staff."

The pain in my head disappeared. I felt my shoulders tightening up. "Did they get a description? Was it . . ."

"No. No description. He was of medium build. He was in town to see a specialist to have some work done on a tooth. Most of his face was covered by a bandage."

I said another four-letter word.

"It was a good enough reason for his being without baggage. Besides, he had the money to pay in advance."

"It could have been Clyde," I breathed. My throat was on fire.

"It could have been almost anybody. If you think Clyde is the one behind all this, let me ask you one thing. Do you honestly think he'd handle the murder end by himself?"

"No," I said with disgust. "The bastard would pay to have it done."

"And the same thing for that deal at the arena."

I smacked the arm of the chair with my fist. "Nuts, Pat. That's only what we surmise. Don't forget that Clyde's been in on murder before. Maybe he has a liking for it now. Maybe he's smart enough not to trust anybody else. Let's see how smart he can get. Let's let it hang just a few days longer and see if he'll hang himself."

I didn't like the look on his face. "Why?"

"The D.A. didn't believe my story about being with you. He has his men out asking questions. It won't take them very long to get the truth."

"Oh, God!"

"The pressure is on the lad. The kind of pressure he can't ignore. Something's going to pop and it may be your neck and my job."

"Okay, Pat, okay. We'll make it quicker then, but how? What the hell are we going to do? I could take Clyde apart but he'd have the cops on my neck before I could do anything. I need some time, damn it. I need those few days!"

"I know it, but what can we do?"

"Nothing. Not a damn thing . . . yet." I lit another butt and glared at him through the smoke. "You know, Pat, you can sit around for a month in a room with a hornet, waiting for him to sting you. But if you go poke at his nest it'll only be a second before you're bit."

"They say if you get bitten often enough it'll kill you."

I stood up and tugged my coat on. "You might at that. What are your plans for the rest of the evening?"

Pat waited for me by the door while I hunted up my hat. "Since you've gotten my schedule all screwed up I have to clean up some work at the office. Besides, I want to find out if Rainey's two pals have been found yet. You know, you called it pretty good. They both disappeared so fast it would make your head swim."

"What did they do about the arena?"

"They sold out . . . to a man who signed the contracts and deeds as Robert Hobart Williams."

"Dinky . . . Clyde! I'll be damned."

"Yeah, me too. He bought it for a song. Ed Cooper ran it in the sports column of the *Globe* tonight with all the nasty implications."

"I'll be damned," I said again. "It tied Rainey in very nicely with Clyde, didn't it?"

Pat shrugged. "Who can prove it? Rainey's dead and the partners are missing. That isn't the only arena Clyde owns. It now appears that he's a man quite interested in sporting establishments."

We started out the door and I almost forgot what I came for. Pat waited in the hall while I went back to the bedroom and pulled out the dresser drawer. The Luger was still there wrapped in an oily rag inside a box. I checked the clip, jacked a shell into the chamber and put it in half cock.

When I slid it into the holster it fit loosely, but nice. I felt a lot better.

The snow, the damned snow. It slowed me to a crawl and did all but stop me. It still came down in lazy fashion, but so thick you couldn't see fifty feet through it. Traffic was thick, sluggish and people were abandoning their cars in the road for the subway. I circled around them, following the cab in front of me and finally hit a section that had been cleared only minutes before.

That stretch kept me from missing Velda. She had her coat and hat on and was locking the door when I stepped out of the elevator. I didn't have to tell her to open up again.

When she threw her coat on top of mine I looked at her and got mad again. She was more lovely than the last time. I said. "Where you going?"

She pulled a bottle out of a cabinet and poured me a stiff drink. It tasted great. "Clyde called me. He wanted to know if that was 'later.' "

"Yeah?"

"I told him it might be."

"Where does the seduction take place?"

"At his apartment."

"You really have that guy going, don't you? How come he's passing up all the stuff at the Inn for you?"

Velda looked at me quickly, then away. I reached for the bottle. "You asked me to do this, you know," she said.

I felt like a heel. All she had to do was look at me when I got that way and I felt like I was crawling up out of a sewer somewhere. "I'm sorry, kid. I'm jealous, I guess. I always figured you as some sort of a fixture. Now that the finance company is taking it away from me I get snotty."

Her smile lit the whole room up. She came over and filled my glass again. "Get that way more often, Mike."

"I'm always that way. Now tell me what you've been doing to the guy."

"I play easy to get but not easy to get at. There are times when sophistication coupled with virtue pays off. Clyde is getting that look in his eyes. He's hinting at a man-and-mistress arrangement with the unspoken plan in mind of a marriage license if I don't go for it."

I put the glass down. "You can cut out the act, Velda. I'm almost ready to move in on Clyde myself."

"I thought I was the boss," she grinned.

"You are . . . of the agency. Outside the office I'm the boss." I grabbed her arm and swung her around to face me. She was damned near as tall as I was and being that close to her did things to me inside that I didn't have time for. "It took me a long time to wise up, didn't it?"

"Too long, Mike."

"Do you know what I'm talking about, Velda? I'm not tossing a pass at you now or laying the groundwork for the same thing later. I'm telling you something else."

My fingers were hurting her and I couldn't help it. "I want you to say it, Mike. You've played games with so many women I won't be sure until I hear you say it yourself. Tell me."

There was a desperate pleading in her eyes. They were asking me please, please. I could feel her breath coming faster and knew she was trembling and not because I was hurting her. I knew something was coming over my face that I couldn't control. It started in my chest and overflowed in my face when the music in my head began with that steady beat of drums and weird discord. My mouth worked to get the words out, but they stuck fast to the roof of my mouth.

I shook my head to break up the crazy symphony going on in my brain and I mumbled, "No . . . no. Oh, good God, I can't, Velda. I can't!"

I knew what the feeling was. I was scared. Scared to death and it showed in my face and the way I stumbled across the room to a chair and sat down. Velda knelt on the floor in front of me her face a fuzzy white blur that kissed me again and again. I could feel her hands in my hair and smell the pleasant woman smell of cleanliness, of beauty that was part of her, but the music wouldn't go away.

She asked me what had happened and I told her. It wasn't that. It was something else. She wanted to know what it was, demanded to know what it was and her voice came through a sob and tears. She gave me back my voice and I said, "Not you, kid . . . no kiss of death for you. There've been two women now. I said I loved them both. I thought I did. They both died, but not you, kid."

Her hands on mine were soft and gentle. "Mike . . . nothing will happen to me."

My mind went back over the years—to Charlotte and Lola.

"It's no good, Velda. Maybe when this is all over it'll be different. I keep thinking of the women who died. God, if I ever have to hold a gun on a woman again I'll die first, so help me I will. How many years has it been since the yellow-gold hair and the beautiful face was there? It's still there and I know it's dead but I keep hearing the voice. And I keep thinking of the dark hair too . . . like a shroud. Gold shrouds, dark shrouds. . . ."

"Mike . . . don't. Please, for me. Don't . . . no more."

She had another drink in my hand and I poured it down, heard the wild fury of the music drown out and give me back to myself again. I said, "All over now, sugar. Thanks." She was smiling but her face was wet with tears. I kissed her eyes and the top of her head. "When this is settled we'll take a vacation, that's what we'll do. We'll take all the cash out of the bank and see what the city looks like when there's not murder in it."

She left me sitting there smoking a cigarette while she went into the bathroom and washed her face. I sat there and didn't think of anything at all, trying to put a cap over the raw edges of my nerves that had been scraped and pounded too often.

Velda came back, a vision in a tailored gray suit that accentuated every curve. She was so big, so damn big and so lovely. She had the prettiest legs in the world and there wasn't a thing about her that wasn't beautiful and desirable. I could see why Clyde wanted her. Who wouldn't? I was a sap for waiting as long as I had.

She took the cigarette from my mouth and put it in her own. "I'm going to see Clyde tonight, Mike. I've been wondering about several things and I want to see if I can find out what they are."

"What things?" There wasn't much interest in my words.

She took a drag on the cigarette and handed it back. "Things like what it is he holds over people's heads. Things like blackmail. Things like how Clyde can influence people so powerful they can make or break judges, mayors or even governors. What kind of blackmail can that be?"

"Keep talking, Velda."

"He has conferences with these big people. They call him up at odd hours. They're never asking . . . they're always giving. To Clyde. He takes it like it's his due. I want to know those things."

"Will they be found in Clyde's apartment, baby?"

"No, Clyde has them . . ." she tapped her forehead, "here. He isn't smart enough to keep them there."

"Be careful, Velda, be damn careful with that guy. He might not be the pushover you think he is. He's got connections and he keeps his nose too damn clean to be a pushover. Watch yourself."

She smiled at me and pulled on her gloves. "I'll watch myself. If he goes too far I'll take a note from that Anton Lipsek's book and call him something in French."

"You can't speak French."

"Neither can Clyde. That's what makes him so mad. Anton calls him things in French and laughs about it. Clyde gets red in the face but that's all."

I didn't get it and I told her so. "Clyde isn't one to take any junk from a guy like Anton. It's a wonder he doesn't sic one of his boys on 'im."

"He doesn't, though. He takes it and gets mad. Maybe Anton has something on him."

"I can't picture that," I said. "Still, those things happen."

She pulled on her coat and looked at herself in the mirror. It wasn't necessary; you can't improve on perfection. I knew what it was like to be jealous again and tore my eyes away. When she was satisfied with herself she bent over and kissed me. "Why don't you stay here tonight, Mike?"

"Now you ask me."

She laughed, a rich, throaty laugh and kissed me again. "I'll shoo you out when I get in. I may be late, but my virtue will still be intact."

"It had damn well better be."

"Good night, Mike."

" 'Night, Velda."

She smiled again and closed the door behind her. I heard the elevator door open and shut and if I had had Clyde in my hands I would have squeezed him until his insides ran all over the floor. Even my cigarettes tasted lousy. I picked up the phone and called Connie. She wasn't home. I tried Juno and was ready to hang up when she answered.

I said, "This is Mike, Juno. It's late, but I was wondering if you were busy."

"No, Mike, not at all. Won't you come up?"

"I'd like to."

"And I'd like you to. Hurry, Mike."

Hurry? When she talked like that I could fly across town.

There was an odd familiarity about Juno's place. It bothered me until I realized that it was familiar because I had been thinking about it. I had been there a dozen times before in my mind but none of the eagerness was gone as I pushed the bell. Excitement came even with the thought of her, a tingling thrill that spoke of greater pleasures yet to come.

The door clicked and I pushed it open to walk into the lobby. She met me at the door of Olympus, a smiling, beautiful goddess in a long hostess coat of some iridescent material that changed color with every motion of her body.

"I always come back, don't I, Juno?"

Her eyes melted into the same radiant color as the coat. "I've been waiting for you."

It was only the radio playing, but it might have been a chorus of angels singing to form a background of splendor. Juno had prepared Olympus for me, arranging it so a mortal might be tempted into leaving Earth. The only lights were those of the long waxy tapers that flickered in a dancing yellow light, throwing wavy shadows on the wall. The table had been drawn up in the living room and set with delicate china, arranged so that we would be seated close enough to want to be closer, too close to talk or eat without feeling things catch in your throat.

We spoke of the little things, forgetting all the unpleasantness of the past few days. We spoke of things and thought of things we didn't speak of, knowing it was there whenever we were ready. We ate, but the taste of the food was lost to me when I'd look at her in that sweeping gown that laughed and danced in the rising and falling of the lights. The cuffs of her sleeves were huge things that rose halfway to her elbows, leaving only her hands visible. Beautiful large hands that were eloquent in movement.

There was a cocktail instead of coffee, a toast to the night ahead, then she rose, and with her arm in mine, the short wisps of her hair brushing my face, took me into the library.

Cigarettes were there, the bar set was pulled out and ice frosted a crystal bowl. I put my crumpled pack of Luckies alongside the silver cigarette box to remind me that I was still a mortal, took one and lit it from the lighter she held out to me.

"Like it, Mike?"

"Wonderful."

"It was special, you know. I've been home every minute since I saw you last, waiting for you to come back."

She sat next to me on the couch and leaned back, her head resting on the cushion. Her eyes were beginning to invite me now. "I've been busy, goddess. Things have been happening."

"Things?"

"Business."

One of her fingers touched the bruise on the side of my jaw. "How'd you get that, Mike?"

"Business."

She started to laugh, then saw the seriousness in my face. "But how . . ."

"It makes nasty conversation, Juno. Some other time I'll tell you about it."

"All right, Mike." She put her cigarette down on the table and grabbed my hand. "Dance with me, Mike?" She made my name sound like it was something special.

Her body was warm and supple, the music alive with rhythm, and together we threw a whirling pattern of shadows that swayed and swung with every subtle note. She stood back from me, just far enough so we could look at each other and read things into every expression. I could only stand it so long and I tried to pull her closer, but she laughed a little song and twisted in a graceful pirouette that sent the gown out and up around her legs.

The music stopped then, ending on a low note that was the cue to a slow waltz. Juno floated back into my arms and I shook my head. It had been enough . . . too much. The suggestion she had put into the dance left me shaking from head to foot, a sensation born of something entirely new, something I had never felt. Not the primitive animal reflex I was used to, not the passion that made you want to squeeze or bite or demand what you want and get it even if you had to fight for it. It made me mad because I didn't know what it was and I didn't like it, this custom of the gods.

So I shook my head again, harder this time. I grabbed her by the arm and heard her laugh again because she knew what was going on inside me and wanted it that way.

"Quit it, Juno. Damn it, quit fooling around. You make me think I want you and I lose sight of everything else. Cut it out."

"No." She drew the word out. Her eyes were half closed. "It's me that wants *you,* Mike. I'll do what I can to get you. I won't stop. There's never been anyone else like you."

"Later."

"Now."

It might have been now, but the light caught her hair again. Yellow candlelight that changed its color to the gold I hated. I didn't wait to have it happen to me. I shoved her on the couch and reached for the decanter in the bar set. She lay there languidly, waiting for me to come to her and I fought it and fought it until my mind was my own again and I could laugh a little bit myself.

She saw it happen and smiled gently. "You're even better than I thought," she said. "You're a man with the instincts of some jungle animal. It has to be when *you* say so, doesn't it?"

I threw the drink down fast. "Not before," I told her.

"I like that about you too, Mike."

"So do I. It keeps me out of trouble." When I filled the glass I balanced it in my hand and sat on the arm of the couch facing her. "Do you know much about me, Juno?"

"A little. I've been hearing things." She picked one of her long cigarettes out of the box and lit it. Smoke streamed up lazily from her mouth. "Why?"

"I'll tell you why I'm like I am. I'm a detective. In spirit only, now, but I used to have a ticket and a gun. They took it away because I was with Chester Wheeler when he used my gun to commit suicide. That was wrong because Chester Wheeler was murdered. A guy named Rainey was murdered too. Two killings and a lot of scared people. The one you know as Clyde is a former punk named Dinky Williams and he's gotten to be so big nobody can lay a finger on him, so big he can dictate to the dictators.

"That isn't the end of it, either. Somebody wants me out of the way so badly they made a try on the street and again in my apartment. In between they tried to lay Rainey's killing at my feet so I'd get picked up for it. All that . . . because one guy named Chester Wheeler was found dead in a hotel room. Pretty, isn't it?"

It was too much for her to understand at once. She bit her thumbnail and a frown crept across her face. "Mike . . ."

"I know it's complicated," I said. "Murder generally *is* complicated. It's so damn complicated that I'm the only one looking for a murderer. All the others are content to let it rest as suicide . . . except Rainey, of course. That job was a dilly."

"That's awful, Mike! I never realized . . ."

"It isn't over yet. I have a couple of ideas sticking pins in my brain right now. Some of the pieces are trying to fit together, trying hard. I've been up too long and been through too much to think straight. I thought that I might relax if I came up here to see you." I grinned at her. "You weren't any help at all. You'll probably even spoil my dreams."

"I hope I do," she said impishly.

"I'm going someplace and sleep it off," I said. "I'm going to let the clock go all the way around, then maybe once more before

I stir out of my sack. Then I'm going to put all the pieces together and find me a killer. The bastard is strong . . . strong enough to twist a gun around in Wheeler's hand and make him blow his brains out. He's strong enough to take me in my own joint and nearly finish it for me. The next time will be different. I'll be ready and I'll choke the son-of-a-bitch to death."

"Will you come back when it's over, Mike?"

I put on my hat and looked down at her. She looked so damn desirable and agreeable I wanted to stay. I said, "I'll be back, Juno. You can dance for me again . . . all by yourself. I'll sit down and watch you dance and you can show me how you have fun on Olympus. I'm getting a little tired of being a mortal."

"I'll dance for you, Mike. I'll show you things you never saw before. You'll like Olympus. It's different up there and there's nothing like it on this earth. We'll have a mountaintop all to ourselves and I'll make you want to stay there forever."

"It'd take a good woman to make me stay anywhere very long."

Her tongue flicked out and left her lips glistening wetly, reflecting the desire in her eyes. Her body seemed to move, squirm, so the sheen of the housecoat threw back the lithe contours of her body, vivid in detail. "*I* could," she said.

She was asking me now. Demanding that I come to her for even a moment and rip that damn robe right off her back and see what it was that went to make up the flesh of a goddess. For one second my face must have changed and she thought I was going to do it, because her eyes went wide and I saw her shoulders twitch and this time there was woman-fear behind the desire and she was a mortal for an instant, a female crouching away from the male. But that wasn't what made me stop. My face went the way it did because there was something else again I couldn't understand and it snaked up my back and my hands started to jerk unconsciously with it.

I picked up my butts and winked good night. The look she sent me made my spine crawl again. I walked out and found my car half buried in a drift and drove back to the street of lights where I parked and checked into a hotel for a long winter's nap.

I SLEPT THE sleep of the dead, but the dead weren't disturbed by dreams of the living. I slept and I talked, hearing my own voice in the stillness. The voice asked questions, demanded answers that couldn't be given and turned into a spasm of rage. Faces came to me, drifting by in a ghostly procession, laughing with all the fury the dead could command, bringing with their laughter that weird, crazy music that beat and beat and beat, trying to drive my senses to the furthermost part of my brain from which they could never return. My voice shouted for it to stop and was drowned in the sea of laughter. Always those faces. Always that one face with the golden hair, hair so intensely brilliant it was almost white. The voice I tried to scream with was only a hoarse, muted whisper saying, "Charlotte, Charlotte . . . I'll kill you again if I have to! I'll kill you again, Charlotte!" And the music increased in tempo and volume, pounding and beating and vibrating with such insistence that I began to fall before it. The face with the gold hair laughed anew and urged the music on. Then there was another face, one with hair a raven-black, darker than the darkness of the pit. A face with clean beauty and a strength to face even the dead. It challenged the golden hair and the music, commanding it to stop, to disappear forever. And it did. I heard my voice again saying over and over, "Velda, thank God! Velda, Velda, Velda."

I awoke and the room was still. My watch had stopped and no light filtered in under the shade. When I looked out the sky was black, pinpointed with the lights of the stars that reflected themselves from the snow-covered street below.

I picked up the phone and the desk answered. I said, "This is Hammer in 541. What time is it?"

The clerk paused, then answered, "Five minutes to nine, sir."

I said thanks and hung up. The clock had come mighty close to going around twice at that. It didn't take me more than ten minutes to get dressed and checked out. In the restaurant that adjoined the hotel I ate like I was famished, took time for a slow smoke and called Velda. My hand trembled while I waited for her to answer.

I said, "Hello, honey, it's Mike."

"Oh . . . Mike, where have you been? I've been frantic."

"You can relax, girl. I've been asleep. I checked into a hotel and told them not to disturb me until I woke up. What happened with you and Clyde? Did you learn anything?"

She choked back a sob and my hand tightened around the receiver. Clyde was dying right then. "Mike . . ."

"Go on, Velda." I didn't want to hear it but I had to.

"He almost . . . did."

I let the phone go and breathed easier. Clyde had a few minutes left to live. "Tell me," I said.

"He wants me in the worst way, Mike. I—I played a game with him and I was almost sorry for it. If I hadn't gotten him too drunk . . . he would have . . . but I made him wait. He got drunk and he told me . . . bragged to me about his position in life. He said he could run the city and he meant it. He said things that were meant to impress me and I acted impressed. Mike . . . he's blackmailing some of the biggest men in town. It's all got to do with the Bowery Inn."

"Do you know what it is?"

"Not yet, Mike. He thinks . . . I'm a perfect partner for him. He said he'd tell me all about it if . . . if I . . . oh, Mike, what shall I do? What shall I do? I hate that man . . . and I don't know what to do!"

"The lousy bastard!"

"Mike . . . he gave me a key to his apartment. I'm going up there tonight. He's going to tell me about it then . . . and make arrangements to take me in with him. He wants me, Mike."

A rat might have been gnawing at my intestines. "Shut up! Damn it, you aren't going to do anything!"

I heard her sob again and I wanted to rip the phone right off the wall. I could barely hear her with the pounding of the blood in my head. "I have to go, Mike. We'll know for sure then."

"No!"

"Mike . . . please don't try to stop me. It isn't nearly as . . . serious as what you've done. I'm not getting shot at . . . I'm not giving my life. I'm trying to give what I can, just like you . . . because it's important. I'm going to his apartment at midnight and then we'll know, Mike. It won't take long after that."

She didn't hear me shout into the phone because she had hung up. There was no stopping her. She knew I might try to, and would be gone before I could reach her.

Midnight. Three hours. That's all the time I had.

It wasn't so funny any more.

I felt in my pocket for another nickel and dialed Pat's number. He wasn't home so I tried the office and got him. I told him it was me without giving my name and he cut me off with a curt hello and said he'd be in the usual bar in ten minutes if I wanted to see him. The receiver clicked in my ear as he hung up. I stood there and looked at the phone stupidly.

The usual bar was a little place downtown where I had met him several times in the past and I went there now. I double-parked and slid out in front of the place to look in the windows, then I heard, "Mike . . . Mike!"

I turned around and Pat was waving me into my car and I ran back and got in under the wheel. "What the hell's going on with you, Pat?"

"Keep quiet and get away from here. I think there's been an ear on my phone and I may have been followed."

"The D.A.'s boys?"

"Yeah, and they're within their rights. I stopped being a cop when I lied for you. I deserve any kind of an investigation they want to give me."

"But why all the secrecy?"

Pat looked at me quickly, then away. "You're wanted for murder. There's a warrant out for your arrest. The D.A. has found himself another witness to replace the couple he lost."

"Who?"

"A local character from Glenwood. He picked you out of the picture file and definitely established that you were there that night. He sells tickets at the arena as a sideline."

"Which puts you in a rosy red light," I said.

Pat muttered, "Yeah. I must look great."

We drove on around the block and on to Broadway. "Where to?" I asked.

"Over to the Brooklyn Bridge. A girl pulled the Dutch act and I have to check it myself. Orders from the D.A. through higher headquarters. He's trying to make my life miserable by pulling me out on everything that has a morgue tag attached to it. The crumb hopes I slip up somewhere and when I do I've had it. Maybe I've had it already. He's checked my movements the night I was supposed to have been with you and is getting ready to pull out the stops."

"Maybe we'll be cellmates," I said.

"Ah, pipe down."

"Or you can work in my grocery store . . . while I'm serving time, that is."

"I said, shut up. What've you got to be cheerful about?"

My teeth were clamped together, but I could still grin. "Plenty, kid. I got plenty to be cheerful about. Soon a killer will be killed. I can feel it coming."

Pat sat there staring straight ahead. He sat that way until we reached the cutoff under the bridge and pulled over to the curb. There was a squad car and an ambulance at the wharf side and another squad car pulling up when Pat got out. He told me to sit in the car and stay there until he got out. I promised him I'd be a good boy and watched him cross the street.

He took too long. I began to fidget with the wheel and chain-smoked through my pack of butts. When I was on the last one I got out myself and headed toward the saloon on the corner. It was a hell of a dive, typically waterfront and reeking with all the assorted odors you could think of. I put a quarter in the cigarette machine, grabbed my fresh deck and ordered a beer at the bar. Two guys came in and started talking about the suicide across the street.

One was on the subject of her legs and the other took it up. Then they started on the other parts of her anatomy until the bartender said, "Jeez, cut it out, will ya! Like a couple ghouls ya sound. Can the crap."

The guy who liked the legs fought for his rights supported by the other one and the bartender threw them both out and put their change in his pockets. He turned to me and said, "Ever see anythin' like that? Jeez, the dame's dead, what do they want of her now? What ghouls!"

I nodded agreement and finished my beer. Every two minutes I'd check my watch and find it two minutes later and start cursing a slimy little bastard named Clyde.

Then the beer would taste flat.

I took it as long as I could and got the hell out of the saloon and crossed the street to see what was taking Pat so long. There was a handful of people grouped around the body and the ambulance was gone. The car from the morgue had taken its place. Pat was bending over the body looking for identification without any success and had the light flashed on her face.

He handed one of the cops a note he fished out of her pocket and the cop scowled. He read, "He left me." He scowled some more and Pat looked up at him. "That's all, Captain. No signature, no name. That's all it says."

Pat scowled too and I looked at her face again.

The boys from the morgue wagon moved in and hoisted the body into a basket. Pat told them to put it in the unidentified file until they found out who she was.

I had a last look at her face.

When the wagon pulled away the crowd started to break up

and I wandered off into the shadows that lined the street. The face, the face. Pale white to the point of transparency, eyes closed and lips slightly parted. I stood there leaning up against a plank wall staring at the night, hearing the cars and the trolley rattle across the bridge, hearing the cacophony of noises that go to make up the voice of the city.

I kept thinking of that face.

A taxi screamed past and slid to a stop at the corner. I backed up and a short fat figure speaking a guttural English shoved some bills in the driver's hand and ran to the squad cars. He spoke to the cop, his arms gesticulating wildly; the cop took him to Pat and he went through the same thing again.

The crowd that had turned away turned back again and I went with them, hanging on the outside, yet close enough so I could hear the little fat man. Pat stopped him, made him start over, telling him to calm himself down first.

The fat man nodded and took the cigarette that was offered him but didn't put it in his mouth. "The boat captain I am, you see?" He said. "The barges I am captain of. We go by two hours ago under the bridge and it is so quiet and peaceful then I sit on the deckhouse and watch the sky. Always I look up at the bridge when I go by. With my night glasses I look up to see the automobiles and marvel at such things as we have in this country.

"I see her then, you understand? She is standing there fighting and I hear her scream even. She fights this man who holds his hand over her mouth and she can't scream. I see all this, you understand, yet I am not able to move or do a thing. On the barge we have nothing but the megaphone to call with. It happens so fast. He lifts her up and over and she goes into the river. First I thought she hit the last barge on the string and I run and shout quickly but it is not so. I must wait so long until I can get somebody to take me off the barge, then I call the police.

"The policeman, he told me here to come. You were here. The girl has already been found. That is what I have come to tell you. You understand?"

Pat said, "I understand all right. You saw this man she fought?"

The guy bobbed his head vigorously.

"Could you identify him?"

Everyone's eyes were on the little guy. He lifted his hands out and shrugged. "I could tell him from someone else . . . no. He had on a hat, a coat. He lifted this girl up and over she goes. No, I do not see his face for I am too excited. Even through the night glasses I could not see all that so well."

Pat turned to the cop next to him. "Take his name and address. We'll need a statement on it."

The cop whipped out a pad and began taking it down. Pat prompted him with questions until the whole thing was straight then dismissed the batch of them and started asking around for other witnesses. The motley group hanging around watching didn't feel like having any personal dealings with the police department for any reason at all and broke up in a hurry. Pat got that grim look, muttered something nasty and started across the street to where I was supposed to be.

I angled over and met him. "Nice corpse," I said.

"I thought I told you to stay in the car. Those cops have you on their list."

"So what. I'm on a lot of lists these days. What about the girl?"

"Unidentified. Probably a lovers' quarrel. She had a couple of broken ribs and a broken neck. She was dead before she hit the water."

"And the note . . . did the lover stuff that in her pocket before he threw her overboard?"

"You have big ears. Yes, that's what it looks like. They probably argued previously, he invited her for a walk, then gave it to her."

"Strong guy to mess her up like that, no?"

Pat nodded. I opened the door and he got in, sliding over so I could get behind the wheel. "He had to be to break her ribs."

"Very strong," I mused. "I'm not a weak sister myself and I know what it's like to come up against one of those strong bastards." I sat there and watched him.

A look of incredulity came over his face. "Now wait a minute. We're on two different subjects, feller. Don't try to tell me that he was the same . . ."

"Know who she was, Pat?"

"I told you she was unidentified at present. She had no handbag but we'll trace her from her clothes."

"That takes time."

"Know a better way?"

"Yeah," I said. "As a matter of fact I do." I reached behind the seat and dragged out an envelope. It was crammed with pictures and I dumped them into my lap. Pat reached up and turned on the overhead light. I shuffled through them and brought out the one I was looking for.

Pat looked a little sick. He glanced at me then back to the picture. "Her name is Jean Trotter, Pat. She's a model at Anton Lipsek's agency. Several days ago she eloped."

I thought he'd never stop swearing. He fanned out the pictures in his hand and squinted at them with eyes that blazed hot as the fires of hell. "Pictures. Pictures. Goddamn it, Mike, what are we up against? Do you know what that burned stuff was that you found in Emil Perry's house?"

I shook my head.

"Pictures!" he exploded. "A whole mess of burned photographs that didn't show a thing!"

The steering wheel started to bend under my fingers. I jammed my foot on the starter and roared away from the curb. Pat looked at the picture again in the light of the dash. His breath was coming fast. "We can make it official now. I'll get the whole department on it if I have to. Give me a week and we'll have that guy ready to face a murder trial."

I glowered back at him. "Week hell, all we have is a couple of hours. Did you trace that piece of fabric I gave you?"

"Sure, we traced it all right. We found the store it came from . . . over a year ago. It was from a damn good suit the owner remembered selling, but the guy had no recollection for faces. It was a cash transaction and he didn't have a record of the size or any names or addresses. Our killer is one smart Joe."

"He'll trip up. They all do."

I cut in and out of traffic, my foot heavy on the accelerator. On the main drag I was lucky enough to make the lights and didn't have to stop until I was in front of the Municipal Building. I said, "Pat, use your badge and check the marriage bureau for Jean Trotter's certificate. Find out who she eloped with and where she was married. Since I can't show my nose you'll have to do this on your own."

"Where'll you be?"

I looked at my watch. "First I'm going to see what I can get on the girl myself. Then I'm going to stop a seduction scene before it starts."

Pat was still trying to figure that one out when I drove off. I looked in the rear-vision mirror and saw him pocket the photograph and walk away up the street.

I stopped at the first drugstore I came to and had a quarter changed into nickels then pushed a guy out of the way who was getting into the booth. He was going to argue about it until he saw my face then he changed his mind and went looking for another phone. I dropped the coin in and dialed Juno's number. I was overanxious and got the wrong number. The second time I hit it right, but I didn't get to speak to Juno. Her phone was connected to one of those service outfits that take messages and a girl told me that Miss Reeves was out, but expected home shortly. I said no, I didn't want to leave a message and hung up.

I threw in another nickel and spun the dial. Connie was home. She would be glad to see me no matter what the hour was. My voice had a rasp to it and she said, "Anything wrong, Mike?"

"Plenty. I'll tell you about it when I get there."

I set some sort of a record getting to her place, leaving behind me a stream of swearing-mad cab drivers who had tried to hog the road and got bumped over to the side for their pains.

A guy had his key in the downstairs door so I didn't have to ring the bell to get in. I didn't have to ring the upstairs bell either, because the door was open and when Connie heard me in the hall she shouted for me to come right in.

I threw my hat on the chair, standing in the dull light of the hall a moment to see where I was. Only a little night light was on, but a long finger of bright light streamed from the bedroom door out across the living room. I picked my way round the furniture and called, "Connie?"

"In here, Mike."

She was in bed with a couple of pillows behind her back reading a book. "Kind of early for this sort of thing, isn't it?"

"Maybe, but I'm *not* going out!" She grinned and wiggled under the covers. "Come over here and sit down. You can tell me all your troubles." She patted the edge of the bed.

I sat down and she put her fingers under mine. I didn't have to tell her something bad had happened. She could read it in my eyes. Her smile disappeared into a frown. "What is it, Mike?"

"Jean Trotter . . . she was murdered tonight. She was killed and thrown off the bridge. It was supposed to look like suicide, but it was seen."

"No!"

"Yes."

"God, when is it going to stop, Mike? Poor Jean . . ."

"It'll stop when we have the killer and not before. What do you know about her, Connie? What was she like . . . who was this guy she married?"

Connie shook her head, her hair falling loosely around her shoulders. "Jean . . . she was a sweet kid when I first met her. I—I don't know too much about her, really. She was older than the teen-age group of course, but she modeled clothes for them. We . . . never did the same type work, so I don't know about that."

"Men . . . what men did she go with? Ever see them?"

"No, I didn't. When she first came to work I heard that she was engaged to a West Point cadet, then something happened. She was pretty broken up for a while. Juno made her take a vacation and when she came back she seemed to be all right, though she didn't take much interest in men. One time at an office party she and I were talking about what wolves some men are and she was all for hanging every man by their thumbs and making it a woman's world."

"Nice attitude. What changed her?"

"Now you've got me. We sort of lived in different parts of the world and I never saw too much of her. I know she had a good sum of money tied up in expensive jewelry she used to wear and there was talk about a wealthy student in an upstate college taking her out, but I never inquired about it. As a matter of fact, I was very surprised when she eloped like that. True love is funny, isn't it, Mike?"

"Not so funny."

"No, I guess not."

I put my face in my hand, rubbing my head to make things come out right. "Is that all . . . everything you know about her? Do you know where she was from or anything about her background?"

Connie squinted at the light and raised her forefinger thoughtfully. "Oh . . . think . . ."

"Come on, come on . . . what?"

"I just happened to think. Jean Trotter wasn't her right name. She had a long Polish name and changed it when she became a model. She even made it legal and I cut the piece out of the paper that carried a notation about it. Mike . . . over there in the dresser is a small leather folder. Go get it for me."

I slid off the bed and started through the top drawer until Connie said, "No . . . the other one, Mike."

I tried that one too but couldn't find it. "Damn it, Connie, come over here and get it, will you!"

"I can't." She laughed nervously.

So I started tossing all her junk to the floor until she yipped and threw back the covers to run over and make me stop. Now I knew why she didn't want to get out of bed. She was as naked as a jaybird.

She found the folder in the back of a drawer and handed it to me with a scowl. "You ought to have the decency to close your eyes, at least."

"Hell, I like you like that."

"Then do something about it."

I tried to look through the folder, but my eyes wouldn't stand still. "For Pete's sake, put something on, will you!"

She put her hands on her hips and leaned toward me, her tongue sticking out. Then she turned slowly, with all the sultry motion she could command, and walked to the clothes closet. She pulled out her fur coat and slipped into it, holding it closed around her middle. "I'll teach you," she said. Then she sat in a low boudior chair with her legs crossed, making it plain that I could look and be tempted, but that was all, brother, that was all.

When I went back to pawing through the folder she let the coat slip open and I had to turn my back and sit down. Connie laughed, but I found the clipping.

Her name had been Julia Travesky. By order of the court she was now legally Jean Trotter. Her address was given at a small hotel for women in an uptown section. I stuffed the clipping in my wallet and put the folder in the dresser drawer. "At least it's something," I said. "We can find out the rest from the court records."

"What are you looking for, Mike?"

"Anything that will tell me why she was important enough to kill."

"I was thinking . . ."

"Yeah?"

"There are files down at the office. Whenever a girl applies for work at the agency she has to leave her history and a lot of sample photos and press clippings. Maybe Jean's are still there."

I whistled through my teeth and nodded. "You've got something, Connie. I called Juno before I came up, but she wasn't home. How about Anton Lipsek?"

Connie snorted and pulled the coat back to bare her legs a little more. "That drip is probably still sleeping off the drunk he worked up last night. He and Marion Lester got crocked to the ears and they took off for Anton's place with some people from the Inn about three o'clock in the morning. Neither of them showed up for work today. Juno didn't say much, but she was plenty burned up."

"Nuts. Who else might have keys to the place then?"

"Oh, I can get in. I had to once before when I left my pocketbook in the office. I kissed the janitor's bald head and he handed over his passkey."

The hands of my watch were going around too fast. My insides were beginning to turn into a hard fuzzy ball again. "Do me a favor, Connie. Go up and see if you can get that file on her. Get it and come right back here. I have something to do in the meanwhile and you'll be helping out a lot if you can manage it."

"No," she pouted.

"Cripes, Connie, use your head! I told you . . ."

"Go with me."

"I can't."

The pout turned into a grin and she peeked at me under her eyelashes. She stood up, put a cigarette between her lips, and in a pose as completely normal as if she had on an evening gown, she pushed back the coat and rested her hands on her hips and swayed over until she was looking up into my face.

I had never seen anything so unnaturally inviting in all my life.

"Go with me," she said, "then we'll come back together."

I said, "Come here, you," and grabbed her as naked as she was and squeezed her against my chest until her mouth opened. Then I kissed her good. So good she stopped breathing for long seconds and her eyes were glazed.

"Now do what I told you to do or you'll get the hell slapped out of your hide," I said.

She lowered her eyes and covered herself up with the coat. The grin she tried so hard to hide slipped out anyway. "You're the boss, Mike. Any time you want to be my boss, don't tell me. I'll know it all by myself."

I put my thumb under her chin and lifted her face up. "There ought to be more people in this world like you, kid."

"You're an ugly so-and-so, Mike. You're big and rough just like my brothers and I love you ten times as much."

I was going to kiss her again and she saw it coming. She shed that coat and flew into my arms and let her body scorch mine. I had to shove her away when it was the one thing I didn't want to do, because it reminded me that soon something like this might be happening to Velda and I couldn't let it happen.

The thought scared the hell out of me. It scared me right down to my shoes and I was damning the ground Clyde walked on. I practically ran out of the apartment and stumbled down the stairs in my haste. I ran to the corner and into a candy store where the owner was just turning out the lights. I was in the phone booth before he could tell me the place was closed and my fingers could hardly hold the nickel to drop it in the slot.

Maybe there was still time, I thought. God, there had to be

time. Minutes and seconds, what made them so important? Little fractions of eternity that could make life worth living. I dialed Velda's number and heard it ring. It rang a long time and no one answered, so I let it go on ringing and ringing and ringing. It rang for a year before she answered it. I said it was me and she wanted to hang up. I shouted, and she held it, and cautiously asked me where I was.

I said, "I'm nowhere near your place, Velda, so don't worry about me pulling anything funny. Look, hold everything. Don't go up there tonight . . . there's no need to now. I think we have the thing by the tail."

Velda's voice was soft, but so firm, so goddamn firm I could have screamed. She said, "No, Mike. Don't try to stop me. I know you'll think of every excuse you can, but please don't try to stop me. You've never really let me do anything before and I know how important this is. Please, Mike . . ."

"Velda, listen to me." I tried to keep my voice calm. "It isn't a stall. One of the agency girls was murdered tonight. Things are tying up. Her name was Jean Trotter . . . before that she was Julia Travesky. The killer got her and . . ."

"Who?"

"Jean . . . Julia Travesky."

"Mike . . . that was the girl Chester Wheeler told his wife he had met in New York. The one who was his daughter's old school chum."

"What!"

"You remember. I spoke of it after I came back from Columbus."

My throat got dry all of a sudden. It was an effort to speak. "Velda, for God's sake, don't go up there tonight. Wait . . . wait just a little while," I croaked.

"No."

"Velda . . ."

"I said no, Mike. I'm going. The police were here earlier. They were looking for you. They want you for murder."

I think I groaned. I couldn't get the words out.

"If they find you we won't have a chance, Mike. You'll go behind bars and I couldn't stand that."

"I know all about that, Velda. I was with Pat tonight. He told me. What do I have to do, get on my knees . . ."

"Mike . . ."

I couldn't fight the purpose in her voice. Good Lord, she thought she was helping me and I couldn't tell her differently! I was trying to protect her and she was going ahead at all costs! Oh, Lord think of a way to stop her, I couldn't! She said, "Please don't bother to come up, Mike. I'll be gone, and besides, there are policemen watching this building. Don't make it any harder for me, please."

She hung up on me. Just like that. Damn it, she hung up and left me cooped up in that two-by-four booth staring at an inanimate piece of equipment. I slammed the receiver back on the hook and ran past the guy who held the pull cord of the light in his hand, ready to turn it out. Lights out. Lights out for me too.

I ran back to the car and started it up. Time. Damn it, how *much* time? Pat said give him a week. A while ago I needed hours. Now minutes counted. Minutes I couldn't spare just when things were beginning to make sense. Jean Trotter . . . she was the one Wheeler met at that dinner meeting. She was the one he went out with. But Jean eloped and got out of the picture very conveniently and Marion Lester took over the duty of saying Wheeler was with her, and Marion Lester and Anton Lipsek were very friendly.

I needed a little talk with Marion Lester. I wanted to know why she lied and who made her lie. I'd tell her once to talk, and if she wouldn't I'd work her over until she'd be glad to talk, glad to scream her guts out and put the finger on the certain somebody I was after.

chapter eleven ▄▄▄▄▄▄▄▄▄▄▄▄▄▄▄▄▄▄

I TRIED HARD to locate Pat. I tried until my nickels were spent and there wasn't any place else to try. He was out chasing a name that didn't matter anymore and I couldn't find him at the time when I needed him most. I left messages for him to either stay in his office or go home until I called him and they promised to tell him when, and if, he came in. My shirt was soaked through with cold sweat when I got finished.

The sky had loosened up again and was letting more flakes of snow sift down. Great. Just great. More minutes wasted getting around. I checked the time and swore some big curses then climbed in the car and turned north into traffic. Jean Trotter and Wheeler. It all came back to Wheeler after all. The two were murdered for the same reason. Why . . . because he saw and recognized her as an old friend? Was it something he knew about her that made him worth killing? Was it something she knew about him?

There was blackmail to it, some insidious kind of blackmail that could scare the pants off a guy like Emil Perry and a dozen other big shots who couldn't afford to leave town when it pleased them. Photographs. Burned photographs. Models. A photographer named Anton Lipsek. A tough egg called Rainey. The brains named Clyde. They added.

I laughed so loud my chest hurt. I laughed and laughed and promised myself the skin of a killer. When I had the proof I could collect the skin and the D.A., the cops and anybody else could go to hell. I'd be clean as a whistle and I'd make them all kiss my rear end. The D.A. especially.

I had to park a block away from the Chadwick Hotel and walk back. My coat collar was up around my face like everyone else's and I wasn't worried about being seen. A patrolman swinging a night stick went by and never gave me a tumble. The lobby of the hotel was small, but crowded with a lot of faces taking a breather from the weather outside.

The Mom type at the desk gave me a smile and a nasal hello when I went to the desk. "I'd like to see Miss Lester," I said.

"You've been here before, sonny. Go ahead up."

"Mind if I use your phone first?"

"Nah, go ahead. Want me to connect you with her room?"

"Yeah."

She fussed with the plugs in the switchboard and triggered her button a few times. There was no answer. The woman shrugged and made a sour face. "She came in and I didn't see her go out. Maybe she's in the tub. Them babes is always taking baths anyway. Go on up and pound on her door."

I shoved the phone back and went up the stairs. They squeaked, but there was so much noise in the lobby nobody seemed to mind. I found Marion's room and knocked twice. A little light was seeping out from under the door so I figured the clerk had been right about the bath. I listened, but I didn't hear any splashing.

I knocked again, louder.

Still no answer.

I tried the door and it opened easily enough.

It was easy to see why she couldn't answer the door. Marion Lester was as dead as a person could get. I closed the door quietly and stepped in the room. "Damn," I said, "damn it all to hell!"

She had on a pair of red satin pajamas and was sprawled out face down. You might have thought she was asleep if you didn't notice the angle of her neck. It had been broken with such force the snapped vertebra was pushed out against the skin. On the opposite side of the neck was a bluish imprint of the weapon. When I put the edge of my palm against the mark it almost fit and the body was stone-cold and stiff.

The only weapon our killer liked was his strong hands.

I lifted the phone and when the clerk came on I said, "When did Miss Lester come in?"

"Hell, she came in this morning drunk as a skunk. She could hardly navigate. Ain't she there now?"

"She's here now, all right. She won't be going out again very soon either. She's dead. You better get up here right away."

The woman let out a muffled scream and started to run without bothering to break the connection. I heard her feet pounding on the stairs and she wrenched the door open without any formalities. Her face went from white to gray then flushed until the veins of her forehead stood out like pencils. "Lawd! Did you do this?"

She practically fell into a chair and wiped her hand across her eyes. I said, "She's been dead for hours. Now take it easy and think. Understand, think. I want to know who was up here today. Who called on her or even asked for her. You ought to know, you've been here all day."

Her mouth moved, the thick lips hanging limp. "Lawd!" she said.

I grabbed her shoulders and shook her until her teeth rattled. A little life came back into her eyes. "Answer me and stop looking foolish. Who was up here today?"

Her head wobbled from side to side. "This tears it, sonny. The joint'll be ruined. Lawd, there goes my job!" She buried her face in her hands and moaned foolishly.

I slapped her hands away and made her look at me. "Listen. She isn't the first. The same guy that killed her killed two others and unless he's stopped there's going to be more killing. Can you understand that?"

She nodded dumbly, terror creeping into her eyes.

"All right, who was up here to see her today?"

"Nobody. Not nobody atall."

"Somebody was here. Somebody killed her."

"H—how do I know who killed her?"

"I didn't say that. I said somebody was here."

She pulled her thick lips together and licked them. "Look, sonny, I don't take a count of who comes and goes in this place. It's easy to get in and it's easy to get out. Lotsa guys come in here."

"And you don't notice them?"

"No."

"Why?"

"I ain't . . . I ain't supposed to."

"So the dump's a whorehouse. Nothing but a whorehouse."

She glared at me indignantly, the terror fading. "I ain't no madam, sonny. It's just a place where the babes can stay with no questions asked, is all. I ain't no madam."

"Do you know what's going to happen around here?" I said. "In ten minutes this place will be crawling with cops. There's no sense running because they'll catch up with you. When they find out what's going on . . . and they will . . . you'll be up the creek. Now you can either start thinking and maybe have a little while to get yourself a clear story to offer them or you can take what the cops have to hand out. What will it be?"

She looked me straight in the eye and told the God's honest truth. "Sonny," she said, "if my life depended upon it I couldn't tell you anything different. I don't know who was in here today. The place was crawling with people ever since noontime and I read a book most of the day."

I felt like I fell through a manhole. "Okay, lady. Maybe there's somebody else who would know."

"Nobody else. The girls who clean the halls only work in the morning. The guests take care of their own rooms. Everyone who lives here is a regular. No overnighters."

"No bellboys?"

"We ain't had 'em for a year. We don't need 'em."

I looked back at the remains of Marion Lester and wanted to vomit. Nobody knew a thing. The killer had no face. Nobody saw him. They felt him and didn't live to tell about it. Only me. I was lucky, I got away. First the killer tried to shoot me. It didn't work. Then he tried an ambush and slipped up there. I was the most important one in the whole lot.

And I couldn't make a target of myself because there wasn't time to play bait.

I looked at Marion and talked to the woman who sat there trembling from head to foot. "Go on downstairs and put me through to the police department. I'll call them from here but I won't be here when they come. You can tell them the same thing you told me. Go on, beat it."

She waddled out, her entire body bearing the weight of the calamity. I held the phone to my ear and heard her call the police. When the connection was through I asked for homicide and got the night man. I said, "This is Mike Hammer. I'm in the Chadwick Hotel with a dead woman. No, I didn't kill her, she's been dead for hours. The D.A. will want to hear about it so you better call him and mention my name. Tell him I'll drop by later. Yeah, yeah. No, I won't be here. If the D.A. doesn't like that he can put my name on his butt-kissing list. Tell him I said that, too. Good-by." I walked downstairs and out the front door with about a minute to spare. I was just starting up my car when the police came up with their sirens wide open, leading a black limousine that skidded to a halt as the D.A. himself jumped out and started slinging orders around.

When I drove by I beeped the horn twice, but he didn't hear it because he was too busy directing his army. Another squad car came up and I looked it over hoping to see Pat. He wasn't with them.

My watch said twenty minutes to twelve. Velda would be leaving her apartment about now. My hands were shaking when I reached for a Lucky and I had to use the dashboard lighter to get it lit, a match wouldn't hold still. If there was any fight left inside me it was going fast, draining out with each minute, and in twenty minutes there wouldn't be a thing left for me, not one damn thing.

I stopped at a saloon and pulled the phone book from its rack and fingered through the L's until I came to Lipsek, Anton. The address was right on the fringe of the Village in a section I knew pretty well. I went back to the car and crawled down Broadway.

Twenty minutes. Fifteen now, Tempus Fugit. Tempus Fugits fast as hell. Twelve minutes. It started to snow harder. The wind picked it up and whipped the stuff into parallel, oblique lines across the multicolored lights that lined the street. Red lights. I made like I was skidding and went through. Cars honked and I cursed back, telling them to be quiet. The gun under my arm was burning a hole in my side and my finger under the glove kept tightening up expectantly.

Fourteenth Street went by and two cabs were bumper-locked in the middle of the road. I followed a pickup truck onto the sidewalk and off again to get around them. A police whistle blew and I muttered for the cop to go to the devil and kept on my way behind the truck.

Five minutes. My teeth were making harsh, grinding noises I could feel through my jaw. I came to my street and pulled into a parking space. Another minute went by while I oriented myself and followed the numbers in the right direction. Another two minutes went by before I found it.

Three minutes. She should almost be there by now. The name on the bell read, ANTON LIPSEK, Esq., and some kid had written a word under it. The kid had my sympathy. I felt the same way myself. I pushed the bell and heard it tinkle someplace upstairs.

Nothing happened. I pushed it again and kept my finger on it. The tinkling went on and on and on and still nothing happened. I pushed one of the other bells and the door clicked open. A voice from the rear of the first floor said, "Who is it?"

"Me," I said. "I forgot my key."

The voice said, "Oh . . . okay," and the door closed. Me, the magic password. Me, the sap, the sucker, the target for a killer. Me, the stupid bastard who was going around in circles while a killer watched and laughed. That was me.

I had to light a match at every door to see where I was. I found Anton's on the top floor with another Esq. after it. There was no sound and no light, and when I tried the knob it was locked.

I was too late. I was too late all around. It was five after twelve. Velda would be inside. The door would be closed and the nuptial couch laid. Velda would know all about it the hard way.

I kicked the door so hard the lock snapped and the door flew open. I kicked it shut the same way and stood there hoping the killer would come at me out of the darkness, hoping he'd run right into the rod I held in my fist. I prayed that he'd come, listened hard hoping to hear him. All I heard was my own breathing.

My hand groped for the wall switch and found it, bathing the place with a brilliant white light. It was some place. Some joint. The furniture was nothing but wooden porch furniture and the lamps were rigged up from discarded old floodlights. The rug on the floor must have been dragged out of an ash can.

But the walls were worth a million dollars. They were hung with canvas painted by the Masters and must have been genuine, otherwise their lavish frames and engraved brass nameplates were going to waste. So Anton had money and he didn't spend it on dames. No, it went into pictures, something with a greater permanent value than money. The inscriptions were all in French and didn't mean a thing to me. Although the rest of the room was littered with empty glasses and cigarette butts, not a speck of dust nested on the frames or the pictures, and the brass plates had been recently polished.

Could this be Anton's reward for wartime collaboration? Or was it his own private enterprise?

I picked some of the trash out of the way and prowled around the apartment. There was a small studio filled with the usual claptrap of a man who brings his work home with him, and adjoining, a tiny darkroom. The sinks were filled and a small red light burned over a table. That was all there was to it. I would have left, but the red light winked at me from a reflected image in a shiny bit of metal against the wall and I ran my hand over the area.

It wasn't a wall, it was a door. It was set flush with the wall and had no knob. Only the scratch on the concealed hinge showed me where it was. Someplace a hidden latch opened it and I didn't waste time looking for it. I braced my back against the sink and kicked out as hard as I could.

Part of the wall shook and cracked.

I kicked again and my foot went through the partition. The third time I had made a hole big enough to crawl into. It was an empty clothes closet that faced into another apartment.

Here was where Anton Lipsek lived in style. A wall had separated two worlds. There was junk lying around here, just the evidence of a recent and wild party. One side was a bar, stocked to the hilt with the best that money could buy. The rest of the room was the best that money could buy too. There were couches and tables that didn't come from any department store and they matched the drapes and color scheme perfectly. Someone with an eye for good taste had done a magnificent job of decorating. Someone like an artist-photographer named Anton Lipsek. The only things out of place were the cheap prints that were framed in bamboo. They belonged outside with the junk. Anton was as cracked as the Liberty Bell.

Maybe.

There were other rooms, a whole lot of rooms. Apparently he had rented two apartments back to back and used the darkroom as a secret go-between. There was a hall that led into three beautiful bedrooms, each with its own shower stall and toilet. Each bedroom had ash trays filled with cigarette butts, some plain, some stained with lipstick. In one room there were three well-chewed cigar stubs squashed out in a glass coaster beside the bed.

Something was wrong. There had to be something wrong. I
would have seen it if my mind wasn't twisted and dead. The
whole thing was as unnatural as it was possible to be. Why the
two apartments? Why the one place crawling with dirt and decorated with a fortune in pictures and the other lavish in furnishings
and nothing else?

Anton was a bachelor. Until recently he didn't mess with women,
so why all the bedrooms? He wasn't so popular that he was
overloaded with guests. I sat on the edge of the bed and shoved
my hat back on my head. It was a nice bed, soft, firm and quiet.
It made me want to lean back and sleep forever to wash the
fatigue from my mind. I lay back and stared at the ceiling.

It was a white ceiling with faint lines crisscrossing in the cal-
cimine. My eyes followed the lines to the wall where they disappeared into the molding. Those lines were like the tracks the
killer made. They started at no place and went everywhere, disappearing just as effectively. A killer who was strong as he was
vicious.

I stared at the molding some more then picked out the pictures
that hung over the bed and stared at them. They were funny little
pictures painted on glass, seascapes, with the water a shimmering
silver. The water had tiny palms. I got up off that bed slowly and
looked at the lines crisscrossing it too, reflecting the cracks in the
ceiling.

My breath was hot in my throat and my eyes must have been
little slits. I could feel my nails bite into my palms. The water
was shiny and silver because the water part was a mirror. It made
a lovely, decorative picture.

Lovely, but very practical. I tried to wrench the frames loose,
but they were screwed into the wall. All I could do was swear
and claw at the damn things and it didn't do any good. I ran
back through the living room, opened the door of the closet and
wiggled through the hole in the wall. The splinters grasped at my
coat and held me back until I smacked at them with my hand.

The pictures. Those beautiful canvases by the Old Masters. They
were worth a million as they stood and they had another million
dollars' worth behind them. I grabbed the one with the two nudes
playing in the forest and lifted it from the hook. It came away
easily and I had what I was looking for.

On the other side a hole had been cut into the wall and I saw
the little seascape in its frame on the other side. The shore line
and the sky were opaque under the paint, but where the glass

had been silvered you could see everything that went on in the room.

What a blackmail setup that was! One-way glass set above a bed! Oh, brother!

It took me about ten seconds to locate the camera Anton used. It was a fancy affair that would take shots without missing a single detail of expression. It had been tucked in a cabinet along with a tripod whose legs were still set at the proper level to focus the camera into the bedroom.

I threw it all on the floor and hauled out everything else that was in that cabinet. I was looking for pictures, direct evidence that would be hanging evidence. Something that would give me the big excuse when I pumped a slug into his guts.

It was simple as hell now, as simple as it could ever get. Anton Lipsek was using some of the girls to bait the big boys into the bedroom. He took pictures that set him up for life. It was the best kind of blackmail I could think of. The public could excuse anything else, but coarse infidelity, no.

Even Chester Wheeler fitted it. He was money, big money. He was in town alone and a little bit drunk. He walked into the trap, but he made one mistake that cost him his life. He recognized the girl. He recognized her as a girl that went to school with his daughter. The girl got scared and told Anton so Anton had to see to it that Wheeler died. But the girl was still scared and eloped, grabbing the first guy who was handy. She did fine until the killer caught up with her again and didn't take any chances with her getting so scared she *would* talk.

Yeah, it all was so simple now. Even Marion. Anton was afraid of me. The papers had it down that I was a cop and my ticket had been lifted. If I had never shown my face around neither Jean nor Marion would have died, but it was too late to think of that now. Anton made Marion pick up the story and say she was the one who went out with Wheeler, but she gave it an innocent touch that couldn't be tracked down. It should have stopped there.

What happened? Did Marion get too big for her pants and want a pay-off for the story she told? Sure, why not? She was in this thing. When those pictures turned up her face would be there. All she could lose would be her character and her job, but if she had something on somebody too, she didn't stand to lose a thing. So she died. Pretty? You bet your life it was!

I started to grin and my breath came fast through my teeth. Even right back to the beginning it checked. It didn't start from the night Wheeler died, it started a few days before, long enough to give the killer time to register in the hotel and take Wheeler at a convenient moment. I was just there by accident. I was a witness who didn't matter because I was out cold, and if I had been anybody else but me it made the killing so much the better. Whiskey-drunk and out like a light with no memory of what happened. The cops would have tagged me and I would have tagged myself.

All the killer forgot was my habit of keeping that .45 loaded with six shots. He took back the extra slug and shell case and overlooked that one little item. If the killer had had sense enough to go through my pockets he would have found a handful of loose shells and replaced that one bullet that went into the mattress.

But it only takes one mistake to hang a guy. Just one. He made it.

The killer must have been scared witless when he found out I was a cop. He must have known I'd been looking to get my ticket back, and he must have gone even further . . . he'd want to know what I was like. He'd check old papers and court records and ask questions, then he'd *know* what I was like. He'd know that I didn't give a damn for a human life any more than he did. I was just a bit different. I didn't shoot anything but killers. I loved to shoot killers. I couldn't think of anything I'd rather do than shoot a killer and watch his blood trace a slimy path across the floor. It was fun to kill those bastards who tried to get away with murder and did sometimes.

I started to laugh and I couldn't stop. I pulled the Luger out and checked it again when it didn't need it. This time I pulled the trigger off half cock and let it sit all the way back ready to nudge a copper-covered slug out of the barrel and into a killer's face.

It was later than ever, late enough to make my blood turn cold as ice. I had to make myself stop thinking. I couldn't look for those pictures and think too.

If ever a room got torn apart, this was it. I ripped and I smashed and I tore looking for those damn photographs and there wasn't a damn thing to see except some unexposed plates. I pulled the room apart like Humpty Dumpty and started on the darkroom when I heard the steps outside.

They came from the hall that led into the good apartment, the one with the bedrooms. The key turned in the lock and the door opened. For one second I had a glimpse of Anton's face, a pale face suddenly gone stark white, then the door slammed shut and the feet pounded down the stairs.

I could have killed myself for leaving the lights on when they had been out!

My coat caught on the sink and ripped. It caught again when I crawled through the hole in the partition. I ripped it loose and felt it tear clear up to the collar. I screamed my rage and took plaster and lath with me when I burst through.

Damn that son-of-a-bitch, he was getting away! I twisted the lock and tumbled into the hall without bothering to close the door. I heard feet slamming on the stairs and the downstairs door smash shut. I started down the steps and fell. I ran and fell again and managed to reach the bottom without breaking any bones. All over my body were spots that would wait until later to hurt, raw spots that stuck to my clothes with my own blood.

My gun was in my hand when I ran out on the street and it was nothing more than a useless weight because Anton's car was screaming up the street toward the intersection.

How important can a guy get? What does he have to do to please the fates that hamstring him every inch of the way? I saw the red dot of his tail-light swing to the right as a cruising cab cut him off. I heard the grinding of metal and the shouts of the drivers and Anton Lipsek was up on the sidewalk trying to back off.

It was too far to run, too much of a chance to take. I wheeled and dashed into the alleyway that passed between the buildings and leaped for the fence at the end and pulled myself over. I climbed in my car and turned the key, felt the motor cough and catch, and I said a prayer that the snow under the wheels would hold long enough for me to get away.

The fates laughed a little and gave me a push. I pulled away from the curb and sped down the street. Just as I turned the corner Anton drove across the sidewalk and back into the street while the cab driver ran after him waving his arms and yelling at the top of his lungs. I had to lean on my horn to get him out of the way.

Anton must have heard the horn because he stepped on the gas and the big, fat sedan he was using leaped ahead like it had a rocket on it. That sedan was the same one that was used as a gun platform when I was shot at on Thirty-third Street. Rainey. I hoped he was burning in hell where he belonged. He did the shooting while Anton drove.

I was glad to see the snow now. It had driven the cars into

garages and the cabs to the curbs. The streets were long funnels of white stretched out under the lights. I was catching up to him and he stepped down harder on the pedal. Red lights blinked on and were ignored. The sedan started to skid, came out of it safely and tore ahead.

Now he could get scared. Good and scared. He could sit there behind the wheel with the spit drooling out of the corner of his mouth and wonder why he couldn't get away. He would curse that big, fat sedan and ask it why the hell it couldn't shake an old rattletrap like mine. Anton could curse and he'd never know about the oversized engine under my hood. I was only fifty yards away and coming closer.

The sedan tried to make a turn, yawed into a skid and slammed against the curb. It seemed to come out of it for a moment and my stomach suddenly turned sour because I knew I'd never make it if I tried too. This time the fates laughed again and gave me Anton. They gave me Anton with a terrible crash that threw the sedan into the wall of a building and left it upside down on the sidewalk like a squashed bug.

I drove my heel into the brake and did a complete circle in the street. I backed up and stopped in the middle of the road and ran to the sedan with my gun out.

I put the gun back and grunted some obscene words. Anton was dead. His neck was topped with a bloody pulp that used to be a head. All that was left were his eyes and they weren't where they were supposed to be. The door was wrenched open and I took a quick look around, hoping to find what I was after. The only thing in the car was Anton. He was a couple of bucks' worth of chemicals now. One of the dead eyes watched me go through his pockets. When I opened his wallet I found a sheaf of five-hundred-dollar bills and a registered mail receipt. There was a penciled notation on it that said "Sent Special Delivery" and it was dated this morning.

It was addressed to Clyde Williams.

Then it wasn't Anton after all . . . it was Clyde. That ratty little punk *was* the brains. Clyde was the killer and Velda was with him now. Clyde was the brains and the killer and Velda was trying to pump a guy who knew every angle.

I was an hour and a half too late.

Time had marched on. It marched on and trampled me underfoot into the mud and slime of its passing. But I could get up and follow it. I could catch up with that lost hour and a half and make it give back what it had stolen, by God!

People were screaming at me from the windows when I jumped in my car. From down the block came the low wailing of a siren and a red eye that winked on and off. The screaming came from both directions then, so I cut down a side street and got out of their path. Somebody was sure to have grabbed my license number. Somebody was sure to relay it to the police and when they found out it was me the D.A. would eat his hat while his fat head was still in it. Suicide, he had said. He gave his own, personal opinion that Chester Wheeler had been a suicide.

Smart man, our D.A., smart as a raisin on a bun.

The sky agreed with a nod and let loose more tiny flakes of snow that felt the city out and called for reinforcements. There was still a mile to go and the snow was coming down harder than ever. My fate snickered.

chapter twelve ▰▰▰▰▰▰▰▰▰▰

I CHECKED THE address on the mail receipt against the one on the apartment. They both read the same. The building was a yellow brick affair that towered out of sight into the snow, giving only glimpses of the floors above.

A heavy blue canvas canopy sheltered the walk that led into the lobby, guarded by a doorman in an admiral's uniform. I sat in the car and watched him pace up and down, flapping his arms to keep him warm. He took the admiral's hat off and pressed his hands against his cauliflowered ears to warm them and I decided not to go in the front way after all. Guys like him were too eager to earn a ready buck being tough.

When I crossed the street I walked to the next building until the snow shielded me, then cut back to the walk that took me around the rear. A flight of steps led down to a door that was half open and I knocked on it. A voice with a Swedish accent called back and an old duck with lip whiskers that reached to his ears opened the door and said "Ya?"

I grinned. The guy waited. I reached in my pocket and pulled out a ten-spot. He looked at it without saying anything. I had to nudge him aside to get in and saw that the place was part of the boiler room in the basement. There was a table under the solitary bulb in the place and a box drawn up to it. I walked over to the table and turned around.

The old boy shut the door and picked up a poker about four feet long.

I said, "Come here, pop." I laid the ten on the table.

He hefted the poker and came over. He wasn't looking at the ten-spot. "Clyde Williams. What's his apartment number?"

Whatever I said made his fingers tighten around the poker. He didn't answer. There wasn't time to be persuasive. I yanked out the Luger and set it next to the ten. "Which one, pop?"

His fingers got tighter and he was getting ready to take me. First he wanted to ask a question. "Why you want him?"

"I'm going to break him in little pieces, pop. Anybody else that stops me might get it too."

"Poot back your gun," he said. I shoved it in the holster. "Now poot back your money." I stuck the ten in my pocket. He dropped the poker to the floor. "He is the penthouse in. There is elevator in the back. You use that, ya? Go break him, ya?"

I threw the ten back on the table. "What's the matter, pop?"

"I have daughter. She was good girl. Not now. That man . . ."

"Okay, pop. He won't bother you again. Got an extra key for that place?"

"No penthouse key." The ends of his whiskers twitched and his eyes turned a bright blue. I knew exactly how he felt.

The elevator was a small service job for the tradesmen delivering packages. I stepped in and closed the gate, then pressed the button on top marked "UP." The cable tightened and the elevator started up, a slow, tedious process that made me bite my lip to keep from yelling for it to hurry. I tried counting the bricks as they went by, then the floors. It dragged and dragged, a mechanical object with no feeling for haste. I wanted to urge it, lift it myself, do anything to hurry it, but I was trapped in that tiny cubicle while my watch ticked off the precious seconds.

It had to stop sometime. It slowed, halted and the gate rattled open so I could get at the door. My feet wanted to run and I had to force them to stand still when I turned the handle and peered out into the corridor.

There was a stillness about the place you would expect in a tomb, a dead quiet that magnified every sound. One side of the hall was lined with plate-glass windows from ceiling to floor, overlooking a city asleep. Only the safety light over the elevator showed me the hall that stretched along this enclosed terrace to the main hall farther down. I let the door close softly and began walking. My gun was in my hand and cocked, ready to blast the first person I saw into a private hell of their own. The devil didn't get any assistants because the hall was empty. There, around the bend, was a lobby that would have overshadowed the best room in the executive mansion, and all it was used for was a waiting room for the elevator.

On the walls were huge framed pictures, magnificent etchings, all the gimmicks of wealth. The chairs were of real leather, enough of them to seat twenty people. On the end tables beside the chairs were huge vases of fresh-cut roses that sent their fragrance through the entire room. The ash trays were sterling silver and clean. Beside each ash tray was a sterling silver lighter. The only incongruous thing was the cigar butt that lay right in the middle of the thick Oriental rug.

I stood there a moment taking it all in, seeing the blank door of the elevator that faced the lobby, seeing the ornate door of the apartment and the silver bell that adorned the opposite wall. When I stepped on the rug there was no sound of my feet except a whisper that seemed to hurry me forward until I stood in front of the door wondering whether to shoot the lock off or ring the bell.

Neither was necessary. Right on the floor close to the sill was a small gold-plated key and I said thanks to the fate that was standing behind me and picked it up. My mouth was dry as a bone, so dry that my lips couldn't pull over my teeth when I grinned.

Velda had played it smart. I never thought she'd be so smart. She had opened the door and left the key there in case I came.

I'm here, Velda. I came too late, but I'm here now and maybe somehow I can make it all up to you. It didn't have to be this way at all, but I'll never tell you that. I'll let you go on thinking that you did what was right; what you had to do. You'll always think you sacrificed something I wanted more than anything else in the world, and I won't get mad. I won't get mad when I want to slap the hell out of the first person that mentions it to me, even if it's you. I'll make myself smile and try to forget about it. But there's only one way I can forget about it and that's to feel Clyde's throat in my hand, or to have him on the end of a gun that keeps going off and off until the hammer clicks on an empty chamber. That way I'll be able to smile and forget.

* * *

I turned the key in the lock and walked in. The door clicked shut behind me.

The music stole into the foyer. It was soft music, deep music with a haunting rhythm. The lights were low, deliberately so to create the proper effect. I didn't see what the room was like; I didn't make any attempt to be quiet. I followed the music through the rooms unaware of the splendor of the surroundings, until I saw the huge phonograph that was the source of the music and I saw Clyde bending over Velda on the couch. He was a dark shadow in a satin robe. They both were shadows there in the corner, shadows that made hoarse noises, one demanding and the other protesting. I saw the white of Velda's leg, the white of her hand she had thrown over her face, and heard her whimper. Clyde threw out his arm to toss off the robe and I said, "Stand up, you stinking bastard!"

Clyde's face was a mask of rage that turned to fear in the single instant he saw me.

I wasn't too late after all. I was about one minute early.

Velda screamed a harried "Mike!" and squirmed upright on the couch. Clyde moved in slow motion, the hate . . . the unbounding hate oozing out of him. The skin of his face was drawn tight as a bowstring as he looked at her.

"Mike, you said. You know him then! It was a frame!" He spoke every word as though it was being squeezed out of him.

Velda came out of the chair and under my arm. I could feel her trembling as she sobbed against my chest. "She knows me, Dinky. So do you know me. You know what's going to happen now?"

The red hole that had been his mouth clamped shut. I lifted Velda's face and asked, "Did he hurt you, kid?"

She couldn't speak. She shook her head and sobbed until it passed. When it was over she mumbled, "Oh, Mike . . . it was awful."

"And you didn't learn a thing, did you?"

"No." She shuddered and fumbled with the buttons of her suit coat.

I saw her handbag on the table and pointed to it. "Did you carry that thing with you, honey?"

She knew I meant the gun and nodded.

"Get it," I said.

Velda inched away from me, loath to leave the protection of my arm. She snatched the bag and ripped it open. When she had the gun in her hand I laughed at the expression on Clyde's face.

"I'm going to let her kill you, Dinky. I'm going to let Velda put a slug in you for what you tried and for what you've done to other girls."

He stuttered something I didn't get and his lower lip hung away from his teeth. "I know all about it, Dinky. I know why you did it and how you did it. I know everything about your pretty little blackmail setup. You and Anton using the girls to bring in the boys who counted. When the girls had them in bed Anton took the pictures and from then on you carried the ball. You know something, Dinky . . . you got a brain. You got a bigger brain than I've ever given you credit for.

"It just goes to show you how you can underrate people. Here I've been figuring you for a stooge and you're the brain. It was clever as hell the way you killed Wheeler, all because he recognized one of the kids. Maybe he was going to have his little affair and keep quiet, but you showed up with the pictures and wanted the pay-off. He wired for five grand and handed it over, didn't he? Then he got sore and got in touch with Jean Trotter again and told her who he was. So Jean ups and tells you, which put the end to Wheeler."

Clyde looked at me speechlessly, his hands limp at his sides.

"That really started things. You had Wheeler planned for a kill and Wheeler grabbed my gun and tried to hand it to you. Only two things stump me. What was it you had planned for Wheeler before he reached for my rod and gave you the bright idea of suicide? And why kill Rainey? Was it because he wasn't the faithful dog you thought he was? I have an idea on that . . . Rainey missed his first try at me on the street and you gave him the whip, hard enough so that Rainey got sore and made off with the dough he got for the photos from Emil Perry. You went out there to the arena to kill him and spotted me. You saw a nice way to drop it in my lap and promised the two witnesses a six-gun pay-off unless they saw it your way.

"Brother, did you get the breaks. Everything went your way. I bet you even have a dandy alibi rigged up for that night. Velda told me you were out until midnight . . . supposedly at a conference. It was enough time, wasn't it?"

Clyde was staring at the gun in my hand. I held it at him level, but he was looking right down the barrel. Velda's was aimed right at his stomach.

"What did you do with Jean, Clyde? She was supposed to have eloped. Did you stash her away in a rooming house somewhere planning to get rid of her? Did she read the papers and find out about Rainey and break loose until you ran her down and tossed her over the bridge? Did Marion Lester put the heat on you for cash when she had you over the barrel until she had to be killed too?"

"Mike . . ." he said.

"Shut up. I'm talking. I want to know a few things, Clyde. I want to know where those pictures are. Anton can't tell me because Anton's dead. You ought to see his head. His eyes were where his mouth was supposed to be. He didn't have them so that puts it on you."

Clyde threw his arms back and screamed. Every muscle of his face contorted into a tight knot and the robe fell off his shoulders to the floor. "You aren't hanging murder on me, you shamus! I'm not going to hang for any murder, not me!"

Velda grabbed my arm and I shrugged her off. "You called it, Clyde. You won't hang for any murder, and you know why? Because you're going to die right here in this room. You're going to die and when the cops come I'll tell them what happened. I'll tell them that you had this gun in your hand and I took it away from you and used it myself. Or I can let Velda do it and put this gun in your hand later. It came from overseas . . . nobody will ever trace it to me. How do you like those apples, Clyde?"

The voice behind me said, "He don't like 'em, mister. Drop that gun or I'll give it to you and the broad both."

No, it couldn't happen to me again. Not again. Please, God, not this time. The hard round snout of a gun pressed against my spine. I dropped the Luger. Velda's hit the floor next to it. Clyde let out a scream of pure joy and staggered across the room to fall on it. He didn't talk. He lifted that rod by the butt and slashed it across my jaw. I tried to grab him and the barrel caught me on the temple with a jolt that dropped me to my knees. The voice with the gun took his turn and the back of my head felt like it flew to pieces.

I don't know how long I lay there. Time didn't mean a thing anymore. First I was too late, then I was early, now I was too late again. I heard Clyde through the fog ordering Velda into another room. I heard him say to the guy, "Drag him in with her. It's soundproof in there, nobody'll hear us. I'll fix him good for this when I get through with her. I want him to watch it. Put him in a chair and make him watch it."

Then there were hands under my arms and my feet dragged across the floor. A door slammed and I felt the arms of a chair

digging in the small of my back. Velda said, "No . . . oh, God
. . . NO!"

Clyde said, "Take it off. All of it." I got my eyes open. Clyde
was standing there flexing his hands, his face a picture of lust
unsatisfied. The other guy stood to one side of me watching Velda
back away until she was against the wall. He still had the gun in
his hand.

They all saw me move at the same time. My heart hammered
me to my feet and I wanted to kill them both. Clyde rasped,
"Shoot him if he tries anything." He said it knowing I was going
to try it anyway, and the guy brought the gun up.

There was only a single second to see it happen. Clyde and the
guy had their eyes off Velda just long enough. Her hand went
inside her suit jacket and came out with a little hammerless
automatic that barked a deadly bark and the guy with the gun
grabbed his stomach and tried to swear.

The pain in my head wouldn't let me stand. I tried to reach
her and fell, seeing Clyde grab her arm and wrestle for the rod
even as I was dragging myself toward the snubnosed revolver that
was still clutched in the other guy's hand.

Velda screamed, "Mike . . . get him! *Mike!*" She was bent
double trying to hold on to the gun. Clyde gave a wrench and
she tumbled to the floor, her jacket ripping wide open. Velda
screamed again and the gun clattered across the floor. Clyde
wouldn't have had time to get it before I reached the other one
and he knew it. He swore obscenely and ran for the door and
slammed it shut after him. A bolt clicked in the lock and furniture
was rammed into it to block the way. Then another door jarred
shut and Clyde was gone.

Velda had my head in her lap rocking me gently. "Mike, you
fool, are you all right? Mike, speak to me."

"I'm okay, kid. I'll be fine in a minute." She touched the cuts
on my face, healing them with a kiss. Tears streamed down her
cheeks. I forced a grin and she held me tighter. "Shrewdie, a
regular shrewdie, aren't you?" I fingered the straps of the miniature
shoulder holster she was wearing under the ruins of her jacket.
"You'll do as a partner. Who'd ever think a girl would be wearing
a shoulder rig?"

She grinned back and helped me to my feet. I swayed and held
on to the chair for support. Velda tried the door, rattling the knob
with all her strength. "Mike . . . it's locked! We're locked in."

"Damn it!"

The guy on the floor coughed once and twitched. Blood spilled out of his mouth and he gave one final, convulsive jerk. I said, "You can put a notch on your gun, Velda."

I thought she was going to get sick, but that animal look screwed her face into a snarl. "I wish I had killed them both. Mike, what are we going to do? We can't get out."

"We have to, Velda. Clyde . . . "

"Did he . . . is he the one?"

My head hurt. My brain was a soggy mass that revolted against thought. "He's the one. Try that door again." I finally picked the gun up off the floor and stood with it in my hand. It was almost too heavy to hold.

"Mike . . . that night that Rainey was killed . . . Clyde was at a conference. I heard them talking about it in the Bowery Inn. He was there."

My stomach heaved. The blood was pounding in my ears. I put the gun to the lock and pulled the trigger. The crack of it sent it spinning out of my hand. The lock still didn't give. Velda repeated, "Mike . . ."

"I heard you, goddam it! I don't care what you saw or what anybody said. It was Clyde, can't you see that? It was Clyde and Anton. They had the pictures and . . . "

I stopped and stared at the door. "The pictures . . . Clyde's gone after those pictures. If he gets them he'll have the protection he needs and he'll get out of this sure as grass grows in the springtime!"

I found the gun and leveled it at the lock, pulling the trigger until the room reeked with fumes of burned powder. Damn his soul! Those pictures . . . they weren't in Anton's apartment and they weren't here . . . the outside door had slammed shut too fast to give him time to pick anything up on the way. That left only one other place, the agency office.

Thinking about it gave me the strength I needed to bash it with my shoulder until it budged. Velda pushed with me and the furniture on the other side moved. We leaned against the dead weight, harder, working until the cords stood out in our necks. Something toppled from the pile and the door moved back far enough to let us out.

There was utter silence.

I threw the revolver on a chair and picked the Luger off the floor and stuffed it under my arm. I waved my thumb to the phone. "Call Pat. Try until you get him and if you can't, call the D.A.'s office. That'll get action quick enough. Make them put out a call for Clyde and we might be able to stop him in time." I half-ran, half-stumbled to the door and held it open. Velda shouted something after me that I didn't hear and I scrambled out to the lobby. The elevator pointer was the bottom floor, the basement. But the service car was still in place. It took its own, agonizing time about going down and I stopped it at the main hall and ran out the front. The admiral gave me a queer look, tried to grab me and got a fist in the mouth. He lost me in the snow before he could get up, but I could hear him yelling as I got in my car. I was two blocks away from the apartment building when the first squad car shot by. I was five blocks farther on when I remembered that Connie had gone up to the office that night.

I got that funny feeling back in my stomach again and jammed my foot down on the throttle and weaved across town so I could intersect Thirty-third Street without wasting a minute.

When I came to the cemetery of buildings I slowed down and parked. A light was on behind the entrance doors and an old fellow sat under it reading a paper. He was just checking his turnip watch when I pulled the door open. He shook his head and waved for me to go away.

I kicked the door so hard it shook violently. The old guy threw his paper down and turned the lock. "It's too late. You can't go in. We closed up half-hour ago. Not even late visitors. Go on, scram."

He didn't get a chance to close it on me. I rammed it with the heel of my hand and stepped inside. "Anybody been here in the last few minutes?"

His head jerked nervously. "Ain't been nobody here for over an hour. Look, you can't come in, so why don't you . . . "

Clyde hadn't shown up. Hell, he had to come here! He should be here! "Is there another way in this place?"

"Yes, the back way. That's locked up tight. Nobody can get in that way unless I unbolt it. Look, mister . . . "

"Oh, keep quiet. Call the cops if you want to."

"I don't understand . . . what you after?"

I let him have the nastiest look I could work up. "A killer. A guy with a gun."

He swallowed hard. "Nobody's been in . . . you're kidding, ain't you?"

"Yeah, I'm kidding so hard it hurts. You know who I am, Mac? My name is Mike Hammer. The cops want me. The killer wants me. Everybody wants my skin and I'm still walking around loose. Now answer my question, who was in here tonight?"

This time he gulped audibly. "Some . . . a guy from the first

. . . floor. He came back and worked. A few people from the insurance came in. Some others were with Roy Carmichael when he came in. They got some likker out of the office and left. I saw some others standing around the register later. Maybe if you looked there . . . "

"Sure, he wrote his name down. Take me upstairs, pop. I want to get in the Anton Lipsek Agency."

"Oh, say now. Young girl went in there while back. Nice kid. Sure I let her in there. Don't remember seeing her come back. Must've been making my rounds."

"Take me upstairs."

"You better use the self-service elevator . . . "

I shoved him in one of the main cars and he dropped his time clock. He glared at me once and shut the door. We got out and walked down the hall to the office and my gun was in my hand. This time there wouldn't be anybody coming up behind me.

The light was on and the doors were open, wide open. I went in running with my gun waist-high and covered the room. The watchman was wheezing in the doorway, bug-eyed with fright. I combed the rooms until the place was lit up like it was a working day. There were dressing rooms and minor offices, closets for supplies and closets for clothes. There were three neat darkrooms and one not so neat. I found the room I was looking for branching off a layout studio.

I found it and I opened the door and stood there with my mouth open to let me breathe up all the insane hatred that was stored up in my chest.

Connie was lying in the middle of the room with her eyes wide open. Her back had been bent to form a "V" and she was dead.

The room was ceiling-high with storage cabinets, covered with dust that revealed its infrequent use. The drawer of one of those cabinets gaped wide open and a whole section of folders had been removed.

I was too late again.

The watchman had to hold on to me to keep from fainting. He worked his mouth, trying to keep his eyes from the body. He made slobbering noises and shouted his fear and he held on tighter. He was still holding my arm when I kneeled down to look at Connie.

No marks, just that look of incredible pain on her face. The whole thing had been done with one swift, clean stroke. I opened her fingers gently and lifted out the piece of shipping tag she had clutched so tightly. The part that was left said, "To attach magnifier to screen . . ." the rest had been torn off. In the dust of the floor was the outline of where a crate had stood. Another fine line in the dust showed where the same crate had been tipped on end and dragged out in the hall. There were no marks after that and no crate either.

I left the door open and went back to the foyer, the little watchman blubbering behind me. After I tried a half-dozen combinations in the switchboard I got an outside wire. I said, "Give me the police." The watchman sat down and trembled while I told the desk man at the precinct station where to look for a body. When I hung up I steered the little guy back to the elevator and made him run me down to the basement.

It was just what I had expected. The door that was supposed to have been bolted so tightly to keep people out was swinging wide where a killer had gotten out.

The watchman didn't want to be left alone, and begged me not to go. I shoved him away and walked up the stairs and around the building.

I knew where the killer was hiding now.

chapter thirteen ▬▬▬▬▬▬▬▬▬▬

THE SNOW THAT had tried so hard to block me wasn't something to be fought any longer. I leaned back against the cushions of the car in complete relaxation and had the first enjoyable cigarette I'd had in a long time. I sucked the smoke down deep into my lungs and let it go reluctantly. Even the smoke looked pretty as it drifted out the window into the night.

Everything was so white, covering up so much filth. Nature doing its best to hide its own. I drove slowly, carefully, staying in the tracks of the cars ahead. When I turned on the radio I heard my name mentioned on the police broadcast band and turned the dial until I had some late music.

When I reached my destination I backed in between two cars and even went to the trouble of locking the door like any good citizen would who expects to go home and to bed for the rest of the night. There were a few lights on in the apartment building, but whether they came from the one I wanted or not, I couldn't tell.

I took one last drag on the butt and flipped it into the gutter. It lay there a moment fizzling before it went out. I walked in the lobby and held my finger on the buzzer until the door clicked, then I walked in.

Why hurry? Time had lost its value. My feet took each step carefully, one after the other, bringing me to the top. I walked straight down the hall to the door that stood open and said, "Hello, Juno."

I didn't wait for her answer. I brushed right past her and walked inside. I walked through the room and pulled chairs from their corners. I walked into the bedroom and opened the closet doors. I walked into the bathroom and ripped the shower curtain down. I walked into the kitchen and poked around the pantry.

My hands were ready to grab and my feet were ready to kick and my gun was ready to shoot. But nobody was there. The fires began in my feet and licked up my body until they were eating into my brain. Every pain that had been ignored up to this moment gave birth to greater pains that were like teeth gripping my flesh apart. I held the edge of the door and spun around to face her with all that pain and hatred laid bare on my face.

My voice was a deadly hiss. "Where is he, Juno?"

The hurt that spoke to me from her eyes was eloquent. She stood there in a long-sleeved gown, her hands clutching her throat as my madness reached her. "Mike . . ." that was all she could say. Her breasts rose under the gown as her breath caught.

"Where is he, Juno?" I had the Luger in my hand now. My thumb found the hammer and dragged it back.

Her lips, her beautiful lips, quivered and she took a step away from me. One step then another until she was standing in the living room. "You're hiding him, Juno. He came here. It was the only place the crazy bastard could come. Where is he?"

Ever so slowly she closed her eyes, shaking her head. "Oh, please, please, Mike. What have they done to you! Mike . . ."

"I found Connie, Juno. She was in the storeroom. She was dead. I found the files gone. Clyde might have had just enough time to get in and tear those files out after he killed Connie. I found something else, the same thing she found. It was part of a shipping ticket for a television set. That was the set you were supposed to deliver to Jean Trotter, but you knew she wasn't going to need that so you had it stacked in the storeroom until you could get rid of it. You were the only one who knew it was there . . . until tonight. Did Clyde find it and take it away so you wouldn't get tied into this?"

Her eyes opened wide, eyes that said it wasn't true, not any part of it. I didn't believe them. "Where is he, Juno?" I grabbed the gun up until it pointed at a spot midway between those laughing, youthful breasts under the gown.

"Nobody is here, Mike. You saw that. Please . . ."

"Seven people are dead, Juno. Seven people. In this whole crazy scheme of things you have a part. It's a beautiful scheme though, hand-tailored to come apart whenever you try to get a look at it. Don't play games with me, Juno. I know why they were killed and how they were killed. It was trying to guess *who* killed them that had me going in circles. Your little blackmail cycle would have remained intact. Just one of those seven would have died if I hadn't been in the room with Wheeler that night. Who knew that I'd do my damndest to break it open?"

She watched me, her hands still at her throat. She shook her head and said, "No, Mike, no!" and her knees trembled so she fought to keep her balance. It was too much. Juno reached out her hand to steady herself, holding the back of a chair. Slowly, gracefully even now, she sat down on the edge of it, her lower lip between her teeth.

I nodded yes, Juno, yes. The gun in my hand was steady. The hatred I had inside me bubbled over into my mouth and spilled out. "I thought it was Anton at first. Then I found a mail receipt to Clyde. Anton had sent him some pictures. The Bowery Inn was a great place to draw the girls. It was designed specifically for that. It got the girls and with them the suckers.

"Who led the girls there in the first place, Juno? Who made it a fad to hang out down there where Clyde could win at his gambling tables and insure his business with photos that gave him the best coverage in the world? Did you do that, Juno? Did Clyde have a crush on you at one time and figure a good way of being able to stay in business? Was it Clyde who saw the possibilities of getting blackmail evidence on the big shots? Or was it you? It wasn't Anton, for sure. That goon had rocks in his head. But he co-operated, though, didn't he? He co-operated because he saw a way to purchase all those expensive paintings he had in his place."

Her eyes were dull things, all the life gone from them. She sat with her head down and sobbed, one hand covering her face.

I spit the words out. "That's the way it was, all right. It worked fine for a while. Clyde had his protection and he was using it for all he was worth. But you, Juno . . . you wanted to go on with it. It wasn't so hard to do because money is easy to like. You were the brains of the outfit . . . the thinking brains. Clyde was the strong-arm boy and he had his little army to help him out."

I stopped and let it sink in. I waited a full minute. "Juno . . ."

She raised her head slowly. Her eyes were red, the mascara streaking her cheeks. "Mike . . . can't you . . ."

"Who killed them all, Juno? Where is he?"

Her hands dropped to her lap, folded across her stomach in despair. I raised the gun. "Juno." Only her eyes looked at me. "I'm going to shoot you, Juno, then I'm going to go out and get him all by myself. I'm going to shoot you where it will hurt like hell and you won't die quickly . . . if you don't tell me. All you have to do is tell me where I can find him and I'll give him the chance to use his hands on me like he tried to do before and like he did to some of the others. Where is he, Juno?"

She didn't speak.

I was going to kill her, so help me God. If I didn't she could fake her way out because I was the only one who knew what had happened. There wasn't a single shred of evidence against her that could be used in court and I knew it. But I could kill her. She had a part in this! The whole thing was her doing and she was as guilty as the killer!

The gun in my hand wavered and I clamped down on the butt to keep it lined up. It was in my face, I could feel it. She could see it. The poison that is hate was dripping out of me and scoring my face. My eyes burned holes in my head and my whole body reeled under the sickening force that pulled me toward her.

I pointed the gun at her head and sighted along the barrel and said, "My God, I can't!" because the light was in her hair turning it into a halo of white that brought the dead back to life and I was seeing Charlotte's face instead of hers.

I went crazy for a second. Stark, raving mad. My head was a throbbing thing that laughed and screamed for me to go on, bringing the sounds out of my mouth before I could stop it. When the madness went away I was panting like a dog, my breath coming in short, hot gasps.

"I thought I could do it. I thought I could kill you, Juno. I can't. Once there was another woman. You remind me of her. You've seen me when I was hating something . . . I was hating her. I loved her and I killed her. I shot her in the stomach. Yeah, Juno . . . I didn't think it would be this much trouble to kill another woman but it is.

"So you don't die tonight. I'll take you down to the police and do what I said. Go on, sit there and smile. You'll get out of it, but I'm going to do everything I can to see that you don't."

I stuck the gun back under my arm and reached for her hand. "Come on, Juno. I have a friend on the force who will be happy to book you on my word, even if it means his job."

She came up out of the chair.

Then all hell broke loose. She grabbed my arm and a fist smashed into my nose and I staggered back. There wasn't time to get my hands up before I crashed into the wall, stunned. A devil had me by the throat and a knee came up into my groin. I screamed and doubled over, breaking the grip on my neck. Something gave me the sense to lash out with my feet and the next second she was on top of me clawing for my eyes.

I jerked my head away feeling the skin go with it and brought my fist up and saw it split her nose apart. The blood ran into her mouth and choked off a yell. She tried to get away, fought, kicked and squirmed to get away, but I held on and hammered until she rolled off me.

She didn't stay off. The room echoed with a torrent of animal noises and my arm was wrenched back in a hammerlock that pulled me completely off my feet. A knee went into my spine and pushed, trying to split me in half. My madness saved me. It flowed into my veins giving me the strength for a tremendous, final effort that hurled me out of her arms and tumbled her in front of me. She came back for another try and I leaped in to meet her and got my hands on her clothes to jam her in close.

But she twisted away and there was a loud whispering tear of cloth and the gown came away in my hands. Juno went staggering across the room stark naked except for the high-heel shoes and sheer stockings. She rammed an end table, her hands reaching for the drawer, and she got it open far enough for me to see the gun she was trying to get at.

I had mine out first and I said harshly, "Stand still, Juno."

She froze there, not a muscle in that beautiful body moving. I looked at all that white bare skin, seeing it in contrast with the shoes and the stockings. Her hands were still on the drawer and inches away from the gun. She didn't have to be told that it couldn't be done.

I let her stand in that position, that ridiculous, obscene position while I lifted the phone off its hook. I had to be sure of just one thing. I went through Information and gave her an address, and I heard Clyde's phone ring. It took a little persuasion to get the cop off the line and Velda on it. I asked her one question and she answered it. She said Clyde was down in the basement out cold. The janitor had gotten him with a poker for some reason or other when he tried to get out. Clyde had never been near the office! She was still asking questions when I hung up.

It was all over now. I had found out *why,* I had found out *how,* now I knew *who.* The dead could go back to being dead forever.

I said, "Turn around, Juno."

No dancer of ballet could have been more poised. Juno balanced delicately on tiptoe and stared at me, the devils of the pit alive in her eyes. The evil of murder was a force so powerful that I could feel it across the room. Juno, queen of the goddesses, standing naked before me, her skin glistening in the light.

Tomorrow I'd get my license back from the D.A. with a note of apology attached. Tomorrow Ed Cooper would have his scoop. Tomorrow would be tomorrow and tonight was tonight. I looked across Olympus and stared at Juno.

"I should have known, Juno. It occurred to me every time you rolled those big beautiful eyes at me. I knew it every time you suggested one of your little love games, then got scared because you knew you didn't dare go through with it. Damn it, I knew it all along and it was too incredible to believe. Me, a guy what likes women, a guy who knows every one of their stunts . . . and I fall for this. Yeah, you and Clyde had a business arrangement all right. You had a lot more than that too. Who kept who, Juno? Are you the reason why Velda went over so big with Clyde? God, what an ass I was! I should have caught it the day you hauled me into that Village joint for dinner. There was a Lesbian who followed you into the ladies' room. I bet she could have kicked herself when she found out you were no better than she was. It was a part that fitted you to perfection. You played it so well that only the ones who didn't dare talk knew about it. Well, Juno, I know about it. Me. Mike Hammer, I know all about it and I'll talk. I'll tell them you killed Chester Wheeler because he got mad enough to try to expose the girl who framed him, and you killed Rainey because he tried to clip you out of some dirty dough, and Jean Trotter died for knowing the truth, and Marion Lester for the same reason. You couldn't have anybody knowing a truth that could be held over your head. Then Connie died because she discovered the truth when she found that television set in the storeroom and knew you never delivered it because Jean Trotter was no more married than you were. Yeah, I'm going to talk my fool head off, you slimy bastard, but first I'm going to do something else."

I dropped the Luger to the floor.

It was too impossible for her to comprehend and she missed her chance. I had the Luger back in my hand before she could snatch the gun out of the drawer. I forgot all my reservations about shooting a woman then. I laughed through the blood on my lips and brought the Luger up as Juno swung around with eyes blazing a hatred I'll never see again. The rod was jumping in my hand, spitting nasty little slugs that flattened the killer against the wall with periods that turned into commas as the blood welled out of the holes. Juno lived until the last shot had ripped through flesh and intestines and kicked the plaster from the wall, then died with those rich, red lips split in a snarl of pain and fearful knowledge.

She lived just long enough to hear me tell her that she was the only one it could have been, the only one who had the time. The only one who had the ability to make her identity a bewildering impossibility. She was the only one who could have taken that first shot at me on Broadway because she tailed me from the minute I left her house. She was the one all the way around because the reasons fit her perfectly as well as Clyde and Clyde didn't kill anybody. And tomorrow that was tomorrow would prove it when certain people had their minds jarred by a picture of what she really looked like, with her short hair combed back and parted on the side.

Juno died hearing all that and I laughed again as I dragged myself over to the lifeless lump, past all the foam rubber gadgets that had come off with the gown, the inevitable falsies she kept covered so well along with nice solid muscles by dresses that went to her neck and down to her wrists. It was funny. Very funny. Funnier than I ever thought it could be. Maybe you'd laugh, too. I spit on the clay that was Juno, queen of the gods and goddesses, and I knew why I'd always had a resentment that was actually a revulsion when I looked at her.

Juno was a queen, all right, a real, live queen. You know the kind.

Juno was a man!

The Big Kill

chapter one ▀▀▀▀▀▀▀▀▀▀▀▀▀▀

IT WAS ONE of those nights when the sky came down and wrapped itself around the world. The rain clawed at the windows of the bar like an angry cat and tried to sneak in every time some drunk lurched in the door. The place reeked of stale beer and soggy men with enough cheap perfume thrown in to make you sick.

Two drunks with a nickel between them were arguing over what to play on the juke box until a tomato in a dress that was too tight a year ago pushed the key that started off something noisy and hot. One of the drunks wanted to dance and she gave him a shove. So he danced with the other drunk.

She saw me sitting there with my stool tipped back against the cigarette machine and change of a fin on the bar, decided I could afford a wet evening for two and walked over with her hips waving hello.

"You're new around here, ain't ya?"

"Nah. I've been here since six o'clock."

"Buy me a drink?" She crowded in next to me, seeing how much of herself she could plaster against my legs.

"No." It caught her by surprise and she quit rubbing.

"Don't gentlemen usually buy ladies a drink?" she said. She tried to lower her eyelids seductively but one came down farther than the other and made her look stupid.

"I'm not a gentleman, kid."

"I ain't a lady either so buy me a drink."

So I bought her a drink. A jerk in a discarded army overcoat down at the end of the bar was getting the eye from the bartender because he was nursing the last drop in his glass, hating to go outside in the rain, so I bought him a drink too.

The bartender took my change with a frown. "Them bums'll bleed you to death, feller."

"I don't have any blood left," I told him. The dame grinned and rubbed herself against my knees some more.

"I bet you got plenty of everything for me."

"Yeah, but what I got you ain't getting because you probably got more than me."

"What?"

"Forget it."

She looked at my face a second, then edged away. "You ain't very sociable, mister."

"I know it. I don't want to be sociable. I haven't been sociable the last six months and I won't be for the next six if I can help it."

"Say, what's eatin' you? You having dame trouble?"

"I never have dame trouble. I'm a misanthropist."

"You *are?*" Her eyes widened as if I had something contagious. She finished her drink and was going to stick it out anyway, no matter what I said.

I said, "Scram."

This time she scowled a little bit. "Say, what the hell's eatin' you? I never. . . ."

"I don't like people. I don't like any kind of people. When you get them together in a big lump they all get nasty and dirty and full of trouble. So I don't like people including you. That's what a misanthropist is."

"I coulda sworn you was a nice feller," she said.

"So could a lot of people. I'm not. Blow, sister."

She gave me a look she kept in reserve for special occasions and got the hell out of there so I could drink by myself. It was a stinking place to have to spend the night but that's all there was on the block. The East Side doesn't cater to the uptown trade. I sat there and watched the clock go around, waiting for the rain to stop, but it was as patient as I was. It was almost malicious the way it came down, a million fingers that drummed a constant, maddening tattoo on the windows until its steady insistence rose above the bawdy talk and raucous screams of the juke box.

It got to everybody after a while, that and the smell of the damp. A fight started down at the other end and spread along the bar. It quit when the bartender rapped one guy over the head with an ice stick. One bum dropped his glass and got tossed out. The tomato who liked to rub herself had enough of it and picked up a guy who had enough left of his change to make the evening profitable and took him home in the rain. The guy didn't like it, but biology got the better of common sense again.

And I got a little bit drunk. Not much, just a little bit.

But enough so that in about five minutes I knew damn well I was going to get sick of the whole mess and start tossing them the hell out the door. Maybe the bartender too if he tried to use the stick on me. Then I could drink in peace and the hell with the rain.

Oh, I felt swell, just great.

I kept looking around to see where I'd start first, then the door opened and shut behind a guy who stood there in his shirt sleeves, wet and shivering. He had a bundle in his arms with his coat over it, and when he quit looking around the place like a scared rabbit he shuffled over to one of the booths and dropped the bundle on the seat.

Nobody but me had paid any attention to him. He threw a buck on the bar, had a shot then brought the other shot over to his table. Still nobody paid any attention to him. Maybe they were used to seeing guys who could cry.

He set the drink down and took the coat off the bundle. It was quite a bundle, all right. It was a little kid about a year old who was sound asleep. I said something dirty to myself and felt my shoulders hunch up in disgust. The rain, the bar, a kid and a guy who cried. It made me sicker than I was.

I couldn't take my eyes off the guy. He was only a little squirt who looked as if he had never had enough to eat. His clothes were damp and ragged, clinging to him like skin. He couldn't have been any older than me, but his face was seamed around the mouth and eyes and his shoulders hung limply. Whatever had been his purpose in life, he had given up long ago.

But damn it, he kept crying. I could see the tears running down his cheeks as he patted the kid and talked too low to be heard. His chest heaved with a sob and his hands went up to cover his face. When they came away he bent his head and kissed the kid on top of his head.

All of a sudden my drink tasted lousy.

I turned around to put a quarter in the cigarette machine so I wouldn't have to look at him again when I heard his chair kick back and saw him run to the door. This time he had nothing in his arms.

For about ten seconds I stood there, my fingers curled around the deck of Luckies. Something crawled up my spine and made my teeth grind together, snapping off a sound that was a curse at the whole damn world. I knocked a drunk down getting around the corner of the bar and ripped the door open so the rain could lash at my face the way it had been wanting to. Behind me somebody yelled to shut the door.

I didn't have time to because I saw the guy halfway down the street, a vague silhouette under the overhead light, a dejected figure of a man too far gone to care any more. But he was worth caring about to somebody in the Buick sedan that pulled away from the curb. The car slithered out into the light with a roar and I heard the sharp cough of the gun over the slapping of my own feet on the sidewalk.

It only took two of them and the guy slammed forward on his face. The back door flew open and another shadow ran under the light and from where I was I could see him bend over and frisk the guy with a blurred motion of his hands.

I should have waited, damn it. I shouldn't have tried a shot from where I was. A .45 isn't built for range and the slug ripped a groove in the pavement and screamed off down the block. The guy let out a startled yell and tore back toward the car with the other guy yelling for him to hurry. He damn near made it, then one of the ricochets took him through the legs and he went down with a scream.

The other guy didn't wait. He jammed the gas down and wrenched the wheel over as hard as he could and the guy shrieking his lungs out in the gutter forgot the pain in his legs long enough to let out one final, terrified yell before the wheels of the car made a pulpy mess of his body. My hand kept squeezing the trigger until there were only the flat echoes of the blasts that were drowned out by the noise of the car's exhaust and the futile gesture as the gun held opened, empty.

And there I was standing over a dead little guy who had two holes in his back and the dried streaks of tears on his face. He didn't look tired any more. He seemed to be smiling. What was left of the one in the gutter was too sickening to look at.

I opened the cigarettes and stuck one in my mouth. I lit it and breathed out the smoke, watching it sift through the rain. The guy couldn't hear me, but I said, "It's a hell of a city, isn't it, feller?"

A jagged streak of lightning cut across the sky to answer me.

The police cars took two minutes getting to the spot. They converged from both ends of the street, howling to a stop under the light and the boys next to the drivers were out before the tires stopped whining.

One had a gun in his hand. He meant business with it too. It was pointed straight at my gut and he said, "Who're you?"

I pointed my butt at the thing on the sidewalk. "Eyewitness."

The other cop came behind me and ran his hand over my pockets. He found the gun, yanked it out of the holster and smelled the barrel. For a second I thought he was going to clip me with it, but this cop had been around long enough to ask questions first. He asked them with his eyes.

"Look in my side pocket," I said.

He dipped his hand in my coat and brought out my wallet. The badge was pinned to the flap with my P.I. ticket and gun license inside the cardcase. He looks them both over carefully, scrutinizing my picture then my face. "Private Investigator, Michael Hammer."

"That's right."

He scowled again and handed the gun and wallet back. "What happened?"

"This guy came in the bar back there a few minutes ago. He looked scared as hell, had two drinks and ran out. I was curious so I tagged after him."

"In this rain you were curious," the cop with the gun said.

"I'm a curious guy."

The other cop looked annoyed. "Okay, go on."

I shrugged. "He ran out and a Buick came after him. There were two shots from the car, the guy fell and one punk hopped out of the car to frisk him. I let loose and got the guy in the legs and the driver of the car ran over him. Purposely."

"So you let loose!" The lad with the gun came in at me with a snarl.

The other cop shoved him back. "Put that thing away and call the chief. I know this guy."

It didn't go over big with the young blood. "Hell, the guy's dead, isn't he? This punk admits shooting, don't he? Hell, how do we know there was a Buick?"

"Go take a look at the corpse over there," the cop said patiently.

Laddie boy with the gun shoved it back on his hip and walked across the street. He started puking after his first look and crawled back in the prowl car.

So at one o'clock in the morning Pat got there with no more fanfare than the winking red light on the top of the police car. I watched him step out and yank his collar up against the rain. The cops looked smart when he passed because there wasn't anything else to do. A killing in this neighborhood was neither important nor interesting enough to drag out the local citizenry in a downpour, so the harness bulls just stood at attention until the brass had given his nod of recognition.

The cop who had frisked me said, "Good evening, Captain Chambers."

Pat said hello and was led out to look over the pair of corpses. I stayed back in the shadows smoking while he bent over to look at the one on the sidewalk. When he finished his inspection he straightened up, listened to the cop a minute and wrinkled up his forehead in a perplexed frown.

My cigarette arched through the night and fizzled out in the gutter. I said, "Hi, Pat."

"What are you doing here, Mike?" Two cops flanked him as he walked over to me. He waved them away.

"I'm the eyewitness."

"So I've heard." Behind Pat the eager beaver cop licked his lips, wondering who the hell I was and hoping I didn't sound off about his gun-waving. "What's the whole story, Mike?"

"That's it, every bit of it. I don't know any more about it than you do."

"Yeah." He made a sour face. "Look, don't screw me. Are you on a case?"

"Chum, if I was I'd say so then keep my trap closed. I'm not on a case and I don't know what the hell happened. This guy got shot, I nicked the other guy and the boy in the car finished him off."

Pat shook his head. "I hate coincidence. I hate it especially when you're involved. You smell out murder too well."

"Sure, and this one stinks. You know either of them?"

"No. They're not carrying any identification around either."

The morgue wagon rolled up with the Medical Examiner about fifty feet in the rear. The boys hopped out and started cleaning up the mess after the verdict was given and the pictures taken. I ambled out to the middle of the street and took a look at the body that was squashed against the roadbed.

He looked like an hourglass.

Fright and pain had made a distorted death mask of his face, but the rain had scrubbed away the blood leaving him a ghostly white in contrast with the asphalt of the street. He was about forty-five and as medium as you can get. His clothes had an expensive look about them, but one shoe had a hole in the bottom and he needed a haircut bad.

The driver of the wagon splashed the light of a flash over him and gave me a toothy grin. "He's a goodie, ain't he?"

"Yeah, a real beaut."

"Not so much, though. You shoulda seen what we had last week. Whole damn trailer truck rolled over that one and we had to scrape him away from between the tires. Coulda put him in a shoe box."

"Do you sleep good nights?" I gave him my best disgusted look.

"Sure, why?" He even sounded surprised.

"Forget it. Put that light on his face again."

The guy obliged and I had a close look this time. I walked around and had a squint from the other side then told him to knock off the light. Pat was a vague figure in a trench coat, watching me closely. He said, "Know him?"

"I've seen him before. Small-time hardcase, I think."

"The M.E. remembered him. He was a witness at a coroner's inquest about twelve years ago. The guy was one of Charlie Fallon's old outfit."

I glanced at Pat then back to the corpse again. The guy had some odd familiarity I couldn't place and it wasn't Fallon I was thinking of. Fallon died of natural causes about the same time I was opening up shop and what I knew of him came strictly from the papers.

"Nope, can't quite place him," I said.

"We'll get him tagged. Too bad they couldn't've had the decency to carry a lodge card or something. The one on the sidewalk there only had forty cents in change and a house key in his pocket. This guy had a fin and two ones and nothing else."

I nodded. "A buck must have been all that first lad had then. He bought two drinks in the bar before he left."

"Well, let's go back there and check. Maybe somebody'll know him there."

"Nobody will," I said.

"Never can tell."

"Nuts. They didn't know him when he came in, I'm telling you. He just had two drinks and left."

"Then what're you getting excited about?" He had his hands shoved down in his pockets and was watching me with eyes that were half shut.

"Skip it."

"The hell I'll skip it. Two guys are murdered and I want to know what the hell goes on. You got another wild hair up your tail, haven't you?"

"Yeah." The way I said it brought the scowl back to his face. "Spill it, Mike."

"Let's go back to the bar. I'm getting so goddamn sick of the things that happen in this town I have to take a bath every time I even stick my head out the door."

The rain stopped momentarily as if something had amazed it, then slashed down with all the fury it could muster, damning me with its millions of pellets. I took a look around me at the two rows of tenements and the dark spots on the pavement where the dead men were a minute ago and wondered how many people behind the walls and windows were alive today who wouldn't be alive tomorrow.

Pat left a moment, said something to the M.E. and one of the cops, then joined me on the sidewalk. I nudged a brace of Luckies out of the pack, handed him one and watched his face in the light. He looked teed off like he always did when he came face to face with a corpse.

I said, "This must gripe the pants off you, Pat. There's not one blasted thing you can do to prevent trouble. Like those two back there. Alive one minute, dead the next. Nice, huh? The cops get here in time to clear up the mess, but they can't move until it happens. Christ, what a place to live!"

He didn't say anything until we turned into the bar. By that time most of the customers were so helplessly drunk they couldn't remember anything anyway. The bartender said a guy was in for a few minutes awhile back, but he couldn't help out. Pat gave up after five minutes and came back to me. I was sitting at the booth with my back to the bundle in the corner ready to blow up.

Pat took a long look at my face. "What's eating you, Mike?"

I picked the bundle up and sat it on my knee. The coat came away and the kid's head lolled on my shoulder, his hair a tangled wet mop. Pat pushed his hat back on his head and tucked his lip under his teeth. "I don't get it."

"The dead guy . . . the one who was here first. He came in with the kid and he was crying. Oh, it was real touching. It damn near made me sick, it was so touching. A guy bawling his head off, then kissing his kid good-by and making a run for the street.

"This is why I was curious. I thought maybe the guy was so far gone he was deserting his kid. Now I know better, Pat. The guy knew he was going to die so he took his kid in here, said so long and walked right into it. Makes a nice picture, doesn't it?"

"You're drawing a lot of conclusions, aren't you?"

"Let's hear you draw some better ones. Goddamn it, this makes me mad! No matter what the hell the guy did it's the kid who has to pay through the nose for it. Of all the lousy, stinking things that happen. . . ."

"Ease off, Mike."

"Sure, ease off. It sounds real easy to do. But look, if this was his kid and he cared enough to cry about it, what happens to him?"

"I presume he has a mother."

"No doubt," I said sarcastically. "So far you don't know who the father is. Do we leave the kid here until something turns up?"

"Don't be stupid. There are agencies who will take care of him."

"Great. What a hell of a night this is for the kid. His old man gets shot and he gets adopted by an agency."

"You don't know it's his father, friend."

"Who else would cry over a kid?"

Pat gave me a thoughtful grimace. "If your theory holds about the guy knowing he was going to catch it, maybe he was bawling for himself instead of the kid."

"Balls. What kind of a kill you think this is?"

"From the neighborhood and the type of people involved I'd say it was pretty local."

"Maybe the killer hopes you'll think just that."

"Why?" He was getting sore now too.

"I told you he ran over his own boy deliberately, didn't I? Why the hell would he do that?"

Pat shook his head. "I don't think he did."

"Okay, pal, you were there and I wasn't. You saw it all."

"Damn it, Mike, maybe it looked deliberate to you but it sounds screwball to me! It doesn't make sense. If he did swerve like you said he did, maybe he was intending to pick the guy up out of the gutter and didn't judge his distance right. When he hit him it was too late to stop."

I said something dirty.

"All right, what's your angle?"

"The guy was shot in the legs. He might have talked and the guy in the car didn't want to be identified for murder so he put the wheels to him."

Suddenly he grinned at me and his breath hissed out in a

chuckle. "You're on the ball. I was thinking the same thing myself and wanted to see if you were sure of yourself."

"Go to hell," I said.

"Yeah, right now. Let's get that kid out of here. I'll be up half the night again on this damn thing. Come on."

"No."

Pat stopped and turned around. "What do you mean . . . 'no'?"

"What I said. I'll keep the kid with me . . . for now anyway. He'll only sit down there at headquarters until morning waiting for those agency people to show up."

Maybe it's getting so I can't keep my face a blank any more, or maybe Pat had seen that same expression too often. His teeth clamped together and I knew his shoulders were bunching up under the coat. "Mike," he told me, "if you got ideas about going on a kill-hunt, just get rid of them right now. I'm not going to risk my neck and position because of a lot of wild ideas you dream up."

I said it low and slow so he had to listen hard to catch it. "I don't like what happened to the kid, Pat. Murder doesn't just happen. It's thought about and planned out all nice and neat, and any reason that involves murder and big fat Buicks has to be a damn good one. I don't know who the kid is, but he's going to grow up knowing that the guy who killed his old man died with a nice hot slug in the middle of his intestines. If it means anything to you, consider that I'm on a case. I have me a legal right to do a lot of things including shooting a goddamn killer if I can sucker him into drawing first so it'll look like self-defense.

"So go ahead and rave. Tell me how it won't do me any good. Tell me that I'm interfering in police work and I'll tell you how sick I am of what goes on in this town. I live here, see? I got a damn good right to keep it clean even if I have to kill a few bastards to do it. There's plenty who need killing bad and if I'm electing myself to do the job you shouldn't kick. Just take a look at the papers every day and see how hot the police are when politics can make or break a cop. Take a look at your open cases like who killed Scottoriggio . . . or Binnaggio and his pal in Kansas City . . . then look at me straight and say that this town isn't wide open and I'll call you a liar."

I had to stop and take a breath. The air in my lungs was so hot it choked me.

"It isn't nice to see guys cry, Pat. Not grown men. It's worse to see a little kid holding the bag. Somebody's going to get shot for it."

Pat knew better than to argue about it. He looked at me steadily a long minute, then down at the kid. He nodded and his face went tight. "There's not much I can do to stop you, Mike. Not now, anyway."

"Not ever. Think it's okay to keep the kid?"

"Guess so. I'll call you in the morning. As long as you're involved the D.A. is probably going to want a statement from you anyway. This time keep your mouth shut and you'll keep your license. He's got enough trouble on his hands trying to nail the big boys in the gambling racket and he's just as liable to take it out on you."

My laugh sounded like trees rubbing together. "He can go to hell for all I care. He got rough with me once and I bet it still hurts when he thinks about it. What's the matter with him now . . . can't he even close up a bookie joint?"

"It isn't funny, Mike."

"It's a scream. Even the papers are laughing."

A slow burn crept into his face. "They should. The same guys who do the laughing are probably some of the ones who keep the books open. It's the big shots like Ed Teen who laugh the loudest and they're not laughing at the D.A. or the cops . . . they're laughing at Joe Citizen, guys like you, who take the bouncing for it. It isn't a bit funny when Teen and Lou Grindle and Fallon can go on enjoying a life of luxury until the day they die while you pay for it."

He got it out of his system and remembered to hand me a good night before he left. I stared at the door swinging shut, my arms tight around the kid, hearing his words come back slowly with one of them getting louder every time it repeated itself.

Lou Grindle. The arm. Lou Grindle who was a flashy holdover from the old days and sold his services where they were needed. Lou Grindle, tough boy de luxe who was as much at home in the hot spots along the Stem as in a cellar club in Harlem.

Lou Grindle who was on his hands and knees in the back of Lake's joint a week ago shooting crap with the help while two of his own boys stood by holding his coat and his dough and the one who held his coat was the dead guy back in the gutter who looked like an hourglass.

I wrapped the coat around the kid and went out in the doorway where I whistled at cabs until one stopped and picked me up. The driver must have had kids of his own at home because he gave me a nasty sneer when he saw the boy in my arms.

I told him where to make his first stop and he waited until I came back. Then I had him make seven others before I got any results. A bartender with a half a bag on mistook me for one of the boys and told me I might find Lou Grindle on Fifty-seventh Street in a place called the Hop Scotch where a room was available for some heavy sugar card games once a week. I threw him a buck and went back to the cab.

I said, "Know where the Hop Scotch is on Fifty-seventh?"

"Yeah. You goin' there now?"

"Looks that way, doesn't it?"

"Don't you think you better take that kid home, buddy? It ain't no good fer kids to be up so late."

"Chum, there's nothing I'd like to do better, but first I got business to take care of."

If I was drunk the cabbie might have tossed me out. As it was, he turned around in his seat to make sure I wasn't, then rolled across to Fifty-seventh.

I left the kid in the cab with a fin to keep the driver quiet and got out. The Hop Scotch was a downstairs gin mill that catered to crowds who liked dirty floor shows and a lot of noise and didn't mind footing the bill. It was hopping with drunks and half drunks who ganged up around the dance floor where a stripper was being persuaded not to stay within the limits prescribed by New York law and when they started throwing rolled-up bills out she said to hell with the law, let go her snaps and braces and gave the customers a treat when she did a two-handed pickup of all the green persuaders.

A waiter was watching the show with a grin on his fat face and I grabbed him while he was still gone over the sight of flesh. I said, "Where's Lou?" just like we were real pals.

"Inside. Him and the others're playin'." His thumb made a vague motion toward the back.

I squeezed through the crowd to where a bus boy was clearing off an empty table and pulled out a chair. The boy looked at the five in my fingers and waited. "Lou Grindle's inside. Go tell him to come out."

He wanted the five, but he shook his head. "Brother, nobody tells Lou nothing. You tell 'im."

"Say it's important business and he'll come. He won't like it if he doesn't get to hear what I have to tell him."

The guy licked his lips and reached for the five. He left the tray on the table, disappeared around a bend that led to the service bar and kitchen, came back for his tray and told me Lou was on his way.

Out on the floor another stripper was trying to earn some persuasion dough herself so the outside of the room was nice and clear with no big ears around.

Lou came around the bend, looked at the bus boy who crooked a finger my way, then came over to see who the hell I was. Lou Grindle was a dapper punk in his forties with eyes like glass marbles and a head of hair that looked painted on. His tux ran in the three-figure class and if you didn't look for it you'd never know he was packing a gun low under his arm.

The edges of his eyes puckered up as he tried to place me and when he saw the same kind of a gun bulge on me as he had himself he made the mistake of taking me for a cop. His upper lip twitched in a sneer he didn't try to hide.

I kicked another chair out with my foot and said, "Sit down, Lou."

Lou sat down. His fingers were curled up like he wanted to take me apart at the seams. "Make it good and make it quick," he said. He hissed when he talked.

I made it good, all right. I said, "One of your butt boys got himself killed tonight."

His eyes unpuckered and got glassier. It was as close as he could come to looking normally surprised. "Who?"

"That's what I want to find out. He was holding your coat in a crap game the other night. Remember?"

If he remembered he didn't tell me so.

I leaned forward and leaned on the table, the ends of my hand inside the lapel of my coat just in case. "He was a medium-sized guy in expensive duds with holes in his shoes. A long time ago he worked for Charlie Fallon. Right now I'm wondering whether or not he was working for you tonight."

Lou remembered. His face went tight and the cords in his neck pressed tight against his collar. "Who the hell are you, Mac?"

"The name's Mike Hammer, Lou. Ask around and you'll find what it means."

A snake wore the same expression he got just then. His eyes went even glassier and under his coat his body started sucking inward. "A goddamn private cop!" He was looking at my fingers. They were farther inside my coat now and I could feel the cold butt of the .45.

The snake look faded and something else took its place. Something that said Lou Grindle wasn't taking chances on being as fast as he used to be. Not where he was alone, anyway. "So what?" he snarled.

I grinned at him. The one with all the teeth showing.

"That boy of yours, the one who died . . . I put a slug through his legs and the guy who drove the car didn't want to take a chance on him being picked up so he put the wheels to him. Right after the two of 'em got finished knocking off another guy too."

Lou's hand moved up to his pocket and plucked out a cigar. Slowly, so I could watch it happen. "Nobody was working for me tonight."

"Maybe not, Lou, maybe not. You better hope they weren't."

He stopped in the middle of lighting the cigar and threw those snake eyes at me again. "You got a few things to learn, shamus, I don't like for guys to talk tough to me."

"Lou . . ." His head came back an inch and I could see the hate he wore like a mask. ". . . if I find out you had a hand in this business tonight I'm going to come back here and take that slimy face of yours and rub it in the dirt. You just try playing rough with me and you'll see your guts lying on the floor before you die. Remember what I said, Lou. I'd as soon shoot your goddamn greasy head off as look at you."

His face went white right down to his collar. If he had lips they didn't show because they were rolled up against his teeth. The number on the floor ended and the people were coming back where they belonged, so I stood up and walked away. When I looked back he was gone and his chair was upside down against the wall.

The cab was still there with another two bucks chalked up on the meter. It was nearly three o'clock and I had told Velda I'd meet her at two-thirty. I said, "Penn Station," to the driver, held the kid against me to soften the jolts of the ride and paid off the driver a few minutes later.

Velda isn't the kind of woman you'd miss even in Penn Station. All you had to do was follow the eyes. She was standing by the information booth tall and cool-looking, in a light gray suit that made the black of her hair seem even deeper. Luscious. Clothes couldn't hide it. Seductive. They didn't try to hide it either. Nobody ever saw her without undressing her with their eyes, that's the kind of woman she was.

A nice partner to have in the firm. And someday. . . .

I came up behind her and said, "Hello, Velda. Sorry I'm late."

She swung around, dropped her cigarette and let me know she thought I was what I looked like right then, an unshaven bum wringing wet. "Can't you ever be on time, Mike?"

"Hell, you're big enough to carry your own suitcases to the platform. I got caught up in a piece of work."

She concentrated a funny stare on me so hard that she didn't realize what I had in my arms until it squirmed. Her breath caught in her throat sharply. "Mike . . . what . . ."

"He's a little boy, kitten. Cute, isn't he?"

Her fingers touched his face and he smiled sleepily. Velda didn't smile. She watched me with an intensity I had seen before and it was all I could do to make my face a blank. I flipped a butt out of my pack and lit it so my mouth would have a reason for being tight and screwed up on the side. "Is this the piece of work, Mike?"

"Yeah, yeah. Look, let's get moving."

"What are you doing with him?"

I made what was supposed to be a laugh. "I'm minding him for his father."

She didn't know whether to believe me or not. "Mike . . . this Florida business can wait if there's something important."

The speaker system was calling off that the Miami Limited was loading. For a second I debated whether or not I should tell her and decided not to. She was a hell of a woman but a woman just the same and thought too goddamn much of my skin to want to see me wrapped up in some kind of a crazy hate again. She'd been through that before. She'd be everything I ever wanted if she'd just quit making sure I stayed alive. So I said, "Come on, you got five minutes."

I put her on the train downstairs and made a kiss at her through the window. When she smiled with that lovely wide mouth and blew a kiss back at me I wanted to tell her to get off and forget going after a punk in Miami who had a hatful of stolen ice, but the train jerked and slipped away. I waved once more and went back upstairs and caught another cab home.

Up in the apartment I undressed the kid, stuffed the ragged overalls in the garbage pail and made him a sack on the couch. I backed up a couple of chairs to hold him in and picked him up. He didn't weigh very much. He was one of those little bundles that were probably scattered all over the city right then with nobody caring much about them. His pale hair was still limp and damp, yet still curly around the edges.

For a minute his head lolled on my shoulder, then his eyes came open. He said something in a tiny voice and I shook my head. "No, kid, I'm not your daddy. Maybe I'll do until we find you another one, though. But at least you've seen the last of old clothes and barrooms for a while."

I laid him on the couch and pulled a cover up over him. Somebody sure as hell was going to pay for this.

chapter two ▪▪▪▪▪▪▪▪▪▪▪▪▪▪▪▪▪

THE SUN WAS there in the morning. It was high above the apartments beaming in through the windows. My watch read a few minutes after ten and I unpiled out of bed in a hurry. The phone let loose with a startling jangle at the same time something smashed to the floor in the living room and I let out a string of curses you could have heard on the street.

If I yelled it got stuck in my throat because the kid was standing barefooted in the wreckage of a china-base table lamp reaching up for my rod on the edge of the end table. Even before I got to him he dragged it out of the clip by the trigger guard and was bringing his other hand up to it.

I must have scared the hell out of him the way I whisked him off the floor and disentangled his mitt from the gun. The safety was off and he had clamped down on the trigger while I was thanking the guy who invented the butt safety on the .45.

So with a gun in one hand and a yelling kid in the other I nudged the phone off the hook to stop the goddamn ringing and yelled hello loud enough so the yowls wouldn't drown me out.

Pat said, "Got trouble, Mike?" Then he laughed.

It wasn't funny. I told him to talk or hang up so I could get myself straightened out.

He laughed again, louder this time. "Look, get down as soon as you can, Mike. We have your little deal lined up for you."

"The kid's father?"

"Yeah, it was his father. Come on down and I'll tell you about it."

"An hour. Give me an hour. Want me to bring the kid along?"

"Well . . . to tell the truth I forgot all about him. Tell you what, park him somewhere until we can notify the proper agency, will you?"

"Sure, just like that I'll dump the kid. What's the matter with you? Oh, forget it, I'll figure something out."

I slammed the phone back and sat down with the kid on my knee. He kept reaching for the gun until I chucked it across the room in a chair. On second thought I called the doorman downstairs and told him to send up an errand boy. The kid got there about five minutes later and I told him to light out for the avenue and pick up something a year-old kid could wear and groceries he could handle.

The kid took the ten spot with a grin. "Leave it to me, mister. Me, I got more brudders than you got fingers. I know whatta get."

He did, too. For ten bucks you don't get much, but it was a change of clothes and between us we got the boy fed. I gave the kid five bucks and got dressed myself. On the floor downstairs was an elderly retired nurse who agreed to take the kid days as long as I kept him nights and for the service it would only cost me one arm and part of a leg.

When she took the kid over I patted his fanny while he tried to dig out one of my eyes with his thumb. "For a client," I said, "you're knocking the hell out of my bank roll." I looked at the nurse, but she had already started brushing his hair back and adjusting his coveralls. "Take good care of him, will you?"

"Don't you worry a bit now. As a matter of fact, I'm glad to have something to do with my time." The kid yelled and reached his hand inside my coat and when I pulled away he yelled again, this time with tears. "Do you have something he wants?" she asked me.

"Er . . . no. We were . . . er, playing a game with my coat before. Guess he remembered." I said so long and got out. She'd eat me out if she knew the kid wanted the rod for a toy.

Pat was at ease in his office with his feet up on the desk, comparing blown-up photos of prints in the light that filtered in the windows. When I came in he tossed them aside and waved me into a chair.

"It didn't take us long to get a line on what happened last night."

I sat back with a fresh cigarette in my fingers and waited. Pat slid a report sheet out of a stack and held it in front of him.

"The guy's name was William Decker," he said. "He was an ex-con who had been released four years ago after serving a term for breaking and entering. Before his arrest he had worked for a safe and lock company in a responsible position, then, probably because of his trade, was introduced to the wrong company. He quit his job and seemed to be pretty well off at the same time a wave of safe robberies were sweeping a section of the city. None of those crimes were pinned on him, but he was suspected of it. He was caught breaking into a place and convicted."

"Who was the bad company?" I cut in.

"Local boys. A bunch of petty gangsters, most of whom are now up the river. Anyway, after his release, he settled down and got married. His wife died less than a year after the baby was born. By the way, the kid's name is William too.

"Now . . . we might still be up in the air about this if something hadn't happened last night that turned the light on the whole thing. We put Decker's prints through at the same time another investigation was being made. A little before twelve o'clock last night we had a call to investigate a prowler seen on a fire escape of one of the better apartment buildings on Riverside Drive. The squad car that answered the call found no trace of the prowler, but when they investigated the fire escape they came across a broken window and heard a moan from inside.

"When they entered they found a woman sprawled on the floor in a pretty battered condition. Her wall safe was open and the contents gone. There was one print on the dial that the boys were able to lift and it was that of William Decker. When we pulled the card we had the answers."

"Great." My voice made a funny flat sound in the room.

Pat's head came up, his face expressionless. "Sometimes you *can't* do what you want to do, Mike. You were all steamed up to go looking for a killer and now you're getting sore because it's all so cut and dried."

"Okay, okay, finish reading. I want to hear it."

He went back to the report. "Like I said, his wife died and in all likelihood he started going bad again. He and two others planned a safe robbery with Decker opening the can while the others were lookouts and drove. It's our theory that Decker tried to get away with the entire haul without splitting and his partners overtook and killed him."

"Nice theory. How'd you reach it?"

"Because it was a safe job where Decker would have to handle the thing alone . . . because he went home long enough after the job to pick up his kid . . . and because you yourself saw the man you shot frisking him for the loot before you barged in on the scene."

"Now spell it backwards."

"What?"

"Christ, can't you see your own loopholes? They're big enough."

He saw them. He stuck his tongue in the corner of his cheek and squinted at the paper. "Yeah, the only catch is the loot. It wasn't."

"You hit it," I agreed. "And something else . . . if he was making a break for it he would have taken the dough along. This guy Decker knew he was damn well going to die. He walked right out into it like you'd snap your fingers."

Pat nodded. "I thought of that too, Mike. I think I can answer it. All Decker got in that haul was three hundred seventeen dollars and a string of cultured pearls worth about twenty bucks. I think that when he realized that was all there was to be had, he knew the others wouldn't believe him and took a powder. Tried to, at least."

"Then where's the dough?"

Pat tapped his fingernails against his teeth. "I think we'll find it in the same place we'll find the pearls . . . if anybody's honest enough to turn it in . . . and that's on top of a garbage pail somewhere."

"Aw, nuts. Even three hundred's dough these days. He wouldn't chuck it."

"Anger and disgust can make a person do a lot of things."

"Then why did he let himself get knocked off?"

Pat waited a moment then said, "I think because he realized that they might try to take out their revenge on the child."

I flipped the butt into the wastebasket. "You sure got it wrapped up nice and tight. Who was the other guy?"

"His name was Arnold Basil. He used to work for Fallon and had a record of three stretches and fourteen arrests without convictions. We weren't able to get much of a line on him so far. We do know that after Fallon died he went to Los Angeles and while he was there got drunk and was picked up for disorderly conduct. Two of our stoolies reported having seen him around town the last month, but hadn't heard about him being mixed up in anything."

"Did they mention him sticking close to Lou Grindle?"

Pat scowled. "Where'd you get that?"

"Never mind. What about it?"

"They mentioned it."

"What're you doing about it?"

"Checking."

"That's nice."

He threw the pencil across the desk. "Don't get so damn sarcastic, Mike." He caught the stare I held on him and started tapping his teeth again. "As much as I'd like to pin something on that cheap crook, I doubt if it can be done. Lou doesn't play for peanuts and you know it. He has his protection racket and he manages to stay out of trouble."

"You could fix that," I said. "Breed 'im some trouble he can't get out of."

"Yeah, try it."

I stood up and slapped on my hat. "I think maybe I will just for the hell of it."

Pat's hands were flat on the desk. "Damn it, Mike, lay off. You're in a huff because the whole thing works out and you're not satisfied because you can't go gunning for somebody. One of these days you're going to dig up more trouble than you can handle!"

"Pat, I don't like orphan-makers. There's still the driver of that car and don't forget it."

"I haven't. He'll be in the line-up before the week is out."

"He'll be dead first. Mind if I look at this?" I picked up the report sheet and scanned it. When I finished remembering a couple of addresses I tossed it back.

He was looking at me carefully now, his eyes guarded. "Mike, did you leave something out of what you've told me?"

"Nope, not a thing."

"Then spill it."

I turned around and looked at him. I had to put my hand in my pocket to keep it still. "It just stinks, that's all. The guy was crying. You'd have to see him to know what he looked like and you didn't see him. Grown men don't cry like that. It stinks."

"Your're a crazy bastard," Pat said.

"So I've been told. Does the D.A. want to see me?"

"No, you were lucky it broke so fast."

"See you around then, Pat. I'll keep in touch with you."

"Do that," he said. I think he was laughing at me inside. I wasn't laughing though. There wasn't a damn thing to laugh about when you saw a guy cry, kiss his kid, then go out and make him an orphan.

Like I said, the whole thing stunk.

To high heaven.

It took me a little while to get over to the East Side. I cruised up the block where the murder happened, reached the corner and swung down to the street where Decker had lived. It was one of those shabby blocks a few years away from condemnation. The sidewalks were littered with ancient baby buggies, a horde of kids playing in the garbage on the sidewalks and people on the stoops who didn't give a damn what the kids did so long as they could yap and slop beer.

The number I had picked from Pat's report was 164, a four-story brownstone that seemed to tilt out toward the street. I parked the car and climbed out, picking my way through the swarm of kids, then went up the steps in to the vestibule. There wasn't any door, so I didn't have to ring any bells. One mailbox had SUPT scratched into the metal case under the 1-C. I walked down the dark channel of the hallway until I counted off three doors and knocked.

A guy loomed out of the darkness. He was a big guy, all right, about two inches over me with a chest like a barrel. There might have been a lot of fat under his hairy skin, but there was a lot of muscle there too.

"Watta ya want?" The way he said it you could tell he was used to scaring people right off.

I said, "Information, friend. What ya bet you give it to me?"

I watched his hands. They looked like they wanted to grab me. I stood balancing myself on my toes lightly so he'd get the idea that whatever he had I had enough to get away from him. Just like that he laughed. "You're a cocky little punk."

"You're the first guy who ever called me little, friend."

He laughed again. "Come on inside and have some coffee and keep your language where it belongs. I got all kinds of visitors today."

There was another long hallway with some light at the end that turned out be a kitchen. The big guy stood in the doorway nodding me in and I saw the priest at the table nibbling at a hard roll. The big guy said, "Father, this is . . . uh, what's the name?"

"Mike Hammer. Hello, Father."

The priest held out a big hand and we shook. Then the super tapped his chest with a forefinger. "Forgot myself, I did. John Vileck's the name. Sit down and have a bite and let's hear what you got on your mind." He took another cup and saucer off the shelf and filled it up. "Sugar'n milk's on the table."

When I was sugared and stirred I put my cards on the table. "I'm a private investigator. Right now I'm trying to get a line on a guy who lived here until last night."

Both the priest and the super exchanged glances quickly. "You mean William Decker?" the priest asked.

"That's right."

"May I ask who is retaining you?"

"Nobody, Father. I'm just sore, that's all. I was there when Decker was knocked off and I didn't like it. I'm on my own time and my own capital." I tried the coffee. It was strong as acid and hot as hell.

Vileck stared at his cup, swirling it around to cool it off. "Decker was an all-right guy. Had a nice wife, too. The cops was here last night and then morning again."

"Today?"

He looked up at me, his teeth tight together. "Yeah, I called 'em in about an hour before you come along. Couple cops in a patrol car. Me and the Father here went upstairs to look around and somebody'd already done a little looking on their own. The place's a wreck. Turned everything upside down."

The priest put his cup down and leaned back in his chair. "Perhaps you can make something of it, Mr. Hammer."

"Maybe I can. If the police have the right idea, whoever searched Decker's place was looking for a pile of dough that he was supposed to have clipped during a robbery last night. The reason he was bumped was because he never got that dough to start with and knew his pals wouldn't believe him. He tried to get out but they nailed him anyway. Apparently they thought that when he came back to get his kid he stashed the money figuring to pick it up later."

Vileck said, "The bastards!" then looked across the table. "Sorry, Father."

The priest smiled gently. "Mr. Hammer . . . do you know anything at all about William Decker?"

"I know he had a record. Did you?"

"Yes, he told me about that some time ago. You see, what puzzles me is the fact that William was such a straight-forward fellow. He was doing his best to live a perfect life. It wasn't easy for him, but he seemed to be making a good job of it."

Vileck nodded agreement. "That's right, too. Me and the Father here was the only ones around here that knew he had a record. When he first moved here he made no bones about it, then he started having trouble keeping a job because guys don't like for ex-cons to be working for them. Tell you somethin' . . . Decker was as honest as they come. None of this wrong stuff for him, see? Wouldn't even cheat at cards and right on time with his rent and his bills. Never no trouble at all. What do you make of it?"

"Don't you know?"

There was genuine bewilderment in his eyes. "For the love of me, I sure don't see nothing. He was okay all the way. Always doing things fer his kid since his wife died of cancer."

"Then he had it tough, eh?"

"Yeah, real tough. Doctors come high and he couldn't afford much. She was supposed to have an operation and he finally got her lined up for it, but by that time it was too late and she died a few days after they cut her apart. Decker was in bad shape for a while."

"He drink much?" I asked.

"Nope. Never had a drop all that time. He didn't want to do nothin' that might hurt his kid. He sure was crazy about that boy. That's why he was strictly on the up and up."

The priest had been listening, nodding occasionally. When Vileck finished he said, "Mr. Hammer, a week ago William came to church to see me and asked me if I would keep his insurance policies. They are all made out to the child, of course, and he wanted to be sure that if ever anything happened to him the child would be well provided for."

That one stopped me for a second. I said, "Tell me, was he jumpy at the time? I mean, now that you look back, did he seem to have anything on his mind at all?"

"Yes, now that I look back I'd say that he *was* upset about something. At the time I believed it was due to his wife having died. However, his story was plausible enough. Being that he had to work, he wanted his important papers in safe hands. I never believed that he was intending to . . . to . . ."

Vileck balled his hands up and knocked his knuckles together. "Nuts. I don't believe he done it because he was going to rob a joint. The guy was straight as they come."

"Some things happen to make a guy go wrong," I said. "Did he need dough at all?"

"Sure he needed dough. He'd get in maybe two, three days a week on the docks . . . pier 51 it was, but that was just enough to cover his eats. He lived pretty close, but he got by."

"Any friends?"

The super shrugged. "Sometimes a guy from the docks would come up awhile. He played chess with the blind newsie down the block every Monday night. Both of 'em picked it up in the big house. Nope, can't say that he had any other friends 'cept me. I liked the guy pretty much."

"No reason why he needed money . . . nothing like that?"

"Hell, not now. Before the wife died, sure. Not now though."

I nodded, finished my coffee and turned to the priest. "Father, did Decker make any tentative plans concerning the boy at all?"

"Yes, he did. It was his intention that the boy be brought up by one of our church organizations. We discussed it and he went so far as to make a will. The insurance money will take care of the lad until he finishes school, and what else Decker had was to be held in trust for his boy. This whole affair is very distressing. If only he had come to me with his problem! Always before he came to the church for advice, but this time when he needed to most he failed. Really, I. . . ."

"Father, I have the boy. He's being well cared for at present and whenever you're ready I'll be glad to turn him over to you. That kid is the reason I'm in this and when I get the guy that made him an orphan they can get another grave ready in potter's field. This whole town needs its nose wiped bad. I'm sick of having to live with some of the scum that breeds here and in my own little way I'm going to do something about it."

"Please . . . my son! I . . ."

"Don't preach to me now, Father. Maybe when it's over, but not now."

"But surely you can't be serious."

Vileck studied my face a second, then said, "He is, Father. If I can help ya out, pal . . . lemme know, will ya?"

"I'll let you know," I said. "When you make arrangements for the boy, Father, look me up in the phone book. By the way, who was the friend of Decker's . . . the one on the docks?"

"Umm . . . think his name was Booker. No, Hooker, that's it. Hooker. Mel Hooker."

I pushed the cup back and shoved away from the table.

"That's all then. Any chance of taking a look around the apartment?"

"Sure, go on up. Top floor, first door off the landing. And it won't do no good to ask them old biddies nothin'. They was all doing the weekly wash when whoever took the place apart was there. Once a week they get hot water and their noses were all in the sinks."

"Thanks," I said. "For the coffee too."

"Don't mention it."

"So long, Father. You'll buzz me later?"

He nodded unhappily. "Yes, I will. Please . . . no violence."

I grinned at him so he'd feel better and walked down the tunnel to the hall.

Vileck hadn't been wrong about somebody taking the place apart. They had started at one end of the three tiny rooms and wound up at the other leaving a trail of wreckage behind them that could have been sifted through a window screen. It was one hell of a mess. The bag of garbage beside the door that had been waiting to get thrown out had been scattered with a kick and when I saw it I felt like laughing because whatever they were looking for they didn't get. There was no stopping place in the search to indicate that the great *It* had been located.

For a while I prowled through the ruin of poverty, picking up a kid's toy here and there, a woman's bauble, a few work-worn things that had belonged to Decker. I even did a little probing in a few spots myself, but there wasn't a damn thing of any value around. I finished my butt and flipped it into the sink, then closed the door and got out of there.

I had a nasty taste in my mouth because so far it looked like Pat was right all along the line. Decker had gotten himself loused up with a couple of boys and pulled a job that didn't pay off. The chances were that they had cased the joint so well they wouldn't have believed him when he gave them the story of the nearly empty safe.

I sat there in the car and thought about it. In fact, I gave it a hell of a lot of thought. I thought so much about it I got playing all the angles against each other until all I could see was Decker's face with the tears rolling down his cheeks as he bent over to kiss the kid.

So I said a lot of dirty words.

The goon who drove the car was still running around loose and if I had to go after somebody it'd might as well be him. I stepped on the starter, dragged away from the curb and started back across town.

It was more curiosity than anything else that put me on Riverside Drive. When I finally got there I decided that it might be a good idea to cruise around a little bit and see if anybody with a pair of sharp eyes might have spotted the boys who cased the joint before they pulled the job.

I didn't have any more luck than you could stuff in your eye. That section of town was a money district, and the people who lived there only had eyes for the dollar sign. They were all sheer-faced apartment buildings with fancy doormen doing the honors out front and big, bright Caddies hauled up close to the curb.

One of the janitors thought he remembered a Buick and a couple of men that hung around the neighborhood a week back but he couldn't be sure. For two bucks he took me through an underground alley to the back court and let me have a look around.

Hell, Decker had had it easy. Every one of the buildings had the same kind of passageway from front to back, and once you were in the rear court it was a snap to reach up and grab the bottom rung of the fire ladder. After I had my look I told the guy thanks and went back to the street.

Two doors down was the building where Decker had pulled the job so I loped in past the beefy doorman and went over the bellboard until I found LEE, MARSHA and gave the button a nudge. There was a phone set in a niche in the wall that gave the cliff dweller upstairs a chance to check the callers before unlocking the door and I had to stand with it at my ear a full minute before I heard it click.

Then heaven answered. What a voice she had. It made the kind of music song writers try to imitate and can't. All it said was, "Yes?" and I started getting mental images of LEE, MARSHA that couldn't be sent through the mail.

I tried hard to sound like a gentleman. "Miss Lee?"

She said it was.

"This is Mike Hammer. I'm a private investigator. Could I speak to you a few minutes?"

"Oh . . . about the robbery?"

"That's right," I said.

"Why . . . yes. I suppose you may. Come right up."

So I went up to heaven in a private elevator that let me out in a semi-private foyer where cloud 4D had a little brass hammer instead of a doorbell. I raised it, let it drop and a ponderous nurse with a mustache scowled me in.

And there was my angel in a big chair by the window. At least the right half of her was angel. The left half sported a very human mouse under the eye and a welt as big as a fist across her jaw.

My face must have been doing some pretty funny things trying to keep from laughing, because she tapped her fingers on the end of the chair and said, "You had better be properly sympathetic, Mr. Hammer, or out you go."

I couldn't hold it back and I laughed anyway, but I didn't go out. "Half of you is the most beautiful girl I ever saw," I grinned.

"I half thank you," she grinned back. "You can leave if you

want to, Mrs. Ross. You'll be back at five?"

The nurse told her she would and picked up her coat. When she made sure her patient was all right she left. I was hoping she'd get herself a shave while she was out.

"Please sit down, Mr. Hammer. Can I get you a drink?"

"No, I'll get it myself. Just tell me where to find the makings."

My angel got up and pulled the filmy housecoat around her like a veil. "Hell, I'll get it myself. This leading the life of a cripple is a pain. Everybody treats me like an invalid. The nurse is the 'compliments of the management' hoping I don't sue them for neglecting to keep their property properly protected. She's a good cook, otherwise I would have told them to keep her."

She walked over to a sideboard and I couldn't take my eyes off her. None of this fancy hip-swinging business; just a nice plain walk that could do more than all the fancy wriggling a stripper could put out. Her legs brushing the sheer nylon of the housecoat made it crackle and cling to her body until every curve was outlined in white with pink undertones.

She had tawny brown hair that fell loosely about her shoulders, with eyes that matched perfectly, and a mouth that didn't have to go far to meet mine. Marsha must have just come from a bath, because she smelt fresh and soapy without any veneer of perfume.

When she turned around she had two glasses in her hands and she looked even prettier coming toward me than going away. Her breasts were precocious things that accentuated the width of her shoulders and the smooth contours of her stomach, rising jauntily against the nylon as though they were looking for a way out.

I thought she was too busy balancing the glasses to notice what I was doing, but I was wrong. She handed me a highball and said, "Do I pass?"

"What?"

"Inspection. Do I pass?"

"If I could get my mouth unpuckered I'd let out a long low whistle," I told her. "I'm getting tired of seeing dames in clothes that make them look like a tulip having a hard time coming up. With all the women wearing crew cuts with curled ends these days it's a pleasure to see one with hair for a change."

"That's a left-handed compliment if ever I heard one. What a lover you'd make."

I looked at her a long time. "Don't fool yourself."

She looked at me just as long. "I'm not."

We raised the glasses in a silent toast and sipped the top off them. "Now, Mr. Hammer . . ."

"Mike."

Her lips came apart in a smile. "Mike. It fits you perfectly. What was it you wanted to see me about?"

"First I want to know why you seem so damn familiar. Even with the shiner you remind me of somebody I've seen before."

Her hands smoothed the front of the housecoat. "Thank you for remembering." She let her eyes drift to the piano that stood in the corner and the picture on top of it. I picked up my drink and walked over to it and this time I did let out a long low whistle.

It was a big shot of Marsha in a pre-Civil War dress that came up six inches above her waist before nature took over. The make-up artist had to do very little to make her the most beautiful woman I had ever seen. She had been younger when it was taken, but me . . . I'd take Marsha like she was now. Time had only improved her. Almost hidden by the frame was a line that said the photo was released by the Allerton Motion Picture Company.

Marsha was familiar because I had seen her plenty of times before. So have you. Ten years ago she was an up-and-coming star in Hollywood.

"Yesteryear, those were the days," she said.

I put the picture back and sat down opposite her so I could see her better. She was well worth looking at and she didn't have to cross her legs to attract attention, either. They were nice legs, too.

"It's a wonder I forgot you," I said.

"Most people do. The public has a short memory."

"How come you quit?"

"Oh, it's a sad but brief story. Perhaps you read about it. There was a man, a bit player but a charming heel if ever I saw one. He played up to me to further his own career by picking up a lot of publicity. I was madly in love with him until I found that he was making a play for my secretary in his spare time. In my foolishness I made an issue of it and he told me how he was using me. So, I became the woman scorned and said if he saw her again I'd see that he was blacklisted off every lot in Hollywood. At the time I carried enough potential importance to let me get away with it. Anyway, he told my secretary that he'd never see her after that and she promptly went out and drove her car off a cliff.

"You know Hollywood. It was bad publicity and it knocked

me back plenty. Before they could tear my contract up I resigned and came back East where I stuck my savings in investments that allow me to live like I want to."

I made a motion with my head to take in the room. The place held a fortune in well-chosen furniture and the pictures on the wall weren't any cheap copies, either. Every one of them must have cost four figures. If this was plain living, I'd like to take a crack at it myself.

I pulled out a smoke and she snapped the catch on a table lighter, holding the flame out to me. "Now . . . you didn't come up here for the story of my life," she said. Her eyes danced for me.

"Nope, I want to know about the robbery."

"There's little to tell, Mike. I left here a few minutes before seven to pick up one of the Little Theater members who broke his arm in a fall, drove him home, stopped off at a friend's for a while then came in about a quarter to twelve. As I was about to turn on the lights I saw the beam of a flashlight inside here and like a fool ran right in. For a second I saw this man outlined against the window and the next thing I knew I was flat on my back. I got up and tried to scream, then he hit me again and the world turned upside down. I was still there on the floor when the police came."

"I got that much of the story from Captain Chambers. Did they tell you the guy is dead?"

"No, they haven't gotten in touch with me at all. What happened?"

"One of his partners killed him. Ran right over him with the car."

"Did they . . . recover the money?"

"Nope, I'm beginning to think they never will, either."

"But . . ."

I dragged on the butt and flipped the ashes off in the tray. "I'm willing to bet that the guy chucked the cash and your pearls on the top of some rubbish pile. He didn't come in here for any three hundred bucks. That kind of job isn't worth the trouble."

She bit her lips and frowned at me. "You know something, Mike, I was thinking the same thing."

I looked at her curiously. "Go on."

"I think this . . . this robber knew what he was doing, but got his floors mixed. Do you know Marvin Holmes?"

"The playboy who keeps a stable of blondes?"

"That's right. He has the apartment directly above me. The

rooms are laid out exactly the same and even the wall safe is in the identical spot as mine. He always keeps a small fortune on hand and he wasn't home last night either. I met him just as I was going out and he mentioned something about a night club."

"You've been up there?"

"Several times. He's always throwing parties. I don't rate because I'm not a blonde," she added as an afterthought.

It made sense, all right. Just to see how much sense it did make I picked Marvin Holmes' number out of the phone book and dialed it. A butler with a German accent answered, told me yes, Mr. Holmes was at home and put him on. I lied and said I was from the insurance company and wanted to know if he kept a bundle at his fingertips. The sap sounded half looped and was only too happy to tell me there was better than ten grand in his safe and tacked on that he thought the guy who opened the safe on the floor below him had made a mistake. I thanked him and hung up.

Marsha said, "Did he . . ."

"The guy has the same idea as you, chick. He thinks there was a one-floor error and for my money you're both right."

Her shoulders made a faint gesture of resignation. "Well, I guess there's little that can be done then. I had hoped to recover the pearls for sentimental reasons. I wore them in my first picture."

If I grinned I couldn't have been nice to look at. My lips felt tight over my teeth and I shook my head. "It's a dirty mess, Marsha. Two guys are dead already and there'll be another on the way soon. The guy who robbed your place left a baby behind, then went right out to get chopped down. Hell, it isn't what he took, it's why he took it. He was on the level for a long time then just like that he went bad and no guy like him is going to pull something that'll let his own kid get tossed to the dogs.

"Damn it, I was there and saw it! I watched him cry and kiss his kid good-by and go out and cash in his chips. Now I have the kid and I know what he must have felt like. Goddamn it anyway, there's a reason why these things happen and that's what I want. Maybe it's only a little reason and maybe it's a big one, but by God, I'm going to get it."

Her eyes were square and steady on mine, a deep liquid brown that got deeper as she stared at me. "You're a strange kind of guy," she said. I picked up my hat and stood up. She came forward to meet me, holding her hand out. "Mike . . . about the child . . . if I can help out with it, well I'm pretty well set up financially . . ."

I squeezed her hand. "You know, you're a strange kind of guy yourself."

"Thanks, Mike."

"But I can take care of the kid okay." She gave me a lopsided smile that made her look good even with the shiner. "By the way . . . would you happen to have an extra picture around . . . like that one?" I nodded toward the piano.

For a long space of time she held on to my hand and ran her eyes over my face. "What for, won't I do in person?"

I let my hat drop and it stayed on the floor. My hands ran up her arms until my fingers were digging into her shoulders and I drew her in close. She was all woman, every bit of her. Her body was taut, her breasts high and firm with all the vitality of youth, and I could feel the warm outlines of her legs as I pressed her against me. She raised herself on her toes deliberately, tantalizing, a subtle motion that I knew was an invitation not lightly given.

I wanted to kiss her, but I knew that when I did I'd want to make it so good and so hard it would hurt long enough to be remembered and now wasn't the time. Later, when her mouth was smooth and soft again.

"You'll be back, Mike?" she whispered.

She knew the answer without being told. I pushed her away and picked up my hat.

There were things in this city that could be awfully nasty.

There were things in this city that could be awfully nice too.

chapter three ▰▰▰▰▰▰▰▰▰

I STOPPED BY the office that afternoon. The only one in the building to say hello was the elevator operator and he had to look twice to recognize me. It was a hell of a feeling. You live in the city your whole life, take off for six months and you are unknown when you come back. I opened the door and felt a little better when I saw the same old furniture in the same old place. The only thing that was missing was Velda. Her desk was a lonely corner in the anteroom, dusted and ready for a new occupant.

I said something dirty. I was always saying something dirty these days.

She had left a folder of correspondence she thought I might want to see on my desk. It wasn't anything important. Just a record of bills paid, my bank statements and a few letters. I closed the folder and stowed it away in a drawer. There was a fifth of good whiskey still there with the wrapper on. I stripped off the paper, uncorked the bottle and looked at it. I worked the top off and smelled it. Then I put it back and shut the drawer. I felt stinking and didn't like the feeling.

Outside on Velda's desk the phone started ringing. I went out in a hurry hoping it might be her, but a rough voice said, "You Mike Hammer?"

"Yeah, who's this?"

"Johnny Vileck. You know, the super down in Decker's building. I had a hell of a time tryin' to get you. Lucky I remembered your name."

"What's up?" I asked.

"I was thinking over what we was speaking about this morning. Remember you asked me about Decker needin' dough?"

"Uh-huh."

"When I went out to get the paper I got talking to the blind newsie on the corner. The old guy was pretty busted up about it. Him and Decker was pretty good friends. Anyway, one night after the old lady died, he was up there playing chess when this guy come around. He wanted to know when Decker was going to get the cash he owed. Decker paid him something and the guy left and after it he mentioned that he had to borrow a big chunk to cover the wife's operation. Mentioned three grand."

I let it jell in my head for a minute, twisting it around until it made sense. "Where could he get that kind of dough?"

Vileck grunted and made a shrug I couldn't see. "Beats me. He never borrowed nuthing and it's damn sure he didn't go to no bank."

"Anybody in the neighborhood got it?"

"Not in this neighborhood, pal. Once somebody'll hit a number or a horse, but he ain't lending it out, you can bet. There's plenty of tough guys around here who show up with a roll sometimes, but it's flash money and they're either gone or in jail the next day. Nope, he didn't get it around here."

"Thanks for the dope, John. If you ever need a favor, let me know."

"Sure, pal, glad to let you know about it."

"Look . . . did you mention this to the cops?"

"Naw. I found out after they left. Besides, they don't hear from me unless they ask. Cops is okay long as they stay outa my joint."

I told him so-long and put the receiver back. There was the reason for murder and it was a good one. Three grands' worth. Now it was coming out right. Decker went into somebody for three grand and he had to bail himself out by stealing it. So he made a mistake when he raids the wrong apartment and his pals didn't believe it. They thought he was holding out. So they bump him figuring to lift a jackpot and all they got was a measly three hundred bucks and a string of pearls.

Damn it, the whole thing made me boil over! Because a guy couldn't wait to get his dough back a kid is made an orphan. My city, yeah. How many places around town was the same thing going on?

I sat down on the edge of the desk to think about it and the whole thing hit me suddenly and sharply and way back in my head I could hear that crazy music start until it was beating through my brain with a maddening frenzy that tried to drive away any sanity I had left. I cursed to myself until it was gone then went back to my desk and pulled out the bottle. This time I had a drink.

It took me all afternoon to find what I wanted. I went down to the docks and let my P.I. ticket and my badge get me inside the gates until I reached the right paymaster who had handled William Decker's card. He was a little guy in his late fifties with an oversize nose built into a face that was streaked with little purple veins.

He made me wait until he finished tallying up his report, then stuck the clipboard on a nail in the wall and swung around in his chair. He said, "What's on your mind, buddy?"

I offered him a smoke and he waved it away to chew on a ratty cigar. "Remember a guy named Decker?"

He grunted a Yes and waited.

"He have any close friends on the docks here?"

"Might have. What'cha want to know for?"

"I heard he died. I owed him a few bucks and I want to see that it goes to his estate."

The guy clucked and sucked his tongue a minute. He opened his desk drawer and riffled through a file of cards until he came to the one he wanted. "Well, here's his address and he's got a kid. Got him down for two dependents, but I think his wife died awhile back."

"I found that out. If I can dig up a pal of his maybe he'll know something more about him."

"Yeah. Well, seems like he always shaped in with a guy named Hooker. Mel Hooker. Tall thin guy with a scar on his face. They got paid off today so they'll be in the joints 'cross the way cashing their checks. Why don'cha go over an' try?"

I stuffed the butt in the ash tray on the desk. "I'll do that. Give me his address in case I miss him."

He scratched something on a pad and handed it over. I said thanks and left.

It wasn't that easy. I thought I hit every saloon on the street until a guy told me about a couple I had missed and then I found him. The place was a rattrap where they'd take the drunks that had been kicked out of other places and make them spend their last buck. You had to go down a couple of steps to reach the door and before you reached it you could smell what you were walking into.

The place was a lot bigger than I expected. They were lined up two deep at the bar and when they couldn't stand any more they sat down at the bench along the wall. One guy had passed out and was propped up against a partition with his pockets turned inside out.

Mel Hooker was down the back watching a shuffleboard game. He had half a bag on and looked it. The yellow glare of the overhead lights brought out the scar that ran from his forehead to his chin in bold relief almost as if it was still an ugly gash. I walked over and pulled out the chair beside him.

He looked at me enough to say, "Beat it."

"You Mel Hooker?"

"Who wants to know?" His voice had a nasty drunken snarl to it.

"How'd you like to get the other side of your face opened up, feller?"

He dropped his glass like it was shot out of his hand and tried to get up off his chair. I shoved him back without any trouble. "Stay put, Mel. I want to talk to you."

His breathing was noisy. "I don't wanna talk to you," he said.

"Tough stuff, Mel. You'll talk if I tell you to. It's about a friend of yours. He's dead. His name was William Decker."

The flesh around the scar seemed to get whiter. Something changed in his eyes and he half twisted his head. One of the guys at the shuffleboard was taking a long time to make his play. Mel unfolded himself and nodded to an empty table over in the corner. "Over . . . here. Make it quick."

I got up and went back to the bar for a pair of drinks and brought them back to the table. When Mel took his his hand wasn't too steady. I let him take half of it down in one gulp before I asked, "Who'd he owe dough to, Mel?"

He almost dropped this glass, too. In time, he recovered it and set it down very deliberately and wiped his mouth with the back of his hand. "You a cop?"

"I'm a private investigator."

"You're gonna be a dead investigator if you don't get the hell outa here."

"I asked you a question."

His tongue flicked out and whipped over his lips. "Get this, I don't know nothing about nothing. Bill was a friend of mine but his business was his own. Now lemme alone."

"He needed three grand, Mel. He borrowed it from somebody. He didn't get it around home so he must have got it someplace around here."

"You're nuts."

"You're a hell of a friend," I said, "one hell of a friend."

Hooker dropped his head and stared at his hands. When he looked up his mouth was drawn back tight. His voice came out barely a whisper. "Listen, Mac, you better quit asking questions. Bill was my friend and I'd help him if I could, but he's dead and that's that. You see this scar I got? I'd sooner have that than be dead. Now blow and lemme alone."

He wouldn't look back at me when he left. He staggered out to the bar and through the mob around it until he reached the door, then disappeared up the stairs. I polished my drink off and waved the waiter over with another. He gave me a frozen look and snatched the buck out of my hand.

The place got too damn quiet. The weights weren't slamming on the shuffleboard and everybody at the bar seemed to have taken a sudden interest in the television set over the bar. I sat there and waited for my change, but I had the drink gone without seeing it.

This I liked. This I was waiting for because the stupid bastards should have known better. My God, did I look like some flunkey from the sticks or did the wise boys lose their memories too?

I pushed the glass back and got up. I found the men's room in the back by the smell and did what I had to do and started to wash my hands. That's how long they gave me.

The guy in the double-breasted suit in the doorway spoke out of the corner of his mouth to somebody behind him. His little pig eyes looked like he was getting ready to enjoy himself. "He's a big one, ain't he?"

"Yeah." The other guy stepped in and seemed to fill up the doorway.

The little guy's hand came out of his pocket with a sap about a foot long and he swung it against his knee waiting to see if I was going to puke or start bawling. The big guy took his time about slipping on the knucks. Outside the volume on the television went up so loud it blasted its way all the way back there.

I dropped the paper towel and backed off until my shoulders were up against the doors of the pot. The little guy was leering. His mouth worked until the spit rolled down his chin and his shoulder started to draw back the sap. His pal closed in on the side, only his eyes showing that there might be some human intelligence behind that stupid expression.

The goddamn bastards played right into my hands. They thought they had me nice and cold and just as they were set to carve me into a raw mess of skin I dragged out the .45 and let them look down the hole so they could see where sudden death came from.

It was the only kind of talk they knew. The little guy stared too long. He should have been watching my face. I snapped the side of the rod across his jaw and laid the flesh open to the bone. He dropped the sap and staggered into the big boy with a scream starting to come up out of his throat only to get it cut off in the middle as I pounded his teeth back into his mouth with the end of the barrel. The big guy tried to shove him out of the way. He got so mad he came right at me with his head down and I took my own damn time about kicking him in the face. He smashed into the door and lay there bubbling. So I kicked him again and he stopped bubbling. I pulled the knucks off his hand then went over and picked up the sap. The punk was vomiting on the floor, trying to claw his way under the sink. For laughs I gave him a taste of his own sap on the back of his hand and felt the bones go into splinters. He wasn't going to be using any tools for a long time.

They moved aside and let me get in to the bar. They moved aside so far you'd think I was contaminated. The bartender looked at me and his thick lips rubbed together. I dropped the knucks and the sap on the bar and waved the bartender over with my forefinger. "I got some change coming," I said.

He turned around and rang up a no sale on the register and handed me fifty-five cents.

If somebody breathed before I left I didn't hear it. I got out of there feeling like myself again and went back to the car. I only had one thing to do before I saw Pat. I checked the slip the timekeeper gave me and saw that Mel Hooker lived not too far from where Decker had lived. I got snarled up in traffic halfway there and it was dark by the time I found his address.

The place was a rooming house with the usual sign outside advertising a lone vacancy and a landlady on the bottom floor using her window for a crow's nest. She was at the door before I got up the steps waiting to smile if I was a renter or glare if I was a visitor.

She glared when I asked her if Mel Hooker had come in yet. Her finger waved up the stairs. "Ten minutes ago and drunk. Don't you two raise no ruckus or out you both go."

If she had been nicer I would have soothed her feelings with a bill. All she got was a sharp thanks and I went upstairs. I heard him shuffling around the room and when I knocked all sound stopped. I knocked again and he dragged across the floor and snapped the lock back. I don't know who he expected to see. It sure wasn't me.

I didn't ask to come in; I gave the door a shove and he reeled back. His face had lost its tenseness and was dull, his mouth sagging. There was a table in the middle of the room and I perched on it, watching him close the door, then turn around until he faced me.

"Christ!" he said.

"What'd you expect, Mel?" I lit a Lucky and peered at him through the smoke. "You're a hell of a guy," I told him. "I guess you knew those boys would tag after me and you didn't want to stick around to see the blood."

"Wh . . . what happened?"

I grinned at him. "I've been messing around with bastards like that for a long time. They should have remembered my face. Now they're going to have trouble remembering what they used to look like before. Did you pull the same stunt on your friend Decker, Mel? Did you beat it when they went looking for him?"

He staggered over to a chair and collapsed in it. "I don't . . . know . . . what'cha talking about."

I leaned forward on the edge of the table and spit the words out. "I'm talking about the loan shark racket. I'm talking about a guy named William Decker who used to be your friend and needed dough bad. He couldn't get it from a legitimate source so he hit up a loan shark and got what he needed. When he couldn't pay off they put the pressure on him probably through his kid so he tries to cop a bank roll from a rich guy's safe. He miffed the job and they gave him the works. Now do you know what I'm talking about?"

Hooker said, "Christ!" again and grabbed the arms of the chair. "Friend, you gotta get outa here, see? You gotta leave me alone!"

"What's the matter, Mel? You were a tough guy when I met you tonight. What's getting you so soft?"

For a minute a crazy madness passed over his face, then he let out a gasp and buried his head in his hands. "Damn it, get outa here!"

"Yeah, I'll get out. When you tell me who's banking the soaks along the dock I'll get out."

"I . . . I can't. Oh, Lord, lemme alone, will ya!"

"They're tough, huh?" He read something in my words and his eyes came up in a series of little jerks until they were back on mine. "Are they tougher than the guys you pushed on me?"

Mel swallowed hard. "I didn't . . ."

"Don't crap me, friend. Those guys weren't there by accident. They weren't there just for me, either. Somebody's got a finger on you, haven't they?"

He didn't answer.

"They were there for you," I said, "only you saw a nice way to shake them loose on me. What gives?"

His finger moved by itself and traced the scar that lay along the side of his jaw. "Look, I got cut up once, I did. I don't want to fool around with them guys no more. Honest, I didn't do nothing! I don't know why they was there but they was!"

"So you're in a trap too," I said.

"No I ain't!" He shouted it. His face was a sickly white and he drooled a little bit. "I'm clean and I don't know why they're sticking around me. Why the hell did you come butting in for?"

"Because I want to know why your pal Decker needed dough."

"Christ, his wife was dying. He had to have it. How'd I know he couldn't pay it back!"

"Pay what back to who?"

His tongue flashed over his lips and his mouth clammed shut.

"You have a union and a welfare fund for that, don't you?"

This time he spit on the floor.

"Who'd you steer him to, Mel?"

He didn't answer me. I got up off the edge of the table and

jerked him to his feet. "Who was it, Mel . . . or do you want to find out what happened to the tough boys back in the bar?"

The guy went limp in my hands. He didn't try to get away. He just hung there in my fist, his eyes dead. His words came out slow and flat. "He needed the dough. We . . . thought we had a good tip on the ponies and pooled our dough."

"So?"

"We won. It wasn't enough so we threw it back on another tip, only Bill hit up a loan shark for a few hundred to lay a bigger bet. We won that one too and I pulled out with my share. Bill thought he could get a big kill quick and right after he paid the shark back, knocked him down for another grand to add to his stake and this time he went under."

"Okay, so he owed a grand."

Mel's head shook sadly. "It was bigger. You pay back one for five every week. It didn't take long to run it up into big money."

I let him go and he sank back into the chair. "Now names, Mel. Who was the shark?"

I barely heard him say, "Dixie Cooper. He hangs out in the Glass Bar on Eighth Avenue."

I picked up my deck of smokes and stuffed them in my pocket. I walked out without closing the door and down past the landlady who still held down her post in the vestibule. She didn't say anything until Mel hobbled to the door, glanced down the stairs and shut it. Then the old biddy humphed and let me out.

The sky had clouded up again, shutting out the stars and there was a damp mist in the air. I called Pat from a candy store down the corner and nobody answered his phone at home, so I tried the office. He was there. I told him to stick around and got back in my car.

Headquarters building was like a beehive without any bees when I got there. A lone squad car stood at the curb and the elevator operator was reading a paper inside his cab. The boys on the night stand had that bored look already and half of them were piddling around trying to keep busy.

I got in the elevator and let him haul me up to Pat's floor. Down the corridor a typewriter was clicking busily and I heard Pat rummaging around the drawers of his file cabinet. When I pushed the door open he said, "Be right with you, Mike."

So I parked and watched him work for five minutes. When he got through at the cabinet I asked him, "How come you're working nights?"

"Don't you read the papers?"

"I didn't come up against any juicy murders."

"Murders, hell. The D.A. has me and everybody else he can scrape together working on that gambling probe."

"What's he struggling so hard for, it isn't an election year for him. Besides, the public's going to gamble anyway."

Pat pulled out his chair and slid into it. "The guy's got scruples. He has it in for Ed Teen and his outfit."

"He's not getting Teen," I said.

"Well, he's trying."

"Where do you come in?"

Pat shrugged and reached for a cigarette. "The D.A. tried to break up organized gambling in this town years ago. It flopped like all the other probes flopped . . . for lack of evidence. He's never made a successful raid on a syndicate establishment since he went after them."

"There's a hole in the boat?"

"A what?"

"A leak."

"Of course. Ed Teen has a pipeline right into the D.A.'s office somehow. That's why the D.A. is after his hide. It's a personal affront to him and he won't stand for it. Since he can't nail Teen down with something, he's conducting an investigation into his past. We know damn well that Teen and Grindle pulled a lot of rough stuff and if we can tie a murder on them they'll be easy to take."

"I bet. Why doesn't he patch that leak?"

Pat did funny things with his mouth. "He's surrounded by men he trusts and I trust and we can't find a single person who's talking out of turn. Everybody's been investigated. We even checked for dictaphones, that's how far we went. It seems impossible, but nevertheless, the leak's here. Hell, the D.A. pulls surprise raids that were cooked up an hour before and by the time he gets there not a soul's around. It's uncanny."

"Uncanny my foot. The D.A. is fooling with guys as smart as he is himself. They've been operating longer too. Look, any chance of breaking away early tonight?"

"With this here?" He pointed toward a pile of papers on his desk. "They all have to be classified, correlated and filed. Nope, not tonight, Mike. I'll be here for another three hours yet."

Outside the racket of the typewriter stopped and a stubby brunette came in with a wire basket of letters. Right behind her was another brunette, but far from stubby. What the first one didn't have she had everything of and she waved it around in front of you like a flag.

Pat saw my foolish grin and when the stubby one left said, "Miss Scobie, have you met Mike Hammer?"

I got one of those casual glances with a flicker of a smile. "No, but I've heard the District Attorney speak of him several times."

"Nothing good, I hope," I said.

"No, nothing good." She laughed at me and finished sorting out the papers on Pat's desk.

"Miss Scobie is one of the D.A.'s secretaries," Pat said. "For a change I have some help around here. He sent over three girls to do the manual labor."

"I'm pretty good at that myself." I think I was leering.

The Scobie babe gave me the full voltage from a pair of deep blue eyes. "I've heard that too."

"You should quit getting things secondhand."

She packed the last of the papers in a new pile and tacked them together with a clip. When she turned around she gave me a look Pat couldn't see but had a whole book written there in her face. "Perhaps I should," she said.

I could feel the skin crawl up my back just from the tone of her voice.

Pat said, "You're a bastard, Mike. You and the women."

"They're necessary." I stared at the door that closed behind her.

His mouth cracked in a grin. "Not Miss Scobie. She knows her way around the block without somebody holding her hand. Doesn't her name mean anything to you?"

"Should it?"

"Not unless you're a society follower. Her family is big stuff down in Texas. The old man had a ranch where he raised horses until they brought oil in. Then he sat back and enjoyed life. He raises racing nags now."

"The Scobie Stables?"

"Uh-huh. Ellen's his daughter. When she was eighteen she and the old boy had a row and she packed up and left. This department job is the first one she ever had. Been here better than fifteen years. She's the gal the track hates to see around. When she makes a bet she collects."

"What the hell's she working for then?"

"Ask her."

"I'm asking you."

Pat grinned again. "The old man disinherited her when she wouldn't marry the son of his friend. He swore she'd never see a penny of his dough, so now she'll only bet when a Scobie horse is running and with what she knows about horses, she's hard to fool. Every time she wins she sends a telegram to the old boy stating the amount and he burns up. Don't ask her to tip you off though. She won't do it."

"Why doesn't the D.A. use her to get an inside track on the wire rooms?"

"He did, but she's too well known now. A feature writer for one of the papers heard about the situation, and gave it a big play in a Sunday supplement a few years ago, so she's useless there."

I leaned back in my chair and stared at the ceiling. "Texas gal. I like the way they're built."

"Yeah, big." Pat grunted. "A big one gets you every time." His fingers rapped on the desk. "Let's come back to earth, Mike. What's new?"

"Decker."

"That's not new. We're still looking for the driver who ran down his buddy. They found the car, you know."

I sat up straight.

"You didn't miss everything that night. There were two bullet holes in the back. One hit the rear window and the other went through the gas tank. The car was abandoned over in Brooklyn."

"Stolen heap?"

"Sure, what'd you expect? The slugs came from your gun, the tires matched the imprints in the body and there wasn't a decent fingerprint anywhere."

"Great."

"We'll wrap it up soon. The word's out."

"Great."

Pat scowled at me in disgust. "Hell, you're never satisfied."

I shook a cigarette out and lit up. Pat pushed an ash tray over to me. I said, "Pat, you got holes in your head if you think that this was a plain, simple job. Decker was in hock to a loan shark for a few grand and was being pressured into paying up. The guy was nuts about his kid and they probably told him the kid would catch it if he didn't come across."

"So?"

"Christ, *you* aren't getting to be a cynic like the rest of the cops, are you? You want things like this to keep on happening? You like murder to dirty up the streets just because some greaseball wants his dirty money! Hell, who's to blame . . . a poor jerk like

Decker or a torpedo who'll carve him up if he doesn't pay up?
Answer me that."

"There's a law against loan sharks operating in this state."

"There's a law against gambling, too."

Pat's face was dark with anger.

"The law has been enforced," he snapped.

I put the emphasis on the past tense. "It *has?* That's nice to
know. Who's running the racket now?"

"Damn it, Mike, that isn't my department."

"It should be; it caused the death of two men so far. What I
want to know is the racket organized or not?"

"I've heard that it was," he replied sullenly. "Fallon used to
bank it before he died. When the state cracked down on them
somebody took the sharks under their wing. I don't know who."

"Fallon, Fallon, hell, the guy's been dead since 1940 and he's
still making news."

"Well, you asked me."

I nodded. "Who's Dixie Cooper, Pat?"

His eyes went half shut. "Where do you get your information
from? Goddamn, you have your nose in everywhere."

"Who is he?"

"The guy's a stoolie for the department. He has no known
source of income, though he claims to be a promoter."

"Of what?"

"Of everything. He's a guy who knows where something is that
somebody else wants and collects a percentage from the buyer
and seller both. At least, that's what he says."

"Then he's full of you know what. The guy is a loan shark.
He's the one Decker hit up for the money."

"Can you prove it?"

"Uh-huh."

"Show me and we'll take him into custody."

I stood up and slapped on my hat. "I'll show you," I said. "I'll
have him screaming to talk to somebody in uniform just to keep
from getting his damn arms twisted off."

"Go easy, Mike."

"Yeah, I'll do just that. I'll twist 'em nice and easy like he
twisted Decker. I'll go easy, all right."

Pat gave me a long look with a frown behind it. When I said
so long he only nodded, and he was reaching for the phone as I
shut the door.

Down the hall another door slammed shut and the stubby
brunette came by, smiled at me politely and kept on going to the

elevator. After she got in I went back down the corridor to the office, pushed the door open and stuck my head in. Ellen Scobie had one foot on a chair with her dress hiked up as far as it would go, straightening her stocking.

"Pretty leg," I said.

She glanced back quickly without bothering to yank her dress down like most dames would. "I have another just like it," she told me. Her eyes were on full voltage again.

"Let's see."

So she stood up in one of those magazine poses and pulled the dress up slowly without stopping until it couldn't go any further and showed me. And she was right. The other was just as pretty if you wasted a sight like that trying to compare them.

I said, "I love brunettes."

"You love anything." She let the dress fall.

"Brunettes especially. Doing anything tonight?"

"Yes . . . I was going out with you, wasn't I? Something I should learn about manual labor?"

"Kid," I said, "I don't think you have anything to learn. Not a damn thing."

She laughed deep in her throat and came over and took my arm. "I'm crazy about heels," she said. "Let's go."

We passed by Pat's office again and I could still hear him on the phone. His voice had a low drone with a touch of urgency in it but I couldn't hear what he was saying. When we were downstairs in the car Ellen said, "I hope you realize that if we're seen together my boss will have you investigated from top to bottom."

"Then you do the investigating. I have some fine anatomy."

Her mouth clucked at me. "You know what I mean. He's afraid to trust himself these days."

"You can forget about me, honey. He's investigated me so often he knows how many moles I got. Who the hell's handing out the dope, anyway?"

"If I knew I'd get a promotion. Right now the office observes wartime security right down to burning everything in the wastebaskets in front of a policeman. You know what I think?"

"What?"

"Somebody sits in another building with a telescope and reads lips."

I laughed at her. "Did you tell the D.A. that?"

She grinned devilishly. "Uh-huh. I said it jokingly and damned if he didn't go and pull down the blinds. Everybody hates me now." She stopped and glanced out the windows, then looked back at me curiously. "Where're we going?"

"To see a guy about a guy," I said.

She leaned back against the cushions and closed her eyes. When she opened them again I was pulling into a parking lot in Fifty-second Street. The attendant took my keys and handed me a ticket. The evening was just starting to pick up and the gin mills lining the street were starting to get a play.

Ellen tugged at my hand. "We aren't drinking very fancy tonight, are we?"

"You come down here much?"

"Oh, occasionally. I don't go much for these places. Where are we going?"

"A place called the Glass Bar. It's right down the block."

"That fag joint," she said with disgust. "The last time I was there I had three women trying to paw me and a guy with me who thought it was funny."

"Hell, I'd like to paw you myself," I laughed.

"Oh, you will, you will." She was real matter-of-fact about it, but not casual, not a bit. I started to get that feeling up my back again.

The Glass Bar was a phony name for a phonier place. It was all chrome and plastic, and glass was only the thing you drank out of. The bar was a circular affair up front near the door with the back half of the place given over to tables and a bandstand. A drummer was warming up his traps with a pair of cuties squirming to his jungle rhythm while a handful of queers watched with their eyes oozing lust.

Ellen said, "The bar or back room?"

I tossed my hat at the redhead behind the check booth. "Don't know yet." The redhead handed me a pasteboard with a number on it and I asked her, "Dixie Cooper been in yet?"

She leaned halfway out of the booth and looked across the room. "Don't see him. Guess he must be in back. He came in about a half hour ago."

I said thanks and took Ellen's arm. We had a quick one at the bar, then pushed through the crowd to the back room where the babes were still squirming with the drummer showing no signs of tiring. He was all eyes for the wriggling hips and the table with the queers had been abandoned for one closer to the bandstand.

Only four other tables were occupied and the kind of people sitting there weren't the kind I was looking for. Over against the wall a guy was slouched in a chair reading a late tabloid while he sipped a beer. He had a hairline that came down damn near to his eyebrows and when his mouth moved as he read his top teeth stuck out at an angle. On the other side of the table a patsy was trying to drag him into a conversation and all he was getting was a grunt now and then.

The guy with the bleached hair looked up and smiled when I edged over, then the smile froze into a disgusted grimace when he saw Ellen. I said, "Blow, Josephine," and he arched his eyebrows and minced off.

Buck teeth didn't even bother to look at me.

Ellen didn't wait to be invited. She plunked herself in a chair with a grin and leaned on the table waiting for the fun to start.

Buck teeth interrupted his reading long enough to say, "Whatta you want?"

So I took the .45 out and slid it down between his eyes and the paper and let him stare at it until he went white all the way back of his ears. Then I sat down too. "You Dixie Cooper?"

His head came around like somebody had a string on it. "Yeah." It was almost a whisper and his eyes wouldn't come away from the bulge under my coat.

"There was a man," I said. "His name was William Decker and he hit you up for a loan not long ago and he's dead now."

Cooper licked his lips twice and tried to shake his head. "Look . . . I . . ."

"Shut up."

His eyes seemed to get a waxy film over them.

"Who killed him," I said.

"Honest to God, Mac, I . . . Christ . . . I didn't kill 'im. I swear . . ."

"You little son of a bitch you, when you put the squeeze on him for your lousy dough he had to pull a robbery to pay off!"

This time his eyes came away from my coat and jerked up to mine. His upper lip pared back from his teeth while his head made funny shaking motions. "I . . . don't get it. He . . . didn't get squeezed. He paid up. I give 'im a grand and two days later he pays it back. Honest to God, I . . ."

"Wait a minute. He paid you back all that dough?"

His head bobbed. "Yeah, yeah. All of it."

"You know what he used it for?"

"I . . . I think he was playing the ponies."

"He lost. That means he paid you back and his losses too. Where'd he get it?"

"How should I know? He paid me back like I told you."

Dixie started to shake when I grinned at him. "You know what'll happen to you if I find out you're lying?"

He must have known, all right. His buck teeth started showing gums and all. Somehow he got his lips together enough to say, "Christ, I can prove it! He . . . he paid me off right in Bernie Herman's bar. Ask Bernie, he was there. He saw him pay me and he'll remember because I bought the house a drink. You ask him."

I grinned again and pulled out the .45 and handed it to Ellen under the table. Dixie couldn't seem to swallow his own spit any more. I said, "I will, pal. You better be right. If he tries to scram, put one in his leg, Ellen."

She was a beautiful actress. She never changed her smile except to give it the deadly female touch and it wasn't because she meant it, but because she was having herself a time and was enjoying every minute of it.

I went out to the phone and looked up Bernie Herman's number and got the guy after a minute or so and he told me the same thing Dixie had. When I got back to the table they were still in the same position only Dixie had run out of spit altogether.

Ellen handed me the rod and I slipped it back under my coat. I nodded for her to get up just as a waiter decided it was about time to take our order. "Your friend cleared you, Dixie. You better stay cleared or you'll get a slug right in those buck teeth of yours. You know that, don't you?"

A drop of sweat rolled down in his eye and he blinked, but that was all.

I said, "Come on, Kitten," and we left him sitting there. When I passed the waiter I jerked my thumb back to the table. "You better bring him a whiskey. Straight. Make it a double."

He jotted it down and went over to the service bar.

Outside a colored pianist was trying hard to play loud enough to be heard over the racket of the crowd that was four deep around the bar. I pushed Ellen behind me and started elbowing a path between the mob and the booths along the side and if I didn't almost trip over a foot stuck out in the aisle I wouldn't have seen Lou Grindle parked in the booth across from a guy who looked like a Wall Street banker.

Only he wasn't a banker, but the biggest bookie in the business and his name was Ed Teen.

Lou just stopped talking and stared at me with those snake eyes of his. I said, "Your boy's still in the morgue, Lou. Don't you guys go in for big funerals these days?"

Ed Teen smiled and the creases around his mouth turned into deep hollows. "Friends of yours, Lou?"

"Sure, we're real old buddies, we are," I said. "Some day I'm gonna kick his teeth in."

Lou didn't scare a bit. The bastard looked almost anxious for me to try it. Ellen gave me a little push from behind and we got through the crowd to the checkroom where I got my hat, then went outside to the night.

Her face was different this time. The humor had gone out of it and she watched me as though I'd bite her. "Lord, Mike, a joke's a joke, but don't go too far. Do you know who they were?"

"Yeah, scum. You want to hear some dirty words that fit 'em perfectly?"

"But . . . they're dangerous."

"So I've heard. That makes it more fun. You know them?"

"Of course. My boss would give ten years off his life to get either one of them in court. Please, Mike, just go a little easy on me. I don't mind holding your gun to frighten someone like that little man back there, but those two . . ."

I slipped my arm around her shoulders and squeezed. "Kitten, when a couple of punks like that give me the cold shivers I'll hang up. They're big because they have money and the power and guns that money can buy, but when you take their clothes off and there's no pockets to hold the money or the guns they're just two worms looking for holes to hide in."

"Have it your way, but I need a drink. A big one and right now. My stomach is all squirmy."

She must have been talking about the inside. I felt her stomach and it was nice and flat. She poked me with her elbow for the liberty and made me take her in a bar.

Only this one was nearly empty and the only dangerous character was a drunk arguing with the bartender about who was going to win the series. When we had our drink I asked her if she wanted another and she shook her head. "One's enough on top of what happened tonight. I think I'd like to go home, Mike."

She lived in the upper Sixties on the top floor of the only new building in the block. About a half-dozen brownstones had been razed to clear an area for the new structure and it stood out like a dame in a French bathing suit at an old maids' convention. It was still a pretty good neighborhood, but most of the new convertibles and sleek black sedans were lumped together in front of her place.

I got in line behind the cars at the curb and opened the door for her. "Aren't you coming up for a midnight snack, Mike?"

"I thought I was supposed to ask that," I laughed.

"Times have changed. Especially when you get my age."

So I went up.

There was an automatic elevator, marble-lined corridors under the thick maroon rugs, expensive knickknacks and antique furniture all for free before you even hit the apartment itself. The layout wasn't much different inside, either. For apartment-hungry New York, this was luxury. There were six rooms with the best of everything in each as far as I could see. The living room was one of these ultra modern places with angular furniture that looked like hell until you sat in it. All along the mantle of the imitation fireplace was a collection of genuine Paul Revere pieces that ran into big dough, while the biggest of the pieces, each with its own copper label of historical data, was used beside the front windows as flowerpots.

I kind of squinted at Ellen as I glanced around. "How much do they pay you to do secretarial work?"

Her laugh made a tinkling sound in the room. "Not this much, I'll tell you. Three of us share this apartment, so it's not too hard to manage. The copper work you seem to admire belongs to Patty. She was working for Captain Chambers with me tonight."

"Oh, short and fat."

"She has certain virtues that attract men."

"Money?"

Ellen nodded.

"Then why does she work?"

"So she can meet men, naturally."

"Cripes, are all the babes after all the men?"

"It seems so. Now, if you'll just stay put I'll whip up a couple of sandwiches. Want something to drink?"

"Beer if you have it."

She said she had it and went back to the kitchen. She fooled around out there for about five minutes and finally managed to get an inch of ham to stay between the bread. A lanky towheaded job in one of those shortie nightgowns must have heard the raid on the icebox, because she came out of the bedroom as Ellen came in and snatched the extra sandwich off the plate. Just as she was going to pop it in her mouth she saw me and said, "Hi."

I said "Hi" back.

She said, "Ummm," but that was before she bit into the sandwich.

Moving her arms jerked the shortie up too far. Ellen blocked the view by handing me my beer and called back over her shoulder, "Either go put some more clothes on or get back in bed."

The towhead took another bite and mumbled, "With you around I need a handicap." She took another bite and shuffled back to the bedroom.

"See what I have to put up with?"

"I wish I had to put up with it."

"You would."

So we sat and finished the snack and dawdled over a beer until I said it was time to scram and she looked painfully unhappy with an expression that said I could stay if I wanted to badly enough. I told her about the kid and the arrangements I had made with the nurse, tacking on that I should have tucked him into bed long ago.

The same look she had in the office stole into her face. "Tuck me into bed too, Mike," she said. With the lithe grace of an animal she slid out of the chair past me and in the brief second that our eyes met I felt the heat of the passion that burned behind those deep blue irises.

Not much more than a minute could have passed. Her voice was a husky whisper calling, "Mike . . ." and I went to her.

There was no light except that which seeped in from the other room, a faint glow that made a bulky shadow of the bed with lesser shadows outlining the furniture against the deeper blackness of the room itself. I could hear the rhythmic sigh of her breathing, too heavy to be normal, and my hands shook when I stuck a cigarette in my mouth.

She said, "Mike . . ." again and I struck the match.

Her hair was a smooth mass of bronze on the pillow, her mouth full and rich, showing the shiny white edges of her teeth. There was only the sheet over her that rose and dipped between the inviting hollows of her breasts. Ellen was beautiful as only a mature woman can be beautiful. She was lustful as only a mature woman can be lustful.

"Tuck me in, Mike."

The match burned closer to my fingers. I reached down and got the corner of the sheet in my fingers and flipped it all the way back. She lay there beautiful and naked and waiting.

"I love brunettes," I said.

The tone of my voice told her no, not tonight, but her smile didn't fade. She just grinned impishly because she knew I'd never be able to look at her again and say no. "You're a heel, Mike."

The match went out. "You told me that once tonight."

"You're a bigger heel than I thought." Then she laughed. When I backed out of the room she was still chuckling, but that thing was running up my back again.

I was thinking of her all the way back to my apartment and thinking of her when I put my car away. I was thinking too damn much to be careful. When I stabbed my key in the lock and turned it there was a momentary catch in the tumblers before it went all the way around and I swore out loud as I rammed the door with my shoulder and hit the floor. Something swished through the air over my head and I caught an arm and pulled a squirming, fighting bundle of muscle down on top of me.

If I could have reached my rod I would have blown his guts out. His breath was in my face and I brought my knee up, but he jerked out of the way bringing his hand down again and my shoulder went numb after a split second of blinding pain. He tried again with one hand going for my throat, but I got one foot loose and kicked out and up and felt my toe smash into his groin. The cramp of the pain doubled him over on top of me, his breath sucking in like a leaky tire.

Then I got cocky. I thought I had him. I went to get up and he moved. Just once. That thing in his hand smashed against the side of my head and I started to crumple up piece by piece until there wasn't anything left except the sense to see and hear enough to know that he had crawled out of the room and was falling down the stairs outside. Then I thought about the lock on my door and how I had a guy fix it so I could tell if it had been jimmied open so I wouldn't step into any blind alleys without a gun in my hand, but because of a dame who lay naked and smiling on a bed I wouldn't share I had forgotten all about it.

And that was all.

chapter four ▰▰▰▰▰▰▰▰▰

I THOUGHT I was in a boat that was sinking and I tried to get over the side before it turned over on me. I clawed for the railing that wouldn't stand still while the screaming of the bells and mechanical pounding of laboring engines blasted the air with frantic insistence.

Somehow I got my eyes open and saw that I wasn't in a boat, but on the floor of my own apartment trying to grab the edge of the table. My head felt like a huge swollen thing that throbbed with a terrible fury, sending the pain shooting down to the balls of my feet. I choked on my tongue and muttered thickly, "God . . . my head . . . my head!"

The phone didn't let up and whoever was pounding on the door wouldn't go away because they could hear me inside.

I staggered to the door first and cursed. It was still unlocked; nobody had to pound like that. The damn thing was almost too heavy for me to open with one hand.

I guess I must have looked pretty bad. The elderly nurse took one look at me and her arms tightened protectively around the kid. He didn't scare so easily though, or maybe he was used to seeing a bloated, unshaven face. He laughed.

"Come on in," I said.

The old lady didn't like the idea, but she came in. Mad, too. "Mr. Hammer . . ." she started.

"Look, get off my back. I wasn't drunk or disorderly. I damn near got my skull smashed in . . ." I looked at the light streaming in the windows, "last night. Right here. I'm sorry you were inconvenienced, but I'll pay for it. Goddamn that phone . . . hello, hello!"

"Mike?"

I recognized Pat's voice. "Yeah, it's me. What's left of me."

"What happened?" He sounded sharp and impatient.

"Nothing. I just got jumped in my own joint and nearly brained, that's all. The bastard got away."

"Look, you get down here as fast as you can, understand? On the double."

"Now what's up?"

"Trouble, and it's all yours, friend. Damn it, Mike, how many times do I have to remind you to keep your nose out of police business!"

"Wait a minute . . ."

"Wait my foot. Get down here before the D.A. sends somebody after you. There's another murder and it's got your name on it."

I hung up and told my head to go right ahead and explode if it wanted to.

Then the old lady let out a short scream and nearly broke her neck running for the kid. He was on his hands and knees reaching for my gun that lay under the table on the floor. She kicked it away and snapped him back on her lap.

Lord, what a day this was going to be!

Somebody else was at the door this time and all they had to do was rap just once more before I got it opened and they'd get a rap right in the teeth. The guy in the uniform said, "You Michael Hammer?"

Nodding my head hurt, so I grunted that I was.

He handed me a box about two feet long and held out a pad. "Package from the Uptown Kiddie Shop. Sign here, please."

I scrawled my name, handed him a quarter and took the package inside. There was a stack of new baby clothes under the wrappings with a note on top addressed to me. It said,

> Dear Mike:
>   Men are never much good at these things, so I picked up some clothes for the little boy. Let me know if they fit all right.
>
>   Marsha

The nurse was still eyeing me suspiciously. I handed her the boy and edged back to a nice soft chair. "Before you say anything, let me explain one thing. The kid's old man was bumped. Murdered. He's an orphan and I'm trying to find out who made him that way. Somebody doesn't like the idea and they got funny ways of telling me so, but that isn't stopping me any. Maybe this'll happen again and maybe it won't, but you'd be doing me and the kid a big favor if you'll put up with it until this mess is cleaned up. Will you?"

Her face was expressionless a moment, then broke into a smile. "I . . . think I understand."

"Good. Arrangements are being made now so the kid'll be taken care of permanently. It won't be long." I patted the back of my head and winced.

"You'd better let me take a look at your scalp," she said.

She let me hold the kid while she probed around the lump awhile. If she had found a hole to stick her finger in, I wouldn't have been at all surprised. Finally she stood back satisfied and picked the kid up. "There doesn't seem to be anything wrong, but if I were you I'd see a doctor anyway."

I told her I would.

"You know, Mr. Hammer, in my time I've seen a great deal of suffering. It isn't new to me, not by a long sight. All I ask is that you don't bring any of it home to the child."

"Nothing will bother the kid. I'll see to that. He'll be all right with you then?"

"I'll take perfect care of him." She paused and her face creased in a frown. "This town is full of rabid dogs and there's not a dogcatcher in sight."

"I kill mad dogs," I said.

"Yes, I've heard that you do. Good morning, Mr. Hammer." I handed her the box of clothes, picked the rod up from the floor and ushered her out.

My head was still booming away and I tried to fix it up with a hot shower. That helped, but a mess of bacon and eggs helped even more. It woke me up enough to remember Pat said my name was on a murder and I didn't have the sense to ask who he was talking about.

I gave it a try on the phone anyway, but they couldn't locate Pat in the building anywhere. I held the receiver down for a second, long enough to check Marsha's number in the book, then punched out her call. The nurse with the mustache answered and told me that Miss Lee had just left for a morning rehearsal of the Little Theater Group and wasn't expected back until later that afternoon.

Nuts. So now I had to go down to police headquarters and face an inquisition. My legs had more life in them by the time I reached the street, and when I had pulled up in front of the building downtown I was back to normal in a sense. At least I felt like having a beer and a butt without choking over the thought.

They were real happy to see me, they were. They looked like they hoped I wouldn't come so they could go drag me down by the neck, but now that I was there everything was malicious, tight smiles and short, sharp sentences that steered me into a little room where I was supposed to sit and sweat so I'd blab my head off when they asked me questions.

I spit on the floor, right in the middle, to be exact, and had the Lucky I wanted. The college boy with the pointed face who rated as the D.A.'s assistant glared at me but didn't have the guts to back it up with any words. He parked behind a desk and tried to look important and tough. It was a lousy act.

When I started wondering how long they were going to let me cool my heels the corridor got noisy and I picked out Pat's voice raising Cain with somebody. The door slammed open and he stalked in with his face tight in anger.

I said, " 'lo, Pal," but he didn't answer.

He walked up to the desk and leaned on it until his face wasn't an inch away from the D.A.'s boy and he did a good job of keeping his hands off the guy's neck. "Since when do you take over the duties of the Police Department? I'm still Captain of Homicide around here and when there's murder I'll handle it myself, personally, understand? I ought to knock your ears off for pulling a stunt like that!"

The boy got a blustery red and started to get up. "See here, the District Attorney gave me full permission . . ."

"To butt into my business because a friend of mine is suspected of murder!"

"Exactly!"

Pat's voice got dangerously low. "Get your ass out of this office before I kick hell out of you. Go on, get out. And you tell the D.A. that I'll see him in a few minutes."

He practically ran to the door. I could see the D.A. getting a sweet version of the story, all right. I said, "What'd he do to you, kid?"

"Crazy little bastard. He thinks because I'm a friend of yours I'll do a little whitewashing. He got me out of the building on a phony call right after I spoke to you."

"You're not going to be very popular with the D.A. for that."

"I'm sick of that guy walking all over this office. They pulled a raid on a wire room last night and all they got was an empty apartment with a lot of holes in the walls and a blackboard that still showed track results and a snotty little character who said he was thinking of opening a school for handicappers. The guy was clean and there wasn't a thing the D.A. could do."

"Sounds like a good business. Whose wire room was it?"

"Hell, who else has wire rooms in this town? The place was run by one of Ed Teen's outfit."

"Or so your information said."

"Yeah. So now the D.A. gets in a rile and raises hell with everyone from the mayor down. He's pulled his last rough sketch on me with this deal though. Let him try getting rough just once and the news boys are going to get a lot of fancy stuff that won't do a thing for him when election time comes."

"Where is he now?"

"Inside waiting for you."

"Let's see the guy then."

"Just a minute. Tell me something straight. Did you kill a guy named Mel Hooker?" he asked.

"Oh, God!"

Pat's eyes got that squinty look. "What's the matter?"

"Your corpse was the friend of William Decker . . . That beautiful local-type kill the police seem to be ignoring so well."

"The police aren't ignoring anything."

"Then they're not looking very hard. Mel and Decker were playing the ponies and Mel introduced him to a loan shark that financed his little escapades. There was a catch in it. Mel said Decker lost his shirt, but the loan shark, that Dixie Cooper guy, said Decker paid him off in full and was able to prove it."

Pat muttered something under his breath. He nodded for me to follow him and started for the door. This time the tight smiles loosened up and nobody seemed to want to get in our way. From the way Pat was glowering it looked like he was ready to take me and anybody else apart and had already started.

Pat knocked on the door and I heard the D.A. call out for somebody to see who it was. The door opened, a pair of thick-lensed glasses did a quick focus on the two of us and the D.A. said, "Show them in, Mr. Mertig."

It was quite a gathering. The D.A. straddled his throne with two assistant D.A.'s flanking him, a pair of plainclothes men in the background and two more over by the window huddled together for mutual protection apparently.

"Sit down, Hammer," the D.A. said.

Everybody watched me with the annoyed look you see when the king isn't obeyed pronto. I walked up to his desk, planted my hands on the top and leaned right down in his face. I didn't like the guy and he didn't like me, but he wasn't getting snooty now or any other time. I said, "You call me *Mister* when you use my name. I don't want any crap from you or your boys and if you think you can make it tough for me just go ahead and try it. I came in here myself to save you the trouble of getting a false arrest charge slapped against your office and right now I'm not above walking out just to see what you'd do. It's about time you learned to be polite to your public when you're not sure of your facts."

The D.A. started to get purple. In fact, a lot of people started to get purple. When they all got a nice livid tinge I sat down.

He made a good job of keeping his voice under control. "We are sure of the facts . . . *Mister* Hammer."

"Go on."

"A certain Mel Hooker has been found dead. He was shot to death with a .45."

"I suppose the bullet came from my gun?" I tried to make it sound as sarcastic as possible.

The purple started to fade into an unhealthy red. Unhealthy for me, I mean. "Unfortunately, no. The bullet passed through the man and out the window. So far we haven't been able to locate it."

I started to interrupt, but he held up his hand. "However, you were very generous with your fingerprints. They're all over the place. The landlady identified your picture and vouched that she heard threats before you left, so it is quite a simple matter to see what followed."

"Yeah, I went back later and shot him. I'm really that stupid."

"Yes, you really are." His eyes were narrow slits in his face.

"And you got rocks in your head," I said. He started to get up but I beat him to it. I stood there looking down at him so he could see what I thought of him. "You're a real bright boy, you are. Brother, the voters sure must be proud of you! Christ, you're ready to kick anything around because your vice racket business is getting the works. It's got you so far down you're all set to slap me in the clink without having the foresight to ask me if I got an alibi or not for the time of the shooting. So it happened last night and I don't know what time and without bothering to find out I'll hand you my alibi on a platter and you can choke on it."

I pointed to the intercom on his desk. "Get Ellen Scobie in here."

The D.A.'s face was wet with an angry sweat. His finger triggered the gadget and when Ellen answered he told her to come in.

Before the door opened I had a chance to look at Pat and he was shaking his head slowly trying to tell me not to go overboard so far I couldn't get back. Ellen came in, smiled at me through a puzzled frown and stood there waiting to see what was going on. From the look that passed between us, the D.A. caught on fast, but he wasn't letting me get in any prompting first. He said, "Miss Scobie, were you with this . . . with *Mister* Hammer last night at, say eleven-thirty?"

She didn't have to think to answer that one. "Yes, I did happen to be with him."

"Where were you?"

"I should say that we were sitting in a bar about then. A place on Fifty-second Street."

"That's all, Miss Scobie."

Everybody ushered her out of the room with their eyes. When

the door clicked shut the D.A.'s voice twanged like a flat banjo string. "You may go too, *Mister* Hammer. I'm getting a little tired of your impertinence." His face had turned a deadly white and he was speaking through his teeth. "I wouldn't be a bit surprised if your license was revoked very shortly."

My voice came out a hiss more than anything else. "I'd be," I said. "You tried that once before and remember what happened?"

That's all I had to say and for a few seconds I was the only one who didn't stop breathing in the room. Nobody bothered to open the door for me this time. I went out myself and started down the corridor, then Pat caught up with me.

We must have been thinking the same things, because neither one of us bothered to speak until we were two blocks away in Louie's place where a quick beer cooled things down to a boil.

Pat grinned at me in the mirror behind the bar. "You're a lucky bastard, Mike. If the press wasn't so hot on the D.A.'s heels you'd be out of business if he lost the election over it."

"Aw, he gives me a pain. Okay, he's got it in for me, but does he have to be so goddamn stupid about it? Why didn't he do some checking first. Christ, him and his investigators are making the police look ridiculous. I'm no chump. I got as much on the ball as any of his stooges and in my own way maybe I got as many scruples too."

"Ease off, Mike. I'm on your side."

"I know, but you're tied down too. Who has to get murdered before the boob will put some time in on the case? Right now you got three corpses locked together as nicely as you please and what's being done?"

"More than you think."

I sipped the top of my beer and watched his eyes in the mirror. "It wasn't any news that Decker and Hooker were tied up. The lab boys lifted a few prints out of his apartment. Some of them were Hooker's."

"He have a record?"

Pat shook his head. "During the war he had a job that required security and he was printed. We picked up the blind newspaper dealer's prints too. He had a record."

"I know. They graduated from the same Alma Mater up the river."

Pat grinned again. "You know too damn much."

"Yeah, but you do it the easy way. What else do you know?"

"You tell me, Mike."

"What?"

"The things you have in that mind of yours, chum. I want your angle first."

I ordered another round and lit a cigarette to go with it. "Decker needed dough. His wife was undergoing an operation that cost heavy sugar and he had to get it from someplace. He and Hooker got some hot tips on the nags and they pooled their dough to make some fast money. When they found out the tips were solid ones they went in deeper. Hooker pulled out while he was ahead, but Decker wanted to make the big kill so he borrowed a grand from Dixie Cooper. According to Hooker, he lost everything and was in hock to Cooper for plenty, but when I braced the guy he proved that Decker had paid him back.

"Okay, he had to get the dough from somebody. He sure as hell didn't work for it because the docks have been too slow the past month. He had to do one of two things . . . either steal it or borrow it. It could be that when he went back to his old trade he found it so profitable he couldn't or didn't want to give it up. If that was the case then he made a mistake and broke into the wrong apartment. He and his partners were expecting a juicy haul and if Decker spent a lot of time casing the joint a gimmick like breaking into the wrong apartment would have looked like a sorry excuse to the other two who were expecting part of the proceeds. In that case he would have tried to take a flyer and they caught up with him."

Pat looked down into his glass. "Then where does Hooker come in?"

"They were friends, weren't they? First Decker gets bumped for pulling a funny stunt, the driver of the car gives the second guy the works so he won't be captured and squeal, then he goes and gets Hooker because he's afraid Decker might have spilled the works to his friend."

"I'll buy that," Pat said. "It's exactly the way I've had it figured."

"You buy it and you'll be stuck," I told him. I finished my beer and let the bartender fill it up again. Pat was making wry faces now. He was waiting for the rest of it.

I gave it to him. "William Decker hadn't been pulling any jobs before that one. He was going straight all along the line. He must have known what might happen and got his affairs in order right down to making provisions for his kid. If Decker paid off Cooper then he borrowed the dough from somebody else and the somebody put on the squeeze play. For my money they even knew where the dough could be had and laid it out so all Decker had to do was go up the fire escape and open up the safe.

"That's where he made his mistake. He got into the wrong place and after all the briefing he had who the hell would believe his story. No, Decker knew he jimmied the wrong can and didn't dare take a chance on correcting the error because Marsha Lee could have come to at any time and called the cops. In the league where he was playing they only allow you one mistake. Decker knew they would believe that he had stashed the money thinking to come back later and get it, so he took off by himself.

"What happened was this . . . he had to go home for his kid. When they knew he had taken a powder they put it together and beat it back to his place. By that time he was gone, but they picked him up fast enough. When he knew he was trapped he kissed his kid good-by and walked out into a bullet. That boy of Grindle's searched him for the dough and when he didn't find it, the logical thought was that he hid it in his apartment. He didn't have much chance to do anything else. So the driver of the car scooted back there and got into the place and messed it up."

Pat's teeth were making harsh grating noises and his fingers rasped against the woodwork of the bar. "So you're all for nailing the driver of the murder car, right?"

The way I grinned wasn't human. It tied my face up into a bunch of hard knots. "Nope," I said, "that's your job. You can have him. I want the son of a bitch who put the pressure on him. I want the guy who made somebody decent revert back to a filthy crime and I want him right between my hands so I can squeeze the juice out of him."

"Where is he, Mike?"

"If I knew I wouldn't tell you, friend. I want him for myself. Someday I want to be able to tell that kid what his face looked like when he was dying."

"Damn it anyway, Mike, you can stretch friendship too far sometimes."

"No, I'll never stretch it, Pat. Just remember that I live in this town too. Besides having what few police powers the state chooses to hand me, I'm still a citizen and responsible in some small way for what happens in the city. And by God, if I'm partly responsible then I have a right to take care of an obligation like removing a lousy orphan-maker."

"Who is he, Mike?"

"I said I didn't know."

"But you know where to find out."

"That's right. It isn't too hard if you want to take a chance on getting your head smashed in."

"Like you did last night?"

"Yeah. That's something else I have to even up. I don't know why or how it happened, but I got a beaut of an idea, I have."

"Something like looking for a guy named Lou Grindle whom you called all sorts of names and threatened to shoot on sight if you found out he was responsible for Decker's death?"

My mouth fell open. "How the hell did you get that?"

"Now you're taking me for the chump, Mike. I checked the tie-up Arnold Basil had with Grindle thoroughly, and from the way Lou acted I knew somebody had been there before me. It didn't take long to guess who it was. Lou was steamed up to beat hell and told me what happened. Let me tell you something. Don't try anything with that boy. The D.A. has men covering him every minute he's awake trying to get something on him."

"Where was he last night then?"

A thundercloud rolled over Pat's face. "The bastard skipped out. He pulled a fastie and skipped his apartment and never got back until eleven. In case you're thinking he had anything to do with Hooker's death, forget it. He couldn't have gotten back at that time."

"I'm not thinking anything. I was just going to tell you he was in a place called the Glass Bar on Eighth Avenue with Ed Teen somewhere around ten. The D.A. ought to get new eyes. The old ones are going bad."

Pat swore under his breath.

I said, "What made you say that, Pat?"

"Say what?"

"Oh, connect Lou and Hooker."

"Hell, I didn't connect anything. I just said . . ."

"You said something that ought to make you think a lot more, boy. Grindle and Decker and Hooker don't go together at all. They're miles apart. In fact, they're so far apart they're backing into each other from the ends."

He set his glass down with a thump. "Wait a minute. Don't go getting this thing screwed up with a lot of wacky ideas. Lou Grindle isn't playing with anything worth a few grand and if he is, he doesn't send out blockheads to do the job. You're way the hell out of line."

"Okay, don't get excited."

"Good Lord, who's getting excited? Damn it, Mike . . . "

My face was as flat as I could make it. I just sat there with the beer in my hand and stared at myself in the mirror because I started thinking of something that was like a shadow hovering in the background. I thought about it for a long time and it was still a shadow when I finished and it had a shape that was so curious I wanted to go up closer for another look.

I didn't hear Pat because his voice was so low it was almost a whisper, but he repeated it loud enough so I could hear it and he made me look at him so I wouldn't forget it. His hands were a nervous bunch of fingers that opened and shut with every word and his mouth was all teeth with sharp biting edges.

"Mike, you try pulling a smart frame that will pull Grindle into that damn murder case of yours and you and I are finished! We've worked too damn long and hard to nail that punk and his boss to have you slip over a cutie that will stink up the whole works. Don't give me the business, friend. I know you and the way you work. Anything appeals to you just as long as you can point a gun at somebody. For my money Lou Grindle is as far away from this as I am and because one of his boys tried to pick up some extra change you can't fix him for it. All right, I'll give you the benefit of the doubt and say that if you tried hard enough and lived through it you'd do it, but Lou's got Teen and a lot more behind him. He'd get out of that charge easy as pie and only leave the department open for another big laugh. When we get those two, we want them so it'll stick, and no frame is going to do it. You lay off, hear?"

I didn't answer him for a long minute, then; "I wasn't thinking of any frame, Pat."

Pat's hands were still jerking on the bar. "The hell you weren't. Remember what I told you, that's all." He spilled his beer down and fiddled with the empty glass until the bartender moved in and filled it up again. I didn't say a damn thing. I just sat. Pat's fingernails were little firecrackers going off against the wood while his coat rippled as the muscles bunched underneath the fabric.

It lasted about five minutes, then he drained the glass and shoved it back. He muttered, "Goddamn!"

I said, "Relax, chum."

Then he repeated what he said the first time, told me to take it easy, and swung off the stool. I waited until he was out the door, then started to laugh. It wasn't so easy to be a cop. At least not a city cop. Or maybe it was the years that were getting him down. Six years ago you couldn't get him excited about anything, not even a murder or a naked dame with daisies in her hair.

The bartender came over and asked me if I wanted another. I said no and shoved him a quarter to make into change, then picked up a dime and walked back to the phone booth. The book listed the Little Theater as being on the edge of Greenwich Village and a babe with a low-down voice told me that Miss Lee was there and rehearsing and if I was a friend I could certainly come up.

The Little Theater was an old warehouse with a poster-decorated front that was a lousy disguise. The day had warped into a hot afternoon and the air inside the place was even hotter, wetter and bedded down with the perfumed smell of make-up. A sawed-off babe in a Roman toga let me in, locked the door to keep out the spies, then wiggled her fanny in the direction of all the noise to show me where to go. A pair of swinging doors opened and two more dames in togas came through for a smoke. They stood right in the glare of the only light in the place looking too cool to be real and lit up the smokes without seeing me there in the shadows.

Then I saw why they were so cool. One of them flipped the damn thing open and stood with her hands on her hips and she didn't have a thing on underneath it. Sawed-off said, "Helen, we have a visitor."

And Helen finally saw me, smiled, and said, "How nice."

But she didn't bother to do anything about the toga. I said, "The play's the thing," and sawed-off grinned a little like she wished she had thought of the open-toga deal first herself and sort of pushed me into the swinging doors.

Inside, a pair of floor fans moved the air around enough to make you think you were cool, at least. I opened my shirt and tie, then stood there for a moment getting used to the artificial dusk. All around the place were stacks of funeral parlor chairs with clothes draped over them. Up front a rickety stage held up some more togas and a few centurians in uniform while a hairy-legged little squirt in tennis shorts screamed at them in a high falsetto as he pounded a script against an old upright piano.

It wasn't hard to find Marsha. There was a baby spot behind her outlining a hundred handfuls of lovely curves through the white cotton toga. She was the most beautiful woman in the place even with a touched-up shiner, and from where I stood I could see that there was plenty of competition.

The squirt with the hairy legs called for a ten-minute break and sawed-off called something up to Marsha I didn't catch. She tried to peer past the glare of the footlights, didn't make out too well, so came off the stage in a jump and ran all the way back to where I was.

Her hands were warm, friendly things that grabbed mine and held on. "Did you get my package, Mike?"

"Yup. Came down to thank you personally."

"How is the boy?"

"Fine, just fine. Don't ask me how I feel because I'll give you a stinking answer. Somebody tried to break my head open last night."

"Mike!"

"I got a hard head."

She moved up close and ran her hand over my hair to where the bump was and wrinkled her nose at me. "Do you know who it was?"

"No. If I did the bastard'd be in the hospital."

Marsha took my arm and nodded over to the side of the wall. "Let's sit down a few minutes. I can worry better about you that way."

"Why worry about me at all?"

The eye with the shiner was closed just enough to give it the damnedest look you ever saw. "I could be a fool and tell you why, Mike," she said. "Shall I be a fool?"

If ever I had wanted to kiss a woman it was then, only she had too much make-up on and there were too many people for an audience. "Later. Tonight, maybe," I told her. "Be a fool then." I was grinning and her lips went into a smile that said a lot of things, but mostly was a promise of tonight.

When we had a pair of cigarettes going I tipped my chair back against the wall and stared at her. "We have another murder on our hands, kitten."

The cigarette stopped halfway to her lips and her head came around slowly. "Another? Oh, no!"

I nodded. "Guy named Mel Hooker. He was Decker's best friend. You know, Marsha, I think there's a hell of a lot more behind this than we thought."

"Chain reaction," she said softly.

"Sort of. It didn't take much to start it going. Three hundred bucks and a necklace, to be exact."

Marsha nodded, her lips between her teeth. "My playboy friend in the other apartment was coerced into keeping his money in a bank instead of the wall safe. The management threatened to break his lease unless he co-operated. Everybody in the building knows what happened and raised a fuss about it. Apparently the idea of being beaten up by a burglar doesn't sound very appealing, especially when the burglar is wild over having made a mistake in safes."

"You got off easy. He might have killed you."

Her shoulders twitched convulsively. "What are you going to do, Mike?"

"Keep looking. Make enough stink so trouble'll come looking for me. Sometimes it's easier that way."

"Do you . . . have to?" Her eyes were soft, and her hand on my arm squeezed me gently.

"I have to, kid. I'm made that way. I hate killers."

"But do you have to be so . . . so damned reckless about it?"

"Yeah. Yeah, I do. I don't have to be but that's the way I like it. Then I can cut them down and enjoy it."

"Oh, Lord! Mike, please . . ."

"Look, kid, when you play with mugs you can't be coy. At first this looked all cut-and-dried-out and all there was to it was nailing a bimbo who drove a car with a hot rod in the back seat. That's the way it looked at first. Now we got names creeping into this thing, names and faces that don't belong to any cheap bimbos. There's Teen and Grindle and a guy who died a long time ago but who won't stay buried . . . his name was Charlie Fallon and I keep hearing it every time I turn around."

Somebody said, "Charlie Fallon?" in a voice that ended with a chuckle and I turned around chewing on my words.

The place was getting to look like backstage of a burlesque house. The woman in the dress toga did a trick with the oversize cigarette holder and stood there smiling at us. She was medium in height only. The rest of her was over done, but that's the way they liked them in Hollywood. Her name was Kay Cutler and she was right in there among the top movie stars and it wasn't hard to see why.

Marsha introduced us and I stood there like an idiot with one of those nobody-meets-celebrity grins all over my pan. She held my hand longer than was necessary and said, "Surprised?"

"Hell, yes. How come all the talent in this dump?"

The two of them laughed together. Kay did another trick with the holder. "It's a hobby that gets a lot of exciting publicity. Actually we don't play the parts for the audience. Instead we portray them so the others can use our interpretation as a model, then coach them into giving some sort of a performance. You wouldn't believe it, but the theater group makes quite a bit of money for itself. Enough to cover expenses, at least."

"You come for free?"

She laughed and let her eyes drift to one of the centurians who was giving me some dark looks. "Well, not exactly."

Marsha poked me in the back so I'd quit leering. I said, "You mentioned Charlie Fallon before. Where'd you hear of him?"

"If he's the one I'm thinking of a lot of people knew him. Was he the gangster?"

"That's right."

"He was a fan-letter writer. God, how that man turned them out! Even the extras used to get notes and flowers from the old goat. I bet I've had twenty or more."

"That was a long time ago," I reminded her.

She smiled until the dimples showed in her cheeks. "You aren't supposed to mention the passage of time so lightly. I still claim to be in my early thirties."

"What are you?"

I got the dimples again. "I'm a liar," she said. "Marsha, didn't you ever get mail from that character?"

"Perhaps. At the time I didn't handle my own correspondence and it was all sorted out for me." She paused and squinted a little. "Come to think of it, yes. I did. I remember talking about it to someone one day."

I pulled on the butt and let the smoke out slowly. "He was like that. The guy made plenty and didn't know how to spend it, so he threw it away on the girlies. I wonder if he ever followed it up?"

"Never," Kay stated flatly. "When he was still news some of the columnists kept up with his latest crushes and slipped in a publicity line now and then, but nobody ever saw him around the Coast. By the way, what's so important about him now?"

"I wish I knew. For a dead man he's sure not forgotten."

"Mike is a detective, Kay," Marsha said bluntly. "There have been a couple of murders and Mike's conducting an investigation."

"And not getting far," I added.

"Really?" Her eyebrows went up and she cocked the holder between her teeth and gave me a look that was sexy right down to her sandals. "A detective. You sound exciting."

"You're not going to sound at all if you don't get back to your warrior, lady," Marsha cut in. "Now scram."

Kay faked a pout at her and said so long to me after another long hand-clasp. When she was across the room Marsha slipped her arm through mine. "Kay's a wonderful gal, but if you have it and it wears pants she wants it."

"Good old Kay," I said.

"Luckily, I know her too well."

"Any more around like that?"

"Well, if it's a celebrity you'd like to meet, I can take you backstage and introduce you to a pair of Hollywood starlets, a television sensation, the country's biggest comic and . . . "

"Never mind," I said. "You're enough for me."

She gave me another one of those squeezes with a laugh thrown in and I wanted to kiss her again. The kid with an arm in a sling who tapped her on the shoulder as he murmured, "Two minutes more, Marsha," must have read my mind, because his eyes went limp and sad.

Marsha nodded as he walked off and I pointed my cigarette at his back. "The kid's got a crush on you."

She watched him a moment, then glanced at me. "I know it. He's only nineteen and I'm afraid he has stars in his eyes. A month ago he was in love with Helen O'Roark and was so far down in the dumps when he found out she was married he almost starved himself to death. He's the one I took to the hospital the night the Decker fellow broke into my apartment."

"What happened to him?"

"He was setting up props and fell off the ladder."

Down at the end of the hall hairy legs in short pants was banging on the piano again screaming for everyone to get back on the stage. Togas started to unravel from the floor, chairs and the scenery and if I had a dozen more pairs of eyes I could have enjoyed myself. Those babes didn't give a damn what they showed and I seemed to be the only one there who appreciated the view. The overhead lights went out and the stage spots came on and I was doing good watching the silhouettes until Marsha said, "I'm getting jealous, Mike."

It wasn't so much what she said as the way she said it that made me jerk around. And there she was leaning on the stack of chairs like a nymph under a waterfall with her own toga wide open down the middle and an impish little grin playing with her mouth. She was barely a reflection of light and shadow, a vague white statue of warm, live flesh that moved with her breathing, then the toga came shut slowly before I could move and she was out of reach.

"You don't have to be jealous of anybody," I said.

She smiled again, and in the darkness her hand touched mine briefly and the cigarette fell out of my fingers to the floor where it lay like a hot red eye. Then she was gone and all I could think about was tonight.

chapter five ∎∎∎∎∎∎∎∎∎∎∎∎∎∎∎∎∎∎∎∎●

AFTER THE LITTLE theater the glare of the sun was almost blinding. I fired up another butt and climbed back into the car where I finished smoking it before I had myself in line again. All the while I kept seeing Marsha in that white toga until it was branded into my brain so deeply that it blotted out everything else. Marsha and Kay and Helen of Troy or something in a lot of white togas drifting through the haze like beautiful ghosts.

Like the ghost of a killer I was after. I threw the butt out the window and hit the starter.

I let my hands and my eyes drive me through traffic while the rest of me sat and thought. It should have been so damn easy. Three guys dead and a killer running loose looking for his lousy split of a robbery that didn't happen. Decker dead on the sidewalk. Arnold Basil dead in the gutter. Hooker dead in his own room and me damn near dead on the floor. Sure it was easy, just like an illiterate doing acrostics.

Then where the hell was the big puzzle? Was it because Basil had been Lou Grindle's boy, or because Fallon's name kept cropping up? I jammed the horn down at the guy in front of me and yelled as I pulled around him. He gave me a scared grimace and plenty of room and I shot by him swearing at the little things that piled up one after the other.

Then I grinned because that was where the puzzle was. In all the little things.

Like the boys who tried to take me when I was putting the buzz on Hooker.

Like the money that Decker had picked up from somewhere to pay off Dixie Cooper.

Like Decker putting his affairs in order before he walked out and got himself bumped.

Now I knew where I was going and what I wanted to do, so I got off the avenue onto a street and headed west until I could smell the river and see the trucks pulling into their docks for the night and hear the mixture of tongues as the longshoremen streamed out of the yards.

The nearest of them were still ten minutes away when I pulled up outside the hole-in-the-wall saloon and there weren't any early birds inside when I pushed the door open. The bartender was perched on a stool watching the television and his hand automatically went out for a glass as he heard me slide up to the bar.

I didn't let him waste his beer. I said, "Remember me, buddy?"

He had a frown all set and his mouth shaped to tell me off when his memory came back with a jolt. "Yeah." His frown had a twisted look now.

I leaned on the bar so my coat hung loose enough for him to see the leather of the gun sling and he knew I wasn't kidding around. "Who were they, buddy?"

"Look, I . . ."

"Maybe I ought to ask it different. Maybe I ought to ask it with the nose of a gun shoved down your throat. You can get it that way if you want."

He choked up a little and his eyes kept darting toward the door hoping someone would come in. He licked his lips to bring the words out and said, "I . . . don't know . . . who the hell they were."

"You like it the hard way, don't you? Now just once I'm going to tell you something and I want an answer. Scarface Hooker is dead. He was shot last night and because you know who they were you might be sitting on top of a powder keg. In case you're not sure, let me tell you that you are right now . . . with me. I'm going to bust you wide open or leave you for those babies to handle."

The guy started to sweat. It formed in little cold drops along the ridges of his forehead and rolled down his cheeks. He made a swipe with the back of his hand across his mouth and swallowed hard. "They was private detectives."

"They were like hell."

"Look, I'm telling ya, I saw their badges."

"Tell me some more."

"They come in here looking for Hooker. They said he was working against the union and pulling a lot of rough stuff. Hell, how'd I know? I'm a union man myself. If that's what he was doing he shoulda got beat up. They showed me their badges and said they was working for the union so I played along."

"Ever see them before?"

"No."

"Anybody else see them?"

"Yeah."

"Goddamn it, say something! Don't give me one word."

"One guy says they was uptown boys. They was roughs . . . strong-arm boys. The little guy . . . I heard the other one call him Nocky."

"What else?"

"That's all. I swear to God I don't know no more."

I slid my elbows off the bar and gave him a tight grin. "Okay, friend, you did fine. Let me give you a word of advice. If either of those boys come in here again you pick up the phone and call the nearest precinct station."

"Sure. I'll ask 'em to blow my crazy head off, too."

"They might do it before you reach the phone, mister. Those lads were after Hooker and it might have been them who got to him. They won't like anybody who can put the finger on 'em. Remember what I told you."

He started to sweat again. All along his neck the cords were standing out against the layer of fat. He didn't look a bit happy. A couple of longshoremen pushed in through the door and lined up at the rail and he had one hell of a time trying to keep the glasses under the beer tap. He didn't want to look up when I left, but he had to and I could feel his eyes on my back.

So they were private dicks and one's name was Nocky. Anybody could pick up a badge to flash if he wanted to, but there was just the chance that they were the real thing, so the first pay station I came to I changed two bucks into nickels and started dialing all the agencies I knew of.

None of them picked up the description, but one of them did hear of a Nocky something-or-other but was sure it was a nickname. He couldn't give me any further information so I tried a couple precincts uptown where I had an in at the desk. A Sergeant Bellew came on and told me the name was familiar, but that was all. He had the idea that the guy was a private dick too but couldn't be sure.

On the off-chance that Pat might know, I called his office. He picked up his phone on the first ring and his voice had a snap to it that wasn't too nice. I said, "It's Mike, Pat. What's eating you now?"

"Plenty. Listen, I'm pretty busy now and . . ."

"Nuts. You're not that busy."

"Damn it, Mike, what is it now?"

"Ever hear of a private cop called Nocky? It's a nickname."

"No."

"Can you check on it for me?"

"Hell no!" His voice had an explosive crack to it. "I can't do a damn thing except obey orders. The D.A.'s working up another stink ever since this afternoon and he's got us nuts up here."

"What happened, another raid go sour?"

"Ah, they all go sour. He closed down a wire room and pulled in a couple of punks when he was looking for something big. Ed Teen came down with a lawyer and a bondsman and got them both out within the hour."

"No kidding? So Ed's taking a personal interest in what goes on now."

"Yeah. He doesn't want 'em to talk before he does a little coaching first. You know, I think we're onto something this time. We had to pull a Gestapo act and check on our own men, but I think we have that leak located."

"How does it look?"

"Lousy. He's a first-grade detective and up to his ears in hock. He's one of three who have been in on every deal so far and money might be a powerful persuader to get him to pass a sign along somehow."

"Have you picked up the tip-off yet?"

"Nope. If he's doing it he's got a damn good system. Keep shut about this. The only reason I mentioned it is because I may need you soon. The guy knows all the other cops and I may have to stick a plant along the line to see who's picking up the flash from him."

"Okay, I'll be around any time you need me. If you run into anything on that Nocky character, let me know."

"Sure, Mike. Wish I could help you out now, but we're all tied up."

I said so long and hung up. I still had a handful of nickels to go so I made a blind stab at a barroom number downtown and asked if Cookie Harkin was there. I had to wait while the guy looked and after a minute or so a voice said, "Cookie speaking."

"Mike Hammer."

"Hey, boy. Long time no see. How's tricks?"

"Good enough. You still got wide-open ears?"

"Sure. See all, hear all and say plenty if the pay's right. Why?"

"Ever hear of a private dick named Nocky? He's a wise runt who has an oversize partner. Supposedly a couple of tough boys from somewhere uptown."

I didn't get any answer for a minute, so I said, "Well?"

"Wait a minute, Mike. You know what you're asking about, don't you?" He spoke in next to a whisper. I heard him pull the door of the booth closed before he said anything else. "What're you working on?"

"Murder, friend."

"Brother!"

"Who is he?"

"I'll have to do a little checking around first. I think I know who you mean, all right. I'll see what I can do, but if it's the guy I think it is, I'm not sticking my neck out too far, understand?"

"Sure, do what you can. I'll pay you for it."

"Forget the pay. All I want is some inside stuff I can pass along for what it's worth. You know my angle."

"How long will it take?"

"Gimme a coupla hours. Suppose I meet you at the Tucker Bar. It's a dive, but you can get away with anything in there."

It was good enough. I told him I'd be there and put the rest of the nickels back in my pocket. They make a big lump and a lot of noise so I went across town to an Automat and spent them all on a supper I needed bad.

It was dark when I finished and had started to rain again. The Tucker Bar was built under a neon sign that put out more light in advertising than was used up inside. It was off on a side street in a place nobody smart went to even on a slumming party, but it was a place where people who knew people could be found and gotten drunk enough to spill over a little excess information if the questions were put right.

I saw Cookie in the back room edging through the tables with a drink in his hand, stopping at a table here and there to say hello. He was small and skinny with a big nose, bigger ears and loose pockets that could spill out the right kind of dough when he needed it. The guy looked and acted like a cheap hood when he was the head legman for one of the biggest of the syndicated columnists. I waited at the bar nursing a beer until the act on the dance floor was finished. A couple of strippers were trying to see how fast they could shed their clothes in time to the same music. They got down to bare facts in a minute's time and there was a lot of noise around the ringside. The rest of the crowd was having a hard time trying to see what they were paying for.

There was a singer and a solo pianist after that before the management decided to let the customers go back to drinking. I picked up my glass and squeezed through the bunch standing under the arch that led to the back room and worked my way to the table where Cookie was sitting.

He had two chicks with him, a pair of phony blondes with big bosoms and painted faces and he was showing them a coin trick so they had to lean forward to see what he was doing and he could leer down their necklines. He was having himself a great time. The blondes were drinking champagne. They were having a great time too.

I said, "Hello, ape man."

He looked up and grinned from one big ear to another until he looked like a clam just opened. "How do ya like that, my old pal, Mike Hammer! What're you doin' down here where people are?"

"Looking for people."

"Well, sit right down, sit right down. Here's one all made to order for you. Meet Tolly and Joan."

I said, "Hi," and pulled out the fourth chair.

"Mike's a friend of mine from way back, kids. A real good skate." He nodded at the blonde who was giving me the eye already. "You take Tolly, Mike. Joan and me's already struck up a conversation. She's a French maid from Brooklyn who works for the Devoe family. Wait'll you catch her accent. She sure fooled them. Gawd, what a family of jerks they are!"

I caught his expression and the slight wink that went with it. Tomorrow the stuff Joan was handing out would turn up in print and the hell would get raised in the Devoe household. She gave us a demonstration of her accent with giggles and launched into a spiel of how the old man had tried to make her and how she refused and I almost wanted to ask her how she got the mink cape that was draped over the back of her chair on a maid's salary.

Tolly turned out to be the better of the two. She was a juicy eyeful with a lot of skin showing and nothing on under the dress she wore just to be conventional. She told me she had been posing for an artist down in the village until she caught him using a camera instead of a paintbrush. She found he was peddling the prints and made him kick in with a fifty-fifty cut or get the pants knocked off him by an ex-boy friend in the Bronx, and now she was living off the cream of the land.

"Your artist friend sure mixes pleasure with business, honey," I told her. "Hell, I wouldn't mind seeing you undraped a bit."

She snapped open her purse and tossed me a wallet-sized print with a laugh. "Get right to it." She had a body that would make a statue drool, and with the poses the artist got her into it was easy to see why she wasn't hurting for dough. She let me look at it a little while, asked me if I wanted to dance and laughed when I said maybe later, but not right then.

Finally we got up and danced while Cookie sat and yapped with the French maid from Brooklyn. Tolly didn't have any trouble giving me the business because the mob on the dance floor had us pressed together like the ham in a sandwich.

Every bit of her was pressed against every bit of me and her mouth was right next to my ear. Every once in a while she'd stick her tongue out and send something chasing down my spine. "I like you, Mike," she said.

I gave her a little squeeze until her eyes half closed and she said something through her teeth. I slapped her fanny for it. We got back to the table and played kneesies while we talked until the girls decided to hit the powder room.

As they walked away Cookie said, "Cute kids, hey?"

"Real cute. Where the devil do you find them?"

"I get around. I don't look like much, but I get around. With a pair like them on my arms it's a ticket to anyplace I want to go so long as a guy's taking up the tickets."

I picked a smoke out of my pack and handed one to him. "What about our deal?"

His eyes crawled up my arm to my face. "I know them. The boys are hurting right now. You do that?"

"Uh-huh."

"What a mess. The little one wants your guts."

"Who are they?"

"Private dicks. That's what the little piece of paper says in their wallets. They're hoods who'll do anything for some cash."

"If they're cops they aren't making any money unless they're hired to protect somebody."

"They are. You know anything about the rackets, Mike?"

"A little."

"The town's divided into sections, see. Like the bookies. They pay off to the local big boy who pays off to Ed Teen."

The cigarette froze in my fingers. "Where's Teen in this?"

"He's not, but one of his local boys is the mug who uses your two playmates for a bodyguard. His name is Toady Link. Ever hear of him?"

"Yeah."

"Then you didn't hear much. He keeps his nose clean. The bodyguards are to keep the small-timers moving and not to protect him. As bookies go, the guy's okay. Now how about coming across with something I can sell."

I squashed the butt out and started on another. Cookie's ears were pinned and he leaned across the table with a grin like we were telling dirty stories. I said, "There was a little murder the other night. Then there was another. In the beginning they looked little, but now they're starting to look pretty big. I haven't got a damn thing I can tell you . . . yet. When it happens you'll get it quick. How's that?"

"Fair enough. Who got killed?"

"A guy named William Decker, Arnold Basil, then the next day Decker's friend Mel Hooker."

"I read about that."

"You'll be reading more about it. Where'll I find this Toady Link?"

Cookie rattled off a couple of addresses where I might pick him up and I let them soak in so I wouldn't forget them. "Just one thing, Mike," he added, "you don't know from nothing, see? Keep me out of it. I stay away from them boys. My racket takes dough but no rough stuff, and when it comes to rods or brass knucks you can count me out. I don't want none of them hoods after my hide."

"Don't worry," I said. I stood up and threw a fin on the table to cover some of Tolly's champagne.

Cookie's eyebrows went up to his hairline. "You aren't going now, are you? Hell, what about Tolly? She's got a yen for you already and I can't make out with two dames."

"Sure you can. Nothing to it."

"Aw, Mike, what a guy you are, and after I hand you such a sweet dish too."

My mouth twisted into a lopsided smile. "I can get all the dishes I want without having them handed to me. Tell Tolly that maybe I'll look her up someday. She interests me strangely."

He didn't say anything, but he looked disappointed. He sat there wiggling those big ears and I cleared out of the place before the blonde came back and twisted my arm into staying.

Dames.

It was turning into a night just like that first one. The sidewalks and pavements were one big wet splash reflecting the garish lights of the streets and throwing them back at you. I pulled my raincoat out of the back and slipped into it, then climbed behind the wheel.

My watch read a few minutes after nine and it was tonight. Marsha said tonight. But there were other things first and Marsha could wait. It would be all the better for the waiting.

So I got in line behind the other cars and headed uptown. On the edge of the Bronx I turned off and looked for the bar that was one of the addresses Cookie had given me and found it in the middle of the block. I left the engine going while I asked around inside, but neither the bartender nor the manager had seen the eminent Mr. Link so far that night. They obliged with his home address and I thanked them politely even though I already had it.

Toady Link was at home.

Maybe it would be better to say he was occupying his Bronx residence. That's the kind of place it was. All fieldstone and picture windows on a walled-in half-acre of land that would have brought a quarter-million at auction. There were lights on all three floors of the joint and nobody to be seen inside. If it weren't for the new Packard squatting on the drive I would have figured the lights to be burglar protection.

I slid my own heap in at the curb and walked up the gravel to the house and punched the bell. Inside there was a faraway sound of chimes and about a minute later the door opened on a chain and a face looked at me waiting to see what I wanted.

You could see why he was called Toady. It was a big face, bigger around the jowls than it was on top with a pair of protuding eyes that seemed to have trouble staying in their sockets.

I said, "Hello, Toady. Do I get asked in?"

Even his voice was like a damned frog. "What do you want?"

"You maybe."

The frog face cracked into a wide-mouthed smile, a real nasty smile and the chain came off the lock. He had a gun in his hand, a big fat revolver with a hole in the end big enough to get your finger into. "Who the hell are you, bub?"

I took it easy getting my wallet out and flipped it back so he could see the tin. I shouldn't have bothered. His eyes never came off mine at all. I said, "Mike Hammer. Private Investigator, Toady. I think you ought to know me."

"I should?"

"Two of your boys should. They tried to take me."

"If you're looking for them . . ."

"I'm not. I'm looking for you. About a murder."

The smile got fatter and wider and the hole in the gun looked even bigger when he pointed it at my head. "Get in here," he said.

I did like he said. I stood there in the hall while he locked the door behind me and I could feel the muzzle of that rod about an inch behind my spine. Then he used it to steer me through the foyer into an outsized living room.

That much I didn't mind. But when he lowered the pile of fat he called a body into a chair and left me standing there on the carpet I got a little bit sore. "Let's put the heater away, Toady."

"Let's hear more about this murder first. I don't like people to throw murder in my face, Mr. Investigator. Not even lousy private cops."

Goddamn, that fat face of his was making me madder every second I had to look at it.

"You ever been shot, fat boy?" I asked him.

His face got red up to his hairline.

"I've been shot, fat boy," I said. "Not just once, either. Put that rod away or I'm going to give you a chance to use it. You'll have time to pump out just one slug and if it misses you're going to hear the nastiest noise you ever heard."

I let my hand come up so my fingertips were inside my coat. When he didn't make a move to stop me I knew I had him and he knew it too. Fat boy didn't like the idea of hearing a nasty noise a bit. He let the gun drop on the chair beside him and cursed me with those bug eyes of his for finding out he was as yellow as they come.

It was better that way. Now I liked standing in the middle of the room. I could look down at the fat slob and poke at him with a spear until he told me what I wanted to hear. I said, "Remember William Decker?"

His eyelids closed slowly and opened the same way. His head nodded once, squeezing the fat out under his chin.

"Do you know he's dead?"

"You son of a bitch, don't try tagging me with that!" Now he was a real frog with a real croak.

"He played the ponies, Toady. You were the guy who picked up his bets."

"So what! I pick up a lot of bets."

"I thought you didn't fool around with small-time stuff."

"Balls, he wasn't small-time. He laid 'em big as anybody else. How'd I know how he was operating? Look, you . . ."

"Shut up and answer questions. You're lucky I'm not a city cop or you'd be doing your talking with a light in your face. Where'd Decker get the dough to lay?"

He relaxed into a sullen frown, his pudgy hands balled into tight fists. "He borrowed it, that's where."

"From Dixie Cooper if you've forgotten." He looked at me and if the name meant anything I couldn't read it in his face. "How much did Decker drop to you?"

"Hell, he went in the hole for a few grand, but don't go trying to prove it. I don't keep books."

"So you killed him."

"Goddamn you!" He came out of the chair and stood there shaking from head to foot. "I gave him that dough back so he could pay off his loan! Understand that? I hate them creeps who can't stand a loss. The guy was ready to pull the Dutch act so I gave him back his dough so's he could pay off!"

He stood there staring at me with his eyes hanging out of that livid face of his sucking in his breath with a wheezy rasp. "You're lying, Toady," I said. "You're lying through your teeth." My hands twisted in the lapels of his coat and I pulled him in close so I could spit on him if I felt like it. "Where were you when Decker was killed?"

His hands fought with mine to keep me from choking him. "Here! I was . . . right here! Let go of me!"

"What about your boys . . . Nocky and that other gorilla?"

"I don't know where they were. I . . . didn't have anything to do with that! Goddamn, that's what I get for being a sucker! I should've let them work on the bastard. I should've kept his dough and kicked him out!"

"Maybe they did work over somebody. They had Decker's buddy all lined up for a shellacking until he shook 'em off on me. I thought I taught 'em to keep their noses out of trouble, but I guess I didn't teach 'em hard enough. The guy they were going to give the business to died with a bullet in him the same night. I hear tell those boys work for you, and they weren't out after the guy on their own."

"You . . . you're crazy!"

"Am I? Who put them on Hooker : . . you?"

"Hooker?" He worked his head into a frown that wouldn't stick.

"Don't play innocent, damn it. You know who I'm talking about. Mel Hooker. The guy who teamed up with Decker to play the nags."

An oversize tongue made a quick pass over his lips. "He . . . yeah, I know. Hooker. Nocky and him got in a fight. It was when he picked up his dough and cleared out. He was drunk, see? He started shooting off his mouth about how it was all crooked and he talked enough to keep some dough from coming across the board. That's how it was. Nocky tried to throw him out and he nearly brained him."

"So your boy picked him off?"

"No, no. He wouldn't do that. He was plenty mad, that's why he was laying for him. He didn't knock anybody off. I don't go for that. Ask anybody, they'll tell you I don't go for rough stuff."

I gave him a shove to get him away from me. "For a bookie you're a big-hearted son of a bitch. You're one in a million and, brother, you better be telling the truth, because if you aren't you're going to get a lot of that fat sweated off you. Where's these two mugs?"

"How the hell do I know?"

I didn't play with him this time. I backhanded him across the mouth and did it again when he stumbled away and tried to grab the gun on the chair. His big belly shook so hard he swayed off balance and I gave it to him again. Then he just about fell into the chair and with the rod right under his hand he didn't have the guts to make a play for it.

I asked him again. "Where are they, Toady?"

"They . . . have rooms over the . . . Rialto Restaurant."

"Names, Pal."

"Nocky . . . he's Arthur Cole. The other one's Glenn Fisher." He had to squeeze the words out between lips that were no more than a thin red gash in his face. The marks of my fingers were across his cheek, making them puff out even farther. I could tell that he was hoping I'd turn my back, even for a second. The crazy madness in his eyes made them bulge so far his eyelids couldn't cover them.

I turned my back. I did it when I picked up the phone, but there was a mirror right in front of me and I could stand there and watch him hate me while I thumbed through the directory until I found the number listed under "Cole" and dialed it.

The phone rang, all right, but nobody answered it. Then I called the Rialto Restaurant and went through two waiters before the manager came on and told me that the boys didn't live there any more. They had packed their bags about an hour before, climbed into a cab and scrammed. Yeah, they were all paid up and the management was glad to be rid of them.

I hung up and turned around. "They beat it, Toady."

Link just sat.

"Where'd they go?"

His shoulders hunched into a shrug.

"I have a feeling you're going to die pretty soon, Toady," I said. And after I said it I looked at him until it sank all the way in and put his eyes back in place so the eyelids could get over them. I picked up the gun that lay beside him, flipped out the cylinder and punched the shells into my hand. They were .44's with copper-covered noses that could rip a guy in half. I tossed the empty rod back on the chair beside him and walked out of the room.

Somehow the night smelled cleaner after Toady. The rain was a light mist washing the stink of the swamp away. It shaded part of the monstrous castle the ugly frog sat in as though it were ashamed of it. I looked back at the lights and I could see why they were all on. They were the guy's only friends.

When I got back in my car I drove down to the corner, swung around and came back up the street. Before I got as far as the house the Packard came roaring out of the drive and skidded halfway across the road before it straightened out and went tearing off down the street. I had to laugh because Toady wasn't going anyplace at all. Not driving like that he wasn't. Toady was so goddamn mad he had to take it out on something and tonight the car took the beating.

I would have kept right on going myself if he hadn't left the door wide open so that the light made a streaming yellow invitation down the gravel. I jammed on the brakes and left the car sitting, the motor turning over and picked up the invitation.

The house was Toady's attempt at respectability, but it was only an attempt. The upstairs lights were turned on from switches at the foot of the stairs and only one set of prints showed in the dust that lay over the staircase. There were three bedrooms, two baths and a sitting room on the top floor, a full apartment-sized layout on the second and the only places that had been used were one bedroom and a shower stall. Everything else was neat and dormant, with the dust-mop marks last week's cleaning woman had left. Downstairs the kitchen was a mess of dirty dishes and littered newspapers. The pantry was stocked to take care of a hundred people who never came and the only things in the guest closet were Toady's hat and coat that he hadn't bothered to wear when he dashed out.

I rummaged around in the library and the study without touching anything then went down the cellar and had a drink of private stock at his bar. It was a big place with knotty pine walls rimmed with a couple hundred beer steins that were supposed to give it the atmosphere of a beer garden. Off to one side was the poolroom with the balls neatly racked and gathering more dust. He even had a cigarette machine down there. The butts were on the house and all you had to do was yank the lever, so I had a pack of Luckies on Toady too.

There were two other doors that led off the poolroom. One

went into the furnace room and I stepped into a goddamned rattrap that nearly took my toes off. The other was a storeroom and I almost backed out of it when the white clothes that shrouded the stockpile of junk took shape. I found the light switch and turned it on. Instead of an overhead going on, a red light blossomed out over a sink on the end of the wall, turning everything a deep crimson.

The place was a darkroom. Or at least it had been. The stuff hadn't been touched since it was stored here. A big professional camera was folded up under wraps with a lot of movie-screen type backdrops and a couple of wrought-iron benches. The processing chemicals and film plates had rotted away on a shelf next to a box that held the gummy remains of tubes of retouching paints. Off in the corner was a screwy machine of some sort that had its seams all carefully dust-proofed with masking tape.

I put the covers back in place and turned the light off. When I closed the door I couldn't help thinking that Toady certainly tried hard to work up a hobby. In a way I couldn't blame him a bit. For friends all that repulsive bastard had was a lot of toys and dust. The louse was rich as sin with nobody to spend his money on.

I left the door open like I found it and climbed in under the wheel of my heap. I sat there feeling a little finger probing at my mind, trying to jar something into it that should already be there and the finger was still probing away when I got back to Manhattan and started down Riverside Drive.

So damn many little things and none of them added up. Some place between a tenement slum that had belonged to Decker and Toady's dismal swamp castle a killer was whistling his way along the street while I sat trying to figure out what a finger nudging my mind meant.

Lord, I was tired. The smoke in the car stung my eyes and I had to open the window to let it out. What I needed was a long, natural sleep without anything at all to think and dream about, but up there in the man-built cliffs of steel and stone was Marsha and she said she'd wait for me. The back of my head started to hurt again and even the thought of maybe sleeping with somebody who had been a movie star didn't make it go away.

But I went up.

And she was still waiting, too.

Marsha said, "You're late, Mike."

"I know, I'm sorry." She picked the hat out of my hand and waited while I peeled off my coat. When she had them stowed in the closet she hooked her arm under mine and took me inside.

There were drinks all set up and waiting beside a bowl that had held ice but was now all water. The tall red candles had been lit, burned down a few inches, then had been blown out.

"I thought you would have been here earlier. For supper perhaps."

She handed me a cigarette from a long narrow box and followed it with a lighter. When I had my lungs full of smoke I leaned back with my head pillowed against the chair and looked at her close up. She had on a light green dress that swirled up her body, over her shoulder and came down again to a thin leather belt at her waist. The swelling around her eye had gone down and in the soft light of the room the slight purple discoloration almost looked good.

I watched her a second and grinned. "Now I'm nearly sorry I didn't. You're nice to look at, kitten."

"Just half?"

"No. All this time. From top to bottom too."

Her eyes burned softly under long lashes. "I like it when you say it, Mike. You're used to saying it too, aren't you?"

"Only to beautiful women."

"And you've seen plenty of them." The laugh was in her voice now.

I said, "You've got the wrong slant, kid. Pretty is what you mean. Pretty and beautiful are two different things. Only a few women are pretty, but even one who's not so hot to look at can be beautiful. A lot of guys make mistakes when they turn down a beautiful woman for one who's just pretty."

Her eyebrows went up in the slightest show of surprise, letting the fires of her irises leap into plain view. "I didn't know you were a philosopher, Mike."

"There're a lot of things you don't know about me."

She uncurled from the chair and picked up the glasses from the table. "Should I?"

"Uh-huh. They're all bad." I got that look again, the one with the smile around the edges, then she brought in some fresh ice from the kitchen and made a pair of highballs. The one she gave me went down cold and easy, nestling there at the bottom of my stomach with a pleasant, creeping kind of warmth that tiptoed silently throughout my body until it was the nicest thing in the world to just sit there with my eyes half shut and listen to the rain drum against the windows.

Marsha's hand went to the switch on the record payer, flooding the room with the soft tones of the "Blue Danube." She filled the glasses again, then drifted to the floor at my feet, laying her head back against my knees. "Nice?" she asked me.

"Wonderful. I'm right in the mood to enjoy it."

"You still . . ."

"That's right. Still." I closed my eyes all the way for a minute. "Sometimes I think I'm standing still too. It's never been like this before."

Her hand found mine and pulled it down to her cheek. I thought I felt her lips brush my fingers, but I wasn't sure. "Do you have the boy yet?"

"Yeah, he's in good hands. Tomorrow or maybe the next day they'll come for him. He'll be all right."

"I wish there was something I could do. Are you sure there isn't? Could I keep him for you?"

"He'd be too much for you. Hell, he's only a little over a year old. I have a nurse for him. She's old, but reliable."

"Then let me take him out for a walk or something. I really do want to help, Mike, honest."

I ran my fingers through the sheen of her hair and across the soft lines of her face. This time I knew it when her lips parted in a kiss on my palm.

"I wish you could, Marsha. I need help. I need something. This whole thing is getting away from me."

"Would it help to tell me about it?"

"Maybe."

"Then tell me."

So I told her. I sat there staring at the ceiling with Marsha on the floor and her head on my knees and I told her about it. I lined up everything from beginning to end and tried to put them together in the right order.

When you strung them out like that it didn't take long to tell. They made a nice neat pile of facts, one on top of the other, but there was nothing there to hold them together. One little push scattered them all over the place. Before I finished my jaws ached from holding my teeth together so tightly.

"Being so mad won't help you think," Marsha said.

"I gotta be mad. Goddamn, you can't go at a thing like this unless you are mad. I never knew much about kids, but when I held the Decker boy in my hands I could see why a guy would give his insides to keep his kid alive. Right there is the thing that screws everything up. Decker knew he was going to die and didn't try to do a single thing about it. Three days before, he knew it was going to happen too. He got all his affairs put right and waited. God knows what he thought about in those three days."

"It couldn't have been nice."

"Oh, I don't know. I don't get it at all." I rubbed my face disgustedly. "Decker and Hooker tie in with Toady Link and he ties in with Grindle and Teen and it was one of Grindle's boys who shot Decker. There's a connection there if you want to look for one."

"I'm sorry, Mike."

"You don't have to be."

"But I am. In a way it started with me. I keep thinking of the boy."

"It would have been the same if Decker had broken into the other apartment. The guy knew he was going to die . . . but why? Whether or not he got what he was after he was still planning to die!"

Marsha lifted her face and turned around "Couldn't it have been . . . a precaution? Perhaps he *was* planning to run out with the money. In that case he would know there *was* a possibility that they might catch up with him. As it was, it turned out to be the same thing. He knew they'd never believe his story about the wrong apartment so he ran anyway, bringing about the same results."

My eyes felt hot and heavy. "It's crazy as hell. It's a mess no matter how I look at it, but someplace there's an answer and it's lost in my head. I keep trying to work it loose and it won't come. Every time I stop to think about it I can feel it sitting here and if the damn thing was human it would laugh at me. Now I can't even think any more."

"Tired, darling?"

"Yeah."

I looked at her and she looked at me and we were both thinking the same thing. Then her head dropped slowly and her smile had a touch of sadness in it.

"I'm a fool, aren't I?" she said.

"You're no fool, Marsha."

"Mike . . . have you ever been in love?"

I didn't know how to answer that so I just nodded.

"Was it nice?"

"I thought so." I was hoping she wouldn't ask me any more. Even after five years it hurt to think about it.

"Are you . . . now?" Her voice was low, almost inaudible. I caught the brief flicker of her eyes as she glanced at my face.

I shrugged. I didn't know what to tell her.

She smiled at her hands and I smiled with her. "That's good," she laughed. Her eyes went bright and happy and she tossed her head so that her hair fell in a glittering dark halo around her shoulders. "I had tonight all planned. I was going to be a fool anyway and make you want me so that you'd keep wanting me."

"It's been like that."

She came up off the floor slowly, gracefully, reaching for my hand to pull me out of the chair. Her mouth was warmer than it should have been. Her body was supple and lovely, like a fluid filling in the gaps between us. I ran my fingers through her hair, pulling her face away while still wanting to keep her crushed against me.

"Why, Marsha?" I asked. "Why me? You know what I'm like. I'm not fancy and I'm not famous and I work for my dough. I'm not in your class at all."

She looked up at me with an expression you don't try to describe. A sleepy expression that wasn't a bit tired. Her hands slid up my back and tightened as she leaned against me. "Let me be a woman, Mike. I don't want those things you say you're not. I've had them. I want all the things you are. You're big and not so handsome, but there's a devil inside you that makes you exciting and tough, yet enough of an angel to make you tender when you have to be."

My hands wanted to squeeze right through her waist until they met and I had to let her go or she would have felt the way they were shaking. I turned around and reached for the bottle and glass on the table and while I was pouring one there was a click and the light dimmed to a pale glow.

Behind me I heard her say softly, "Mike . . . you never told me whether I was . . . just pretty or beautiful."

I turned around and was going to tell her that she was the most lovely thing I had ever seen, but her hands did something to her belt and the fold of the dress that came up over one shoulder dropped away leaving her standing there with one hand on the lamp like a half-nude vision and the words got stuck in my throat.

Then the light disappeared altogether and I could only drink the drink quickly, because although the vision was gone it was walking toward me across the night and somewhere on the path there was another whisper of fabric and she was there in my hands without anything to keep her from being a woman now, an invisible, naked dream throwing a mantle of desire around us both that had too great a strength to break and must be burned through by a fire that leaped and danced and towered in a blazing crescendo that could only be dampened and never extinguished.

And when the mantle was thrown back I left the dream there in the dark, warm and soft, breathing quickly to tell me that it was a dream that would come back on other nights too, disturbing and at the same time satisfying.

She was beautiful. She was pretty, too.

She was in my mind all the way home.

chapter six ▬▬▬▬▬▬▬▬▬

AT A QUARTER past ten I got up, dressed and made myself some breakfast. Right in the middle of it the phone rang and when I answered it the operator told me to hold on for a call from Miami. Velda's husky voice was a pleasure to hear again. She said, "Mike?"

And I said, "Hello, sweetheart. How's everything?"

"Fine. At least it's partly fine. Our boy got out on a plane, but he left all the stuff behind. The insurance investigator is here making an inventory of the stuff now."

"Great, great. Try to promote yourself a bonus if you can."

"That wouldn't be hard," she laughed. "He's already made a pass. Mike, miss me?"

I felt like a heel, but I wasn't lying when I said, "Hell yes, I miss you."

"I don't mean as a business partner."

"Neither do I, kitten."

"You won't have to miss me long. I'm taking the afternoon train out."

My fingers started batting out dots and dashes on the table. I wanted her back but not too soon. I didn't want anybody else climbing all over me. "You stay there," I told her. "Stay on that guy's tail. You're still on salary from the company and if you can get a line on him now they'll cut us in for more business later. They're as interested in him as they are in recovering the stuff."

"But, Mike, the Miami police are doing all they can."

"Where'd he hop to?"

"Some place in Cuba. That's where they lost him."

"Okay, get over to Cuba then. Take a week and if it's no dice forget it and come on home."

She didn't say anything for a few seconds. "Mike . . . is something wrong up there?"

"Don't be silly."

"You sound like it. If you're sending me off . . ."

"Look, kid," I cut her off, "you'd know about it if anything was wrong. I just got up and I'm kind of sleepy yet. Be a good girl and stay on that case, will you?"

"All right. Love me?"

"You'll never know," I said.

She laughed again and hung up. She knew. Women always know.

I went back and finished my breakfast, had a smoke then turned on the faucet in the bathroom sink to bring the hot water up. While I shaved I turned on the radio and picked up the commentator who was just dropping affairs in Washington to get back to New York and as far as he was concerned the only major problem of the day was the District Attorney's newest successes in the gambling probe. At some time last night a series of raids had been carried out successfully and the police dragnet had brought in some twenty-five persons charged with bookmaking. He gave no details, but hinted that the police were expecting to nail the kingpins in the near future.

When I finished shaving I opened my door and took the tabloid out of the knob to see what the press had to say about it. The front page carried the pictures of those gathered in the roundup with appropriate captions while the inside double spread had a layout showing where the bookies had been operating.

The editorial was the only column that mentioned Ed Teen at all. It brought out the fact that Teen's personal staff of lawyers were going to bat for the bookies. At the same time the police were finding that a lot of witnesses were reluctant to speak up when it came to identifying the boys who took their money or paid off on wins, places and shows. At the end of the column the writer came right out with the charge that Lou Grindle had an organization specially adept at keeping witnesses from talking and demanded that the police throw some light on the subject.

I went through the paper again to make sure I didn't miss anything, then folded it up and stuck it in the bottom of my chair until I got around to reading it. Then I went downstairs and knocked on the door of the other apartment and stood there with my hat in my hands until the door opened and the nurse said, "Good morning, Mr. Hammer. Come on in."

"I can only stay a minute. I want to see how the kid is."

"Oh, he's a regular boy. Right now he's trying to see what's inside the radio."

I walked in behind her to the living room where the kid was doing just that. He had the extension cord in his fists and the set teetered on the edge of the table a hair away from complete ruin. I got there first and grabbed the both of them.

The kid knew me, all right. His face was sunny with a big smile and he shoved his hand inside my coat and then chattered indignantly when I pulled it out. "How's the breakage charge coming?"

"We won't count that," the nurse said. "As a matter of fact, he's been much better than I expected."

I held the kid out where I could look at him better. "There's something different about him."

"There ought to be. I gave him a haircut." I put him back on the floor where he hung on my leg and jabbered at me. "He certainly likes you," she said.

"I guess I'm all he's got. Need anything?"

"No, we're getting along fine."

"Okay, anything you want just get." I bent down and ruffled the kid's hair and he tried to climb up my leg. He yelled to come with me so I had to hand him back and wave good-by from the door. He was so damn small and pathetic-looking I felt like a heel for stranding him, but I promised myself I'd see that he got a lot of attention before he was dropped into some home for orphans.

The first lunch shift was just hitting the streets when I got to Pat's office. The desk man called ahead to see if he was still in and told me to go right up. A couple of reporters were coming out of the room still jotting down notes and Pat was perched on the edge of a desk fingering a thick Manila folder.

I closed the door behind me and he said, "Hi Mike."

"Making news?"

"Today we're heroes. Tomorrow we'll be something else again."

"So the D.A.'s making out. Did you find the hole?"

He turned around slowly, his face expressionless. "No, if that cop is passing out the word then he wised up. Nothing went out on this deal at all."

"How could he catch on?"

"He's been a cop a long time. He's been staked out often enough to spot it when he's being watched himself."

"Did he mention it?"

"No, but his attitude has changed. He resents the implication apparently."

"That's going to make pretty reading. Now the papers'll call for the D.A. to make a full-scale investigation of the whole department, I suppose."

"The D.A. doesn't know a damn thing about it. You keep it to yourself too. I'm handling the matter myself. If it is the guy there's no sense smearing the whole department. We still aren't sure of it, you know."

He tossed the folder on top of the filing cabinet and sat down behind the desk with a sigh. There were tired lines around his eyes and mouth, little lines that had been showing up a lot lately.

I said, "What came of the roundup?"

"Oh, hell, Mike." He glanced at me with open disgust, then realized that I wasn't handing him a dig. "Nothing came of it. So we closed down a couple of rooms. We got a hatful of small-timers who will probably walk right out of it or draw minimum sentences. Teen's a smart operator. His lawyers are even smarter. Those boys know all the angles there are to know and if there are any new ones they think them up.

"Teen's a real cutie. You know what I think? He's letting us take some of his boys just to keep the D.A. happy and get a chance to put in a bigger fix."

"I don't get it," I said.

"Look, Teen pays for protection. That is, if it takes money to keep his racket covered. If it takes muscle he uses Lou Grindle. But supposing it does take dough . . . then all the chiselers, petty politicians and maybe even the big shots who are taking his dough are going to want more to keep his personal fix in because things are getting tougher. Okay, he pays off, and the more those guys rake in the deeper in they are too. Suddenly they realize that they can't afford to let Teen get taken or they'll go along with him, so they work overtime to keep the louse clean."

"Nice."

"Isn't it though?" He sat there tapping his fingers on the desk, then: "Mike, for all you've heard, read and seen of Ed Teen, do you know what we actually have on him?"

"Tell me."

"Nothing. Not one damn thing. Plenty of suspicions, but you don't take suspicions to court. We know everything he's hooked up with and we can't prove a single part of it. I've been upside down for a month backtracking over his life trying to tie him into something that happened a long time ago and for all I've found you could stuff in your ear." Pat buried his face in his hands and rubbed his eyes.

"Have you had time to do anything about Decker and Hooker?"

At least it made him smile a little. "I haven't been upside down *that* long, Pal," he said. "I was going to call you on that. Routine investigation turned up something on Hooker. For the last four months he made bank deposits of close to a thousand bucks each time. They apparently came in on the same date and were all for the same amount, though he spent a little of each wad before he deposited it. That sort of ties in with your story about him hitting the winning ponies."

I rolled a cigarette between my fingers slowly then stuck it in my mouth. "How often were the deposits made?"

"Weekly. Regular as pie."

"And Decker?"

"Clean. I had four men cover every minute of his time as far back as they could go. As far as we could find out he didn't even associate with any shady characters. The kind of people who vouched for him were the kind who knew what they were talking about too. Incidentally, I talked to his parish priest personally. He's made all the arrangements for the boy and cleared them with the authorities, so he'll pick him up at the end of the week."

He stopped and watched my face a moment. The silence was so thick you could slice it with a knife. "All right, now what are you thinking, Mike?"

I let a lazy cloud of smoke sift up toward the ceiling. "It might scare you," I said.

The tired lines got deeper when his mouth clamped shut. "Yeah? Scare me then."

"Maybe you've been closer to nailing Teen than you thought, chum."

His fingers stopped their incessant tapping.

"After Decker was killed a lot of awfully funny things started to happen. Before they didn't seem to make much sense, but just because you can't actually see what's holding them together doesn't mean that they're not there. Wouldn't it be a scream if the guy who killed Decker could lead you to Teen?"

"Yeah, I'd laugh myself sick." Now Pat's eyes were just thin shiny slits in his head.

I said, "Those bank deposits of Hooker's weren't wins. Hooker was being paid off to do something. You got any idea what it was?"

"No," sullenly.

"I'd say he was being paid to see that a certain guy was put in a certain spot where he was up the creek."

"Damn it, Mike, quit talking in riddles!"

"Pat, I can't. It's still a puzzle to me, too, but I can tell you this. You've been routine on this case all along. It's been too small-time to open up on but I think you'd damn well better open up on it right now because you're sitting on top of the thing that can blow Teen and his racket all to hell. I don't know how or why . . . yet. But I know it's there and before very long I'm going to find the string that's holding it together. As far as Ed Teen's concerned I don't care what happens to him, only someplace in there is the guy who made an orphan out of a nice little kid and he's the one I want. You can take it for what it's worth or I can go it alone. Just don't shove the Decker kill down at the bottom of the page and hope something turns up on it because you think grabbing Teen is more important."

He started to come up out of his chair and his face was strictly cop without tired lines anymore. He got all set to give me the business, then, like turning on the light, the scowl and the tired lines went away and he sat back smiling a little with that excited, happy look I hadn't seen him wear for so long.

"What's it about, Mike?"

"I think the Decker murder got away from somebody. It was supposed to be nice and clean and didn't happen that way."

"What else?"

"A lot of scrambled facts that are going to get put right fast if you help out. Then I'll give it to you so there's sense to it."

"You know, you're damn lucky I know what makes you tick, Mike. If you were anybody else I'd hammer out every last bit of information you have. I'm only sorry you didn't get on the force while you were still young enough."

"I don't like the hours. The pay either."

"No," he grinned, "you'd sooner work for free and get me all hopped up whenever you feel like it. You and the D.A. Okay, spill it. What do you need?"

"A pair of private detectives named Arthur Cole and Glenn Fisher."

He jotted the names down and stared at them blankly a second. "Nocky . . .?"

"That's Cole."

"You should have given me their names before."

"I didn't know them before."

He reached out and flipped the switch on the intercom. "Tell Sergeant McMillan to come in a moment, please."

A voice rasped that it would and while we waited Pat went to the filing cabinet and pawed through the drawers until he had what he wanted. He tossed the stuff in my lap as a thick-set plain-clothesman came in chewing on a dead cigar.

Pat said, "Sergeant, this is Mike Hammer."

The cop shifted his cigar and held out his hand. I said, "Glad to know you."

"Same here. Heard lots about you, Mike."

"Sergeant McMillan has the inside information on the up-town boys," Pat said. He turned to the plain-clothesman with, "What do you know about two supposedly private detectives named Cole and Fisher?"

"Plenty. Fisher lost his license about a month ago. What do you want to know?"

Pat raised his eyebrows at me. "Background stuff," I said.

"The guys are hoods, plain and simple. Especially Fisher. You ever see them?"

I nodded. Pat pointed to the folder in my lap and I pulled out a couple of candid shots taken during a strike-breaking melee on the docks. My boys were right there in the foreground swinging billies.

The cop said, "They're troublemakers. About a year ago some-body with a little pull had them tagged with badges so what they did would be a little bit legal. Neither one of 'em have records, but they've been pulled in a few times for minor offenses. Brawling mostly. They'll work for anybody who pays off. You want me to put out a call for 'em, Captain?"

"What about it, Mike?" Pat asked.

"It wouldn't be a bad idea, but you won't find them in New York. Stick them on the teletype and see if they aren't holing up in another city. You might try alerting the railroads dicks to keep an eye out for them. They skipped out last night and might still be traveling. Cole has a broken hand and Fisher's face is a mess. They ought to be easy to identify."

"You want to do that, sergeant?"

He nodded at Pat. "I have everything I need. They shouldn't be too hard to trace." He said so long to me and went back the way he came.

Pat picked the photo up and studied it. "What's with these two?"

"They worked for Toady Link." Pat's head came up quickly.

"They were on to Hooker for some reason until I started buzzing the guy, then they went into me. I didn't get the pitch in time or Hooker might still be alive. Last night I paid a visit to our friend Link and he was happy to tell me who the boys were."

"Mike, damn it . . ."

"If you're wondering how I found out who they were when the cops didn't know . . . I have a friend who gets around. With blondes."

"I'm not wondering that at all! I'm wondering how the hell I could have been so negligent or stupid, whatever you want to call it." He grinned wryly. "I used to be a bright boy. A year ago I would have seen the connection or let you talk me into something a lot sooner. Everything you do is tying right in with this Teen affair. Did you know that we had Link slated to go through the mill this week?"

"No."

"Well, we had. He and four others. While the D.A.'s been getting pushed around he's been doing one hell of a job on the organization's working men. Toady's about a month away from a man-sized stretch up the river. Every move you make you step on my toes."

"Why didn't you pick it up sooner?"

"Because it's no novelty to be tied up with Teen or Grindle, especially when there's money or murder concerned. Some of the help those two employ have turned up on more than one offense. It wasn't too difficult to suppose that Basil was just out for extra cash when he went in on that robbery and shot Decker afterward."

"Are you positive that he's the one who did the shooting?"

"As positive as the paraffin test. Of course, he may have discharged the bullet prior to the killing, but if he did I don't know where. If this Decker thing has even the slightest tie-up with the boys we want then we'll get to it."

"Hang on, Pat. I'm not saying that it has."

"I'll damn soon find out."

I tried to be unconcerned as I pulled on my smoke. "How about letting me find out for you. So far Decker has been my party."

"Nix, Mike. I know what you want. All you have in your head is the idea that you want to tangle with that killer. Not this time. Taking that one guy out of play could screw up this whole thing so nicely we'll be left with nothing at all."

"Okay, Pal," I grinned, "go right to it. Just try to get an identification out of me. Just try it."

"Mike . . ."

"Aw, nuts, Pat. I'm as critical to this thing as those two mugs are. It was me who saw them and me who pushed them around. Without my say-so you don't have a thing to haul them in on. You're taking all the gravy for yourself . . . or at least you're trying to."

"What do you want, Mike?"

"I want three or four days to make my own play. Things are just beginning to look up. I'd like a file on Toady Link too."

"That's impossible. The D.A. has it classified top secret. That's out."

"Can't *you* get it, kid?"

"Nope. That would mean an explanation and I'm not giving blue boy a chance to climb up my back again."

"Well, hell . . . do you know anything about the guy at all?"

He leaned back in the chair and shook his head slowly. "Probably no more than you know, Mike. I haven't done anything more than listen in and supply a little information I had when Toady's name came up. The D.A. had his own men doing the legwork."

I looked out the window and while I watched the people on the roof across the street Pat studied my face and studied it hard. I could feel his eyes crawl across me and make everything I was thinking into thoughts and words of his own.

He said, "You're thinking Toady Link's the last step in the chain, aren't you?"

I nodded.

"Spell it out for me."

So I spelled it out. I said, "Big-money boys like to splurge. They say they go for wine, women and song but whoever said it forgot to add the ponies too. Go out to the races and take a look around. Take a peek at the limousines and convertibles and the bank rolls that own them."

"So?"

"So there was a big-money boy named Marvin Holmes who likes his blondes fast and furious and very much on hand. He spends his dough like water and keeps plenty of it locked up in a safe on his wall. He plays the nags through a bookie named Toady Link and doesn't like the way the ponies run so he won't pay off his bet. He's too big to push around, but Link can't take a welch so he looks around for a way to get his dough. Somebody tips him about a former safe expert named Decker, but the guy is honest and wants to stay that way. Okay so Toady waits until the guy needs dough. He finds out who his friend is . . . a guy named Mel Hooker, and pays him to steer Decker his way. They use a rigged-up deal to make it look like they're winning a pot and everybody is happy. Then Decker goes in over his head. He borrows from a loan shark to make the big kill and loses everything. That's where the pressure starts. He's not a big shot and he's got a kid and he's an easy mark to push around. He knows what happens on this loan-shark deal and he's scared, so when Toady comes up with the proposition of opening a safe . . . a simple little thing like that . . . Decker grabs it, takes a pay-off from Link to keep the shark off his neck and goes to it.

"It would have been fine if Decker had hit the right apartment, but he made a mistake he couldn't afford. He had to take a powder. Maybe he had even planned on taking a powder and arranged for his kid to be taken care of if things didn't go right. I don't know about that. He had something planned anyway. The only trouble was that he didn't plan well enough, or the guys who went out with him in the job were too sharp. They had him cold. Basil shot him then went over him for the dough. He must have yelled out that Decker was clean just before I started shooting. When he went down the driver couldn't afford to let him be taken alive and ran over him.

"Just take it from there . . . he already knew where Decker lived and thought that maybe when he went back for his kid he stashed the dough he was supposed to have. The guy searched the place and couldn't find it. Then he got the idea that maybe Basil had been too hurried when he searched Decker's corpse . . . but I had been right there and figured that I wouldn't overlook picking up a pile from a corpse if I got the chance. So while I was out my apartment was searched and I came back in time to catch the guy at it. I was in too damn much of a hurry and he beat the hell out of me.

"Now let's suppose it *was* Toady. Two guys are dead and he can be right in line for the hot seat if somebody gets panicky and talks. After all, Hooker didn't know the details of the kill so he could have thought that Toady was getting him out of the way to keep him from talking. That puts him in the same spot and he's scared stiff. Evidently he did have one run-in with the tough boys before and carried the scar around on his face to prove it.

"So Hooker spots two of Toady's boys and gets the jumps. They're sticking around waiting for the right spot to stick him. When Hooker got confidential with me they must have thought that Mel was asking for protection or trying to get rid of what I knew so they tried to take me. They muffed that one and went back to get Hooker. They didn't muff that one.

"Up to there Toady didn't have too much to worry about, but when I showed my face he got scared. Just before that he packed his boys out of town because he couldn't afford to have them around, so if we can get them back we ought to finger Toady without any trouble at all. Not the least little bit of trouble."

There was a silence that lasted for a full minute and I could hear Pat breathing and my own watch ticking. Pat said, "That's supposing you got all this dealt out right."

"Uh-huh."

"We can find out soon enough." He picked up the phone and said, "Give me an outside line, please," and while he waited riffled through the phone book. I heard the dial tone come on and Pat fingered out a number. The phone ringing on the other end made a faraway hum. Then it stopped. "I'd like to speak to Mr. Holmes," Pat said. "This is Captain Chambers, Homicide, speaking."

He sat there and frowned at the wall while he listened, then put the receiver back too carefully. "He's gone, Mike. He left for South America with one of his blondes yesterday morning."

"That's great," I said. My voice didn't sound like me at all.

Pat's mouth got tight around the corners. "That's perfect. It proves your point. The guy isn't too big to push around after all. Somebody's scared him right out of the city. You called every goddamn move right on the nose."

"I hope so."

I guess he didn't like the way I said it.

"It looks good to me."

"It looks too good. I wish we had the murder weapons to back it up."

"Metal doesn't rot out that fast. If we get those two we'll get the gun and we'll get Toady too. It doesn't matter which one we get him for."

"Maybe. I'd like to know who drove the car that night."

"Toady certainly wouldn't do it himself."

I stopped watching the people on the roof across the way and turned my face toward Pat. "I'm thinking that he did, Pat. If it was the kind of haul he expected he wasn't going to let it go through a few hands before it got back to him. Yeah, feller, I think I'll tag Toady with this one."

"Not you, Mike . . . *we'll* tag him for it. The police. The public. Justice. You know."

"Want to bet?"

Suddenly he wasn't my friend any more. His eyes were too gray and his face was too bland and I was the guy in the chair who was going to keep answering questions until he was done with me. Or that's what he thought.

I said, "A few minutes ago I asked you if you'd like to nail the whole batch of them at once."

"So there's more to it?"

"There could be. Lots more. Only if I get a couple extra days first."

Something you might call a smile threw a shadow around his mouth. "You know what will happen to me if you mess things up?"

"Do you know what will happen to me?"

"You might get yourself killed."

"Yeah."

"Okay, Mike, you got your three days. God help you if you get in a jam because I won't."

He was lying both times and I knew it. I'd no more get three days than he'd give me a boot when I needed a hand, but I played it like I didn't catch the drift and got up out of my chair. He was sitting there with the same expression when I closed the door, but his hand had already started to reach for the phone.

I went down the corridor to where a bunch of typewriters were banging out a madhouse symphony and asked one of the stenos where I could find Ellen Scobie. She told me that she had gone out to lunch at noon and was expected back that afternoon, but I might still find her in the Nelson Steak House if I got over there right away.

It took me about ten minutes to make the four blocks and there was Ellen in the back looking more luscious than the oversize T-bone steak she was gnawing on.

She saw me and waved and I wondered what it was going to cost who to get hold of that file on Toady Link.

It made nice wondering.

chapter seven ███████████████

SHE WAS ALL in black, but without Ellen inside it the dress would have been nothing. The sun had kissed her skin into a light toast color, dotting the corner of her eyes with freckles. Her hair swept back and down, caressing her bare shoulders whenever she moved her head.

She said, "Hello, man."

I slid in across the table. "Did you eat yourself out of company?"

"Long ago. My poor working friends had to get back to the office."

"What about you?"

"You are enjoying the sight of a woman enjoying the benefits of working overtime when the city budget doesn't allow for un-authorized pay. They had to give me the time off. Want something to eat?"

A waitress sneaked up behind me and poised her pencil over her pad. "I'll have a beer and a sandwich. Ham. Plenty of mustard and anything else you can squeeze on."

Ellen made a motion for another coffee and went back to the remains of the steak. I had my sandwich and beer without benefit of small talk until we were both finished and relaxing over a smoke.

She was nice to look at. Not because she was pretty all over, but because there was something alive about everything she did. Now she was propped in the corner of the booth with one leg half up on the bench grinning because the girl across the way was talking her head off to keep her partner's attention. The guy was trying, but his eyes kept sliding over to Ellen every few seconds.

I said, "Give the kid a break, will you?"

She laughed lightly, way down in her throat, then leaned on the table and cupped her chin in her hands. "I feel real wicked when I do things like that."

"Your friends must love you."

"Ooh," her mouth made a pouty little circle, ". . . they do. The men, I mean. Like you, Mike. You came in here especially to see me. You find me so attractive that you can't stay away." She laughed again.

"Yeah," I said. "I even dream about you."

"Like hell."

"No kidding, I mean it."

"I can picture you going out of your way for a woman. I'd

give my right arm to hear you say that in a different tone of voice, though. There's something about you that fascinates me. Now that we have the love-making over with, what do I have that you want?"

I shouldn't have let my eyes do what they did.

"Besides that, I mean," she said.

"Your boss has a certain file on Toady Link. I want a look at it."

Her hands came together to cover her eyes. "I should have known. I spend every waking hour making myself pretty for you, hoping that you'll pop in on me and when you do you ask me to climb up a cloud."

"Well?"

"It's . . . well, it's almost impossible, Mike."

"Why?"

Her eyes drifted away from mine reluctantly. "Mike, I . . ."

"It isn't exactly secret information with me, Ellen. Pat told me about the D.A. getting ready to wrap Link up in a gray suit."

"Then he should have told you that those files are locked and under guard. He doesn't trust anybody."

"He trusts you."

"And if I get caught doing a thing like that I'll not only lose this job and never be able to get another one, but I'll get a gray suit too. I don't like the color." She reached out and plucked a Lucky from my pack and toyed with it before accepting the light I held out.

"I only want a look at it, kid. I don't want to steal the stuff and I won't pass the information along to anybody."

"Please, Mike."

I bent the match in my fingers and threw it on my plate. "Okay, okay. Maybe I'm asking too damn much. You know what the score is as well as I do. Everything is so almighty secret with the D.A. that he doesn't know what he has himself. If he'd open up on what he knows he'd get a little more action out of the public. Right now he's trying to squelch the big-time gambling in the city and what happens? Everybody thinks it's funny. By God, if they had a look behind the scenes at what's been going on because of the same gambling they condone they'd think twice about it. They ought to take a look at a corpse with some holes punched in it. They ought to take a look at some widows crying at a funeral or a kid who was made an orphan crying for his father who's one of the corpses."

The cigarette had burned down in her fingers without being

touched, the long ash drooping wearily, ready to fall. Ellen's eyes were bright and smoky at the same time; languid eyes that hid the thoughts behind them.

"I'll get it for you, Mike."

I waited and saw the richness of her lips grow richer with a smile.

"But it'll cost you," she said.

I didn't get it for a second. "Cost me what?"

"You."

And that thing on my spine started crawling around again.

She reached out for my hand and covered it with hers. "Mike . . . you're only incidental in the picture this time. It's the only way I'll ever be able to get you and it's worth it even if I have to buy you. But it's because of what you said that I'm doing it."

There was something new about her, something I hadn't noticed before. I said, "You'll never have to buy me, Ellen."

It was a long minute before I could take my eyes off her face and get rid of the thing chasing up my back. The waitress dropped the check on the table and I put down a bill to cover them both and told her to keep the change. When we came out of the booth together the guy across the room looked at me enviously and Ellen longingly. His lunch date looked relieved.

We went back to the street and got as far as the bar on the corner. Ellen stopped me and nodded toward the door. "Wait here for me. I can't go back upstairs or somebody's likely to think it peculiar."

"Then how are you going to get the file out?"

"Patty—my short and stout roommate, if you remember—is on this afternoon. I'll call her and have her take them when she leaves this evening. The way my luck runs, if I took them any earlier he'd pick just this day to want to see them."

"That's smart," I agreed. "You know her well enough so there won't be a hitch, don't you?"

She made an impatient gesture with her hand. "Patty owes me more favors than I can count. I've never asked her for anything before and I had might as well start now. I'll be back in about ten minutes. Stay at the bar and wait for me, will you?"

"Sure. Then what?"

"Then you're going to take me to the races. Little Ellen cleans up today."

I gave her my fattest smile and jingled a pocketful of coins. "Pat told me about that. You're not going to be selfish about the thing, are you?"

"I think we're both going to have a profitable day, Mike," she said impishly. She wasn't talking about money, either. I watched her cross the street and admired her legs until she was out of sight, then went into the bar and ordered a beer.

The television was tuned to the game in Brooklyn and the bets were flowing heavy and fast. I stayed out of the general argument and put my beer away. A tall skinny guy came in and stood next to me and did the same thing himself. A kid came in peddling papers and I bought one before the bartender told him to scram and quit annoying the customers.

But it didn't do any good. The guys on my left were arguing batting averages and one poked me to get my opinion. I said he was right and the other guy started jawing again and appealed to the tall skinny guy. He shrugged and tapped his ear, then took a hearing aid out of his shirt pocket and made indications that it wasn't working. He was lucky. They turned back to me again, spotted my paper and I handed it over to settle the argument. The one guy still wouldn't give in and I was about to become the backstop of a beautiful brawl.

But Ellen walked in just then and baseball switched to sex in whispers. I got her out so they could see her going away and really have something to talk about.

She cuddled up under my arm all the way back to the car and climbed in next to me looking cool and lovely and very pleased with herself. When I had about as much silence as I could take I asked, "Did it work out?"

"Patty was glad to help out. She was a little nervous about it, but she said she'd wait until everyone had cleared out and put it in her briefcase. She's taking some work home with her tonight and it shouldn't be hard to do at all."

"Good girl."

"Don't I deserve a kiss for effort?" She timed it as the light turned red.

Her mouth wasn't as cool as it looked. It was warm, a nice soft, live warmth with a delicate spicy sweetness that was excited into a heady wine by the tip of her tongue.

Then the car behind me blasted that the light was green again and I had to put my cup of wine down not fully tasted.

I hit three winners that afternoon. The two of us crowded the railing and yelled our heads off to push the nags home and when the last one slowed up in the stretch my heart slowed up with it because I had a parlay riding on his nose that was up in four figures. Fifty yards from the finish the jock laid on the whip and he crossed the line leading by a nostril.

Ellen shook my arm. "You can open your eyes now. He won."

I checked the board to make sure and there it was in big square print. I looked at the tickets that had gotten rolled up in the palm of my hand. "I'll never do that again! How the hell do the guys who bet all their lives stand this stuff! You know what I just won?"

"About four thousand dollars, didn't you?"

"Yeah, and before this I worked for a living." I smoothed out the pasteboards with my thumb and forefinger. "You ought to be a millionaire, kitten."

"I'm afraid not."

"Why? You cleaned up today, didn't you?"

"Oh, I did very well."

"So?"

"I don't like the color of the money."

"It's green, isn't it? You got a better color than that?"

"I have a cleaner kind of green," she said. Her body seemed to stiffen with a tension of some sort, drawing her hands into tight little fists. "You know why I like to see the Scobie horses win. It's the only way and the best way I can get back at my father. Just because of me he tries to run them under other colors, but I always learn about it before the races. He pays me a living whether he wants to or not and it hurts him right where he should be hurt. However, it's still money that came from him, even if it was indirectly given, and I don't want any part of it."

"Well, if you're going to throw it away, I'll take it."

"It doesn't get thrown away. You'll see where it goes."

We walked back to the ticket window and picked up a neat little pile of brand-new bills. They felt crisp as new lettuce and smelled even better. I folded mine into my wallet and stowed it away with a fond pat on the leather and started thinking of a lot of things that needed buying bad. Ellen threw hers in the wallet as if it happened every day. Thinking about it like that put a nasty buzz in my head.

"Why can't somebody follow you play for play? If anybody used your system and put a really big bundle down the odds would go skittering all over the place."

She gave me a faint smile and took my hand going up the ramp to the gate. "It doesn't work that way, Mike. All Scobie horses don't win by a long sight. It just happens that I know the ones that will win. It isn't that I'm a clever handicapper either.

Dad has a trainer working for him who taught me all I know about horses. Whenever a winner is coming up I'm notified about it and place my bets."

"That's all there is to it?"

"That's all. Once the papers did a piece about it and according to them I did all the picking and choosing. I let them get the idea just to infuriate the old boy. It worked out fine."

"You're a screwball," I said. She looked hurt. "But you're nice," I added. She squeezed my arm and rubbed her face against my shoulder.

On the way back to the city the four G's in my pocket started burning through and it was all I could do to keep it there and let it burn. I wanted to stop off at the fanciest place we could find and celebrate with a drink, but Ellen shook her head and made me drive over to the East Side, pointing out the directions every few minutes.

Everything was going fine until we got stuck behind a truck and I had a chance to see where we were. Then everything wasn't so fine at all. There was a run-down bar with the glass cracked across the center facing the sidewalk. The door opened and a guy walked out, and before it shut again the familiarity of it came back with a rush and I could smell the rain and the beer-soaked sawdust and almost see a soggy little guy kissing his kid good-by.

My throat went dry all of a sudden and I breathed a curse before I wrenched the wheel and sent the heap screaming around the truck to get the hell out of the neighborhood.

We went straight ahead for six blocks, then Ellen said, "Turn right at the next street and stop near the corner."

I did as I was told and parked between a beer truck and a dilapidated sedan. She opened the door and stepped out, looking back at me expectantly. "Coming, Mike?"

I said okay and got out myself.

Then she walked me into a settlement house that was a resurrected barn or something. The whole business took about five minutes. I got introduced to a pair of nice old ladies, a clergyman and a cop who was having a cup of tea with the old ladies. Everybody was all smiles and joy and when Ellen gave one of the women a juicy wad of bills I thought they were going to cry.

Ellen, it seemed, practically supported the establishment.

I had a chance to look through the door at a mob of raggedy kids playing in the gym and I got rid of a quarter of the bundle of my wallet. I avoided a lot of thanks and got back to the car as fast as I could and looked at Ellen like I hadn't seen her before.

"Boy, am I a big-hearted slob," I said.

She laughed once and leaned over and kissed me. This time I had a long sip of the wine before she took my cup away. "It was worth it at that," I mused.

"You know something, Mike . . . you're not such a heel. I mean, such a *very* big heel."

I told her not to come to any hasty conclusions and backed the car out. It was a quarter to six and both of us were pretty hungry, so I drove up Broadway to a lot, left the car and walked back to a place that put out good food as well as good dinner music. While we waited for our orders Ellen bummed a nickel from me and went back to the phone booth to call Patty.

I could hardly wait for her to sit down again. "Get her?"

"Uh-huh. Everything's all set. Most of the office crew have left already. She'll leave the stuff at the house for us."

"Could we meet her somewhere? It would save time."

"Too risky. I'd rather not. Patty seemed a little jittery on the phone and I doubt if she'd like it either. I only hope they can be put back as easily as they're taken out."

"You won't have any trouble." Maybe I didn't put enough conviction in my voice, because she just looked at me and bent down to her salad. I said, "Now quit worrying. There won't be anything there that I couldn't find out if I had the time to look for it."

"All right, Mike, it's just that I've never done anything like that before. I won't worry."

She wrinkled her nose at me and dug into her supper.

It was eight-ten when we left the place. A thunderhead was moving up over Jersey blotting out the stars, replacing them with the dull glow of sheet lightning. I let Ellen pick up a couple quarts of beer while I rolled the car out and met her on the corner. She hopped in as the first sprinkle of rain tapped on the roof.

Sidewalks that were just damp a moment before took on a black sheen of water and drained it off into the gutter. Even with the wipers swatting furiously like a batter gone mad I could hardly see out. The car in front of me was a wavering shadow with one sick red eye, the neon signs and window fronts on either side just a ghostly parade of colors.

It was another night like that first one. The kind that made you run anywhere just to get away from it. You could see the vague shapes that were people huddled under marquees and jammed into doorways, the braver making the short dash to waiting cabs and wishing they hadn't.

By the time we reached Ellen's apartment it had slacked off into a steady downpour without the electrical fury that turned the night into a noisy, deafening day.

A doorman with an oversize umbrella led Ellen into the foyer and came back for me. Once we were out of it we could laugh. I was only making sloshing noises with my shoes but Ellen had gotten rained on down the back and her dress was plastered against her skin like a postage stamp. Going up in the elevator she stood with her back against the wall and edged sidewise after making me walk ahead of her.

I was going to knock first, but she poked her key in the lock and waved me inside.

"Nobody home?"

"Don't be silly. Tonight's date night . . . or haven't you noticed the couples arm in arm dashing for shelter."

"Yeah." I kicked my shoes off and carried them out to the kitchen. Ellen dumped the beer on the table and showed me where the glasses were.

"Pour me, Mike. I'll be back as soon as I get these wet things off."

"Hurry up."

She grinned at me and waltzed out while I was uncorking the bottles. I just finished topping the glasses off when she waltzed right back in again wrapped up in a huge terrycloth bathrobe, rubbing the rain out of her hair with a towel.

I handed her a glass and we clinked them in a toast we didn't speak. I drank without taking my eyes from hers, watching the deep blue swirl into a smoky gray that seemed to come up from the depths of a fire.

It got to be a little more than I could take. She knew it when I said, "Let's look at the files, Ellen."

"All right." She tucked the bottle under her arm and I trailed after her into the living room. A large console set took up a corner of the room and she pulled it away from the wall and worked her hand into the opening.

"Your private safe?"

"For intimate letters, precious nylons and anything else a nosy cleaning woman might take home with her."

She pulled out another of those Manila folders held together with a thick rubber band and handed it to me. My hand started to shake when I worked the band off it. The thing snapped and flew across the room.

I took it sitting down. I reached in and pulled out a stack of official reports, four photographs and more affidavits than I could count. I spread them out across the coffee table and scanned them to see what I could pick up, laying the discards on top of the empty folder. When I tried to do it carefully I got impatient, and when I went faster I got clumsy and knocked the whole batch on the floor. Ellen picked them up and sorted them out again and I went on from there.

I was cursing myself and the whole damn mess long before I was finished because it was ending in a blank, a goddamn stone wall with nothing there but a fat ha-ha and to hell with you, bub. My hand went out of its own accord and spilled everything all across the room while Ellen let out a little scream and stepped back with her hand to her mouth.

"Mike!"

"I'm sorry, kid. It's a dud. Goddamn it, there's not a thing in there!"

"Oh, Mike . . . it can't be! The D.A. has been working on that a month!"

"Sure, trying to tangle Link up in that lousy gambling probe of his. So he proves he's a bookie. Hell, anybody can tell you that. All he had to do was go in and lay a bet with the guy himself. I'll say he's worked a month on it. Link doesn't stand a chance of getting out of this little web, but for all the time he'll draw for it, it will be worth it."

I scooped up a couple of the reports and slammed them with my fingers. "Look at this stuff. Two official reports that give any kind of background on the guy at all and those were turned in while Roberts was the D.A. What was going on in all the years until a month ago?"

Ellen glanced at the reports curiously and took them out of my hand, tapping the rubber-stamped number in the upper right-hand corner with her finger. "This is a code number, Mike. These reports are part of a series."

"Where are the rest of them then?"

"Either in the archives or destroyed. I won't say so for certain, but it's more likely that they were discarded. I've been with the department long enough to have seen more than one new office holder make a clean sweep of everything including what was in the files."

"Damn!"

"I'll check on it the first thing in the morning, Mike. There's a possibility that they're stored away someplace."

"Nuts on tomorrow morning. There isn't that much time to waste. There has to be another way."

She folded the sheets up carefully, running her nail along the edges. "I can't think of anything else unless you want to contact Roberts. He might remember something about the man."

"That's an idea. Where does he live?"

"I don't know . . . but I can find out." She looked at me pensively. "Does it have to be tonight?"

"Tonight."

I caught up with her before she reached the phone. I put my arms around her and breathed the fragrance that was her hair. "I'm sorry, Kitten."

Ellen let her head fall back on my shoulder and looked up at me. "It's all right, Mike, I understand."

She had to make three separate calls to locate Roberts' number. It was an address in Flushing and when she had it she handed me the phone to do the calling. It was a toll call, so I put it through the operator and listened to it ring on the other end. When I was about ready to hang up a woman came on and said, "Hello, this is Mrs. Roberts."

"Can I speak to Mr. Roberts, please?"

"I'm sorry, but he isn't home right now. Can I take a message?"

Somebody had bottled up all my luck and thrown it down the drain. I said, "No, but can you tell me when he'll be back?"

"Not until tomorrow sometime. I expect him about noon."

"Well, thanks. I'll call him then. 'By."

I tried not to slam the receiver back in its cradle. I tried to sit on myself to keep from exploding and if it hadn't been for Ellen chuckling to herself from the depths of the couch I would have kicked something across the room. I spun around to tell her to shut up, but when a woman looks at you the way she was doing you don't say anything at all. You just stand there and look back because a toast-colored body that is all soft, molded curves and smooth hollows makes a picture to take your breath away, especially when it is framed against the thick texture of white terrycloth.

She laughed again and said, "You're trapped, Mike."

I wanted to tell her that I wasn't trapped at all, but there wasn't any room for words in my throat. I walked across the room and stood there staring at her, watching her come up off the couch into my arms to prove that she was real and not just a picture after all.

The cup was full this time, the wine mellow and sweet, and

she was writhing in my arms fighting to breathe, yet not wanting me to stop holding her. I heard her say, "Mike . . . I'm sorry you're trapped, but I'm glad . . . glad." And I kissed her mouth shut again letting the rain slashing against the window pitch the tempo, hearing it rise and rise in a crescendo of fury, shrieking at me because the minutes were things not to be wasted.

It took all I had to shove her away. "Texas gal, don't make it rough for me. Not now."

She opened her eyes slowly, her fingers kneading my back. "I can't even buy you, can I?"

"You know better than that, sugar. Let me finish what I have to do first."

"If I let you get away you'll never come back, Mike. There are too many others waiting for you. Every week, every month there will be someone new."

"You know too much."

"I know I'm a Texas gal who likes a Texas man."

My grin was a little flat. "I'm a city boy, kid."

"An accident of birth. Everything else about you is Texas. Even a woman doesn't come first with you."

She stretched up on her toes, not far because she didn't have to go far, and kissed me lightly. "Sometimes Texas men do come back. That's why there are always more Texas men." She smiled.

"Don't forget to take those files in," I reminded her. Then there was nothing more to say.

I went back to the rain and the night, looking up just once to see her silhouetted against the window waving to me. She didn't see me, but I waved back to her. She would have liked it if she'd known what I was thinking.

On the way back I stopped off for a drink and a sandwich and tried to think it out. I wanted to be sure of what I was doing before I stuck my neck out. I spent an hour going over the whole thing, tying it into Toady Link and no matter how I looked at it the picture was complete.

At least I tried to tell myself that it was.

I said it over and over to myself the same way I told Pat, but I couldn't get it out of my mind that some place something didn't fit. It was only a little thing, but it's the little things that hold bigger things together. I sat there and told myself that it was Toady who drove the murder car and Toady who gave the orders to Arnold Basil because he couldn't afford to trust anybody else to do the job right. I told myself that it was Toady who engineered Hooker's death and tried to engineer mine.

Yet the more I told myself the more that little voice inside my head would laugh and poke its finger into some forgotten recess and try to jar loose one fact that would make me see what the picture was really like.

I gave up in disgust, paid my bill and walked out.

I walked right into trouble, too. Pat was slouched up against the wall outside my apartment with the friendliness gone completely from his face.

He didn't even give me a chance to say hello. He held out his hand with an abruptness I wasn't used to. "Let's have your gun, Mike."

I didn't argue with him. He packed it open, checked the chamber and the slide, then smelled the barrel.

"You already know when I shot it last," I said.

"I do?" It didn't sound like a question at all.

It started down low around my belly, that squeamish feeling when something is right there ready to pop in your face. "Quit being a jerk. What's the act for?"

He came away from the door frame with a scowl. "Goddamn it, Mike, play it straight if you have to play it at all!"

I said a couple of words.

"You've had it, Mike," he told me. He put it flat and simple as if I knew just what he meant.

"You could tell me about it."

"Look, Mike, I'm a cop. You were my friend and all that, but I'm not getting down on my knees to anybody. I did everything but threaten you to lay off and what happened? You did it your way anyhow. It doesn't go, feller. It's finished, washed up. I hated to see it happen, but it was just a matter of time. I thought you were smart enough to understand. I was wrong."

"That isn't telling me about it."

"Cut it, Mike. Toady's dead. He was shot with a .45," he said.

"And I'm tagged."

"That's right," Pat nodded. "You're tagged."

SOMETIMES YOU GET mad and sometimes you don't. If there was any of that crazy anger in me it had all been drained out up there in Ellen's apartment. Now it's making sense, I thought. Now it's where it should be.

Pat dropped my gun in his pocket. "Let's go, Mike."

So I went as far as the front door and watched the rain wash through under the sill. Before Pat opened the door I said, "You're sure about this, aren't you?"

He *was* sure. Two minutes ago he had been as sure of it as the day he was born and now he wasn't sure of it at all. His mouth hardened into a gash that pushed his eyes halfway shut with some uncontrollable emotion until they seemed to focus on something right behind me.

I didn't want him to answer me before he knew. "I didn't kill him, Pat. I was hoping I would, but somebody beat me to it."

"The M.E. sets the time of death around four o'clock last night." His voice asked for an explanation.

I said, "You should have told me, Pat. I was real busy then. Real busy."

His hand came away from the door. "You mean you can prove it?"

"I mean just that."

"Mike . . . if you're lying . . ."

"I've never been that stupid. You ought to know that."

"I ought to know a lot of things. I ought to know where you were every minute of last night."

"You know how to find out."

"Show me."

I didn't like the way he was looking at me at all. Maybe I'm not so good at lying any more, and I was lying my head off. Last night I was busy as hell sleeping and there wasn't one single way I could prove it. If I tried to tell him the truth it would take a month to talk my way clear.

I said, "Come on," and headed for the phone in the lobby. I shoved a dime in the slot and dialed a number, hoping that I could put enough across with a few words to say what I wanted. He stood right there at my elbow ready to take the phone away as soon as I got my party and ask the question himself.

I couldn't mistake her voice. It was like seeing her again with the lava green of her dress flowing from her waist.

"This is Mike, Marsha. A policeman . . . wants to ask you something. Mind?"

That was as far as I could get. Pat had the phone while she was still trying to figure it out. He gave me a hard smile and turned to the phone. "Captain Chambers speaking. I understand you can account for Mr. Hammer's whereabouts last night. Is that correct?"

Her voice was music pouring out of the receiver. Pat glanced at me sharply, curiously, then muttered his thanks and hung up. He still didn't quite know what to make of it. "So you spent the night with the lady."

I said a beautiful thanks to Marsha under my breath. "That's not for publication, Pat."

"You better stop tomcatting around when Velda gets back, friend."

"It makes a good alibi."

"Yeah, I'd like to see the guy who'd sooner kill Toady than sleep with a chick like that. Okay, Mike, you got yourself an alibi. I have a screwy notion that I shouldn't believe it, but Link isn't Decker and if you're in this there'll be hell to pay and I'll find out about it soon enough."

I handed him a butt and flipped a light with my thumbnail. "Can I hear about the deal or is it secret info like everything else?"

"There's not much to it. Somebody walked in and killed him."

"Just like that?"

"He was in bed asleep. He got it right through the head and whoever killed him went through the place like a cyclone. I'm going back there now if you want to come along."

"Blue boy there?"

"The D.A. doesn't know about it yet. He's out with the vice squad again," Pat said tiredly.

"You checked the bullet, didn't you?"

Pat squirmed a little. "I didn't wait for the report. I was so goddamned positive it was you that I came right over. Besides, you could have switched barrels if you felt like it. I've seen the extras you have."

"Thanks. I'm a real great guy."

"Quit rubbing it in."

"Who found the body?"

"As far as we know, the police were the first on the scene. A telegraph boy with a message for Toady saw the door open and went to shut it. Enough stuff was kicked around inside to give him the idea there was a robbery. He was sure of it when he rang the bell and nobody answered. He called the police and they found the body."

"Got any idea what they were looking for . . . or if they found it?"

Pat threw the butt at the floor. "No. Come on, take a look at it yourself. Maybe it'll make you feel better."

What was left of Toady wouldn't make anybody feel better. Death had taken the roundness from his body and made an oblong slab of it. He lay there on his back with his eyes closed and his mouth open, a huge, fat frog as unlovely dead as he was alive. Right in the center of his forehead was the hole. It was a purplish-black hole with scorched edges flecked by powder burns. Whoever held the gun held it mighty close. If there was a back to his head it was smashed into the pillow.

Outside on the street a couple more prowl cars screamed to a stop and feet came pounding into the house. A lone newshawk was sounding off about the rights of the press and being told to shut up. Pat left me there with a plain-clothesman while he got things organized and started the cops going through the rooms in a methodical search for anything that might be a lead.

When I had enough of Toady I went downstairs and followed Pat around, watching him paw through the wreckage of the living room. "Somebody didn't make a lot of noise, did they?"

I got a sharp grin. "Brother, this place was really searched."

I picked up a maple armchair and looked at it closely. There wasn't a scratch on it. There weren't any scratches on anything for that matter. For all the jumble that it seemed to be, the room had been carefully and methodically torn apart and the pieces put down nice and gently. You could even see some order in the way it was done. The slits in the seat cushions were evenly cut all in the same place. Anything that could be unscrewed or pulled out was unscrewed or pulled out. Books were scattered all over the floor, some with the back linings ripped right out of them.

Pat had one in his hand and waved it at me. "It wasn't very big if they went looking for it here."

I thought I said something to myself, but I said it out loud and Pat's head swiveled around at me. "What?"

I didn't tell him the second time. I shook my head, knowing the leer I was wearing had pulled my face out of shape and if Pat had good eyes he could read what I was thinking without looking any farther than my eyes. He might have done it if a cop hadn't come up to tell him about the junk in the basement, and he left me standing in the middle of the room right where Toady had made me stand, only this time I wasn't after Toady's hide any more because he wasn't the end at all.

Another cop came in looking for Pat. I told him he was downstairs and would be right back. The cop spread out the stuff in his hand and flashed it at me. "Look at the pin-ups I found." He gave a short laugh. "I guess he didn't go for this new stuff. Don't blame him. I like the pre-war crop better myself."

"Let's see them."

He handed them over to me as he looked through them.

Half of them were regular studio stills and the rest were enlargements of snapshots taken during stage shows. Every one of them was personally autographed to Charlie Fallon with love and sometimes kisses from some of the biggest stars in Hollywood.

When he was done with the pictures the cop let me look at a couple of loose-leaf pads that had scrawled notations of appointments to be made for more photos of more lovelies and the list of private phone numbers he had accumulated would have made any Broadway columnist drool. Every so often there was a reminder after a name . . . *introduction to F.*

And there it was again. Fallon. No matter where I turned the name came up. Fallon, Fallon, Fallon. Arnold Basil was an old Fallon boy. All the dames knew Fallon, Toady had some connection with Fallon. Damn it, the guy was supposed to be dead!

I didn't wait for Pat to come back. I told the cop to tell him I'd left and would call up tomorrow. Before I got to the door the reporter who was trying to make the most of being first on the scene tried to corner me for a story and I shook my head no. He dropped me for the cop and got the same story.

Something had gentled the rain, taking the madness out of it. The curious were there in a tight knot at the gate shrinking together under umbrellas and raincoats to gape at the death place and speculate among themselves. I managed to push myself through to the outer fringes of the crowd with about a minute to spare. Just as I broke clear the D.A. came in from the other side with his boys doing the blocking. His face was blacker than the night itself and I knew right away that somebody had crossed him up on another deal. His boat still had a hole in the bottom and if it leaked any more he was going to get swamped.

If it hadn't been so late I would have called Marsha to kiss her hand for pulling me out of a spot, but tonight I didn't want to see anybody and speak to anybody. I wanted to stretch out in bed and think. I wanted to start at the beginning and chew my way through it slowly until I found the tough hunk that didn't chew so easily and put it through the grinder.

Then I'd have my killer.

Two blocks down a hackie tooted his horn at me and I ran for the door he held open. I gave him my address and settled back into the seat. The guy was one of those Dodger fans who couldn't keep quiet about how the bums were doing and talked my ear off until I climbed out in front of my apartment and handed over a couple of bucks.

I got all the way upstairs and there they were again. Two of them this time. One was big as a house and the other wasn't much smaller. The little guy closed in with a badge flashing in his palm while the other one stood by ready to take me if I didn't act right. Both of them kept one hand in their pockets just to let me know that the play was theirs all the way.

The guy said, "Police, buddy," and stowed the badge back in his pants.

"What do you want with me?"

"You'll find out. Get moving."

The other one said, "Wait a minute," and yanked my gun out of the holster. Under his flat smile his teeth were yellowed from too much smoking. "You're supposed to have a bad temper. Guns and guys with bad tempers don't go together."

"Neither do badges without those leather wallets a cop keeps them in."

I caught the quick look that passed between them, but I caught the nose of a gun in my back at the same time. The big guy smiled again. "Wise guy. You wanta do it the hard way."

"That rod'll make a big boom in here. A nice quiet joint like this people'll want to know what all the noise is about."

The gun pressed in a little deeper. "Maybe. You won't hear it, buddy. Move."

Those two were real pros. Not the kind of hoods who pick up some extra change with nickel-plated rods either. These were delivery boys, the real McCoy. They knew just where to stand so I couldn't move in and just how to look so nobody would get the pitch. One had a pint bottle of whisky outlined in his inside jacket pocket to pour over me so I'd smell like a drunk in case they had to carry me out. And they had that look. Somebody had given the orders to bump me fast if I tried to get rough.

That look was enough for me. Besides, I was curious myself.

We got downstairs and big boy said, "Where's your car?"

I pointed it out. He snapped his fingers for my keys and got them. The other one did something with his hand and a car down the block pulled away from the curb and shot by us without looking over.

It didn't take much to see what was going to happen. I was getting a one-way ride in my own car. After I was delivered someplace first. I wasn't supposed to know about it. I was supposed to be a real good boy and act nice and polite so they wouldn't have any trouble with me. I was supposed to be a goddamn fool and let myself get killed with no fuss at all while a couple of pros congratulated themselves on their technique.

My head started banging with that insane music that was all kettledrums and shrill flutes blended together in wild discord until my hands shook with the madness of it. What kind of a simple jerk did they take me for? Maybe they thought they were the only ones who were pros in this game. Maybe they thought this had never happened before and if it had I wouldn't be ready for it to happen again.

By God, if they played this the way a pro would play it they were going to get one hell of a jolt. I had a .32 hammerless automatic in a boot between the seat and the door right where I could get at it if I had to.

They played it that way too. Big boy said, "You drive, shamus. Take it nice and easy or we'll take it for you." He held the door open so I could get in and was right there beside me when I slid under the wheel. He didn't crowd me. Not him, he was an old-timer. He kept plenty of room between us, sitting jammed into the corner with his arm on the sill. His other arm was in his lap pointing my own gun at me. The little guy didn't say much. He climbed in back and leaned on the seat behind my head like he was talking to me confidentially. But it was the gun he had pressed against my neck that was doing all the talking.

We took a long ride that night. We were three happy people taking a cruise out to the shore. To keep everybody happy I switched on the radio and picked up a disk jockey and made a habit of lighting my cigarettes from the dashboard lighter so they'd get used to seeing my arms move around.

My pal beside me was calling the turns and someplace before we came to Islip he said, "Slow down." Up ahead a macadam road intersected the highway. "Go right until I tell you to turn."

I swung around the corner and followed the black strip of road. It lasted a half-mile, butting against an oiled-top dirt road that went the rest of the way. We made a few more turns after that and I started to smell the ocean coming in strong with the wind.

The houses had thinned out until they were only black shapes on spindly legs every quarter-mile or so. The road curved gently away from the shore line, threading its way through the knee-high sawgrass that bent with the breeze and whisked against the fender of the car with an insidious hissing sound.

Nobody had to tell me to stop. I saw the shaded lights of the house and the bulk of the sedan against its side and I eased on the brakes. Big boy looked pleased with himself and the pressure of the gun on my neck relaxed. The guy behind me got out and stood by the door while the other one tucked the keys in his pocket and came up stepping on my shadow.

"You got the idea good," he told me. "Let's keep it that way. Inside and take it slow."

I practically crawled. The boys stayed behind me and to the right and left, beautiful spots in case I tried to run for it. Either one of them could have cut me down before I got two feet. I picked the last smoke out of my pack and dropped the empty wrapper. Shortie was even smart enough to pick that up. I didn't have a match and nobody offered me one, so I let it droop there between my lips. It was a little too soon to start worrying. This wasn't the time nor the place. A body doesn't hide so easy and neither does a car. When we went we'd go together. I could almost draw a picture of the way it would happen.

The door opened and the guy was a thin dark shadow against the light. I said, "Hello, scrimey."

I should have kept my mouth shut. Lou Grindle backhanded me across the mouth so that my teeth went right through my lips. Two guns hit me in the spine at the same time ramming me right into him and I couldn't have gotten away with it in a million years but I tried anyway. I hooked him down as low as I could then felt my knuckles rip open when I got him in the mouth.

Neither of the guys behind me dared risk a shot, but they did just as well. One of them brought a gun barrel around as hard as he could. There wasn't even any pain to it, just a loud click that grew into a thunderous wave of sound that threw me flat on the floor and rolled over me.

The pain didn't come until later. It wasn't there in my head where I thought it would be. It was all over, a hundred agonizing points of torture where the toe of a shoe had ripped through my clothes and torn into the skin. Something dripped slowly and steadily like a leaky faucet. Every movement sent the pain shooting up from my feet and if screaming wouldn't have only made it worse I would have screamed. I got one eye open. The other was covered by a puffy mass of flesh on my cheekbone that kept it shut.

Somebody said, "He's awake."

"He'll get it worse this time."

"I'll tell you when." The voice was so decisive that nobody gave it to me worse.

I managed to focus the one good eye then. It was pointed at the floor looking at my feet. They were together at attention strapped to the rungs of a chair. My arms weren't there at all so I guess that they were tied someplace behind the same chair. And the drip wasn't from the faucet at all.

It was from something on my face that used to be a nose.

Somehow, I dragged myself straight up. It didn't hurt so bad then. When the fuzziness went away I squinted my one good eye against the light and saw them sitting around like vultures waiting for the victim to die. The two boys with the rods over by the door and Lou Grindle holding a bloody towel to his mouth.

And Ed Teen perched on the edge of the leather armchair with his chin propped on a cane. He still looked like a banker, even to the gray Homburg.

He stared at me very thoughtfully for a minute. "Feel pretty bad?"

"Guess." The one word almost choked me.

"It wasn't necessary, you know. We just wanted to talk to you. Everything would have been quite friendly." He smiled. "Now we have to tie you down until we're finished talking."

Lou threw the towel at me. "Christ, quit stalling around with him. I'll make him talk in a hurry."

"Shut up." Ed didn't even stop smiling. "You're lucky I'm here. Lou is rather impulsive."

I didn't answer him.

He said, "It was too bad you had to kill Toady, Mr. Hammer. He was very valuable to me."

I got the words out. "You're nuts."

He pushed himself up off the cane and leaned back in the chair. "Don't bother with explanations. I'm not the police. If you killed him that's your business. What I want is what's my business. Where is it?"

My lips felt too thick to put any conviction in my voice. "I don't know what the hell you're talking about."

"Remind him, Lou."

Then he sat back chewing on a cigar and watched it. Lou didn't use his foot this time. The wet towel around his fist was enough. He was good at the job, but I had taken so much the first time that even the half-consciousness I had left went fast.

I tried to stay that way and couldn't. My head twitched and Teen said metallically, "Now do you remember?"

I only had to shake my head once and that fist clubbed it again. It went on and on and on until there was no pain at all and I could laugh when he talked to me and try to smile when the delivery boy in the corner got sick and turned his head away to puke.

Ed rapped the cane on the floor. "Enough. That's enough. He can't feel it any more. Let him sit and think about it a few minutes."

Lou was glad to do that. He was breathing hard through his mouth and his chin was covered with blood. He went over and sat down at the table to massage his hand. Lou was very happy.

The cane kept up a rhythm on the floor. "This is only the beginning you know. There's absolutely no necessity for it."

I managed to say, "I didn't . . . kill Link."

"It doesn't matter whether you did or not. I want what you took from his apartment."

Lou started to cough and spat blood on the floor. He gagged, put his hand to his mouth and pushed a couple of teeth into his palm with his tongue. When he brought his head up his eyes bored into mine like deadly little black bullets. "I'm going to kill that son of a bitch!"

"You sit there and shut up. You'll do what I say."

He was on his feet with his hands apart fighting to keep himself from tearing Teen's throat out with his fingers. Ed wasn't so easy to scare. The snub-nosed gun in his hand said so.

Lou's face was livid with rage. "Damn you anyway. Damn you and Fallon and Link and the whole stinking mess of you!"

"You're lisping, Lou. Sit down." Lou sat down and stared at his teeth some more. He was proud of those teeth. They were so nice and shiny.

They lay where they were dropped on the table and seemed to fascinate him. He kept feeling his gums as though he couldn't believe it, cursing his heart out in black rage. Ed's gun never left him for a second. Right then Lou was in a killing rage and ready to take it out on anybody.

He kept saying over and over, "Goddamn every one of 'em! Goddamn 'em all!" His mouth drew back baring the gap in his teeth and he slammed the table with his fist. "Goddamn, this wouldn't've happened if you'd let me do it my way! I would've killed Fallon and that lousy whore he kept and Link and this wouldn't've happened!" I got the eyes this time. They came around slow and evilly. "I'll kill you for it, too."

"You'll get new teeth, Lou," Ed said pleasantly. Everything he said was pleasant.

Grindle gagged again and walked out of the room. Water started to run in a bowl somewhere and he made sloshing noises as he washed out his mouth. Ed smiled gently. "You hit him where he hurts the most . . . in his vanity."

"Where does it hurt you the most, Ed?"

"A lot of people would like to know that."

"I know." I tried to grin at him. My face wouldn't wrinkle. "It's going to hurt you in two places. Especially when they shave the hair off your head and leg."

"I think," he told me, "that when Lou comes back I'll let him do you up right."

"You mean . . . like old times when Fallon pulled the strings . . . with cigar butts and pliers?"

His nostrils flared briefly. "If you have to say something at all, tell me where it is."

"Where what is?"

The water was still running inside. Without turning his head Ed called, "Johnny. Give it to him."

The big guy came over. Under his shirt his stomach made peculiar rolling motions. His techniques stunk. His fist made a solid chunk against my chin and I went out like a light. They poured cold water over me so I'd wake up and watch it happen all over again.

It started to get longer between rounds. I would come only partially back out of that jet-black land of nowhere and hang there limply. The big guy's voice was a hoarse croak. "He's done, Ed. I don't think he knows what you're talking about."

"He knows." His cane tapped the floor again. "Give him another dousing."

I got the water treatment again. It washed the blood out of my eyes so I could see again and the shock of it cleared my mind enough to think.

Ed knew when I was awake. He had a cigar lit and gazed at the cherry-red end of it speculatively. "You can hear me?"

I nodded that I could.

"Then understand something. I shall ask you just once more. Remember this, if you're dead you can't use what you have."

"Tell . . . me what the hell . . . you want."

Only for a second did his eyes go to the pair leaning on the window sill. If they weren't there I would have had it, but whatever I was supposed to know was too much for their big ears. "You know very well what I mean. You've been trouble from the very first moment. I know you too well, Mr. Hammer. You're only a private investigator, but you've killed people before. In your own way you're quite as ruthless as I am . . . but not quite as smart. That's why I'm sitting here and you're sitting there. Keep what you have. I've no doubt that it's hidden some place you alone can get it, and after you're dead nobody else will find it. Not in my time at least. Johnny . . . go see what's keeping Lou."

The guy walked inside and came right back. "He's lying down. He puked on the bed."

"Let him stay there then. Untie this man."

The straps came off my hands and legs, but I couldn't get up. They let me sit there until the circulation came back, with it the flame that licked at my body. When I could move Johnny hauled me to my feet.

"What'll I do with him, Ed?"

"That's entirely up to you. Martin, drive me back to the city. I've had enough of this."

The little guy saluted with his two fingers and waited until Ed had picked up his topper. He made a beautiful flunky. He opened the door and probably even helped him down the steps. I heard the car purr into life and drag back on the road.

Johnny let go my coat collar and jammed the gun in my back. "You heard what the man said." He started me off with a push to the door.

The long walk. The last ride. The boys call it a lot of things. You sit there in the car with your head spinning around and around thinking of all the ways to get out and every time you think of one there's a gun staring you in the face. You sweat and try to swallow. All your joints feel shaky and though you want a cigarette more than anything in the world you know you'll never be able to hold one in your mouth. You sweat some more. Your mouth wants to scream for help when you see somebody walking along the street. A gun pokes you to keep quiet. There's a cop on the corner under the arc light. A prayer gets stuck in your throat. He'll recognize them . . . he'll see the glint of their guns . . . his hand will go up and stop the car and you'll be safe. But he looks the other way when the car passes by and you wonder what happened to your prayer. Then you stop sweating because your body is dried out and your tongue is a thick rasp working across your lips. You think of a lot of things, but mostly you think of how fast you're going to stop living.

I remembered how I thought of all those things the first time. Now it was different. I was beat to hell and too far gone to fight. I had the strength to drive and that was all. Johnny sat there in his corner watching me and he still had my own gun.

This time I wanted a cigarette and he gave me one. I used the dash lighter again. I finished that and he gave me another while he laughed at the way my hand shook when I tried to get it in my mouth. He laughed at the way I kept rolling the window up first to get warm then to get cooled off. He laughed at the way I made the turns he told me to take, creeping around them so I'd have seconds longer to live.

When he told me to stop he laughed again because my arms seemed to relax and hang limply at my sides.

He took his eyes off me for one second while he searched for the door handle and he never laughed again.

I shot him through the head five times with the .32 I had pulled out of the boot and kicked him out in the road after I took my gun from his hand. When I backed around the lights of the car swept over him in time to catch one final involuntary twitch and Johnny was getting his first taste of hell.

The gray haze of morning was beginning to show in the sky behind me when I reached the shack again. It was barely enough to show me the road through the grass and outline the car against the house. I killed the engine, backed into the sand and opened the door.

This time the car wasn't any big sedan. It was the same coupé that had brought the boys to get me then pulled away at their signal. I knew who was in there. The little guy Ed called Martin had come back for Lou.

I made a circuit of the house and stopped under the bedroom window. Lou was cursing the guy, telling him to stop shaking him. I straightened up to look in, but there was no light and the curtains made an effective blind. Somebody started running the water and there was more talk I couldn't catch. It faded away until it was in the back of the house and I grabbed at the chance.

I hugged the wall climbing up on the porch, squeezing myself into the shadows. The wood had rotted too soft to have any squeak left in it but I wasn't taking any chances. I got down low with the gun in one hand and reached up for the knob with the other.

Somebody had oiled it not so long ago. It turned noiselessly and I gave the door a shove. The guy with the oilcan was nice people. He had oiled the hinges too.

My breath stuck in my lungs until I was inside with the door closed behind me, then I let it out in a low hiss and tried to breathe normally. The blood was pounding through my body making noise enough to be heard throughout the house. My legs wanted to drag me down instead of pushing me forward and the .45 became too heavy to hold steadily.

I had to fight against the letdown that was sweeping over my body. It couldn't come now! The answer was there in Lou's bloody mouth waiting to be squeezed out. I started to weave a little bit and reached out to grab the wall and hang on. My hand hit the door of a closet and slammed it shut.

Silence.

A cold, black silence.

A tentative voice calling, "Johnny?"

I couldn't fake an answer. My knees started to go.

Again, "Johnny, damn it!"

Lou cursed and a tongue of flame lashed out of a doorway.

There was no faking about the way I hit the floor. Lou had heard too many men fall like that before. It was real, but only because my legs wouldn't hold me any longer. I still had the .45 in my mitt and I let the feet come my way just so far before I squeezed the trigger.

The blasting roar of the gun echoed and shattered on the walls. I rolled until I hit something and stopped, my free hand clawing my one good eye to keep it open. The remnants of a scream were still in the air and the pin points of light were two guns punching holes in the woodwork searching for me. I got my hand around the leg of an end table and let it go. The thing bounced on the floor and split under the impact of the bullets. They were shouting at each other now, calling each other fools for wasting shots. So they stopped wasting shots. They thought I was hit and waited me out.

Somebody was breathing awfully funny. It made a peculiar racket when you took time to listen to it. I could hear them changing position, getting set. I went as quietly as I could and changed position myself.

It had to come soon. A few more minutes and the light would come through the curtains and they could see better than I could. It went on like a kid's game, that incessant crawling, the fear that you'd be caught, the deliberate motions of stealth that were so hard to make.

The funny breathing was real close. I could reach out and touch it. It was there on the other side of the chair. It heard me too, but it didn't change its tone. From across the room came the slightest sound and a whisper from only five feet away. "He's over there."

Orange flame streaked across the room and the sound jolted my ears even before the scream and the hoarse curse. The answer was two shots that pounded into the floor and a heavy thud as a body toppled over.

Lou's voice said, "I got the son of a bitch." He still lisped.

He moved out past the chair and I saw him framed in the window.

I said, "You got your own man, Lou."

Lou did too many things at once. He tried to drop, shoot and curse me at the same time. He got two of them done. He dropped because I shot him. His gun went off because a dead hand pulled the trigger. He didn't curse because my bullet went up through his mouth into his brain taking the big answer with it.

There was nothing left there for me at all.

Outside the gray haze had brightened into morning, very early morning. It took me a long time to get back to the car, and much, much longer to get to the highway.

Fate allowed me a little bit of luck. It gave me a hitchhiker stranded between towns. I picked him up and told him I'd been in a fight and that he could drive.

The hiker was glad to. He felt sorry for me.

I felt sorry for myself too.

chapter nine ▰▰▰▰▰▰▰▰▰▰

WE WERE ON a side street just off Ninth Avenue and the guy beside me was pulling my arm to wake me up. He tugged and twisted until I thought the damn thing would come off. I got the one eye open and looked at him.

"You sure were dead to the world, brother. Took me a half-hour to get you out of it."

"What time is it?"

"Eight-thirty. Feel pretty rotten?"

"Lousy."

"Want me to call somebody?"

"No."

"Well, look, I have to catch a bus. You think you're going to be all right? If you're not I'll stick around awhile."

"Thanks . . . I'll make out."

"Okay, it's up to you. Sure appreciate the ride. Wish I could do something for you."

"You can. Go get me a pack of butts. Luckies."

He waved away the quarter I handed him and walked down to the corner to the newsstand. He came back with the pack opened, stuck one in my mouth and lit it. "You take care now. Better go home and sleep it off."

I said I would and sat there smoking the butt until a cop came along slapping tickets on car windows. I edged over behind the wheel, kicked the starter in and got out of there.

Traffic wasn't a problem like it usually was. I was glad to get behind a slow-paced truck and stay there. Every bone and muscle in my body ached and I couldn't have given the wheel a hard wrench if I wanted to. I got around the corner somehow and the truck crossed over to get in the lane going through the Holland Tunnel. I dropped out of position, squeezed through the intersection as the light changed and got on the street that led up to police headquarters.

Both sides of the street were lined with people going to work. They all seemed so happy. They walked alone or in couples, thousands of feet and legs making a blur of motion. I envied them the sleep they had had. I envied their normal unswollen faces. I envied a lot of things until I took time to think about it. At least I was alive. That was something.

The street in front of the red brick building was a parade ground of uniformed patrolmen. Some were walking off to their beats and others were climbing in squad cars. The plain-clothes men went off in pairs, separating at the corner with loud so-longs. Right in front of the main entrance three black sedans with official markings were drawn up at the curb with their drivers reading tabloids behind the wheel. Directly across from them a pair of squad cars pulled out and the tan coupé in front of me nosed into the space they left. I followed in behind him, did a better job of parking than he did and was up against the bumper of the car behind me so the guy would have room to maneuver.

I guess the jerk got his license wholesale. He tried to saw his way in without looking behind him and I had to lean on the horn to warn him off. Maybe I should have planted a red flag or something. He ignored the horn completely and slammed into me so hard I wrapped my chest around the wheel.

That did it. That was as much as I could take. I opened the door with my elbow and got out to give him hell. You'd think with all the cops around one of them would have jumped him, but that's how it goes. The guy was getting out of his heap with a startled apology written all over him. He took a look at my face and forgot what he was going to say. His mouth hung open and he just looked.

I said, "You deaf or something? What the devil do you think a horn's for?"

His mouth started to say something, but he was too confused to get it out. I took another good look at him and I could see why. He was the guy who stood next to me in the bar the afternoon before with the busted headset. He was making motions at his ears and tapping the microphone or whatever it was. I was too disgusted to pay any attention to him and waved him off. He still smacked the bumper twice again before he got himself parked.

This was starting off to be a beautiful day too.

When I got in the building I started to attract a little attention. A cop I know pretty well passed right by me with no more than a cursory glance. One asked me if I was there to register a complaint and looked surprised when I shook my head no. The place was a jumble of activity with men going in and out of the line-up room, getting their orders at the desk or scrambling to get off on a case.

Too much was popping in the morning to hope Pat would be in his office, so I waited my turn at the information desk and told the cop at the switchboard that I wanted to see Captain Chambers.

He said, "Name?"

And I said, "Hammer, Michael Hammer."

Then his hand paused with the plug in it and he said, "Well, I'll be damned."

He tried about ten extensions before he got Pat, said Yes, sir a few times and yanked the plug out. "He'll be right down. Wait here for him."

By the clock I waited exactly one minute and ten seconds. Pat came out of the elevator at a half-run and when he saw me his face did tricks until it settled down in a frown.

"What happened to you?"

"I got took, pal. Took good, too."

He didn't ask me any more questions. He looked down at his shoes a second then put it to me hard and fast. "You're under arrest, Mike."

"What?"

"Come on upstairs."

The elevator was waiting. We got on and went up. We got off at the right floor and I started to walk toward his office automatically, but he put out his hand and stopped me.

"This way, Mike."

"Say, what's going on?"

He wouldn't look at me. "We've had men covering your apartment, your office and all your known places of entertainment since six this morning. The D.A. has a warrant out for your arrest and there's not a damn thing you can do about it."

"Sorry. I should have stayed home. What's the charge?"

We paused outside a stained-oak door. "Guess."

"I give up."

"The D.A. looked for Link's personal file last night and found it missing. He was here when Ellen Scobie tried to put it back this morning. You have two girls on the carpet right this minute who are going to lose their jobs and probably have charges preferred against them too. You're going in there yourself and take one hell of a rap and this time there's no way out. You finished yourself, Mike. You'll never learn, but you're finished."

I dropped my hands in my pockets and made like I was grinning at him.

"You're getting old, son. You're getting set in your ways. For the last two years all you've done is warn me about this, that, and the next thing. We used to play a pretty good game, you and me, now you're starting to play it cautious and for a cop who handles homicide that's no damn good at all."

Then just for the hell of it that little finger that was probing my brain deliberately knocked a couple of pieces together that made lovely, beautiful sense and I remembered something Ellen had told me not so long ago. I twisted it around, revamped it a little and I was holding something the D.A. was going to pay for in a lot of pride. Yep, a whole lot of pride.

I reached for the knob myself. "Let's go, chum. Me and the D.A. have some business to transact."

"Wait a minute. What are you pulling?"

"I'm not pulling a thing, Pat. Not a thing. I'm just going to trade him a little bit."

Everything was just like it was the last time. Almost.

There was the D.A. behind his desk with his boys on either side. There were the detectives in the background, the cop at the door, the little guy taking notes and me walking across the room.

Ellen and her roommate were the exceptions this time. They sat side by side in straight-back chairs at the side of the big desk and they were crying their eyes out.

If my face hadn't been what it was there would have been a formal announcement made. As it was, everybody gave me a kind of horrified stare and Ellen turned around in her seat. She stopped crying abruptly and put her hand to her mouth to stifle a scream.

I said, "Take it easy, kid."

Her teeth went into her lip and she buried her face in her hands.

The District Attorney was very sarcastic this time. "Good morning, *Mister* Hammer."

"I'm glad you remembered," I told him.

Any other time his face would have changed color. Not now. He liked this cat-and-mouse stuff. He had waited a long time for it and now he was going to enjoy every minute of it while he had an audience to appreciate it. "I suppose you know why you're here?" He leaned back in his chair and folded his arms across his chest. The two assistants did the same thing.

"I've heard about it."

"Shall I read the charges?"

"Don't bother." My legs were starting to go again. I pulled a chair across the floor and sat down. "Start reading me off any time you feel like it," I said. "Get it all off your chest at once so you'll be able to listen to somebody else except your yes men for a change."

The two assistants came to indignant attention in their seats.

It was so funny I actually got a grin through.

The D.A. didn't think it was so funny. "I don't intend to take any of your nonsense, *Mister* Hammer. I've had about all I can stand of it."

"Okay, you know what you can do. Charge me with conspiracy and theft, toss me in the pokey and I catch hell at the trial. So I'll go up."

"You won't be alone." He glanced meaningly at the two women.

There were no tears left in Ellen any more, but her friend was sobbing bitterly.

I said, "Did you stop to think why the three of us bothered to take a worthless file out of here?"

"Does it matter?"

Ellen had nudged her companion and the crying stopped. I took the deck of cigarettes out of my pocket and fiddled with it to keep my hands busy. The white of the wrapper flashed the light back at the sun until attention seemed to be focused on it rather than me.

"It matters," I said. "As the charge will state, it was a deliberate conspiracy all right, perpetrated by three citizens in good standing who saw a way to accomplish something that an elected official couldn't manage. The papers will have a field day burying you."

He smiled. The damn fool smiled at me! "Don't bother going through that song and dance again."

He was getting ready to throw the book in my face when Pat spoke from the back of the room. His voice held a strained note, but it had a lot of power behind it. "Maybe you better hear what he has to say."

"Say it then." The smile faded into a grimace of anger. "It had better be good, because the next time you say anything will be to a judge and jury."

"It's good. You'll enjoy hearing about it. We," and I emphasized that "we," "found the hole in the boat."

I heard Pat gasp and take a step nearer.

"Ellen suggested it to you at one time and the full possibilities of the thing never occurred to you. We know how information is getting out of this office."

The D.A.'s eyes were bright little beads searching my face for the lie. They crinkled up around the edges when he knew I was telling the truth and sought out Pat for advice. None came so he said, "How?"

Now I had the ball on his goal line and I wasn't giving it up. "I won't bother you with the details of how we did it, but I can tell you how it was being done."

"Damn it . . . How!"

I gave him his smile back. On me it must have looked good. "Uh-uh. We trade. You're talking to three clams unless you drop all those charges. Not only drop 'em, but forget about 'em."

What else could he do? I caught Pat's reflection in the window glass behind the D.A.'s head and he was grinning like an idiot. The D.A. tapped his fingers on the desk-top, his cheeks working.

When he looked up he took in the room with one quick glance. "We'll finish this privately if you gentlemen don't mind. You say stay, Captain Chambers."

As far as the two assistants were concerned, it was the supreme insult. They hid their tempers nicely though and followed the others out. I laughed behind their backs and the thing that was working at the D.A.'s cheeks turned into a short laugh. "You know, there are times when I hate your guts. It happens that it's all the time. However, I admire your precocity in a way. You're a thorn in my skin, but even a thorn can be used to advantage at times. If what you have to say is true, consider the charges dropped completely."

"Thanks," I said. The women couldn't say anything. They were too stunned. "I understand you have a man in the department who is suspected of carrying information outside."

He frowned at Pat. "That is correct. We're quite sure of it. What we don't know is his method of notifying anyone else."

"It isn't hard. There's a guy with a tin ear who stands across the street. He wears a hearing aid that doesn't work. He reads lips. A good dummy can read lips at thirty feet without any trouble at all. Your man gets to the street, moves his mouth silently like he's chewing gum or something, but actually calls off a time and place, gets in a car and goes off on a raid. Meanwhile the guy had time to reach a phone and pass the word. Those places are set up for a quick scramble and are moved out before you get there. It's all really very simple."

"Is he there now?"

"He was when I came in."

The D.A. muttered a damn and grabbed the phone.

You know how long it took? About three minutes. He started to blab the second they had him inside the building. The voice on the phone got real excited and the D.A. slammed the phone back. His face had happy, happy smeared all over it and he barely had time to say thanks again and tell the women that their efforts were appreciated before he was out the door.

I got to Ellen and tried to put my arms around her. She put her hands on my chest and pushed me away. "Please, Mike, not now. I . . . I'm much too upset. It was . . . horrible before you came."

"Can I call you later?"

"Yes . . . all right."

I let go of her and she hurried out, dabbing at her mouth with a damp handkerchief.

"Well," Pat said, "you're a smart bastard anyway. You certainly made life miserable for them for a while even if you did get them off the hook in the end."

He held the door open and came out behind me. We walked down the corridor to his office without saying anything and when we were inside he waved me into a chair I needed worse than ever and slumped into his own in back of the desk.

Pat let me get a smoke going. He let me have one long drag, then: "I'm not the D.A., Mike. You don't have anything to trade with me so let's have it straight. That business with the dummy outside was strictly an accident. If the D.A. wasn't so damn eager to grab Teen and Grindle he would have seen it. Two good questions would have put you right back on the spot again."

"And I still would have had something to trade."

"Like what?"

"Lou Grindle is dead. I killed him a few hours before I walked in here. Not only that, but two of his boys are dead. I got one and Lou bumped the other by mistake thinking he was me."

"Mike . . ." Pat was drumming his fists on the arms of the chair.

"Shut up and listen. Teen had me picked up. He thought I killed Link and took something from the apartment. It was kidnapping and I was within the law when I shot them so don't worry about it. There's a body in the road out near Islip someplace and the local police ought to have it by now. The other two are in a house I can locate for you on a map and you better hop to it before they get turned up.

"Ed Teen gave the orders to bump me but you can bet your tail you aren't picking him up for it. He probably had an alibi all set for an emergency anyway, and now that he no doubt knows what happened he'll insure it."

"Why the hell didn't you tell me this earlier? Good Lord, we can break any alibi he has if he's involved!"

"You're talking simple again, friend. I'd like to see you break his alibi. Whoever stands up for him has a chance of being dead if he talks. All you can offer is a jail cell. Nope, you won't put anything down on Teen. He's been through this mill before."

Pat slammed his head with his open palm. "So you waste an hour playing games with the D.A. Damn, you should have said something."

"Yeah, I had plenty of time to talk. You would have heard all about it if you didn't give me that under arrest business."

"I wish I knew what was going on, Mike."

"That makes two of us."

He dragged out a map of the Island and handed it to me. I penciled in the roads and marked the approximate spot where the house was and handed it back. Pat had the thing on the wires immediately. Downstairs somebody checked with the police in Islip and verified the finding of the body on the road.

I said, "Pat . . ."

He covered up the mouthpiece of the phone and looked at me.

"Go through the motions of finding Lou's body before you hand the story to the D.A., will you?"

The phone went back into its cradle slowly. "What's the score, Mike?"

"I think I know how we can get Teen."

"That's not a good reason at all." His voice was soft, dangerous.

"You tell him now and I'll get the treatment again, Pat. Look . . . you've been working this from the wrong angle. You would have gotten there, but it would have taken longer. I'm hot now. I can't stop while I'm hot. You said I could have three days."

"The picture's changed."

"Nix . . . it's just hanging a little crooked, that's all. With all your cops and all your equipment, you're still chasing after shadows."

"You know it all, is that it?"

"No . . . but I got the shadows chasing me now. I know something I shouldn't know. I wish to God I knew where and how I picked it up. I've been wandering through this thing picking up a piece here and there and it should have ended when Toady died. I thought he was the one I was after."

"He was."

Pat said it so flatly that I almost missed it.

"What'd you say?"

"He drove the car when Decker was killed."

It was like a wave washing up the beach, then receding back into itself, the way my body was suddenly flushed before it was drained completely dry. I couldn't get my hands unclenched. They were the only live part of me, balled up in my lap doing the cursing my throat wanted to do. The killer was supposed to be mine, goddamn it. I promised the kid and I promised myself. He wasn't supposed to die in bed never knowing why he died. He should have gone with his tongue hanging out and turning black while I choked the guts out of him!

"How do you know?"

"Cole and Fisher were apprehended in Philadelphia. They decided to shoot it out and lost. Cole lived long enough to say a few things."

"What things?"

"You were right about Hooker and Decker. Toady gave the orders to get Mel. He was going to put Cole and Fisher out with Decker, changed his mind and went himself instead. That was all they knew."

"You mean they were supposed to bump Decker?"

"No . . . just go with him when they pulled the job."

I got up slowly. I put my hat back on and dropped my butt in the ash tray on the desk. "Okay, Pat, get Teen your own way. I still want you to give me a break with the D.A. I want to get some sleep. I need it bad."

"If Grindle's dead he'll stay dead. Make yourself scarce. When you wake up give me a ring. I'll hold things as long as I can."

"Thanks."

"And Mike . . ."

"Yeah?"

"Do something about your face. You look like hell."

"I'll cut it off at the neck and get a new one," I said.

Pat said seriously, "I wish you would."

chapter ten ▬▬▬▬▬▬▬▬▬▬▬▬▬

I HAD COMPANY again. I had a whole hall full of company. Everybody was coming to see me. I was the most popular guy in town and everybody was standing in front of my door dying to get a look at me. One of my company gasped in a huge breath of air before she said, "Oh . . . oh, thank heavens, there he is."

The super's wife was a big fat woman no corset could contain properly and with all that air in her she looked ready to burst. But she was smiling as she recognized my walk and then the smile froze on her face. The super stopped poking a key in the lock on my door, pushed through the small knot and he froze too.

Then there was Marsha. She shoved them all out of the way. The laugh she had ready for me twisted to dismay and she said, "Mike!"

"Hello, sugar."

"Oh, Mike, I knew something happened to you!" She ran into my arms and the tears welled into her eyes. Her fingers touched my cheek gently and I felt them tremble. "Darling, darling . . . what was it . . ."

"Oh, I'll tell you about it sometime. What's all the excitement about?"

She choked and gasped the words out. "I kept calling you and calling you all last night and this morning. I . . . thought something happened . . . like that last time in your apartment. Oh, Mike . . ."

"It's all right now, honey. I'll be back to normal soon."

"I . . . came up and you didn't answer. I told the superintendent you might be hurt . . . and he . . . he was going to look. Mike, you scared me so."

The super was nodding, licking his lips. The others crowded in for a last look at me before going back to their apartments. His wife said, "You scared us all, Mr. Hammer. We were sure you were dead or something."

"I almost was. Anyway, thanks for thinking of me. Now if you don't mind, I'd just like to be left alone for a while. I'm not feeling any too hot."

"Is there anything . . ."

"No, nothing, thanks." I took out my key and opened the door. I had to prop myself against the sill for a minute before I could go in. Marsha grabbed my arm and held me steady, then guided me inside to a chair and helped me down.

The day had been too long . . . too much to it. A guy can't take days like that one and stay on his feet. I let my head fall back and closed my eyes. Marsha sobbed softly as she untied my shoes and slid them off. The aches and pains came back, a muted throbbing at first, taking hold slowly and biting deeper with each pulse beat.

Marsha had my tie off and was unbuttoning my shirt when the knock came. It didn't make any difference any more who it was. I heard her open the door, heard the murmur of voices and the high babble of a child's voice in the background.

"Mike . . . it's a nurse."

"The superintendent asked me to look in on you," the other voice said.

"I'm all right."

Her voice became very efficient. "I doubt it. Will you watch

the child, please? Thank you." Her hand slipped under my arm.
"You'll do better lying down."

I couldn't argue with her. She had an answer for everything.
Marsha was on the couch still crying, playing with the kid. I got
up and went to the bedroom. She had me undressed and in bed
before I realized it. The sting of the iodine and the cold compresses
on my face jerked me out of immediate sleep and I heard her
telling Marsha to call a doctor. It seemed like only seconds before
he was there, squeezing with hands that had forgotten how to be
gentle, then gone as quickly as he had come. I could hear the
two women discussing me quietly, deciding to stay until I had
awakened. The kid squealed at something and it was the last thing
I heard.

There were only snatches of dreams after that, vague faces that
had an odd familiarity and incomprehensible mutterings about
things I didn't understand. It took me away from the painful
present and threw me into a timeless zone of light and warmth
where my body healed itself immediately. It was like being inside
a huge beautiful compound where there was no trouble, no misery
and no death. All that was outside the transparent walls of the
compound where you could see it happen to everyone else without
being touched yourself.

They were all there, Decker with his child, listening intently to
what Mel Hooker had to say, and Toady Link in the background
watching and nodding to make sure he said it right, his boys
ready to move in if he said the wrong thing. Lou and Teen were
there too, standing over the body of a man who had to be Fallon,
their heads turned speculatively toward Toady. A play was going
on not far away. Everybody was dressed in Roman togas. Marsha
and Pat held the center of the stage with the D.A. and Ellen was
standing in the open wings waiting to come on. They turned and
made motions to be quiet to the dozens of others behind them
. . . the women. Beautiful women. Lovely women with faces you
could recognize. Women whose faces I had seen before in photographs.

When the players moved it was with deliberate slowness so you
could watch every move. I stood there in the center of the
compound and realized that it was all being done for my benefit
without understanding why. It was a scene of impending action
the evil of it symbolized by the lone shadow of the vulture wheeling
high above in a gray, dismal sky.

I waited and watched, knowing that it had all happened before
and was going to happen again and this time I would see every

move and understand each individual action. I tried to concentrate on the players until I realized that I wasn't the only audience they had. Someone else was there in the compound with me. She was a woman. She had no face. She was a woman in black hovering behind me. I called to her and received no answer. I tried to walk to her, but she was always the same distance away without seeming to move at all. I ran on leaden feet without getting any closer, and tiring of the chase turned back to the play.

It was over and I had missed it again.

I said something vile to the woman because she had caused me to miss it and she shrank back, disappearing into the mist.

But the play wasn't over, not quite. At first I thought they were taking a curtain call, then I realized that their faces were hideous things and in unreal voices of pure silences they were all screaming for me to stop her and bring her back. Teen and Grindle and Link were slavering in their fury as they tried to break through the transparent wall and were thrown back to the ground. Their faces were contorted and their hands curved into talons. I laughed at them and they stopped, stunned, then withdrew out of sight.

The gray and noiseless compound dissolved into sound and yellow light. I was rocked gently from side to side and a voice said, "Mike . . . please wake up."

I opened my one eye and the other came open with it a little bit. "Marsha?"

"You were talking in your sleep. Are you awake, Mike?"

She looked tired. The nurse behind her looked tired too. The boy in her arms was smiling at me. "I'm awake, honey." I made a motion for her to pull down the shade. "Same day?"

"No, you slept all through yesterday, all night and most of today."

I rubbed my face. Some of the puffiness had gone down. "Lord. What time is it?"

"Almost four-thirty. Mike . . . that Captain Chambers is on the phone. Can you answer him?"

"Yeah, I'll get it. Let me get something on."

I struggled into my pants, swearing when I hit a raw spot. I was covered with adhesive tape and iodine, but the agony of moving was only a soreness now. I padded outside and picked up the phone. "Hello . . ."

"Where've you been, Mike? I told you to call me."

"Oh, shut up. I've been asleep."

"I hope you're awake now. The D.A. found Grindle."

"Good."

"Now he wants you."

"What's it this time, a homicide charge?"

"There's no charge. I explained that away. He wants Teen and he thinks you're pulling a fast one again."

"What's the matter with the guy?"

"Put yourself in his shoes and you'll see. The guy is fighting to hang onto his job."

"Christ, I gave him enough. What does he want . . . blood? Did he expect me to get Teen the hard way for him?"

"Don't be a jerk, Mike. He doesn't want Teen dead. He doesn't want a simple obit in the papers. He wants Teen in court so he can blow the whole thing wide open before the public. That's the only thing that will keep him in office."

"What happened to tin ear?"

"All the guy had was the telephone number of a booth in Grand Central Station. If he didn't call in every hour it meant there was trouble. We traced the number and there was nobody around. The guy worked through an intermediary who passed the information on to the right people. Both of them got paid off the same way . . . a bundle of cash by mail on the first of every month."

"I suppose Ed Teen's laughing his head off."

"Not exactly, but he's grinning broadly. We checked his alibi for the night before last and it's perfect. You know and I know that it's phoney as hell, but nobody is breaking it down in court. According to Teen the entire thing is preposterous. He was playing cards with a group of friends right through the night."

"Nuts. His story is as old as his racket. One good session under the lights and he'll talk."

"You don't put him under lights."

"There're other things you can do," I suggested.

"You don't do that either, Mike. Teen's going around under the watchful eye of a battery of lawyers well protected by a gang of licensed strong-arm boys. You try anything smart and it'll be your neck."

"Great. Now what's with the D.A.?"

It was a moment before he said anything. "Mike . . . are you on the level with me?"

"You know everything I know, Pat. Why?"

"You're going to be tied up with our boy for a long time if you don't get a move on," he said. "And by the way, call Ellen when you have time. She wants to talk to you."

"She there now?"

"No, she left a little while ago. I got something else for you. The playboy is back."

"Marvin Holmes?"

"Yeah. Customs passed the word on to us but it was too late to stop him. We traced him as far as New York and lost him here. The last lead we had said he was with a foreign-looking blonde and was doing his damnedest to stay under cover."

I let it run through my mind a minute. "He's still scared of something."

"It looks that way. I'm hoping to pick him up some time today. He's too well known to stay hidden long. Look, you give me a call when you have time. I have to get going now. This place is a madhouse. I wish the D.A. would operate out of his own office for a change."

I heard the click of his receiver cutting off the connection. Good old Pat. We still played on the same ball team. He was still worrying about me enough to want me to pick my own time and place when I had a long talk with the District Attorney.

Marsha was propped against the corner of the couch yawning. "We have to scram, kid."

Her mouth came shut. "Something wrong?"

"People want to talk to me and I can't afford the time. I want to go someplace and think. I want to be where nobody'll bother me for a week if I don't feel like seeing them."

"Well . . . we can go to my place. I won't bother you, Mike. I just want to crawl in bed and sleep forever."

"Okay. Get your things on. I'll get dressed."

I went back to the bedroom and finished putting on my clothes. There was a light tap on the door and I yelled come on in. The nurse opened the door and stood there holding the boy's hand. He would have been content to stay there, only he spotted the sling of the shoulder holster dangling from the dresser and made a dash for it.

This time she grabbed him before he was halfway there and dragged him back.

"I wish he liked his toys that way," she said.

"Maybe he'll grow up to be a cop."

I got a disapproving look for that. "I hope not!" she paused. "Miss Lee tells me you have to leave again."

"That's right."

"Then perhaps you'll do me a favor."

"Sure."

"They came to repaint my apartment this morning. I was

wondering if you'd mind my staying here tonight."

"Go right ahead. You'll be doing me the favor if you stay. If anybody calls tell them I'm out, you don't know where I am, nor when I'll be back. Okay?"

A frown creased her forehead. "You . . . expect callers?" There was a tremulous note in her voice.

I laughed at her and shook my head. "Not that kind. They'll be respectable enough."

She sighed uncertainly and took the kid back to the living room with her. I finished tying my shoes, strapped the gun around my chest and picked my jacket off a coat hanger in the closet. My other suit was draped over the back of the chair and a quick inspection said that it wasn't worth wearing any more. I emptied out the pockets on the dresser, rolled them up in a tight ball and carried them out to the kitchen. I stuffed them into the garbage can on top of the kid's old clothes, pressed the lid down tight and shoved the can back into the corner.

Marsha was waiting for me inside trying to hide her red-rimmed eyes with some mascara. We said good-by to the nurse and the kid and picked up the elevator going down. She fell asleep almost immediately and I had a hell of a time trying to wake her up when we got to her place.

I tried shaking her, pinching her and when that didn't work I bent over and kissed her.

That worked.

She wrinkled her nose and fought her eyes open. I said. "We're here. Come on, snap out of it."

"You did this to me," she smiled.

"That mustached bodyguard you got upstairs will wring my neck for it."

Her lips crinkled in a grin. "So that's why you came so readily. You thought you were going to be chaperoned. I'm sorry, Mike, but I'm all alone. The nurse is gone."

I gave her a playful rap on the chin and scooted her out of the car. She took my hand and we went up together. The guy on the elevator gaped at me until I said, "Up," twice, then he swallowed hard and slid the door shut. It was too bad he didn't see me yesterday.

We were so far away from everything up there. The evening filtered through the blinds, the late, slanting rays of the sun forming a crosshatch pattern on the rug. She settled me back in a big chair and disappeared in the kitchen where she made all the pleasant sounds of a woman in her element. I smelled the coffee and heard the bacon and eggs sizzling in the pan. My stomach remembered how long it was since it had been filled, and churned in anticipation.

I was out there before she called me, trying to be helpful by making the toast. She said, "Hungry?"

"Starving."

"Me too, I finished a box of stale crackers in your place and haven't eaten since."

That was all we said. You just don't talk when you don't leave room between bites. The coffee was hot and strong the way I like it and I finished it before I picked up a smoke.

Marsha turned the small radio on to a local station and picked up a supper orchestra and everything was perfect. It stayed that way until the band went off on the hour and a news commentator came on. It was the same boy who got all worked up over affairs in the city and this time he was really running over.

He gushed through his usual routine of introducing himself to the public and said, "Tonight has seen the end of an era. The man known to the police, the press, and the underworld as Lou Grindle has been found dead in a summer cottage near Islip, Long Island. Two men known to have been Grindle's associates were found shot to death, one in the same house and another twenty miles east of the spot. The house was the scene of violent gunplay and according to police ballistics experts, it was a bullet from Grindle's own gun that killed one of his men. An early reporter on the scene claims that the house had been used as some sort of inquisition chamber by Grindle and his men, but when questioned on the point the police refused to comment. Because of the significance of Grindle's death, the District Attorney has issued a No comment statement, but it is hinted that he is in full possession of the facts.

"Lou Grindle was a product of the racketeering of the early Twenties. Since the repeal of Prohibition he has been suspected of being a key figure in . . ."

I reached out and tuned in another station. I got a rhumba band that was all drums filling in behind a piano and let it beat through the room. But Marsha wasn't listening to it. Her mouth held a fixed position of surprise that matched the startled intensity of her eyes.

"Mike . . . that was . . . you?"

So I grinned at her. My mouth twisted up on the side and I

said, "They were going to kill me. They worked me over then took me for a ride."

Her hands were flat on the table, pushing her up from her chair. "Good heavens, Mike, no!" She trembled all over.

"They won't do it again, kid."

"But . . . why, Mike?"

"I don't know. Honest to God, I don't know."

She sat down limply and pushed her hair back from her face. "All this . . . all this started . . . from that night . . ."

"That's right. From a loused-up robbery. You got beat to hell, I got beat to hell. A kid's an orphan. A big-shot racketeer and two of his boys are dead. Arnold Basil's dead. Toady Link is dead and so are a pair of phony private investigators who tried to shoot it out with the cops. Mel Hooker's dead. Goddamn, there won't be anybody alive before you know it!"

"Supposing they come back?"

"They won't. I'm not going to give them the chance. If anybody goes after anybody else I'll do the going." I snubbed the butt out in my saucer. "Mind if I use your phone?"

She told me to go ahead and came inside with me. I checked the directory again and dialed Marvin Holmes' number. It buzzed at steady intervals and just as somebody picked it up there was a knock at the door and Marsha grabbed my arm. It rattled me for a second too. Then I picked the .45 out of the holster, thumbed the safety off and handed it to her while I answered the hellos that were making a racket in my ear.

She opened the door with the gun pointed straight ahead, stared a moment then began to shake in a soft hysterical laugh. I said, "Is Mr. Holmes there?"

It was the butler with the accent. "If this is the police again may I say that he has not come in during the last five minutes. You are being very annoying. He is not expected back, but if he comes I will give him your message."

I slammed the phone back the same time he did and walked over to Marsha who was still laughing crazily. The kid with his arm in a sling was trying to comfort her and shake the gun loose at the same time. I picked it out of her fingers, put it back where it belonged and shook her until she snapped out of it.

The laughing left her and she leaned against my shoulder. "I . . . I'm sorry, Mike. I thought . . ."

The kid said, "Gee, Marsha . . ."

"Come on in, Jerry." He stepped inside and shut the door. "This is Mr. Hammer . . . Jerry O'Neill."

Jerry said "Hi," but didn't make any effort to shake hands. Jerry didn't like me very much. It was easy to see why.

Marsha gave my hand a little squeeze. "Mike, I need a drink. Do you mind?"

"Not a bit, kitten. How about you, Jerry?"

"No. No, thanks. I gotta go right away. I . . ." he looked at Marsha hoping for some sign of jealousy, ". . . gotta date tonight."

She disappointed him. The stars in his eyes blinked out when she said, "Why, that's fine, Jerry. Is there something you wanted to see me about?"

"Well," he hesitated and shot me a look that was pure disgust, "we were all kind of worried when you didn't show up today. We called and all that and I kinda thought, well, they didn't want me to, but I came up anyway. To make sure. Nobody was home then."

"Oh, Jerry, I'm sorry. I was with Mr. Hammer all day."

"I see."

"You tell them they can stop worrying."

"I'll do that." He reached for the knob. "By, Marsha."

"Good-by, Jerry."

He didn't say anything to me. I handed Marsha the drink. "You shouldn't have done that. He's crazy mad in love with you."

She sipped and stared at the amber liquid thoughtfully. "That's why I have to do it, Mike. He's got to learn sometime."

I raised my glass and toasted her. "Well, I don't blame the kid much at that."

"I wish you felt the same way," she said.

It was a statement that needed an answer, but she didn't let me give it. She smiled, her face reflecting the fatigue of her body, finished her drink in a long draught and walked away to the bedroom. I sat down on the arm of the chair swirling the ice around in the glass. I was thinking of the kid with the busted wing, knowing how he must have felt. Some guys got everything, I thought. Others have nothing at all. I was one of the lucky ones.

Then I knew how lucky I was because she was standing in the doorway bathed in the last of the light as the sun went down into the river outside. The soft pink tones of her body softened the metallic glitter of the nylon gown that outlined her in bronze, flowing smoothly up the roundness of her thighs, melting into the curve of her stomach, then rising higher into rich contours to meet the dagger point of the neckline that dropped into the softly shaded well between her breasts.

She said simply, "Good night, Mike," and smiled at me because she knew she was being kissed right then better than she had ever been kissed before. The sun said good night too and drowned in the river, leaving just indistinct shadows in the room and the sound of a door closing.

I waited to hear a lock click into place.

There wasn't any.

chapter eleven ▬▬▬▬▬▬▬▬▬

I THOUGHT IT would be easy to sit there with a drink in my hand and think, staring into the darkness that was a barrier against any intrusion. It wasn't easy at all. It was comfortable and restful, but it wasn't easy. I tried to tell myself that it was dark like this when Decker had come through the window and gone to the wall directly opposite me and opened the safe. I tried like hell to picture the way it started and see it through to the way it ended, but my mind wouldn't accept the continuity and kept throwing it back in jumbled heaps that made no sense. The ice in my glass clinked against the bottom four times and that didn't help either.

Someplace, and I knew it was there, was an error in the thought picture. It was a key that could unlock the whole thing and I couldn't pick it out. It was the probing finger in my brain and the voice that nagged at me constantly. It made me light one butt after another and throw them away after one drag. It got to me until I couldn't think or sit still. It made my hands want to grab something and break it into a million fragments and I would have let myself go ahead and do it if it weren't for Marsha asleep in the room, her breathing a gentle monotone coming through the door.

I wasn't the kind of guy who could sit still and wait for something to happen. I had enough of the darkness and myself. Maybe later I'd want it that way, but not now.

I snapped the latch on the lock that kept it open and closed the door after me as quietly as I could. Rather than go through another routine with the elevator operator I took the stairs down and got out to the street to my car without scaring anybody. I rolled down the window and let the breeze blow in my face, feeling better for it. I sat there watching the people and the cars go by, then remembered that Pat had told me Ellen had wanted me to call her.

Hell, I could do better than that. I shoved the key in the lock and hit the starter.

My finger found the bell sunk in the framework of the door and pushed. Inside a chair scraped faintly and heels clicked on the woodwork. A chain rattled on metal and the door opened.

"Hello, Texas."

She was all bundled up in that white terrycloth robe again and she couldn't have been lovelier. Her mouth was a ripe red apple waiting to be bitten, a luscious curve of surprise over the edges of her teeth. "I . . . didn't expect you, Mike."

"Aren't you glad to see me?"

It was supposed to be a joke. It went flat on its face because those eyes that seemed to run through the full colors of the spectrum at times suddenly got cloudy with tears and she shook her head.

"Please come in."

I didn't get it at all. She walked ahead of me into the living room and nodded to a chair. I sat down. She sat down in another chair, but not close. She wouldn't look directly at me either.

I said, "What's the matter, Ellen?"

"Let's not talk about it, Mike."

"Wait a minute . . . you *did* tell Pat that you wanted me to call, didn't you?"

"Yes, but I meant . . . oh, never mind. Please, don't say anything more about it." Her mouth worked and she turned her head away.

That made me feel great. Like I kicked her cat or something.

"Okay, let's hear about it," I said.

She twisted out of the chair and walked over to the radio. It was already pulled out so she didn't have to fool with it. Then she handed me another one of those Manila folders.

This one had seen a lot of years. It was dirty and crisp with years. The string that held it together had rotted off leaving two stringy ends dangling from a staple. Ellen went back to her chair and sat down again. "It's the file on Toady Link. I found it buried under tons of other stuff in the archives."

I looked at her blankly. "Does the D.A. know you have this?"

"No."

"Ellen . . ."

"See if it's what you want, Mike." Her voice held no emotion at all.

I turned up the flap only to have it come off in my hand, then reached in for the sheets of paper that were clipped together. I leaned back and took my time with these. There wasn't any hurry now. Toady was dead and his file was dead with him, but I could look in and see what his life had been like.

It was quite a life.

Toady Link had been a photographer. Apparently he had been a good one because most of the professional actresses had come to him to have their publicity pictures made. Roberts hadn't missed a trick. His reports were full of marginal notes speculating on each and every possibility and it was there that the real story came out.

Because of Toady's professional contacts he had been contacted by Charlie Fallon. The guy was a bug on good-looking female celebrities and had paid well for pictures of them and paid better when an introduction accompanied the photographs.

But it wasn't until right after Fallon died that Toady became news in police circles. After that time there was no mention made of photography at all. Toady went right from his studio into big-time bookmaking and though he had little personal contact with Ed Teen it was known that, like the others, he paid homage and taxes to the king and whenever he took a step it was always up.

There was a lot of detail stuff there that I didn't pay any attention to, stuff that would have wrapped Toady up at any time if it had been put to use. Roberts would have used it, that much was evident by the work put in on collecting the data for the dossier. But like Ellen had said, a new broom had come in and swept everything out including months and miles of legwork.

Ellen had to speak twice before I heard her. "Does it . . . solve anything?"

I threw them on the coffee table in disgust. "Fallon. It solves him. He's still dead and so is Toady. Goddamn it anyway."

"I'm sorry. I thought it would help."

"You tried, kid. That was enough. You can throw these things away now. What the D.A. never saw he won't miss." I picked up my cigarettes from the table and stuffed them in my pocket. She still watched me blankly. "I'd better be going," I told her.

She didn't make any motion to see me out. I started to pass her and stopped. "Texas . . . what the hell goes on? Tell me that at least, will you? It wasn't so long ago that you were doing all the passing and I thought you were a woman who knew what was going on. All right, I asked you to do me a favor and I put you in a spot. It wasn't so bad that I couldn't get you off it."

"That's not it, Mike." She still wouldn't look at me.

"So you're a Texas gal who likes guys that look like Texas men. Maybe I should learn to ride a horse."

She finally looked up at me from the depths of the couch. Her eyes were blue again and not clouded. They were blue and hurt and angry all at once. "You're a Texas man, Mike. You're the kind I dreamed of and the kind I want and the kind I'll never have, because your kind are never around long enough. They have to go out and play with guns and hurt people and get themselves killed.

"I was wrong in wanting what I did. I read too many stories and listened to too many old men telling big tales. I dreamed too hard, I guess. It isn't so nice to wake up suddenly and know somebody you're all gone over is coming closer to dying every day because he likes it that way.

"No, Mike. You're exactly what I want. You're big and strong and exciting. While you're alive you're fun to be with but you won't be any fun dead. You're trouble and you'll always be that way until somebody comes along who can make bigger trouble than you.

"I'm afraid of a Texas man now. I'm going to forget all about you and stop looking for a dream. I'll wait until somebody nice and safe comes along, somebody peaceful and quiet and shy and I'll get all those foolish romanticisms out of my head and live a bored and relatively normal life."

I planted my feet apart and looked down at her with a laugh that came up from my chest. "And you'll always wonder what a Texas man would have been like," I said.

The change stole over her face slowly, wiping out the bitterness. Her eyes half closed and the blue of her irises was gray again. The smile and the frown blended together like a pleasant hurt. She leaned back with a fluid animal motion, her head resting languidly against the couch. The pink tip of her tongue touched her lips that were parted in a ghost of a smile making them glisten in the light of the single lamp. Then she stretched back slowly and reached out her arms to me, and in reaching the entire front of the robe came open and she made no move to close it.

"No," she said, "I'll find out about that first."

We said good-by in the dim light of morning. She said good-by, Texas man, and I said so long, Texas gal, and I left without looking back because everything she had said was right and I didn't want to hear it again by looking back at her eyes. I got in the car, drove over to Central Park West and cruised along until I found a parking place. It was right near an entrance so I left it there and walked off the pavements to the grass and sat on a hill where I could see the sun coming up over the tops of the buildings in the background.

The ground still held the night dampness, letting it go slowly in a thin film of haze that was suspended in mid-air, rising higher as the sun warmed it. The whole park had a chilled eerie appearance of something make-believe. An early stroller went by on the walk, only the top half of him visible, the leash in his hand disappearing into the fog yet making all the frantic motions of having some unseen creature on its end.

When the wind blew it raised the gray curtain and separated it into angry segments that towered momentarily before filtering back into the gaps. There were other people too, half-shapes wandering through a dream world, players who didn't know they had an audience. Players buried in their own thoughts and acts on the other side of a transparent wall that shut off all sound.

I sat there scowling at it until I remembered that it was just like my dream even to the colors and the synthetic silence. It made me so uncomfortable that I turned around expecting to see the woman in black who had no face.

She was there.

She wasn't in black and she had a face, but she stopped when she saw me and turned away hurriedly just like the other one did. This one seemed a little annoyed because I blocked her favorite path.

And I knew who the woman was in the compound with me that night. She had a name and a face I hadn't seen yet. She was there in the compound trying to tell me something I should have thought of myself.

I waited until the sun had burned off the mist and made it a real world again. I went back to the daylight and searched through it looking for a little guy with big ears and a brace of dyed blondes on his arms. The sun made an arc through the sky and was on its way down without me finding him.

At three-thirty I made a call. It went through three private secretaries and a guy who rumbled when he talked. He was the last man in front of Harry Bailen, the columnist, and about as high as I was going to get.

I said, "This is a friend of Cookie Harkin's. I got something for him that won't keep and I can't find the guy. I want his address if you have it."

He had it, but he wasn't giving it out. "I'm sorry, but that's private information around here."

"So is what I got. Cookie can have it for your boss free or I can sell it to somebody else. Take your pick."

"If you have anything newsworthy I'll be glad to pass it on to Mr. Bailen for you."

"I bet you would, feller, only it happens that Cookie's a friend of mine and either he gets it or the boss'll get scooped and he isn't gonna like that a bit."

The phone dimmed out a second as he covered up the mouthpiece. The rumble of his voice still came through as he talked to somebody there in the office and when he came back to me he was more sharp than before.

"Cookie Harkin lives in the Mapuah Hotel. That's M-A-P-U-A-H. Know where it is?"

"I'll find it," I told him. "And thanks."

He thanked me by slamming the phone back.

I looked up the Mapuah Hotel in the directory and found it listed in a crummy neighborhood off Eighth Avenue in the upper Sixties. It was as bad as I expected, but just about the kind of a place a guy like Cookie would go for. The only rule it had was to pay the rent on time. There was a lobby with a couple of old leather chairs and a set of wicker furniture that didn't match. The clerk was a baldheaded guy who was shy a lower plate and he was bent over the desk reading a magazine.

"Where'll I find Cookie Harkin?"

"309." He didn't look up and made no attempt at announcing me.

The only concession to modernization the place made was the automatic elevator. Probably they couldn't get anybody to run a manual job anyway. I closed the door, pushed the third button in the row and stood there counting bricks until the car stopped.

Cookie had a good spot. His room took up the southwest corner facing the rear court where there was a reasonable amount of quiet and enough of a breeze that wasn't contaminated by the dust and exhaust gases on the street side.

I knocked twice, heard the bedsprings creak inside, then Cookie yelled, "Yeah?"

"Mike, Cookie. Get out of the sack."

"Okay, just a minute."

The key rattled in the lock and Cookie stood there in the top half of his pajamas rubbing the sleep out of his eyes. "This is a hell of an hour to get up," I said.

"I was up late."

I looked at the second pillow on his bed that still had the fresh imprint of a head, then at the closed door that led off the room. "Yeah, I'll bet. Can she hear anything in there?"

He came awake in a hurry. "Nah. Whatcha got, Mike?"

"What would you like to have?"

"Plenty. Did you see the papers?" I said no. "I'm not so dumb, Mike. The D.A.'s giving out a song and dance about that triple kill in Islip. Me, I know what happened. The rags gotta clam up because no names are mentioned, but you let me spill it and I'll clean up."

I sat down and pulled out a butt. "I'll swap," I said.

"Now wait a sec, Mike . . ."

"There aren't any rough boys this time. Do something for me and you'll get the story. Right from the beginning."

"You got a deal."

So I told him straight without leaving anything out and he was on the phone before I was finished talking. Dollar bills were drooling out of his eyes and the thing was big enough to get a direct line to Harry Bailen himself. I told him not to play the cops down and when he passed it down with the hint that more was yet to come if it was played right, the big shot agreed and his voice crackled excitedly until he hung up.

Cookie came back rubbing his hands and grinning at me. "Just ask me, Mike. I'll see that you get it."

I dragged in on the smoke. "Go back a ways, Cookie. Remember when Charlie Fallon died?"

"Sure. He kicked off in a movie house on Broadway, didn't he? Had a heart attack."

"That's right."

"He practically lived in them movies. Couldn't tell if he was in the classiest playhouse or the lousiest theater if you wanted to go looking for him."

I nodded that I knew about it and went on, "At the time he was either married or living with a woman. Which was it?"

"Umm . . ." he tugged at one ear and perched on the edge of the bed. "Nope, he wasn't married. Guess he was shacking with somebody."

"Who?"

"Hell, how'd I know? That was years ago. The guy was woman-happy."

"This one must have been special if he was living with her."

His eyes grew shrewd. "You want her?"

"Yep."

"When?"

"As soon as you can."

"I dunno, Mike. Maybe she ain't around no more."

"She'll be around. That kind never leaves the city."

Cookie made a face like a weasel and started to grin a little bit. "I'll give it a spin. Supposing I gotta lay out cash?"

"Go ahead. I'll back it up. Spend what you have to." I stood up and scrawled a number on the back of a match-book cover. "I'll be waiting for you to call. You can reach me here anytime and if anybody starts buzzing you about that story your boss is going to print, tell them you picked it up as a rumor and as far as I'm concerned, you haven't seen me in a month of Sundays."

"I got it, Mike. You'll hear from me."

He was reaching for his shorts when I closed the door and I knew that if she was still there he'd find her. All I had to do was wait.

I went back to Marsha's apartment, went in and made myself a drink. She was still asleep. I knew how she felt.

It wasn't so bad this time because somebody else was doing the work. At least something was in motion. I picked up the phone, tried to get Pat and missed him by a few minutes. I didn't bother looking for him. The liquor was warm in my stomach and light in my head; the radio was humming softly and I lay there stretched out watching the smoke curl up to the ceiling.

At a quarter to eight I opened the door to the bedroom and switched on the light. She had thrown back the covers and lay there with her head pillowed on her arm, a dream in copper-colored nylon who smiled in her sleep and wrinkled her nose at an imaginary somebody.

She didn't wake up until I kissed her, and when she saw me I knew who it was she had been dreaming of. "Don't ever talk about me, girl, you just slept the clock around too."

"Oh . . . I couldn't have, Mike!"

"You did. It's almost eight P.M."

"I was supposed to have gone to the theater this afternoon. What will they think?"

"I guess we're two of a kind, kid."

"You think so?" Her hands met behind my head and she pulled my face down to hers, searching for my mouth with lips that were soft and full and just a little bit demanding. I could feel my fingers biting into her shoulders and she groaned softly asking and wanting me to hold her closer.

Then I held her away and looked at her closely, wondering if she would be afraid like Ellen too. She wrinkled her nose at me this time as if she knew what I had been thinking and I knew that she wouldn't be afraid of anything. Not anything at all.

I said, "Get up," and she squirmed until her feet were on the floor. I backed out of the room and made us something to eat while she showered, and after we ate there was an hour of sitting comfortably watching the sun go back down again, completing its daily cycle.

At five minutes to ten it started to rain again.

I sat in the dark watching it slant against the lights of the city. Something in my chest hammered out that this, too, was the end of a cycle. It had started in the rain and was going to end in the rain. It was a deadly cycle that could start from nothing, and nothing could stop it until it completed its full revolution.

The Big Kill. That's what Decker had wanted to make.

He made it. Then he became part of it himself.

The rain tapped on the window affectionately, a kitten scratching playfully to be let in. A jagged streak of lightning cut across the west, a sign that soon that playful kitten would become a howling, screaming demon.

At seven minutes after ten Cookie called.

There was a tenseness in my body, an overabundance of energy that had been stored away waiting for this moment before coming forward. I felt it flow through me, making the skin tighten around my jaws before it seeped into my shoulders, bunching the muscles in hard knots.

I picked up the phone and said hello.

"This is Cookie, Mike." He must have had his face pressed into the mouthpiece. His voice had a hoarse uncertain quality.

"Go ahead."

"I found her. Her name is Georgia Lucas and right now she's going under the name of Dolly Smith."

"Yeah. What else?"

"Mike . . . somebody else is after her too. All day I've been crossing tracks with somebody. I don't like it. She's hot, Mike."

The excitement came back, all of it, a hot flush of pleasure because the chase was still on and I was part of it. I asked him, "Who, Cookie? Who is it?"

"I dunno, but somebody's there. I've seen signs like these before.

I'm telling you she's hot and if you want her you better do something quick."

"Where is she?"

"Not twenty-five feet away from where I'm standing. She's got on a red and white dress and hair to match. Right now she's doing a crummy job of singing a torch song."

"Where, dammit!"

"It's a place in the Village, a little night club. Harvey's."

"I know where it is."

"Okay. The floor show goes off in about ten minutes and won't come on for an hour again. In between times she's doubling as a cigarette girl. I don't like some of the characters around this place, Mike. If I can I'll get to her in the dressing room. And look, you can't get in the back room where she is if you're stag, so I better call up Tolly and have her meet us."

"Forget Tolly. I'll bring my own company. You stick close to her." I slapped the phone back, holding it in place for a minute. I was thinking of what her face would be like. She was the woman in the compound with me, the other one watching the play. She was the woman Lou Grindle found worth cursing in the same breath with Fallon and Link and me. She was the woman somebody was after and the woman who could supply the answers.

From the darkness Marsha said, "Mike . . ."

My hands were sweating. It ran down my back and plastered my shirt to my skin. I said, "Get your coat on, Marsha. We have to go out."

She did me the favor of not asking any questions. She snapped on the lights and took her coat and mine out of the closet. I helped her into it, hardly knowing what I was doing, then opened the door and walked out behind her.

We got on Broadway and drove south while the windshield wipers ticked off the seconds.

The rain had grown. The kitten was gone and an ugly black panther was lashing its tail in our faces.

The bars were filling up, and across town on the East Side an overpainted redhead in last year's clothes would be rubbing herself up against somebody else.

A guy would be nursing a beer down at the end of the bar while a pair of drunks argued over what to play on the juke box.

The bartender would club somebody who got out of line. The floor would get damper and stink of stale beer and sawdust.

Maybe the door would open and another guy would be standing

there with a bundle in his arms. A little wet bundle with a wet, tousled head.

Maybe more people would die.

"You're quiet, Mike."

"I know. I was remembering another night like this."

"Where are we going?"

I didn't hear the question. I said, "All the way it's been Fallon. Whenever anything happened it was his name that came up. He was there when Decker was killed. He was there when Toady died. He was there when Grindle died. He was there at the beginning and he's right here at the end. There was a woman in it. She disappeared after Fallon died and she's the one we're going to see. She's going to tell us why she disappeared and why Toady Link got so important and when she tells that I'll know why Decker made his own plans to die and kissed his kid good-by. I'll know why Teen sat there and watched me being cut up and know what was so important in Toady's apartment. I'll know all that and I'll be able to live with myself again. I went out hunting a killer and I missed him. I never missed one before. Somebody else had a bigger grudge and cut him down before I had a chance, but at least I have the satisfaction of knowing he's dead. Now I want to know why it happened. I want to make sure I did miss. I've been thinking and thinking . . . and every once in a while when I think real hard I can see a hole no bigger than a pinhead and I begin to wonder if it was really Toady I was after at all."

Her hand tightened over mine on the wheel. "We'll find out soon," she told me.

A rain-drenched canopy sagging on its frame braced itself against the storm. Lettered on the side was HARVEY'S. The wind had torn a hole in the top and the doorman in the maroon uniform huddled in the entrance to stay dry. I parked around the corner and locked the car, then dragged my raincoat over the two of us for the run back to the joint.

The doorman said it was a bad night and I agreed with him.

The girl in the cloakroom said the same thing and I agreed with her too.

The headwaiter who was the head bouncer with a carnation didn't say anything. I saw Cookie over at a corner table with another bleach job and let muscles make a path through the crowd for us until we reached him.

Somewhere, Cookie had lost his grin. We went through the introductions and ordered a drink. He looked at me, then at

Marsha and I said, "You can talk. She's part of it."

The blonde who looked like a two-bit twist caught my attention. "Don't mind my getup. I can get around better when I act like a floozie. I've been on this thing with Cookie ever since he started."

"Arlene's one of Harry's stenos. We use her once in a while. She's the one who dug up the dame."

"Where is she, Cookie?"

His head made a motion toward the back of the bandstand. "Probably changing. The act goes on again in a few minutes." He was scowling.

The blonde had a single sheet of paper rolled up in her hand. She spread it out and started checking off items with her fingernail.

"Georgia . . . or Dolly . . . is forty-eight and looks like it. She was Fallon's girl friend and then his mistress. At one time she was a looker and a good singer, but the years changed all that. After Fallon died she went from one job to another and wound up being a prostitute. We got a line on her through a guy who knows the houses pretty well. She took to the street for a while and spent some time in the workhouse. Right after the war she was picked up on a shoplifting charge and given six months. Not two weeks after she got out she broke into an apartment and was caught at it. She got a couple years that time. She got back in the houses after that to get eating money, broke loose and got this job. She's been here a month."

"You got all that without seeing her?"

The blonde nodded.

"I thought you were going to speak to her, Cookie."

"I was," he said. "I changed my mind."

He was staring across the room to where Ed Teen was sitting talking to four men. Only two of them were lawyers. The other two were big and hard-looking. One chewed on a match-stick and leered at the dames.

My drink slopped over on the table.

Cookie said, "I thought you told me there wouldn't be any rough stuff."

"I changed my mind too." I had to let go of the glass before I spilled the rest of it. "They see me come in?"

"No."

"They know you or why you're here?"

Cookie's ears went back, startled. "Do I look like a dope?" His tongue licked his lips nervously. "You think . . . that's who I been crossing all day."

I was grinning again. Goddamn it, I felt good! "I think so, Cookie," I said.

And while I was saying it the lights turned dim and a blue spot hit the bandstand where a guy in a white tux started to play. A girl with coal-black hair stepped out from behind the curtains and paused dramatically, waiting for a round of applause before going into her number.

I couldn't wait any longer. It was coming to a head too fast. I said, "I'm going back there. Cookie, you get over to the phone and call the police. Ask for Captain Chambers and tell him to get down here as fast as he can move. Tell him why. I don't know what's going to happen, but stick around and you'll get your story."

I could see Cookie's face going white. "Look, Mike, I don't want no part of this. I . . ."

"You won't get any part of it unless you do as you're told. Get moving."

I started to get up and Marsha said, "I'm going with you, Mike."

All the hate and excitement died away and there was a little piece of time that was all ours. I shook my head. "You can't, kid. This is my party. You're not part of the trouble any more." I leaned over and kissed her. There were tears in her eyes.

"Please, Mike . . . wait for the police. I don't want you . . . to be hurt again."

"Nobody's going to hurt me now. Go home and wait for me."

There was something final in her voice. "You won't . . . come back to me, Mike."

"I promise you," I said. "I'll be back."

A sob tore into her throat and stayed there, crushed against her lips by the back of her hand. Part of it got loose and I didn't want to stay to see the pain in her face.

I nudged the .45 in the holster to kick it free of the leather and tried to see across the room. It was much too dark to see anything. I started back and heard Marsha sob again as Cookie led her to the front. The blonde had disappeared somewhere too.

chapter twelve ▰▰▰▰▰▰▰▰▰▰▰▰

A CURTAIN COVERED the arch. It led into a narrow, low-ceilinged alcove with another curtain at the far end. The edges of it overlapped and the bottom turned up along the floor, successfully cutting out the backstage light that could spoil an effective entrance.

I stepped through and pulled it back to place behind me. The guy tilted back in the chair put his paper down and peered at me over his glasses. "Guests ain't allowed back here, buddy."

I let him see the corner of a sawbuck. "Could be that I'm not a guest."

"Could be." He took the sawbuck and made it vanish. "You look like a fire inspector to me."

"That'll do if anybody asks. Where's Dolly's room?"

"Dolly? That bag? What you want with her?" He took his glasses off and waved them down the hall. "She ain't got no room. Under the stairs is a supply closet and she usually changes in there." The glasses went back on and he squinted through them at me. "She's no good, Mac. Only fills in on an empty spot."

"Don't worry about it."

"I won't." He tilted the chair back again and picked up the paper. His eyes stayed on me curiously, then he shrugged and started reading.

There was a single light hanging from the ceiling halfway down and a red exit bulb over a door at the end. A pair of dressing rooms with doors side by side opened off my right and I could hear the women behind them getting ready for their act. In one of them a man was complaining about the pay and a woman told him to shut up. She said something else and he cracked her one.

The other side was a blank beaverboard wall painted green that ran down to the iron staircase before meeting a cement-block wall. It must have partitioned off the kitchen from the racket that was going on in back of it.

I found the closet where the guy said it would be. It had a riveted steel door with an oversize latch and SUPPLIES stenciled across the top. I stepped back in the shadows under the staircase and waited.

From far off came the singer's voice rising to the pitch of the piano. Down the hall the guy was still tilted back reading. I knocked on the door.

A muffled voice asked who it was. I knocked again.

This time the door opened a crack. I had my foot in the opening before she could close it. She looked like she was trying hard to scream. I said, "I'm a friend, Georgia."

Stark terror showed in her eyes at the mention of her name. She backed away until the fear reached her legs, then collapsed on a box. I went all the way in and shut the door.

Now the figure from the mist had a face. It wasn't a nice face. Up close it showed every year and experience in the tiny lines that crisscrossed her skin. At one time it had been pretty. Misery and fear had wiped all that out without leaving more than a semblance of a former beauty. She was small and fighting to hold her figure. None of the artifices were any good. The red hair, the overly mascaraed eyes, the tightly corseted waist were too plainly visible. I wondered why the management even bothered with her. Maybe she sang dirty songs. That always made a hit with the customers who were more interested in lyrics than music.

The kind of terror that held her was too intense to last very long. She managed to say, "Who . . . are you?"

"I told you I was a friend." There was another box near the door and I pulled it over. I wanted this to be fast. I sat down facing the door, a little behind it. "Ed Teen's outside."

If I thought that would do something to her I was wrong. Long-suffering resignation made a new mask on her face. "You're afraid of him, aren't you?"

"Not any more," she replied simply. The mascara on her lashes, suddenly wet, made dark patches under her eyes. Her smile was a wry, twisted thing that had no humor in it. "It had to come sometime," she said. "It took years to catch up with me and running never put it behind me."

"Would you like to stop running?"

"Oh, God!" Her face went down into her hands.

I leaned on my knees and made her look at me. "Georgia . . . you know what's happened, don't you?"

"I read about it."

"Now listen carefully. The police will be here shortly. They're your friends too if you'd only realize it. You won't be hurt, understand! Nobody is going to hurt you." She nodded dumbly, the dark circles under her eyes growing bigger. I said, "I want to know about Charlie Fallon. Eveything. Tell me about Fallon and Grindle and Teen and Link and anybody else that matters. Can you do that?"

I lit a cigarette and held it out to her. She took it, holding her eyes on the tip while she passed her finger through the column of smoke. "Charlie . . . he and I lived together. He was running the rackets at the time. He and Lou and Ed worked together, but Charlie was the top man.

"It . . . it started when Charlie got sick. His heart was bad. Lou and Ed didn't like the idea of doing all the work so they . . . they looked for a way to get rid of him. Charlie was much too smart for them. He found out about it. At the time, the District Attorney was trying his best to break up the organization and Charlie saw a way to . . . to keep the two of them in line. He was afraid they'd kill him . . . so he took everything he had that would incriminate Ed and Lou, things that would put them right in the chair, and brought them to Toady Link to be photographed. Toady put them on microfilms.

"Charlie told me about it that night. We sat out in the kitchen and laughed about it. He thought . . . he had his partners where they could never bother him again. He said he was going to put the microfilms in a letter addressed to the District Attorney and send it to a personal friend of his to mail if anything ever happened to him.

"He did it, too. He did it that same night. I remember him sitting there doing all his correspondence. It was the last letter he ever wrote. He intended to wait awhile, then tell Lou and Ed about it, but something else happened he didn't foresee. Toady Link saw a way to work himself into the organization. He went to Ed and told him what Charlie had done.

"That's . . . where I came into it. Lou came for me. He threatened me. I was afraid. Honest, it wasn't my fault . . . I couldn't help myself. Lou . . . would have killed me if I didn't do what he said! They wanted to kill Charlie so they wouldn't be suspected at all. They knew he had frequent attacks and had to take nytroglycerin tablets and they made me steal the tablets from his pockets. God, I couldn't help myself! They made me do it! Charlie had an attack the next day and died in the theater. God, I didn't mean it, I had to do it to stay alive!"

"The bastards!" The word cut into her sobbing. "The lousy miserable bastards. Toady pulled a double-cross as long as your arm. He must have made two prints of those films. He kept one himself and let the boys know about it, otherwise they would have knocked him off long ago. That was his protection. That's what Teen thought I took out of his apartment!"

Georgia shook her head, not knowing what I was talking about, but it made sense to me. It made a damn lot of sense now.

I said, "After Fallon died . . . what happened? What did the District Attorney do?"

"Nothing. Nothing happened."

The evil of it was like the needle-point of a dagger digging into my brain. The incredible evil of it was right there in front of my face and needed nothing more than a phone call to make it a fact.

All along I had tripped over that one stumbling block that threw me on my face. I had missed it because it had been so goddamn small, but now it stuck out like a huge white rock with a spotlight on it.

I grabbed Georgia by the arm and lifted her off the box. "Come on, we're getting out of here. Anything you want to take with you?"

She reached out automatically for her hat and purse, then I shoved her out the door. The hallway was empty. There was no guy in the chair down under the light. A pair of tomtoms made the air pulsate with a harsh jungle rhythm that seemed to enjoy echoing through the corridor as if it were in its natural element.

I didn't like it a bit.

The red exit light pointed the way out. If Ed Teen was waiting to see Georgia he was going to have a long wait. Maybe he thought he was the only one looking for her and he didn't have to hurry. I pulled the door open and stepped out ahead of her, feeling for the step.

The voice behind the gun said, "This the one, Ed?"

And Ed said, "That's the one. Take him."

I was keyed up for it. There was no surprise to it except for them. A gun is a gun and when one is rammed in your ribs you aren't supposed to scream your guts out while you slam into a woman in the darkness and hit the pavement as the flame blasts out above your head.

The .45 was a living thing in my hand cutting its own lightning and thunder in the rain. I rolled, scrambled to my feet and ran in a crouch only to roll again. They were shouting at each other, running for the light that framed the end of the alley. The bright flashes of gunfire at close range made everything blacker than before. I saw the legs go past my face and grabbed at them, slashing at a head with the barrel of my gun. Back in the shadows Georgia's voice was a wail of terror. There was the sound of other feet hugging the wall and for an instant a shape was there in the frame. I had time to get in one shot that sparked off the brick wall then a body slammed into mine that was all feet and something heavy that pounded at my head.

The cursing turned into a hoarse wheeze when my fingers raked across a throat and held on. But a foot found my stomach and my fingers slid off. They had me down on my back; an arm was under my chin wrenching my head to the side and the guy was telling the other one to give it to me.

Before he could a siren moaned and wheels screamed on the pavement. There was only that one way out. They ran for it and I saw them stop completely when the beams of three torches drenched them. Georgia was still a shrill voice buried under the shadows and Pat was calling to me. His light picked me out of the rubble and he jerked me to my feet.

I said, "She's back there. Go find her."

"Who?"

"Fallon's old girl friend."

He said something I couldn't catch and went back for her, letting me lean up against the wall until my breath came back. I heard him in there behind the garbage can, then he came back with her in his arms. She hung there limply, completely relaxed.

I didn't want to ask it. "Is she . . . dead?"

"She's all right. Passed out, I think."

"That's good, Pat. You don't want anything to happen to her. Right now she's the most precious thing you have. The D.A. is going to love her."

"Mike, what the hell is this about?"

"She'll tell you, Pat. Treat her nice and she'll tell you all about it. When you hear her story you're going to have Ed Teen just a step away from the chair. He was an accomplice before the fact of Fallon's murder and she's the girl who's going to prove it."

I followed him back to the street, my feet dragging. The two boys were trying to explain things to a cop who didn't want to listen. Pat passed Georgia into a car and told the driver to get her down to headquarters. He looked at the big boys and they started to sweat. The rain was beating in their faces, but you could still tell they were sweating.

I said, "They're Teen's men, Pat. Ed was here to supervise things himself. He was real smart about it too. I had a man trying to run down the woman while Ed was doing the same thing. He guessed who was doing it. He came to make sure I didn't get away with it. He's gone now, but you won't have any trouble picking him up. An hour ought to do it."

The crowd had gathered. They fought for a look, standing on

their toes to peer over shoulders and ask each other what had happened. Cookie was on the edge and I waved him over. He had my coat in his hand and I put it on. "Here's the guy I was telling you about, Pat. I'd appreciate it if you'd let him in on the story before it gets out to the papers. Think you can?"

"Who's going to tell the story . . . you?"

"No . . . I'm finished, kid. It's all over now. Let Georgia tell it. She had to live with it long enough; she ought to be glad to get it off her chest. I'm going home. When you get done come on up and we'll talk about it."

Pat made a study of my face. "All this . . . it had something to do with Decker?"

"It had a lot to do with Decker. We just couldn't see it at first."

"And it's finished now?"

"It's finished."

I turned around and walked through the crowd back to my car. The rain didn't matter now. It could spend its fury on me if it wanted to. The city was a little bit cleaner than it was before, but there was still some dirt under the carpet.

Back uptown I found a drugstore that was open all night and went into the phone booth. I dialed the operator and got a number out on the Island. It rang for a few minutes and the voice that answered was that of a tired man too rudely awakened. "Mr. Roberts?"

"Speaking."

"This is Mike Hammer. I was going to call you earlier but something came up. If you don't mind, there's something I'd like to ask you. It's pretty important."

His voice was alert now. "I don't mind a bit. What is it?"

"During your term in office you conducted a campaign to get rid of Fallon and his gang. Is that right?"

"Yes, quite right. I wasn't very successful."

"Tell me, did you ever have any communication from Fallon about that?"

"Communication?"

"A letter."

He thought a moment, then: "No . . . no, I didn't." Then he thought again. "Now that you mention it . . . yes, there was a peculiar incident at one time. An envelope was in my wastebasket. It was addressed to me and had Fallon's home address on it. I recognized the address, of course, but since he lived in an apartment

hotel that was fairly prominent I didn't give it another thought.
Besides, Fallon was dead at that time."

"I see. Well, thanks for your trouble, Mr. Roberts. Sorry I had
to bother you." It was a lie. I wasn't a bit sorry at all.

"Perfectly all right," he said, and hung up.

And I had the answer.

I mean I had all of it and not just part of it like I had a minute
before and my brain screamed a warning for me to hurry before
it was too late even though I knew that it was already too late.

I cursed the widow-makers and the orphan-makers and every
goddamn one of the scum that found it so necessary to kill because
their god was a paper one printed in green. But I didn't curse
the night and the rain any more. It kept the cars off the street
and gave me the city for my own where red lights and whistles
didn't mean a thing.

It gave me a crazy feeling in my head that pushed me faster
and faster until the car was a mad dervish screaming around
corners in a race with time. I left it double-parked outside my
apartment and ran for the door. I took the stairs two at a time,
came out on my floor with the keys in my hand reaching out for
the lock.

I didn't stop to feel the gimmick on the lock. I turned the key,
shoved the door open and pushed in with my gun in my fist and
she was there like I knew she'd be there and it wasn't too late
after all. The nurse was face down on the floor with her scalp
cut open, but she was breathing and the kid was crying and pulling
at her dress.

"Marsha," I said, "you're the rottenest thing that ever lived and
you're not going to live long."

There was never any hate like hers before. It blazed out of
those beautiful eyes trying to reach my throat and if ever a maniac
had lived she was it. She dropped the knife that was cutting so
neatly into the sofa cushion and got up from her crouch like the
lovely deadly animal she was.

I looked at the partial wreckage of the room and the guts of
the chairs that were spread over the floor. "I should have known,
kid. God knows it slapped me in the face often enough. No man
would cut up a cushion as neat as that. You're doing almost as
nice a job here as you did in Toady's place. You're not going to
find what you're looking for, Marsha. They were never hidden.
You couldn't believe that everybody's not like yourself, could you?
You had to think that anybody who saw those films would try
to make them pay off like you did."

She started to tremble. Not from fear. It was an involuntary spasm of hate suffusing her entire body at once. I laughed at her. Now I could laugh.

Her mouth wasn't soft and rich now. It was slitted until it bared her teeth to the gums. "You don't like me to laugh, do you? Hell, you must have laughed at me plenty of times. Woman, when you were alone you must have laughed your damned head off. You know, it *was* funny the way this thing went. I based everything I had on a false premise yet I wound up with the right answers in the long run. You had me talked into it as nicely as you please.

"All this time I thought Decker had made a mistake in apartments. Like hell! Decker knew what he was doing. They had your place cased too well to make any mistake.

"But just to see if I'm right, let's go back to the beginning. I haven't got a damn thing to stand on but speculation, yet I bet I can call every turn right on the button. What I have got will hold you until we can dig up the real stuff though. We may have to go back a way, but we'll get it and you'll burn for it.

"You were even nice enough to give me a lot of hints. There you were out in Hollywood in a spot most girls would give their right arms to be in and there was only one drawback. You weren't big time. You weren't going to get to be big time, either. You were one of that big middle class of actors who were okay, but not for the feature films. Then a man came along who gave you a hard time and you got sour on the world.

"Right then you were ripe for the kicker. You were shaking hands with the devil and didn't know it. Back in New York a guy named Charlie Fallon was writing a batch of letters. One was a fan letter to you. The other was to the District Attorney with enough evidence on microfilms to put a couple of racketeers where they belonged. Old Charlie was feeling good that night. He felt so good that he got his envelopes mixed and those films came to you.

"That was just before your secretary died, wasn't it? Yeah, I can tell that much by your face. She was all for turning them in to the authorities and you put the kibosh on that. You saw a way to get yourself a lot of easy dough. That man came in handy too. When you knocked off that secretary you made it look like a suicide and it wasn't hard to explain away at all.

"Now let me speculate on what happened right here in New York. The D.A. got a letter, all right. It was from Fallon, but it contained a fan letter to you. Teen and Grindle put out a lot of cash to have a pipeline in where it counted and they had a slick cop watching the mail for that letter. When they got it they must have turned green because it didn't take much thought to figure out what had happened. All they could do was to sit back and see what you would do.

"You did it. You came around with your hand out and they greased it to whatever tune you called. For ten years that went on. Even the time checks. It's a lot of years, too. Hell, you know what blackmail is like. It grows and grows like a damned fungus. Ed and Lou had two of you on their necks. When Toady Link made those films for Fallon he made a copy for himself. But at least he added something to the outfit. Then one day one of you put too much pressure on the boys. One of you had to go. Toady probably pulled the squeeze play. Since he knew all about it anyway they told him that if he could lift those copies you had he'd make out better himself.

"That's where Decker came in. Good safe men are hard to get for those jobs. Toady located Decker somehow and had Mel Hooker steer him right into a trap where he had to play ball with Toady or else. They figured it out nice as you please and never stopped to figure out what can go on inside a guy's mind.

"Decker had been through the mill and he wasn't setting his kid up to have any part of it. In his own way he was a martyr. He knew what he was going to do and knew he'd die for it. When he lifted that stuff from your place I think he planned to take it straight to the police. He didn't move fast enough though. So he did the next best thing. He stuck those films where they'd probably be found and went out and died.

"You know the rest of it from there, Marsha. I don't have to tell you anymore, do I? I shot my mouth off to you and spilled it about Toady, so you went up there to see him yourself. You did a nice job of bumping him. Nice and clean. Maybe in those ten years you figured it all out for yourself, and if you didn't think Toady had those films you were going to get his copy. Yeah, me and my big mouth. You hung on like a leech and kept giving me the old sex treatment just to know where you stood. And I fell for it. You sure learned how to act these last ten years, all right. I thought it was pretty real.

"What gets me is the way you thought that I had them all this time. You couldn't get that out of your head. You thought I had them and Teen thought I had them. They were worth a million bucks on the open market and I didn't look like a guy who'd throw it away. You even went to the trouble of getting a copy made of my keys while I was asleep, didn't you? Tonight you used them. Tonight you had to take a look to be sure because you knew that when I talked to Fallon's old girl I was going to know the truth!

"Yeah, everybody was looking for those pictures. That's what should have tipped me off. Toady searched Decker's apartment and I thought Toady or his boys searched mine. That was where I kept tripping up. That was the one fault in the whole picture. *When Toady drove that car he never had time to see who I was at all, so how could he know where I lived? You, Marsha, were the only other person at the time who knew I had gone over Decker's body right after he was shot because I told you that myself.*

"That was a nice set-up here that night. Want me to guess who it was? It was that jerk from the theater . . . the kid with the broken arm who's so much in love with you that he'd do anything you ask. He got me with that damn cast.

"Where is he tonight? He'd like to be in on this, wouldn't he?"

All that pent-up hate on her face turned into a cunning sneer and she said, "He's here, Mike."

I started to move the same time she started to talk and I wasn't fast enough. I had a glimpse of something white streaking toward my head just before it smashed the consciousness from my body.

Long before my eyes could see again I knew what would be there when I opened them. I heard the kid crying, a series of terror-stricken gasps because the world was too much for him. I pushed up from the floor, forced my eyes open and saw him huddled there in the corner, his thin body shivering. Whatever I did with my face made him stop, and with the quick switch of emotions a child is capable of, he laughed. He climbed to his feet and held on to the arm of the chair babbling nonsense at the wall.

I raised my head and caught her looking at me, a spiteful smile creasing her face. She was a big beautiful evil goddess with a gun in her hand ready to take a victim and there wasn't a thing I could do about it. My .45 was over there on the table and I didn't have the strength to go for it.

Jerry was in a chair holding his broken arm to his chest, rocking back and forth from the pain in it. One side of the cast was split halfway.

Then I saw the junk on the floor. The suit I had thrown away and the kid's overalls that had been stuffed in the bottom of the can. And Marsha smiled. She opened her palm and there were the films, four thin strips of them. "They were in the pocket of the overalls." She seemed amazed at the simplicity of it.

"They won't do you any good, Marsha. Teen's finished and so are they. Your little racket's over." I had to stop for breath. Something sticky ran down my neck.

"They'll serve their purpose," she said. "Somebody else might guess like you did, but they'll never know now. Those Toady had I destroyed. These will go too and only you will be left, Mike. I really hate having to kill you, but it's necessary, you know."

There was none of the actress in her voice now. There was only death. She had finished acting. The play was over and she could put away the smiles and tears until the next time.

I swung my head around until my eyes were fixed on Jerry. He stopped rocking. I said, "Then I guess you'll have to marry Jerry, won't you? He'll have you trapped like you had Ed and Lou trapped. He'll have something you'll pay dearly for, won't he?"

I think she laughed again. It was a cold laugh. "No, Mike. Poor Jerry will have to go too. You see, he's my alibi." Her hand went out and picked up my gun. "Everyone knows how crazy he is about me. And he's so jealous he's liable to do anything . . . especially if he came up here and caught us together . . . like tonight. There would have been gunplay. Unfortunately, you killed each other. The nurse was in the way and she died too. Doesn't that make a good story, Mike?"

Jerry came out of his chair slowly. He had time to whisper incredulously, "Marsha!" The .45 slammed in her hand and blasted the night to bits. She watched the guy jerking on the floor and threw the gun back on the table. The rod she held on me was a long-barreled revolver and it didn't tremble in her hand at all. She held it at her hip slanting it down enough to catch me in the chest.

She was going to get that shot off fast for the benefit of the people who were listening. She was killing again because murder breeds murder and when she had killed she was going to put the guns in dead hands and go into her act. She'd be all faints and tears and everyone would console her and tell her how brave she was and damn it all to hell, her story would stand up! There wouldn't be a hole in it because everything was working in her favor just like when she killed her secretary! It would be a splash in the papers and she could afford that.

The hate was all there in my face now and she must have known what I was thinking. She gave me a full extra second to

see her smile for the last time, but I didn't waste it on the face
of evil.

I saw the kid grab the edge of the table and reach up for the
thing he had wanted for so long, and in that extra second of time
she gave me his fingers closed round the butt safety and trigger
at the same instant and the tongue of flame that blasted from the
muzzle seemed to lick out across the room with a horrible vengeance that ripped all the evil from her face, turning it into a ghastly
wet red mask that was really no face at all.

My Gun Is Quick

TO ALL MY FRIENDS
PAST, PRESENT, AND FUTURE

chapter one ━━━━━━━━━━━━━━━

WHEN YOU SIT at home comfortably folded up in a chair beside a fire, have you ever thought what goes on outside there? Probably not. You pick up a book and read about things and stuff, getting a vicarious kick from people and events that never happened. You're doing it now, getting ready to fill in a normal life with the details of someone else's experiences. Fun, isn't it? You read about life on the outside, thinking of how maybe you'd like it to happen to you, or at least how you'd like to watch it. Even the old Romans did it, spiced their life with action when they sat in the Colosseum and watched wild animals rip a bunch of humans apart, revelling in the sight of blood and terror. They screamed for joy and slapped each other on the back when murderous claws tore into the live flesh of slaves, and cheered when the kill was made. Oh, it's great to watch, all right. Life through a keyhole. But day after day goes by, and nothing like that ever happens to you, so you think that it's all in books and not in reality at all and that's that. Still good reading, though. Tomorrow night you'll find another book, forgetting what was in the last, and live some more in your imagination. But remember this: there *are* things happening out there. They go on every day and night, making Roman holidays look like school picnics. They go on right under your very nose and you never know about them. Oh, yes, you can find them all right. All you have to do is look for them. But

465

I wouldn't if I were you, because you won't like what you'll find. Then, again, I'm not you, and looking for these things is my job. They aren't nice things to see because they show people up for what they are. There isn't a Colosseum any more, but the city is a bigger bowl and it seats more people. The razor-sharp claws aren't those of wild animals, but man's can be just as sharp and twice as vicious. You have to be quick, and you have to be able, or you become one of the devoured, and if you can kill first, no matter how and no matter who, you can live and return to the comfortable chair and the comfortable fire. But you have to be quick—and able. Or you'll be dead.

At ten minutes after twelve I tied a knot in my case and delivered Herman Gable's lost manuscript to his apartment. To me, it was nothing more than a sheaf of yellow papers covered with barely legible tracings, but to my client it was worth twenty-five hundred bucks. The old fool had wrapped it up with some old newspapers and sent it down the dumbwaiter with the garbage. He sure was happy to get it back. It took three days to run it down and practically snatch the stuff out of the city incinerator; but when I fingered the package of nice, crisp fifties he handed me I figured it was worth going without all that sleep.

I made him out a receipt and took the elevator downstairs to my heap. As far as I was concerned the dough would live a peaceful life until I had a good, long nap. After that, maybe, I'd cut loose a little bit. At that hour of the night traffic was light. I cut across town, then headed north to my own private cave in the massive cliff I called home.

But the first time I hit a red light I fell asleep across the wheel and woke up with a dozen horns blasting in my ears. A couple of cars banged bumpers backing up so they could swing around me, and I was too damned pooped even to swear back at some of the stuff they called me. The hell with 'em. I pulled the jalopy over to the curb and chilled the engine. Right up the street under the el was an all-night hash joint, and what I needed was a couple of mugs of good java to bring me around.

I don't know how the place got by the health inspectors, because it stunk. There were two bums down at one end of the counter taking their time about finishing a ten-cent bowl of soup, making the most out of the free crackers and catsup in front of them. Half-way down, a drunk concentrated between his plate of eggs and hanging on to the stool to keep from falling off the world. Evidently he was down to his last buck, for all his pockets had been turned inside out to locate the lone bill that was putting a roof on his load.

Until I sat down and looked in the mirror behind the shelves of pie segments, I didn't notice the fluff sitting off to one side at a table. She had red hair that didn't come out of a bottle, and looked pretty enough from where I was sitting.

The counterman came up just then and asked, "What'll it be?" He had a voice like a frog's.

"Coffee—black."

The fluff noticed me then. She looked up, smiled, tucked her nail tools in a peeling plastic handbag and hipped it in my direction. When she sat down on the stool next to me she nodded towards the counterman and said, "Shorty's got a heart of steel, mister. Won't even trust me for a cup of joe until I get a job. Care to finance me to a few vitamins?"

I was too tired to argue the point. "Make it two, feller."

He grabbed another cup disgustedly and filled it, then set the two down on the counter, slopping half of it across the washworn linoleum top.

"Listen, Red," he croaked, "quit using this joint fer an office. First thing I get the cops on my tail. That's all I need."

"Be good and toddle off, Shorty. All I want from the gentleman is a cup of coffee. He looks much too tired to play any games tonight."

"Yeah, scram, Shorty," I put in. He gave me a nasty look, but since I was as ugly as he was and twice as big, he shuffled off to keep count over the cracker bowl in front of the bums. Then I looked at the redhead.

She wasn't very pretty after all. She had been once, but there are those things that happen under the skin and are reflected in the eyes and set of the mouth that take all the beauty out of a woman's face. Yeah, at one time she must have been almost beautiful. That wasn't too long ago, either. Her clothes were last year's old look and a little too tight. They showed a lot of leg and a lot of chest; nice white flesh still firm and young; but her face was old with knowledge that never came out of books. I watched her from the corner of my eye when she lifted her cup of coffee. She had delicate hands, long fingers tipped with deep-toned nails perfectly kept. It was the way she held the cup that annoyed me. Instead of being a thick, cracked mug, she gave it a touch of elegance as she balanced it in front of her lips. I thought she was wearing a wedding band until she put the cup down. Then I saw that it was just a ring with a fleur-de-lis design of blue enamel and diamond chips that had turned sideways slightly.

Red turned suddenly and said, "Like me?"

I grinned. "Uh-huh. But, like you said, much too tired to make it matter."

Her laugh was a tinkle of sound. "Rest easy, mister, I won't give you a sales talk. There are only certain types interested in what I have to sell."

"Amateur psychologist?"

"I have to be."

"And I don't look the type?"

Red's eyes danced. "Big mugs like you never have to pay, mister. With you it's the woman who pays."

I pulled out a deck of Luckies and offered her one. When we lit up I said, "I wish all the babies I met thought that way."

She blew a stream of smoke towards the ceiling and looked at me as if she were going back a long way. "They do, mister. Maybe you don't know it, but they do."

I don't know why I liked the kid. Maybe it was because she had eyes that were hard, but could still cry a little. Maybe it was because she handed me some words that were nice to listen to. Maybe it was because I was tired and my cave was a cold empty place, while here I had a redhead to talk to. Whatever it was, I liked her and she knew it and smiled at me in a way I knew she hadn't smiled in a long time. Like I was her friend.

"What's your name, mister?"

"Mike. Mike Hammer. Native-born son of ye old city, presently at loose ends and dead tired. Free, white and over twenty-one. That do it?"

"Well, what do you know! Here I've been thinking all males were named Smith or Jones. What happened?"

"No wife to report to, kid," I grinned. "The tag's my own. What do they call you besides Red?"

"They don't."

I saw her eyes crinkle a little as she sipped the last of her coffee. Shorty was casting nervous glances between us and the steamed-up window, probably hoping a cop wouldn't pass by and nail a hustler trying to make time. He gave me a pain.

"Want more coffee?"

She shook her head. "No, that did it fine. If Shorty wasn't so touchy about extending a little credit I wouldn't have to be smiling for my midnight snacks."

From the way I turned and looked at her, Red knew there was

more than casual curiosity back of the remark when I asked, "I didn't think your line of business could ever be that slow."

For a brief second she glared into the mirror. "It isn't." She was plenty mad about something.

I threw a buck on the counter and Shorty rang it up, then passed the change back. When I pocketed it I said to Red, "Did you ever stop to think that you're a pretty nice girl? I've met all kinds, but I think you could get along pretty well . . . any way you tried."

Her smile even brought out a dimple that had been buried a long while ago. She kissed her finger, then touched the finger to my cheek. "I like you, Mike. There are times when I think I've lost the power to like anyone, but I like you."

An el went by overhead just then and muffled the sound of the door opening. I felt the guy standing behind us before I saw him in the mirror. He was tall, dark and greasy looking, with a built-in sneer that passed for know-how, and he smelled of cheap hair oil. His suit would have been snappy in Harlem, edged with sharp pleats and creases.

He wasn't speaking to me when he said, "Hullo, kid!"

The redhead half turned and her lips went tight. "What do you want?" Her tone was dull, flat. The skin across her cheeks was drawn taut.

"Are you kidding?"

"I'm busy. Get lost."

The guy's hand shot out and grabbed her arm, swinging her around on the stool to face him. "I don't like them snotty remarks, Red."

As soon as I slid off the stool Shorty hustled down to our end, his hand reaching for something under the counter. When he saw my face he put it back and stopped short. The guy saw the same thing, but he was wise about it. His lip curled up and he snarled, "Get the hell out of here before I bust ya one."

He was going to make a pass at me, but I jammed four big, stiff fingers into his gut right above the navel and he snapped shut like a jack-knife. I opened him up again with an openhanded slap that left a blush across his mouth that was going to stay for a while.

Usually a guy will let it go right there. This one didn't. He could hardly breathe, but he was cursing me with his lips and his hand reached for his armpit in uncontrollable jerks. Red stood with her hand pressed against her mouth, while Shorty was croaking for us to cut it out, but too scared to move.

I let him almost reach it, then I slid my own .45 out where everybody could get a look at it. Just for effect I stuck it up against his forehead and thumbed back the hammer. It made a sharp click in the silence. "Just touch that rod you got and I'll blow your damn greasy head off. Go ahead, just make one lousy move towards it," I said.

He moved, all right. He fainted. Red was looking down at him, still too terrified to say anything. Shorty had a twitch in his shoulder. Finally she said, "You . . . didn't have to do that for me. Please, get out of here before he wakes up. He'll . . . kill you!"

I touched her arm gently. "Tell me something, Red. Do you really think he could?"

She bit her lip and her eyes searched my face. Something made her shudder violently. "No. No, I don't think so. But please go. For me." There was urgent appeal in her voice.

I grinned at her again. She was scared, in trouble, but still my friend. I took out my wallet. "Do something for me, will you, Red?" I shoved three fifties in her hand. "Get off this street. Tomorrow you go uptown and buy some decent clothes. Then get a morning paper and hunt up a job. This kind of stuff is murder."

I don't ever want anybody to look at me the way she did then. A look that belongs in church when you're praying or getting married or something.

The greaseball on the floor was awake now, but he wasn't looking at me. He was looking at my wallet that I held open in my hand. His eyes were glued to the badge that was pinned there, and if I still didn't have my rod dangling by the trigger guard he would have gone for his. I reached down and pulled it out of the shoulder holster, then grabbed his collar and dragged him out the door.

Down on the corner was a police call-box and I used it. In two minutes a squad car pulled up to the curb and a pair of harness bulls jumped out. I nodded to the driver. "Hullo, Jake."

He said, "Hi ya, Mike. What gives?"

I hoisted the greaseball to his feet. "Laughing boy tried to pull a gun on me." I handed over the rod, a short-barrelled .32. "I don't think he has a license for it, so you can lock him up on a Sullivan charge. I'll press charges in the morning. You know where to reach me."

The cop took the gun and prodded the guy into the car. He was still cursing when I walked up to my heap.

* * *

It was early morning when I woke up to stay. Those forty-eight hours were what I needed. I took a hot and cold shower to shake the sleep out of my eyes, then stood in front of the mirror and shaved. I certainly was a mess. My eyes were still red and bleary and I felt like I was ploughing my whiskers under instead of shaving them off. At least I felt better. A big plate of bacon and eggs made my stomach behave to the point where I could get dressed and start the rest of the day off with a decent meal.

Jimmy had a steak in the broiler as soon as I entered the door of his snack bar. Luckily, I liked it rare and it was on deck before it was fully warmed through. While I was shoveling it down Jimmy said, "That dame in your office has been on the phone all day. Maybe you better call her back."

"What'd she want?"

"Wondered where you were. Guess she thinks you were out with a broad somewhere."

"Nuts! She's always thinking something." I finished my dessert and threw a bill down. "If she calls up again, tell her I'm on my way up to the office, will you?"

"Sure, Mr. Hammer, glad to."

I patted my meal in place, lit up a smoke and hopped into my car. The trip downtown didn't take long, but I was a half-hour finding a parking place. When I finally barged into the office, Velda looked up with those big brown eyes starting to give me hell before she even opened her mouth. When I got a girl to hold down the office I figured I might as well get a good-looking one as a bean head, and I sure skimmed the cream off the top. Only, I didn't figure she'd turn out to be so smart. Good-looking ones seldom are. She's big and she's beautiful, and she's got a brain that can figure angles while mine only figures the curves.

"About time you got in." She looked me over carefully for lipstick stains or whatever those tip-offs are that spell trouble for a guy. I could tell by the way she let a slow grin play around with her mouth that she decided that my time was on the job and not on the town.

When I shucked out of my coat I tossed most of the package of fifties on her desk. "Meal money, kiddo. Take expenses out of that and bank the rest. Any callers?"

She tucked the cabbage in a file and locked it. "A couple. One wanted a divorce set-up and the other wanted himself a bodyguard. Seems like his girl-friend's husband is promising to chill him on sight. I sent both of them over to Ellison's where they'd get proper treatment."

"I wish you'd quit making up my mind for me. That bodyguard job might have been all right."

"Uh-uh. I saw a picture of the girl friend. She's the bosomy kind you go for."

"Ah, bugs! You know how I hate women."

I squeezed into the reception chair and picked up the paper from the table. I ruffled through it from back to front, and as I was going to lay it down I caught the picture on the front page. It was down there on the corner, bordered by some shots of the heavyweight fights from the night before. It was a picture of the redhead lying cuddled up and against the curbstone. She was dead. The caption read HIT-AND-RUN DRIVER KILLS, ESCAPES.

"The poor kid! Of all the rotten luck!"

"Who's that?" Velda asked me.

I shoved the paper over to her. "I was with that kid the other night. She was a street-walker and I bought her a coffee in a hash joint. Before I left I gave her some dough to get out of the business, and look what happened to her."

"Fine company you keep." Her tone was sarcastic.

I got sore. "Damn it, she was all right. She wasn't after me. I did her a favor and she was more grateful than most of the trash that call themselves people. The first time in a month of Sundays I've done anything half-way decent and this is the way it winds up."

"I'm sorry, Mike. I'm really sorry, honest." It was funny how she could spot it when I was telling the truth. She opened the paper and read the news item, frowning when she finished. "She wasn't identified. Did you know her name?"

"Hell, no. She was a redhead, so I called her Red. Let's see that." I went over the item myself. She was found in the street at half-past two. Apparently she had been there for some time before someone had sense enough to call the cop on the beat. A guy who had passed her twice as she lay there told the cop that he thought she was a drunk who had passed out. It was reasonable enough. Over there you find enough of them doing just that. But the curious part was the complete lack of identification on her.

When I folded the paper up I said, "Look, stick around a while; I have a little walking to do."

"That girl?"

"Yeah. Maybe I can help identify her some way. I don't know. Call Pat and tell him I'm on my way down."

"O.K., Mike."

I left the car where it was and took a cab over to the red-brick building where Pat Chambers held down his office. You want to see that guy. He's a Captain of Homicide and all cop, but you couldn't tell it to look at him. He was young and charged with knowledge and the ambition to go with it, the best example of efficiency I could think of. It isn't often that you see cops hob-nobbing with private dicks, but Pat had the sense to know that I could touch a lot of places outside the reach of the law, and he could do plenty for me that I couldn't do for myself. What started out as a modest business arrangement turned into a solid friendship.

He met me over in the lab where he was running a ballistics test. "Hullo, Mike, what brings you around so early?"

"A problem, chum." I flipped the paper open in front of him and pointed to the picture. "This. Have you found out about her?"

Pat shook his head. "No . . . but I will. Come on in the office." He led me into the cubbyhole off the lab and nodded to a chair. While I fired a cig he called an extension number and was connected. He said, "This is Chambers. I want to find out if that girl who was killed by a hit-and-run driver last night has been identified." He listened a little bit, then frowned.

I waited until he hung up, then: "Anything?"

"Something unusual—dead of a broken neck. One of the boys didn't like the looks of it and they're holding the cause of death until a further exam is made. What have you?"

"Nothing. But I was with her the night before she was found dead."

"So?"

"So she was a tramp. I bought her a coffee in a hash house and we had a talk."

"Did she mention her name?"

"Nope, all I got out of her was 'Red.' It was appropriate enough."

Pat leaned back in his chair. "Well, we don't know who she is. She had on all new clothes, a new handbag with six dollars and change in it, and not a scar on her body to identify her. Not a single laundry mark either."

"I know. I gave her a hundred and fifty bucks to get dressed up and look for a decent job. Evidently she did."

"Getting big-hearted, aren't you?" He sounded like Velda, and I got mad.

"Damn it, Pat, don't you give me that stuff, too! Can't I play saint for five minutes without everyone getting smart about it? I've seen kids down on their luck before, probably a damn sight more than you have. You think anyone would give them a break? Like hell! They play 'em for all they can get and beat it. I liked the kid; does that make me a jerk? All right, she was a hustler, but she wasn't hustling for me and I did her a favor. Maybe she gets all wrapped up in a new dream and forgets to open her eyes when she's crossing the street, and look what happens. Any time I touch anything it gets killed!"

"Hey, wait up, Mike, don't jump me on it. I know how you feel . . . it's just that you seemed to be stepping out of character."

"Aw, I'm sorry, Pat. It's kind of got me loused up."

"At least you've given me something to go on. If she bought all new clothes we can trace them. If we're lucky we can pick up the old stuff and check them for laundry marks."

He told me to wait for him and took off down the corridor. I sat there for five minutes and fidgeted, and cursed people who let their kids run loose. A hell of a way to die. They just lower you into a hole and cover you up, with nobody around but the worms, and the worms don't cry. But Pat would find out who she was. He'd put a little effort behind the search and a pair of parents would turn up and wring themselves dry with grief. Not that it would do much good, but at least I'd feel better.

Pat came back looking sour. I guess I knew what was coming when he said, "They covered that angle downstairs. The sales clerks in the stores all said the same thing . . . she took her old clothes with her and wore the new ones."

"Then she must have left them at home."

"Uh-huh. She wasn't carrying them with her when she was found."

"Nope, I don't like that, either, Pat. When a girl buys a new outfit, she won't look at the old one, and what she had on when I met her was a year out of date. She probably chucked them somewhere."

Pat reached into his desk and came up with a notepad. "I think the best we can do is publish her picture and hope someone steps up with an identification. At the same time we'll get the bureau checking up in the neighborhood where you met her. Does that suit you?"

"Yeah. Can't do more than that, I guess."

He flipped the pages over but, before I could tell him where the hash house was, a lab technician in a white smock came in and handed over a report sheet. Pat glanced at it, then his eyes squinted and he looked at me strangely.

I didn't get it, so I stared back. Without a word he handed me the sheet and nodded to dismiss the technician. It was a report on Red. The information was the same that Pat had given me, but down at the bottom was somebody's scrawled notation. It said very clearly that although there was a good chance that death could have been accidental, the chance was just as good that she had been murdered. Her neck had been broken in a manner that could have been caused only by the most freakish accident.

For the first time since I'd known him, Pat took a typical cop's attitude. "A nice story you gave me, Mike. How much of it am I supposed to believe?" His voice was dripping with sarcasm.

"Go to hell, Pat!" I said it coldly, burning up inside.

I knew damn well what was going on in that official mind. Just because we had tangled tails on a couple of cases before, he thought I was pitching him a fast one. I got it off my chest in a hurry. "You used to be a nice guy, Pat," I said. "There was a time when we did each other favors and no questions asked. Did I ever dummy up a deal on you?"

He started to answer, but I cut him off. "Yeah, sure, we've crossed once or twice, but you always have the bull on me before we start. That's because you're a cop. I can't withhold information . . . all I can do is protect a client. Since when do you figure me to be putting the snear on you?"

This time Pat grinned. "O.K., that makes me sorry twice today. Do me another favor and admit I had a half-way decent reason to be suspicious. You're usually in something up to your neck, and you aren't above getting a little free info even from me, and I can't blame you. It's just that I have to look out for my own neck once in a while. You know the pressure that's being put on our department. If we get caught short we have a lot of people to answer to."

He kept talking, but I wasn't listening to him. My eyes kept drifting back to that report sheet until that one word, MURDERED, kept jumping at me like it was alive. I was seeing Red standing there with the dimples in her cheeks, kissing her finger and smiling a smile that was for me alone. Just a two-bit tramp who could have been a lady, and who was, for a few short minutes, a damn decent friend.

And I had jinxed her.

My guts were a tight little ball under my belt, because Red wasn't the only one I remembered. There was the greaseball with the rod and the dirty sneer. There was the way Red had looked at him with terror in her eyes, and I felt my fingernails bite into my palms, and I started cursing under my breath. It always starts that way, the crazy mad feeling that makes me want to choke the life out of some son of a bitch, and there's nothing to grab but air. I knew damn well what it was then.

They could cross all the probable words off in front of murder and let it stand alone.

Pat said, "Give, Mike."

"There's nothing to give," I told him. "I'm teed off. Things like this give me the pip. I might as well have killed her myself."

"What makes you think it's murder?" He was watching me closely again.

I flipped the sheet to his desk. "I don't know, but she's dead and what difference does it make how she died. When you're dead you're dead and it doesn't matter much to you any more how you got that way."

"Let's not have any tangents, Mike. What do you know that I don't?"

"What she looked like when she was alive. She was a nice kid."

"Go on."

"Nuts! There isn't any place to go. If she was killed accidentally, I feel like hell. If she was murdered . . ."

"Yeah, Mike, I've heard it before . . . if she was killed you're going to go out all by yourself and catch the bastard and rub his nose in the dirt. Maybe so hard that you break his neck, too."

"Yeah," I said. Then I said it again.

"Mike."

"What?"

"Look, if it's a kill it belongs to my department. It probably isn't, but you get me so damn excited I'm getting positive that it is, and I'm getting mad, too, because you have thoughts in that scrambled brain of yours that will make the track nice and muddy if it's another race. Let's not have any more of that, Mike. Once was enough. I didn't mind so much then, but no more of it. We've always played it square, though only God knows why I set myself up to be knocked down. Maybe I'm the jerk. Are you levelling with me on what you know?"

"I'm levelling, Pat." I wasn't lying. What I had told him was the truth. I just hadn't told him the rest. It's awfully nice to get so goddamn mad at something you want to bust wide open, and it's a lot better to take that goddamn something you're mad at and smash it against the wall and do all the things to it you wanted to do, wishing it could have been done before it was too late.

Pat was playing cop with his notebook again. "Where did you meet her?" he asked me.

"A joint under the el on Third Avenue. I came off the bridge and ran down Third and stopped at this joint along the way. I don't remember the street because I was too tired to look, but I'll go back and check up again and find it. There's probably a thousand places like it, but I'll find it."

"This isn't a stall, is it?"

"Yeah, it's a stall. Lock me up for interfering with the process of the law. I should have remembered every detail that happened that night."

"Can it, Mike."

"I told you I'd find it again, didn't I?"

"Good enough. Meanwhile, we'll pull an autopsy on her and try to locate the old clothes. Remember, when you find the place, let me know. I'll probably find it without you anyway, but you can make it quicker . . . if you want to."

"Sure," I said. I was grinning, but nothing was funny. It was a way I could hold my mouth and be polite without letting him know that I felt as if ants were crawling all over me. We shook hands and said civilized "so longs" when I wanted to curse and swing at something instead.

I don't like to get mad like that. But I couldn't help it. Murder is an ugly word.

When I got downstairs I asked the desk sergeant where I could get in touch with Jake Larue. He gave me his home number and I went into a pay station just off the main corridor and dialed the number. Jake's wife answered, and she had to wake him up to put him on, and his voice wasn't too friendly when he said hullo.

I said, "This is Mike Hammer, Jake. What happened to that punk I gave you the other night?"

Jake said something indecent. Then, "That was some deal you handed us, Mike."

"Why?"

"He had a license for that gun, that's why. You trying to get me in a jam or something?"

"What are they doing, giving licenses away in New York State, now?"

"Nuts! His name is Feeney Last and he's a combination chauffeur and bodyguard for that Berin-Grotin guy out on the Island."

I whistled through my teeth and hung up. Now they were giving out licenses to guys who wanted to kill people. Oh, great! Just fine!

chapter two ▰▰▰▰▰▰▰▰▰▰▰▰▰▰▰

IT WAS A little after four when I got back to the office. Velda was licking envelopes in an unladylike manner and glad of an excuse to stop. She said, "Pat called me a little while ago."

"And told you to tell me to behave myself like a good boy, I suppose."

"Or words to that effect. Who was she, Mike?"

"I didn't find out. I will though."

"Mike, being as how you're the boss, I hate to say this, but there are a few prosperous clients knocking on the door and you're fooling around where there isn't any cash in sight."

I threw my hat on the desk. "Wherever there's murder there's money, chick."

"Murder?"

"I have that idea in mind."

It was nice sitting there in the easy chair, stretched out in comfort. Velda let me yawn, then: "But what are you after, Mike?"

"A name," I said. "Just a name for a kid who died without one. Morbid curiosity, isn't it? But I can't send flowers with just 'Red' on them. What do you know about a guy called Berin-Grotin, Velda?" I watched a fly run across the ceiling upside down, making it sound casual.

After a moment she told me: "That must be Arthur Berin-Grotin. He's an old society gent about eighty, supposedly one of the original Four Hundred. At one time he was the biggest sport on the Stem, but he got tangled with old age and became almighty pious trying to make up for all his youthful escapades."

I remembered him then, mostly from stories the old-timers like to pass out when they corner you in a bar for a hatful of free drinks. "Why would a guy like that need a bodyguard?" I asked her.

Velda dug back into her memory. "If I remember correctly, his estate out on the Island was robbed several times. An old man would be inclined to be squeamish, and I can't say that I blame him. I'd hire a bodyguard, too. The funny part is that the burglar could have had what he wanted for the asking by simply knocking on the door. Arthur Berin-Grotin is a sucker for hard-up stories . . . besides being one of the city's biggest philanthropists."

"Lots of money, hey?"

"Umm."

"Where did you get the dope on him?"

"If you'd read anything but the funnies, you'd know. He's in the news as often as a movie star. Apparently he has a fierce sense of pride, and if he isn't suing somebody for libel, he's disinheriting some distant relative for besmirching the fair name of Berin-Grotin. A month ago he financed a million-dollar cat and dog hospital or something. Oh, wait a minute . . ."

She got up and began ruffling through a heap of newspapers on top of the file. After a brief search she pulled out a rotogravure section, a few weeks old, and folded it back. "Here's something about him."

It was a picture taken in a cemetery. Amid a background of tombstones and monuments was the half-built form of a mausoleum. There were two workers on the scaffolding laying marble slabs in place, and from the looks of it money was being poured into the job. Next to it was the artist's conception of the finished job, a classic Greek-temple arrangement. Arthur Berin-Grotin was playing it safe. He was making sure he'd have a roof over his head after he died.

Velda put the paper back on the pile. "Is he a client, Mike?"

"Nope. I happened to run across his name and was interested."

"You're lying."

"And you're getting fresh with the boss," I grinned at her. She stuck out her tongue and went back to her desk. I got up and told her to knock off early, then jammed on my hat. There were a few things that I had in mind, but I needed a little time to pass before I could get started.

Downstairs I found a bar and called for a beer. I was on my third when the paperboy came in with the evening edition. I flipped him a dime and spread it on the bar. Pat had done a good job. Her picture was on the front page. Under it was the question "Do you know this girl?" Sure, I knew her. Red. I couldn't forget her. I was wondering if anybody else was having trouble forgetting her, too.

I tucked the paper in my pocket and walked down to my car.

The taxis and commuters were jamming traffic all the way downtown, and by the time I had crossed over to Third Avenue it was nearly six o'clock. I didn't have a bit of trouble finding that hash house again. There was even a place to park right outside it. I went in and climbed on a stool and laid the paper down in front of me with the picture up. Down at the end Shorty was pushing crackers and soup over to another bum. He hadn't seen me yet.

When he did he went a little white around the nostrils and he couldn't seem to take his eyes off my face. He said, "Whatta ya want?"

"Eggs. Bacon and eggs . . . over light. And coffee."

He sort of sidled down the counter and fished in a basket for the eggs. One dropped and splattered all over the floor. Shorty didn't even seem to notice it. The bum was making a slobbering noise with his soup and the bacon on the griddle started to drown him out. Behind the grill was a stainless steel reflector, and twice I caught Shorty looking in it at me. The spatula was big enough to handle a cake, yet he couldn't balance an egg on it. He made each on the third try.

Shorty was suffering badly from the shakes. It didn't help any when he had to push the paper away to set the plate down and saw Red's picture staring at him.

I said, "One thing about eggs: you can't spoil them with bum cooking. No matter what you do they still taste like eggs." Shorty just stared at me. "Yeah, eggs are eggs. Once in a while you get a bad one, though. Makes me mad as hell to get hold of one. Did you ever smash a bad egg wide open? They make a noisy pop and stink like hell. Bad eggs can be poison, too."

I was half-way done before Shorty said, "What are you after, mister?"

"You tell me."

Both of us looked down at the paper at the same time.

"You're a copper, ain't'cha?"

"I carry a badge . . . and a rod."

"A private snooper, eh?" He was going tough on me.

I laid my fork down and looked at him. I can make pretty nasty faces when I have to. "Shorty, maybe just for the hell of it I'll take you apart. You may be a rough apple, but I can make your face look like it's been run through a grinder, and the more I think of the idea the more I like it. The name is Mike Hammer, chum . . . you ought to know it down here. I like to play games with wise guys."

He was white around the nostrils again.

I tapped the picture, then let my finger stay on the question underneath. Shorty knew damn well I wasn't fooling around any more. I was getting mad and he knew it, and he was scared. But just the same he shrugged. "Hell, I don't know who she is."

"It wasn't the first time she had been in here. Quit holding out."

"Ah, she came in for about a week. Sometimes she tried to make pick-ups in here and I threw her out. She was Red to me and everybody else. That's all I knew about her."

"You got a record, haven't you, Shorty?"

His lips drew back over his teeth. "You bastard!"

I reached out and grabbed his shirt and held him against the counter. "When a guy gets out of stir he goes straight sometimes. Sometimes he don't. I'm betting that if the cops decided to look around a little bit they could find you had a finger in some crooked pie, and it wouldn't take them a week to put you back up the river."

"H-honest, Mac, I don't know nothing about the dame. Look, I'd tell you if I did. I ain't no trouble-maker and I don't want no trouble around here! Why don't'cha lemme alone?"

"There was a greaseball in here that night. His name is Feeney Last. How often has he been in?"

Shorty licked his thick lips nervously. "Hell, maybe twice. I dunno. He went for the redhead, that's all. He never even ate in here. Lay off, will ya."

I dropped the handful of shirt. "Sure, pal, I'll lay off." I threw a half buck on the counter and he was glad to grab it and get over to the register away from me. I swung off the stool and stood up. "If I find out you know any more than you told me, there's going to be a visitor in here looking for you. A guy in a pretty blue uniform. Only when he finds you he's going to have a tough time making any sense out of what you tell him. It's not easy to talk when you've just choked on your own teeth."

Just before I reached the door he called, "Hey, Mac."

I turned around.

"I-I think she had a room some place around the corner. Next block north."

He didn't wait for an answer. He got real busy swabbing the broken egg off the floor.

Outside I started the car, changed my mind, then walked up Third to the street corner. It would have taken a week to comb the dingy apartments that sprawled along the sidewalks and I wasn't in the mood for any leg work.

On one corner was a run-down candy store whose interior was obscured by flyspecked signs, but for all its dirt it served as a neighborhood hangout. In front of the paper stand were three young punks in sharp two-tone sports outfits making dirty cracks at the girls passing by. A husky blonde turned and slapped one across the jaw and got a boot in the tail for her trouble. This time she kept going.

I angled across the street and walked up to the kid holding his jaw, trying to rub out the red blotch. I opened the button on my jacket and reached back for a handkerchief, just enough so the sling on the shoulder holster was visible across my shirt for a second. They knew I was carrying a rod and looked at me as if I were a tin god. The kid even forgot to rub his face any more. Nice place to live.

"There's a cute little redhead who has a room around here, Buster. Know where I can find her?"

The kid got real important with the man-to-man line I was handing him and gave me a wink. "Yeah, she had a place upstairs in old-lady Porter's joint." He jerked his head down the street. "Won't do ya no good to go there. That little bitch got herself killed last night. All the papers got her pitcher on the front page."

"You don't say! Too bad."

He edged me with his elbow and slipped me a knowing look. "She wasn't no good anyway, buddy. Now, if you want a real woman, you go up to Twenty-third Street and . . ."

"Some other day, feller. While I'm here I'll look around this end of town." I slipped him a fin. "Go buy a beer for the boys."

I walked away hoping they'd choke on it.

Martha Porter was an oversize female in her late fifties. She wore a size dress that matched her age and still she peeked out in places. What hair wasn't yanked back in a knot straggled across her face and down the nape of her neck, and she was holding the broom ready to use it as a utensil or a club.

"You looking for a room or a girl?" she said.

I let a ten-spot talk for me. "I saw the girl. Now I want to see the room."

She grabbed the bill first. "What for?"

"Because she copped a wad of dough and some important papers from the last place she worked and I have to find it."

She gave me an indifferent sneer. "Oh, one of them skiptracers. Well, maybe the papers is there, but you won't find no dough. She came here with the clothes on her back and two bucks in her pocketbook. I took the two bucks for room rent. Never got no more from her neither."

"Where'd she come from?"

"I don't know and I didn't ask. She had the two bucks and that's what the room cost—in advance, when you don't have no bags."

"Know her name?"

"Why don't you grow up, mister! Why the hell should I ask when it don't mean nothing. Maybe it was Smith. If you want to see the room it's next floor up in the back. I ain't even been in there since she got killed. Soon as I seen her face in the papers I knew somebody would be around. Them broads give me a pain in the behind."

The broom went back to being a broom and I went up the stairs. There was only one door on the landing and I went in, then locked it behind me.

I always had the idea that girls were kind of fussy, even if they were living in a cracker barrel. Maybe she was funny at that. It was a sure thing that whoever searched the room wasn't. The bed was torn apart and the stuffing was all over the place. The four drawers of the chest lay upside down on the floor where someone had used them as a ladder to look along the wall molding just below the ceiling. Even the linoleum had been ripped from the floor, and two spots on the wall where the plaster had been knocked off were poked out to let a hand feel around between the partitions. Oh, it was a beautiful job of searching, all right. A real dilly. They had plenty of time, too. They must have had, because they would have had to be quiet or have the young elephant up here with the broom, and the place wouldn't have looked like that if they had been hurried.

One hell of a mess, but I started to grin. Whatever caused the wreckage certainly wasn't found, because even after they had looked in the obvious places they tore apart everything else, right down to the mouse-hole in the baseboard.

I kicked aside some of the junk on the floor, but there wasn't much to see. Old magazines, a couple of newspapers, some underwear and gadgets that might have been in the drawers. What had once been a coat lay in strips with all the hems ripped out and the lining hanging in shreds. A knife had been used on the collar to split the seams. On top of everything was a film of dust from a spilled powder box, giving the place a cheaply perfumed odor.

Then the wind blew some of the mattress stuffing in my face

and I walked over to close the window. It faced on a fire-escape and the sash had been forced with some kind of tool. It couldn't have been simpler. On the floor by the sill was a white plastic comb. I picked it up and felt the grease on it. A few dark hairs were tangled around the teeth. I smelled it.

Hair oil. The kind of hair oil a greaseball would use. I wasn't sure, but there were ways of finding out. The hag was still in the corridor sweeping when I went out. I told her somebody had crashed the place before I got there and liked to knock it apart. She gave one unearthly shriek and took the steps two at a time until the building shook.

It was enough for one day. I went home and hit the sack. I didn't sleep too well, because the redhead would smile, kiss her finger and put it on my cheek and wake me up.

At half-past six the alarm went off with a racket that jerked me out of a wild dream and left me standing on the rug shaking like a kitten in a dog kennel. I shut it off and ducked into a cold shower to wash the sleep out of my eyes, then finished off the morning's ceremonies with a close shave that left my face raw. I ate in my shorts, then stacked the dishes in the sink and laid out my clothes.

This had to be a new-suit day. I laid the tweeds on the bed and, for a change, paid a little attention to the things that went with it. By the time I had climbed into everything and ran a brush over my shoes I even began to look dignified. Or at least sharp enough to call on one of the original Four Hundred.

I found Arthur Berin-Grotin's name in the Long Island directory, a town about sixty miles out on the Island that was a chosen spot for lovers, trapshooters and recluses. Buck had my car gassed up and ready for me when I got to the garage, and by the time nine-thirty had rolled around I was tooling the heap along the highway, sniffing the breezes that blew in from the ocean. An hour later I reached a cut-off that sported a sign emblazoned with Old English lettering and an arrow that pointed to Arthur Berin-Grotin's estate on the beach.

Under the wheels the road turned to macadam, then packed crushed gravel, and developed into a long sweep of a drive that took me up to one of the fanciest joints this side of Buckingham Palace. The house was a symbol of luxury, but utterly devoid of any of the garishness that goes with new wealth. From its appearance it was ageless, neither young nor old. It could have stood there a hundred years or ten without a change to its dignity.

Choice fieldstone reached up to the second floor, supporting smooth clapboard walls that gleamed in the sun like bleached bones. The windows must have been imported; those on the south side were all stained glass to filter out the fierce light of the sun, while the others were little lead-rimmed squares arranged in patterns that changed from room to room.

I drove up under the arched dome of a portico and killed the engine, wondering whether to wait for a major-domo to open the door for me or do it myself. I decided not to wait.

The bell was the kind you pull—a little brass knob set in the door-frame—and when I gave it a gentle tug I heard the subtle pealing of electric chimes inside. When the door opened I thought it had been done by an electric eye, but it wasn't. The butler was so little and so old that he scarcely reached above the door-knob and didn't seem strong enough to hold it open very long, so I stepped in before the wind blew it shut, and turned on my best smile.

"I'd like to see Mr. Berin-Grotin, please."

"Yes, sir. Your name, please?" His voice crackled like an old hen's.

"Michael Hammer, from New York."

The old man took my hat and led me to a massive library panelled in dark oak and waved his hand towards a chair. "Would you care to wait here, sir. I'll inform the master that you have arrived. There are cigars on the table."

I thanked him and picked out a huge leather-covered chair and sank into it, looking around to see how Society lived. It wasn't bad. I picked up a cigar and bit the end off, then looked for a place to spit it. The only ashtray was a delicate bowl of rich Wedgwood pottery, and I'd be damned if I'd spoil it. Maybe Society wasn't so good after all. There were footsteps coming down the hall outside so I swallowed the damn thing to get rid of it.

When Arthur Berin-Grotin came into the room I stood up. Whether I wanted to or not, there are some people to whom you cannot help but show respect. He was one of them. He was an old man, all right, but the years had treated him lightly. There was no stoop to his shoulders and his eyes were as bright as an urchin's. I guessed his height to be about six feet, but he might have been shorter. The shock of white hair that crowned his head flowed up to add inches to his stature.

"Mr. Berin-Grotin?" I asked.

"Yes, good morning, sir." He held out his hand and we clasped firmly. "I'd rather you use only the first half of my name," he added. "Hyphenated family names have always annoyed me, and since I am burdened with one myself I find it expedient to shorten it. You are Mr. Hammer?"

"That's right."

"And from New York. It sounds as though one of you is important," he laughed. Unlike his butler, his voice had a good solid ring. He pulled a chair up to mine and nodded for me to be seated.

"Now," he said, "what can I do for you?"

I gave it to him straight. "I'm a detective, Mr. Berin. I'm not on a case exactly, but I'm looking for something. An identity. The other day a girl was killed in the city. She was a redheaded prostitute, and she doesn't have a name."

"Ah, yes! I saw it in the papers. You have an interest in her?"

"Slightly. I gave her a handout, and the next day she was killed. I'm trying to find out who she was. It's kind of nasty to die and not have anyone know you're dead."

The old man closed his eyes slightly and looked pained. "I understand completely, Mr. Hammer." He folded his hands across his lap. "The same thought has occurred to me, and I dread it. I have outlived my wife and children and I am afraid that when I pass away the only tears to fall on my coffin will be those of strangers."

"I doubt that, sir."

He smiled. "Thank you. Nevertheless, in my vanity I am erecting a monument that will bring my name to the public eye on occasions."

"I saw the picture of the vault in the papers."

"Perhaps I seem morbid to you?"

"Not at all."

"One prepares a house for every other phase of living . . . why not for death. My silly hyphenated name will go to the grave with me, but at least it will remain in sight for many generations to come. A bit of foolishness on my part, yes; I care to think of it as pride. Pride is a name that has led a brilliant existence for countless years. Pride of family. Pride of accomplishment. However, the preparations concerning my death weren't the purpose of your visit. You were speaking of this . . . girl."

"The redhead. Nobody seems to know her. Just before she was killed your chauffeur tried to pick her up in a joint downtown."

"My chauffeur?" He seemed amazed.

"That's right. Feeney Last, his name is."

"And how did you know that?"

"He was messing with the redhead and I called him on it. He tried to pull a rod on me and I flattened him. Later I turned him over to the cops in a squad car to haul him in on a Sullivan charge and they found out he had a license for the gun."

His bushy white eyebrows drew together in a puzzled frown. "He . . . would have killed you, do you think?"

"I don't know. I wasn't taking any chances."

"He was in town that night, I know. I never thought he'd act like that! Had he been drinking?"

"Didn't seem that way to me."

"At any rate, it's inexcusable. I regret the incident extremely, Mr. Hammer. Perhaps it would be better if I discharged him."

"That's up to you. If you need a tough boy around maybe he's all right. I understand you need protection."

"That I do. My home has been burgled several times, and although I don't keep much money on hand, I do have a rather valuable collection of odds and ends that I wouldn't want stolen."

"Where was he the night the girl was killed?"

The old gent knew what I was thinking and shook his head slowly. "I'm afraid you can dismiss the thought, Mr. Hammer. Feeney was with me all afternoon and all evening. We went to New York that day and I kept several appointments in the afternoon. That night we went to the Albino Club for dinner and from there to a show, then back to the Albino Club for a snack before returning home. Feeney was with me every minute."

"Your chauffeur?"

"No, as a companion. Here in the country Feeney assumes servant's garb when I make social calls, because others expect it. However, when we go to the city I prefer to have someone to talk to, and Feeney wears mufti, so to speak. I'm afraid I have to tell you that Feeney was in my company every minute of the time."

"I see." There was no sense in trying to break an alibi like that. I knew damn well the old boy wasn't lying, and the hardest guy to shake was one whose character was above reproach. I had a nasty taste in my mouth. I was hoping I could tag the greaseball with something.

Mr. Berin said, "I can understand your suspicion. Certainly, though, the fact that Feeney saw the girl before she died was coincidence of a nature to invite it. From the papers I gathered that she was a victim of a hit-and-run driver."

"That's what the papers said," I told him. "Nobody saw it happen, so how could you be sure? She was somebody I liked

. . . I hate like hell to see her buried in a potter's field."

He passed a hand over his face, then looked up slowly. "Mr. Hammer . . . could I help in some way . . . for instance, could I take care of decent funeral arrangements for her? I . . . would appreciate it if you would allow me to. Somehow I feel as though I should. Here I have everything, while she . . ."

I interrupted with a shake of my head. "I'd rather do it; but thanks anyway. Still, it won't be like having her family take care of her."

"If you do need assistance of any sort, I wish you would call on me, Mr. Hammer."

"I might have to at that."

The butler came in then with a tray of brandy. We both took one, toasted each other with a raised glass and downed it. It was damn good brandy. I put the glass on a side table, hating myself because it looked like everything stopped here. Almost, I should say. The greaseball was still in it, because he might possibly know who the redhead was. So I made one last stab at it.

"Where did you get this Last character?"

"He came well recommended to me by a firm who had used his services in the past. I investigated thoroughly and his record is excellent. What connection could he have had with the deceased girl, do you suppose?"

"I don't know. Maybe he was only making use of her services. Where is he now, Mr. Berin?"

"He left for the cemetery with the nameplate for the tomb early this morning. I instructed him to stay and see that it was properly installed. I doubt if he will be back before late this afternoon."

There was as much here as I wanted to know. I said. "Maybe I'll run out and see him there. Where's the cemetery?"

He stood up and together we started walking towards the door. The little old butler appeared from out of nowhere and handed me my hat. Mr. Berin said, "Go back towards the city for ten miles. The cemetery lies west of the village at the first intersection. The gate-keeper will direct you once you reach it."

I thanked him for his time and we shook hands again. He held the door open for me and I ran down the steps to the car. He was still there when I pulled away and I waved so-long. In the rear-view mirror I saw him wave back.

The gate-keeper was only too happy to show me all the pretty tombstones and the newly dug graves. He took over the right seat of the car like a tour guide on a sightseeing bus and started a spiel that he hardly interrupted by taking a breath. It was quite a joint, quite a joint. From the names on all the marble it seemed as if only the rich and famous died. Apparently there were three prerequisites necessary before they'd let you rot under their well-tended sod: Fortune, Fame or Position. Nearly everyone had all three. At least very few went to their reward with just one.

It was easy to see that the winding road was leading to a grand climax. In the north-east corner of the grounds was a hillock topped by a miniature Acropolis, and the guide was being very particular to keep my attention diverted the other way so it would come as a complete surprise. He waited until we were at the foot of the hill, then pointed it out with a flourish, speaking with awed respect in his voice.

"This," he said, "is to be a great tribute to a great man . . . Mr. Arthur Berin-Grotin. Yes, a fitting tribute. Seldom has one done so much to win a place in the hearts of the people." He was almost in tears.

I just nodded.

"A very sensible man," he continued. "Too often those final preparations are hurried and a person's name is lost to posterity. Not so with Mr. Berin-Grotin."

"Mr. Berin," I corrected.

"Ah, you know him then."

"Somewhat. Do you think it would be O.K. if I looked at the place close up?"

"Oh, certainly." He opened the door. "Come, I'll take you there."

"I'd rather go alone. I may never have another chance to get back, and . . . well, you understand."

He was sympathetic at once. "Of course. You go right ahead. I'll walk back. I must see to certain plots at this end, anyway."

I waited until he was lost among the headstones, then lit a cigarette and walked up the path. The men were working on the far side of the scaffolding and never saw me come up. Or else they were used to sightseers. The place was bigger than it looked. Curved marble columns rose upwards for fifteen feet, oversha-dowing huge solid-bronze doors that were embellished with hand-crafted Greek designs.

The lintel over the doors was a curved affair held in place with an engraved keystone. Cut in the granite was the three-feather emblem of the royal family, or a good bottle of American whisky. Each plume, the tall center one and the two outward-curving side plumes, was exact in detail until they could have passed for fossil impressions. There were words under it in Latin. Two of them were Berin-Grotin. Very simple, very dignified. The pride of a name; and the public could draw its own conclusions from the grandeur of the structure.

I started to walk around the side, then flattened against a recess in the wall. The greaseball was there, jawing out the workman for something or other. His voice had the same nasty tone that it had had the other night, only this time he had on a brown gabardine chauffeur's uniform instead of a sharp suit. One of the workmen told him to shut up and he threw a rock at the scaffolding.

Just on a hunch I reached in my pocket and took out the plastic comb, and slid it down the walk so that it stopped right by his feet. He didn't turn around for a minute, but when he did he kicked the comb and sent it skittering back in my direction. Instinctively, his hand went to his breast pocket, then he bent over and picked it up, wiped it on his hand and ran it through his hair, then returned it to his shirt.

I didn't need any more after that. The greaseball was the guy who'd made a mess out of the redhead's room.

He didn't see me until I said, "Hullo, Feeney."

Then his lips drew back over his teeth and his ears went flat against the side of his head. "You dirty son of a bitch," he snarled.

Both of us saw the same thing at the same time. No guns. Feeney must have liked it that way because the sneer turned into a sardonic smile and he dropped his hand casually into his pocket. Maybe he thought I was dumb or something. I was just as casual when I flicked open the buttons of my nice new jacket and slouched back against the wall.

"What do you want, shamus?"

"You, greaseball."

"You think I'm easy to take?"

"Sure."

He kept on grinning.

I said, "I went up to the redhead's room last night. What were you looking for, Feeney?"

I thought he'd shake apart, he got so mad. There was a crazy light going in his eyes. "There was a comb on the floor by the window. When you doubled over to get out it dropped out of your pocket. That comb you just picked up."

He yanked his hand out of his pocket and the partially opened blade of the knife caught on cloth and snapped into place. I had my jacket off one arm and flipped it into his face. For a second it blinded him and the thrust missed my belly by an inch. He jumped back, then came in at me again, but my luck was better.

The knife snagged in the jacket and I yanked it out of his hand.

Feeney Last wasn't easy. He ripped out a curse and came into me with both fists before I could get the coat all the way off. I caught a stinger on the cheek and under the chin, then smashed a right into his face that sent him reeling back to bounce off one of the columns. I tore the sleeve half off the jacket shucking it, and rushed him. That time I was a damn fool. He braced against the pillar and lashed out with a kick that landed in my gut and turned me over twice. If I hadn't kept rolling, his heels would have broken my back. Feeney was too anxious; he tried it again. I grabbed his foot and he landed on the stone flooring with a sickening smash.

No more chances. I could hardly breathe, but I had enough strength left to get a wristlock and make him scream with pain. He lay like that, face down and yelling, while I knelt across his back and dragged his hand nearly to his neck. Little veins and tendons stretched in bas-relief under his skin, and the screams died to a choking for air.

"Who was she, Feeney?"

"I dunno!"

The arm went up another fraction. His face was bleeding from pressing it into the stone. "What were you after, Feeney? Who was she?"

"Honest to God . . . I dunno. God . . . stop!"

"I will . . . when you talk." A little more pressure on the arm again. Feeney started talking. I could barely hear him.

"She was a whore I knew from the Coast. I went up there and fell asleep. She stole something from me and I wanted it back."

"What?"

"Something I had on a guy. He was paying off and she stole it. Pictures of the guy and a broad in a hotel room."

"Who was the redhead?"

"I swear it, I dunno! I'd tell you, only I dunno. Oh, God, oh, God!"

For the second time Feeney fainted. I heard footsteps behind me and looked up to see the two workers standing there in coveralls. One had a newly smashed nose and a black eye and he was carrying a stonemason's hammer. I didn't like the way he held it.

"You in on this, chums?"

The guy with a black eye shook his head. "Just wanted to make sure he got it good. He's a wise guy . . . too quick to use his hands. Always wants to play boss. If we weren't getting plenty for this job we would have chucked it long ago." The other agreed with a nod.

I stood up and pulled on what remained of my new suit, then picked Feeney up and hoisted him on my shoulder. Just across from my car was a newly opened grave with the canopy up and chairs all set, waiting for a new arrival. I leaned forward and Feeney Last dropped six feet to the bottom of the grave and never moved. I hoped they'd find him before they lowered the coffin, or somebody was going to get the hell scared out of him.

The gate-keeper came to the side of my car as I was pulling out to say a friendly word and be complimented on his handiwork. He took one look at me and froze there with his mouth open. I put the car in gear. "Mighty unfriendly corpses you have in this place," I said.

chapter three ▰▰▰▰▰▰▰▰▰▰

I HIT NEW YORK in the middle of a rainstorm and drove straight to my apartment to change my clothes and down a bottle of beer. As soon as I finished I grabbed a quick bite in a luncheonette and headed back towards the office. The rain was still coming down when I found a parking space two blocks away, so I hopped a cab to save my only remaining suit.

It was after five, but Velda was still there. So was Pat. He looked up with a grin and waved hullo. "What are you doing here?" I asked.

"Oh, just stopped by to give you some news. Velda makes good company. Too bad you don't appreciate her more."

"I do, but I don't have a chance to show it." She wrinkled her nose at me. "What news?"

"We found the guy that killed the redhead."

My heart started hammering against my ribs. "Who?"

"Some young kid. He was drunk, speeding, and beat out the red light. He remembered hitting somebody and knew he was in the wrong, whole hog, and kept on going. His father turned him in to us."

I had to sit down after that. "You sure, Pat?"

"As sure as you were that she was killed deliberately." He laughed, and said, "I was all hopped up for a while, but it's been turned over to another department and I can relax. Every time I'm on the same trail as you I get the jumps. You ought to be a city cop, Mike. We could use you."

"Sure, and I'd go bats trying to stay within all the rules and regulations. Look, what makes you so sure the kid did it?"

"Well, as far as we can determine, it was the only accident along the avenue that night. Then, too, we have his confession. The lab checked the car for fender dents and paint chips on her clothing, but the kid had anticipated that before he confessed and did a good job of spoiling any traces that might have been left. We had a good man on the job and he seems to think that the unusual nature of the accident was caused because she was hit a glancing blow and broke her neck when she struck the edge of the curb."

"It would have broken the skin, then."

"Not necessarily. Her coat collar prevented that. All the indications point that way. The only abrasions were those caused by the fall and roll after she was hit. Her cheek and knees were skinned up, but that was all."

"What about identification."

"Nothing yet. The Bureau of Missing Persons is checking on it."

"Horse manure!"

"Mike," he said, "just why are you so damn upset about her name? There are thousands of kids just like her in the city and every day something happens to some of them."

"Nuts, I told you once. I liked her. Don't ask me why, because I don't know, but I'll be damned if I'm not going to find out. You aren't going to stick her in a hole in the ground with an 'X' on a slab over her head!"

"O.K., don't get excited. I don't know what you can do about it when there's a full-staffed bureau working on it."

"Horse manure to the bureau, too."

I jammed the butt in my mouth and Pat waited until I lit it, then he got up and walked over to me. He wasn't laughing any more. His eyes were serious and he laid an arm on my shoulder and said, "Mike, I kind of know you pretty well. You still got a bug up your tail that says she's been murdered, right?"

"Uh-huh!"

"Got the slightest reason why?"

"No."

"Well, if you find out, will you let me know about it?"

I blew a stream of smoke at the ceiling and nodded my head. I looked up at him and the old friendship was back. Pat was one of those guys with sense enough to know that other people had hunches besides the cops. And not only hunches. There's a lot of experience and know-how that lies in back of what people call hunches.

"Is she in the morgue now?" I asked him. Pat nodded. "I want to see her."

"All right, we'll go down now."

I looked at Velda, then the clock, and told her to blow. She was putting on her coat when we went out the door. On the way Pat didn't say much. I fought the traffic up to the old brick building and slid out to wait for Pat.

It was cold inside there. Not the kind of cold that comes with fresh air and wintry mornings, but a stale cold that smelt of chemicals and death. It was quiet, too, and it gave me the creeps. Pat asked the attendant for the listing of her personal belongings, and while he ruffled through a desk drawer we waited, not speaking.

There wasn't much. Clothes—but everybody wears clothes. Lipstick, powder and some money; a few trinkets of no account every girl totes in a handbag. I handed the listing back. "Is that all?"

"All I got, mister," the attendant yawned. "Want to see her?"

"If you don't mind."

The attendant went down the row of file cases, touching them with his finger like a kid does with a stick on a picket fence. When he came to the "Unidentified" row he checked a number with a slip in his hand and unlocked the second case from the bottom. For all he was concerned, Red could have been a stack of correspondence.

Death hadn't changed her, except to erase some of the hardness from her face. There was a bruise on the side of her neck and abrasions from the fall, neither seemingly serious enough to be fatal. But that's the way it is. People go under subway cars and get back on the platform, scared but laughing; others pile a car over a cliff and walk away. She gets clipped lightly and her neck is broken.

"When's the autopsy, Pat?"

"There won't be one now. It hardly seems necessary when we have the driver. It isn't murder any more."

Pat didn't see me grimace then. I was looking at her hands folded across her chest, thinking of the way she held that cup of coffee. Like a princess. She had had a ring, but there wasn't one now. The hand it had graced was scratched and swollen, and the marks where some bastard had forced the ring off went unnoticed among the others.

No, it wasn't stolen. A thief would have taken the handbag and not the ring while she had lain in the gutter. And girls aren't ones to forget to wear rings, especially when they're dressed up.

Yeah, Pat was wrong. He didn't know it, and I wasn't about to tell him . . . yet. It was murder if ever I saw one. And it wasn't just a guess now.

"Seen enough, Mike?"

"Yep. I've seen everything I want to see." We went back to the desk and for a second time I checked the listing of her belongings. No ring. I was glad to get out of there and back into fresh air. We sat in the car a few minutes and I lit up a cigarette.

"What's going to happen to her now, Pat?"

He shrugged. "Oh, the usual thing. We'll hold the body the regular time while we check information, then release it for burial."

"You aren't burying her without a name."

"Be reasonable, Mike. We'll do everything we can to trace her."

"So will I." Pat shot me a sidewise look. "Anyway," I said, "whatever happens, don't put her through the disposal system. I'll finance a funeral for her if I have to."

"Uh-huh. But you're thinking you won't have to again. All right, Mike, do what you want to. It's officially out of my hands now, but damn it, man . . . if I know you, it will be back in my hands again. Don't try to cut my throat, that's all. If you get anything, let me know about it."

"Of course," I said, then started up the car and pulled away from the curb.

The letter was three days late. The address had been taken from the telephone book, which hadn't been revised since I moved to my new apartment. The post office had readdressed it and forwarded it to me. The handwriting was light and feminine, touched with a gracious Spencerian style.

My hand was shaking when I slit it open; it shook even more when I started to read it, because the letter was from the redhead.

Dear Mike,
What a lovely morning, what a beautiful day and I feel so new all over I want to sing my way down the street. I can't begin to tell you "thank you" because words are so small and my heart is so big that anything I could write would be inadequate. When I met you, Mike, I was

tired . . . so tired of doing so many things . . . only one of which had any meaning to me. Now I'm not tired at all and things are clear once more. Some day I may need you again, Mike. Until now there has been no one I could trust and it has been hard. It isn't a friendship I can impose upon because we're really not friends. It's a trust, and you don't know what it means to me to have someone I can trust.

You've made me very happy.

Your Redhead.

Oh, damn it to hell, anyway. Damn everybody and everything. And damn me especially because I made her happy for half a day and put her in a spot where living was nice and it was hard to die.

I folded the letter up in my fist and threw it at the wall.

A bumper bottle of beer cooled me off and I quit hating myself. When I killed the quart I stuck the empty under the sink and went back and picked up the letter, smoothing it out on the table top. Twice again I read it, going over every word. It wasn't the kind of letter a tramp would write; the script and the phrasing had a touch of eloquence that wasn't used by girls who made the gutter their home. I've seen a lot of bums, and I've fooled around with them from coast to coast, and one thing I know damn well . . . they're a definite type. Some give it away and some sell it, but you could pick out those who would and those who wouldn't. And those who would had gutter dirt reflected in everything they did, said and wrote.

Red had been a decent kid. She had to give up her decency to do something important. Something had a meaning for her . . . and some day she was going to need me again. She needed me more now than she ever did. O.K., I was hers, then.

They don't start walking the streets until midnight, if that's what you're after. But if you're in a hurry there are guys you can see who will steer you straight to a house and pick up their cut later. Usually they're sallow-faced punks with sharp pointed faces and wise eyes that shift nervously, and they keep toying with change in their pockets or a key chain hooked to high-pleated pants as they talk out of the corner of their mouths.

Cobbie Bennett was like that. As long as there are girls who make a business out of it, you'll find guys like Cobbie. The only shadow he cast was by artificial light, and he looked it. I found him in a dirty bar near Canal Street, his one hand cupped around a highball and his other hooked in his belt, in earnest conversation with a couple of kids who couldn't have been more than seventeen. Both of them looked like high-school seniors out to spend a week's allowance.

I didn't wait for them to finish talking. Both kids looked at me once when I nudged in beside them, turned a little white and walked away without a word.

"Hullo, Cobbie," I said.

The pimp was more like a weasel backed into a corner than a man. "What do you want?"

"Not what you're selling. By the way, who are you selling these days?"

"Try and find out, banana nose."

I said O.K. and grabbed a handful of skin around his leg and squeezed. Cobbie dropped his drink and started cursing. When spit drooled out of the corner of his mouth I quit and ordered him another drink. He could hardly find his face with it. "I could punch holes in you and make you talk if I felt like it, pal." I grinned.

"Damn it, what'd you do that for?" His eyes were squinted almost shut, chopping me up into little pieces. He rubbed his leg and winced. "I don't have to draw you pitchers, you know what I'm doing. Same thing I been doing right along. What's it to you?"

"Working for an outfit?"

"No, just me." His tone was sullen.

"Who was the redhead who was murdered the other night, Cobbie?"

This time his eyes went wide and he twitched the corner of his mouth. "Who says she was murdered?"

"I do." The bartender drew a beer and shoved it at me. While I sipped it I watched the pimp. Cobbie was scared. I could see him try to shrink down inside his clothes, making himself as unobtrusive as possible, as though it weren't healthy to be seen with me. That put him in a class with Shorty . . . he had been scared, too.

"The papers said she was hit by a car. You call that murder?"

"I didn't say what killed her. I said she was murdered."

"So what am I supposed to do?"

"Cobbie . . . you wouldn't want me to get real sore at you, would you?" I waited a second, then, "Well . . .?"

He was slow in answering. His eyes sort of crawled up to meet mine and stayed there. Cobbie licked his lips nervously, then he turned and finished his drink with a gulp. When he put the glass down he said, "You're a dirty son of a bitch, Hammer. If I was one of them hop-heads I'd go get a sniff and a rod and blow your goddam guts out. I don't know who the hell the redhead was except another whore and I don't give a damn either. I worked her a couple of times, but mostly she wasn't home to play ball and I got complaints from the guys, so I dropped her. Maybe it was lucky for me that I did, because right after it I got word that she was hot as hell."

"Who passed the word?"

"How should I know? The grapevine don't come from one guy. Enough people said it, so I believed it and forgot her. One of the other babes told me she wasn't doing so good. The trade around here ain't like it is uptown. We don't get no swells . . . some kids maybe, like them you loused up for me, but the rest is all the jerks who don't care what they get so long as they get it. They heard the word and laid off, too. She wasn't making a nickel."

"Keep talking." He knew what I was after.

Cobbie rapped on the bar for another drink. He wasn't talking very loud now. "Get off me, will you! I don't know why she was hot. Maybe some punk gun-slinger wanted her for a steady and was getting rough. Maybe she was loaded three ways to Sunday. All I know is she was hot and in this business a word is good enough for me. Why don't'cha ask somebody else?"

"Who? You got this end sewed up pretty tight, Cobbie. Who else is there to ask? I like the way you talk. I like it so much that I might spread it around that you and me have been pretty chummy and you've been yapping your greasy little head off. Why should I ask somebody else when I got you to tell me. Maybe I don't know who to ask."

His face was white as it could get. He hunched forward to get his drink and almost spilled that one too. " . . . Once she said she worked a house . . ." He finished the highball and muttered the address as he wiped his mouth.

I didn't bother to thank him; it was favor enough to throw my drink down silently, pick up my change and walk out of there. When I reached the street I crossed over and stood in the recess of a hallway for a few minutes. I stuck a butt between my lips and had just cupped my hands around a match when Cobbie came out, looked up and down the street, jammed his hands in his pockets and started walking north. When he rounded the corner I got in the car and sat there a few minutes, trying to figure just what the hell was going on.

One red-headed prostitute down on her luck. She was killed,

her room was searched, and her ring was missing.

One trigger-happy greaseball who searched her room because she stole his blackmail set-up. He said.

One ex-con who ran a hash house the redhead used for a hangout. He was scared.

One pimp who knew she was hot but couldn't say why. Maybe he could, but he was scared, too.

It was a mess no matter how you looked at it, and it was getting messier all the time. That's why I was so sure. Death is like a bad tooth . . . no matter what's wrong with it, you pull it out and it's all over. That's the way death usually is; after that people can talk all they want, they even do things for dead joes that they wouldn't do for the living. Death is nice and clean and antiseptic. It ends all trouble. Someone gathers up your belongings, says a word of praise, and that's it. But the redhead's was a messy death. There was something unclean about it like a wound that has healed over on top, concealing an ugly, festering sore brewing a deadly poison that will kill again.

When the butt burned down to my fingers I started the car and shoved off, threading my way across town to the address Cobbie had given me. New York had its sinkholes, too, and the number of this one placed it smack in the middle of the slime. It was a one-way street of rats' nests, with the river at one end and a saloon on each corner, peopled with men and women that had the flat vacant look of defeat stamped on their faces.

I checked the numbers and found the one I wanted, but all it was was a number, because the house was gone. Unless you can call a flame-gutted skeleton of masonry a house. The doorway yawned open like a leper's mouth and each window had its scar tissue of peeling paint.

The end of the trail. I swore and kicked at the curb.

A kid about ten looked at me and said, "Some jerk t'rew a match out the winder inta the garbage coupla weeks ago. Most of the dames got killed."

These kids knew too much for their age nowadays. I needed a drink bad this time. The joint on the left was closer, so I went in and stood at the bar making tight fists with my hands until the nails cut into my palms. Now this, I kept thinking, now this! Did every corner to this have a blank wall I couldn't hurdle. The bartender didn't ask . . . he shoved a glass and a bottle under my nose and drew a chaser from the beer tap, then made change from my buck. When I had the second he put all the change in the register, then came back and waited.

"One more?"

I shook my head. "Just beer this time. Where's your phone?"

"Over in the corner." He jerked his head towards the end of the bar while he pulled the beer. I went down to the booth and dropped a nickel in, then dialed Pat at his home.

This time I had a little luck because he answered. I said, "This is Mike, chum. Need a favor done. There was a fire in one of the bawdy houses down the street here and I want to know if there has been an investigation made. Can you check it?"

"Guess so, Mike. What's the number?" I gave it to him and grunted when he checked it back to me. "Hang up while I call and I'll buzz you back. Give me your number there."

He got that, too, and I hung up. I went down and got my beer, then went back to the seat in the phone booth and sat there sipping the stuff slowly. The minute it rang I snatched it off the hook.

"Mike?"

"Yeah."

"The fire happened twelve days ago. A complete investigation was made because the place had been condemned for occupancy a month before and nothing had been done about it. The fire started accidentally and the guy who flipped the lit match out the window is still in the hospital recovering. Apparently, he was the only one who got out alive. The flames blocked the front door and the rear was littered with junk so as to be impassable.

"Three girls perished on the roof, two in the rooms and two jumped to their deaths before the firemen could get the nets up. Destruction was complete because the floors caved in completely."

Pat didn't give me a chance to thank him. Before I could say a word his voice thinned out and had an edge on it. "Give me what you know, Mike. You aren't there out of curiosity and if you're still thinking in terms of murder I want a trade. And right now, too."

"O.K., sharp guy," I laughed. "I'm still trying to find out who the redhead was. I met a guy who knew where she had worked before she free-lanced and I wound up here."

This time Pat was the one who laughed. "Is that all? I could have told you that if you'd called me." I froze on the phone. "Her name was Sanford, Nancy Sanford. She used several first names, but seemed to stick to Nancy most of the time, so we picked it as her own."

My teeth grinding together made more sound than my voice. "Who said so?"

"We have a lot of men on the Force, Mike. A couple of the patrolmen got on to her."

"Maybe you know who killed her, too."

"Sure. The kid did. The lab finally found traces of fender paint on her clothes, and strands of fibres from her dress on the car. It was as simple as that."

"Was it?"

"Uh-huh. Besides, we have a witness. At least a witness who saw her just a few minutes before she was killed. A janitor was putting out the ashes and saw her staggering up the street, dead drunk. She fell, got up again and staggered some more. Later she was discovered a half-block away in the gutter where she was hit."

"Did you trace her parents—anybody at all who knew her?"

"No, we couldn't get that far. She did a good job of wiping out all traces of her past."

"So now she gets the usual treatment . . . pine box and all."

"What else, Mike? The case is closed except for the kid's trial."

I snarled into that mouthpiece, "So help me, Pat, if you lower her coffin before I'm ready, I'll beat the hell out of you, cop or no cop!"

Pat said quietly, "We're not in a hurry, Mike. Take your time, take your time."

I set the receiver back in its cradle gently and stood up, saying her name over and over again. I must have said it too loud, because the willowy brunette at the corner table looked up at me with a quizzical expression in eyes that had seen through too many bottles of liquor. She was a beaut, all right, not part of this section of town at all. She had on a black satin dress with a neckline that plunged down to her belt buckle, and she sat there with her legs crossed, unconscious of what she was giving away for free.

The heavy rouged lips parted in a smile and she said, "Nancy . . . always Nancy. Everybody's looking for Nancy. Why don't they pay a little attention to pretty Lola?"

"Who was looking for Nancy?"

"Oh, just everybody." She tried to lean her chin on her hand, but her elbow kept slipping off the table. "I think they found her, too, because Nancy isn't around any more. Nancy's dead. Did you know Nancy was dead? I liked Nancy fine, but now she's dead. Won't pretty Lola do, mister? Lola's nice and alive. You'll like Lola lots when you get to know her."

Hell, I liked Lola already.

chapter four ▮▮▮▮▮▮▮▮▮▮▮▮

WHEN I SAT down beside the brunette the bartender watched me so hard the three drunks at the rail turned around too. The drunks didn't matter, they couldn't see that far, so I turned on my best nasty look and the bartender went about his business. Just the same he stayed down at the end where he could hear things if they were said too loud.

Lola uncrossed her long, lovely legs and leaned towards me. The big, floppy hat she was wearing wobbled an inch away from my eyes. "You're a nice guy, mister. What's your name?"

"Mike."

"Just Mike?"

"It's enough. How would you like to go for a ride and sober up a little."

"Ummm. You got a nice shiny convertible for Lola to ride in? I love men with convertibles."

"All right."

She stood up and I held her arm to keep her straight. Nice, very nice. Deep-dish apple pie in a black satin dress. I steered her towards the door, hardly taking my eyes off her. Tall, and as long as you didn't look too close, as pretty as they come. But close looks were what counted. She had that look around the eyes and a set of the mouth that spelled just one thing. She was for sale cheap.

My heap wasn't what she expected, but it was comfortable and she leaned back against the cushions and let the breeze blow across her face and fluff out her hair. Her eyes closed and I thought she was asleep until she reached up and tugged off the floppy hat. Then she did go to sleep.

I wasn't going anywhere . . . just driving, taking it easy along the main Stem, following anybody that was ahead of me. Somehow we got to the approach of the Manhattan Bridge and it was easier to go across than to cut out of traffic. This time I was behind a truck that led the way down Flatbush Avenue at a leisurely pace. Evidently he was in no hurry because he didn't bother going through light changes and never jumped the reds. He set such a nice pace that when he parked at Beverley Road for ten minutes I sat behind him and waited until he came back and followed him some more. The first thing I knew we had the lights of the city behind us and were skirting Floyd Bennett Field, and the air was carrying the salty tang of the ocean with it. We crossed the

502

bridge then and he turned left, but I didn't follow. The winding macadam on the right led in the direction of the breezes and I took it to a gate and on into Rockaway Point.

We had been parked for an hour before Lola woke up. The radio was turned low, making music that mingled with the air and the stars and if murder hadn't led me here it could have been pretty nice.

She looked at me sleepily and said, "Hullo, you."

"Hi, kid."

"Where is Lola this time?"

"At the beach."

"And who with?"

"A guy called Mike . . . that's me. I found you back in the city under a rock. Remember?"

"No, but I'm glad you're with me." She twisted on her hip, and slouched back, looking at me. No remorse, no bewilderment. Just curiosity.

"What time is it?"

I said, "After midnight. Want to go home?"

"No."

"Want to take a walk, then?"

"Yes. Can I take off my shoes and walk in the sand?"

"Take off everything if you want to."

"Maybe I will when we get down on the beach, Mike."

"Don't do anything of the kind. I'm too damn susceptible."

It was pretty good strolling down that narrow lane, jumping the cracks in the sidewalk and making faces at the moon. Lola slipped her hand into mine and it was warm and soft, but holding tight as though I was something worth holding on to. I was remembering what Red said about guys like me never having to pay, and I wondered how true it was.

She took off her shoes like she wanted to and walked in the sand, kicking at mounds with her toes. When we reached the bulkhead we jumped down and walked to the water, and I took off my shoes too. It was cold, but it was nice, too nice to spoil by talking yet, and we waded up the beach, stepping up the wooden jetties and jumping to the other side, until there was nothing left but straight sandy beach, and even the houses were in the background.

"I like it here, Mike," she said. She let go my hand and picked up a clamshell, looking at it as if it were a rare specimen. I put my arm around her and we stepped out of the water that licked at our feet and walked to the rolling hillocks of the dunes. After we sat down I handed her a cigarette, and in the light of the flame I saw that her face had changed and was at peace with itself.

"Cold?" I asked.

"A little chilly. I haven't much on under the dress."

I didn't question it; I just gave her my coat, then leaned back on my elbows while she hugged her knees, staring out at the ocean.

When she took a long last drag on the cigarette she turned around and said, "Why did you bring me out here, Mike?"

"To talk. I need somebody to talk to."

She leaned back on the sand. "My mind's unfogging, Mike," she said. "Was it about Nancy?"

I nodded.

"She's dead, Mike. I liked her, too."

"Who killed her?"

There was a long moment of silence while Lola searched my face. "You're a cop, aren't you?"

"A private dick. And I'm not hired by anybody, either."

"And you think she was murdered instead of being killed by a hit-and-run driver."

"Lola, I don't know what to think. Everything's going around in circles right now. Let's say I didn't like the way she died."

"Mike . . . what if I said I thought she was murdered, too?"

I jumped at that. "What makes you think so?"

"Oh, I don't know. Lots of things, maybe. If she wasn't murdered, she was killed accidentally before she *could* be murdered. Let's say that, Mike."

I turned on my side and my hand covered hers. The moonlight on the white V of the plunging neckline made it hard to concentrate. Her skin was white and smooth, in sharp contrast to the black satin. The only thing I could think of was the kind of bra she would be wearing under a dress like that. It would have to be an engineering marvel.

"How did you get to know her, Lola?"

Her answer was simple enough. "We worked together."

"You?" It didn't seem right.

"Don't I look the type?"

"Maybe . . . if a guy had dough and a convertible and was looking for an interesting sideline in life. But not down in that section. What were you doing there?"

"I worked in a house up the street."

"I thought all the girls were killed in the fire."

"They were, but I wasn't there at the time. I was . . . in a hospital. I had been there quite a while. I left today."

She looked at the sand and traced two letters in it—V.D.

"That's why I was in the hospital. That's why I was working down there instead of playing for guys with dough and convertibles. I had that once and lost it. I'm not very smart, am I, Mike?"

"No," I told her, "you're not. Anybody can do what you're doing and make a living at it. You never had to go in for that, neither did Nancy. There's no excuse for it. No matter what happens, there's only one way you wind up. No, Lola, there's no excuse for it."

"Sometimes there is."

She ran her fingers through my hair, then dropped her hand to cover mine. "Maybe that's why Nancy and I were so close . . . because there was some excuse for it. I was in love, Mike . . . terribly in love with a guy who was no damn good. I could have had anybody I wanted, but no, I had to fall for a guy who was no damn good at all. We were going to get married when he ran away with a two-bit bum who hung around all the saloons in town. I was pretty disgusted, I guess. If that was all men wanted I figured on playing the game. I played it pretty good, too. After that I had everything, but I never fell for anybody.

"At first I was bitter about it, but living became too easy. I had something men wanted, and they were willing to supply the overhead charges. It got so good that it wasn't worth while playing one sucker at a time. Then one day I met a smart girl who introduced me to the right people, and after that the dates were supplied and I made plenty of money, and had a lot of time to spend it in, too.

"I had a name and phone number, and if they had the dough all they had to do was call. That's why they called us call-girls. The suckers paid plenty, but they got what they wanted and were safe. Then one day I got drunk and slipped up. After that I wasn't safe to be with any more and the suckers complained, and they took away my name and my phone number, so all I had left was to go on the town.

"There's always people looking for left-overs like me. One got me set with an outfit that had a house and a vacancy and I worked there, then they set me down a couple of notches until I wound up in the place where I met Nancy. Most of the girls in the racket just drifted into it, that's why Nancy and I became friends. She had a reason for being there, too. It wasn't the same reason, but it was a reason and it put us above the others.

"One day I got smart. I pulled out of it and went to the hospital. When I was there Nancy was killed, and when I got back to the house it was burned. I came back to get Nancy, but she was gone, and she was the only friend I had left, so I went down to Barney's and got drunk."

"Where you made a very professional pass at me."

"I didn't mean to, Mike. I was drunk and I couldn't get out of the habit, I guess. Forgive me?"

When she turned the neckline fell away and I was ready to forgive her for anything. But first there was more I had to find out.

"Nancy . . . what about Nancy . . . did she follow the same route you did? About working her way down the ladder, I mean."

"It happens to the best of them sooner or later, Mike. Yes, Nancy was a call-girl too, only she had made the grade before me."

"And did she have to go to the hospital, too?"

A puzzled frown tugged at her forehead. "No, that was the strange part about it. She was very careful. First she was in the big money, then suddenly she quit it all and dropped out of sight. She was for ever running into people that hadn't seen her for a long time, and it frightened her. She stayed in the business as though it were a place to hide."

"Hiding from what?"

"I never found out. Those were things you didn't ask about."

"Did she have anything worth hiding?"

"If she did I didn't see it, though she was mighty secretive about her personal belongings. The only expensive thing she had was a camera, an imported affair that she used when she had a job once. You know, taking pictures of couples on the street and handing them a card. They would send the card in with a quarter and get their picture."

"When was that . . . recently?"

"Oh, no, quite some time ago. I happened to see some of the cards she had left over and asked about them. I think the name was QUICK PIC . . . or something like that."

I put a cigarette in my mouth and lit it, then gave her a drag from it. "What's your whole name, Lola?"

"Does it matter?"

"Maybe."

"Bergan. Lola Bergan, and I come from a little town called Byeville down in Mississippi. It isn't a big town, but it's a nice town, and I still have a family there. My mother and father think

I'm a famous New York model and I have a little sister that wants to grow up and be just like me, and if she does I'll beat her brains out."

There wasn't any answer to that. I said, "Lola, there's just one thing more. Answer me yes or no fast, and if you lie to me I'll know it. Does the name Feeney Last mean anything to you?"

"No, Mike. Should it?"

"No, perhaps not. It meant something to Red and some other people, but it shouldn't involve you. Maybe I'm on the wrong trolley."

"Mike . . . did you love Nancy?"

"Naw, she was a friend. I saw her once and spoke to her a few minutes and we got to be buddies. It was one of those things. Then some son of a bitch killed her."

"I'm sorry, Mike. I wish you could like me like that. Do you think you could?"

She turned again, and this time she was closer. Her head nestled against my shoulder and she moved my hand up her body until I knew that there was no marvel of engineering connected to the bra because there was no bra. And the studded belt she wore was the keynote to the whole ensemble, and when it was unsnapped the whole affair came apart in a whisper of black satin that folded back against the sand until all of her reflected the moonlight from above until I eclipsed the pale brilliance, and there was no sound except that of the waves and our breathing. Then soon even the waves were gone, and there was only the warmth of white skin and little muscles that played under my hand and the fragrance that was her mouth.

The redhead had been right.

At one-fifteen I awoke with the phone shrilling in my ears. I kicked the cover off the bed and shuffled over to the stand, wiping the sleep from my eyes. Then I barked a sharp hullo into the phone.

Velda said, "Where the devil have you been? I've been trying to get you all morning."

"I was here. Sleeping."

"What were *you* doing last night?"

"Working. What did ya want?"

"A gentleman came in this morning, a very wealthy gentleman. His name was Arthur Berin-Grotin and he wants to see you. I made an appointment for two-thirty here in the office and I suggest you keep it. In case you didn't know, the bank balance can stand relining."

"O.K., kid, I'll be there. Was his stooge with him?"

"He came alone. Maybe he had someone waiting, but he didn't come up."

"Good! Stick around until I show up. Won't be long. 'Bye, honey."

For ten minutes I splashed around in the shower, then made a bit to eat without drying off. A full pot of coffee put me back in shape and I started to get dressed. My suit was a mess, wrinkled from top to bottom, with the pockets and cuffs filled with sand. There were lipstick smears on the collar and shoulders, so it went back into the closet behind the other until I could get it to the tailor's. That left me with the custom-built tweed that was made to be worn over a rod, so I slapped on the shoulder holster and filled it with the .45, then slipped on the jacket. I looked in the mirror and grunted. A character straight out of a B movie. Downstairs I got a shave and a haircut, which left me with just enough time to get to the office a few minutes before the old gent.

Mr. Berin-Grotin came in at exactly two-thirty. My switch box buzzed and Velda called in from the waiting-room, "A gentleman here to see you, Mike."

I told her to send him in and sat back in my swivel chair, waiting. When he opened the door I got up and walked over with my mitt out. "Glad to see you again, Mr. Berin. Come over and park."

"Ah, thank you." He took an overstuffed leather chair by the desk and leaned forward on his cane. In the light from the window I could see a troubled look about his eyes.

"Young man," he said, "since you left me I have given more and more thought to the plight of the girl you were so interested in. The one that was found dead."

"The redhead. Her name was Nancy Sanford."

His eyebrows went up. "You discovered that already?"

"Hell, no, the cops got that angle. All I ever found out was some junk that makes no sense." I leaned back and fired up a smoke, wondering what he wanted. He told me soon enough.

"Did they find her parents . . . anyone who would take care of . . . the body?"

"Nah. There's not much they can do, anyhow. The city is filled with a thousand girls like her. Ten to one she's from out of the state and has been away from home so long nobody gives a damn any more. The only one who's trying to give her back her past is me. Maybe I'll be sorry for it."

"That is exactly what I came to see you about, Mr. Hammer."

"Mike . . . I hate formalities."

"Oh, yes . . . Mike. At any rate, when you left I thought and thought about the girl. I made a few judicious calls to friends I have with the newspapers, but they couldn't help in the least. They said the girl was just a . . . a drifter. It seems a shame that things like that must happen. I believe that we're all to blame somehow.

"Your deep concern has transferred itself to me, and I think I may be of some help to you. I am continually giving to charities of some sort . . . but that's a rather abstract sort of giving, don't you think? Here is a chance for me to help someone, albeit a trifle late, and I feel I must."

"I told you once, I'll take care of the funeral arrangements myself," I said.

"I realize you intend to . . . but that's not what I mean. What I wish to do is to employ you. If you carry on an investigation you must be financed, and since I am as anxious as you to have her remains properly cared for, I would be deeply grateful if you would let me give you the means of locating her relatives. Will you do it?"

It was a break I hadn't expected. I took my feet off the desk and swung the chair around. "It's all right with me," I told him. "I would have poked around anyway, but this makes it a lot easier."

He reached in his jacket pocket for his wallet and thumbed it open. "And what are your rates, Mike?"

"A flat fifty a day. No expense account. The fifty takes care of it all."

"Have you any idea how long it may take?"

I shrugged my shoulders. "Who can tell. Sometimes chasing a name is easy, sometimes not."

"In that case, let me do this . . . ." He laid a sheaf of crisp new bills on my desk. The top one was a beautiful fifty. "Here is one thousand dollars. Not a retainer . . . but payment in full. Please stay with it until you think it has been spent. If you find out about the girl quickly, good. If you don't locate her history in twenty days, then it is probably a hopeless task and not worth your time. Is that a satisfactory arrangement?"

"I'm stealing your money, Mr. Berin."

His face brightened into an easy smile and the trouble lines were gone. "I don't think so, Mr. Hammer. I have become familiar with your record and know how far you are capable of going. With an added incentive of having an interest in the girl yourself, you should make excellent progress. I hope so. It isn't a pleasant thing to see someone go like that . . . no one to know or care. . . ."

"I care."

"Yes, I know you do, Mike, and I care, too, because yours is a genuine, unselfish interest to restore some touch of decency to her. She couldn't have been all bad. Do whatever you think is necessary, and in the interim, if there is a need for more money you will call on me, won't you?"

"Certainly."

"The whole affair makes me feel so very small. Here I am preparing for a grand exit from this life, spending thousands that will be a memorial to my name, and this girl dies as if she had never existed. You see, I *know* what aloneness is; I *know* the feeling of having no one to call your own, not even an entombed memory to worship. My wife, as you may know, was an ardent sportswoman. She loved the sea, but she loved it too much. During one of her cruises aboard a yacht that should never have been out of still waters she was washed overboard. My only son was killed in the First World War. His daughter was the dearest thing to my heart, and when she died I knew what it was like to be utterly, completely alone in this world. Like my wife, she loved the sea too dearly, too. It finally took her during a storm off the Bahamas. Perhaps you understand now why I have erected a memorial to myself . . . for there is not even so much as a headstone for the others, except perhaps a cross over my son's grave in France. And that, too, is why I want no one else to share my burden of having nothing left, nothing at all. I am thankful that there are people like you, Mike. My faith in the kindnesses of man was extremely low. I thought that all people cared about was money, now I know I was quite wrong."

I nodded, blowing a streamer of smoke at the ceiling. "Money is great, Mr. Berin, but sometimes a guy gets pretty damn sore and money doesn't matter anymore. A guy can get just plain curious, too . . . and money doesn't matter then either."

My new client stood up, giving me an old-fashioned bow. "That takes care of the matter, then?"

"Almost. Where do you want me to send my report?"

"I never gave it a thought. It really doesn't matter, but if you come across anything you might feel is interesting, call or write to me at my home. It's entirely up to you. I'm more interested in results than the procedure."

"Oh . . . one other thing. Is Feeney Last still with you?"

His eyes twinkled this time and a grin crossed his face. "Fortunately, no. It seems that he had quite a scare. Quite a scare. He saved me the task of discharging him, by resigning. At present my gardener is serving in his capacity. Good day, Mike."

I stood up and led him to the door and shook hands there. On the way out he gave Velda a gentlemanly bow and strode out the door. She waited until the door had shut and said, "He's nice, Mike. I like him."

"I like him, too, kid. You don't have many around like him anymore."

"And he's got money, too. We're back in business again, huh?"

"Uh-huh." I looked at the intercom box. She had the switch up and had overheard the conversation. I frowned at her the way a boss should, but it didn't scare her a bit.

"Just curious, Mike. He was such an interesting guy." She smiled.

I faked a punch at her jaw and sat on the desk, reaching for the phone. When I got the dial tone I poked out Pat's number and held on until he got on the wire. He gave me a breezy hullo and said, "What's new, kid?"

"A few things here and there, but nothing that you can call withholding evidence. Look, have you had lunch yet?"

"An hour ago."

"Well, how about some coffee and Danish. I want to know a few things, if you care to tell me."

"What kind of things?"

"Stuff the police ought to know and the general public shouldn't. Or would you rather have me find out for myself?"

"Nuts to you! It's better to have you obligated to me. I'll meet you in Mooney's as soon as you can make it. How's that?"

"Fine," I said, then hung up.

Pat beat me to the beanery by five minutes. He already had a table over in the back and was sipping coffee from an oversize mug the place used as a trademark. I pulled out a chair and sat down. I didn't have time to waste; as soon as the waiter came over with my coffee and pastry I got right down to cases. "Pat, what's the angle on the call-girl racket in this town?"

The cup stopped half-way to his mouth. "Now, that's a hell of a question to ask me. If I tell you, it implies that I'm crooked and I'm looking the other way. If I don't, I look stupid for not knowing what goes on."

I gave him a disgusted grunt, then: "Pat, there are certain things that are going to happen in every town no matter how strait-laced the citizens are or how tough the cops are. It's like taxes. We got 'em and we can't get rid of 'em. And who likes taxes except the small group of bureaucrats that handle the mazuma?"

"Now you've made me feel better," he chuckled. "There isn't too much I can tell you because those outfits are good at keeping things to themselves. We rarely get complaints because their clientele isn't in a position to lay themselves open to criticism by entering a complaint. However, the police are well aware of the existing situation and try to enforce the letter of the law. But remember one thing—politics. There are ways of bogging the police down and it's a hurdle hard to jump.

"Then there's the matter of evidence. The higher-ups don't run houses or keep books where they can be found. It's a matter of merely suggesting to someone just who is available and letting him do the rest. I think the girls come across with a cut of the take or the proper persons aren't steered in their direction. They may get shoved around a little, too. In fact, there have been several deaths over the years that point suspiciously in that direction."

"That they got shoved too hard, you mean?" I asked.

"Exactly."

"How did the coroner call them?"

"Suicides, mainly . . . except for Russ Bowen. You know about him . . . he was the guy who ran a chain of houses and tried to buck the combine. We found him shot full of holes a couple of months ago and his houses closed out. We never could get a line on the killing. Even the stoolies clammed up when we mentioned his name. Yes, Russ was murdered, but the others were all called suicides."

"And you?"

"Murder, Mike. The cases are still open, and some day we're going to nail the goons that are behind them. Not only the hired hands that did the dirty work, but the ones that run the organizations. They're the ones we want . . . the ones that turn decent kids into a life of filth and despair while they sit back and collect the big money. The ones that can kill and get away with it and sit back and laugh while the papers call it suicide!"

His face was a mask of hate. My eyes caught his and held for a long moment. "Suicide . . . or accident, Pat?" I queried.

"Yes, both. We've had them that looked that way, too, and . . ."

Now the hate was gone and his face was friendly again, but

there was something different about the eyes that I had never seen before. "You're a bastard, Mike. You set me up very pretty."

"I did?" I tried to play innocent, but it didn't work.

"Cut it and get to the redhead. Nancy, I believe her name was. What are you handing me?"

I took my time about finishing the Danish. After it soaked long enough in the coffee I fished it out and ate it, licking the sugar from my fingers. When I lit a butt I said, "I'm not handing you a thing, Pat. You just told me something I've been trying to tell you right along. I've always said Red was murdered. Now, what do you think?"

Pat wrapped his fists into hard knots and pressed them into the table. He had a hard time talking through clenched teeth. "Damn your soul, Mike, we had that case nicely wrapped up. She was killed accidentally beyond a shadow of doubt, and I'm positive of it. I'm so positive of it I'd bet my right arm against a plugged nickel I couldn't be wrong! Maybe people make mistakes, but the sciences of the laboratory don't!"

It was fun watching him beat his head against the wall. His words turned into a torrent of sharp sounds and he leaned against the edge of the table with fire leaping from his eyes.

"I saw the evidence. I checked on the evidence. I'm certain of the evidence as is everyone else concerned with the case. In the beginning you had me dancing on hot coals because I thought that maybe you were right. Then I knew what had happened and I knew you were wrong. Mind you, I didn't say think—I said *knew!* And right now I still *know* you are wrong and I am *right.*"

"But . . ." I protested.

"But you, you bastard, you've got me all crazied up again and I'm thinking I'm wrong even when I know I'm right! Why don't you drop dead!"

It had been a long time since I had seen Pat like that. I grinned at him and blew a wreath of smoke around his head. The draft made a halo of it and I said, "The smoke it encircled his head like a wreath."

"What?"

"Excerpt from the 'Night Before Christmas.' You probably can't go back that far."

Pat ran his fingers through his hair and shook his head. "You give me the pip. Maybe I'm nuts. What makes me get all excited about things like this? Ordinarily I'm cool, calm and collected. I run my office with precision and great efficiency, then you come along and I get like a rookie on his first beat with a gang war going on in the back alleys."

I shoved the deck of Luckies towards him and he stuck one in his mouth. When I thumbed a match and lit him I said very quietly, "Pat, offices like yours are great things. You take one lousy little clue and make a case out of it and somebody pays society for a misdeed. Sure, you serve justice. You do more good than a million guys working separately, but there's one thing you miss."

"Tell me what." He was getting sarcastic again.

"The excitement of the chase, Pat. The thrill of running something down and pumping a slug into it. Right now you are so damn fond of indisputable proof you can't figure an angle anymore. Since when can't murder be made to look like an accident?"

"She was hit by the car, Mike. The driver admits he hit somebody but he was too fuzzy to remember who. The lab found traces on the car. They found traces on her. We had witnesses who saw her staggering down the street dead drunk a little while before she got it. The guy that hit her is ordinarily an upstanding citizen with no underworld connections. We checked."

I nodded. "Yet now you're beginning to entertain doubts. Right?"

He said something obscene.

"Right is right! Entertain is no word for it. You have me refuting everything I ever learned and I'll wind up being a stupe. Do you know why?"

"Yeah, but tell me again, Pat."

This time he leaned on the table and practically hissed through his teeth. "Because right in here"—he tapped the side of his head—"you're a sharp article. You could be a good crook, but you're a better cop. You get something and hang on to it longer than anybody else and make something of it. You got a brain and the sense to use it and you have something I haven't got which is a feeling for things. Damn it, I'd like to poke you in the ear."

"Stop hating yourself. You were going to tell me something. Who's behind the racket?"

"I wish I knew. All I know is a few names of the guys we suspect of having a hand in it."

"They'll do."

"Oh, no! First let's hear what you have. Remember, please, that I'm the one who should know things. Of all the crazy things that happen, imagine a cop and a private eye chumming up like we do. Give out, Mike, sing me a song."

It was going to take a while, so I ordered some more coffee for us both, and when it came I started at the beginning and didn't stop until I brought Pat up to date—all but a few of the more intimate details. He didn't bother to jot anything down; his mind was filing away each item for future reference and I could see him laying the facts side by side, trying to make something of them.

When I finished he put a cigarette in his mouth and sat back thinking. When he fully absorbed everything, he said, "You have a nice accumulation of events, Mike. Now theorize."

"I can't," I told him. "There's no place to start."

"Start with Red."

"She was killed. That means she was killed for a reason."

"The same reason she had for being in the racket?"

"Maybe . . . or maybe the reason developed afterwards. What would a girl in her position have that would make it worthwhile being killed. Blackmail? I've thought of that, but it doesn't fit. Who would take her word in court? Maybe she had proof of someone's misconduct, but I doubt it. That's a tough racket and she wasn't mingling with anybody who counted. If she was playing against small stuff that same small stuff was tough enough to take care of her clean and simple without a lot of dummying. I have that feeling, as you call it, that the reason was a big one. I'm mad at somebody, Pat, and that person is going to answer to me for her death."

"Find the motive and you find the murderer," Pat said. "What about this Feeney Last character?"

"To me he looks like a punk. When he hit the city he went off on a spree and wound up in Red's neighborhood. He's the kind of a guy that would pull off a blackmail stunt all right. He said Red swiped his pay-off material and as long as she was what she was I wouldn't put it past her. But there's always another angle to that. He could have lost it, or whoever was being black-mailed paid off to see that it was destroyed. If Red was paid enough she might have lifted it from him while he was with her."

"Could he have killed her?"

"Sure, but not with any fancy trimmings. Feeney's no artist. He likes knives and guns. The only trouble is . . . he doesn't seem to expect to run into any opposition. No, Feeney didn't kill her. If he did, Red would have died quick and messy."

Pat dragged on the cigarette again. "What about your client, Mike?"

"Berin-Grotin? Hell, he couldn't have a hangnail without the papers knowing about it. He's from another generation, Pat. Money, position, good manners . . . everything you could expect of a gentleman of the old school. He's fiercely proud of his name, you know . . . constantly alert that nothing should cloud the escutcheon of his family. The old boy's no fool, either. He wanted protection so he hired Feeney, but he was ready to get rid of him as soon as the jerk got himself in trouble. It seemed to me that he was a little leery of Feeney, anyway. I got the impression that he was happy over what had happened up there in the cemetery."

"Which brings us to Lola. What there?"

"Nothing. She knew Red."

"Come on, Mike, she wasn't a complete nonentity, was she?"

"You can say that again." I let out a little laugh. "Marvellous personality, Pat. A body that'd make your hair stand on end. Lola's another of the decent kids you were speaking about, that went wrong. Only this one wised up in time."

"O.K., then let's go back a step. You told me the guy in the hash house and that Cobbie Bennett were afraid of something. Think around that."

"It doesn't think right, Pat. Shorty was a con and he was more than anxious to stay away from murder. Cobbie's in a racket where nothing looks good except dough. Anything could scare him. Both those guys scare too damn easily, that's why I can't attach too much significance to either one. I've thought it over a dozen times and that's how it shapes up."

Pat grunted, and I could feel his mind working it over, sorting and filing, trying for an answer. When none came he shrugged his shoulders and said, "The guys I know who may be part of the game are small fry. They run errands and do the legwork. I've made my own guesses before this, but I won't pass them on to you, for if I do you'll go hog wild and get me in a jam. Yourself, too, and like I said, they were only guesses with nothing to back them up."

"You usually guess pretty good, Pat. I'll take them."

"Yeah, but you're not going to get them. But I will do this: I'll see if I can make more out of it than guesses. We have ways of finding out, but I don't want to scare off the game."

"Good deal! Between the two of us we ought to make something of it."

Pat snubbed the butt out and stared into the ashtray. "Now for the sixty-four dollar question, Mike. You got me into this, so what do you expect me to do?"

"You got men at your fingertips. Let them scout around. Let

them rake in the details. Work at it like it was a murder and something will show up. Details are what we need."

"All right, Mike, my neck is out so far it hurts. I'm going against everything I know by attaching a murder tag to this and I expect some cooperation from you. All the way, understand?"

"You'll get it."

"And since I'm putting men on it, what *can* I expect from you?"

"Hell," I said, "I have a date with Lola tonight. Maybe she's got a girlfriend."

chapter five ▰▰▰▰▰▰▰▰▰▰▰▰

IT WAS NICE to get back to Lola. I found her apartment on West Fifty-ninth Street and walked up two flights to 4-C. Even before I could get my finger off the buzzer she had the door open and stood there smiling at me as if I were somebody. She was dressed in black again and there was no plunging neckline. There didn't need to be. It was easy to see that not even calico or homespun could be demure on her.

Her voice was soft as kitten's fur. "Hullo, Mike. Aren't you coming in?"

"Just try to keep me out."

I walked into the foyer, then followed her into a tiny livingroom that had been dressed up with all the gimcracks women seem to collect when they live alone. The curtains were starched stiff and the paint was fresh enough to have a lingering smell of turpentine. When I slid into an overstuffed chair I said, "New place?"

She nodded and sat down opposite me and began mixing highballs from a miniature bar set. "Brand new, Mike. I couldn't stay in . . . the old place. Too many sordid memories. I have a surprise for you."

"Yeah, what?"

"I'm a model again. Department store work at a modest salary, but I love it. Furthermore, I'm going to stay a model."

There was a newness about her as well as the apartment.

Whatever she had been was forgotten now and the only thing worth looking at was the future.

"Your former—connections, Lola. How about that?"

"No ghosts, Mike. I've put everything behind me. What people I knew will never look for me here and it's a thousand-to-one chance they'll run into me anywhere else. If they do I can pass it off."

She handed me the drink and we toasted each other silently. I lit up a Luckie and threw the deck to the coffee table and watched her while she tapped one on a fingernail. As she lit it her eyes came up and caught me watching her.

"Mike," she said, "it was nice last night, wasn't it?"

"Wonderful." It had been—very.

"But tonight you didn't come up . . . just for that, did you?"

I shook my head slowly. "No. No, it was something else."

"I'm glad, Mike. What happened was awfully fast for me. I— I like you more than I should. Am I being bold?"

"Not you, Lola. I'm the one who was off on the wrong foot. You got under my skin a little bit and I couldn't help it. You're quite a gal."

"Thanks, pal." She grinned at me. "Now tell me what you came up for. First, I thought you were only fooling about coming to see me and I got kind of worried. Then I thought maybe I was only good for one thing. Now I feel better again."

I hooked an ottoman with my toe and got it under my feet. When I was comfortable I dragged in on the butt and blew smoke out with the words: "Nancy was killed, Lola. I have to find out why, then I'll know who. She was in the oldest racket in the world. It's a money racket; it's a political racket. Everything about it is wrong. The only ones who don't give a damn whether school keeps or not are the girls. And why should they? They're as far down as they can go and who cares? So they develop an attitude. Nothing can hurt them, but they can hurt others very easily . . . if they wanted to. I'm thinking of blackmail, Lola. Would Nancy have tried a stunt like that?"

Her hand was shaking so she had to put the glass down. There were tears in her eyes, too, but she managed a rueful smile and brushed them away. "That was rough, Mike."

"It wasn't meant for you, kid."

"I know, I'm just being silly. No, I don't think Nancy would do that. She might have been a—been no good, but she was honorable. I'd swear to that. If she wasn't what she was she could have been a decent woman. As far as I know she had no vices, but, like I told you, she had a reason for doing what she did. Perhaps it was the money. I don't know. It *is* a quick way to get rich if you have no moral scruples."

"Supposing money was her reason. Any idea why she might have needed it?"

"That I can't tell you. We had no confidences, merely a bond that held us together."

The circle was getting me dizzy. "Look, let's go back further. Go back to the call-girl system. Who ran it?"

For the first time her face went white. She looked at me with fear in her eyes and her lips tight against her teeth. "No, Mike!" Her voice was barely audible. "Keep away from them, please."

"What's scaring you, honey?"

It was the way I said it that made her shrink back into her seat, her fingers digging into the arms.

"Don't make me tell you things I don't want to remember!"

"It isn't things you're afraid of, Lola. It's people . . . what people? Why does it scare you to think of them?"

I was leaning forward now, anxious, trying to make something out of every word she spoke. She was hesitant at first, turning her head from side to side as though someone else could be listening.

"Mike . . . they're vicious. They don't care what they do. They . . . wreck lives . . . as easily as they'd spend a dollar. If they knew I ever said anything they'd kill me. Yes, they would. It wouldn't be the first time, either!"

It might have been Pat talking. The fear left her face and anger took its place, but there was still a quiver in her voice.

"Money is all they're after and they get it. Thousands . . . millions . . . who knows. It's dirty money, but it's good to spend. It isn't like the houses . . . it's bigger. One tight little group has it so organized nobody else can move, and if you try to operate alone something happens to you. Mike, I don't want anything to happen to me!"

I got up and sat on the arm of her chair, then ran my fingers through her hair, "Nothing's going to happen, baby. Keep talking . . . all of it."

For an answer she buried her face in her hands and sobbed uncontrollably; I could afford to wait. In five minutes she was cried out, but still shaking. There was a haunted look in her eyes that went with the tenseness in her shoulders and her nails had drawn blood from her palms. I lit another butt and handed it to her, watching while she sucked on it gratefully, taking the smoke down deep, seeking a relief of some sort.

Then she turned those haunted eyes on me and said, "If they find out I told you . . . or anybody, anything at all, they'll kill me, Mike. They can't afford to have people talk. They can't afford to have people even suspect. I'm afraid! And what could you do . . . it's been going on forever and it will keep going on as long as there are people. I don't want to die for something like that."

I picked my words carefully because I was getting mad again. "Kid," I told her, "you don't know me very well. You don't, but there are plenty of guys who do. Maybe they're able to scare the hell out of decent citizens, but they'll drop a load when I come around. They know me, see? They know damn well I won't take any crap from them, and if they get tough about it they'll get their guts opened up for them. I got a gun and I've used it before . . . plenty. I got a license to use it, which they don't have and if somebody gets killed I go to court and explain why. Maybe I catch hell and get kicked out of business, but if *they* pull the trigger they sit in the hot seat. I'm calling the plays in this game, kid. I like to shoot those dirty bastards and I'll do it every chance I get and they know it. That's why they scare easy.

"And don't you worry about anything happening to you. Maybe they'll know where it came from, but they won't do anything about it, because I'm going to pass the word that I want somebody's skin and the first time they get rough they'll catch a slug in the front or back or even in the top of the head. I don't care where I shoot them. I'm not a sportsman. I'd just as soon get them from a dark alley as not, and they know it. I play it their way, only worse, and somebody is going to worry himself into a grave over it."

My hand was resting on her shoulder, and she turned her head and kissed my fingers. "You're kind of wonderful, even if you do tell me yourself," she said.

The haunted look in her eyes was gone now.

Lola took another drag on the cigarette and snubbed it out, then reached for the glasses. When they were filled she handed me mine and we touched them briefly and drank deep. She finished hers with one breath in between, then set it back on the table. She was ready to talk now.

"Nobody seems to know who's behind the system, Mike. It may be one person or it may be several. I don't know the details of the pay-off, but I do know how the racket operates. It isn't a haphazard method at all, and you'd probably fall flat on your face if you knew who was involved. Right now there are some girls with an amazing social standing who were, at one time, no better than me. They got out in time. They made the right contacts between 'appointments' and married them.

"You see, the real call-system is highly specialized. The girls are of only the highest calibre. They must be beautiful, well educated, with decorum enough to mingle with the best. Their 'clients' are the wealthy. Generally an appointment means a weekend at some country estate or a cruise along the coastline on some luxurious yacht. Of course, there are other appointments less fancy, but equally as lucrative, as when somebody wants to entertain a business associate. Apparently tactics like that pay off to the extent that the money involved means nothing.

"A girl is carefully investigated before she is approached to take part in the racket. It starts when she is seen around town too often with too many men. In the course of her travels she meets other girls already in the racket who seem to have everything they want without having to do much to earn it. These acquaintances ripen into easy friendships and a few hints are passed and the girl begins to take the attitude of why should she do the same things for free when she can get paid for it.

"So she mentions the fact and introductions are made to the right people. She is set up in a nice apartment, given an advance and listed in the book as a certain type. When a party wants that type he calls, or makes the arrangement with an in-between, and you're off on your date. Whatever gifts the girl gets she is allowed to keep and some of them make out pretty well. The money that is paid for her services is passed in advance and the girl gets a cut from that, deposited to her account in a bank.

"Oh, it's all very nice and easy, a beautiful deal. There aren't any ties on the girl either. If she happens to run across someone she cares for, she's free to quit the racket and get married, and she can expect a juicy bonus for the time in service. That's one reason why there's no kick-back. The girls never talk because they can't have anyone know of their associations, and the system won't force them to stay because there's nothing more dangerous than a hysterical woman.

"But there are times when one of the girls becomes dangerous. She can develop a conscience, or take to drink and find herself with a loose tongue, or get greedy and want more money on the threat of exposure. Then the system takes care of itself. The girl simply disappears . . . or has an accident. If we hear of it, it's a lesson to us to do one thing or another . . . keep quiet or get out . . . and keep quiet then, too.

"I learned my lesson well. When I got careless and became a disease carrier I lost my place in the system. Oh, they didn't mention the fact . . . one of the other girls did. I suddenly had an expensive apartment on my hands and no income, so I cashed in what I had and moved on down the ladder. I was too ashamed to go to a doctor and I didn't know what else I could do, so I started drinking. I met some more people again. Those people didn't care what I had. They got me a room in a house and I was in business again. It took me a long time to get smart, but I did, and I went to the hospital. After I came out the house was gone, Nancy was dead and you were there."

She slumped back in the chair and closed her eyes as though she were exhausted. I said, "Now some names, Lola."

Her eyes were mere slits, her voice practically a whisper. "Murray Candid. He owns some night clubs, but he's always at the Zero Zero Club. He is the contact man I met. He made all the arrangements, but he isn't the top man. The town is worked in sections and he covers the part I worked. He's dangerous, Mike."

"So am I."

"What are you going to do now?"

"I don't know, kid. You can't go in and accuse a guy without proof, even if you know you're right. The law's on his side then. I need proof . . . what could I use to stick him?"

"There are books, Mike . . . if you could find them. They'd love to do without books because they'd be almost clean then, but they can't because they can't trust each other."

"Would this Candid guy have them?"

"I doubt it. He'd keep temporary records, but the big boy has the important data."

I stood up and finished my drink. "O.K., Lola, you did fine," I said. "It's something to work on . . . a place to start. You don't have to worry because I won't bring you into it. Sit tight around here and I'll call you from time to time. There are still things you probably know that I don't, but I can't tell what they are yet."

Lola came up from her seat slowly and slid her arms around my waist. She laid her head on my shoulder and nuzzled her face into my neck. "Be careful, Mike, please be careful."

I tilted her chin up and grinned at her. "I'm always careful, sugar. Don't worry about me."

"I can't help it. Maybe I ought to have my head examined, but I'm crazy about you."

She stopped me before I could speak by putting her finger on my lips. "Not a word, Mike. Let me do the liking. I'm no good and I know it. I'm not going to mess into your life a bit so you can let me go on liking you if I please. No obligations, Mr. Hammer, I'll just sit on the side lines and throw kisses your way, and wherever you are you'll always know that where I am is a girl you'll always have to yourself. You're a nice guy, you big lug. If I had the sense to lead a normal life you'd never get away from me."

This time I shut her up. Her body was a warm thing in my hands and I pressed her close to me, feeling tremors of excitement run across her back. Her lips were full and ripe, and whatever she had been was cleansed and there was no past for a brief instant. When I kissed her, her mouth was like a flame that fluttered from a feeble glow into a fiery torch.

I had to shove her away roughly before everything else was forgotten. We stood there, two feet apart, and my voice didn't want to come. When it did I said, "Save yourself for me, Lola, just me."

"Just you, Mike," she repeated.

She was still there in the middle of the room, tall and beautiful, her breasts alternately rising and falling with a craving neither of us could afford, when I went out the door.

The Zero Zero Club was a cellar joint off Sixth Avenue that buried itself among the maze of other night spots with nothing more than two zeros done in red neon to proclaim its location. But it was doing a lively business. It had atmosphere; plenty of it . . . that's why they called it the Zero Zero. Both visibility and ceiling were wiped out with cigar smoke.

Down the stairs a cauliflower-eared gent played doorman with a nod, a grunt and an open palm. I gave him a quarter so he wouldn't remember me as a piker. The clock on the wall read eleven-fifteen and the place was packed. It wasn't a cheap crowd because half of them were in evening clothes. Unlike most joints, there was no tinsel or chrome. The bar was an old solid mahogany job set along one wall, and the tables were grouped around a dance floor that actually had room for dancing. The orchestra was set into a niche that could double as a stage for the floor show if necessary.

The faces around me weren't those of New Yorkers—at least

those of the men. Most could be spotted as out-of-towners looking for a good time. You could tell those who had their wives along. They sat at the bar and tables sipping drinks, with one eye on the wife and the other on the stray babes, wondering why they had been talked into taking the little woman along.

Yeah, the atmosphere was great, what you could see of it. The Zero Zero Club took you right back to the saloons of a western mining camp, and the patrons loved it. Scattered throughout the crowd were half a dozen hostesses that saw to it that everyone had a good time. I got a table back in one corner that was partially screened by a group of potted plants, and waited. When the waiter came over I ordered a highball, got it and waited some more.

Five minutes later a vat-dyed blonde hostess saw me there and undulated over to my table.

She gave me a big smile from too-red lips and said, "Having fun?"

"Not so much."

I leaned over and pulled out a chair for her. She looked around once and sat down with a sigh, using me as a breather between courses. I signalled the waiter and he brought her a Manhattan without asking. She said, "It isn't tea, friend. You're paying for good whisky."

"Why tell me?"

"The farmers out there have read too much about hostesses drinking cold tea. They always want to taste it. So we don't drink at all, or have a small cola."

There wasn't much sense fooling around with chitchat here. I finished my drink, called for another, and while I waited I asked, "Where's Murray?"

The blonde squinted her eyes at me a moment, checked her watch and shook her head. "Beats me. He hardly ever gets here before midnight. You a friend of his?"

"Not exactly. I wanted to see him about something."

"Maybe Bucky can help you. He's the manager when Murray's away."

"No, he couldn't help me. You remember Nancy Sanford, don't you?"

She set her glass down easily and made little rings on the table with the wet bottom. She was looking at me curiously. "Yes, I remember her. She's dead, you know."

"I know. I want to find out where she lived."

"Why?"

"Look, honey. I'm an insurance investigator. We have reason

to believe that Nancy Sanford was actually somebody else. She was using a phoney name. Oh, we know all about her, all right. But if she was this somebody else, we have a policy on her we'd like to clear up. The beneficiaries stand to collect five thousand dollars."

"But why come here?"

"Because we heard she used to work here."

There was a sad look in the blonde's eyes this time. "She was working in a house. . . ."

"It burned down," I interrupted.

"Then she moved over to an apartment, I think. I don't know where, but . . ."

"We checked there. That's where she lived before she died. Where was she before either one?"

"I don't know. I lost track of her after she checked out of here. Once in a while someone would mention seeing her, but I never did. I'm afraid I can't help you at all. Perhaps Murray could tell you."

"I'll ask him," I said. "Incidentally, there's a reward that goes with finding the place. Five hundred bucks."

Her face brightened at that. "I don't get it, Mac. Five bills to find out where she lived and not who she was. What's the angle?"

"We want the place because there's someone in the neighborhood who can positively identify her. We're having trouble now with people putting in phoney claims for the money, and we don't want to lead them to anybody before we get there first, see?"

"In other words, keep all this under my hat until I find out. If I can find out."

"You got it."

"I'll buy it. Stop back again soon and see if I learned anything. I'll ask around." She finished her drink and turned on her "having fun?" smile, waved to me and went back to the rest of the party. The kid wanted money, all right. She'd keep it under her hat and ask around. It wasn't exactly what I had come for, but it might give me a lead sometime.

Five drinks and an hour and a half later Murray Candid came in. I had never seen him before, but when the waiters found something to do in a hurry and the farmers started chucking hullos over, looking for a smile of recognition that might impress the girlfriend, I knew the boss had come in.

Murray Candid wasn't the type to be in the racket at all. He was small and pudgy, with red cheeks, a few chins and a face that had honesty written all over it. He looked like somebody's favorite uncle. Maybe he *was* the one to be in the racket at that. The two guys that trailed him in made like they were friends of the family, but goon was the only word that fitted them. They both were young, immaculately dressed in perfectly tailored tuxedos. They flashed smiles around, shook hands with people they knew; but the way they kept their eyes going and the boss under their wing meant they were paid watch-dogs. And they were real toughies, too. Young, strong, smart with a reckless look that said they liked their job. I bet neither one of them smoked nor drank.

The band came on then, with a baby spot focused on the dance floor, and as the house lights were dimming out I saw the trio turn into an alcove over in the far corner. They were heading for the place I wanted to see—Murray Candid's office. I waited through the dance team and sat out a strip act, then paid my check and picked my way through the haze to the alcove and took the corridor that opened from it.

There were two doors at the far end. One was glass-panelled and barred, with EXIT written across it. The other was steel, enamelled to resemble wood, and there was no door-knob. Murray's office. I touched the button in the sill and if a bell rang somewhere I didn't hear it, but in a few seconds the door opened and one of the boys gave me a curt nod.

"He's in. Your name, please?"

"Martin. Howard Martin from Des Moines."

He reached his hand to the wall and pulled down a house phone. While he called inside I felt the door. It was about three inches thick and the interior lining was of some resilient sound-proofing material. Nice place.

The guy hung up and stepped aside. "Mr. Candid will see you." His voice had a peculiar sound: toneless, the ability to speak without accentuating any syllable. Behind me the door closed with a soft click and we were in an anteroom that had but one decoration—another door. This time he opened it and I stepped inside at once.

I was half-way across the room before I heard a cough and looked to see another door about to close. The place was lousy with doors, but not a sign of a window.

Murray Candid was half-hidden by a huge oak desk that occupied most of the wall. Behind his head were framed pictures of his floor-show stars and studio photos of dozens of celebrities, all autographed. There was a couch, a few easy chairs and a small radio and bar combination. That was all, except for the other goon that was stretched out on the couch.

"Mr. Candid?"

He rose with a smile and stretched out his hand. I took it, expecting a moist, soft clasp. It wasn't. "Mr. Martin from, ah, Des Moines, is that correct?"

I said it was.

"Sit down, sir. Now, what can I do for you?"

The goon on the couch hardly turned his head to look at me, but he rasped, "He's got a gun, Murray."

He didn't catch me with my pants down at all. "Natch, brother," I agreed, "I'm a cop. Des Moines police." Just the same, it annoyed the hell out of me. The coat was cut to fit over the rod and you weren't supposed to notice it. These guys were pros a long time.

Murray gave me a big smile. "You officers probably don't feel dressed unless you're armed. Now, tell me, what can I do for you?"

I sat back and lit a cigarette, taking my time. When I flicked the match into a wastebasket I was ready to pop it. "I want a few women for a party. We're having a convention in town next month and we want things set up for a good time."

If there was supposed to be a reaction it was a flop. Murray drew his brow into a puzzled frown and tapped his fingers on the desk. "I don't quite understand. You said . . . girls?"

"Uh-huh."

"But how can I . . .?"

I let him have a grin that was half-leer. "Look, Mr. Candid, I'm a cop. The boys come back home from a big time in the city and tell us all about it; they said you were the one to see about getting some girls."

Murray's face seemed genuinely amazed. "Me? I admit I cater to the tourist crowd, but I can't see the connection. How could I supply you with girls. I'm certainly not a—a——"

"I'm just doing like the boys said, Mr. Candid. They told me to come to you."

He smiled again. "Well, I'm afraid they were mistaken, Mr. Martin. I'm sorry I can't help you." He stood up, indicating that the conversation was over. Only this time he didn't offer to shake hands. I told him so-long and put on my hat, letting the goon open the doors for me.

The boy gave me a polite nod when I went out and let the door hiss shut behind me. I didn't know what to think, so I went to the bar and ordered a drink. When I had it in my hand, cold and wet, I watched the bubbles fizz to the top and break.

Cold and wet. That was me all over. There wasn't a floor or

wall safe in the office, nothing, for that matter, where my nice Mr. Candid could hide any books if he kept any. But at least it was an elimination, supposing there *were* some books. If they weren't here they were somewhere else. Good enough . . . it was an angle worth playing.

When I finished the drink I got my hat and got clear of the joint. The air above ground wasn't very clean, but it smelled like a million bucks after the fog in the Zero Zero. Directly across the street was the Clam Hut, a tiny place that specialized in seafood and had a bar where a guy could keep one eye on his beer and the other on the street. I went in and ordered a dozen of the things and a brew and started the wait.

I had it figured for a long one, but it wasn't. Before I had half the clams down Murray Candid came out of his place alone and started walking west. His pace was more businesslike than leisurely, a cocky strut that took him up the street at a good clip. I stayed on the other side and maybe fifty feet behind him. Twice he stopped to gas with some character and I made like I was interested in a menu pasted on the window of a joint. Not that I was worried about being seen . . . there were too many people making the rounds for me to be singled out.

By the time we had walked half-way across town and cut up a few streets I figured where Murray was heading. There was a parking lot down the street on my side and he jay-walked across, angling towards it, and I had to grin. Even if he *did* spot me I had the best excuse in the world. My heap was parked in the same lot, too.

I let him go in, then trailed him by twenty feet. The attendant took my ticket and handed me my car keys, trying to keep his eyes open long enough to take his tip.

My car was down in the corner and I hugged the shadows going to it. There was no sound except that of my feet in the gravel. Somewhere a door should be slamming or a car starting, but there was nothing. There was just the jungle noise of the city hanging in the air, and the stillness you would find when the tiger crouches ready to spring.

Then I heard it, a weak cry from between a row of cars. I froze, then heard it again and in a second I was pounding towards the spot.

And I ran up a dark alley of chrome and metal into the butt end of a gun that sent me flat on my face with a yell choked off in my throat. There was no time to move, no room to move before I was being smashed across the head and shoulders. Feet were plowing into my ribs with terrible force and the gun butt came down again and again.

I heard the sounds that got past my lips, low sounds of pain that bubbled and came out in jerks. I tried to reach up to grab something, anything at all, then a hard toe lashed out and into my cheek and my head slammed against metal and I couldn't move any more at all.

It was almost nice lying there. No pain now. Just pressures and the feeling of tearing flesh. There was no sight, no feeling. Somewhere a monotonous-sounding voice said, "Enough this time."

Then another voice argued a little quietly that it wasn't enough at all, but the first voice won and the pounding ceased, then even the hearing stopped. I lay there, knowing that I was asleep, yet awake, dreaming a real dream but not caring at all, enjoying a consciousness that was almost like being dead.

chapter six

IT WAS THE first slanting rays of the sun that wakened me. They streaked across the rooftops and were reflected from the rows of plate-glass windows in the cars, bringing a warmth that took away the blessed numbness and replaced it with a thousand sharp pains.

My face was in the gravel, my hands stretched out in front of me, the fingers curled into stiff talons that took excruciating effort to straighten. By the time I had dragged myself out from under the car the sweat that bathed my face brought down rivulets of dried blood, mixing with the flesh as cuts reopened under the strain.

I sat there, swaying to the beat of thunder in my head, trying to bring my eyes into focus. Perception returned slowly, increasing proportionately with the ache that started all over and ended nowhere. I could think now, and I could remember, but remembering brought a curse that split my swollen lips again so I just sat there and thought.

The weight that was dragging me down was my gun. It was still there under my arm. A hell of a note. I never had a chance to get to it. What a damn fool I was, running into a trap like that! A plain, stupid jerk who deserved to get his head knocked off.

Somehow my watch survived with nothing more than a scratched crystal, and the hands were standing at 6:15 a.m.; I had been there the whole night. Only then did it occur to me that the cars parked there were all-nighters. Those boys had picked their spot well, damn well!

I tried to get up, but my feet didn't move well enough yet, so I slumped back to the gravel and leaned against the car gasping for breath. It hurt like hell to move even so much as an inch. My clothes were a mess, torn by their feet and the gun. One whole side of my face had been scraped raw and I couldn't touch the back of my head without wincing. My chest was on fire from the pounding my ribs had taken. I couldn't tell if any were broken . . . they felt as if there wasn't a whole one left.

I don't know how long I sat there sifting the gravel through my fingers and thinking. It might have been a minute, maybe an hour. I had a little pile of stones built up at my side, then I picked them off the pile and flicked them at the chrome wheel hub of the car opposite me. They made ping sounds when they hit.

Then one of them didn't make a ping sound and I reached out and picked it up to try again. But it wasn't a stone. It was a ring. A ring with a peculiar fleur-de-lis design, scratched and battered where it had been ground into the gravel and trampled on.

Suddenly I wasn't tired anymore. I was on my feet and my lips were split into a wide-mouthed grin because the ring I was holding was the redhead's ring and somebody was going to die when they tried to get it away from me. They were going to die slower and harder than any son of a bitch had ever died before, and when they died I'd laugh my goddamn head off!

My car was where I had left it, against the back wall. I opened the door and climbed in, easing myself into a comfortable position where it wouldn't hurt so much to drive. I jerked it out of the slot and turned around, then when I went past the gate I threw two bucks into the window to pay for the overtime. The guy took the dough and never even looked up.

I thought I could make it home. I was wrong. Long before I had reached the Stem the knifing pains in my side started again and my legs could barely work the pedals. Somehow, I worked the heap across town without killing anybody, and cut up Fifty-sixth Street. There was a parking space outside Lola's place and I swung into it and killed the motor. When a couple of early risers got past me I squirmed out of the seat, slammed the door and clawed my way into the building.

The steps were torture. I was wishing I could die by the time I got to the door and punched the bell. Lola opened the door and her eyes went wide as saucers.

"My God, Mike, what happened?" She grabbed my arm and steered me inside where I could slide down on the couch. "Mike . . . are you all right?"

I swallowed hard and nodded. "Yeah. It's O.K. now."

"I'll call a doctor!"

"No."

"But, Mike . . ."

"I said no, damn it! Just let me rest up. I'll be all right." The words came out hard.

She came over and unlaced my shoes, then lifted my feet on to the cushions. Except for her worried expression she was at her loveliest best, with another black dress that looked painted on. "Going somewhere, kid?"

"To work, Mike. I won't now."

"The hell you won't," I said. "Right now, that's more important than me. Just let me stay here until I feel better. I'm in one piece as far as I can tell and it isn't the first time I've been this way either. Go on, beat it."

"I still have an hour yet." Her hands went to my tie and unloosened it and took it off. She got me out of the wreck of my jacket and shirt without doing me much damage and I looked at her with surprise. "You got a professional touch, honey," I told her.

"Patriotism. I was a nurse's aid during the war. I'm going to clean you up."

She lit a cigarette and stuck it between my lips, then went out to the kitchen and I heard water splashing in a pan. When she came back she carried a bowl of steaming water and an armful of towels.

My muscles were beginning to stiffen up and I couldn't take the butt out of my mouth until she did it for me. When I had a couple of deep drags she snubbed it out, then took a pair of scissors and cut through my undershirt. I was afraid to look, but I had to. There were welts along my side that were turning a deep purple. There were spots where the flesh was bruised and torn and still oozing blood. She pressed above the ribs, searching for breaks, and even that gentle pressure made me tighten up. But when she got done we both knew there were no sharp edges sticking out and I wasn't quite ready for a cast or casket yet.

The water was hot and bit deep, but it was soothing, too. She wiped my face clean and touched the cuts with a germicide, then patted it dry. I just lay there with my eyes closed and let her rub my shoulders, my arms, then my chest, grimacing when she hit a soft spot. I was almost asleep again when I felt her fingers open my belt, then my eyes opened half-way.

I said, "Hey . . . nix . . . ," but it was an effort to speak and she wouldn't stop. It hurt too much to move and there wasn't a damn thing I could do but let her undress me, so I closed my eyes again until even my socks were on the pile in the chair and her fingers were magic little feathers that were brushing the dirt and the pain away in a lather of hot, soapy water being massaged in with a touch that was almost a caress.

It was wonderful. It was so good that I fell asleep at the best part and when I woke up it was almost four o'clock in the afternoon and Lola was gone. There was a sheet over me and nothing else. At the table by my elbow was a pitcher of water with nearly melted ice cubes, a fresh deck of Luckies and a note.

When I reached out and plucked it from the ashtray I wasn't hurting so bad. It said: "Mike, Dear, Stay right where you are until I get home. All but your unmentionables went in the trash can anyway, so don't expect to run off on me. I took your keys and I will pick up clothes for you from your apartment. Your gun is under the sofa, but please don't shoot it off or the super will put me out. Be good. Love, Lola."

The clothes! Hell, she couldn't have thrown them away . . . that ring was in the pocket! I tossed back the sheet and pushed myself up and began to ache again. I should have stayed there. My wallet, change and the ring were in a neat little huddle on the table behind the water pitcher.

But at least I was in a position to reach for the phone without an extra effort. I dialed the operator, asked for information, then gave her my client's name and address. The butler took the call, then put me on an extension to Mr. Berin-Grotin.

His voice was cheery and alive; mine sort of crackled. "Mike Hammer, Mr. Berin."

"Oh! Good evening, Mike. How are you?"

"Not what you'd call good. I just had the crap beat out of me."

"What—what was that?"

"I fell for a sucker trap and got taken but good. My own fault . . . should have known better."

"What happened?" I heard him swallow hard. Violence wasn't up his alley.

"I was steered to a guy named Murray Candid. I didn't get what I was looking for, so I followed him to a parking lot and got jumped. One of the punks thought he was being kind when he let me go on living, but I'm beginning to doubt his kindness. I'd be better off dead."

He exploded with, "My goodness, Mike . . . perhaps you had better not . . . I mean . . ."

If I put a laugh in my voice I was faking it. "No dice, Mr. Berin. They hurt me, but they didn't scare me. The next time I'll be on my toes. In one way I'm glad it happened."

"Glad? I'm afraid I don't enjoy your viewpoint, Mike. This sort of thing is so . . . so uncivilized! I just don't understand. . . ."

"One of the bastards was the guy who killed the redhead, Mr. Berin."

"Actually? Then you have *made* progress! But . . . how do you know?"

"He dropped the ring that he took from Red's finger before he killed her. I have it now."

There was eagerness in his voice this time. "Did you see him, Mike? Will you be able to identify him?"

I hated to give the bad news. "The answer is no to both. It was darker than dark and all I saw was stars."

"That *was* too bad. Mike . . . what do you intend doing now?"

"Take it easy for a while, I guess." I was beginning to get tired. I said, "Look, I'll call you back again later. I want to think about this a little while, O.K.?"

"Certainly, Mike. But please . . . this time be more careful. If anything should happen to you I would feel directly responsible."

After I told him to quit worrying, I hung up and flopped back on the couch again, this time with the phone in my hand so I could do my talking on my back. I dialed Pat at his office, was told he had left, then picked him up at home. He was glad to hear from me and kept quiet while I went through the story for him. I gave him everything except the news of the ring.

Even at that he guessed at it. "There's more to it than that, isn't there?"

"What makes you think so, Pat?" I asked him.

"You sound too damn satisfied for a guy who was cleaned."

"I'm satisfied because I think I'm getting into something now."

"Who were the guys . . . Candid's boys?"

"Could be, Pat, but I'm not sure. Maybe they had it figured

out and got there ahead of us, but maybe that wasn't it at all. I have another idea."

"Go on."

"When I went in his office someone was just leaving . . . someone who saw me. I was following Murray and the other was following me. When he knew where Murray was going he scooted ahead in a cab with some boys and waited."

Pat added, "Then why didn't Murray horn in when things started to pop?"

"Because he's in a position . . . I think . . . where he has to keep his nose clean and strictly out of anybody else's business. If he knew what was going to happen he didn't care. Of course, that's figuring that he had nothing to do with it in the first place."

"Could be," Pat agreed. "If we were working on more than a vague theory we could move in and find out for sure. Listen . . . you're getting more help with this than you expected."

He made me curious. "Yeah?"

"Uh-huh. The kid who ran into her with the car was insured. The company is positive of the cause of death and wants to pay off. Right now they're tracking down the next of kin."

"Did you tell them anything, Pat?"

"Not a thing. They looked for themselves, got the official police report and that's that. I didn't want to make a fool of myself by telling them I let a jerky private eye talk me into murder. Those boys are pretty sharp, too. And something else. I've had tracers out on your pal."

"Pal! . . . who?"

"Feeney Last."

I was tingling all over and I damn near dropped the phone. Even the mention of the greaseball's name set me off.

Pat said, "He's got a good rep . . . as far as we can tell. Not even an arrest. We found two cities on the West Coast where he was known. In both cases he was employed by businesses who needed strong-arm boys. Feeney's a trouble kid, but good. The local cops informed me that the lesser punks in town were scared stiff of him because, somehow, they got the notion he was a gunslinger from the old school and would go out of his way to find something to shoot at. Right out of a grade-B western. Feeney played it smart by carrying a license for the gun and the only time he was ever fingerprinted was for the application."

"But nothing you can hang on him, eh?"

"That's right, Mike."

"What happened to the license he had for the job with Berin-Grotin?"

"He even thought of that. It was returned in the mail. The lad isn't taking any chances."

"So now he sticks to a chiv."

"What?"

"You don't need a license for a knife, chum, and Feeney likes cold steel."

My back was aching and I was getting too tired to talk any more so I told Pat I'd call him later and hung up. I put the phone on the table and rolled into a more comfortable position, then lay there a while trying to think. The redhead's ring was in my hand and her face was in my mind, but now all the hard lines were gone and it was a pretty face that could smile with relief and anxiety.

The ring was large enough to fit my little finger. I slipped it on.

At half-past four I heard a key slide into the lock and I came out of my half-sleep with a gun in my hand and the safety kicked off. Across the knuckles was a thin red line of blood where I had caught on a nail under the sofa going for it.

But it was only Lola.

My expression scared the hell out of her and she dropped the package she was carrying. "Mike!"

"Sorry, kid. I'm jumpy." I dropped the rod on the table.

"I . . . brought your clothes." She picked up the package and came over to me. When she sat down on the edge of the sofa I pulled her head down and kissed her ripe lips.

She smiled, running her fingers across my forehead. "Feel all right?"

"Fine, honey. That sleep was just what I needed. I'll be sore for a few days, but nothing like somebody else is going to be. It's been a long time since I was jumped like that, but maybe it did me good. I'll keep my eyes open the next time and sink a slug into somebody's gut before I run up a blind alley."

"Please don't talk like that, Mike." A little worried frown tugged at the corners of her eyes.

"You're a beautiful girl."

She laughed, a throaty laugh of pleasure. Then she stood up quickly, grabbed the sheet and flicked it off. "You're beautiful, too." She grinned devilishly.

I let out a yell and got my toga back and she only laughed again. When she started for the kichen I opened the package and took out my clothes. I was knotting my tie when she called that soup was on. I walked into the kitchen and she said, "I like you better the other way."

"Quit being so fresh and feed me."

I sat down at the table while she pulled pork chops from the pan and filled my plate. It wasn't the kind of a meal you'd expect a city girl to cook . . . there was just too much of it. I thought that maybe the whole works was for me until Lola piled it on her plate, too.

She caught my expression and nodded towards the stove. "That's how I grew so big. Eat up and you'll get the same way."

I was too hungry to talk at the table until I was finished. She topped it with some pie, gave me seconds while she finished her own, then took a cigarette I offered her.

"Good?" she asked.

"The best. Makes me feel almost new."

She dragged on the cigarette hungrily. "Where away, Mike?"

"I'm not sure. First I want to find out why I was worked over. Then I want to find out who did it."

"I told you Candid was dangerous."

"That fat monkey isn't dangerous, honey. It's his dough. That's dangerous. It hires people to get things done he can't do himself."

"I still wouldn't trust him too far. I've heard stories about Murray that weren't nice to hear. You looked for the books, didn't you?"

"No," I told her. "He wouldn't keep them in sight. I looked for a place he could stash 'em, but there wasn't even a sign of a safe in the joint. No, that trip was just reconnoitering. Those boys aren't dummies by a long shot. *If* they have any books—and I still think it's a big 'if'—they're someplace that will take a lot of heavy digging to root out."

I leaned back in the chair and pulled on the butt. It still hurt to sit up straight, but I was getting over it fast. "Supposing I do get something on Candid . . . where does it get me? It's a killer I want, not a lot of sensational stuff for the papers."

This time I was talking to myself rather than to Lola, trying to get things straight in my mind. So far it was just a jumble of facts that could all be important, but it was like going up an endless ladder. Each rung led to the next one with the top nowhere in sight.

"So the redhead was killed. She was killed for a reason. She had a ring on while she was alive, but it wasn't there when she was dead. It was a beautiful kill, too . . . how the hell it happened

I don't know, but I'll find out. The killer has a perfect cover-up and it's listed as accidental death. If she was pushed somebody would have seen her get it, or even in his damn drunken stupor the kid who ran her down would have remembered it. But no . . . he thought he did it all alone and took off from there. He remembered enough to cover it up so he would have remembered if she were pushed. But what dame is going to take her ring off? Women aren't like that! And one of those jokers who jumped me had it, so it makes it a legitimate kill and not an accidental one.

"Bats! If it wasn't murder, nobody would give a damn any more, but why did she have to get it? What made her so all-fired important that she had to die? So Feeney Last had his blackmail junk lifted . . . yet you say she wouldn't buy that kind of stuff. She was hot, according to another guy, and nobody would go near her. Feeney's a tough character and has the bull on guys to the extent that they won't talk. But what are they afraid of? Getting beat up, maybe? Or getting shot? Hell's bells, nobody can go around shooting people up in this town. Sure, it's a rough place to be in trouble, but pull a rod and see how far you get! Maybe you can scare somebody for a while, but after a bit the scare wears off and you got to prove you're not kidding. So who would be the guy that could do it and get away with it? Just one—a jerk who thinks he's got enough protection to carry him through."

For the first time Lola interrupted. "Is that Feeney Last?"

"Maybe. He's supposed to be a gunman. But he's still no dummy. He proved that by turning in his gun license when he lost his job with Berin."

She agreed with a slight nod. "You think, then, that he might have killed Nancy?"

"That, sugar, is something I'd give a lot to know," I answered. "It's a screwy affair, but there's something pretty big at the bottom of it. For somebody to be wiped out, the cause has to be a heavy one. There's too many ways of doing business without being eligible for the chair—unless the risk is worth it."

"And Nancy was a good risk?"

"What do you think, Lola?"

"You might be right. At least you have her death to prove you're right, but poor Nancy . . . I still can't see why she could be so important . . . to have to die. I told you she had a secretive side . . . but still, if she weren't what she was, Nancy could have been a decent kid. By that I mean she had all the aspects of quality. She was a gentle, kind, considerate . . . oh, you know what I mean."

"But she seemed to be in the business for a reason. Correct?"

"That's right."

"You don't think she was getting back at a man . . . doing it to spite a former lover or something?"

"Of course not! She had more sense than that!"

"All right, I was just asking."

She leaned on the table and looked at me, long and hard. Her voice was husky again. "Mike . . . just what kind of people are they that kill?"

"Dirty people, kid," I said. "They have minds that don't care anymore. They put something else above the price of human life and kill to get it, then kill to keep it. But no matter what it is it's never worth the price they have to pay for it."

"You've killed people, Mike."

I felt my lips pulling back. "Yeah, and I'm going to kill some more, Lola. I hate the lice that run the streets without even being scratched. I'm the guy with the spray gun and they hate me, too, but even if I am a private cop I can get away with it better than they can. I can work the bastards up to the point where they make a try at me and I can shoot in self-defense and be cleared in a court of law. The cops can't go that far, but they'd like to, don't forget it. People are always running down the police, but they're all right guys that are tied down by a mass of red tape and they have to go through channels. Sure, there are bum cops, too—not many of them. They get disgusted maybe, because things happen that they have to let happen, yet any one of them boils over inside when he sees mugs get away with stuff that would hang a decent citizen."

Her eyes were looking past me now with an eager, intense look. "What can I do to help?" she whispered.

"Think, Lola. Think over every conversation you ever had with Nancy. Think of the things she might have said or implied. See if you can pick out just one thing that may be important. Then tell me."

"I will, Mike, I will. But how will I know if it's important?"

I reached over and laid my hand on hers. "Look, kid . . . I hate to bring it up, but you were in a money racket. It was a no-good racket, but it brought in the dough. Anything that might have interfered with that income to certain people could be a cause of death, even if it was something they just suspected. When you think of anything that *could* be that something, you're getting warm."

"I think I understand, Mike."

"Good girl!" I stood up and stuffed my butts back into my pocket. "You know where to call me. Don't go out of your way for anything unless it's mighty important. I don't want you to get on anybody's list."

Lola pushed her chair back and came to me. Together we walked towards the door. "Why?" she asked. "Do I mean that much to you, Mike?"

She was lovelier than ever, tall and graceful, with a hidden depth to her eyes as she looked at me. I could feel the firm roundness of her pressing against my body and I folded my arms around her. "You mean more than you think to me, Lola. Anybody can be wrong. Not everybody can be right again. You're one in a million."

Her eyes swirled in a film of tears then, and her face was soft as she touched her cheek to mine. "Please don't, darling. I've got so far to go before I'll ever be right for anyone. Just be nice to me . . . but don't be too nice. I—I don't think I could stand it."

There was no answering her with words. I reached for her mouth and felt the fire in her lips that ran like a fuse down her body until she curved inward against me with a fierce undulation, and I knew my hands were hurting her and she didn't care.

It was hard to push her away; it was hard for her to let go. I shoved my hat on my head and squeezed her hand without saying anything, but we both knew of the promise it held and I went out of there walking as if there had been no last night at all and my body wasn't stiff and sore nor my face battered and swollen.

chapter seven ▆▆▆▆▆▆▆▆▆▆▆▆▆▆▆▆▆▆

THERE WAS A parking ticket under the windshield wiper of the car, staring me in the face. I pulled it off, read it over and stuck it in the glove compartment. Another few hours to be wasted in a police court. I sat there a minute, my hands on the wheel, trying to line things up in order. Hell, there was no order. I was like the chairman of a meeting trying to rap for quiet with a rubber gavel, when the whole assembly was on its feet shouting to be heard.

Red's ring was there on my finger, a tiny circlet of gold that had slipped around until it looked like a wedding band. I straightened it, held it out in the dimming light to look at it better, wishing the thing could speak. All right, maybe it could—maybe. I jammed the car in gear, pulled up to Ninth Avenue and turned south.

By the time I reached the downtown section most of the smaller shops had closed. I cruised the avenue slowly, looking for a jewelry shop run by an old friend of mine. I found it by luck, because the front had been done over and the lights were out and he was getting ready to go home.

When I banged on the door he twitched the shade aside, recognized me with a big grin and unlocked the door. I said, "Hullo, Nat. Got time for a few words?"

He was all smiles, a small pudgy man who took prosperity in the same alpaca coat and shiny pants as he did the leaner years. His hand was firm around mine as he waved me in. "Mike," he laughed, "for you I have plenty of time. Come in the back. We talk about old times."

I put my arm around his shoulders. "About times now, Nat. I need some help."

"Sure, sure! Here, sit down." He pulled out a chair and I slid into it while he opened a bottle of wine and poured a drink for us both.

We toasted each other, then spilled it down. Good wine. He filled the glasses again, then leaned back and folded his hands across his stomach.

"Now, Mike, what is it that I can do for you? Something not so exciting like the last when you made me be bait to trap those chiselling crooks, I hope."

I grinned and shook my head as I pulled off the redhead's ring and handed it to him. Automatically, his fingers dipped into his vest pocket and came up with a jeweler's glass that he screwed into his eye.

I let him turn it over several times, look at it carefully, then told him, "That's the job, Nat. Can that ring be traced?"

He was silent for several minutes as he examined every detail of the band, then the glass dropped into his palm and he shook his head. "Antique. If it has a peculiar history maybe. . . ."

"No history."

"That is too bad, Mike. It is very important that you should know?"

"Very."

"What I should say, I don't know. I have seen many rings of this type before, so I am quite certain I am right. However, I am just one man. . . ."

"You're good enough for me, Nat. What about it?"

"It is a woman's ring. Never inscribed as far as I can see, but maybe an inscription has been worn off. Notice the color of the gold, see? The composition of the metal is not what is used today to harden gold. I would say that this ring is perhaps three hundred years old. Maybe more, even. It is more durable than most rings, otherwise the pattern would have been worn off completely. However, it is not as pretty as the gold nowadays. No, I am sorry, Mike, but I cannot help you."

"The pattern, Nat; know anybody who could trace that?"

"If you found the company that made it . . ." He shrugged. "Their records might go back. But see . . . three hundred years means it was made in the Old Country. What with the war and the Nazis. . . ." He shrugged again, hopelessly this time. I nodded agreement and he went on, "In those days there were no big companies, anyway. It was a father-and-son business. For a ring like this it was a special order and that is all."

I took the ring back and slipped it on my finger again. "Well, Nat, it was a good try just the same. At least I cut down a lot of unnecessary footwork."

His pudgy face warped into a quizzical frown. "Do not the police have methods to bring out inscriptions that have been worn off, Mike?"

"Yeah, they can do it, but suppose I do find a set of initials. Those would belong to the original owner, and since it's a woman's ring, and no doubt passed down through the family, how often would the name have changed? No, the inscription wouldn't do much good, even if I did find the original owner. It was just an idea I had." If it hadn't been an antique it might have solved the problem. All it did was set me up in the other alley wondering where the hell I was.

I stood up to leave and stuck my hand out. Nat looked disappointed. "So soon you must go, Mike? You could come home with me and maybe meet the wife. It has been a year since the last time."

"Not tonight, Nat. I'll stop back some other time. Say hullo to Flo for me, and the kids."

"I'll do that. Them kids, they be pretty mad I don't bring you home."

I left him standing there in the doorway and climbed back in the car. Red's ring was winking at me, and I could see it on her finger again as she graced a battered old coffee cup.

Damn it! . . . I had the key and I couldn't find the lock! Why the devil would a killer take this thing off her finger? What good was it to him if it couldn't be traced? And who was the goon that carried it around with him until he lost it? Hell's bells, it couldn't be a red herring across the path or it never would have turned up again!

My mind was talking back to me then. One part of me drove the car away from the curb and stopped for red lights. The other part was asking just why I got beat up at all? Yeah, why did I? And why was it planned so nicely? Oh, it was planned quick, but very, very nice! I wasn't important enough to kill, but I did warrant a first-class going-over. A warning?

Sure! What else?

Murray and his boys didn't know me from Adam, but they spotted a phoney in my story and figured me as a wise guy, or somebody with an angle, so it was a warning to steer clear. And one of the goons who had done this warning had killed the redhead or was tied up with it some way.

I was uptown without knowing it. I had crossed over and was following a path I had taken once before, and when I slowed down outside the parking lot I knew what I was after.

I made a U-turn and parked at the curb across the street, then walked to the corner, waited for the light to change and strolled to the other side. I couldn't be sure if the attendant was the same one who was on the other night; at least this one was awake.

He opened the window when I rapped on it and I said, "Anybody lose anything in here recently, bud?"

The guy shook his head. "Just a guy what lost his car keys. Why, find something?"

"Yes, but there's no money involved. A little trinket a dame might like to have back. Just thought I'd ask."

"Check the ads in the papers. If she wants it bad enough maybe she'll advertise. Got it with you?"

"Naw. Left it home."

He said, "Oh!" shut the window and went back to his chair. I started to walk away, but before I reached the building that bordered the lot a car turned in and its lights cut a swath down the rows. I saw a pair of legs jump back from the glare and duck in among the cars.

I stopped flat.

The legs had gone up the same row I had run into last night.

My heart started doing a little dance and the other part of me was saying go to it, that's why you came here in the first place. Maybe you got your hands on something, only don't botch it up this time. Take it easy and keep your eyes open and a gun in your fist.

The car turned its lights out and a door slammed. Feet started walking back towards the gate, and a fat guy in a Homburg said something to the man in the booth, laughed and angled across the street. I waited a second, then put my hands on the fence and hopped over.

This time I didn't take any chances. I stayed between the cars and the wall, keeping my head down and my footsteps soft. Twice the gravel crunched under my shoes and I stopped dead, listening. Two rows up I heard a soft shuffling sound and a shoe kick metal.

I reached inside my coat and loosened the gun in the holster.

The guy was too busy to hear me. He was down on one knee sifting the gravel through his fingers, his back towards me. I stood up from the crouch I was in and waited as he inched his way back.

Another car turned into the lot and he froze, holding his position until it had parked and the driver had left the lot, then he went back to his sifting. I could have reached out and touched him then.

I said, "Lost something?"

He tried to get up so fast he fell flat on his face. He made it on the second try and came up swinging, only this time I was ready. I smashed one into his mouth and the guy slammed against the car, but that didn't stop him. I saw his left looping out and got under it and came into him with a sharp one-two that doubled him over. I didn't try to play it clean. I brought my knee up and smashed his nose to a pulp and when he screamed he choked on his own blood.

I bent over and yanked him up and held him against the car, then used my fist on his face until his hands fell away and he was out with his eyes wide open.

When I let go he folded up and sat in the gravel staring into the dark.

I lit a match and cupped it near his face, or what was left of it. Then I swore under my breath. I had never seen the guy in my life before. He was young, and he might have been handsome, and the clothes he wore weren't the ready-made type. I swore again, patted his sides to see if he had a rod, and he didn't. Then I lifted his wallet. It was hand-tooled morocco, stuffed with dough, a few cards and a driver's license issued to one Walter Welburg. Out of curiosity I tapped his pockets and there weren't any keys in them. Maybe the guy *was* looking for that.

Damn! I blew the match out, went down past the cars and hopped over the fence feeling like a dummy.

I left the car where it was and headed across town on the same walk that had taken me into the trap, only this time I wasn't tailing anybody. The street was getting lousy with taxis, and the evening crowd was just beginning to show its face. Already the dives had their doors open like gaping mouths swallowing the suckers, and the noise of a dozen bands reached the sidewalk. Ahead of me the Zero Zero Club was a winking eye of invitation, and the flunky was opening taxi doors, picking himself a hatful of quarters. He didn't see me duck in, so he lost a two-bit tip.

The hat-check girl gave me a bored smile and a ticket, then when she saw the marks on the side of my face she grinned, "What's the matter . . . she say no and you didn't believe her?"

I grinned right back. "I was fighting her off, kid."

She leaned over on the counter and propped her chin in her hands, giving me a full view of what went on down the neckline of her blouse. It was plenty. "I don't blame her for fighting for it, feller," she said. "I'd fight, too."

"You wouldn't have to."

I blew her a kiss and she made like she caught it and stuffed it down her neckline. Her eyes got dark and sensuous and she said, "You have to come back for your hat. Maybe I'll trade you . . . even."

A couple in evening clothes came in and she turned to them while I went inside. Most of the tables around the dance floor were filled, and a baby spot played over a torch singer who was making more music with her hips than her throat. Neither Murray nor his boys were anywhere around so I found a table in the back and ordered a highball and watched the show.

The waiter brought the drink and before I sipped it half-way through a hand went through my hair and I looked up to see my blonde hostess smiling at me. I started to rise but she pushed me back and pulled the other chair out and sat down.

"I've been looking for you," she said.

She leaned over and took a cigarette from my pack and tapped it on the table. When I lit it for her she blew a stream of smoke into the air. "You spoke of five hundred bucks the last time . . ."

"Go on."

"Maybe I can deliver."

"Yeah?"

"But not for five hundred bucks."

"Holding me up?"

"Could be."

"What have you got? Five hundred can get me a lot of things."

The torch singer was coming to the end of the number and the blonde took another drag on the butt, then rubbed it out in the ashtray. "Look, get out of here before the lights go on. I'll be through here at one o'clock and you can pick me up on the corner. We can go up to my place and I'll tell you about it."

"O.K."

"And you better bring more than five hundred."

"I'll see what I can do," I told her.

She smiled at me and laid her hand over mine. "You know, you seem like a pretty nice joe, mister. See you at one."

I didn't wait for the lights to go on. I threw the rest of the drink down, waved the waiter over and paid him, then went out to the foyer. The kid at the hat window gave me a mock scowl. "You're too eager. I don't get off for hours yet."

I threw a half in the cup while she retrieved my hat, and when she handed it to me she took that stance that showed me where she put the kiss I threw at her. And she didn't mind my looking.

I took out a bill, folded it lengthwise and poked it down there out of sight. "If the boss doesn't find it you can keep it."

"He'd never think of looking there," she grinned devilishly. She stood up and there was no trace of the green at all. "But you can have it back if you want to chase it."

This time I pushed my hat on my head and started for the door. Hell, I was no Indian giver. But maybe the Indians had something if they played games like that.

My watch said I had a long while to wait, so I cut over two blocks and found a bar that had a few empty stools. I ordered a beer and a sandwich twice, then started in to enjoy a mild evening, but I kept drifting back to the blonde. Something was going to cost me and I hoped it was worth it. Five hundred bucks, just half my fee. It took me two hours to make up my mind, then I went to the phone booth in the back, dropped in a nickel and asked for long-distance.

The operator came on and I gave her my client's number. The gnome squeaked out a hullo, told me Mr. Berin had retired for the night, but when I insisted I wanted to speak to him, put the phone down and shuffled off muttering to himself. I had just finished putting in another handfull of dimes when Mr. Berin gave me a sleepy "Good evening."

"This is Mike, Mr. Berin. Sorry I had to disturb you, but something important has come up."

"It did? Is it something I should know?"

"Well, yes. It concerns money."

He chuckled, the tiredness out of his voice. "Then I'm glad to be of use to you, Mike. What is it?"

"I may have a line on the redhead. For a dodge I offered a dame five bills. . . ."

"What was that?"

"Five hundred bucks . . . if she did some successful snooping. Apparently she did. But now she wants more. Shall I go for it or do I try to get it out of her some other way?"

"But . . . what is it? Did she . . .?"

"She wouldn't talk. Wants me to meet her later."

"I see." He thought a moment. Then, "What do you think, Mike?"

"It's your show, Mr. Berin, but I'd say look it over and if it's worth anything, buy it."

"Then you think it's worth something?"

"I'd take that chance. The dame's a hostess in the Zero Zero and she knew Nancy. At least she knew her quite a while ago and it looks as if that's where the bones lie buried."

"Then do it, Mike. The sum is trivial enough . . . at least to me. You, er, look it over, and do what you think is best."

"O.K., but she wants the dough right away."

"Very well. You write her a check, then call me, and I'll wire that amount to your bank so it will be there in the morning to cover it."

"Right. I'll buzz you later. Take it easy."

I stuck the phone back in its cradle and went back to the bar. At twelve-thirty I gathered up my change, whistled at a cab outside and had him drive me over to where I left my heap.

It was five minutes past one when I cruised past the corner and saw the blonde coming towards the curb. I rolled the window down and yelled for her to hop in. She recognized me, opened the door and slid on to the seat.

"Nice timing. Where to?" I pulled away from the curb and got into the line of traffic going uptown.

"Straight ahead. I have a place on Eighty-ninth."

She had a beat-up overnight bag between her feet and I indicated it with a nod. "That the stuff?"

"Uh-huh." The blonde opened her purse and pulled out a lipstick. There wasn't much light, but she seemed to be getting it on straight. When I stopped for a red I took a good look at her. Not a bad number at all. The curves looked real and in some spots too good to be true.

She turned her head and looked straight into my eyes, then let a little grin play with the corners of her mouth. "Curious?"

"About the bag?"

"About me?"

"I'm always curious about blondes."

She waited to see what I was going to do then, but the light turned green and I rolled with the traffic. At Eighty-ninth I turned over until she told me to stop, then pulled into the curb and killed the engine. When I opened the door for her I picked up the bag and let her step out.

"You wouldn't think of running off with that, would you?" She hooked her arm in mine.

"I thought of it, then I got curious."

"About the bag?"

"About you." Her hand squeezed mine and we walked to the apartment. At the door she fished out a key, opened it, then led me upstairs two flights to a front apartment and flicked on the light.

It was an old high-ceilinged affair done over in a welter of curves and angles the designers call modern. Each wall was a different color of pastel with tasteful but inexpensive pictures in odd groupings. The furniture looked awkward, but it was comfortable enough.

When I threw my hat over a lamp the blonde said, "Shouldn't we introduce ourselves? I'm Ann Minor." She shrugged out of her coat, looking at me peculiarly.

"Mike Hammer, Ann. I'm not an insurance investigator. I'm a private cop."

"I know. I was wondering if you were going to tell me." Her laugh was one of relief.

"Who told you that?"

"Me. I knew damn well I had seen you or your picture somewhere before. It didn't come to me until tonight, though."

"Oh!"

"It was your picture."

"Was that why you shooed me out of the joint so fast?"

"Yes. Murray isn't fond of cops, not even private ones."

"What has a legitimate businessman got to be afraid of?"

"Say that again and leave out one word."

I didn't. I sat there on the arm of a chair and watched her. She hung her coat in a closet, took my hat from the lamp and put it on the shelf and closed the door. Then she turned around fast and walked over to me.

"I'm no kid," she said. "I don't think I ever was a kid. You weren't in the club looking for a good time and I knew it. When you mentioned Nancy I had a pretty good idea what you were after, and I get the wim-wams when I think about getting mixed up in anything. Tell me something, how good are you?"

I had a .45 out and pointed at her stomach almost before she finished the sentence. When she had a good look at it I slid it back in the leather and waited. Her eyes were wider than before.

"I hate Murray. There are other guys I hate too, but he's the only one I can point to and say I'm sure I hate. Him and his butt boys."

"What have *you* got against him?"

"Don't play coy, Mike. He's a rat. I don't like what he does to people. You know what he is or you wouldn't be here now."

"What did he do to you?"

"He didn't do anything to me. But I saw what he did to other kids. He pays my salary and that's all, but I have to stand by and watch what happens in that place. He's a smooth talker, but he always gets what he wants."

My fingers were itching to get to the bag on the floor and she knew it. Ann smiled again, reading my mind, then she tapped the wallet in my inside pocket. "Bring the money?"

"As much as I could get."

"How much?"

"That depends on what's in it. What are you going to do with the stake?"

"Take a long trip, maybe. Anything to get away from this town. I'm sick of it."

I walked over and picked up the bag. It wasn't very heavy. There were paint splotches across the top and long scuffed streaks down the side. Maybe here was the answer. Maybe this was the reason the redhead was killed. I ran my hand across the top, tried the catch, but it was locked. "Yours?" I asked her.

"Nancy's, Mike. I came across it this morning. We have a small prop-room behind the bandstand that's full of junk. I was hunting for some stuff for the dressing-room when I came across it. There was a bus tag on the handle with Nancy's name on it and I knew it was hers."

"How did it get in there?"

"A long time ago Murray remodelled the place. Probably Nancy was off at the time and when they cleaned out they tossed all the odds and ends in the prop-room. I imagine she figured she lost it."

Ann went outside and came back with a bottle and two glasses. We both had a drink in silence, then she filled the glasses again and settled into the corner of a sofa and watched me. The way she sat there reminded me of a cat, completely at ease, yet hiding the tension of a coiled spring. Her dress was loose at the shoulders, tapering into a slim waist that was a mass of invitation. She sipped her drink, then drew her legs up under her, letting me see that not even the sheerest nylon could enhance the firm roundness of her thighs. When she breathed, her breasts fought the folds of her dress and I waited to see the battle won.

"Aren't you going to open it?" Her voice was taunting.

"I need an ice pick . . . a chisel—something." It wasn't easy to speak.

She put her drink on the end table and uncoiled from the couch. She passed too close and I reached out and stopped her, but I didn't have to make the effort because she was in my arms, her mouth burning on mine, pulling herself so close that I could feel every part of her rubbing against me deliciously. I tangled my fingers in her hair and pulled her head back to kiss her neck and shoulders, and she moaned softly, her body a live, passionate thing that quivered under my hands.

When I let her go her eyes were smouldering embers ready to flame; then she gave me that quick smile that showed her teeth white and even, and she drew her tongue deliberately over full, ripe lips that wanted to be kissed some more, until they glistened wetly and made me want to reach out and stop her again.

Before I could, she went out through an archway and I heard her rummage around in a drawer, pawing through cutlery until she found what she wanted. The drawer closed, but she didn't come right back. When she did the dress was gone and she had on a clinging satin robe and nothing else, and she passed in front of the lamp to be sure I knew it.

"Like it?" she asked me.

"On you, yes."

"And on someone else?"

"I'd still like it."

She handed me one of those patented gadgets that was supposed to solve every household mechanical difficulty, even to a stuck window. I took it while she fished in my pocket for a cigarette and fired it from a table-lighter. She blew the smoke in my face and said, "Can't that wait?"

I kissed the tip of her nose. "No, honey, it can't."

When I turned around and stuck the edge of the gadget under the clasp of the lock she walked away from me. I pried at the metal until the tool bent in my hand, then reversed it and used the other end. This time I was in luck. The hasp made a sharp snapping sound and flew open. The outside snaps were corroded where the plating hadn't peeled off, but they opened easily enough; but before I could open the bag the light snapped off and there was only the dim glow from the table-lamp at the other end of the room.

Ann whispered, "Mike?"

I looked around to bark something at her, but nothing would come out because Ann had thrown the robe over the back of the couch and stood there in the center of the room, a living statue in high-heeled shoes smoking a cigarette that reflected orange-colored lights from her eyes. She stood with her feet spread apart and her hand on her hip, daring me with every muscle in her body.

She stood there until I grabbed her and squeezed so hard she breathed into my mouth, then she bit me on the neck and slid out of my hands to the couch. I had to follow her.

My hand shook when I reached for a cigarette. Ann grinned up at me, and her voice was soft, almost musical. "I was wondering if I could be important to anybody any more."

I kissed her again. "You can be important any time. You happy now that you steered me right off the track?"

"Yes."

She didn't say a word when I stood up and went back to the table, but her eyes followed me every second. I dragged on the cigarette again, but it caught in my chest and I put it out. This time I laid the case down and flipped open the lid.

I whistled softly under my breath. The bag was crammed full of baby clothes, every one brand-new. I fingered them slowly, the tiny sweaters, boots, caps, other things I had no name for. At the bottom of the bag were two soft cotton blankets, neatly folded, waiting to be used.

A dozen thoughts were going through my head, but only one made any sense. The redhead was a mother. Somebody was the father. A wonderful, beautiful set-up for blackmail and murder if ever I saw one. Only Nancy wasn't that kind of a girl. Then there was one other thing. All the clothes were new. Some of them showed where price tags had been glued on. What about that?

I ran my hand through the pockets of the lining. The ones on the side brought up an assortment of safety pins, a lipstick and a small mirror. The lid pocket held a folder of snapshots. I opened them out and looked at them, seeing a Nancy different from the one I had known. Here was a young girl, sixteen perhaps, on the beach with a boy. Then another with a different boy. Several had been taken on an outing or a picnic, but Nancy seemed to show no special preference for any one fellow.

She was different then, with the freshness of a newly opened flower. There were no harsh lines in her face, no wise look about the eyes. She was new then, new and lively. Her mouth and eyes seemed to smile at me, as if knowing that some day these pictures would be here in front of me. There were only two that showed her hands clearly, but in each one I saw the same thing. She was wearing her ring.

I looked over the background carefully, hoping to spot some landmark, but there was none. They showed only stretches of water or sand. When I flipped them over there were no marks indicating date or the outfit that developed them. Nothing. Now my blind alley had a wall at the end. A nice high wall that I couldn't get over without a ladder.

I heard Ann speak to me then. She asked, "Does it help you?"

An idea was beginning to jell and I nodded. I pulled out my checkbook and wrote on it, then laid the slip on the table. I made up my mind as to the value, but just the same I queried, "What are you asking for it?"

When she didn't answer I turned around and looked at her, still lying there naked and smiling. Finally she said, "Nothing. You've paid for it already."

I snapped the bag shut and went over to the closet for my hat, then opened the door. The redhead had been right all along the line; but Mr. Berin still owed me five hundred bucks, to be deposited in the morning. Ann would get that trip she wanted.

I winked at her and she winked back, then the door clicked shut behind me.

chapter eight ▄▄▄▄▄▄▄▄▄▄▄

I DIDN'T GET to sleep that night. Instead, I laid the contents of the bag out in front of me and sat there smoking one cigarette after another, trying to figure out what it meant. Baby clothes. Some pictures. A battered overnight bag. All of them the redhead's. How long ago? Where? Why?

There was beer in the refrigerator and I finished off bottle after bottle, sipping it slowly, thinking, letting my mind wander back and forth over the facts I had. They were mighty little when you tried to put them all together.

The sun came up over the windowsill chasing the night out, and I remembered to call Mr. Berin. He answered the phone himself and this time the sleep was in my voice. "Mike again."

"Good morning! You're up early."

"I haven't been to bed yet."

"You'll pay for lack of self-discipline in later years, young man."

"Maybe," I said tonelessly, "but tonight you pay. I left my friend a check for five hundred bucks."

"Fine, Mike. I'll take care of it at once. Did you learn anything from your—shall I say, source?"

"Not a damn thing, but I will, I will."

"Then I can consider the money well spent. But please be careful. I don't want you running into any more trouble."

"Trouble's an occupational hazard in this racket, Mr. Berin. I can usually take care of it one way or another. But what I got here won't mean trouble for me. I haven't got the angle lined up yet, but I can see it coming."

"Good! You've got my curiosity aroused now. Is it a secret or can you . . .?"

"No secret. I have an overnight bag that had been packed with baby clothes. That and a folder of pictures."

"Baby clothes?"

"They were the redhead's—or her baby's."

He mulled over it a moment and admitted that it presented quite a puzzle, quite a puzzle. I agreed with him.

"What do you intend to do now?" he asked me.

"I don't know. I'm too sleepy to do much, that's for sure."

"Then go to bed by all means. Keep in touch with me whenever you think I can be of use."

I said all right and hung up. My eyes were burning holes in my head and too much beer had me stumbling over things. I took a last drag on the butt and clinched it, then lay back on the couch and let the sleep come, wonderful, blessed sleep that pulled a curtain over all the ugly things and left me with nothing but a nebulous dream that had no meaning or importance.

There was a bell. It kept ringing insistently and I tried to brush it away like a fly and it wouldn't leave. Finally I opened my eyes and came back to the present with the telephone going off behind my head. I squirmed around and picked it up, wanting to throw it against the wall.

Velda said hullo twice and when I didn't answer right away, "Mike . . . is that you? Mike, answer me!"

"It's me, sugar. What do you want?"

She was mad, but there was relief in her voice. "Where the devil have you been? I've been calling every saloon in town all morning."

"I've been right here."

"I called there four times."

"I've been asleep."

"Oh, out all night again. Who was she?"

"Green eyes, blue hair, purple skin. What do you want, or aren't I the boss any more?"

"Pat called early this morning. Something to do with Feeney Last. He wants you to call him back when you can."

"Well, why didn't you say so!" I sat up quickly, my hand over the cut-off bar. "See you later, Velda. I'll buzz him right away."

I held the bar down, let it up and dialed police headquarters. The guy at the desk said yes, Captain Chambers had been in, but he wasn't now. No, he couldn't say where he was. Official business, and did I want to leave a message. I wanted to swear, but I couldn't very well so I told him never mind and hung up.

It was five minutes to twelve and the day was half-shot. I gathered up the baby clothes and folded them back into the bag, stuffing the photos in the same top pocket, then I went in and took a shower.

Right in the middle of it the phone rang again and I had to wade back into the living-room. It was Pat, but I didn't lace into him for dragging me out of the tub because I was too anxious to get the news.

He chuckled when I answered and said, "What kind of hours do you keep, pal?"

"If you knew you'd want to change jobs with me. Velda said you have something on Feeney. What gives?"

He got right down to cases. "When I put out feelers on him

they all came back negative. This morning I had one in the mail from the Coast, a return feeler from an upstate sheriff. It seems like Feeney Last answers the description of a guy who is wanted for murder. The only catch is that the guy who could identify him is dead and they have to go from the poop he gave them."

"That's something." I thought it over, knowing that a mug like Feeney wouldn't be hard to describe. A greaseball. "What are you going to do about it?"

"I wrote for the finer details. If it fits we'll put out a call for him. I had copies made of his picture on the gun license and forwarded them to the sheriff to see if Feeney could be identified there."

"At least it's handy to have, Pat. He can always be held for suspicion if we need him . . . and if we can find him."

"O.K., then, I just thought I'd let you know. I have a death on my hands and I have to do the report."

"Anybody we know?" I asked.

"Not unless you hang around the tourist traps. She was a hostess at the Zero Zero Club."

My hand tightened around the receiver. "What did she look like, Pat?"

"Bleached blonde about thirty. Nice looking, but a little on the hard side. The coroner calls it suicide. There was a farewell note in her handbag along with complete identification."

I didn't need to know her name. There might have been a dozen bleached blondes in the Zero Zero, but I was willing to bet anything I had I knew who this one was. I said, "Suicide, Pat?"

He must have liked the flatness of my words. He came back with, "Suicide beyond doubt, Mike. Don't try to steer this one into murder!"

"Was her name Ann Minor?"

"Yes . . . you . . . how did . . .?"

"Is the body in the morgue?"

"That's right."

"Then meet me there in twenty minutes, hear?"

It took me forty-five minutes to get there and Pat was pacing up and down outside the place. When he saw my face his eyes screwed up and he shook his head disgustedly. "I hope they don't try to keep you here," he said. "I've seen better-looking corpses than you."

He went inside, over to the slab where the body was laid out. Pat pulled back the sheet and waited. "Know her?"

I nodded.

"Anything to do with the Sanford case?"

I nodded again.

"Damn you, Mike. One day the coroner is going to beat your head off. He's positive she was a suicide."

I took the corner of the sheet from his hand and covered her face up again. "She was murdered, too, Pat."

"O.K., pal, let's go some place and talk about it. Maybe over lunch."

"I'm not hungry." I was thinking of how she looked last night. She had wanted to be important to someone. To me. She was important to someone else, too.

Pat tugged at my sleeve. "Well, I'm hungry and murder won't spoil my dinner any. I want to know how a pretty suicide like this can be murder."

There was a spaghetti joint a few blocks away so we walked over to it. Pat ordered a big lunch and I had a bottle of red wine for myself. After the stuff was served I started the ball rolling with, "What's your side of it, Pat?"

"Her name is Ann Minor . . . which you seemed to know. She worked for Murray Candid as a hostess four years. Before that a dancing career in lesser clubs, and before that a tour with a carnival as a stripper. Home life, nil. She had a furnished apartment uptown and the super said she was a pretty decent sort.

"The last few months she's been a little down in the dumps, according to her co-workers, but nothing to indicate positively a suicide. The farewell note said she was just tired of it all, life was a bore and she was getting no place, thus the Dutch act. The handwriting checked with the signature on other documents."

"Baloney!"

"No baloney, Mike. The experts checked it."

"Then they'd better check it again."

Pat let his eyes drop when he saw the set of my mouth. "I'll see that they do." He went back to his spaghetti, forked in a mouthful, then reviewed the case. "We reconstruct it this way. Just before dawn she walked down the pier that's being dismantled off Riverside Drive, removed her hat, shoes, jacket . . . laid them down on the planks with her bag on top, and jumped in.

"Apparently she couldn't swim. However, even if she could, she would have drowned because her dress was caught on some bolts below the surface and held her there. About eight-thirty this morning some kids came along to do some fishing and they spotted her stuff first, then her. One of the kids called a cop who called the emergency squad. They didn't bother to work on her."

"How long had she been dead?"

"Roughly, about four to five and a half hours."

I poured another glass of the wine out and spilled it down. "I was with her until two forty-five last night," I said.

Pat's eyes blazed and he stabbed his fork into the pile of spaghetti. It could have been good, but he wasn't tasting it. "Go on," he answered.

"She found an overnight bag that belonged to Nancy. She gave it to me, because before that I had asked her to poke around a little for some history on the redhead. The bag was full of baby clothes, all unused. We went up to her apartment."

He nodded. "Was she frightened . . . or remorseful?"

"When I left her she was a pretty happy girl. She was no suicide."

"Damn it, Mike! I . . ."

"When is the autopsy due?"

"Today . . . right now! You got me dancing again! I wouldn't be surprised to find her full of arsenic, either!" He threw his fork down and pushed away from the table and went over to a wall phone. When he came back he grunted, "Two hours and there'll be an official report. The coroner's pulling the autopsy now."

"I bet he won't change the verdict."

"Why?"

"Because somebody is pretty damn smart."

"Or dumb. Maybe it's you that's dumb, Mike."

I lit a cigarette and grinned at him, thinking of something somebody told me once about persons that drown. "I'm not so dumb, kid. Maybe we'll give the coroner a shock. I liked that blonde."

"You think this is mixed up with Nancy, don't you?"

"Yup."

"Positive?"

"Yup."

"Then get me proof, Mike. I can't move without it."

"I will."

"Yeah, when?"

"When we get our hands on someone who knows enough to talk."

Pat agreed with a flicker of his eyebrows. "I can see us making him talk."

"You don't have to," I reminded him. "When that party gets

to you he'll be so happy to talk he'll spill his guts. You don't have to do a thing."

"You're going to squeeze it out him, I betcha?"

"Damn right, friend."

"You know what you're bucking, of course."

"Yeah, I know. Guys that are paying heavy for protection. Guys who can take care of themselves if that protection doesn't go through. Money boys with private armies maybe."

"We're on touchy ground," Pat grated.

"I know it. We're going to run into a lot of dirt unless I miss my guess. There will be people involved who will raise hell. That's where I have the edge, Pat. They can *make* you smell their stink. Me, I can tell 'em to blow it. They can't take my job away and they can't scare me because I can make more trouble than they can shake a stick at."

"You're telling me!"

Pat went back to his spaghetti while I finished the bottle of wine and I could almost hear the gears clicking in his head. When he finished he put down his napkin, but before he could enjoy a smoke the proprietor called him to the phone. He kicked his chair back and walked away.

Five minutes later he came back wearing a grin. "Your murder theory is getting kicked around. The men rechecked on the note. There is absolutely no doubt that the Minor girl wrote it. We had confirmation from several sources. Not a trace of forgery. You can't break it, Mike."

I scowled at the empty glass in my hand. At least I was smart enough to know that the police labs mean what they say when a positive statement is issued.

Pat was watching me. "This takes it right out of my department, you know."

"There's still the autopsy."

"Want to go watch it?"

I shook my head. "No, I'll take a walk. I want to think. Supposing I call you back later. I'd like to know what's on the report."

"O.K." Pat checked his watch. "Give me a ring in a couple of hours. I'll be at the office."

"One other thing . . ."

Pat grinned. "I was wondering when you were going to ask it."

He was a sharp one, all right. "I haven't got the time, nor the facilities for a lot of leg-work right now. How about having your wire service check the hospitals for me. See if they ever had a

Nancy Sanford as a maternity case. Get the name of the man, family or anything else, will you?"

"I would have done it anyway, Mike. I'll get it off right away."

"Thanks."

I took the check and paid it, then said so-long to Pat outside the door. For a while I strolled up the street, my hands in my pockets, whistling an aimless tune. It was a nice day, a lovely day . . . a hell of a day for murder.

Suicide? Not on your life! They worked it so sweet you couldn't call it murder—yet. Well, maybe you couldn't, but I could. I was willing to bet my shirt that the blonde had asked the wrong questions in the wrong places. Somebody had to shut her up. It fitted, very nicely. She was trying to earn that five hundred. She got too much for her money.

When I made a complete circle around the block I ambled over to the car and got in. For a change, the streets were half empty, and I breezed uptown without having to stop for a red light. When I got to Ninety-sixth Street I turned towards the river, found a place to park and got out.

A breeze was blowing up from the water, carrying with it the partially purified atmosphere of a city at work. It was cool and refreshing, but there was still something unclean about it. The river was grey in color, not the rich blue it should have been, and the foam that followed the wake of the ships passing by was too thick—almost like blood. In close to shore it changed to a dirty brown trying to wash the filth up on the banks. It was pretty if you only stopped to look at it, but when you looked too close, and thought enough, it made you sick.

She removed her hat, shoes, jacket . . . laid them down on the planks with her bag on top, and jumped in. That would be a woman's way of going it . . . a woman who had given suicide a lot of thought. Not a sudden decision, the kind that took a jump and tried to change her mind in mid-air. A suicide like this would be thought out, all affairs put in order to make it easy for those who did the cleaning up—if it was a suicide. Neat, like it had been planned for a long, long time.

My feet had carried me down to the grass that bordered the water, taking me over towards a pier that was partially ripped up. They had a watchman on it now in a brand-new shack. I was conscious of a face curling into a nasty smile. It was still there when the watchman came out, a short fat guy with a beer bottle in his hand. He must have picked me for another cop because he gave me the nod and let me walk down the runway to the end without bothering to ask questions.

I could hear the music going off in my head. It was always like that when I began to get ideas and get excited. I was getting a crazy, wild idea that might prove a point and bring Pat into it after all, then the crap would really fly. Heads would roll. They'd set up the guillotine in Times Square and the people could cheer like at a circus, then slink back and get ready to start the same thing all over again.

There was an empty peanut-butter jar with dead worms in it on top of the piling. I shook the things out and wiped the jar clean with a handkerchief until it shone, then threw the handkerchief away, too. I climbed down the supports and filled the jar nearly full before I worked my way back, then screwed the lid back on and went back to the street.

Instead of calling Pat I drove straight to his office. He shook hands and invited me down the hall, where he picked up a report sheet, then took me back to his cubicle. He handed me the form. "There it is, Mike. She died by suffocation. Drowning. We called the time right, too. No doubt about it now."

I didn't bother to read the report. Instead I tossed it back on his desk. "The coroner around, Pat?"

"He's downstairs, if he hasn't left already."

"Call and find out."

He was about to ask a question, but thought better of it and reached for the phone. After a minute he said, "He's still there."

"Tell him to wait."

"It better be good. He's pretty cranky. Besides, he's with the D.A."

"It's good."

Pat told the operator to hold him, his eyes never leaving mine. When he hung up he leaned forward over his desk. "What is it this time?"

I laid the jar on his desk. "Have him analyze that."

He picked up the jar and scrutinized it, shaking it to bring the sediment to the top, frowning into the murky ooze inside the jar. When he saw I wasn't going to explain it he got up abruptly and went out the door and I heard the elevator take him downstairs.

I went through half a deck of Luckies before I heard the elevator stop again. His feet were coming towards the office fast and hard and I knew he was mad.

He was. He slammed the jar on the desk and swung around with anger written across his face. "What kind of a steer did you call that? He analyzed all right . . . he told me it was nothing but water filled with every kind of mess there was. Then he wanted to know the whys and wherefores. I looked like a damn fool. What was I going to say, that a private cop is using the police for a workbench to figure out a crazy scheme? I didn't know what I expected to find in there, but I thought it would be better than that!"

"Why didn't you ask the coroner if it was the same stuff he found in her lungs? Not her stomach, mind you, but her lungs. When you drown you suffocate because that little valve in your throat tightens up the air passage to keep anything from running into your lungs. It doesn't take much to suffocate a person—just enough water to make that little valve jam. There's water in the stomach, but very little in the lungs. Go ahead, ask him."

Pat's eyes were ready to pop. His teeth bared in an animal-like grin and he said, "You brainy bastard, you!"

He picked up the phone and called downstairs. The conversation didn't take more than a minute, but there was a lot of excited talk going on. He put the phone back and slid into his chair. "They're double-checking now, I think you called it."

"I told you that before."

"Don't go too fast, Mike. We have to wait for the report. Now tell it your own way."

"Simple, Pat. Ann Minor was drowned, most likely in her own place. Then she was tossed into the river."

"That means carrying the body out of the house without being seen, you know."

"What of it? Who's on the street at that hour? Hell, getting her out isn't the hard job. Dumping her wouldn't be a hard job either."

"There's only one catch: the suicide note."

"I got ideas on that, too."

Pat dropped his head in his hand. "You know I'm pretty smart. I've been tied up in police work as long as you have. I love it, I'm good at it. But you come up with the ideas. Do you think I'm getting too set in my ways any more? Am I reverting to type or something? What the hell is wrong with me, Mike?"

The only thing I could do was chuckle at him. "You aren't slowing up, kid. You just forget . . . sometimes a smart crook knows as much as a smart cop. You ought to start thinking like one of *them* sometimes. It helps."

"Nuts!"

"We have two murders now. They both looked like something

else. We haven't proved the first one, but this second shows you the kind of people you're up against. They aren't amateurs by a long shot."

Pat looked up. "You were talking about an idea you had. . . ."

"No dice. Get your own. This one's a little cock-eyed even for you. If it's what I'm thinking it's just another piece in the puzzle. Maybe it's even from a different puzzle."

The phone rang again and Pat answered it. His face stayed blank until he finished the conversation. He wasn't too happy. "My department has it now. The water in her lungs was clear. Traces of soap. She was drowned in a bathtub, probably. Not a sign of contamination."

"Then cheer up."

"Yeah, I'll break out in smiles. They're patting me on the back downstairs, but they want to know how I got wise. What the hell will I tell them?"

I pushed the chair back and stood up. "Tell 'em you made it all up out of your own two little heads."

When I left, Pat said damn, soft like, but he was grinning now.

And I was grinning because I wanted the police in on this thing. Where I was going was too much trouble for one person. Much too much—even for me. The cops had the boys and the guns. They had the brains, too. Pretty soon now those heads were going to roll.

I had my supper in the Automat before I went home. I loaded up a tray with everything they had and picked a table where I was alone and able to think. When I finished I felt better and kept thinking, over a cigarette. All the assorted pieces of the puzzle were clear in my mind, but I couldn't get them together. But at least they were clear and if I couldn't see the picture on the puzzle I knew one thing . . . there would *be* one thing when I got it together. I looked at Nancy's ring again and said, "Soon, Red . . . very soon now."

In an hour the day had lost its brightness and a light rain rolled in with the dusk. I turned up my collar and stayed close to the buildings until I reached my car. Traffic was heavier now, but I got on an express street that was running freely and headed home. By the time I made my apartment the rain was coming down hard with no signs of letting up. I drove into the garage, and ran for it. Just the same, I got soaked before I reached the canopy over the gates.

When I tried to get my key in the lock it jammed. I tried again and it jammed again. Then I saw scratches on the brass. The lock has been jimmied. I hauled out my rod with one hand and kicked at the door. It flew open and I charged in there like a jerk wide open to get myself killed, only there was nobody else in there with me.

The lights were on in every room and the place was turned upside down. Nothing was where it belonged. The cushions in the chairs and couch were ripped apart and the breeze was blowing the stuffing through the air like a field of ragweed.

Drawers were emptied and discarded in the middle of the floor. All my clothes were out of the closet and heaped in a pile, the pockets turned inside out. They didn't even overlook the refrigerator. Bottles, cans and cold cuts were drawing flies and dirt on the table and under the sink.

I grabbed the phone and dialed the house number downstairs and waited for the doorman to answer. When he came on I had to fight to keep my voice down. "This is Mike Hammer in 9-D. Was anybody here looking for me?"

The guy replied in the negative.

"Was anybody hanging around the place today? Anybody who doesn't belong here?"

Another negative. He asked me if there was any trouble.

I said, "No, but there damn soon will be. Somebody's ruined my joint."

He got excited at that, but I told him to keep quiet. I didn't feel like answering questions or scaring the neighbors. I went into the bedroom and started to yank the covers from the heap in the corner. The overnight case was there under the layers of wool, the top gaping open and the baby clothes scattered around it. Some of them hadn't even been unfolded. Both side pockets and the top pocket had been ripped completely off and the lining opened so a hand could search underneath.

And the folder of pictures was gone.

I took an inventory of everything in the house, a search that cost me two hours, but the only thing missing was the pictures. Just to be sure I looked again. I needn't have bothered. Fifty-four bucks and a wristwatch lay on top of the dresser untouched, but an old set of films was gone.

They didn't mean anything to me, but they did to somebody else. That's why Ann died. I sat on the wreckage of a chair with a butt dangling from my lips, tallying things up. A lock lay on the floor, smashed from a heel. A cigarette box was forced open, broken. A socket fixture on the wall had been pried loose, leaving the wire ends hanging out like broken fingers.

I looked around me more carefully this time, noticing the pattern of the search. They took the pictures, but they were looking for something else, a something small enough to hide in almost anything. The inkwell had been emptied on the desk, and I remembered the salt and pepper shaker that had been dumped in the kitchen.

Sure, it was simple enough. I lifted my hand and grinned at the ring. "They'll be back, kid," I told it. "They didn't get you that time, so they'll be back. And we'll be waiting for them."

I could relax now. It was going to cost me, but I could relax. The pattern was taking shape. Nancy was the figurehead. The ring was Nancy. And they wanted her pictures back. What for, I couldn't say. They were old and they didn't show anything, but they were important, too. The baby clothes didn't mean anything to them, but the ring and the pictures did.

My eyes were staring into the distance and I was seeing Nancy's letter to me. Some day she might need me again . . . she was doing many things . . . only one of which had any meaning to her . . . ours was a trust.

Words. Now I had a lot of words. Some of them were tugging at my brain trying to claw their way into the clear. What was it? What the hell was it I was trying to remember? It was shrieking out to be heard and my mind was deaf. I was listening but I couldn't hear it. Damn it, what was there? What was I trying to remember! Somebody said something. It didn't mean a thing then, yet it sank in and stayed there until now. Who said it? What was it?

I shook my head to clear it, hoping to bring it back. The shrill clamor of the phone snapped me out of the fog and I got up and answered it. Pat's voice said hullo with a tone that had a snap to it.

"What's up, Pat?"

"I just want to tell you we went over the thing again. It works out. The coroner and the D.A. are calling it murder. Now they want an answer to the suicide note. It was authentic as hell. What was the idea you had? . . . I'm up the creek without a paddle."

I answered him listlessly. "Go ask some questions of her friends. See if she ever talked about committing suicide. There's a chance she did at one time and wrote the note. Somebody could have talked her out of it, then kept the note for future use."

"You think of everything, don't you?"

"I wish I did, Pat."

"It isn't going to be as easy as that. I put the whole question to the D.A. and it stood him on his ear. He thought the idea was preposterous."

"What do you think?"

"I think we got a snake by the tail."

"That's the only safe way to pick up a snake."

"I hope you're right. You still playing ball, Mike?"

"All the way, kid. You'll hear from me when I have something. Like now. Somebody broke into my apartment and wrecked it. They were looking for Nancy's ring. They didn't get it, but they did take those snapshots I got from the blonde."

"Hell!" Pat exploded. "What made you keep them? You know better than that!"

"Sure, I'll close the barn door after the horse is stolen. I wouldn't have known they were important if they hadn't been lifted. I'm not worried about them. They wanted the ring, why, I don't know. It's impossible to trace the thing, but they wanted it."

Pat was silent, then he said, "I've got news for you, too. I got an answer from a hospital in Chicago. We were lucky to get it back so quickly."

I squeezed the receiver. "Yeah?"

"Nancy Sanford had a baby there four years ago. She was an unwed mother. She refused to divulge the name of the father and she was put in a charity ward sponsored by a group that takes care of those affairs. It was a stillbirth. Nobody knows where she went after that."

My hand was shaking and my voice was almost a whisper when I thanked him for the information. Before I could hang up he said, "That ring . . . better drop it off with me, Mike."

I laughed harshly. "Like hell! Nancy is still an accident on your books. When you call it murder you can have it."

Pat was arguing about it when I interrupted.

"What are you going to do about the blonde? . . . and Murray?"

"He was just picked up at his club. On his way over now. Listen, about the ring, I want . . ."

I said thanks and cradled the receiver. Murray was about to be questioned. That meant a couple of hours at least, unless he had a good lawyer and good connections. It was enough time.

chapter nine ▰▰▰▰▰▰▰▰▰▰▰▰

MURRAY CANDID HAD two listings: one at the club and the other in a fancy residential section of Brooklyn. I didn't like either one of them. I tried the one in Brooklyn, and a butler with an English accent answered and told me Mr. Candid was out and wasn't expected back until the club had closed for the night, and could I leave a message. I told him never mind, and hung up.

A butler yet! Probably golden candelabra and rare Ming vases, too!

I held my hand over the dial, and on second thought punched Lola's number out. She recognized my voice and smiled over the phone. "Hullo, darling. Where are you?"

"Home."

"Am I going to see you?"

She made me feel nice and warm with just a few words. "In a little while maybe. Right now I'm up to my ears in something. I thought you might be able to help."

"Of course, Mike. What . . .?"

"Did you know Ann Minor? She worked for Murray."

"Certainly. I've known her for years. Why?"

"She's dead."

"No!"

"Yes. She was murdered and I know why. It had to do with Nancy, only the cops are in on this one."

"Oh, Mike . . . what makes these things happen? Ann wasn't one—one of us. She never did anything wrong. Why, she used to take care of the kids in the racket . . . try to help them. Oh, Mike . . . why? Why?"

"When I know that I'll know who killed her, honey. But that's not the point. Do you know where Murray might have a private hangout? Not his place in Brooklyn, but some place where he could do some trick entertaining or contact business associates?"

"Y-yes. He used to have a place in the Village. It won't be the same one I knew because he changed his spots regularly. He didn't like to stay in one place too long, but he favored the Village. I . . . was up there once . . . a party. It wasn't nice, Mike; I'd rather not speak about it."

"You don't have to. Where was the place?"

She gave me the location and I scribbled it down. "You'd have to ask around to see where he is now. I could find it, I guess, but . . ."

"You sit pat. I'll find it myself. I don't want you sticking your neck out."

"All right, Mike. Please don't get hurt . . . please."

I grinned. Not many people worried about me, and it was a nice feeling. "I'll be real careful, sugar. In fact, I'll call you back later so you'll know everything is all right. O.K.?"

"If you don't I'll never forgive you. I'll be waiting for you."

I put the phone back easy and patted it.

The evening was well on its way when I finished dressing. I had on the made-to-order suit with space built in for my armory, looking like something out of the prohibition era. I found my raincoat under the rest of the other stuff and climbed into it, stuffing a pack of butts in each pocket.

When I took one last look around the mess I went out the door and down to the garage for my car. It was raining harder than before, slanting down against the sidewalk, driving people into the welcome shelter of the buildings. Cars were going past, their windshield wipers moving like agitated bugs, the drivers crouched forward over the wheels, peering ahead intently.

I backed out of the garage, turned around and cut over to Broadway, following the main stem downtown. The Village should have been crammed with tourists and regulars, but the curbs were empty, and even the taxis were backed up behind their hack stands. Once in a while someone would make a dash for another saloon or run to the subway kiosk with a newspaper over his head, but if life was to be found in the Village this night, it would be found under a roof somewhere.

Down the corner from the address Lola had given me was a joint called Monica's. The red neon sign was a blur through the rain, and when I cruised past I could see a bar with a handful of people on stools, huddled over their drinks. It was as good a place to start as any.

I parked the car and pulled up my coat collar, then ducked out and stepped over puddles, my head bulling a path through the downpour. Before I got to the joint my legs were soaked and my feet squished in my shoes.

The heads at the bar came up and round like a chorus line, looking at me. Three belonged to guys trapped there on their way some place else. They went back to their drinks. Two were dames more interested in each other than men and they went back to low, sensual looks and leg holding. The other two were all smiles that exchanged nasty glances as if they were going to fight over the new arrival. Monica's catered to a well-assorted clientele.

Behind the bar was a big, beefy guy with a scar on his chin
and one ear cauliflowered to look like a dumpling. If his name
was Monica I'd eat my hat. He came down the bar and asked
me what it would be. I said whisky and his top lip curled up into
a grin.

"Annoder normal." His voice was a croak. "The place's gettin'
reformed."

The two patsies made a *moue* at him and looked insulted.

He put the bottle on the bar in front of me. "Even th' dames
is screwy. Odder place I woiked they kicked hell outa each other
to get a guy. Here th' dames don't think of nuttin' but dames."

"Yeah, there's nothing like a dame," I said.

"Inside's a coupla loose ones, bub. Go see if ya like 'em."

He gave me an outsized wink and I picked up my glass, threw
a buck on the bar and walked inside. The two babes were there
like he said, only they were already taken. Two women in man-
tailored suits were showing them a better time than I could have
done.

So I sat down by myself at a table next to a piano and watched
them. One of the boys from the bar came in and sat a drink in
front of me, smirking a little as he pulled out the chair.

He said, "The bartender's too fresh, don't you think?"

I grunted at him and gulped the drink. These guys give me the
pip.

"You're new around here, aren't you?"

"Yeah."

"From uptown?"

"Yeah."

"Oh!" Then he frowned. "You . . . have a date already?"

The guy was asking for a punch in the mouth and he was just
about to get it when I changed my mind and muttered, "I'm
gonna see a guy named Murray Candid. He told me where he
lived, then I forgot."

"Murray? He's a *dear* friend of mine. But he moved again only
a week ago. Georgie told me he has a place over the grocery store
two blocks south. How long have you known him? Why, only
last week I . . . say, you're not leaving yet . . . we haven't . . ."

I didn't bother to look back. If the punk tried to follow me I'd
wrap him around a pole. The bartender looked at me and chirped
that the make-up crowd could spoil the business, and I agreed.

But the guy gave me the steer I wanted. I was lucky. Maybe I
should have patted his behind to make him feel good.

I came down the street slowly, made a U-turn and came back.

There were no lights on in the store and the shades in the apartment above were drawn and dark. A few cars were parked along one side and I wedged in between them, waiting there a minute until a couple of pedestrians lost themselves in the rain.

It was hard to keep from running. I crossed over, walked towards the store, then stepped into the doorway as if to light a butt, but more to look around. There wasn't anything to see, so I stepped back into the gloom of the hallway and tried the door, feeling it give under my hand. I dragged on the butt and looked at the mailboxes. One said "Byle" the name on the store. The other was for the top floor and was blank.

That would be it.

My eyes took a few minutes to become accustomed to the darkness, then I saw the stairs, worn and rickety, covered with sections of old carpet. I stayed on the wall side, trying to keep them from creaking, but even as careful as I was they groaned ominously, waiting to groan again when I lifted my foot.

The first-floor landing was a narrow box flanked by a door and a railing with "Byle" lettered on it in white paint. They should have used green to go with the name. I held on to the rail, using it for a guide, and felt my way to the next flight. These stairs were new. They didn't make a sound. When I reached the door my hand went out for the knob and I stiffened, my ears chasing an elusive sound.

Somebody was inside, somebody moving softly but fast.

I had the knob in my hand, turning it slowly without sound until the catch was drawn completely back. The hinges were well oiled and the door inched open soundlessly, bit by bit until I could see inside. There were no lights on and the shuffling sounds were coming from another room.

When the door was opened half-way I unpacked the .45 and stood there with it in my hand waiting to see what would happen. Something hit the floor and shattered and somebody whispered to somebody else to be quiet for the love of God. That made two of them.

Then the other one said, "Goddamn it, I cut my hand!"

A chair was pushed back and the glass that was lying on the floor went skittering into the wall.

The first voice said, "Didn't I tell you to be quiet?"

"Shut the hell up! You don't tell me anything."

There was the tearing sound of cloth, then it came again. The voice whispered, "I can't bandage this. I'm going inside."

He came in my direction, picking his way around the furniture.

I was pressed back against the wall, hanging on to the rod. His hand felt the opening into the foyer and for a second he just stood there, black silhouetted against a deeper black, then his hand brushed my coat and he opened his mouth to yell.

I smashed the barrel of the gun across his forehead with a sickening dull sound and his knees went out from under him. He fell right in my arms, limp and heavy, his head lolling to one side, and I heard the blood drip onto the floor. It would have been all right if I could have laid him down, but his body rolled in my hands and a gun fell out of a holster and banged along the woodwork.

Inside there was a complete silence. Nothing, not even the sound of his breathing. I moved my feet around and swore under my breath, muttering like a guy who had just bumped into a wall.

In a voice barely audible the guy called out, "Ray . . . was that you, Ray?"

I had to answer. "Yeah, it was me."

"Come back here, Ray."

I threw off my hat, shrugged my coat to the floor. The other guy was about my size and maybe I could get away with it.

Just in time I smartened up and dropped to my hands and knees and went around the corner. The guy was standing there pointing a gun where my belly would have been.

My pal's name wasn't Ray and I answered to it.

He saw me at the same time and a tongue of flame licked out in my direction with a noise that was almost a "plop," but I was rolling before he pulled the trigger and slug thudded into the wall.

Somehow I got my feet under me and squeezed the .45 into a roar that shook the room. I wasn't waiting for any return fire. I saw that shadow of a chair and dived for it, hearing the other guy going for cover only a few feet away.

From where I was, the darkness made it impossible to tell whether or not I was exposed, and I lay there, forcing myself to breathe silently when I wanted to pant like a dog. The other guy wasn't so good at it. He gasped, then moved quickly, afraid that he might have been heard. I let him sweat. I knew where he was now, but I didn't fire. He moved again, deliberately, wondering if his first blast had caught me. My leg began to tighten up in a cramp, and there was a tremor in my arm from leaning on it. I wasn't going to be able to hold the tableau much longer.

The guy was getting up his nerve, but carefully. I fixed my eyes a little to one side of where I thought he'd show and waited, scanning the area, not focusing my gaze on any one spot. I tried to remember what they taught us in basic training. It worked in the jungle. Damn it, it *had* to work now.

I saw his head then. Barely enough light came through the curtained windows to give the background a deeper shade, and against it his face was just a spot of motion. He was creeping right into the line of my rod.

My fingers were starting to squeeze when the boy in the hallway came back to life. His feet slammed the wall and his nails scratched the floor. He must have lain there a second, remembered where he was and what had happened, and then he let out a choked-off curse and scrambled to the door.

It pulled the stop on the tension. The guy behind the chair jerked, his breath coming out in a long wheeze and he sprang out of his crouch into a chair that tipped over on me just as the .45 went off.

He screamed, tripped and fell, then got up and hit the wall before he made the door. I fought the chair and the gun went off into an empty room because I heard the other guy falling down a flight of stairs. By the time I was on my feet an engine roared outside and a car ripped into gear and was gone up the street.

There was no use chasing them. I lit a match, found the light switch and turned it on. It only took one look to see what they had been doing. Along one side of the wall was a bookcase with half the books lying on the floor. Some had closed shut, but at least fifty of them were lying there opened and discarded.

I stuck the gun back under my arm and picked up where they left off, yanking the books down and flipping through them. With the light on I made better time, and was half-way across the next to last shelf when one book opened and another fell out of the well that had been cut into the pages.

Somebody was yelling on the street and a door slammed in the apartment below me. I shoved the book under my belt at the small of my back, ran out to the corridor long enough to grab my hat and coat and made a mad dash down the stairs. When I came to the landing the door started to open but banged shut and a bolt clicked into a hasp.

The open front door was a welcome invitation, even with the rain still coming down outside. I took that last flight two at a time, hit the bottom running and felt my head explode into a whirlwind of spinning lights and crazy sounds as something crashed into the side of my neck.

My body wasn't a part of me at all. It collapsed in a limp heap and my head cracked the floor, but there was no pain, just a numbness that was lit by another light, a brighter red this time, and there was a pressure on my chest, and in that final moment of recollection I knew that I had walked into a trap and somebody had pumped a bullet into me point-blank.

How long I lay there I couldn't tell. There are times when the body has recuperative powers beyond belief. A sound penetrated, a high wailing sound of a siren, and I climbed to my feet, grasping at the banister for support. Unconsciously I got my coat and hat back in my hands, staggered towards the door and came out. There was a crowd down the street pointing in my direction, but if they saw me they didn't show it. I was glad of the rain and the night then, the shadows that wrapped themselves around me as I lurched across the street, looking for my car.

When I found it I half fell across the seat, dragging the door shut behind me. My chest felt crushed and my skull was a throbbing thing that sent tongues of fire lacing down my body. All sensation had been torn loose from my neck, and although I felt nothing there, it hurt to breathe, and hurt even worse to make a sound.

I heard the police car screech to a stop, heard the pounding of feet, the shouts, the excited murmur of a crowd that expanded every minute. I couldn't stay on the seat any longer. The hell with them! The hell with everything! I let my eyes close and my arms relaxed without warning, and I dropped forward on the floor boards, gasping into a puddle of dirt.

I was cold, colder than I had ever been before. I was wet and shivering and I didn't want to raise my head because the Japs were only twenty yards away waiting for me. Some place back of the lines a chow wagon had been rolled up and I could smell hot coffee and stew, hearing the guys line up for chow. I wanted to call for them to come and get me, lay down an artillery barrage so I could get the hell out of the foxhole, but if I yelled the Japs would spot my position and lob a grenade in on top of me. Just to make it worse it started raining harder.

Fighting to get my eyes open was a job in itself. The rain was coming in the open window and I was drenched. I could smell the coffee again, coming from some window. With my hands propped under me I pushed myself back to the seat and got behind the wheel.

The crowd was gone, the police were gone and the street was normal again. Just rain, black squares of windows, a drunk that weaved up the sidewalk. I knew how he felt. My mind was unfogging, bringing with it the throb in my head and chest. I put my hand inside my jacket, felt the tear in the cloth half fearfully, then eased the .45 out. A slug had smashed into the top of the slide mechanism tearing it loose, embedding itself in the blued metal, looking like some nasty amoeba cast in lead. My chest hurt like hell from the impact, but the skin wasn't even broken.

And some place somebody was thinking I was a dead duck.

I reached in back of my belt, feeling for the book. It was still there. I couldn't see what it was so I tossed it in the glove compartment until later.

It was another ten minutes before I felt right enough to drive or strong enough to hold the wheel. I kicked over the motor and turned on my lights.

Right away I got it. The redhead's ring didn't wink back at me in the frosty gleam of the dashboard light. It was gone.

On my little finger was a long pink scratch where it had been yanked off in a hurry. They came back sooner than I expected.

Things were looking up. If they looked higher they'd see the pretty angels.

chapter ten

TIME WASN'T IMPORTANT to Lola. She said she'd wait and she did. Hers was the only light in the apartment building, and I saw her shadow pass the drawn curtains twice, then recede back into the room. I didn't forget that other parking ticket; this time I found a spot that wasn't on an express street and pulled to the curb.

I had to take it easy walking back, wishing the sidewalks were carpeted to ease the shock of my heels pounding the concrete. Every step jarred the balloon of pain that was my head, and when I lit a butt to try to forget it the smoke sent cramps into my lungs that caught and held like a thousand knives digging into my rib cage.

The stairs looked a mile long. The only way I could make them was to go up a couple, rest, then go up a couple more. The outside door was open so I didn't bother ringing until I was at the apartment door, then I punched the bell and held it, leaning against the jamb.

Inside, I heard her heels click on the floor, hurried, then break into a run. Her fingers fumbled with the bolt, got it open and yanked the door back.

I guess I didn't look so hot. She said, "Oh, Mike!" and her fingers went out to my face tenderly, holding my cheeks, then she took my hand and led me inside.

"I almost stood you up." It wasn't easy to grin at her.

Lola looked at me and shook her head. "Some day . . . will you come to see me when you're not a . . . a hospital case?"

Very slowly I turned her around. She was lovely, this woman. Tonight she had dressed up for me, hoping I'd do more than call. She stood almost as tall as me, her body outlined under an iridescent green dress that sent waves of light shimmering down her legs whenever she moved. I held her at arm's length doing nothing but looking at her, smelling the fragrance of a heady cologne. Her hair was a dark frame, soft and feathery, then rolled to her shoulders and made you want to close your eyes and pull it over you like a blanket. Somewhere she had found a new beauty, or perhaps it was there all along, but it was a beauty that was always hers now.

My hand found her waist and I drew her in close, waiting until her eyes half closed and her lips parted, eager to be kissed. Her mouth was a soft bed of fire, her tongue a searching thing asking questions I had to answer greedily. When I pushed her away she stood there a long moment, breathing heavily before she opened her eyes and smiled. She didn't have to tell me that she was mine whenever I wanted it. I knew that.

Her eyes were watching me. "Mike . . ."

I ran my fingers through her hair like I had wanted to. "What, honey?"

"I love you, Mike. No . . . don't love me back. Don't even try. Just let me love you."

I pulled her face to mine and kissed her eyes closed. "That isn't easy. It's hard not to do things."

"You have to do this, Mike. I have a long way to go yet."

"No, you don't, kid. You can forget everything that has ever happened. I don't give a damn what went on this year or last. Who the hell am I to talk, anyway? If there's any shame to attach to the way you run your life, then maybe I ought to be ashamed. I've done the same things you've done, but a man gets away with it. It's not what you do but the way you think. Hell, I've met bums in a saloon who would do more for you than half the churchgoers."

"But I want it to be different with me, Mike. I'm trying so hard to be . . . nice."

"You were always nice, Lola. I haven't known you long, but I bet you were always nice."

She squeezed my hand and smiled. "Thank you, Mr. Hammer. You can make it awfully easy for me. That's why I love you so much." Her finger went to my mouth so I couldn't answer. "But it still works my way. I still have a long way to go. I want to be worth a love that's returned."

I aimed a kiss at her nose, but it was too quick and I winced. Lola didn't need an explanation. Worry lines grew in the corner of her eyes and she pointed to a chair.

After I had let myself into it she said, "Again, Mike?"

"Again."

"Bad?"

"It could have been. A slug that was aimed at my chest ruined my gun. I'll never leave Betsy home after that. The same party must've clubbed me across the neck with a sledgehammer. Like to ripped my damn head off."

"Who . . . who did it?"

"Beats me. It was dark, I was in a hurry, and I never had a chance to be introduced."

She loosened my tie and shirt, sat on the arm of the chair and rubbed my neck and head. Her fingers were long and cool, probing into the hurt and wiping it away. I leaned my head back and closed my eyes, liking the touch of her hand, loving the nearness of her. She hummed a song in a rich, throaty voice, softly, until I was completely relaxed.

I said, "They got Nancy's ring, Lola."

"They did." It wasn't a question; more a statement that meant she was ready to listen when I was ready to talk.

"I found Murray's place and went in there. His two boys were going through his wall library looking for something. He must have told where it was, but didn't have time to give them full details."

"Did they find it?"

"No. I found it."

Her hands were rubbing my shoulders, kneading the muscles. "What was it?"

"A book. A book that was inside another book." Without opening my eyes I reached around and slipped it out of my pocket.

She took it from me with one hand and I heard her flip the cover back.

She stared at it for a while, then ruffled through the pages. "It's gibberish."

"That's what I expected." I took her hand away from my neck and kissed it and she handed me the book, her face a puzzled frown.

It was no bigger than a small notepad, bound in black leather, a size that fitted nicely in an inside jacket pocket, easy to conceal almost anywhere. The writing was small and precise, in a bookkeeper's hand, flowing straight across the page as if underruled by invisible lines.

Letters, numbers. Meaningless symbols. Capital letters, small letters. Some letters backward, deliberately so. Yet there was an order about it all that couldn't be mistaken. I went through the pages rapidly, coming to the end about three-quarters of the way. The rest of the pages were blank.

Lola had been watching over my shoulder. "What is it, Mike?"

"Code."

"Can you read it?"

"No, but there are people who can. Maybe you can. See if there's anything familiar to you in here." I held the book out and began at the beginning again.

She scanned the pages with me, holding her lower lip between her teeth, carefully following my finger as I paced the lines with her. She shook her head at the end of each page and I turned to the next.

But it was always the same. She knew no more about it than I did. I would have closed it right there, except that I felt her hand tighten on my arm and I saw her teeth dig into her lip. She started to say something, then stopped.

"What is it?" I prompted.

"No, it can't be." She was frowning again.

"Tell me, kid."

Her finger was shaking as she pointed to a symbol that looked like a complex word in a steno's notebook. "A . . . long time ago . . . I was in Murray's office when a man phoned him. Murray talked a while, then put down something on a pad. I think . . . I think it was that. He saw me watching and covered it up. Later he told me I had an appointment."

"Who was it?"

"Do . . . I have to?" She was pleading with me not to make her remember.

"Just this once, baby."

"I don't remember his name." She said it fast. "He was from out of town. He was fat and slimy and I hated him, Mike. Oh, please . . . no more, no more."

"O.K., it's enough." I closed the book and laid it on the endtable. The ball had started to roll. The heads would follow. I reached for the phone.

Pat was in bed, but he wasn't sleeping. His voice was wide-awake, tense. "I knew you'd get around to calling about this time," he told me. "What's going on?"

"That's what I'd like to know. Maybe you'd like to tell *me*."

"Sure, I'll tell you. After all, you're the one who started this mess and, brother, I mean mess."

"Trouble, Pat?"

"Plenty. We picked up Murray for questioning. Naturally, he didn't know a thing. According to his story Ann Minor was moody, brooding constantly, and a general pain in the neck. He considered firing her a while ago and thinks she got wind of it and got worse than ever. He took it calmly when we told him she was a suicide."

"He would."

"That's not all. He knew there was more to it than that, but he had a good lawyer. We couldn't hold him at all. About thirty minutes after we let him go, hell started popping. Something's happening and I'm on the receiving end. Until tonight I didn't think the politics in this town were as dirty as they are. You started something, kid."

"I'm going to finish it, too. What about the apartment . . . Ann's. Any prints?"

"None that mattered. The tub was clean as a whistle. On the far side were a few smudges that turned out to be hers, but the rest had been wiped off. We took samples of the water and tested them. It worked. Some traces of the same soap."

"Did you ask around about that suicide note?"

"Hell, I haven't had time. Two of the men on the case started to question some of the employees in the Zero Zero Club, but before they got very far they were called to a phone. A voice told them to lay off if they knew what was good for them."

"What did they do?"

Pat's voice had a snarl in it. "They didn't scare. They tried to have the call traced only to find it came from a subway phone booth—a pay station. They called me for instructions and I gave them to them. I told them to knock some heads together if they have to."

I chuckled at that. "Getting smart, huh?"

"I'm getting mad, damn it! The people pay for protection. What the hell do they take the police for, a bunch of private servants."

"Some do," I remarked sourly. "Look, Pat, I have something for you. I know it's late and all that, but it's important. Get over here as fast as you can, will you?"

He didn't ask questions. I heard him slide out of bed and snap a light on. I gave him Lola's address and he said O.K., then hung up.

Lola rose and went into the kitchen, coming back with a tray and some beer. She opened the bottle and poured it out, giving me the big one. When she settled herself in a chair opposite me she said, "What happens now?"

"We're going to scare the blazes out of some people, I think."

"Murray?"

"He's one."

We sipped the beer, finished it, had another. This time Lola curled up on the end of the couch, her legs crossed, one arm stretched out across the back. "Will you come over here, or do I go over there?" she grinned impishly.

"I'll go over there," I said.

She made room for me on the same cushion, putting a head on the beer. "That's to keep one hand out of trouble."

"What about the other hand?"

"Let it get in trouble."

I laughed at her and hugged her to me so she could nuzzle against my shoulder. "Mike . . . I think the college kids have something. It's nice to neck."

I couldn't disagree with that. When the beer was gone she brought in another bottle and came back into my arm again. I should have been thinking of Nancy or doing something else maybe, but it was nice just sitting there with her, laughing at foolish things. She was the kind of a girl who could give you back something you thought you had lost to the years.

Pat came in too soon. He rang from downstairs and Lola pushed the buzzer to let him in. He must have run up the stairs because he was knocking on the door a few seconds later.

Lola let him in with a smile and I called out, "Lola, meet Pat Chambers, the finest of the finest."

Pat said, "Hullo, Lola," then came over to me and threw his hand on the back of the couch. He didn't waste any time.

"Gimme. What did you get?"

Lola brought the book over from the endtable and I handed it to him. "Part of Murray's collection, Pat. Code. Think you can break it?"

I scanned his face and saw his lips set in a line. He talked to himself. "Memory code. Damn it to hell!"

"What?"

"It's a memory code, I'll bet a fin. He's got a symbol or a structure for everything and he's the only one who knows it."

I set the glass down and inched forward on the couch. "The Washington boys broke the Jap Imperial code, didn't they?"

"Yeah, but that was different." He shook his head helplessly. "Let me give you an example. Suppose you say a word to me, or several of them for that matter. You know what they mean, but I don't. How could I break that? If you strung out sentences long enough there would be repetition, but if you allowed nothing to repeat itself, using different symbol or letter grouping that you committed to memory, there would be nothing to start with."

"That takes a good memory, doesn't it?" I cut in.

"For some things. But there isn't too much to remember in this." He tapped the book. "Probably anyone could do it if he puts his mind to it."

I reached for the glass and filled it, emptying the bottle. "Lola recognized one of the symbols, she thinks. Murray used it to identify one of his 'customers.' That little gadget is Murray's account book with a listing of his clients and his fleshly assets."

Pat jumped to his feet, a light blazing in his eyes. "Son of a bitch, if it is we can rip him apart! We can split this racket right down the middle!"

His language was getting contaminated from hanging around private detectives. "Only temporarily," I reminded him.

"It's better than not at all. It'll pay for people getting killed. Where did you get it, Mike?"

"Your boy Candid has himself a party den in the Village. While you were popping the questions he sent his lads up to get that book, taking no chances. I surprised them at it. The damn thing was worth their trying to knock me off. I just missed having my head handed to me."

"You can identify them, then?"

"Nope. I didn't see their faces. But one will have a cut on his hand and a beauty across his forehead. The other guy is his pal. Ask around the club. I think they were Murray's personal body-guards. We put the squeeze on so fast Murray didn't have time to pull that book himself. He probably figured nobody would question Ann's death except for routine questioning at his joint."

"You might be right. I'll get this thing photostated and hand it around to the experts. I'll let you know what comes of it."

"Good!"

"Where will I get in touch with you?"

"You won't. I'll get in touch with you."

"I don't get it, Mike. Won't you be . . .?"

He stopped when he saw the expression on my face. "I'm supposed to be dead."

"Good Lord!"

"There were three guys at Murray's place. One wasn't in on it. All he wanted was the redhead's ring. He gave it to me square in the chest. So he's gonna drop his load when he sees me again."

Pat caught the implication at once. "He tailed you. The same guy killed the blonde, tailed you home, searched your place and stayed right behind you until he had a clear shot at you."

"Uh-huh. In a dark hallway."

"And he just wanted the ring?"

"That's right. I had the book on me, and he never looked for it."

"That makes two parties. Both after you for a different reason."

"Could be the same reason, but they don't know it."

A grin spread over his face. "They'll be waiting for your body to show. They'll have their ears to the ground and their eyes open. They'll want to know what happened to your body."

I nodded. "Let 'em wonder," I said slowly. "They'll think the cops are keeping it quiet purposely. They'll think you have more than you're giving out. Let's see what happens, Pat."

"Ummm." That was all he said. He went to the door, looking satisfied, his mind pounding out the angles. He turned around once, grinned, waved goodbye and was gone.

Lola picked up the empty bottle and looked at me sideways.

"If you're really dead it's going to be a wonderful wake."

I faked a kick at her and she ducked out for a refill. When she came back she was serious and I knew it. Her eyes questioned me before she asked. "Could you tell me . . . about your place being searched, I mean? If I have to worry about you I want to know what I'm worrying about."

I told her then, skipping some details, just a general outline of what had occurred. She let me bring it up to date, absorbing every word, trying to follow with her mind. When I was through I let her mull it over.

Finally she said, "The baby clothes, Mike . . . it fits."

"How?"

"Nancy had stretch marks on her abdomen. Purplish streaks that come with pregnancy. I never questioned her about it."

"We discovered that. It was a stillbirth."

"The father . . .?"

"No trace."

She was thinking of something else and chewed on her fingernail. "Those pictures that were stolen . . ."

"Only snapshots of her when she was younger."

"That isn't it."

"What then?"

"This person who was so careless . . . you said he just took the ring . . . didn't look for the book you had. . . ."

"He didn't know I had it."

"No, I don't mean that. Maybe he just took the pictures. He didn't look at them, he just *took* them. He would have taken any pictures."

I was beginning to get the point, but I wanted to make sure. "What are you getting at, Lola?"

"Nancy had a camera, I told you that. Maybe it was pictures she took that were wanted. Maybe the others were taken by mistake."

It made sense. I gave her neck a little squeeze and grinned through my teeth. "Now you're the smart one," I told her. "You said Nancy wouldn't go in for blackmail."

"I said I *thought* she wouldn't. I still don't think she would, but who can tell?"

"You know, we're throwing this right in Feeney Last's lap. If he's the bastard behind this he's going to get it right!"

Lola laid her hand over mine, reaching for my fingers.

"Mike, don't get excited too fast. You have to think about it first. If he's not the type . . ."

"Hell, he's the type, all right. Could be that I didn't give him credit for being that smart. You can't tell what goes on behind their heads, Lola. Their faces might be blank as an empty coconut, but up here there's a lot of brain power. Damn! Just follow Feeney with me: he approached Red in the hash house; he had her scared and a lot of other people scared. He was tough and dirty, and decent people are usually scared of that kind. He could carry a gun to push a scare through, even if that wasn't the purpose of the gun. What a nice set-up he had!

"So Nancy had his blackmail stuff . . . he said it was pictures of somebody in a hotel room with a babe. Who was the somebody and who was the babe? Maybe it was Nancy herself. If she had a good camera she could take shots automatically with a time arrangement on the camera. Maybe Feeney knew she had it and wanted it—maybe it was the other way around and he had it and she got it. Hell, maybe they were in it together.

"One thing we know: Feeney searched her room. He's a snotty little bastard who'd take a chance on anything. There's only one trouble. Feeney has an alibi. He was with Berin-Grotin when Nancy was killed, and unless he was able to sneak off without the old boy knowing it he had to have somebody else to do the job."

She reviewed it with an expression that reminded me of Pat, making me eat my own words. "But you said Mr. Berin was positive in his statement . . . and the police were just as positive that the boy ran down Nancy accidentally. How can you get around that?"

My chest started hurting again and I slumped back. "Ah, I don't know. Nothing makes sense. If Nancy was an accident, who took her ring off and why—and why the trouble to get it back? The ring's the thing. If I could find what it meant I'd have it."

I pulled out the cigarettes, stuck two in my mouth and lit them. Lola took hers from between my lips and dragged on it deeply. When I closed my eyes she said, "That's not the point I'm trying to make, Mike. Nancy had pictures of some sort that were important. Her place was searched for them—must have been because then they already had the ring. You say they didn't find them. Then they searched your place and took pictures that apparently had no meaning. All right, suppose they *didn't* have any meaning . . . where are the ones that have?"

Good Lord, how could I be so incredibly stupid! I took the cigarette and squashed it out in my hand and never felt it burn me. The pictures, the pictures! Nancy must have used herself to work up the prettiest blackmail scheme that ever was. She had pictures of everything and everybody and was getting ready to use them when Feeney Last in his visits to her room saw the damn things and wanted them himself.

Of course, how could it be any other way? A cheap gunman with big ideas who saw a way to cash in. But before he could do the job himself Nancy stepped out in front of a car and got herself killed. Maybe Feeney even had a guy trailing her to keep track of things, a guy who knew enough to take the ring off and stall identification. And why? Because when she was identified somebody else might get to the stuff first. The ring was an accident.

And Nancy was just a blackmailer at heart.

Nuts! I still didn't care what she was. For a little while she was my friend. Maybe Feeney didn't kill her, but he had it in mind, which was the same thing to me, and he was going to pay for it. I had liked the blonde, too.

I blew a ring at the ceiling and Lola stuck her finger through it. She was waiting again, giving me time to think. Aloud, I said, "The camera, Lola, where could it be?"

She answered me with a question. "Didn't Nancy imply to you that she was up against it for some reason?"

The redhead had, at that. "Uh-huh. Business was bad, she said. Feeney might have conceivably been driving her customers away purposely. He tried it with me that first night. She needed dough. She hocked the camera."

Each thought brought a newer one. The puzzle that had been scattered all over the place was being drawn in on the table by an invisible vacuum cleaner. Ghostly fingers were picking up the pieces and putting them in place, hesitating now and then to let me make a move. It was a game. First, he'd put in one, then I'd put in one. Then he let me put in two, three, urging me to finish the puzzle myself. But some of the pieces would fit two places, and you'd have to hold them out until you were sure.

The old biddy at Nancy's rooming house said she showed up with a couple of bucks and nothing else. She was broke. Where did she come from? Was she trying to get away from Feeney Last . . . only to have him catch up with her anyway? Like Cobbie Bennett said, the grapevine had a loud voice. It could certainly keep track of a redheaded prostitute. So she moved around trying to get away from him and couldn't. Some place behind her she had left the wealth of pictures he was after, and they were still there. Still there waiting to be found, and right now somebody was looking for them and taking his time because he thought I was dead. Feeney Last was in for a big surprise.

Lola slipped her arm around me. "Is it finished?"

"Almost." I relaxed in peaceful anticipation.

"When?"

"Tomorrow. The next day. It'll be soon. Tomorrow we'll pick up the trail. First, I'll have to get a new gun. Pat'll fix me up. Then we'll begin."

"Who's we?"

"Me and you, sugarpuss. I'm supposed to be dead, remember. A corpse can't go roaming around the streets. Tomorrow you're going to run your poor legs to the bone, checking every hock shop in town, until we find that camera. There will be an address on the ticket, if it's still around, and that's what we want."

Lola showed her teeth in a grin and poked her legs out in front of her. Very temptingly she inched her dress up, letting me see the lush fullness of the calves, bringing it higher over her knees until the smooth white flesh showed over her stocking tops.

Her eyebrows were lifted in a tantalizing way and she whispered, "Won't that take a lot of walking?"

It would take a hell of a lot of walking.

I reached over and pulled her dress down, which wasn't like me at all, but it was worth it because she threw her head back and laughed, and I kissed her before she could close her mouth, and felt her arms tighten around my neck until it hurt again.

I pushed her away roughly, still holding her close, and she said, "I love you, Mike, I love you, I love you, I love you."

I wanted to tell her the same thing, but she knew it was coming, and stopped me with her mouth again. She stood up then, holding out her hands so she could pull me to my feet. While I watched, she transformed the sofa into a bed and brought out a pillow from her bedroom. I kicked off my shoes and tossed my coat and tie on a chair. "You go to bed," I said, "we'll hold the wake some other night."

"Good night, Mike." She blew a kiss. I shook my head, and she came back for a real one. I lay down on the sheets, trying to figure out whether I was a jerk, just plain reformed, too tired, or in love.

I guessed it was because I was too tired, and I fell asleep grinning.

chapter eleven ■■■■■■■■■■■■■■

IT WAS THE sound of coffee bubbling and the smell of bacon and eggs sizzling in a pan that awakened me. I yawned, stretched and came alive as Lola walked in. She was just as lovely in the morning as she had been last night. She crooked her finger at me. "Breakfast is served, my lord."

As soon as she went back to the kitchen I climbed into my clothes and followed. Over the table she told me that she had already called and told her boss that she was sick and was ordered to take the day off. Several, if she needed them.

"You're in solid, I guess."

She wrinkled her nose at me. "They're just being nice to a good worker. They like my modelling technique."

When we finished she went into the bedroom and changed into a suit, tucking her hair up under her hat. She deliberately left off most of the make-up, but it didn't spoil her looks any. "I'm trying to look like I can afford only to do my shopping in hock shops," she explained.

"They'll never believe it, honey."

"Stop being nice to me." She paused in front of the mirror and surveyed the effect, making last-minute adjustments here and there. "Now, what do I do and say, Mike?"

I leaned back in the chair, hooking my feet over the rungs. "Take the phone book . . . the classified section. Make a list of all the joints and start walking. You know the camera . . . it may be in the window, it may be inside. Tell the guy what you want and look them over. If you see it, buy it. Remember, what you want is the address on the ticket. You can make up your own story as you go along . . . just make it good, and don't appear overanxious."

I dragged out my wallet and fingered off some bills. "Here! You'll need taxi fare and grub money, plus what the guy will ask. That is, if you find it."

She tucked the bills in her pocketbook. "Frankly, what do you think of the chances, Mike?"

"Not too good. Still, it's the only out I know of. It won't be easy to run down, but it's the only lead I have right now."

"Will you be here while I'm gone?"

"I may be, I don't know." I wrote down my home and office addresses, then added Pat's number as an afterthought. "In case you find anything, call me here or at these numbers. If you're in a jam and I'm not around, call Pat. Now, have you got everything straight?"

She nodded. "I think so. Does the faithful wife off to work get a farewell kiss from her lazy spouse?"

I grabbed her arm and hauled her down to me, bruising her lips with mine, and felt the fire start all over again. I had to push her away.

"I don't want to go," she said.

"Scram!" She wrinkled her nose again and waved to me from the doorway.

As soon as she left I went over to the phone and dialed the

office. Velda started with, "I'm sorry, but Mr. Hammer isn't here at the moment."

"Where is he?"

"I'm not at liberty to say. He should . . . Mike! Where the devil are you now? Why don't you stop in and take care of your business? I never . . ."

"Off my back, chick. I'm tied up. Look, have I had any calls?"

"I'll say you have. So far I haven't had time to answer the mail!"

"Who called?"

"First off there was a man who wouldn't give his name. Said it was confidential and he'd call back later. Then two prospective clients called, but I told them you were engaged. Both of them thought their business was so urgent you'd drop what you were doing and go with them."

"Get their names?"

"Yes. Both were named Johnson. Mark and Joseph Johnson, neither related."

I grunted. Johnson was about the third or fourth most popular name in the phone directory. "Who else?"

"There was a guy named Cobbie Bennett. I had a hard time getting his name because he was almost hysterical. He said he had to see you right away but wouldn't say why. I told him you'd call back soon as you came in. He wouldn't leave a number. He's called three times since."

"Cobbie! What could he want? He said nothing at all, Velda?"

"Not a thing."

"O.K., continue."

"Your client, Mr. Berin-Grotin, called. He wanted to know if his check got to the bank in time. I didn't know about it so I said you'd check with him. He said not to bother if everything was all right."

"Well, everything's not all right, but it's too late to bother about now. You hold down the phone, kiddo. Give out the same answers to whoever calls. Keep one thing in mind . . . you *don't* know where I am and you *haven't* heard from me since yesterday. Got it?"

"Yes, but . . ."

"No buts. The only one you can feel free to speak to is Pat or a girl called Lola. Take their messages. If they have anything for me try to get me at home or here." I rattled off Lola's number and waited while she wrote it down.

"Mike . . . what is it? Why can't you . . ."

I was tired of repeating it. "I'm supposed to be dead, Velda. The killer thinks he nailed me."

"Mike!"

"Oh, quit worrying. I'm not even scratched. The bullet hit my gun. Which reminds me . . . I got to get a new one. 'Bye baby. See you soon."

I stuck the phone back and sat on the edge of the chair, running my hand across my face. Cobbie Bennett. He was hysterical and he wanted to see me. He wouldn't say why. I wondered which of the Johnson boys was the killer trying to make certain I was gone from the land of the living. And who was the caller with the confidential info? At least I knew who Cobbie was.

I hoped I knew where I could find him.

My coat was wrinkled from lying across the chair, and without a rod under my arm the thing bagged like a zoot suit. The holster helped fill it out, but not enough. I closed the door behind me and walked downstairs, trying to appear like just another resident, maybe a little on the seedy side. In that neighborhood nobody gave me a tumble.

At Ninth Avenue I grabbed a cab and had him drive me over to a gunsmith on the East Side. The guy who ran the shop might have made Daniel Boone's rifle for him, he was so old. At one time guns had been his mainstay, but since the coming of law and order he specialized in locks, even if the sign over the door didn't say so.

He didn't ask questions except to see my license, and when he had gone over it to the extent of comparing the picture with my face, he nodded and asked me what I liked. There were some new Army .45's mounted in a rack on the wall and I pointed them out. He took them down and let me try the action. When I found one that satisfied me I peeled off a bill from my roll, signed the book and took my receipt and a warning to check with the police on the change in gun numbers on my ticket.

I felt a lot better when I walked out of the place.

If the sun had been tucked in bed I would have been able to locate Cobbie in a matter of minutes. At high noon it was going to be a problem. In a cigar store on the corner I cashed in a buck for a handful of nickels and started working the phone book, calling the gin mills where he usually hung out. I got the same answer every time. Cobbie had dropped out of sight. Two wanted to know who I was, so I said a friend and hung up.

Sometimes the city is worse than the jungle. You can get lost in it with a million people within arm's length. I was glad of it now. A guy could roam the streets for a week without being recognized if he were careful not to do anything to attract attention. A cab went by and I whistled it, waited while it braked to a stop and backed up, then got in. After I told the driver where to go, I settled back against the cushions and did exercises to loosen up my neck.

I missed the redhead's ring. I was doing good while I had it. Nancy, a mother . . . a blackmailer? A girl down on her luck. A good kid. I could never forget the way she looked at me when I gave her the dough. I'd never forget it, because I told her that kind of stuff was murder.

I didn't know how right I was.

She must have had fun shopping for those clothes, being waited on, seeing herself in the mirror as a lady again. What had happened to her attitude, her personal philosophy after that? She was happy, I knew that. Her letter was bubbling over with happiness. What was it that meant so much to her? . . . and did I help change her mind about it?

Nancy with the grace of a lady, the veneer of a tramp. A girl who should have been soft and warm, staying home nights to cook supper for some guy, was being terrorized by a gunslinging punk. A lousy greaseball. A girl who had no defense except running, forced to sell herself to keep alive. I did her a favor and her eyes lit up like candles at an altar. We were buddies, damn good buddies for a little while.

The driver said, "Here you are, mister."

I passed a bill through the window and got out, my eyes looking up and down the street until I spotted a familiar blue uniform. I was going to have to do it the quickest way possible. The cop was walking towards me and I stared into a drugstore window until he went by, and when he had a half-block lead I followed him at a leisurely pace.

A lot of people like to run down the cops. They begin to think of them as human traffic lights, or two faces in a patrol car cruising down the street hoping some citizen will start some trouble. They forget that a cop has eyes and ears and can think. They forget that sometimes a cop on a beat likes it that way. The street is his. He knows everyone on it. He knows who and what they are and where they spend their time. He doesn't want to get pulled off it even for a promotion, because then he loses his friends and becomes chained to a desk or an impersonal case. The cop I was following looked like that kind. He was big from the ground up, and almost as big around. There was a purpose in his stride and pride in his carriage, and several times I saw him nod to women sitting in doorways and fake a pass at fresh brats that yelled out something nasty about coppers. Some day those same kids would be screaming for him to hurry up and get to where the trouble was.

When the cop called in at a police phone I picked up on him. He turned into a lunchroom, climbed on a stool and I was right beside him. He took off his coat and hat, ordered corn beef and cabbage and I took the same. The plates came and we both ate silently. Half-way through, the two guys next to me paid up and left, which was the chance I waited for.

One had left a tabloid on the stool and I propped it up in front of me, using it as a shield while I took my badge and identification card from my pocket. I only had to nudge the cop once and he looked over, saw the stuff I palmed and frowned.

"Mike Hammer, private cop." I kept my voice low, chewing as I spoke. "Don't watch me."

The cop frowned again and went back to his lunch. "Pat Chambers will vouch for me. I'm working with him on a case." This time the frown deepened and lines of disbelief touched his cheeks.

"I have to find Cobbie Bennett," I said. "Right away. Do you know where he is?"

He took another mouthful of corn beef and threw a dime on the counter. The chef came over and he asked for change. When he had two nickels he got up, still chewing, and walked over to a phone booth up front and shut the door.

About a minute later he was back and working on the corn beef again. He shoved the plate away, drew his coffee to him and seemed to notice me for the first time.

"Done with the paper, feller?"

"Yeah." I handed it to him. He took a pair of horn-rimmed glasses from his pocket and worked them on, holding the paper open to the baseball scores. His lips worked as if he were reading, only he said, "I think Cobbie's hiding out in a rooming house one block west. Brownstone affair with a new stoop. He looks scared."

The counterman came over and took the plates away. I ordered pie and more coffee, ate it slowly, then paid up and left. The cop was still there reading the paper; he never glanced up once and he probably wouldn't for another ten minutes.

I found the stoop first, then the house. Cobbie Bennett found me. He peered out of a second-story window just as I turned up the stairs and for a split second I had a look at a pale, white face that had terror etched deep into the skin.

The door was open and I walked into the hallway. Cobbie called to me from the head of the stairs. "Here, up here, Mike." This time I watched where I was going. There were too many nice places for a guy to hide with a baseball bat in those damn hallways. Before I reached the landing Cobbie had me by the lapels of my coat and was dragging me into a room.

"Christ, Mike, how'd ya find me? I never told nobody where I was! Who said I was here?"

I shoved him away. "You're not hard to find, Cobbie. Nobody is when they're wanted badly enough."

"Don't say that, Mike, will ya? Christ, it's bad enough having you find me. Suppose . . ."

"Stop jabbering like an idiot. You wanted me, so I'm here."

He shoved a bolt in the door and paced across the room, running his fingers through his hair and down his face. He couldn't stand still and the fact that I parked myself in the only chair in the place and seemed completely at ease made him jumpier still.

"They're after me, Mike. I just got away in time."

"Who's they?"

"Look, ya gotta help me out. Jeez, you got me inta this, now ya gotta help me out. They're after me, see? I can't stick around. I gotta get outa town." He stuck a cigarette in his mouth and tried to light it. He made it with the fourth match.

"Who's they?" I asked again.

Cobbie licked his lips. His shoulder had a nervous twitch and he kept turning his head towards the door as if he were listening for something. "Mike, somebody saw you with me that night. They passed the word and the heat's on. I—I gotta blow."

I just sat there and watched him. He took a drag on the cigarette before he threw it on the worn-out carpet and ground it in with his heel. "Damn it, Mike, don't just sit there. Say something!"

"Who's they?"

For the first time it sank in. He got white around the corners of his mouth. "I dunno, I dunno. It's somebody big. Something's popping in this town and I don't know what it is. All I know is the heat's on me because I got seen messing around with you. What'll I do, Mike? I can't stay here. You don't know them guys. When they're out to get ya they don't miss!"

I stood up and stretched, trying to look bored. "I can't tell you a damn thing, Cobbie, not unless you sound off first. If you don't want to speak, then the hell with you. Let 'em get you."

He grabbed my sleeve and hung on for dear life. "No, Mike, don't . . . I'd tell you what I know only I don't know nothing. I just got the sign, then I heard some things. It was about that redhead. Because of you I'm getting the works. I saw some big boys down the street last night. They wasn't locals. They was here before when there was some trouble, and a couple guys disappeared. I know why they're there . . . they're after me . . . and you maybe."

He was doing better now. "Go on, Cobbie."

"Th' racket's organized, see? We pay for protection and we pay plenty. I don't know where it goes, but as long as we pay there's no trouble. As long as we make like clams there's still no trouble. But, damn it, you came around and somebody saw me shooting my mouth off, now there's plenty of trouble again and it's all for me."

"How do they know what you said?"

His face grew livid. "Who cares? Think they worry about what I said? Some guys is poison and you're one, because you was on that redhead! Why didn't she drop dead sooner!"

I reached out and grabbed his arm and brought him up to my face. "Shut up," I said through my teeth.

"Aw, Mike, I didn't mean nothin', honest. I'm just trying to tell ya."

I let him go and he backed off a step, wiping his forehead with a sleeve. The light glistened on a tear that rolled down his cheek. "I don't know what it's about, Mike. I don't wanna get knocked off. Can't you do something?"

"Maybe."

Cobbie looked up, hopefully. His tongue passed over his parched lips. "Yeah?"

"Think, Cobbie. Think of the boys you saw. Who were they?"

The lines in his face grew deeper. "Hard boys. They were carrying rods. I think they came outa Detroit."

"Who do they work for?"

"The same guy what gets the pay-off jack, I guess."

"Names, Cobbie?"

He shook his head, the hope gone. "I'm only a little guy. Mike. How would I know? Every week I give a quarter of my take to a guy who passes it along in a chain until it reaches the top. I don't even want to know. I'm . . . I'm scared, Mike, scared silly. You're the only one I knew to call. Nobody'll look at me now because they know the heat's on, that's why I wanted to see you."

"Anybody know you're here?"

"No. Just you."

"What about the landlady?"

"She don't know me. She don't care, neither. How'd you find me, Mike?"

"A way your pals won't try. Don't worry about it. Here's what I want you to do. Sit tight, don't leave this room, not even to go downstairs. Keep away from the window and be sure your door is locked."

His eyes widened and his hands went to my arms. "You got an out figgered? You think maybe I can get outa town?"

"Could be. We'll have to do this carefully. You got anything to eat in the place?"

"Some canned stuff and two bottles of beer."

"It'll hold you. Now remember this. Tomorrow night at exactly nine-thirty I want you to walk out of this place. Go down the street, turn right one block, then head west again. Keep walking as if you didn't know a thing was up. Take a turn around your neighborhood and say hullo to anyone you want to. Only keep walking. Got that?"

Little beads of sweat were standing out on his forehead. "Christ, ya want me to get killed? I can't leave here and . . ."

"Maybe you'd sooner get bumped off here . . . if you don't starve to death first."

"No, Mike. I don't even mean that! But, jeez, walking out like that! . . ."

"Are you going to do it or not? I haven't got time to waste, Cobbie."

He sank into the chair and covered his face with his hands. Crying came easy for Cobbie. "Y-yeah. I'll go. Nine-thirty." His head jerked up, tears streaking his face. "What're ya thinking of? Can't you tell me?"

"No, I can't. You just do what I told you. If it works, you'll be able to leave town in one piece. But I want you to remember something."

"What?"

"Don't—ever—come—back."

I left him with his face white and sick-looking. When the door closed I heard him sobbing again.

Outside, a premature dusk was settling over the city as the grey haze of rain clouds blew in from the southeast. I crossed the street and walked north to a subway kiosk. Before I reached it the rain had started again. A train had just pulled out of the station, giving me five minutes to wait, so I found a phone and called Lola's apartment. Nobody answered. No news was good news, or so they say. I tried the office and Velda told me it had been a fairly quiet afternoon. I hung up before she could ask questions. Besides, my train was just rattling past the platform.

At Fifty-ninth I got off, grabbed another cab and had the driver haul me over to where my car was parked. I thought I saw a guy I knew walk past and I went into a knee bend fumbling for my shoelace. It was getting to be a pain in the butt playing corpse.

When I finally got the chance I hopped in and shot away from there as fast as I could. Some chances I couldn't afford, one was being spotted near Lola's place. She was one person I wanted to myself, all nice and safe.

The wind picked up and began throwing the rain around. The few pedestrians left on the sidewalks were huddled under marquees or bellowing for cabs that didn't stop. Every time I stopped for a red light I could see the pale blur of faces behind the glass storefronts, the water running down making them waver eerily. All with that same blank look of the trapped when nothing can be done to help.

I was wondering if Lola was having any trouble. The rain was going to slow her up plenty at a time when speed was essential. That damn camera! Why did Red ever mess with it in the first place?

Lola had said a job, didn't she? A place called Quick Pix or something. It had slipped my mind until now. I spotted a parking place ahead and turned into it, ready to make a dash into a candy store the moment the rain slackened. There was a lull between gusts that gave me a chance to run across the pavement and work my way through the small crowd that had gathered in the doorway out of the wet.

Inside I pulled out the directory and thumbed through it, trying each borough, but nothing like Quick Pix showed up. Not even a variation. I bought a pack of butts and asked the clerk if he had an old directory around and he shook his head, paused, then told me to wait a minute. He went into the back room and came up with a dog-eared Manhattan phone book, covered with dust. "They usually take 'em back, but this was an extra they forgot," he explained. "Saw it the other day at the back of the shelf."

I thanked him and ran through it. The hunch paid off. Quick Pix had a phone number and an address off Seventh Avenue. When I dialed the number there was a series of clicks and the operator asked me who I was calling. I gave her the number and she said it had been discontinued some time ago.

That was that. Or not quite. Maybe they still had an office, but no phone.

One of the boys asked me if I was going uptown and I nodded for him to come along. For ten blocks he kept up an incessant line of chatter that I didn't hear until he poked me to let him out at a subway station. I pulled over, he opened the door and thanked me and ran down the stairs.

Behind me a line of horns blasted an angry barrage in my direction, and over it a cop's whistle shrilled a warning. I came back to the present with a dirty word and my mind in a spin, because on the newsstand by the subway was a pile of the late evening papers and each one screamed to the world that the police were conducting a city-wide clean-up campaign of vice.

Somebody had talked.

I stopped for another red light, yelling to a newsy to bring one over and I gave him a buck for his trouble. It was there, all right, heads, captions, and sub-captions. The police were in possession of information that was going to lead to the biggest round-up of this, that, and the next thing the city ever saw.

Which was fine, great. Just what we wanted in the pig's neck. Pat must be raving mad. The papers were doing a beautiful civic job of chasing the rats out of town. Damn them, why couldn't they keep quiet!

The light changed and I saw my street coming up. I had to circle the block because it was a one-way, then squeeze in between a decrepit delivery truck and a battered sedan. The number I wanted was a weather-beaten loft building with an upholstery shop fronting on the street. On one side was a narrow entrance with a service elevator in the rear and a sign announcing the available vacancies hanging on the door.

I rang the bell and heard the elevator rattle its way downwards and come to a stop. The door opened and a guy with a week's growth of beard looked at me with rheumy eyes and waited for me to say something.

"Where can I find the super of this building?"

"Whatcha want him fer?" He spat a stream of tobacco juice between the grill of the elevator.

I palmed my badge in one hand and a fin in the other and let him see both. "Private cop."

"I'm the super," he said.

He reached for the fin and tucked it in his shirt pocket. "I'm listening."

I said, "I'm looking for an outfit called Quick Pix. They were listed as being here."

"That was a long time ago, buster. They pulled out in a hurry 'most a year ago."

"Anybody there now?"

"Naw. This place's a dive. Who the hell would want to rent here? Maybe another outfit like Q.P. They was a fly-by-night bunch, I think."

"How about a look at the place?"

"Sure, come on."

I stepped aboard and we crept up to the fourth floor and stopped. He left the elevator there and turned the lights on, pointing to the end of the hall. "Room 209."

The door wasn't locked. Where an ordinary house nightlatch should be was a round hole like an eye in a skull. The super did some trick with a switch box in a closet and the lights went on in the room.

It was a mess, all right. Somebody had packed out of there like the devil was on his tail. Finished proofs and negatives littered the floor, covered with spider webs and long tendrils of dust. The two windows had no shades and didn't need them, that's how thick the dirt was. Hypo had blown or was knocked from a box, covering one end with once white powder. Even now a few heel prints were visible in the stuff.

I gathered up a handful of snaps and looked them over. They were all two-by-three prints taken on the streets of couples walking arm-in-arm, sitting on park benches, coming out of Broadway theatres grinning at each other. On the backs were numbers in pencil and scrawled notations of the photogs.

A large packing-box served as a filing cabinet, spilling out blank tickets with a slit built for a quarter. The back half of the box contained other tickets that had been sent in with the mailer's name and address written in the right spot. They were tied in groups of about a hundred, and, all in all, there was a couple thousand dollars represented in cash right there. Quick Pix had done all right for itself.

To one side was a shelf running around the wall lined with shoe boxes and inscribed with names. One said, "N. Sanford" and my interest picked up. In it were cards numbered to correspond with the film in the camera, which looked like a three- or four-day supply. A pencilled note was a reminder to order more film. Neat, precise handwriting. Very feminine. It was Nancy's without a doubt. I plucked it out and tucked it in my pocket.

The guy had been standing near the door watching me silently. I heard him grunt a few times, then: "You know something? This place wasn't like this when they moved out."

I stopped what I was doing. "How's that?"

"I came in to see if they left the walls here and all this junk on the floor was stacked in one corner. Looks like somebody kicked it around."

"Yeah?"

He spat on the floor. "Yeah."

"Who ran the business?"

"Forgot his name." He shrugged. "Some character on his uppers. Guess he did pretty good after a while. One day he packs in here with a new convertible, tells me he's moving out and scrams. Never gimme a dime."

"What about the people that worked for him?"

"Hell, they was all out. They came in here that night and raised a stink. What was I supposed to do, pay their wages? I was lucky I tagged the guy, so I got the rent. Never said nothing to nobody, he didn't."

I stuck a match in my mouth and chewed the end off it. When I gave one last quick glance I walked out. "That does it." He shut the door and played with the switch box again, then stepped into the elevator after me and we started down.

"Get what you come for?" he asked.

"I didn't come for anything special. I'm, er, checking on the owner. He owed some money and I have to collect—for films."

"You don't say! Come to think of it, there's some stuff down in the cellar yet. One of the kids what worked there asked me if she could park it there. I let her when she slipped me a buck."

"She?"

"Yeah, a redhead. Nice kid."

He spat through the grill again and it splattered against the wall. "Do you ever read the papers?" I asked him.

"Funnies sometimes. Just the pictures. Broke my glasses four years ago and never got new ones. Why, what's going on?"

"Nothing. Let's see that stuff downstairs."

Before he could suggest it I came across with another five and it went in the pocket with the other. His grin showed teeth that were brown as mud. We passed the main floor and jolted to a stop at the basement. The air was damp and musty, almost like the morgue, but here was the smell of dirt and decay and the constant whirr of rat feet running along the pipes and timbers. There weren't any lights, but the guy had a flashlight stashed in a joint and he threw the beams around the walls. Little beady eyes looked back at me and ran off, to reappear again farther down. I got the creeps.

He didn't seem to mind it at all.

"Down back, I think." He pointed the flash at the floor and we stepped over crates, broken furniture and the kind of trash that accumulates over a span of years. We stopped by a bin and he poked around with a broom handle, scaring up some rats but nothing else. Beyond that was a row of shelves piled to capacity and he knocked the dust off some of the papers with a crack of the stick. Most of them were old bills and receipts, a few dusty ledgers and a wealth of old paper that had been saved up carefully. I opened a couple of boxes to help out. One was full of pencil stubs; the other some hasty sketches of nudes. They weren't very good.

The light got away from me before I could shove them back and the super said, "Think this is it." I held the light while he dragged out a corrugated cardboard box tied with twine. A big SAVE was written across the front in red crayon. He nodded and pursed his mouth, looking for a rat to spit tobacco juice at. He saw one on a pipe and let loose. I heard the rat squeaking all the way to the end, where he fell off and kicked around in some papers. The stuff he chewed must have been poison.

I pulled the twine off and opened the top. Inside was another box tied with lighter cord that broke easily enough. My hand was shaking a little as I bent back the cover and I pulled the light closer.

There were pictures in this one, all neatly sorted in two rows and protected by layers of tissue paper. Both sides of the box were lined with blotters to absorb any moisture, and between each group of shots was an index card bearing the date they were taken.

Perhaps I expected too much. Perhaps it was the thought of the other pictures that were stolen from me, perhaps it was just knowing that pictures fitted in somewhere, but I held my breath expectantly as I lifted them out.

Then I went into all the curse words I knew. All I had was another batch of street photos with smiling couples waving into the camera or doing something foolish. I was so damn mad I would have left them if I hadn't remembered that they cost me five bucks and I might as well get something for my dough. I tucked the box under my arm and went back to the elevator.

When we got to the street floor the super wanted to know if I felt like signing the after-hours book and I scratched J. Johnson in it and left.

At eight-fifteen I called Pat's home. He still hadn't come in, so I tried the office. The switchboard located him and the minute I heard his voice I knew there was trouble. He said, "Mike? Where are you?"

"Not far from your place. Anything new?"

"Yes." His words were clipped. "I want to speak to you. Can you meet me in the Roundtown Grill in ten minutes?"

"I'll be there. What's up?"

"Tell you then. Ten minutes." Someone called to him and he hung up. Ten minutes to the second I reached the Roundtown and threaded my way to the back and found Pat sitting in the last booth. There were lines of worry across his forehead that hadn't been there before, giving him an older look. He forced a grin when he saw me, and waved me to sit down.

Beside him he had a copy of the evening paper and he spread it out on the table. He tapped the headline. "Did you have anything to do with this?"

I shoved a butt in my mouth and fired it. "You know better than that, Pat."

He rolled the paper up into a ball and threw it aside, his mouth twisting into a snarl. "I didn't think so. I had to be sure. It got out some way and loused things up nice."

"How?"

A waiter set two beers down in front of us and Pat polished his off before the guy left and ordered another, quick. "I'm getting squeezed, pal. I'm getting squeezed nice. Do you know how many rotten little jerks there are in this world? There must be millions. Nine-tenths of them live in the city with us. Each rotten little jerk controls a block of votes. Each rotten little jerk wants something done or not done. They make a phone call to somebody who's pretty important and tell him what they want. Pretty soon that person gets a lot of the same kind of phone calls and decides that maybe he'd better do something about it, and the squeeze starts. Word starts drifting up the line to lay off or go slow, and it's the kind of a word that's blocked up with a threat that can be made good.

"Pretty, isn't it? You get hold of something that should be done and you have to lay off." The second beer followed the first and another was on its way. I had never seen Pat so mad before.

"I tried to be a decent cop," he ranted. "I try to stick to the letter of the law and do my duty. I figure the taxpayers have a say in things, but now I begin to wonder. It's coming from all directions—phone calls, hints that travelled too far to trace back, sly reminders that I'm just a cop and nothing but a captain, which doesn't carry too much weight if certain parties feel like doing something about it."

"Get down to cases, Pat."

"The D.A. called Ann Minor's death murder. He's above a fix and well in the public eye, so there's no pressure on him. The murder can be investigated if necessary, but get off the angles. That's the story. Word got out about the book, but not the fact that it's in code."

I tapped the ashes in the tray and squinted at him. "You mean there are a lot of boys mixed up with call-girls and the prostitution racket who don't want their names to get out, don't you?"

"Yes."

"And what are you going to do about it?"

No, Pat wasn't a bit happy. He said, "Either I go ahead with it, dig up the stuff and then get nicely pushed into a resignation, or I lay off and keep my job, sacrificing this case to give the public their money's worth in future cases."

I shook my head pathetically. "That's what you get for being honest. What'll it be?"

"I don't know, Mike."

"You'll have to make up your mind soon."

"I know. For the first time I wish I were wearing your badge instead of mine. You aren't so dumb."

"Neither are you, kid. The answer's plain, isn't it?" I was sneering myself now. He looked up and met my eyes and nodded. A nasty grin split his lips apart and his teeth were together, tight.

"Call it, Mike."

"You take care of your end. I'll brace the boys who give you trouble. If I have to I'll ram their teeth down their throats and I hope I have to. There's more to it than that. I don't have to tell you how big this racket is. The girls in the flashy clothes and the high-price tags are only one side of it. The same group with its hand on them reaches down to the smaller places, too. It's all tied in together. The only trouble is that when you untie one knot the whole thing can come apart.

"They're scared now. They're acting fast. We have that book, but you can bet it isn't much. There other books, too, nicely ducked out of sight where it'll take a lot of looking to dig up. They'll come. We'll get hold of somebody who will sing, and to save their own necks the others will sing, too. Then the proof will pop up."

I slammed my hand against the table and curled my fingers into a tight knot until the flesh was white around the knuckles. "We don't need proof, Pat. All we have to do is *look* for proof. The kind of boys behind the curtain won't take that. They'll make a move and we'll be ready for them."

"Yeah, but when?"

"Tomorrow night. The big boys are hiring their work done. One of their stoolies is on the list because he sounded off to me. Tomorrow night at exactly nine-thirty, a pimp called Cobbie Bennett is going to walk out of his rooming house and down the street. Some time that night he's going to be spotted and a play will be made. That's all we need. Beat them to the jump and we'll make the first score. It will scare the hell out of them again. Let them know that politics are going to pot. We can get the politicians later if we have to."

"Does this Bennett know about this?"

"He knows he's going to be a clay pigeon of some sort. It's his only chance of staying alive. Maybe he will and maybe he won't. He has to take it. You have your men spotted around ready to wade in when the trouble starts. After it's finished, let Cobbie beat it. He's no good any more. He won't be back."

I wrote the address of the rooming house on the back of an envelope, diagramming the route Cobbie would take, and passed it over. Pat glanced at it and stuck it in his pocket. "This can mean my job, kid."

"It might mean your neck, too," I reminded him. "If it works you won't have any more sly hints and phone calls, and those rotten little jerks with the bloc of votes will be taking the next train out of town. We're not going to stop anything because the game is as old as Eve. What we will do is slow it up long enough to keep a few people alive who wouldn't be alive, and maybe knock off some who would be better off dead."

"And all because of one redheaded girl," Pat said slowly.

"That's right. All because of Nancy. All because she was murdered."

"We don't know that."

"I'm supposing it. I've uncovered a few other things. If it was an accident, she wasn't expected to die that way. Nancy was slated to be killed. Here's something else, Pat. This *looks* like one thing, the part you can't see is tied in with that same redhead. I can't understand it, but I'm kicking a few ideas around that look pretty good."

"The insurance company is satisfied it was an accident. They're ready to pay off if her inheritors can be found."

"Ah, that's the rub, as the bard once said. That, my chum, is the big step."

My watch was creeping up on itself. I stood up and finished the beer that had turned flat while we talked. "I'll call you early tomorrow, Pat. I want to be in on the show. Let me know what comes out of the little black book."

He still wore his sneer. Back of his eyes a fire was burning bright enough to put somebody in hell.

"Something came out of it already. We paid a call on Murray Candid. Among his belongings we found a few doodles and some notes. The symbols compare with some of those in his book. He's going to have to do some tall explaining when we find him."

My mouth fell open at that. "What do you mean . . . find him?"

"Murray Candid has disappeared. He wasn't seen by anybody after he left us," he said.

chapter twelve

As I GOT into my car I thought over what Pat had said. Murray was gone. Why? That damned, ever-present why! Did he duck out to escape what would follow, or was he taken away because he knew too much? A guy like Murray was a slicker. If he knew too much he knew he knew it, and knew what it could cost him, so he'd have to play it smart and have insurance. Murray would let it be known that anybody who tried to plow him under would be cutting their own throats. He'd have a fat, juicy report in a lawyer's hands, ready to be mailed to the police as soon as he was dead. That's double indemnity . . . the bigger boys would have to keep him alive to keep their own noses clean.

No, Murray wasn't dead. The city was big enough to hide even him. He'd show sooner or later. Pat would have covered that angle, and right now there'd be a cop watching every bus terminal, every train station. I bet they'd see more rats than Murray trying to desert the sinking ship.

The rain had turned into a steady drizzle that left a slick on the pavement and deadened the evening crowd. I turned north with the windshield wipers clicking a monotonous tune, and stopped a block away from Lola's apartment. A grocery store was still open and the stack of cold cuts in the window looked too inviting to pass up. When I had loaded my arms with more than I could eat for a month, I used the package to shield my face and walked up to her place.

I kicked the door with my foot and she yelled to come in. I had to peek around the bundle to see her stretched out on the couch with her shoes off and a wet towel across her forehead.

"It's me, honey."

"Do tell. I thought it was a horse coming up the stairs."

I propped the package in a chair and sat down on the edge of the couch, reaching for the towel. She came out from under it grinning. "Oh, Mike! It's so good to see you!"

She threw her arms around my neck and I leaned over and kissed her. She was nice to look at. I could sit there all day and watch her. She closed her eyes and rubbed her hair in my face.

"Rough day, kid?"

"Awful," she said. "I'm tired, I'm wet and I'm hungry. And I didn't find the camera."

"I can take care of the hungry part. There's eats over there. Nothing you have to cook either."

"You're a wonderful guy, Mike. I wish . . . "

"What?"

"Nothing. Let's eat."

I slid my arms under her and lifted her off the couch. Her eyes had a hungry sparkle that could mean many things. "You're a big girl," I said.

"I have to be . . . for you. To the kitchen, James." She scooped up the bag as I passed the chair and went through the doorway.

Lola put the coffee on while I set the table. We used the wrappings for plates and one knife between us, sitting close enough so our knees touched. "Tell me about today, Lola."

"There isn't much to tell. I started at the top of the list and reached about fifteen hock shops. None of them had it, and after a few discreet questions I learned that they never had had it. A few of the clerks were so persuasive that they almost made me buy one anyway."

"How many more to go?"

"Days and days worth, Mike. It will take a long time, I'm afraid."

"We have to try it."

"Uh-huh. Don't worry, I'll keep at it. Incidentally, in three of the places that happened to be located fairly close to each other, someone else had been looking for a camera."

My cup stopped half-way to my mouth. "Who?"

"A man. I pretended that it might have been a friend of mine who was shopping for me and got one clerk to remember that the fellow had wanted a commercial camera for taking street pictures. Apparently the kind I was after. He didn't look any over; just asked, then left."

It was a hell of a thought, me letting Lola run head on into something like that. "It may be a coincidence. He may have shopped just those three places. I don't like it."

"I'm not afraid, Mike. He . . . "

"If it wasn't a coincidence he might shop the other places and find that you were ahead of him. If he guessed what you were doing he could wait up for you. I still don't like it."

She became grim then, letting a shadow of her former hardness cloud her face for an instant. "Like you said, Mike, I'm a big girl. I've been around long enough to stand any guy off if he pulls something on the street. A knee can do a guy a lot of damage in the right places, and if that doesn't work, well . . . one scream will bring a lot of heroes around to take care of any one guy no matter how tough he is."

I had to laugh at that. "O.K., O.K., you'll get by. After that speech I'll even be afraid to kiss you good night."

"Mike, with you I'm as powerless as a kitten and as speechless as a giraffe. Please kiss me good night, huh?"

"I'll think about it. First, we have work to do."

"What kind, I hope . . . ?"

"Look at pictures. I have a batch of pics Nancy had tucked away. They're pictures and I paid for them, so I'll look at them."

We cleared the mess off the table and I went in for the box. I took them out of the box and piled half in front of Lola and half in front of me. When we took our seats I said, "Give every one a going-over. They may mean something, they may not. They weren't where they should have been, that's why I'm thinking there might be something special in the lot."

Lola nodded and picked a snapshot from the top of her pile. I did the same. At first I took in every detail, looking for things out of the ordinary, but the pictures followed such a set pattern that my inspection grew casual and hurried. Faces and more faces. Smiles, startled expressions, deliberate poses. One entire group taken from the same spot on Broadway, always the same background.

In two of them the man in the picture tried to shield his face. The camera was fast enough to stop the motion, but the finger on the shutter trigger was too slow to prevent him getting his hand in the way. I went to put one back on the discard pile, looking at it again carefully and put it aside instead. The portion of the face that showed looked familiar.

Lola said, "Mike . . . "

She had her lip between her teeth and was fingering a snap. She turned it around and showed it to me, a lovely young girl smiling at a middle-aged man who was frowning at the camera. My eyes asked the question. "She was . . . one of the girls, Mike. We . . . went on dates together."

"The guy?"

"I don't know."

I took the snap and laid it face down with the other. Five minutes later Lola found another. The girl was a zoetic creature, about thirty, with the statuesque lines of a mannequin. The guy she was with could have been a stand-in for a blimp. He was short and fat, in clothes that tried to make him look tall and thin and only made him look shorter and fatter.

"She's another one, Lola?"

"Yes. She didn't last long in New York. She played it smart and married one of the suckers. I remember the man, too. He runs a gambling joint uptown. Some sort of a small-time politician, too. He used to call for her in an official car."

It was coming now. Little reasons that explained the *why*. Little things that would be big things before long. My pile was growing nicely. Maybe every picture on the table had a meaning I couldn't see. Maybe most were just camouflage to discourage hasty searchers.

I turned the snap over, and lightly pencilled on the back near the bottom was "See S-5." There was more to it than the picture, evidently.

Could it be nothing more than an office memo . . . or did Nancy have a private file of her own?

My breath started coming in quick, hot gasps. It was like seeing a half-finished picture and recognizing what it would be like when it was finished. If this was an indication . . . I pulled the remaining photos closer and went to work on them.

The next one came out of my deal. I got it because I was lucky and I was hating some people so damn hard that their faces drew an automatic response. The picture was that of a young couple, no more than twenty. They smiled into the camera with a smile that was youth with the world in its pocket and a life to be led. But they're weren't important.

It was the background that was important. The faces in the background. One was that of my client, his hand on the knob of a door, a cane swinging jauntily over his arm. Behind him was Feeney Last in a chauffeur's uniform, closing the door of the car. It wasn't just Feeney, it was the expression on his face. It was a leer of hateful triumph, a leer of expectancy as he eyed a guy in a sports outfit that had been about to step past him.

The guy was pop-eyed with fear, his jaw hanging slack, and even at that moment he had started to draw back as he saw Feeney.

He should have been scared. The guy's name was Russ Bowen and he was found shot full of holes not long after the picture was taken.

I could feel the skin pulling tight around my temples and my lips drew back from my teeth. Lola said something, but I didn't hear her. She grabbed my hand, made me look at her. "What is it. What is it, Mike? Please . . . don't look that way!"

I shoved the picture in front of her and pointed to the little scene in the background. "This guy's dead, Lola. The other guy is Feeney Last."

Her eyes came up slowly, unbelievingly. She shook her head. "Not Feeney . . . it can't be, Mike."

"Don't tell me, kid. That's Feeney Last. It was taken when he worked for Mr. Berin. I couldn't miss that greaseball in a million years."

She stared at me hard. Her eyes drifted back to the picture and she shook her head again. "His name is Miller. Paul Miller. He—he's one of the men who supplies girls to . . . the houses."

"What?"

"That's right. One of the kids pointed him out to me some time ago. He used to work the West Coast, picking them up there and sending them East to the syndicate. I'm positive that's him!"

Nice going, Feeney, I thought, very nice going. Keep a respectable job as a cover-up for the other things. Good heavens, if Berin-Grotin in all his insufferable pride ever knew that, he would have had Feeney hanging by the thumbs! I looked at the snap again, saw my client unaware of the little scene behind him, completely the man-about-town bent on an afternoon of mild pleasure. It was a good shot, this one. I could see the lettering on the door there. BAR ENTRANCE, ALBINO CLUB, it read. Apparently Mr. Berin's favorite haunt. He'd have his cup of good cheer while five feet away a murder was in progress.

"Do you know the other guy?"

"Yes. He ran some houses. They—found him shot, didn't they?"

"That's right. Murdered. This thing goes back a long way."

Lola closed her eyes and dropped her head forward. Her face was relaxed in sadness. She took a deep breath and opened her eyes. "There's something on the back, Mike."

It was another symbol. This one said "See T-9-20." If that dash stood for "to," it meant eleven pages of something was connected with this. The details of the Russ Bowen murder maybe? Could there be a possibility that the redhead had come up with something covering that murder? Ye gods, if that were true, no wonder Feeney was on her neck. How many angles could there be to this thing?

I could not find anything else; I went through my pile twice and nothing showed for me, so I swapped with Lola and started all over again. I didn't find any more, either, but Lola did. When she was through she had half a dozen shots beside her and called my attention to the women. They were her former associates. She knew some of the men by sight, too, and they weren't just pickups. They dipped dough in the cut of their clothes and the sparkle of diamonds on their fingers.

And always there was that notation on the back referring to some other file. There was an envelope on the dish closet and I tucked the prints in it, stowing them in my pocket. The rest I threw back in the box and pushed aside. Lola followed me into the living room, watched me pace up and down the room. When she held out a cigarette I took it, had one deep drag and snuffed it out in a dish.

Feeney Last. Paul Miller. He came from the Coast. He saw a way to get back East without arousing suspicion. He was connected with the racket but good, and he could operate under the cover of old boy's respectability. Feeney was after Nancy and for good reason. If it was blackmail, the plot went pretty deep. She wasn't content to stick to strangers with herself as the catch . . . she used the tie-up with girls already in the racket.

I stopped in the middle of the floor, fought to let an idea battle its way into my consciousness, felt it blocked by a dozen other thoughts. I shook my head and began pacing again.

"I need a drink," I said.

"There's nothing in the house," Lola told me.

I reached for my hat. "Get your coat. We're going out."

"Aren't you supposed to be dead?"

"Not that dead. Come on."

She pulled a raincoat from the closet, stepped into frilly boots that did things for her legs. "All set, Mike. Where are we going?"

"I'll tell you better when we get there."

All the way downtown I put my mind to it. Lola had snuggled up against me and I could feel the warmth of her body soaking through her coat to mine. She knew I was trying to think and kept quiet, occasionally looking up at me with interest. She laid her head on my shoulder and squeezed my arm. It didn't help me think any.

The rain had laid a pall over the city, keeping the spectators indoors. Only the tigers were roaming the streets this night. The taxis were empty hearses going back and forth, the drivers alert for what few fares there were, jamming to a stop at the wave of a hand or a shrill whistle.

We went past the Zero Zero Club and Lola sat up to look. There wasn't much to see. The sign was out and the place in darkness. Somebody had tacked a "Closed" sign on the door. Pat was going whole hog on this thing. I pulled into a half-empty parking lot and we found a small bar with the windows steamed up. Lola had a Martini and I had a beer there, but the place had a rank odor to it and we left. The next bar was three stores down and we turned into it and climbed on the stools at the end.

Four guys at the other end with nothing much to talk about until we came in suddenly found a topic of conversation and eight eyes started looking Lola up and down. One guy told the bartender to buy the lady a drink and she got another Martini and I got nothing.

She was hesitant about taking it at first and I was too deep in thought to argue the point. The redhead's face floated in front of me. She was sipping her coffee again, the ring on her finger half-turned to look like a wedding band. Then the vision would fade and I'd see her hands again, this time folded across her chest, and the ring was gone, leaving only a reddish bruise that went unnoticed among the other bruises. The greaseball would laugh at me. I could hear his voice sneering, daring, challenging me to get the answer.

I ordered another beer. Lola had two Martinis in front of her now and one empty pushed aside. The guys were laughing, talking just loud enough to be heard. The guy on the end shrugged as he threw his leg off the stool, said something dirty and came over to Lola with a cocky strut.

He had an arm around her waist and was pulling out the stool next to her when I rolled the cigarette down between my fingers and flipped it. The lit end caught him right in the eye and his sweet talk changed into a yelp of pain that dwindled off to a stream of curses.

The rest of the platoon came off the stools in a well-timed maneuver that was a second later than mine. I walked around and kicked the wise guy right in the belly, so hard that he was puking his guts out before he hit the floor doubled up like a pretzel. The platoon got back on their stools again without bothering to send a first-aid party out.

I bought Lola the next Martini myself.

The guy on the floor groaned, vomited again, and Lola said, "Let's leave, Mike. I'm shaking so hard I can't lift the glass."

I shoved my change toward the bartender, who was watching me with a grin on his face. The guy retched again and we left.

"When are you going to talk to me?" Lola asked. "My honor has been upheld and you haven't even bestowed the smile of victory on me."

I turned a smile on her, a real one. "Better?"

"You're so ugly you're beautiful, Mike. Some day I want you to tell me about those scars over your eyes . . . and the one on your chin."

"I'll only tell you part of the story."

"The woman in your life, huh?"

When I nodded happily she poked me in the ribs and pretended to be hurt.

One side of the street was fairly well deserted. We waited for a few cars to pass and cut over, our collars turned up against the drizzle. The rain in Lola's hair reflected a thousand lights, each one shimmering separately on its deep-toned background. We swung along with a free stride, holding hands, our shoulders nearly touching, laughing at nothing. It struck me that we were the faces in those pictures, the kind of people the redhead snapped, a sure thing to buy a print to remember the moment.

I wondered what her cut of the quarter was. Maybe she got five cents for every two bits sent in. A lousy nickel. It wasn't fair. Guys like Murray Candid rolling in dough, monkeys with enough capital to finance a week-end with a high-class prostitute. Greaseballs like Feeney Last being paid off to talk a girl into selling her body and soul for peanuts. Even Cobbie Bennett got his. Hell, I shouldn't squawk, I had mine . . . and now I had five hundred bucks too much. Ann Minor certainly didn't have time to cash that check. It should still be in her apartment, nobody else could cash it, not with the newspapers carrying all the tripe about the investigation and her death.

"Where are we going?" Lola had to step up her pace to keep abreast of me.

"The Albino Club. Ever been there?"

"Once. Why there? I thought you didn't want to be seen."

"I've never been there either. I owe my client five bills and there's a chance he might be there. He may want an explanation."

"Oh!"

The club wasn't far off. Ten minutes' walking brought us to the front entrance and a uniformed doorman obviously glad to see a customer for a change. It was a medium-sized place, stepped down from the sidewalk a few feet, lacking the gaudy atmosphere of the Zero Zero. Instead of chrome and gilt, the wall lights reflected the sheen of highly polished oak and brought out the color of the murals around the room. There was an orchestra rather than a band—one that played, soft and low, compositions to instill a mood and never detract from the business of eating and drinking.

As we stepped into the anteroom we both had a chance to look at the place over the partitions. A few tables were occupied by late diners. Clustered in a corner were half a dozen men still in business suits, deep in discussion with occasional references to pictures sketched on the tablecloth. The bar ran the length of the room and behind it four bartenders fiddled with glasses or did something to while away the time. The fifth was pouring whisky into the glasses of the only two patrons.

Lola went rigid and she breathed my name. I saw what she meant. One of the guys at the bar was Feeney Last. I wasn't interested in him right then. The other was the guy I had beat the hell out of in the parking lot. The one I thought *might* have been looking for his car keys. My conscience felt much better when I looked at the wreck of his nose. The bastard was after the ring.

Lola read my mind again. "Are . . . you going in . . . after him?"

I wanted to. God, how I wanted to! I couldn't think of anything I'd sooner do. Feeney Last, right here where I could get to him. Man, oh man, the guy sure felt secure. After all, what did the cops have on him? Not a damn thing . . . and if anything hung over his head he was the only one that had an idea where it could be found. Except me.

And I was supposed to be dead.

We didn't go in the Albino Club after all. I snatched my hat back from the rack and pushed Lola outside. The doorman was cut to the quick yet able to nod good night politely.

On the corner of Broadway a glorified dog-wagon was doing a land-office business in late snacks. When I saw the blue-and-white phone disc on the front I steered Lola in, told her to order us some coffee, then went down the back to the phone booth.

Pat was home. He must have just gotten in because he was breathing hard from the stairs. I said, "This is Mike, kid. I just saw Feeney Last in the Albino Club with a guy I tangled with not long ago. Can you put a man on him? I have things to do or I'd tail him myself."

"You bet!" Pat exploded. "I've had him on the wires for over two hours. Every police car in the city is looking for him."

It puzzled me. "What . . . ?"

"I had a teletype from the Coast. It's Feeney they want out there for that murder. He answers the description in every respect."

Something prompted me to ask, "What kind of a kill was it, Pat?"

"He broke the guy's neck in a brawl. He started off with a knife, lost it in the scuffle, then broke his neck."

A chill crept up my back and I was in that hallway again, feeling the cut of a smashing blow under my ear. There wasn't any doubt about it now, not the slightest. Feeney had more than one technique. He could kill with a rod or a knife, and with his hands if he had to.

"The Albino Club, Pat. You know where it is. He's there. I'm going to race the patrol car and if I win you'll need the dead wagon."

I slammed the phone back and shoved my way through the crowd at the counter. Lola was looking for me and she didn't have to be told that something had happened. When I went past her as though she wasn't there she called after me and spun off her stool, but by that time I was on the street and running, running as fast as I could go and the few people on the sidewalk got out of the way to stare after me with their mouths dropping open.

My gun was in my hand when I took the corner. My chest was a ball of fire that ejected the air in quick, hot gasps and all I could think of was smashing the butt end of the rod in Feeney's face. From far off I heard the wail of a siren, a low moaning that put speed in my feet and craving desire to get there first.

We both lost. In the yellow light of the street I saw a car pull away from the curb and when I got outside the Albino Club Feeney Last and his friend had left.

I found out why in a minute. There was a radio at the bar and Feeney had persuaded the bartender to keep it on police-calls just for laughs. He had the laugh, all right. He was probably howling his goddamn head off.

chapter thirteen ▰▰▰▰▰▰▰▰▰▰▰

PAT ARRIVED SEVEN minutes after the patrol car. By that time, Lola had caught up to me and stood to one side catching her breath. As usual, the curious had formed a tight ring around us and the cops were busy trying to disperse them. Pat said, "It's a hell of a note. You didn't get the make of the car?"

I shook my head. "Only that it was a dark one. The doorman didn't notice either. Goddamn, that makes me mad!"

A reporter pushed his way through the cordon ready to take notes. Pat told him tersely, "The police will issue an official statement later." The guy wouldn't take it for an answer and tried to quiz the cops, but they didn't know any more than the police-call told them, to close in on the Albino Club and hold anyone from leaving.

I stepped back into the crowd and Pat followed. I couldn't press my luck too far. I was still dead and I might as well stay that way for a while if I could. I leaned up against the fender of a car and Pat stayed close. Lola came over and held my hand.

"How's it going, Pat?"

"Not good. I'm catching hell. It's coming at me from all directions now and I don't know which way to turn. Somebody has one devil of a lot of pull in this town. They're talking, too, enough to put the papers wise. The reporters are swarming around headquarters looking for leads. I can't give them anything and they jump me for it. The publicity is going to cause a lot of eyebrow-lifting tomorrow."

There was a determined set to his jaw anyway. Pat could dish it out, too. His time was coming. "What are you doing about it?"

His grin wasn't pleasant. "We staged a couple of raids tonight. Remember what you said about the police knowing things . . . . and still having to let them go on?" I nodded. "I used hand-picked men. They raided two fancy houses uptown and came up with a haul that would make your eyes pop out. We have names now, and charges to go with them. Some of the men we netted in the raid tried to bribe my officers and are going to pay through the nose for it!"

"Brother!"

"They're scared, Mike. They don't know what we have or what we haven't and they can't take chances. Between now and to-morrow the lid will be off City Hall unless I miss my guess. They're scared and worried."

"They should be."

Pat waited, his tongue licking at the corner of his mouth.

"Nancy had been working at a scheme. Oh, it was a pretty little scheme that I thought involved petty blackmail. I think it went further than that."

"How much further?"

I looked at Lola. "In a day or two . . . maybe we can tell you then."

"My legs have a long way to go yet," she said.

"What are you getting at?" Pat asked.

"You'll find out. By the way, have you got things set up for tomorrow night?"

Pat lit a cigarette and flipped the burnt match into the gutter. "You know, I'm beginning to wonder who's running my department. I'm sure as hell not."

But he was smiling when he said it.

"Yeah, we're ready. The men are picked, but they haven't been told their assignments. I don't want any more leaks."

"Good! They'll pull their strings and when they find that doesn't work they'll pull their guns. We beat them at that and they're up the tree, ready for the net. Meanwhile we have to be careful. It's rough, Pat, isn't it?"

"Too rough. The city can be damn dirty if you look in the right places."

I ground out my butt under my heel. "They talk about the Romans. They only threw human beings into a pit with lions. At least, then, the lions had a wall around them so they couldn't get out. Here they hang out in bars and on the street corners looking for a meal."

The crowd had thinned out and the cops were back in the car trying to brush off the reporter. Another car with a press tag on the window swerved to a stop and two stepped out. I didn't want to wait around. Too many knew me by sight. I told Pat so-long and took off up the street with Lola trotting alongside me.

I drove her to the apartment and she insisted I come up for the coffee I didn't have before. It was quiet up here, the absolute early-morning quiet that comes when the city has gone to bed and the earliest risers haven't gotten up yet. The street had quieted down, too. Even an occasional horn made an incongruous sound in that unnatural stillness.

From the river the low cry of dark shapes and winking lights that were ships echoed and re-echoed through the canyons of the avenues. Lola turned the radio on low, bringing in a selection of classical piano pieces, and I sat there with my eyes closed, listening, thinking, picturing my redhead as a blackmailer. In a near sleep I thought it was Red at the piano fingering the keys while I watched approvingly, my mind filled with thoughts. She read my mind and her face grew sad, sadder than anything I had ever seen, and she turned her eyes on me and I could see clear through them into the goodness of her soul, and I knew she wasn't a blackmailer and my first impression had been right. She was a girl who had come face to face with fate and had lost, but in losing hadn't lost all, for there was the light of holiness in her face that time when I was her friend, when I thought that a look like that belonged only in a church when you were praying or getting married or something—a light that was there now for me to see while she played a song that told me I was her friend and she was mine, a friendship that was more than that, it was a trust and I believed it . . . knew it and wanted it, for here was a devotion more than I expected or deserved and I wanted to be worthy of it. But, before I could tell her so, Feeney Last's face swirled up from the mist beside the keyboard, smirking, silently mouthing smutty remarks and leering threats that took the holiness away from the scene and smashed it underfoot, assailing her with words that replaced the hardness and terror that had been ingrown before we met, and I couldn't do a thing about it because my feet were powerless to move and my hands were glued to my sides by some invisible force that Feeney controlled and wouldn't release until he had killed her and was gone with his laugh ringing in the air and the smirk still on his face, daring me to follow when I couldn't answer him. All I could do was stand there and look at my redhead's lifeless body until I focused on her hands to see where he had scratched her when he took off her ring.

Lola said, "The coffee's ready, Mike."

I came awake with a start, my feet and hands free again and I half-expected to see Feeney disappearing around the corner. The radio played on, an inanimate thing in the corner with a voice of deep notes that was the only sound in the night.

"Thinking, honey?"

"Dreaming." I lifted the cup from the tray and she added the sugar and milk. "Sometimes it's good to dream."

She made a wry mouth. "Sometimes it isn't." She kissed me with her eyes then. "My dreams have changed lately, Mike. They're nicer than they used to be."

"They become you, Lola."

"I love you, Mike. I can be impersonal because I can't do a thing about it. It isn't a love like that first time. It's a cold fact. Is it that I'm in love with you or do I just love you?"

She sipped her coffee and I didn't answer her. She wouldn't have wanted me to.

"You're big, Mike. You can be called ugly if you take your face apart piece by piece and look at it separately. You have a brutish quality about you that makes men hate you, but maybe a woman wants a brute. Perhaps she wants a man she knows can hate and kill yet still retain a sense of kindness. How long have I known you: a few days? Long enough to look at you and say I love you, and if things had been different I would want you to love me back. But because it can't be that way I'm almost impersonal about it. I just want you to know it."

She sat there quietly, her eyes half-closed, and I saw the perfection in this woman. A mind and body cleansed of any impurities that were, needing only a freedom of her soul. I had never seen her like this, relaxed, happy in her knowledge of unhappiness. Her face had a radiant glow of unusual beauty; her hair tumbled to her shoulders, alive with the dampness of the rain.

I laid my cup on the end table, unable to turn my head away. "It's almost like being married," she said, "sitting here enjoying each other even though there's a whole room between us."

It was no trouble to walk across the room. She stretched out her hands for me to pull her to her feet and I folded her into my arms, my mouth searching for hers, finding it without trouble, enjoying the honey of her lips that she gave freely, her tongue a warm little dagger that stabbed deeper and deeper.

I didn't want her to leave me so soon when she sidled out of my hands. She kissed me lightly on the cheek, took a cigarette from the table and made me take it, then held up a light. The flame of the match was no more intense than that in her eyes. It told me to wait, but not for long. She blew out the match, kissed me again on the cheek and walked into the bedroom, proud, lovely.

The cigarette had burned down to a stub when she called me. Just one word.

"Mike! . . ."

I dropped it, still burning, in the tray. I followed her voice.

Lola was standing in the center of the room, the one light on the dresser throwing her in the shadow. Her back was towards me and she faced the open window, looking into the night beyond. She might have been a statue carved by the hands of a master sculptor, so still and beautiful was her pose. A gentle breeze wafted in and the sheer gown of silk she wore folded back against her body, accentuating every line, every curve.

I stood there in the doorway hardly daring to breathe for fear she would move and spoil the vision. Her voice was barely audible. "A thousand years ago I made this to be the gown I would wear on my wedding night, Mike. A thousand years ago I cried my heart out and put it away under everything else and I had forgotten about it until I met you."

She swung around in a little graceful movement, taking a step nearer me. "I never had a night I wanted to remember. I want to have this one for my memories." Her eyes were leaping, dancing coals of passion.

"Come here, Mike!" It was a demand that wasn't necessary.

I grabbed her shoulders and my fingers bit into her flesh.

"I want you to love me Mike, just for tonight," she said. "I want a love that's as strong as mine and just as fierce because there may be no tomorrow for either one of us, and if there is it will never be the same. Say it, Mike. Tell me."

"I love you, Lola. I could have told you that before, but you wouldn't let me. You're easy to love, even for me. Once I said I'd never love again, but I have."

"Just for tonight."

"You're wrong. Not just for tonight. I'll love you as long as I please. If there's any stopping to be done I'll do it. You're brand new, Lola . . . you're made for a brand-new guy, somebody more than me. I'm trouble for everything I touch."

Her hand closed over my mouth. My whole body was aching

for her until my head felt dizzy. When she took her hand away she put it over one of mine that squeezed her shoulders and moved it to the neckline of the gown.

"I made this gown to be worn only once. There's only one way to get it off."

A devil was making love to me.

My fingers closed over the silk and ripped it away with a hissing, tearing sound and she was standing in front of me, naked and inviting.

Her voice had angels in it, though. "I love you, Mike," she said again.

She was my kind of woman, one that you didn't have to speak to, for words weren't that necessary. She was honest and strong in her honesty, capable of loving a man with all her heart had to give, and she was giving it to me.

Her mouth was cool, but her body was hot with an inner fire that could only be smothered out.

It was a night she thought she'd never have.

It was a night I'd never forget.

I was alone when I woke up. The tinkling of a miniature alarm-clock on the dresser was a persistent reminder that a new day was here. Pinned to the pillow next to mine was a note from Lola and signed with a lipstick kiss. It read, "It ended too soon, Mike. Now I have to finish the job you gave me. Breakfast is all ready—just warm everything up."

Breakfast, hell! It was after twelve. I ate while I was getting dressed, anxious to get into things. The coffee was too hot to touch and while it cooled I snapped the radio on. For the first time in his life the news commentator seemed genuinely excited. He gave out with a spiel at a fast clip, only pausing to take a breath at the end of each paragraph. The police had staged two more raids after I left Pat, and the dragnet was pulling in every shady character suspected of having dealings with the gigantic vice ring that controlled the city.

The iron fist had made a wide sweep. It closed in on places and persons I never thought of. A grin crossed my face and I ran my hand over the stubble of beard on my chin. I was seeing Pat again, acknowledging the knowledge of the existence of such a ring, yet readily agreeing that there was little that could be done about it. He was eating his own words and liking it.

One thing about a drive like that, it can't be stopped. The papers take up the crusade and the hue and cry is on. The public goes on a fox-hunt in righteous indignation, ready to smash something they had unconcernedly supported with indifference only the day before. To them it was fun to see a public name grovelling in the mud, a thrill to know they were part of the pack.

But the big scenes weren't written yet. They'd come later in a court-room after postponements, stalls, anything to gain time to let the affair cool down. Then maybe a fine would be handed out, maybe a light jail sentence here and there, maybe a dismissal for lack of evidence.

Evidence—the kind that could stick. The police would do their share, but if the evidence didn't stick there would be people walking out of that court with the memory of what had happened and a vow never to let it happen again. They'd be people with power, of course, filthy, rotten squibs who liked the feeling of power and money, determined to let nothing interfere with their course of life. They'd undermine the workings of the law. A little at a time, like the waves lapping at the sand around a piling, uncovering it until it was ready to topple of its own accord. Then they could get in their own kind . . . people who would look the other way and interpret the law to their own advantage.

I got into my coat and went downstairs for a paper, hurrying back to the apartment to read it. The story was there complete with pictures, but it was the columnists that went further than fact. They hinted that more than one prominent personage had been hurriedly called away from town on the eve of the investigation and, if the revelations continued, the number in the Blue Book was going to diminish by many pages. One of the more sensational writers inferred that the police were getting able assistance outside their own circle, a subtle implication that they couldn't handle the situation unless they were prodded into action.

The police themselves had little or nothing to say. There was no statement from higher headquarters as yet, but a few of the lesser politicos had issued fiery blasts that the law was taking too much on its shoulders and was more concerned with smear tactics than law enforcement. I had to laugh at that. I was willing to bet those boys were trying to cover up by making more noise than the police.

I picked up the phone and dialed Pat. He was dog tired and glad to hear from me. "Read the papers yet?" he asked.

"Yeah, and listened to the radio. The exodus has begun."

"You can say that again. We're picking them up left and right trying to beat it. Some of them talked enough to lead us into other things, but all we have are the mechanics, the working group of the outfit—and the customers."

"They're the ones who support the racket."

"They're going to pay more than they expected to. It's getting rougher. A lot of dirty noses are looking for someone to wipe them on."

"And you're the boy?"

"I'm the boy, Mike."

"Who's going bail for all the big names?"

"It's coming in from all over. I've been called more dirty names than any one guy in the city . . ."

"Except me."

"Yeah, except you. But nobody wants your job like they want mine. I've been cajoled, threatened, enticed and what not. It makes me feel ashamed to know that I live within a hundred miles of some people."

He yawned into the phone and muttered, "I have news, friend. Murray Candid has been seen in the city, hopping from one place to another. He's accompanied by an alderman in a downtown district."

"He isn't trying to make a break for it, then?"

"Evidently not. He's keeping out of sight until something happens. I think he wants to see how far we're going to go. He'll be pretty surprised."

"You have a murder warrant out on him?"

"Couldn't make it, Mike. He had an alibi for that. He's ducking out on this investigation. Here's something else that might interest you, but keep it under your hat. There's been an influx of tough guys who are walking around the city just being seen by the right persons. One look and you couldn't make them talk for love or money."

"How do you like that!"

"I don't. They have records, most of them, but they're clean now and we can't touch them. We started holding them for questioning. It didn't work. Every one of them is loaded with dough and sense enough to have a lawyer pull them out fast. None of them was armed or talked back to a cop, so there wasn't a thing we could stick them with."

My hands got sticky with sweat. "That's big money talking again, Pat. The combine is still in business, using its retrenching dough to scare off the talkers. Those babies can do it, too. They aren't just kidding. What the hell is happening . . . are we going back to the Wild West again? Damn it, if they keep that up, you'll have a jugful of claims on your hands and I don't blame them! It's not nice to know that sooner or later you'll get bumped because a guy has already been paid to do the job and he's a conscientious worker."

"Our hands are tied. That's the way it is and we're stuck with it. They know where to go, besides. It seems like they've contacted right parties before we got to them."

Damn! I smacked my fist against the back of the chair. All right, let them play tough. Let them import a gang with smart, knowing faces and minds that weren't afraid of taking a chance. They were just mugs who couldn't think for themselves, but they could feel, and they had emotions, and they could scare just as easily as any one else, and when they saw the blood run in the streets they wouldn't be quite so cocky or eager to reach for a rod. They'd run like hell and keep on running until their feet gave out.

"You still there, Mike?"

"I'm still here. I was thinking."

"Well, I'm going home and get some sleep. You'll be there tonight?"

"I wouldn't miss it for anything."

"Right! Keep out of sight. The D.A. is getting ideas about me and if he finds out that you have a hand in this I'll be on the carpet."

"Don't worry, I'll stay dead until I need resurrection. I told Lola to get in touch with you if it's necessary. Do me a favor and don't ask questions, just do what she asks. It's important."

"She's working on it, too?"

"Lola's handling the most important end of this case right now. If she finds what I think she might find, you cinch your case without kickbacks. See you tonight. I'll be there, but you won't see me."

I said so-long and hung up. The end was near, or at least it was in sight. The showdown was too close to risk spoiling it by getting myself involved. All I wanted was Feeney. I wanted to get his neck in my hands and squeeze. But where the hell would Feeney be now? The city was too big, too peppered with foxholes and caves to start a one-man search. Feeney had to be forced out into the open, made to run so we could get a crack at him.

The catch was, the little guys did the running. The big boys stayed out of sight after they buried their gold, ready to dig it up again when the enemy was gone. Feeney wasn't big. He was the kind that would watch and wait, too, ready to jump out and claim part of the loot. It could be that he wanted more than his share and was ready to take all if he had the chance. Murray Candid, another one content to stay at home, still trusting the devices they had set up to protect themselves. Cobbie Bennett waiting to die. How many more would there be?

I grabbed the phone again and asked for long-distance, waited while the operator took my number and put it into Mr. Berin's address. I asked for my client and the butler told me he had left for the city only a short while before, intending to register at the Sunic House. Yes, he had reservations. He asked who was calling, please, and wanted to take a message, but there wasn't anything I could tell him, so I grumbled goodbye and put the phone back.

Velda must have been out for lunch. I let the phone ring for a good five minutes and nobody picked it up. Hell, I couldn't just sit there while things were happening outside. I wanted to do some hunting of my own, too. I pushed out of the chair and slung my coat on. Something jingled in the pocket and I pulled out a duplicate set of door keys Lola had left for me and each one had lipstick kisses on the shanks, with a little heart dangling from the chain that held them together. I opened the heart and saw Lola smiling up at me.

I smiled back and told her picture all the things she wouldn't let me tell her last night.

There was still a threat of rain in the air. Overhead the clouds were grey and ruffled, a thick, damp blanket that cut the tops off the bigger buildings and promised to squat down on the smaller ones. From the river a chill wind drove in a wave of mist that covered everything with tiny wet globules. Umbrellas were furled, ready to be opened any instant; passengers waiting for buses or standing along the curb whistling at taxis carried raincoats or else eyed the weather apprehensively.

Twice a radio car screamed its way south, the siren opening a swath down the center of the avenue. I passed a paperstand and saw a later edition and an extra, both with banner headlines. A front-page picture showed the alderman and a socially prominent manufacturer in a police court. The manufacturer looked indignant. A sub-caption made mention of some highly important confidential information the police had and wouldn't disclose at the moment. That would be Murray's code book. I wondered how Pat was getting on with it.

At the bar on the corner I found a spot in the rear and ordered a beer. There was only one topic of discussion going on in the place and it was being pushed around from pillar to post. A ratty little guy with a nose that monopolized his face said he didn't like it. The police were out of order. A girl told him to shut up. Every fifteen minutes a special bulletin would come out with the latest developments, making capital of the big names involved, but unable to give information of any special nature.

For a little over two hours I sat there, having one beer after another, hearing a cross-sectional viewpoint of the city. Vice was losing ground fast to the publicity of the clean-up.

When I had enough I crawled into the phone booth and dialed the Sunic House. The desk clerk said Mr. Berin had arrived a few minutes before. I thanked him and hung up. Later I'd go up and refund his dough. I went out where the mist had laid a slick on the streets and found another bar that was a little more cheerful and searched my mind for that other piece to the puzzle.

My stomach made growling noises and I checked my watch. Six-thirty. I threw a buck on the counter for the bartender and walked out and stood in the doorway.

It had started to rain again.

When I finished eating and climbed behind the wheel of the car it was almost eight. The evening shadows had dissolved into night, glossy and wet, the splatter of the rain on the steel roof an impatient drumming that lulled thoughts away. I switched on the radio to a news program, changed my mind and found some music instead.

Some forty-five minutes later I decided I had had enough aimless driving and pulled to the curb between two sheer walls of apartment buildings that had long ago given up any attempt at pretentiousness. I looked out and saw that there were no lights showing in Cobbie Bennett's room and I settled down to wait.

I might have been alone in that wilderness of brick and concrete. No one bothered to look at me huddled there, my coat collar turned up to merge with the brim of my hat. A few cars were scattered at odd intervals along the street, some old heaps, a couple more respectable by a matter of a few years. A man came out of a building across the way holding a newspaper over his head and hurried to the corner where he turned out of sight.

Off in the distance a fire engine screamed, demanding room, behind it another with a harsh, brassy gong backing up the order. I was listening to the fading clamor when the door of Cobbie's house opened and the little pimp stepped out. He was five minutes early. He had a cigarette in his mouth and was trying to light it with a hand that shook so hard the flame went out and, disgusted, he threw the unlit butt to the pavement and came down the steps.

He didn't walk fast, even in the rain, nor a straight course. His choppy stride carried him through a weaving pattern, avoiding the street lights, blacking him out in the shadows. When he came to a store front I saw his head turn to look into the angle of the window to see if he was being followed.

I let him turn the corner before I started the car. If the police were there, they weren't in sight. Nothing was moving this night. I knew the route Cobbie would take, and rather than follow him, decided to go ahead and wait, taking a wide sweep around the one-way street and coming up in the direction he was walking.

There were stores here, some still open. A pair of gin mills operated at a short stagger apart, smelling the block up with the rank odor of flat beer. Upstairs in an apartment a fight was going on. Somebody threw a coffeepot that smashed through the window and clattered down the basement well. Cobbie was part of the night until it hit, then he made a short dash to the safety of a stairway and crouched there determining the origin of the racket before continuing his walk. He stopped once to light a cigarette and made it this time.

He was almost opposite me when a car pulled up the street and stopped in front of the gin mill. Cobbie went rigid with fear, one hand half-way to his mouth. When the driver hopped out and went into the dive he finished dragging on the cigarette.

I had to leave the car where it was, using Cobbie's tactics of hugging the shadows to pass him on the opposite side of the street without being seen. Following did no good. I had to anticipate his moves and try to stay ahead of him. The rain came in handy; it let me walk under awnings, stop in doorways for a breather before starting off again.

A cop went by, whistling under his slicker, his night stick slapping his leg in rhythm to his step. It was ten minutes after ten then. I didn't see Pat or his men. Just Cobbie and me. We were in his own bailiwick now, the street moving with people impervious to the rain and the tension. Beside a vacant store I stopped and watched Cobbie hesitate on the corner, making his decision and shuffling off into a cross street.

I didn't know where I expected it to come from, certainly not from the black mouth of an apartment. Cobbie's weave had been discarded for an ambling gait of resignation. Tension can be borne only so long, then the body and mind reverts to normal. His back suddenly stiffened and I heard a yelp that was plain fear. His head was swivelled around to the building and his hands came up protectively.

If the guy had shot from the doorway he would have had him, but he wanted to do it close up and came down the steps with a rod in his fist. He hadn't reached the third step when Cobbie screamed at the top of his lungs, trying to shrink back against the inevitable. The gun levelled with Cobbie's chest but never went off because a dark blur shot out of the same doorway and crashed into the guy's back with such force that they landed at Cobbie's feet together.

My own rod was in my hand as I ran. I heard the muted curses mingled with Cobbie's screaming as a heavy fist slammed into flesh. I was still fifty yards away when the two separated, one scrambling to his feet immediately. Cobbie had fallen into a crouch and the guy fired, flame lacing towards his head.

The other guy didn't bother to rise. He propped his gun arm on the sidewalk, took deliberate aim and pulled the trigger. The bullet must have gone right through his head because his hat flew off faster than he was running and was still in the air when the man was nothing but a lump of lifeless flesh.

A gun went off farther up the street. Somebody shouted and shot again. I was on top of the guy with the rod and it didn't worry me at all seeing it pointed at my middle. It was a police positive and the guy had big, flat feet.

Just the same, I raised my hands, my .45 up and said, "Mike Hammer, private cop. Ticket's in my pocket, want to see it?"

The cop stood up and shook his head. "I know you, feller."

A prowl car made the corner on two wheels and passed it, the side door already open with a uniformed patrolman leaning out, his gun cocked. The cop and I followed it together, crossing the street diagonally where the commotion was.

Windows were being thrown open, heads shouted down asking what went on and were told to get back in and stay there. A voice yelled, "He's on the roof!" There was another shot, muffled by the walls this time. A woman screamed and ran, slamming a door in her passage.

Almost magically the searchlights opened up, stretching long arms up the building fronts to the parapets, silhouetting half a dozen men racing across the roof in pursuit of someone.

The reflection of the lights created an artificial dawn in the tight group, dancing from the riot guns and blued steel of service revolvers. The street was lousy with cops, and Pat was holding one of the lights.

We saw each other at the same time and Pat handed the light over to a plainclothes man. I said, "Where the hell did you come from? There wasn't a soul on the street a minute ago."

Pat grimaced at me. "We didn't come, Mike . . . we were there. The hard boys weren't too smart. We had men tailing them all day and they never knew it. Hell, we couldn't lay a trap without having everybody and his brother get wise, so the men stuck close and stayed on their backs. Cobbie was spotted before he got off his block. The punks kept in touch with each other over the phone. When they saw Cobbie turn down here one cut behind the buildings and got in front of him. There was another one up the block to cut him off if he bolted."

"Good deal! How many were there?"

"We have nine so far. Seven of them just folded up their tents and came along quietly. We let them pass the word first so there would be no warning. What came of that guy down the block?"

"He's dead."

From the roof there was a volley of shots that smashed into stone and ricochetted across the sky. Some didn't ricochet. A shrill scream testified to that. One of the cops stepped into the light and called down. "He's dead. Better get a stretcher ready, we have a wounded officer up here."

Pat snapped. "Damn! Get those lights in the hallway so they can see what they're doing!" A portable stretcher came out of a car and was carried upstairs. Pat was directing operations in a clear voice, emphasized by vigorous arm movements.

There wasn't anything I could do right then. I edged back through the crowd and went up the street. There was another gang around the body on the sidewalk, with two kids trying to break away from their parents for a closer look.

Cobbie Bennett was nowhere in sight.

chapter fourteen ▰▰▰▰▰▰▰▰▰▰

SEEING A JOB well done can bring a feeling of elation whether you did it yourself or not. There was a sense of pride in me when I climbed behind the wheel of my heap, satisfaction extraordinary because the bastards were being beaten at their own game. I switched on the radio a few minutes later in time to catch the interruption of a program and a news flash of the latest coup. I went from station to station, but it was always the same. The noses for news were right in there following every move. Scattered around town would be other tough boys hearing the same thing. Money wouldn't mean a damn thing now, not if the cops were going to play it their way. It's one thing to jump the law, but when the law is right behind you, ready to jump back even harder, it's enough to make even the most stupid, hopped-up killer think twice.

Ha! They wouldn't be wearing their metallic smiles tonight. The ball was piling up force as it rolled along. The half-ways were jumping on the wagon, eager to be on the winning side. Political injustice and string-pulling were taking one hell of a beating. I *knew* where I stood and I felt good about it.

My route uptown was taking me within a few blocks of the Sunic House, and late as it was I wanted to stop off and see my client. This the old boy would like. He was paying for it. At least he was getting his money's worth. The name of Berin-Grotin would be remembered in places long after the marble tomb was eaten away by the sands of time, and that's what he wanted . . . someone to remember him.

There was a driveway beside the old brownstone structure that curved into a parking space in back. I pulled half-way in and handed the keys over to a bellboy old enough to be my father. As I walked to the door I heard him grind it into gear, then jerk out of sight. I waited to hear him hit something else, but apparently he made it.

The Sunic House was a well-kept relic of yesteryear, reserved for gentlemen guests only. The hushed atmosphere wasn't due to the late hour: it probably was that way all day. The lobby was done in plush, gilt and leather. From the ceiling ancient gas fixtures had been converted to electric whose yellow bulbs did little to brighten the mortuary effect of the mahogany-panelled walls. The pictures spotted around the place showed the city of long ago when it was at peace with itself, and the Sunic House was a name to hold honor among the best.

I asked the desk-clerk if Mr. Berin was in.

He nodded slowly and knit his eyebrows. "I'm certain Mr. Berin does not care to be disturbed, sir. He has been coming here these many years and I know his preferences well."

"This is a very unusual circumstance, pop. Give him a call, will you?"

"I'm afraid that . . . really, now, sir. I don't think it proper to . . ."

"If I suddenly stuck my fingers between my teeth and whistled like hell, then ran up and down the room yelling at the top of my lungs, what would you do?"

His eyebrows ran up to where his hairline used to be. He craned his head to the wall where an old guy was nodding in a chair. "I'd be forced to call the house detective, sir!"

I gave him a great big grin and stuck my fingers between my teeth. With the other hand I pointed to the phone and waited. The clerk got pale, flushed, went white again as he tried to cope with the situation. Evidently, he figured one upset customer would be better than a dozen and picked up the house phone.

He tugged the call bell while watching me nervously, jiggled it again and again until a voice barked hard enough in his ear to make him squirm. "I beg your pardon, sir, but a man insists he should see you. He . . . he said it was very urgent."

The phone barked again and the clerk swallowed hard. "Tell him it's Mike Hammer," I said.

It wasn't so easy to get it in over the tirade my client was handing out. At last he said bleakly, "It's a Mr. Hammer, sir . . . a Mr. Hammer. Yes, sir, Mike Hammer. Yes, he's right here, sir. Very well, sir. I'll send him right up."

With a handkerchief the clerk wiped his face and gave me his look reserved for the most inferior of persons. "Room 406," he said. I waved my thanks and climbed the stairs, ignoring the elevator that stood in the middle of the room, working through a well in the overhead.

Mr. Berin had the door open waiting for me. I pushed it in and closed it behind me, expecting to find myself in just another room. I was wrong, dead wrong. Whatever the Sunic House looked like on the outside, its appearance was deceiving. Here was a complete suite of rooms, and as far as I could see executed with the finest taste possible.

A moment later my client appeared, dressed in a silken smoking jacket, his hair brushed into a snow-white mane, looking for all the world like a man who had planned to receive a guest rather than be awakened out of a sound sleep by an obnoxious employee.

His hand met mine in a firm clasp. "It's good to see you, Mike, very good. Come inside where we can talk."

"Thanks." He led me past the living-room, that centered around a grand piano, into a small study that faced on the street, a room banked with shelves of books, mounted heads of animals and fish, and rows of framed pictures showing himself in his younger days. "Some place you have here, Mr. Berin."

"Yes, I've used it for years as you can see. It's my city residence with all the benefits of a hotel. Here, sit down." He offered me an overstuffed leather chair and I sank into it, feeling the outlines of another person who had made his impression through constant use.

"Cigar?"

"No, thanks." I took out my deck of Luckies and flipped one into my mouth. "Sorry I had to drag you out of bed like this."

"Not at all, Mike. I must admit that I was rather surprised. That all comes of having fixed habits for so many years, I presume. I gathered you had a good reason for wanting to see me."

I breathed out a cloud of smoke. "Nope, I just wanted to talk to somebody. I have five hundred bucks of yours and that's my excuse for picking you as that somebody."

"Five hundred . . ." he began, "you mean that money I sent to your bank to cover that, ah, expense?"

"That's right. I don't need it now."

"But you thought it would be worth spending to secure the information. Did you change your mind?"

"No, the girl didn't live to cash it, that's all." His face showed bewilderment, then amazement. "I was tailed. Like a jerk I didn't think of it and was tailed. Whoever was behind me killed the girl and fixed it to look like suicide. It didn't work. While I was out the same party went through my room and copped some of the stuff."

"You know . . .?" his voice choked off.

"Feeney Last. Your ex-hired hand, Mr. Berin."

"Good Lord, no!"

"Yes."

His fingers were entwined in his lap and they tightened until the knuckles went white. "What have I done, what have I done?" He sat there with his eyes closed, looking old and shrunken for the first time.

"You didn't do a thing. It would have happened anyway. What you did do was stop the same thing from happening again."

"Thank you, Mike."

I stood up and laid my hand on his shoulder. "Look, come off it. You don't have anything to feel bad about. If you feel anything, feel good. You know what's been going on in town all day and night?"

"Yes, I—I've heard."

"That's what your money bought, a sense of decency to this place. It's what the town has needed for a long time. You hired me to find a name for the redhead. We found a package of dirt instead, all because a girl lies in the morgue unidentified. I didn't want her buried without a name, neither did you. Neither of us expected what would come, and it isn't over yet by a long shot. One day the sun is going to shine again and when it does it will be over a city that can hold its head up."

"But the red-headed girl still doesn't have a name, does she?" He glanced at me wryly, his eyes weary.

"No. Maybe she will have soon. Mind if I use your phone?"

"Not at all. It's outside in the living-room. I'll mix a drink in the meantime. I believe I can use one. I'm not used to distressing news, Mike."

There was sadness in his carriage that I hated to see. The old boy was going to take a lot of cheering up. I found the phone and dialed Velda's number at home. She took a long time answering and was mad as hell. "It's me, Velda. Anything doing at the office?"

"Gee whiz, Mike, you call at the most awful hours. I waited in the office all evening for you to call. That girl, Lola, was it? . . . sent up an envelope by special messenger. There was a pawn ticket in it and nothing else."

"A pawn ticket?" My voice hit a high note. "She's found it then, Velda! Hot damn, she's found it! What did you do with it?"

"I left it there," she said, "on top of my desk."

"Damn, that's wonderful. Look, kid, I left my office keys home. Meet me there in an hour . . . make it an hour and a half. I want a drink first to celebrate the occasion. I'll call Pat from there and we can go on together. This is it, Velda, see you in a jiffy!"

I slapped my hand over the bar, holding it a moment before I spun out Lola's number on the dial. Her voice came on before the phone finished ringing. She was breathless with excitement. "Mike, baby! . . . Oh, Mike, where are you? Did you get my envelope?"

"I just called Velda, and she has it at the office. I'm going up to get it in a little while. Where did you find it?"

"In a little place just off the Bowery. It was hanging in the window like you said it might be."

"Great! Where's the camera now?"

"I have it."

"Then why the rigmarole with the pawn ticket."

A new note crept into her voice. "Someone else was looking for it, too, Mike. For a while they were right ahead of me. Five different clerks told me that I was the second party after a camera like that."

The chill went up my back this time. "What happened?"

"I figured that whoever he was had been using the same method . . . going right from the phone book. I started at the bottom and worked backwards."

Mr. Berin came in and silently offered me a highball. I picked it off the tray with a nod of thanks and took a quick swallow. "Go on."

"I found it then, but I was afraid to keep the ticket on me. I addressed an envelope to your office and sent the ticket up with a boy."

"Smart girl! I love you to pieces, little chum. You'll never know how much."

"Please, Mike."

I laughed at her, happy, bubbling over with joy I hadn't known in a long time. "You stow it this time, Lola. When this is done you and I will have the world in our hands and a lifetime to enjoy it. Tell me, Lola. Say it loud and often."

"Mike, I love you, I love you!" She sobbed and said it again.

My voice went soft. "Remember it, sugar . . . I love you, too. I'll be along in just a little while. Wait up for me?"

"Of course, darling. Please hurry. I want to see you so much it hurts."

When I put the phone back I finished the drink in one long pull and went into the den. I wished I could give some of my happiness to Mr. Berin. He needed it badly.

"It's finished," I said.

There was no response save a slow turn of his head. "Will there be more . . . killing, Mike?"

"Maybe. Might be the law will take its course."

His hand lifted the glass to his lips. "I should be elated, I suppose. However, I can't reconcile myself to death. Not when my actions are partly responsible for it." He shuddered and put the glass down. "Care for another? I'm going to have one."

"Yeah, I have time."

He took my glass on the tray, and on the way out opened the lid of a combination radio-phonograph. A sheaf of records was already in the metal grippers, and he lowered the needle to the first one. I leaned back and listened to the pounding beat of a

Wagnerian opera, watching the smoke curl upwards from the red tip of my cigarette.

This time Mr. Berin brought the bottle, the mixer and a bowl of ice with him. When he handed me the drink he sat on the edge of his chair and said, "Tell me about it, Mike, not the details, just the high points, and the reasons for these things happening. Perhaps if I knew I could put my mind at rest."

"The details are what count, I can't leave them out. What I want you to realize is that these things had to be, and it was good to get rid of them. We chased a name and found crime. We chased the crime and we found bigger names. The police dragnet isn't partial to anyone now. The cops are taking a long chance and making it stick. Every minute we sit here the vice and rot that had the city by the tail gets drawn closer to the wringer.

"You should feel proud, Mr. Berin. I do. I feel damn proud. I lost Nancy but I found Lola . . . and I found some of myself, too."

"If only we could have done something for that girl. . . ."

"Nancy?"

"Yes. She died so completely alone. But it was all her own doing. If it was true, as you said, that she had an illegitimate child and went downwards into a life of sin, who can be blamed? Certainly the girl herself." He shook his head, his eyes crinkling in puzzled wonder. "If only they had some pride . . . even the slightest essence of pride, these things would never happen. And not only this girl Nancy . . . how many others are like her? No doubt this investigation will uncover the number.

"Mike, there were times when I believed my own intense pride to be a childish vanity, one I could afford to indulge in, but I am glad now to have that pride. It *can* mean something, this pride of name, of ownership. I can look over my fine estate and say, 'This is my own, arrived at through my own efforts.' I can make plans for the future when I will be nothing but a name and take pride that it will be remembered."

"Well, it's the old case of the double standard, Mr. Berin. You can't blame these kids for the mistakes they make. I think nearly every one makes them, it's just a few that get caught in the web. It's rough then, rough as hell."

Half the bottle was gone before I looked at my watch and came to my feet. I reached for my hat, remembered the check in time and wrote it out. "I'm late already. Velda will chew me out."

"It has been nice talking to you, Mike. Will you stop back

tomorrow? I want to know what happens. You will be careful, won't you?"

"I'll be careful," I said. We shook hands at the door and I heard it shut as I reached the stairway. By the time I reached the main floor the desk-clerk was there, his finger to his lips urging me to be quiet. Hell, I couldn't help whistling. I recovered my car from the lot and roared out to the street. Just a little while longer, I thought.

Velda had nearly given me up. I saw her pacing the street in front of the Hackard Building, swinging her umbrella like a club. I pulled over and honked at her. "I thought you said an hour and a half."

"Sorry, honey, I got tied up."

"You're always getting tied up." She was pretty when she was mad.

We signed the night book in the lobby and the lone operator rode us up to our floor. Velda kept watching me out of the corner of her eye, curiosity getting the better of her. Finally she couldn't hold it any longer. "Usually I know what's going on, Mike."

I told her as briefly as I could. "It was the redhead. She used her camera to take pictures."

"Naturally."

"These weren't ordinary pictures. They could be used for blackmail. She must have had plenty . . . it's causing all the uproar. Pat went ahead on the theory we were right in our thinking. We'll need that stuff for evidence."

"Uh-huh."

She didn't get it, but she made believe she did. Later I'd have to sit down and give her a detailed account. Later, not now.

We reached the office and Velda opened the door with her key and switched on the light. It had been so long since I had been in, that the place was almost strange to me. I walked over to the desk while Velda straightened her hair in front of the mirror.

"Where is it, kid?"

"On the blotter."

"I don't see it."

"Oh, for pity sakes. Here . . ." Her eyes went from the desk to mine, slowly, widening a little. "It's gone, Mike."

"Gone! Hell, it can't be!"

"It is. I put it right here before I left. I remember it distinctly. I put my desk in order . . ." She stopped.

"What is it?" I was afraid to talk.

Her hand was around the memo pad, looking at the blank sheet on top. Every bit of color had drained from her face.

"Damn it, speak up!"

"A page is torn off . . . the one I had Lola's phone number and address on."

"My God!"

I grabbed the front door and swung it open, holding it in the light. Around the key slot in the lock were a dozen light scratches made by a pick. I must have let out a yell, because the noise of it reverberated in my ears as I ran down the hall. Velda shouted after me, but I paid no attention. For once the elevator was where I wanted it, standing with the door back and the operator waiting to take us back down.

He recognized the urgency in my face, slammed the door shut and threw the handle over. "Who was up here tonight?" I demanded.

"Why, nobody I know of, sir."

"Could anyone get up the stairs without being seen?"

"Yes, I guess they could. That is, if the attendant or myself happened to be busy."

"Were you?"

"Yes, sir. We've been swabbing down the floors ever since we came on."

I had to keep my teeth shut to keep the curses in. I wanted to scream at the guy to hurry. Get me down. It took an eternity to reach the bottom floor and by then Velda had her hand on the button and wouldn't take it off. I squeezed out before the door was all the way open and bolted for my car.

"Oh, God!" I kept saying over and over to myself. "Oh, God! . . ."

My foot had the accelerator on the floor, pushing the needle on the speedometer up and around. The tires shrieked at the turns protestingly, then took hold once again until another turn was reached! I was thankful for the rain and the hour again; no cars blocked the way, no pedestrians were at the crossings. Had there been I never would have made it, for I was seeing only straight ahead and my hands wouldn't have wrenched the wheel over for anything.

I didn't check my time, but it seemed like hours before I crowded in between cars parked for the night outside the apartment. My feet thundered up the stairs, picking their way knowingly through the semi-darkness. I reached the door and threw it open and I tried to scream but it crammed in my throat like a hard lump and stayed there.

Lola was lying on the floor, her arms sprawled out. The top of her dress was soaked with blood.

I ran to her, fell on my knees at her side, my arms going to her face. The hole in her chest bubbled blood and she was still breathing. "Lola . . ."

Her eyelids fluttered, opened. She saw me and her lips, once so lusciously ripe with the redness of life, parted in a pale smile. "God, Lola! . . ."

I tried to help her, but her eyes told me it was too late. Too late! Her hand moved, touched me, then went out in an arc, the effort racking her with pain. The motion was so deliberate I had to follow it. Somehow she managed to extend her forefinger, point towards the phone table, then swing her hand to the door.

She made no sound, but her lips moved and said for the last time, "I love you, Mike." I knew what she wanted me to do. I bent forward and kissed her mouth gently, and tasted the salt of tears. "Dear God, why did it have to happen to her? Why?"

Her eyes were closed. The smile was still on her face. But Lola was dead. You'll always know one thing. I love you. No matter where you are or when, you will know that wherever I am I'll be loving you. Just you.

The joy was gone. I was empty inside. I had no feeling, no emotion. What could I feel . . . how was I supposed to act? It happened so fast, this loving and having it snatched away at the moment of triumph. I closed my eyes and said a prayer that came hard, but started with, "Oh, God! . . ."

When I opened my eyes again she was still pointing at the door, even now, in death, trying to tell me something.

Trying to tell me that her killer was outside there and I had come up too fast for him to get away. By all that was holy he'd never get away! My legs acted independently of my mind in racing for the door. I stopped in the hall, my ears tuned for the slightest sound . . . and I heard it. The soft tread of feet walking carefully, step by step, trying to be quiet. Feet that expected me to do the natural thing and call for the doctor first, then the police, and let just enough seconds go by for the killer to make his escape.

Like hell!

I didn't try to be quiet. I hit the stairs, took them two at a time, swinging around the banister at the landing. Below me the killer made no pretense at secrecy any longer and fled headlong into the street. I heard the roar of an engine as I came out the door, saw a car nose out of the line as I was climbing into mine and rip out into the street.

chapter fifteen ▐▇▇▇▇▇▇▇▇▇▇▇

WHOEVER DROVE THAT car was stark mad with terror, a crazy madness that sent him rocketing down the avenue without the slightest regard for life. Maybe he heard my wild laugh as I closed the distance between us. It could be that his mind pictured my face, eyes bright with the kill, my teeth clamped together and lips drawn back, making me lose all resemblance to a human being.

I was just one tight knot of muscle, bunched together by a rage that wanted to rip and tear. I couldn't breathe; I could only take a breath, hold it as long as I could, and let it out with a flat hissing sound. A police car picked up our trail, tried to follow and was lost in the side streets.

Every second saw the distance shorten, every second heaped more coal on the fire that was eating at my guts and blurring my vision until all that was left was a narrow tunnel of sight with that car in front on the other end. We were almost bumper to bumper as we turned across town, and I felt my car start to go over, fighting the speed of the swerve. It was fear that led me out of it and back on four wheels again, fear that I would lose him. The tires slammed back to the pavement, pulled to the side, and when I was straight again, the car in front of me had a half-block lead.

The sharp jolts of trolley tracks almost snatched the wheel from my hands, then it was gone and we were going west towards the river and the distance between us closed to yards, then feet. I knew where he was heading . . . knew he wanted to make the West Side Highway where he could make a run for it without traffic hazard, thinking he might lose me with speed.

He couldn't lose me now or ever. I was the guy with the cowl and the scythe. I had a hundred and forty black horses under me and an hourglass in my hand, laughing like crazy until the tears rolled down my cheeks. The highway was ahead all of a sudden and he tried to run into it, brakes slamming the car into a skid.

If the steep pillar hadn't been there he would have done it. I was on my own brakes as I heard the crash of metal against metal and saw glass fly in all directions. The car rolled over once and came to a stop on its wheels. I had to pull out and around it, brakes and tires adding a new note to that unearthly symphony of destruction.

I saw the door of the other car get kicked open. I saw Feeney Last jump out, stagger, then turn his gun at me. I was diving for the ground when the shot blasted over my head, rolling back of

the pillar, clawing for my gun when Feeney made his break for
it.

Run, Feeney, run. Run until your heart is ready to split open
and you fall in a heap unable to move but able to see how you
are going to die. Run and run and run. Hear the feet behind you
running just a little bit faster. Stop for one second and you'll be
as dead as hell.

He turned and fired a wild one and I didn't bother to answer
him. There was panic in his stride, wild, unreasoning panic as he
ran head down to the shadows of the pier, heading for the black
throat of the shed there. The darkness was a solid wall that shut
him out, then enveloped me because I was right behind him,
pitch-black darkness that threw a velvet cloth over your eyes so
that you might as well be blind.

I hit a packing case with my hands, stopped, and heard a body
trip and fall, curse once and crawl. I wanted to keep my eyes
closed because they felt so bright he couldn't miss them in the
dark. Things took shape slowly, towering squares of boxes heaped
to the ceiling with black corridors between them. I bent down
and untied my shoes, kicked them off and eased into a walk
without sound.

From the other side of the room came the rasp of hoarse
breathing being restrained, Feeney Last, waiting for me to close
the interval, step between himself and the gaping doorway where
I would be outlined against the blue night of the city.

Hurry, I thought, before he gets wise. He'll know in a minute.
He'll understand that rage lasts only so long before giving way to
reason. Then he'll figure it. I stepped around the boxes, getting
behind him, trusting to luck to bring myself through that maze
to the end. I found an alley that led straight to the door, but
Feeney wasn't standing there where he should have been. My foot
sent a board clattering across the concrete and automatically I
pulled back into the protection of the crates.

And I was lucky because Feeney was stretched out on the floor
under an overhang of the boxes and the shot he threw back over
his shoulder missed me by inches.

But I had him spotted. I fired a snap shot around the corner
and heard him scramble farther under the crate. Maybe he thought
he was safe because neither one of us could take the chance of
making the first break.

My fingers searched for handholds, found them, and I pulled
myself up, climbing slowly and silently over the rough frames of
the crates. Splinters worked into my flesh and nails tugged at my

clothes until I disengaged them. A cat couldn't have been more quiet.

The tops formed a platform and I crept across it, inch by inch, my brain measuring distances. When I looked over the edge I saw Feeney's arm protruding from the shadow, a gun in his hand, slowly sweeping up and down the narrow lane, his finger tensed on the trigger ready to squeeze off a shot.

I leaned over and put a bullet right through his goddamn hand and jumped just as he made a convulsive jerk of pain and writhed out from under the box. My feet hit him in the shoulders and cut off his scream and we were one kicking, gouging mass rolling in the dust.

I didn't want my gun . . . just my hands. My fists were slashing into the pale oval of his face, reaching for his throat. He brought his knees up and I turned just in time and took it on my leg. He only had one hand he could use, and he chopped with it, trying to bring the side of his palm against my neck. He kicked me away, pushed with the warm bloody mess that used to be fingers, and swung again, getting me in the ear.

Feeney tried to say "No!" but my hands had his throat, squeezing . . . slamming his head to the concrete floor until he went completely limp. I rolled on top of him and took that head like a sodden rag and smashed and smashed and smashed and there was no satisfying, solid thump, but a sickening squashing sound that splashed all over me.

Only then did I let go and look at Feeney, or what was left of him, before I got sick to my stomach.

I heard the police whistles, the sirens and the shouting around the wreck of the car outside. Dimly I heard voices calling that we were in the shed. I sat on the floor, trying to catch my breath, reaching in Feeney's pockets until my fingers closed about an oblong of cardboard with a rough edge where the stub had been torn off and I knew I had the ticket that had cost Lola's life.

They took me outside into the glare of the spotlights and listened to what I said. The radio car made contact with headquarters, who called Pat, and after that I wasn't a gun-mad killer any more, but a licensed private cop on a legitimate mission. A double check led to Lola, and the clincher was in Feeney's hip pocket, a bloodstained knife.

Oh, they were very nice about it. In fact, I was some sort of hero. They didn't even bother to take me in for questioning. They had my statement and Pat did the rest. I rode home in a patrol wagon while a cop followed in my car. Tomorrow, they said, would be time enough. Tonight I would rest. In a few hours the dawn would come and the light would chase the insanity of the night away. My phone was ringing as I reached the apartment. I answered it absently, hearing Pat tell me to stay put, he'd be right over. I hung up without saying a word, my eyes searching for a bottle and not finding it.

Pat was forgotten, everything was forgotten. I stumbled out again and down the stairs, over a block to the back of Mast's joint where he had his own private party bar and banged on the door to be let in.

After a minute a light went on and Joe Mast opened the door in his pajamas. Men can see things in other men and know enough to keep quiet. Joe waited until I was in, closed the door and pulled down the shades. Without a word he went behind the tiny bar and pulled a bottle down from the shelf, pouring me a double hooker while I forced myself onto a stool.

I didn't taste it; I didn't feel it go down.

I had another and didn't taste that one either.

Joe said, "Slow, Mike. Have all you want, but do it slow."

A voice started speaking, and I knew it was mine. It came of its own accord, a harsh, foreign voice that had no tone to it. "I loved her, Joe. She was wonderful and she loved me, too. She died tonight and the last thing she told me was that she loved me. It would have been nice. She loved me most, and I had just started to love her. I knew that it wouldn't be long before I loved her just as much. He killed her, the bastard. He killed her and I made a mess of his head. Even the devil won't recognize him now."

I reached in my pocket for a butt and felt the pawn ticket. I laid it on the bar next to the glass and the cigarettes. The name said Nancy Sanford and the address was the Seaside Hotel in Coney Island. "He deserved to die. He had a murder planned for my redhead and it didn't come off, but it worked out just as well. He was a big guy in the vice racket with sharp ideas and he killed to keep them sharp. He killed a blonde and he killed Lola. He wanted to kill me once but he got talked out of it. It was too soon to kill me then. Murder unplanned is too easily traced."

My mind went back to the parking lot, then before it, when I had walked into Murray Candid's office and seen the door closing and heard the cough. That was Feeney. He had spotted me in the club and put Murray wise. No wonder they wanted to warn me. Feeney was the smart one, he wanted me dead. He knew I wasn't going to be scared out of it. Too bad for him he got talked out of it. He was there that night. Did he have the ring? Damn it, why did that ring present a problem. Where the hell *did* it tie in? The whole thing started because of it . . . would it end without it?

Vacantly, I stared at the back bar, lost in thought. The ring with the battered fleur-de-lis design. Nancy's ring. Where was it now? Why was it there? The beating of my heart picked up until it was a hammer slamming my ribs. My eyes were centered on the bottles arranged so nicely in a long row.

Yeah! YEAH! I knew where the ring was!

How could I have been so incredibly stupid as to have missed it!

And Lola, who sent me after Feeney, had tried to tell me something else too . . . and I didn't get it until now!

Joe tried to stop me, but I was out the door before he could yell. I found my car and crawled in, fumbling for the ignition switch. I didn't have to hurry because I knew I had time. Not much, but enough time to get to the Seaside Hotel in Coney Island and do what I had to do.

I knew what I'd find. Nancy had left it there with her baggage. She was broke, she had to hock her camera. And being broke she had to get out of the Seaside Hotel without her baggage. But she knew it would be safe. Impounded but safe, redeemable when she had the money.

I found the Seaside Hotel tucked away on a street flanked by empty concession stands. Maybe from the roof it had a view of the sea. There wasn't any from where I stood. I parked a block away and walked up to it, seeing the peeling walls, the shuttered windows, the sign that read CLOSED FOR THE SEASON. Beneath it was another sign that told the public the building was protected by some obscure detective agency.

I took another drag on the cigarette and flipped it into the sand that had piled up in the gutter.

One look at the heavy timbers across the door and the steel bars on the ground-floor windows told me it was no use trying to get in that way. I scaled a fence beside the concession booth and walked around to the back. While I stood there looking at the white sand underneath the darker layer of wet stuff my feet had kicked up, the rain began again, and I smiled to myself. Nice rain. Wonderful, beautiful rain. In five minutes the tracks would be wet, too, and blend in with the other.

The roof of the shack slanted down towards the back. I had to jump to reach it, preferring to chin myself up rather than use any of the empty soda boxes piled there. I left part of my coat on a nail and took the time to unsnag it. The slightest trace would be too much to leave behind.

I was able to reach a window, then tried it and found it locked.

A recession in the wall farther down had stairsteps of bricks making an interlocking joint and I ran my hand over it. I saw I had about ten feet to go to the roof, a vertical climb with scarcely a thing to hang on to.

I didn't wait.

My toes gripped the edges of the brick, holding while I reached up for another grasp, then my hands performed the same duty. It was a tortuous climb, and twice I slipped, scrambling back into position to climb again. When I reached the top I lay there breathing hard a minute before going on.

In the center of the roof was a reinforced glass skylight, next to it the raised outlines of a trapdoor. The skylight didn't give, but the trapdoor did. I yanked at it with my hands and felt screws pull out of weather-rotted wood, and I was looking down a black hole that led into the Seaside Hotel.

I hung down in the darkness, swinging my feet to find something to stand on, and finding none, dropped into a welter of rubbish that clattered to the floor around me. I had a pencil flash in my pocket and threw the beam around. I was in a closet of some sort. On the side, shelves were piled with used paint cans and hard, cracked cakes of soap. Brooms lay scattered on the floor where I had knocked them. There was a door on one side, criss-crossed with spider webs, heavy with dust. I picked them off with the flash and turned the knob.

Under any other conditions the Seaside Hotel would have been a flophouse. Because it had sand around the foundations and sometimes you could smell the ocean over the hotdogs and body odors, they called it a summer hotel. The corridors were cramped and warped, the carpet on the floor worn through in spots. Doors to the rooms hung from tired hinges, eager for the final siege of dry rot, when they could fall and lie there. I went down the hallway, keeping against the wall, the flash spotting the way. To one side a flight of stairs snaked down, the dust tracked with the imprints of countless rat feet.

The front of the building was one story higher, and a sign pointed to the stairs at the other end. As I passed each room I threw the light into it, seeing only the empty bed and springs, the lone dresser and chair.

I found what I was looking for on the next floor. It was a room marked STORAGE, with an oversized padlock slung through the hasps. I held the flashlight in my teeth and reached for the set of picks I always carried in the car. The lock was big, but it was old. The third pick I inserted sent it clicking open in my hand. I laid it on the floor and opened the door.

It had been a bedroom once, but now it was a morgue of boxed sheets, mattresses, glassware and dirty utensils. A few broken chairs were still in clamps where an attempt had been made to repair them. Against the wall in the back an assortment of luggage had been stacked; overnight bags, footlockers, an expensive Gladstone, cheap paper carriers. Each one had a tag tied to the handle with a big price marked in red.

The runner of carpet that ran the length of the room had been laid down without tacks and I turned it over to keep from putting tracks in the dust. I found what I was looking for. It was a small trunk that had Nancy Sanford stencilled on it and it opened on the first try.

With near reverence I spread the folders apart and saw what was in them. I wasn't ashamed of Nancy now, I was ashamed of myself for thinking she was after blackmail. There in the trunk was her reason for living, a complete exposé of the whole racket, substantiated with pictures, documents, notes that had no meaning at the moment but would when they were studied. There were names and familiar faces. More than just aldermen. More than just manufacturers. Lots more. The lid was coming off City Hall. Park Avenue would feel the impact. But what was more important was the mechanics of the thing, neatly placed in a separate folder, enlarged pictures of books the police and the revenue men would want, definite proof of to whom those books belonged. The entire pretty set-up.

My ears picked up the sound, a faint metallic snapping. I closed the lid, locked it, then walked back my original path, taking time to fold the carpet over and study it, and satisfied that I had left no trace, closed the door and snapped the padlock in place. From the baseboard around the wall I scooped a handful of dust and blew it at the lock, restoring to it the age my hands had wiped off.

A yellow flood of light wandered up the hall, centered on the stairs and held. I stepped back into a bedroom, stuffing my watch in my pocket so the luminous face would be out of sight.

The light was poking into the rooms just as I had done. Feet sounded on the stairs, trying to be careful. Whoever stood behind that light was taking no chances, for it went down on the carpet, scanning it for tracks.

Back there in the room I grinned to myself.

The light came up the stairs, throwing the whole corridor into flickering shadows, giving off a hissing noise that meant he carried a naphtha lantern. It came onto the door of the storage room. There was a sigh. He sat the lantern on the floor, directing the beam towards the lock, and I heard him working over it with a pick.

He took longer than I did. But he got it open.

When I heard him enter the room I reached for my rod and stood with it in my hand. The racket he made dragging the trunk into the light covered the sound of my feet carrying me to the door. He was too excited to use a pick in the lock; instead he smashed it open and a low chuckle came out of his throat as he pawed through the contents.

I said, "Hullo, Mr. Berin-Grotin."

I should have shot the bastard in the back and kept quiet. He whipped around with unbelievable speed, smashing at the light and shooting at the same time. Before I could pull the trigger a slug hit my chest and spun me out of the doorway. Then another tore into my leg.

"Damn you anyway!" he screamed.

I rolled to one side, the shock of the bullet's impact numbing me all over. I lay on my face and pulled the trigger again and again, firing into the darkness.

A shot licked back at me and hit the wall over my head, but that brief spurt of flame had death in it. The lantern had over-turned, spilling the naphtha over the floor, and it rose in a fierce blaze right in Berin's face. I saw his eyes, mad eyes, crazy eyes. He was on his hands and knees, shoving himself back, momentarily blinded by the light.

I had to fight to get a grip on the gun, bring it back in line. When I pulled the trigger it bucked in my hand and skittered across the floor. But it was enough. The .45 caught him in the hip and knocked him over backwards.

Everything was ablaze now, the flames licking to the bedding, running up the walls to the ceilings. A paint can and something in a bottle went up with a dull roar. It was getting hard to feel anything, even the heat. Over in the corner Berin groaned and pushed himself erect. He saw me then, lying helpless on the floor, and his hand reached out for his gun.

He was going to kill me if it was the last thing he did. He would have if the wall hadn't blossomed out into a shower of sparks and given way. One of the timbers that had lost the support of rusted nails wavered, and like a falling giant pine tree, crashed into the room and nailed the goddamn killer to the floor under it.

I laughed like a fiend, laughed and laughed, even though I knew I was going to die anyway.

"You lost, Berin, you lost! You could have gotten away, but you lost!"

He fought the heavy timber, throwing his hands against the flame of the wood to push it away and I smelt the acrid odor of burning flesh. "Get it off me, Mike! Get it off . . . please. You can have anything you want! Get it off me!"

"I can't . . . I can't even move. Maybe I would if I could, but I can't even move!"

"Mike! . . ."

"No good, you filthy louse. I'll die with you. I don't give a damn any more. I'll die, but you'll go, too. You never thought it would happen, did you? You had the ring and you thought you'd have time. You didn't know I killed Feeney and got the ticket from him.

"There was Lola waiting for me. You heard me tell her that on the phone. While you got the drinks you called Feeney and covered up by playing the phonograph for me. He must have walked right in on her. She was expecting me and she got a killer. Sure, you stalled me while Feeney went to my office and broke in. He did a good job of it, too. But he had to go back and kill Lola because she knew the address on the ticket, and the camera could have been traced.

"Feeney called you right after he sank his knife in her, but she wasn't dead and saw him do it. You told Feeney to get out of there and wait for you somewhere. Sure, you wouldn't want Feeney to get his hands on that stuff. He got out . . . just as I came in and Lola put the finger on him. She put the finger on you, too, when she pointed to the phone. Feeney got out, but I was coming in and he stepped back to let me pass and I didn't see him. I caught him, though. Yeah, you played it cautious right to the end. You took your time about getting here, careful not to attract attention in any way. Did you sneak out of your hotel or just pretend you were up early as usual?"

"Mike, I'm burning!"

His hair smoked, puffed up in a ball of flame and he screamed again. He looked like a killer, being bald like that. The other wall was a sheet of fire now.

"I didn't get the connection until tonight. It was the ring after all. The ring was very important. I sat there looking at a bottle of whisky. The label had three feathers spread across the front just like the fancy plaque on your private morgue. I happened to think that the spread of feathers looked just like a fleur-de-lis pattern, then I got it. The design on the ring *was* three feathers, battered out enough to make it hard to recognize."

He fought the timber now, his face contorted in agony. I watched him a second and laughed again.

"The three feathers were part of your family crest, weren't they? An imitation of royalty. You and your damn pride, you bastard! Nancy Sanford was your own granddaughter. She was going to have a baby and you kicked her out. What did you think of *her* pride? So she turned from one job to another, working under an assumed name. She became a prostitute on the side. She got to know guys like Russ Bowen and his connection with Feeney. Then one day she saw you two together.

"I can imagine what she thought when she realized you were one of them, living your vain life of wealth on money that came from the bodies of the girls, hiding behind the front of respectability. You had it set up nice until she came along. She only had one thing in mind and that was to break the whole racket to pieces.

"Only she had to leave her baggage behind her until she had money to redeem it. Then you got the breaks. Feeney ran across her, looking for a piece on the side, and saw something. What was it, more pictures? Enough to make you get wise? Did he see the ring and know what it meant?"

Berin rolled from side to side. The timber, out of the flame, wasn't burning. It lay across his chest smoking. His eyes were on the ceiling watching the plaster crack and fall. The fire had spread, eating at everything it touched. Only on the floor was there an escape from the intense heat. But not for long. Soon the flames would come up from the floor, and that would be it. I tried to move, drag myself, but the effort was too great, and all I could do was stare at the man under the timber and be glad to know that I wouldn't die alone.

I laughed and Berin turned his head. A hot spark lit on his cheek and he didn't feel it. "Nancy was murdered, wasn't she?" I said. "It wasn't planned to work out so nice, but who could tell that a girl who had been clubbed so hard by an expert that her neck was broken, would get up from where she was thrown out of a car and stagger down the street and out into the path of another car.

"*You* were Feeney's alibi the night she was killed. You tailed her, forced her into the car, went into your act and heaved her out—and it all very nicely worked into your normal routine!

"Feeney didn't usually miss those shots, but he missed on Nancy and he missed on me. I should have known that sooner, too, when Lola told me Nancy had no vices. No, she didn't drink, but people swore she staggered and assumed she was drunk. I bet you had a big laugh over that.

"Pride! Pride did it to you. In the beginning you were a playboy and spent all your dough, but your pride wouldn't let you become a pauper. The smart operators got hold of you and then you fronted for them until you squeezed them out and had the racket all to yourself. You could work the filthiest racket in the world, but your pride wouldn't let you take back your granddaughter after she made a mistake. Then your pride kept you from letting her interfere with your affairs."

I could hardly talk over the roar of the flames now. Outside the engines were clanging up the streets and far-away voices mingled with crashing walls. Only because the fire had to eat its way down had we stayed alive as long as this.

"But it's all there in that box, mister. You'll die and your fancy hyphenated name will be lost in the mud and slime that'll come out of it."

"It won't, goddamn you! It won't!" Even in pain his eyes grew crafty. "The box will burn and even if it doesn't they'll think I was here with you, Mike. Yes, you're my alibi, and my name *won't* be lost. Nobody will trace that girl now and the world will never know!"

He was right, too. He was so right that the anger welling up in me drove the numbness out of my leg and the pain from my chest and I pulled myself across the room. I reached the trunk, shoved it, shoved it again, my hands brushing aside the hot embers that fell from the ceiling. Berin saw what I was doing and screamed for me to stop. I grinned at him. He was bald and ugly. He was a killer in hell before he died.

Somehow I got the box on edge and heaved, the effort throwing me back to the floor. But it smashed the window out and fell to the ground and I heard an excited shout and a voice yell. "Somebody is in the room up there!"

The sudden opening of the window created a draft that sucked the flames right out of the wall, sent them blasting into my face. I smelled hair burning and saw the legs of Berin's pants smoulder. His gun was lying under my hand.

He should never have spoken to me that way, but he did and it gave me strength to go it all the way. I reached for the gun, a .38, and fitted the butt into my hand.

"Look at your employee, Berin. See what I'm going to do? Now, listen carefully to what I tell you and think about it hard, because you only have a few minutes left. That tomb of yours won't be empty. No, the redhead will live there. The girl your pride kicked out. She'll be in that tomb. And do you know where you'll be? In potter's field next to Feeney Last, or what's left of you. I'll tell the police what happened. It won't be the truth, but it'll fit. I'll tell them the body up here is that of one of your boys you sent to get me. They'll never find you even though they'll never give up looking, and whenever your name is mentioned it will be with a sneer and a dirty memory. The only clean thing will be the redhead. You'll die the kind of death you feared most . . . lost, completely lost. Animals walking over your grave. Not even a marker."

The horror of it struck him and his mouth worked.

"But I won't deprive myself of the pleasure of killing you, mister rat. It will make up for the blonde and Lola. I'll kill you so I can live with myself again. I'll tell them we fought it out and I killed you. But you'll know the truth. It hurts, doesn't it?"

The pain in his eyes wasn't physical any longer.

"They'll be up here in a minute. I'll be waiting for them. I'll let them take me down and tell them there's no use going back in again. I'll let you burn until there isn't a thing left to identify you."

A stream of water hit the side of the wall, centered on the window and turned the room into a steaming inferno.

"A ladder will be pushed up here in just a minute now. When it comes I'll pull the trigger. Think about it, think hard."

A truck was being run into position. The shouts below grew louder. I crouched in the protection of the same timber that had him pinned down. The ceiling over the corridor outside fell in with a crash, dragging the front wall with it. I heard the crackling and looked up. Directly overhead the ceiling began to buckle, sagging in the middle with flame lancing through the cracks.

I looked at Berin and laughed. He turned his head and stared right into the muzzle of his own gun. Minutes—seconds—fractions of time. The ceiling was swaying now. The killer's face was a vile mask of hatred, praying for the ceiling to get us both. He was going to go first if it happened that way.

Something banged against the side of the window and slid over the sill: two prongs with a crossbar between them. A ladder bobbed as someone came up it, covered by the stream of water.

Berin had his mouth open, screaming with all the furies of the gods dethroned, but my laugh was even louder.

He was still screaming when I pulled the trigger.

Kiss Me, Deadly

chapter one ■■■■■■■■■■■■■■■

ALL I SAW was the dame standing there in the glare of the headlights, waving her arms like a huge puppet and the curse I spit out filled the car and my own ears. I wrenched the wheel over, felt the rear end start to slide, brought it out with a splash of power and almost ran up the side of the cliff as the car fishtailed. The brakes bit in, gouging a furrow in the shoulder, then jumped to the pavement and held.

Somehow I had managed a sweeping curve around the babe. For a few seconds she had been living on stolen time because instead of getting out of the way she had tried to stay in the beam of the headlights. I sat there and let myself shake. The butt that had fallen out of my mouth had burned a hole in the leg of my pants and I flipped it out the window. The stink of burned rubber and brake lining hung in the air like smoke and I was thinking of every damn thing I ever wanted to say to a harebrained woman so I could have it ready when I got my hands on her.

That was as far as I got. She was there in the car beside me, the door slammed shut and she said, "Thanks, mister."

Easy, feller, easy. She's a fruitcake. Don't plow her. Not yet. Hold your breath a minute, let it out easy, then maybe bend her over the fender and paddle her tail until she gets some sense in her head. Then boot her the hell out and make her walk the rest of the way home.

I fumbled out another cigarette, but she reached it before I did. For the first time I noticed her hands shaking as hard as mine were. I lit hers, got one out for me and lit that one too. "How stupid can you get?" I said.

She bit the words off. "Pretty stupid."

Behind me the lights of another car were reaching around a curve. Her eyes flicked back momentarily, fear pulling their corners tight. "You going to sit here all night, mister?"

"I don't know what I'm going to do. I'm thinking of throwing you over that cliff over there."

The headlights shone in the car through the rear window, bathed the roadway in light then swept on past. In the second that I had a good look at her she was rigid, her face frozen expressionlessly. When only the red dot of the taillight showed in front of us she let out her breath and leaned back against the seat.

In a way she was good-looking, but her face was more interesting than pretty. Wide-set eyes, large mouth, tawny hair that spilled onto her shoulders like melted butter. The rest of her was wrapped into a tailored trench coat that was belted around her waist and I remembered her standing there in the road like something conjured up too quickly in a dream. A Viking. A damn-fool crazy Viking dame with holes in her head.

I kicked the stalled engine over, crawled through the gears and held on tight to the wheel until my brain started working right. An accident you don't mind. Those you halfway expect when you're holding seventy on a mountain road. But you don't expect a Viking dame to jump out of the dark at you while you're coming around a turn. I opened the window all the way down and drank in some of the air. "How'd you get up here?"

"What does it look like?"

"Like you got dumped." I looked at her quickly and saw her tongue snake out over her lips. "You picked the wrong guy to go out with."

"I'll know better the next time."

"Pull a trick like that last one and there won't be any next time. You damn near became a painting on the face of that rockslide."

"Thanks for the advice," she said sarcastically, "I'll be more careful."

"I don't give a hoot what you do as long as you don't get strained through my radiator."

She plucked the cigarette from her lips and blew a stream of smoke at the windshield. "Look, I'm grateful for the ride. I'm sorry I scared hell out of you. But if you don't mind just shut up and take me somewhere or let me out."

My mouth pulled back in a grin. A dame with nerve like that sure could've made a mess out of a guy before he gave her the boot. "Okay, girl," I said, "now it's my turn to be sorry. It's a hell of a place for anybody to be stranded and I guess I would have done the same thing. Almost. Where do you want to go?"

"Where're you going?"

"New York."

"All right, I'll go there."

"It's a big city, kid. Name the spot and I'll take you there."

Her eyes got cold. The frozen expression came back in her face. "Make it a subway station. The first one you come to will do."

Her tone wiped my grin away. I eased the car around another turn and settled down to a straightway, jamming hard on the gas. "Damn rape-happy dame. You think all guys are the same?"

"I . . ."

"Shut up."

I could feel her watching me. I knew when she dropped her eyes in her lap and knew when she looked back at me again. She started to say something and closed her mouth over the words. She turned to stare out of the window into the blackness of the night and one hand wiped her eyes. Let her bawl. Maybe she'd learn how to be a little polite.

Another car was coming up behind us. She saw it first and pressed back into the seat until it was past. It went on down the long incline ahead of us until its taillight merged and disappeared into the maze of neons that were part of the town below.

The tires whined on a turn and the force of it made her lean across the seat until our shoulders touched. She pulled away at the contact, braced herself until the car rocked back to level and edged into the corner. I looked at her, but she was staring out of the window, her face still cold.

I slowed to fifty coming into the town, then to thirty-five and held it. The sign along the road said HANAFIELD, POP. 3600, SPEED LIMIT 25. A quarter mile up the highway a flashing red light winked in our direction and I got on the brakes. There was a police car in the middle of the road and two uniformed cops stood alongside it checking the cars as they came by. The car that had passed us further back was just getting the okay to go on through and the flashlight was waving at me to make a full stop.

Trouble. Like the smoke over a cake of dry ice. You can't smell it but you can see it and watch it boil and seep around things and know that soon something's going to crack and shatter under the force of the horrible contraction. I looked at the dame and she was stiffly immobile, her lips held so tight her teeth showed, a scream held in her throat ready to let go.

I leaned out the car before I reached the cop and took the beam of his flash in the face before he lowered it. "Trouble, officer?"

His hat was pushed back on his head and a cigarette drooped from his mouth. The gun he wore hung cowboy style, and for effect he draped his hand on its butt. "Where'd you come from, bud?"

A real cop, this guy. I wondered how much he paid for his appointment. "Coming down from Albany, officer. What's up?"

"See anybody along the road? Anybody hitchhiking?"

I felt her hand close over mine before I answered him. It closed and squeezed with a sudden warmth and urgency and in a quick movement she had taken my hand in hers and slid it under the trench coat and I felt the bare flesh of her thigh there, smooth and round, and when my fingers stiffened at the touch she thought I was hesitating and with a fluid motion moved her grip up my forearm and pulled my hand against her body where there was no doubting her meaning, then amplified it by squeezing her legs together gently to keep it there.

I said, "Not a thing, officer. My wife or me have been awake all the way and if anybody was there we sure would know about it. Maybe they came on ahead."

"Nobody came ahead, bud."

"Who were you looking for?"

"A dame. She escaped from some sanitarium upstate and hitched a ride down to a diner with a truck. When they started broadcasting a description she beat it outside and disappeared."

"Say, that's pretty serious. I wouldn't want to be the guy who picks her up. Is she dangerous?"

"All loonies are dangerous."

"What does she look like?"

"Tall blonde. That's about all we got on her. Nobody seems to remember what she was wearing."

"Oh. Well, okay for me to go?"

"Yeah, go on, beat it."

He walked back to the patrol car and I let out the clutch. I took my hand away slowly, keeping my eyes on the road. The town went by in a hurry, and on the other side I stepped on it again.

This time her hand crept up my arm and she slid across the

seat until she was beside me. I said, "Get back where you came from, sister. You didn't have to pull a stunt like that."

"I meant it."

"Thanks. It just wasn't necessary."

"You don't have to drop me at a subway station if you don't want to."

"I want to."

Her foot nudged mine off the gas pedal and the car lost headway. "Look," she said, and I turned my head. She had the coat wide open and was smiling at me. The coat, that's all, all the rest was sleekly naked. A Viking in satin skin. An invitation to explore the curves and valleys that lay nestled in the shadows and moved with her breathing. She squirmed in the seat and her legs made a beautifully obscene gesture and she smiled again.

She was familiar then. Not so much the person, but the smile. It was a forced, professional smile that looks warm as fire and really isn't anything at all. I reached over and flipped the coat closed. "You'll get cold," I said.

The smile twisted crookedly on her mouth. "Or is it that you're afraid because you think I'm not quite sane?"

"That doesn't bother me. Now shut up."

"No. Why didn't you tell him then?"

"Once when I was a kid I saw a dogcatcher about to net a dog. I kicked him in the shins, grabbed the pup and ran. The damn mutt bit me and got away, but I was still glad I did it."

"I see. But you believed what the man said."

"Anybody who jumps in front of a car isn't too bright. Now shut up."

The smile twisted a little more as if it weren't being forced. I looked at her, grinned at what had happened and shook my head. "I sure get some dillies," I said.

"What?"

"Nothing." I pulled the car off the road into the dull glare of the service-station sign and coasted up to the pumps. A guy came out of the building wiping his eyes and I told him to fill it up. I had to get out to unlock the gas cap and I heard the door open, then slam shut. The blonde went up to the building, walked inside and didn't come back until I was counting the money into the guy's hand.

When she got back in the car there was something there that hadn't been there before. Her face had softened and the frost had thawed until she seemed almost relaxed. Another car came by as we rolled off the gravel to the road only this time she didn't pay any attention to it at all. The coat was belted again, the flicker of a smile she gave me was real, and she put her head back against the seat and closed her eyes.

I didn't get it at all. All I knew was that when I hit the city I was going to pull up to the first subway station I saw, open the door, say good-by, then check on the papers until I found where somebody had put her back on the shelf again. I thought that. I wished I could mean it. All I felt was the trouble like the smoke over dry ice and it was seeping all over me.

For five minutes she sat and watched the edge of the road, then said, "Cigarette?" I shook one into her hand and shoved the dashboard lighter in. When it was lit she dragged in deeply and watched the gray haze swirl off the windows. "Are you wondering what it's all about?" she asked me.

"Not particularly."

"I was . . . ," she hesitated, "in a sanitarium." The second pull on the butt nearly dragged the lit end down to her fingers. "They forced me to go there. They took away my clothes to make me stay there."

I nodded as if I understood.

She shook her head slowly, getting the meaning of my gesture. "Maybe I'll find somebody who will understand. I thought maybe . . . you would."

I went to say something. It never came out. The moon that had been hidden behind the clouds came out long enough to bathe the earth in a quick shower of pale yellow light that threw startlingly long shadows across the road and among those dark fingers was one that seemed darker still and moved with a series of jerks and a roar of sound that evolved into a dark sedan cutting in front of us. For the second time I heard the scream of tires on pavement and with it another scream not from the tires as metal tore into metal with a nasty tearing sound as splintering glass made little incongruous musical highlights above it all.

I kicked the door open and came out of the car in time to see the men piling out of the sedan. The trouble was all around us and you couldn't walk away from it. But I didn't expect it to be as bad as that. The gun in the guy's hand spit out a tongue of flame that lanced into the night and the bullet's banshee scream matched the one that was still going on behind me.

He never got another shot out because my fist split his face open. I went into the one behind him as something hissed through the air behind my head then hissed again and thudded against my shoulders. My arm went on that one and I spun around to get him with my foot. It was just a little too late. There was another hiss of something whipping through the air and whatever it was, it caught me across the forehead and for a second before all time and distance went I thought I was going to be sick and the hate for those bastards oozed out of my skin like sweat.

I didn't lie there for long. The pain that pounded across my head was too sharp, too damn deep. It was a hard, biting pain that burst in my ears with every heartbeat, sending a blinding white light flashing into my eyes even though they were squeezed shut.

In back of it all was the muffled screaming, the choked-off sobs, the cadence of harsh, angry voices biting out words that were indistinguishable at first. The motor of a car chewed into the sounds and there was more jangling of metal against metal. I tried to get up, but it was only my mind that could move. The rest of me was limp and dead. When the sense of movement did happen it wasn't by command but because arms had me around the waist and my feet and hands scraped cold concrete. Somewhere during those seconds the screaming had been chopped off, the voices had ceased and a certain pattern of action had begun to form.

You don't think at a time like that. You try to remember first, to collect events that led up to the end, to get things relatively assorted in their proper places so you can look at and study them with a bewildered sort of wonder that is saturated with pain, to find a beginning and an end. But nothing makes sense, all you feel is a madness and hate that rises and grows into a terrible frenzy that even wipes out the pain and you want to kill something so bad your brain is on fire. Then you realize that you can't even do that and the fire explodes into consciousness because of it and you can see once more.

They had left me on the floor. There were my feet and my hands, immobile lumps jutting in front of my body. The backs of the hands and the sleeves were red and sticky. The taste of the stickiness was in my mouth too. Something moved and a pair of shoes shuffled into sight so I knew I wasn't alone. The floor in front of my feet stretched out into other shoes and the lower halves of legs. Shiny shoes marred with a film of dust. One with a jagged scratch across the toe. Four separate pairs of feet all pointing toward the same direction and when my eyes followed them I saw her in the chair and saw what they were doing to her.

She had no coat on now and her skin had an unholy whiteness

about it, splotched with deeper colors. She was sprawled in the chair, her mouth making uncontrollable mewing sounds. The hand with the pliers did something horrible to her and the mouth opened without screaming.

A voice said, "Enough. That's enough."

"She can still talk," the other one answered.

"No, she's past it. I've seen it happen before. We were silly to go this far, but we had no choice."

"Listen . . ."

"I'll give the orders. You listen."

The feet moved back a little. "All right, go ahead. But so far we don't know any more than we did before."

"That's satisfactory. What we do know is still more than anyone else. There are other ways and at least she won't be talking to the wrong ones. She'll have to go now. Everything is ready?"

"Yeah." It was a disgusted acknowledgment. "The guy too?"

"Naturally. Take them out to the road."

"It's a shame to dress her."

"You pig. Do what you're told. You two, help carry them out. We've spent enough time on this operation."

I could feel my mouth working to get some words out. Every filthy name I could think of for them was stuck in my throat. I couldn't even raise my eyes above their knees to see their faces and all I could do was hear them, hear everything they said and keep the sound of their voices spilling over in my ears so that when I heard them again I wouldn't need to look at their faces to know I was killing the right ones. The bastards, the dirty lousy bastards!

Hands went under my knees and shoulders and for a second I thought I would see what I wanted to see, but the hate inside me sent the blood beating to my head bringing back the pain and it was like a black curtain being pulled closed across my mind. Once it drew back hesitatingly and I saw my car on the side of the road, the rear end lifted with a jack and red flares set in front and in back of it.

Clever, I thought. Very clever of them. If anybody passed they'd see a car in trouble with warning signals properly placed and the driver obviously gone into town for help. Nobody would stop to investigate. Then the thought passed into the darkness as quickly as it came.

It was like a sleep that you awaken from because you had been sleeping cramped up. It was a forced awakening that hurts and you hear yourself groan as you try to straignten out. *Then suddenly there's an immediate sharpness to the awakening as you realize that it hadn't been a bad dream after all, but something alive and terrifying instead.*

She was there beside me in the car, the open coat framing her nakedness. Her head lolled against the window, the eyes staring sightlessly at the ceiling. She jerked and fell against me.

But not because she was alive! The car was moving ahead as something rammed into the rear of it!

Somehow I got myself up, looked over the wheel into the splash of light ahead of me and saw the edge of the cliff short feet away and even as I reached for the door the wheels went over the edge through the ready-made gap in the retaining wall and the nose dipped down into an incredible void.

chapter two ▰▰▰▰▰▰▰▰▰▰

"MIKE . . ."

I turned my head toward the sound. The motion brought a wave of silent thunder with it like the surf crashing on a beach. I heard my name again, a little clearer this time.

"Mike . . ."

My eyes opened. The light hurt, but I kept them open. For a minute she was just a dark blur, then the fuzzy edges went away and the blue became beautiful. "Hello, kitten," I said.

Velda's mouth parted in a slow smile that had all the happiness in the world wrapped up in it. "Glad to see you back, Mike."

"It's . . . good to be back. I'm surprised . . . I got here."

"So are a lot of people."

"I . . ."

"Don't talk. The doctor said to keep you quiet if you woke up. Otherwise he'd chase me away."

I tried to grin at her and she dropped her hand over mine. It was warm and soft with a gentle pressure that said everything was okay. I held it for a long time and if she took it away I never knew about it because when I awoke again it was still there.

The doctor was an efficient little man who poked and prodded with stiff fingers while he watched the expression on my face. He seemed to reel off yards of tape and gauze to dress me in and went away looking satisfied, as though he had made me to start with.

Before he closed the door he turned around, glanced at his watch and said, "Thirty minutes, miss. I want him to sleep again."

Velda nodded and squeezed my hand. "Feel better?"

"Somewhat."

"Pat's outside. Shall I ask him to come in?"

". . . Yeah."

She got up and went to the door. I heard her speak to somebody, then there he was grinning at me foolishly, shaking his head while he looked me over.

"Like my outfit?" I said.

"Great. On you white looks good. Three days ago I was figuring I'd have to finance a new tux to bury the corpse in."

Nice guy, Pat. A swell cop, but he was getting one hell of a sense of humor. When his words sunk in I felt my forehead wrinkling under the turban. "Three days?"

He nodded and draped himself in the big chair beside the bed. "You got it Monday. This is Thursday."

"Brother!"

"I know what you mean."

He glanced at Velda. A quick look that had something behind it I didn't get. She bit her lip, her teeth glistening against the magenta ripeness of her mouth, then nodded in assent.

Pat said, "Can you remember what happened, Mike?"

I knew the tone. He tried to cover it but he didn't make out. It was the soft trouble tone, falsely light yet direct and insistent. He knew I had caught it and his eyes dropped while he fiddled with his coat. "I remember."

"Care to tell me about it?"

"Why?"

This time he tried to look surprised. That didn't work either. "No reason."

"I had an accident, that's all."

"That's all?"

I got the grin out again and turned it on Velda. She was worried, but not too worried to smile back. "Maybe you can tell me what's cooking, kid. He won't."

"I'll let Pat tell you. He's been pretty obscure with me too."

"It's your ball, Pat," I said.

He stared at me a minute, then: "Right now I wish you weren't so sick. I'm the cop and you're the one who's supposed to answer questions."

"Sure, but I'm standing on my constitutional rights. It's very legal. Go ahead."

"All right, just keep your voice down or that medic will be hustling me out of here. If we weren't buddies I couldn't get within a mile of you with that watchdog around."

"What's the pitch?"

"You're not to be questioned . . . yet."

"Who wants to question me?"

"Among other law enforcement agencies, some government men. That accident of yours occurred in New York State, but right now you happen to be just over the state line in a Jersey hospital. The New York State Troopers will be looking forward to seeing you, plus some county cops from upstate a ways."

"I think I'll stay in Jersey a while."

"Those government men don't care what state you're in."

And there was that tone again.

"Suppose you explain," I said.

I watched the play of expression across his face to see what he was trying to hide. He looked down at his fingers and pared his nails absently. "You were lucky to get out of the car alive. The door sprung when it hit the side of the drop and you were thrown clear. They found you wrapped around some bushes. If the car hadn't sprayed the place with burning gas you might still be there. Fortunately, it attracted some motorists who went down to see what happened. Not much was left of the car at all."

"There was a dame in there," I told him.

"I'm coming to that." His head came up and his eyes searched my face. "She was dead. She's been identified."

"As an escapee from a sanitarium," I finished.

It didn't catch him a bit off base. "Those county cops were pretty sore about it when they found out. Why did you pass them up?"

"I didn't like their attitude."

He nodded as if that explained it. Hell, it did.

"You better start thinking before you pull stunts like that, Mike."

"Why?"

"The woman didn't die in the crash."

"I figured as much."

Maybe I shouldn't have been so calm about it. His lips got tight all of a sudden and the fingernails he had been tending disappeared into balled-up fists. "Damn it, Mike, what are you into? Do you realize what kind of a mess you've been fooling around with?"

"No. I'm waiting for you to tell me."

"That woman was under surveillance by the feds. She was part of something big that I don't know about myself and she was committed to the institution to recover so she could do some tall talking to a closed session of Congress. There was a police guard outside her door and on the grounds of the place. Right now the Washington boys are hopping and it looks like the finger is pointed at you. As far as they're concerned you got her out of there and knocked her off."

I lay there and looked at the ceiling. A crack in the plaster zigzagged across the room and disappeared under the molding. "What do *you* think, Pat?"

"I'm waiting to hear you say it."

"I already said it."

"An accident?" His smile was too damn sarcastic. "It was an accident to have a practically naked woman in your car? It was an accident to lie your way through a police roadblock? It was an accident to have her dead before your car went through the wall? You'll have to do better than that, pal. I know you too well. If accidents happen they go the way you want them to."

"It was an accident."

"Mike, look . . . you can call it what you like. I'm a cop and I'm in a position to help you out if there's trouble, but if you don't square away with me I'm not going to do a thing. When those Federal boys move in you're going to have to do better than that accident story."

Velda moved her hand up to my chin and turned my head so she could look at me. "It's big, Mike," she said. "Can you fill in the details?" She was so completely serious it was almost funny. I felt like kissing the tip of her nose and sending her out to play, but her eyes were pleading with me.

I said, "It was an accident. I picked her up on the way down from Albany. I don't know a thing about her, but she seemed like a nervy kid in a jam and I didn't like the snotty way that cop acted when he stopped the car. So I went on through. We got down maybe ten miles when a sedan pulled out from the side of the road and nudged me to a stop. Now here's the part you won't believe. I got out sore as hell and somebody took a shot at me. It missed, but I got sapped and sapped so beautifully I never came completely out of it. I don't know where the hell they took us, but wherever it was they tried to force something out of the dame. She never came across. Those lads were anxious to get rid of her and me too so they piled us in the car and gave it a shove over the cliff."

"Who are they?" Pat asked.

"Damned if I know. Five or six guys."

"Can you identify them?"

"Not by their faces. Maybe if I heard them speak."

I didn't mean maybe at all. I could still hear every syllable they spoke and those voices would talk in my mind until I died. Or they did.

The silence was pretty deep. The puzzle was on Velda's face. "Is that all?" She asked me.

Pat spoke out of the stillness, his voice soft again. "That's all he's going to tell anybody." He got up and stood by the bed. "If that's the way you want it, I'll play along. I hope like hell you're telling me the truth."

"But you're afraid I'm not, is that it?"

"Uh-huh. I'll check on it. I can still see some holes in it."

"For instance?"

"The gap in the guardrail. No slow-moving car did that. It was a fresh break, too."

"Then they did it with their car purposely."

"Maybe. Where was your heap while they were working the woman over?"

"Nicely parked off the road with a jack under it and flares set out."

"Clever thought."

"I thought so too," I said.

"Who could ever find anybody who noticed the flares? They'd just breeze right on by."

"That's right."

Pat hesitated, glanced at Velda, then back to me again. "You're going to stick with that story?"

"What else?"

"Okay, I'll check on it. I hope you aren't making any mistakes. Good night now. Take it easy." He started to the door.

I said, "I'll do my own checking when I'm up, Pat."

He stopped with his hand on the knob. "Don't keep asking for trouble, kid. You have enough right now."

"I don't like to get sapped and tossed over a cliff."

"Mike . . ."

"See you around, Pat." He shot me a wry grin and left. I picked up Velda's hand and looked at her watch. "You have five minutes left out of the thirty. How do you want to spend it?"

The seriousness washed away all at once. She was a big, luscious woman smiling at me with a mouth that was only inches away and coming closer each second. Velda. Tall, with hair like midnight. Beautiful, so it hurt to look at her.

Her hands were soft on my face and her mouth a hot, hungry thing that tried to drink me down. Even through the covers I could feel the firm pressure of her breasts, live things that caressed me of their own accord. She took her mouth away reluctantly so I could kiss her neck and run my lips across her shoulders.

"I love you, Mike," she said. "I love everything about you even when you're all fouled up with trouble." She traced a path down my cheek with her finger. "Now what do you want me to do?"

"Get your nose to the ground, kitten," I told her. "Find out what the hell this is all about. Take a check on that sanitarium and get a line into Washington if you can."

"That won't be easy."

"They can't keep secrets in the capital, baby. There will be rumors."

"And what will you do?"

"Try to make those feds believe that accident yarn."

Her eyes widened a little. "You mean . . . it didn't happen that way?"

"Uh-uh. I mean it did. It's just that nobody's going to believe it."

I patted her hand and she straightened up from the bed. I watched her walk toward the door, taking in every feline motion of her body. There was something lithe and animal-like in the way she swung her hips, a jungle tautness to her shoulders. Cleopatra might have had it. Josephine might have had it. But they never had it like she had it.

I said, "Velda . . ." and she turned around, knowing damn well what I was going to say. "Show me your legs."

She grinned impishly, her eyes dancing, standing in a pose no calendar artist could duplicate. She was a Circe, a lusty temptress, a piece of living statuary on display, that only one guy would be able to see. The hem of the dress came up quickly, letting the roundness under the nylon evolve into a magical symmetry, then the nylon ended in the quick whiteness of her thigh and I said, "Enough, kitten. Quit it."

Before I could say anything else she laughed down deep, threw me a kiss and grinned. "Now you know how Ulysses felt."

Now I knew. The guy was a sucker. He should have jumped ship.

chapter three ████████████████████████

IT WAS MONDAY again, a rainy, dreary Monday that was a huge wet muffler draped over the land. I watched it through the window and felt the taste of it in my mouth. The door opened and the doctor said, "Ready?"

I turned away from the window and squashed out the cigarette. "Yeah. Are they waiting for me downstairs?"

His tongue showed pink through his lips for a moment and he nodded. "I'm afraid so."

I picked my hat up from the chair and walked across the room. "Thanks for keeping them off my back so long, doc."

"It was a necessary thing. You had quite a blow, young man. There still may be complications." He held the door open for me, waved toward the elevator down the hall and waited silently beside me for it to crawl up to the floor. He took his place beside me on the way down, once letting his eyes edge over so he could watch me.

We got out in the lobby, shook hands briefly and I went to the cashier's window. She checked my name, told me everything had been paid for by my secretary, then handed me a receipted bill.

When I turned around they were all standing there politely, hats in their hands. Young guys with old eyes. Sharp. Junior executive types. Maybe you could pick them out of a crowd but most likely you couldn't. No gun bulges under the suit jackets, no high-top shoes with arch supports. Not too fat, not too lean. Faces you wouldn't want to lie past. Junior executives all right, but in J. Edgar Hoover's organization.

The tall guy in the blue pin stripe said, "Our car is out front, Mr. Hammer." I fell in beside him with the others bringing up on the flank and went out to get driven home. We took the Lincoln Tunnel across into New York, cut east on Forty-first, then took Ninth Avenue downtown to the modern gray building they used for operational headquarters.

They were real nice, those boys. They took my hat and coat, shoved up a chair for me to sit in, asked if I felt well enough to talk and when I told them sure, suggested that maybe I'd like a lawyer present.

I grinned at that one. "Nope, just ask questions and I'll do what I can to answer them. But thanks anyway."

The tall one nodded and looked over my head at someone else. "Bring in the file," he said. In back of me a door opened and closed. He leaned forward on the desk, his fingers laced together. "Now, Mr. Hammer, we'll get down to cases. You're completely aware of the situation?"

"I'm aware that no situation exists," I said bluntly.

"Really?"

I said, "Look, friend. You may be the F.B.I and I may be up to my ears in something you're interested in, but let's get something straight. I don't get bluffed. Not even by the feds. I came here of my own free will. I'm fairly well acquainted with the law. The reason I didn't squawk about coming down here was because I wanted to get straightened out all the way around and quick because I have things to do when I leave and I don't want any cops tagging me around. That much understood?"

He didn't answer me right away. The door opened and closed again and a hand passed a folder over my shoulder. He took it, flipped it open and glanced through it. But he wasn't reading it. He knew the damn thing by heart. "It says here you're pretty tough, Mr. Hammer."

"Some people seem to think so."

"Several close brushes with the law, I notice."

"Notice the result."

"I have. I imagine your license can be waivered if we want to press the issue."

I dragged out my deck of Luckies and flipped one loose. "I said I'd cooperate. You can quit trying to bluff me."

His eyes came over the edge of the folder. "We're not bluffing. The police in upstate New York want you. Would you sooner talk to them?"

It was getting a little tiresome. "If you want. They can't do anything more than talk either."

"You ran a roadblock."

"Wrong, chum, I stopped for it."

"But you did lie to the officer who questioned you?"

"Certainly. Hell, I wasn't under oath. If he had any sense he would have looked at the dame and questioned her." I let the smoke drift out of my mouth toward the ceiling.

"The dead woman in your car . . ."

"You're getting lame," I said. "You know damn well I didn't kill her."

His smile was a lazy thing. "How do we know?"

"Because I didn't. I don't know how she died, but if she was shot you've already checked my apartment and found my gun there. You've already taken a paraffin test on me and it came out negative. If she was choked the marks on her neck didn't match the spread of my hands. If she was stabbed . . ."

"Her skull was crushed by a blunt instrument," he put in quietly.

And I said just as quietly, "It matched the indentation in my own skull then and you know it."

If I thought he was going to get sore I was wrong. He twisted his smile in a little deeper and leaned back in the chair with his head cradled in his hands. Behind me someone coughed to cover up a laugh.

"Okay, Mr. Hammer, you seem to know everything. Sometimes we can break even the tough ones down without much trouble. We did all the things you mentioned before you regained consciousness. Were you guessing?"

I shook my head. "Hell, no. I don't underestimate cops. I've made a pretty good living in the racket myself. Now if there's anything you'd really like to know I'd be glad to give it to you."

His mouth pursed in thought a minute. "Captain Chambers gave us a complete report on things. The details checked . . . and your part in it seems to fit your nature. Please understand something, Mr. Hammer. We're not after you. If your part was innocent enough that's as far as we need to go. It's just that we can't afford to pass up any angles."

"Good. Then I'm clear?"

"As far as we're concerned."

"I suppose they have a warrant out for me upstate."

"We'll take care of it."

"Thanks."

"There's just one thing . . ."

"Yeah?"

"From your record you seem to be a pretty astute sort of person. What's your opinion on this thing?"

"Since when do you guys deal in guesswork?"

"When that's all we have to go on."

I dropped the cigarette into the ashtray on the desk and looked at him. "The dame knew something she shouldn't have. Whoever pulled it were smart cookies. I think the sedan that waited for us was one that passed us up right after I took her aboard. It was a bad spot to try anything so they went ahead and picked the right one. She wouldn't talk so they bumped her. I imagine it was supposed to look like an accident."

"That's right, it was."

"Now do you mind if I ask one?"

"No. Go right ahead."

"Who was she?"

"Berga Torn." My eyes told him to finish it and he shrugged his shoulder. "She was a taxi dancer, nightclub entertainer, friend of boys on the loose and anything else you can mention where sex is concerned."

A frown pulled at my forehead. "I don't get it."

"You're not supposed to, Mr. Hammer." A freeze clouded up his eyes. It told me that was as much as he was about to say and I was all through. I could go now and thanks. Thanks a lot.

I got up and pulled my hat on. One of the boys held the door open for me. I turned around and grinned at him. "I will, feller," I said.

"What?"

"Get it." My grin got bigger. "Then somebody else is going to get it."

I pulled the door closed and got out in the hall. I stood there a minute leaning up against the wall until the pounding in my forehead stopped and the lights left my eyes. There was a dry sour taste in my mouth that made me want to spit, a nasty hate buzzing around my head that pulled my lips tight across my teeth and brought the voices back in my ears and then I felt better because I knew that I'd never forget them and that some day I'd hear them again, only this time they'd choke out the last sound they'd ever make.

I took the elevator downstairs, called a cab and gave him Pat's office address. The cop on the desk told me to go ahead up and when I walked in Pat was sitting there waiting for me, trying on a friendly smile for size.

He said, "How did it go, Mike?"

"It was a rotten pitch." I hooked a chair over with my foot and sat down. "I don't know what the act was for, but they sure wasted time."

"They *never* waste time."

"Then why the ride?"

"Checking. I gave them the facts they hadn't already picked up."

"They didn't seem to do anything about it."

"I didn't expect them to." He dropped the chair forward on all four legs. "I suppose you asked them some things too."

"Yeah, I know the kid's name. Berga Torn."

"That's all?"

"Part of her history. What's the rest?"

Pat dropped his eyes and stared at his hands. When he was ready to speak he looked up at me, his face a study in caution. "Mike . . . I'm going to give you some information. The reason I'm doing it is because you're likely to fish around and find it yourself if I don't and interference is one thing we can't have."

"Go ahead."

"You've heard of Carl Evello?"

I nodded.

"Evello is the boy behind the powers. The last senatorial investigations turned up a lot of big names in the criminal world, but they never turned up his. That's how big he is. The others are pretty big too, but not like him."

I felt my eyebrows go up. "I didn't know he was that big. Where does it come from?"

"Nobody seems to know. A lot is suspected, but until there's plenty of concrete evidence, no charges are going to be passed around even by me. Just take my word for it that the guy is big. Now . . . they want him. They want him bad and when they get him all the other big boys are going to fall too."

"So what."

"Berga Torn was his mistress for a while."

It started to make sense now. I said, "So she had something on the guy?"

Pat shrugged disgustedly. "Who knows? She was supposed to have had something. She can't talk. When they were giving her the business as you said they were trying to get it out of her."

"You figure they were Carl's men then."

"Evidently."

"What about the sanitarium she was in?"

"She was there under the advice of her doctor," Pat said. "She was going to testify to the committee and under the strain almost had a nervous breakdown. All the committee hearings were tied up until she was released."

I said, "That's a pretty picture, kid. Where do I come in?"

Little light lines seemed to grow around his eyes. "You don't. You stay out of it."

"Nuts."

"Okay, hero, then let's break it down. There's no reason for you to mess around. It was just an accident that got you into it anyway. There's nothing much you can do and anything you *try* to do is damn well going to be resented by all the agencies concerned."

I gave him my best big grin. All the teeth. Even the eyes. "You flatter me."

"Don't get smart, Mike."

"I'm not."

"All right, you're a bright boy and I know how you work. I'm just trying to stop any trouble before it starts."

"Pal, you got it wrong," I said, "it's already started, remember? I got patted between the eyes, a dame got bumped and my car is wrecked." I stood up and looked down at him, feeling things changing in my smile. "Maybe I have too much pride, but I don't let anybody get away with that kind of stuff. I'm going to knock the crap out of somebody for all that and if it gets up to Evello it's okay with me."

Pat's hand came down on the edge of the desk. "Damn it, Mike, why don't you get a little sense in your head? You . . ."

"Look . . . suppose somebody took you for a patsy. What would you do?"

"That didn't happen."

"No . . . but it happened to me. Those boys aren't that tough that they can get away with it. Damn it, Pat, you ought to know me better than that."

"I do, that's why I'm asking you to lay off. What do I have to do, appeal to your patriotism?"

"Patriotism, my back. I don't give a damn if Congress, the President and the Supreme Court told me to lay off. They're only men and they didn't get sapped and dumped over a cliff. You don't play games with guys who pull that kind of stuff. The feds can be as cagey as they like, but when they wrap the bunch up what happens? So they testify. Great. Costello testified and I can show you where he committed perjury in the minutes of the hearing. What happened? Yeah . . . you know what happened as well as I do. They're too big to do anything with. They got too much dough and too much power and if they talk too many people are going to go under. Well, the hell with 'em. There are a bunch of guys who drove a sedan I want to see again. I don't

know what they look like, but I'll know them when I see them.
If the feds beat me to 'em it's okay with me, but I'll wait, pal.
If I don't reach them first I'll wait until they get through testifying
or serving that short sentence those babies seem to draw and when
I do you won't be having much trouble from them again ever."

"You have it all figured?"

"Uh-huh. Right down to the self-defense plea."

"You won't get far."

I grinned at him again. "You know better than that, don't
you?"

For a moment the seriousness left his face. His mouth cracked
in a grin. "Yeah," he said, "that's what I'm afraid of."

"That wasn't any ordinary kill."

"No."

"They were a bunch of cold-blooded bastards. You should have
seen what they did to that kid before they killed her."

"Nothing showed on her body . . . or what was left of it after
the fire."

"It was there. It wasn't very pretty." I stared at him hard. "It
changes something in the way you were thinking."

His eyes came up speculatively.

"They didn't give her the works to see how much she knew.
They were after something she knew and they didn't. She was the
key to something."

Pat's face was grave. "And you're going after it?"

"What did you expect?"

"I don't know, Mike." He wiped his hand across his eyes. "I
guess I didn't expect you to take it lying down." He turned his
head and glanced out of the window at the rain. "But since it's
going to be that way you might as well know this much. Those
government boys are shrewd apples. They know your record and
how you work. They even know how you think. Don't expect
any help from this end. If you cross those boys you're going to
wind up in the can."

"You have your orders?" I asked him.

"In writing. From pretty high authority." His eyes met mine.
"I was told to pass the news on to you if you acted up."

I stood up and fiddled with my pack of butts. "Great guys.
They want to do it all alone. They're too smart to need help."

"They have the equipment and manpower," Pat said defensively.

"Yeah, sure, but they don't have the attitude." A grimace pulled
at my mouth. "They want to make a public example out of those
big boys. They want to see them sweat it out behind bars. Nuts

to that. Those lads in the sedan don't give a hoot for authority. They don't give a damn for you, me or anybody besides themselves. They only respect one thing."

"Say it."

"A gun in their bellies that's going off and splashing their guts around the room. That kind of attitude they respect." I stuck my hat on my head, keeping it back off the blue lump between my eyes. "See you around, Pat," I said.

"Maybe, maybe not," he said to my back.

I went downstairs into the rain and waited there until a cab came along.

Unless you knew they were there you'd never notice it. Just little things out of place here and there. A streak through the dust where a coat sleeve dragged, an ashtray not quite in place, the rubber seal around the refrigerator door hanging because they didn't know it was loose and had to be stuffed back by hand.

The .45 was still hanging in the closet, but this time there was a thumbprint on the side where I knew I had wiped it before I stuck it away. I picked the rig off the hook and laid it on the table. The Washington boys were pretty good at that sort of thing. I started to whistle a tuneless song as I climbed out of my jacket when I noticed the wastebasket beside the dresser. There was a cigarette butt in the bottom with the brand showing and it wasn't my brand. I picked it up, stared at it, threw it back and went on whistling. I stopped when the thought of it jelled, picked up the phone and dialed the super's number downstairs.

I said, "This is Mike Hammer, John. Did you let some men in up here?"

He hedged with, "Men? You know, Mr. Hammer, I . . ."

"It's okay, I had a talk with them. I just wanted to check on it."

"Well, in that case . . . they had a warrant. You know what they were? They were F.B.I. men."

"Yeah, I know."

"They said I shouldn't mention it."

"You're sure about it?"

"Sure as anything. They had a city cop along too."

"What about anybody else?"

"Nobody else, Mr. Hammer. I wouldn't let a soul in up there, you know that."

"Okay, John. Thanks." I hung up the phone and looked around again.

Somebody else had gone through the apartment. They had done a good job too. But not quite as good as the feds. They had left their trademark around.

The smoke that was trouble started to boil up around me again. You couldn't see it and you couldn't smell it, but it was there. I started whistling again and picked up the .45.

chapter four ▰▰▰▰▰▰▰▰▰▰▰▰

SHE CAME IN at half-past eleven. She used the key I had given her a long time ago and walked into the living room, bringing with her the warmth and love for life that was like turning on the light.

I said, "Hello, beautiful," and I didn't have to say anything more because there was more in the words than the sound of my voice and she knew it.

She started to smile slowly and her mouth made a kiss. Our lips didn't have to touch. She flung that warmth across the room and I caught it. Velda said, "Ugly face. You're uglier now than you were but I love you more than ever."

"So I'm ugly. Underneath I'm beautiful."

"Who can dig down that deep?" She grinned. Then added, "Except me, maybe."

"*Just* you, honey," I said.

The smile that played around her mouth softened a moment, then she slipped out of the coat and threw it across the back of a chair.

I could never get tired of looking at her, I thought. She was everything you needed just when you needed it, a bundle of woman whose emotions could be hard or soft or terrifying, but whatever they were it was what you wanted. She was the lush beauty of the jungle, the sleek sophisticate of the city. Like I said, to me she was everything, and the dull light of the room was reflected in the ring on her finger that I had given her.

I watched her go to the kitchen and open a pair of beer cans. I watched while she sat down, took the frosted can from her and watched while she sipped the top off hers and felt a sudden stirring when her tongue flicked the foam from her lips.

Then she said what I knew she was going to say. "This one's too big, Mike."

"It is?"

Her eyes drew a line across the floor and up my body until they were staring hard into mine. "I was busy while you were in the hospital, Mike. I didn't just let things wait until you got well. This isn't murder as you've known it before. It was planned, organizational killing and it's so big that even the city authorities are afraid of it. The thing has ballooned up to a point where it's federal and even then it's touching such high places that the feds have to move carefully."

"So?" I let it hang there and pulled on the can of beer.

"It doesn't make any difference what I think?"

I set the can on the endtable and made the three-ring pattern on the label. "What you think makes a lot of difference, kitten, but when it comes to making the decisions I'll make them on what I think. I'm a man. So I'm just one man, but as long as I have a brain of my own to use and experience and knowledge to draw on to form a decision I'll keep on making them myself."

"And you're going after them?"

"Would you like me better if I didn't?"

The grin crept back through the seriousness on her face. "No." Then her eyes laughed at me too. "Ten million dollars' worth of men and equipment bucking another multi-million outfit and you elect yourself to step in and clean up. But then, you're a man." She sipped from the beer can again, then said, "But what a man. I'll be glad when you step off that bachelorhood pedestal and move over to where I have a little control over you."

"Think you ever will?"

"No, but at least I'll have something to bargain with." She laughed. "I'd like to have you around for a long time without worrying about you."

"I feel the same way myself, Velda. It's just that some things come first."

"I know, but let me warn you. From now on you're going to be up against a scheming woman."

"That's been tried before."

"Not like this."

"Yeah," I said, and finished the beer. I waited until she put hers down too, then shook out a Lucky and tossed the pack over to her. "What did you pick up?"

"A few details. I found a trucker who passed your car where

they had it parked with the flares fore and aft. The guy stopped, and when he saw nobody around he went on. The nearest phone was three miles down the road in a diner and he was surprised when nobody had shown up there because he hadn't seen anyone walking. The girl in the diner knew about an abandoned shack a few hundred yards from the spot and I went there. The place was alive with feds."

"Great."

"That's hardly the word for it." She squirmed in the chair and ran her fingers through her hair, the deep ebony of it rubbed to a soft glow in the pale lamplight. "They held me for a while, questioned me, and released me with a warning that had teeth in it."

"They find anything?"

"From what I could see, nothing. They backtracked the same way that I did and anything they found just supported what you had already told them.

"There's a catch in it though," she said. "The shack was a good fifty yards in from the highway and covered with brush. You could light the place up and it wouldn't be seen, and unless you knew where to look you'd never find it."

"It was too convenient to be coincidental, you mean?"

"Much too convenient."

I spit out a stream of smoke and watched it flow around the empty beer can. "That doesn't make sense. The kid was running away. How'd they know which direction she'd pick out?"

"They wouldn't, but how would they know where that shack was?"

"Who'd the shack belong to?"

A frown creased her forehead and she shook her head. "That's another catch. The place is on state property. It's been there for twenty years. One thing I did learn while I was being questioned was that aside from its recent use the place had no signs of occupancy at all. There were dates carved in the doorpost and the last one was 1937."

"Anything else?"

Velda shook her head slowly. "I saw your car. Or what's left of it."

"Poor old baby. The last of the original hot rods."

"Mike . . ."

I finished the beer and put the empty down on the table. "Yeah?"

"What are you going to do?"

"Guess."

"Tell me."

I had a long pull on the smoke and dropped the butt into the can. "They killed a dame and tried to frame me for it. They wrecked my heap and put me in the hospital. They're figuring us all for suckers and don't give a hang who gets hurt. The slobs, the miserable slobs." I rammed my fist against my palm until it stung. "I'm going to find out what the score is, kid. Then a lot of heads are going to roll."

"One of them might be yours, Mike."

"Yeah, one of 'em might, but it sure won't be the first to go. And you know something? They're worried, whoever they are. They read the papers and things didn't quite happen like they wanted them to. The law of averages bucked 'em for a change and instead of getting a sucker to frame they got me. Me. That they didn't like because I'm not just the average joe and they're smart enough to figure out an angle."

Her face pulled tight and the question was in her eyes. "They were up here looking around," I said.

"Mike!"

"Oh, I don't know what they were after, but I don't think they knew either. But you can bet on this, they went through this place because they thought I had something they wanted and just because they didn't find it doesn't mean they think I haven't got it. They'll be back. The next time I won't be in any emergency ward."

"But what could it be?"

"Beats me, but they tried to kill two people to find out. Whether I like it or not I'm in this thing as deep as that dame was." I grinned at Velda sitting there. "And I like it, too. I hate the guts of those people. I hate them so bad it's coming out of my skin. I'm going to find out who 'they' are and why and then they've had it."

A note of sarcasm crept into her voice. "Just like always, isn't that right?"

"No," I said, "maybe not. Maybe this time I'll do it differently. Just for the fun of it."

Velda's hands were drawn tight on the arms of the chair. "I don't like you this way, Mike."

"Neither do a lot of people. They know something just like their own names. They know I'm not going to sit on my fanny and wait for something to happen. They know from now on they're going to have to be so careful they won't even be able to spit because I'm going to get closer and closer until I have them on the dirty end of a stick. They know it and I know it too."

"It makes you a target."

"Kitten, it sure does and that I go for. If that's one way of pulling 'em inside shooting range I'm plenty glad to be a target."

Her face relaxed and she sat back. For a long minute neither one of us spoke. She sat there with her head against the cushion, staring at the ceiling, then, "Mike, I have news for you."

The way she said it made me look up. "Give."

"Any shooting that's to be done won't be done by you."

A muscle in my face twitched.

Velda reached in her jacket pocket and came out with an envelope. She flipped it across the room and I caught it. "Pat brought it in this morning. He couldn't do a thing about it, so don't get teed off at him."

I pulled the flap out and fingered the sheet loose. It was very brief and to the point. No quibbling. No doubting the source. The letterhead was all very official and I was willing to bet that for the one sheet they sent me a hundred more made up the details of why the thing should be sent.

It was a very simple order telling me I no longer had a license to carry a gun and temporarily my state-granted right to conduct private investigations was suspended. There was no mention of a full or partial refund of my two-hundred-buck fee for said license to said state.

So I laughed. I folded the sheet back into the envelope and laid it on the table. "They want me to do it the hard way," I said.

"They don't want you to do it at all. From now on you're a private citizen and nothing else and if they catch you with a gun you get it under the Sullivan law."

"This happened once before, remember?"

Velda nodded slowly. There was no expression at all on her face. "That's right, but they forgot about me. Then I had a P.I. ticket and a license for a gun too. This time they didn't forget."

"Smart boys."

"Very." She closed her eyes again and let her head drop back. "We're going to have it rough."

"Not we, girl. Me."

"We."

"Look . . ."

Only the slight reflection of the light from her pupils showed that her eyes were open and looking at me. "Who do you belong to, Mike?"

"You tell me."

She didn't answer. Her eyes opened halfway and there was something sad in the way her lips tried to curve into a smile. I said, "All right, kid, you know the answer. It's we and if I stick my neck out you can be there to help me get back in time." I picked the .45 up off the floor beside the chair, slid the clip out and thumbed the shells into my palm. "Your boy Mike is getting on in years, pal. Soft maybe?"

There was laughter in the sad smile now. "Not soft. Smarter. We're up against something that's so big pure muscle won't even dent it. We're up against a big brain and being smart is the only thing that's going to move it. At least you have the sense to change your style."

"Yeah."

"It won't be so easy."

"I know. I'm not built that way." I grinned at her. "Let's not worry about it. Everybody's trying to step on me because they don't want me around. Some of 'em got different reasons, but the big one is they're afraid I'll spoil their play. That happened before too. Let's make it happen again."

Velda said, "But let's not try so hard, huh? Seven years is a long time to wait for a guy." Her teeth were a white flash in the middle of her smile. "I'd like him in good shape when he gets ready to take the jump."

I said, "Yeah," but not so loud that she heard me.

"Where do we take it from here, Mike?"

I let the shells dribble from my fingers into the ashtray. They lay there, deadly and gleaming, but helpless without the mother that could give them birth.

"Berga Torn," I said. "We'll start with her. I want those sanitarium records. I want her life history and the history of anybody she was associated with. That's your job."

"And you?" she asked.

"Evello. Carl Evello. Someplace he comes into this thing and he's my job."

Velda nodded, drummed her fingernails against the arm of the chair and stared across the room. "He won't be easy."

"Nobody's easy."

"Especially Evello. He's organized. While you were under wraps in the hospital I saw a few people who had a little inside information on Evello. There wasn't much and what there was of it was mostly speculation, but it put the finger on a theme you might be interested in."

"Such as?"

She looked at me with a half smile, a beautiful jungle animal sizing up her mate before telling him what was outside the mouth of the den. "Mafia," she said.

I could feel it starting way down at my toes, a cold, burning flush that crept up my body and left in its wake a tingling sensation of rage and fear that was pure emotion and nothing else. It pounded in my ears and dried my throat until the words that came out were scratchy, raspy sounds that didn't seem to be part of me at all.

"How did they know?"

"They don't. They suspect, that's all. The federal agencies are interested in the angle."

"Yeah," I said. "They *would* be interested. They'd go in on their toes, too. No wonder they don't want me fishing around."

"You make too much noise."

"Things happen, don't they?"

Velda didn't answer that one either.

"So now it makes sense," I told her. "They have the idea I'm in the deal someplace but they can't come out and say it. They play twenty questions, hoping I do have a share of it so they'll have someplace to start. They won't give up until the day they die or I do because once the finger touches you it never comes away. There's no such thing as innocence, just innocence touched with guilt is as good a deal as you can get."

Velda's mouth moved slowly. "Maybe it's a good thing, Mike. It's a funny world. Pure innocence as such doesn't enter in much nowadays. There's always at least one thing people try to hide." She paused and ran her finger along the side of her cheek. "If a murderer is hung for the wrong killing, who is wrong?"

"That's a new twist for you, kid."

"I got it from you."

"Then finish it."

Her fingers reached out and plucked a cigarette from the pack. It was a graceful, feminine motion that spoke of soft girlishness, the texture of her skin satiny and amber in the light. You could follow the fingers into the hand and the hand into the arm, watching the curves melt into each other like a beautiful painting. Just watching like that and you could forget the two times that same hand held a snarling, spitting rod that chewed a guy's guts out. "Now innocence touched with guilt pays off," she said. "You'll be one of the baited hooks they'll use until something bites."

"And in the end the public will benefit."

"That's right." She grinned, the corner of her mouth twisting upward a little. "But don't feel badly about it, Mike. They're stealing your stuff. You taught them that trick a long time ago."

My fingers went out and began to play with the slugs that squatted in the bottom of the ashtray where I had dropped them. She watched me from across the room, her eyes half closed in speculation. Then she uncurled, tossed my deck of smokes into the chair beside me and reached for her coat.

I didn't watch her walk away. I sat there dreaming of the things I'd like to do and how maybe if nobody was there to see me I'd do anyway. I was dreaming of a lot of fat faces with jowls that got big and loose on other people's meat and how they'd look with that smashed, sticky expression that comes with catching the butt end of a .45 across their noses. I was dreaming of a slimy foreign secret army that held a parade of terror under the Mafia label and laughed at us with our laws and regulations and how fast their damned smug expressions would change when they saw the fresh corpses of their own kind day after day.

She didn't have to go far to read my mind. She had seen me look like this before. She didn't have to go far to get me back on the track, either. "Isn't it about time you taught them some fresh tricks, Mike?" Velda said softly.

Then she left and the room got a little darker.

chapter five ■■■■■■■■■■■■■■■■

I SAT THERE for a while, staring at the multicolored reflections of the city that made my window a living, moving kaleidoscope. The voice of the monster outside the glass was a constant drone, but when you listened long enough it became a flat, sarcastic sneer that pushed ten million people into bigger and better troubles, and then the sneer was heard for what it was, a derisive laugh that thought blood running from an open wound was funny, and death was the biggest joke of all.

Yeah, it laughed at people like me and you. It was the voice of the guy with the whip who laughed at each stroke to drown out the screams of the victim. A subtle voice that hid small cries, a louder voice that covered the anguished moans.

I sat and heard and thought about it while the statistics ran through my head. So many a minute killed by cars, so many injured. So many dead an hour by out-and-out violence. So many this and so many that. It made a long impressive list that was recited at board meetings and assemblies.

There was only one thing left out. How many were scared stiff? How many lay awake nights worrying about things they shouldn't have to worry about at all? How many wondered where their kids were and what they were doing? *How many knew the army of silent men who made their whispered demands and either got them or extracted payment according to the code?*

Then I knew the voice outside for what it was. Not some intangible monster after all. Not some gigantic mechanical contrivance that could act of its own accord. Not a separate living being with its own rules and decrees. Not one of those things.

People, that's all.

Just soft, pulpy people, most of them nice. And some of them filthy and twisted, who gorged themselves on flesh and puffed up with the power they had so that when they got stuck they popped like ripe melons and splashed their guts all over the ground.

The Mafia. The stinking, slimy Mafia. An oversize mob of ignorant, lunkheaded jerks who ruled with fear and got away with it because they had money to back themselves up.

The Black Hand? You think you can laugh it off? You think all that stuff went out with prohibition? There's a lot of widows around who can tell you differently. Widowers, too.

Like Velda said, it wasn't going to be easy at all. You don't just ask around where you can find the top boy.

First you find somebody to ask and if you're not dead by then, or he's not dead, you ask. Then you ask and look some more, each time coming closer to the second when a bullet or a knife reaches across space and spears you.

There's a code they work by, a fixed unbreakable code. Once the Mafia touches you it never takes its hand away. And if you make one move, just one single, hesitant move to get out from under, it's all over. Sometimes it takes a day or two, even a year maybe, but it was all over from then.

You get dead.

In a sense though, it was funny. Someplace at the top of the heap was a person. From him the fear radiated like from the center of a spiderweb. He sat on his throne and made a motion of his hand and somebody died. He made another motion and somebody was twisted until they screamed. A nod of his head did something that sent a guy leaping from a roof because he couldn't take it any more.

Just one person did that. One soft, pulpy person.

I started to grin a little bit, thinking how he'd act stripped of weapons and his power for a minute or so in a closed room with someone who didn't like him. I could almost see his face behind the glass and my grin got bigger because I was pretty sure of what I was going to do now.

It was late, but only by the clock. The city was yawning and stretching after its supper, waking up to start living. The rain had died, leaving a low grumble in the skies overhead to announce its passing. The air was fresher now, the light a little brighter, and the parade of cabs had slowed down enough so I could whistle one down and hop a ride over to Pat's apartment.

He let me in with a grin and muttered something between the folder of papers he had clamped in his teeth, waved me into the living room and took my coat. His eyes made a casual sweep over my chest and he didn't have to look a second time to tell I wasn't wearing a rig under my arm.

Pat said, "Drink?"

"Not now."

"It's only ginger ale."

I shook my head and sat down. He filled his glass, relaxed into a wing chair and shoved all the papers into an envelope. "Glad to see you traveling light."

"Didn't you expect me to?"

His mouth crooked up at the corner. "I figured you'd know better than not to. Just don't blame me for the deal, that's all."

"You're not too sorry about it, are you?"

"As a matter of fact, no." His fingers tapped the envelope, then his eyes came up to mine. "It puts you on the spot as far as business is concerned, but I don't imagine you'll starve."

"I don't imagine I will either," I grinned back at him. "How long am I supposed to be in solitary for?"

He didn't like the grin at all. He got those wrinkles around his eyes that showed when something was getting under his hide and took a long drag on the drink to muffle what he knew I saw. "When they're ready to lift it they'll lift it and not before."

"They won't have it that soft," I told him.

"No?"

I flicked a butt into my mouth and lit it. "Tomorrow you can remind 'em I'm an incorporated business, a taxpayer and a boy with connections. My lawyer has a judge probably getting up a show cause right now and until they settle the case in court they aren't pulling any bill-of-attainder stuff on me."

"You got a mouthful of words on that one, Mike."

"Uh-huh. And you know what I'm talking about. Nobody, not even a federal agency is going to pull my tail and not get chewed a little bit."

His hands got too tight around the glass. "Mike . . . this isn't just murder."

"I know."

"How much?"

"No more than before. I've been thinking around it though."

"Any conclusions?"

"One." I looked at him, hard. "Mafia."

Nothing changed in his face. "So?"

"I can be useful if you'd quit booting me around." I took a drag on the smoke and let it curl out into the light. "I don't have to pull my record out. You know it as well as I do. Maybe I have shot up a few guys, but the public doesn't seem to miss them any. If your buddies think I'm stupid enough to go busting in on something over my head without knowing what I'm doing then it's time they took a refresher course. They haven't got one guy in Washington that's smarter than I am . . . not one guy. If they had they'd be making more moolah than I am and don't fool yourself thinking they're in there for love of the job. It's about the limit they can do."

"You sure think a lot of yourself."

"I have to, friend. Nobody else does. Besides, I'm still around when a lot of others have taken their last car ride."

Pat finished off the glass and swirled the last few drops around the bottom. "Mike," he said, "if I had my way I'd have you and ten thousand more in on this thing. That's about how many we'd need to fight it. As it is, I'm a city cop and I take orders. What do you want from me?"

"You say it, Pat."

He laughed this time. It was like the old days when neither one of us gave a damn about anything and if we had to hate it was the same thing. "Okay, you want me for your third arm. You're going to dive into this thing no matter who says what and as long as you are we'd might as well use your talents instead of tripping over them."

The grin was real. It was six years ago and not now any longer. The light was back in his eyes again and we were a team riding over anything that stood in our way. "Now I'll tell you something,

Mike," he said, "I don't like the way the gold-badge boys do business either. I don't like political meddling in crime and I'm sick of the stuff that's been going on for so long. Everybody is afraid to move and it's about time something jolted them. For so damn long I've been listening to people say that this racket is over our heads that I almost began to believe it myself. Okay, I'll lay my job on the line. Let's give it a spin and see what happens. Tell me what you want and I'll feed it to you. Just don't hash up the play . . . at least not for a while yet. If something good comes of it I'll have a talking point and maybe I can keep my job."

"I can always use a partner."

"Thanks. Now let's hear your angle."

"Information. Detailed."

He didn't have to go far for it. The stuff was right there in his lap. He pulled it all out of the envelope and thumbed the sheets apart. The light behind his head made the sheets translucent enough so the lines of type stood out and there weren't very many lines.

"Known criminals with Mafia connections," he drawled. "Case histories of Mafia efficiency and police negligence. Twenty pages of arrests with hardly enough convictions to bother about. Twenty pages of murder, theft, dope pushing, and assorted felonies and all we're working with are the bottom rungs of the ladder. We can name some of the big ones but don't fool yourself and think they are the top joes. The boys up high don't have names we know about."

"Is Carl Evello there?"

Pat looked at the sheets again and threw them on the floor in disgust. "Evello isn't anywhere. He's got one of those investigatable incomes but it looks like he'll be able to talk his way out of it."

"Berga Torn?"

"Now we're back to murder. One of many."

"We don't think alike there, Pat."

"No?"

"Berga was special. She was so special they put a crew of boys on her who knew their business. They don't do that for everybody. Why did the committee want her?"

I could see him hesitate a moment, shrug and make up his mind. "There wasn't much to the Torn dame. She was a good-looking head with a respectable mind but engaged in a mucky racket, if you get what I mean."

"I know."

"There was a rumor that Evello was keeping her for a while.

It was during the time he was raking in a pile. The same rumor had he gave her the boot and the committee figured she'd be mad enough to spill what she knew about him."

"Evello wouldn't be that dumb," I said.

"When it comes to dames, guys can be awfully dumb," he grinned at me knowingly.

"Finish it."

"The feds approached her. She was scared stiff, but she indicated that there was something she could give out, but she wanted time to collect her information and protection after she let it out."

"Great." I snuffed the butt out and leaned back in the chair. "I can see Washington assigning her a permanent bodyguard."

"She was going to appear before the committee masked."

"No good. Evello could still spot her from the info she handed them."

Pat confirmed the thought with a nod. "In the meantime," he went on, "she got the jitters. Twice she got away from the men assigned to cover her. Before the month was out she was practically hysterical and went to a doctor. He had her committed to a sanitarium and she was supposed to stay there for three weeks. The investigation was held up, there were agents assigned to guard the sanitarium, she got away and was killed."

"Just like that."

"Just like that only you were there when it happened."

"Nice of me."

"That's what those Washington boys thought."

"Coincidence is out," I said.

"Naturally." His mouth twitched again. "They don't know that you're the guy things happen to. Some people are accident prone. You're coincidence prone."

"I've thought of it that way," I told him. "Now what about the details of her escape?"

He shrugged and shook his head slightly. "Utter simplicity. The kind of thing you can't beat. Precautions were taken for every inconceivable thing and she does the conceivable. She picked up a raincoat and shoes from the nurses' quarters and walked out the main entrance with two female attendants. It was raining at the time and one of them had an umbrella and they stayed together under it the way women will who try to keep their hair dry or something. They went as far as the corner together, the other two got in a bus while she kept on walking."

"Wasn't a pass required at the gate?"

He nodded deeply, a motion touched with sarcasm. "Sure, there was a pass all right, each of the two had a pass and showed it. Maybe the guy thought he saw the third one. At least he said he thought so."

"I suppose somebody was outside the gate too?"

"That's right. Two men, one on foot and one in a car. Neither had seen the Torn girl and were there to stop anyone making an unauthorized exit."

I let out a short grunt.

Pat said, "They thought it *was* authorized, Mike."

I laughed again. "That's what I mean. *They thought.* Those guys are supposed to think right or not at all. Those are the guys who had my ticket lifted. Those are the guys who want no interference. Nuts."

"Anyway, she got away. That's it."

"Okay, we'll leave it there. What attitude are the cops taking?"

"It's murder, so they're working it from that end."

"And getting nowhere," I added.

"So far," Pat said belligerently. I grinned at him and the scowl that creased his forehead disappeared. "Lay off. How do you plan to work it?"

"Where's Evello?"

"Right here in the city."

"And the known Mafia connections?"

Pat looked thoughtful a moment. "Other big cities, but their operational center is here too." He bared his teeth in a tight grimace. His eyes went hard and nasty as he said, "Which brings us to the end of our informative little discussion about the Mafia. We know who some of them are and how they operate, but that's as far as it goes."

"Washington doesn't have anything?"

"Sure, but what good does it do. Nobody fingers the Mafia. There's that small but important little item known as evidence."

"We'll get it," I told him, ". . . one way or another. It's still a big organization. They need capital to operate."

Pat stared at me like he would a kid. "Sure, just like that. You know how they raise that capital? They squeeze it out of the little guy. It's an extra tax he has to pay. They put the bite on guys who are afraid to talk or who can't talk. They run an import business that drives the Narcotics Division nuts. They got their hand in every racket that exists with a political cover so heavy you can't bust through it with a sledge hammer."

He didn't have to remind me. I knew how they operated. I

said, "Maybe, chum, maybe. Could be that nobody's really tried hard enough yet."

He grunted something under his breath, then, "You still didn't say how you were going to work it."

I pushed myself out of the chair, wiping my hand across my face. "First Berga Torn. I want to find out more about her."

Pat reached down and picked the top sheet off the pile he had dropped on the floor beside him. "You might as well have this then. It's as much as anyone has to start with."

I folded it up and stuck it in my pocket without looking at it. "You'll let me know if anything comes up?"

"I'll let you know." I picked up my coat and started for the door.

"And Mike . . ."

"Yeah?"

"This is a two-way deal, remember?"

"Yeah, I remember."

Downstairs, I stood in front of the building a minute. I took the time to stick a Lucky in my mouth and even more time lighting it. I let the flare of the match bounce off my face for a good ten seconds, then dragged in deeply on the smoke and whipped it back into the night air. The guy in the doorway of the apartment across the street stirred and made a hesitant motion of having come out of the door and not knowing which way to walk. I turned east and he made up his mind. He turned east too.

Halfway down the block I crossed over to make it a little easier on him. Washington didn't discount shoe leather as expenses so there was no sense giving the boy a hard time. I went three more blocks closer to the subway station and pulled a few gimmicks that had him practically climbing up my back.

This time I had a good look at him and was going to say hello to add insult to injury when I caught the end of a gun muzzle in my ribs and knew he wasn't Washington at all.

He was young and good-looking until he smiled, then the crooked march of short, stained teeth across his mouth made him an expensively dressed punk on a high-class job. There was no hop behind his pupils so he was a classy workman being paid by an employer who knew what the score was. The teeth smiled bigger and he started to tell me something when I ripped his coat open and the gun in the pocket wasn't pointing at me any more. He was half spun around fighting to get the rod loose as the side of my hand caught him across the neck and he sat down on the sidewalk with his feet out in front of him, plenty alive, plenty awake, but not even a little bit active.

I picked the Banker's Special out of his hand, broke it, dumped the shells into the gutter and tossed the rod back into his lap. His eyes were hurting. They were all watered up like he was ashamed of himself.

"Tell your boss to send a man out on the job the next time," I said.

I walked on down the street and turned into the subway kiosk wondering what the deuce had happened to Washington. Little boy blue back on the sidewalk would have a good story to take home to papa this time. Most likely he wouldn't get his allowance. At least they'd know a pro was in the game for a change.

I shoved a dime in the turnstile, went through, pulled the sheet out of my pocket, glanced at it once and walked over to the downtown platform.

chapter six ▬▬▬▬▬▬▬▬▬▬▬

SOMETHING HAPPENS TO Brooklyn at night. It isn't a sister borough any more. She withdraws to herself and pulls the shades down, then begins a life that might seem foreign to an outsider. She's strange, exciting, tinted with bright lights, yet elusive somehow.

I got off the Brighton Line at De Kalb and went up to the street. A guy on the corner pointed the way to the address I wanted and I walked the few blocks to it.

What I was looking for was an old-fashioned brownstone, a hangover from a half-century past, that had the number painted on the door and looked at the street with dull, blank eyes. I went up the four sandstone steps, held a match to the mailboxes and found what I wanted.

The name CARVER and TORN were there, but somebody had drawn a pencil through the two of them and had written in BERNSTEIN underneath. All I could do was mutter a little under my breath and punch the end button on the line, the one labeled

SUPER. I leaned on it until the door started clicking, then I opened it and went in.

He came to the door and I could almost see his face. Part of it stuck out behind the fleshy shoulder of a woman who towered all around him and glared at me as if I had crawled up out of a hole. Her hair was a gray mop gathered into tiny knots and clamped in place with metal curlers. She bulged through the bathrobe, trying to slow down her breathing enough so she could say something. Her hands were big and red, the knuckles showing as they bit into her hips.

Dames. The guy behind her looked scared to death. She said, "What the hell do you want! You know what time it is? You think . . ."

"Shut up." Her mouth stopped. I leaned against the door jamb. "I'm looking for the super."

"I'm the . . ."

"You're not anything to me, lady. Tell your boy to come out." I thought her face would fall apart. "Tell him," I repeated.

When men learn to be men maybe they can handle dames. There was something simpering in the way she forced a smile and stepped aside.

The boy didn't want to come out, but he did. He made himself as big as he could without it helping much. "Yes?"

I showed him the badge I still had. It didn't mean a thing any more, but it still shined in the light and wasn't something everybody carried. "Get your keys."

"Yessir, yessir." He reached up beside the door, unhooked a ring and stepped back into the hall.

The dame said. "You wait a minute, I'll be right . . ."

He seemed to stand on his toes. "*You* wait right there until I come *back*," he told her. "*I'm* the super." He turned and grinned at me. Behind him his wife's face puffed out and the door slammed.

"Yessir?" he said.

"Berga Torn's place. I want to go through it."

"But the police have already been through there."

"I know."

"Today I rented it already."

"Anybody there now?"

"Not yet. Tomorrow they're supposed to come."

"Then let's go."

First he hesitated, then he shrugged and started up the stairs. Two flights up he fitted a key into the lock of a door and threw it open. He felt around for the light switch, flipped it and stood aside for me.

I don't know what I expected to find. Maybe it was more curiosity than anything that dragged me up there. The place had been gone over by experts and if anything had been worth taking it was gone by now. It was what you might call a functional apartment and nothing more. The kitchen and living room were combined with a bathroom sandwiched between two bedrooms that jutted off the one wall. There was enough furniture to be comfortable, nothing gaudy and nothing out of place.

"Whose stuff is this?"

"We rent furnished. What you see belongs to the landlord."

I walked into the bedroom and opened the door of the closet. A half dozen dresses and a suit hung there. The floor was lined with shoes. The dresser was the same way, filled to the brim. The clothes were good, fairly new, but not the type that came out of exclusive shops.

Stockings were neatly rolled up and packed into a top drawer. Beside them were four envelopes, two with paid-up receipts, one a letter from the Millburn Steamship Line saying that there were no available berths on the liner *Cedric* and how sorry they were, and the other a heavier envelope holding about a dozen Indianhead pennies.

The other small drawer was cluttered with half-used lipsticks and all the usual junk a dame can collect in hardly any time at all.

It was the other bedroom that gave me the surprise. There was nothing there at all. Just a made-up bed, a cleaned-out closet and dresser drawers lined with old sheets of newspaper.

The super watched me until I backed out into the living room, saying nothing.

"Whose room?" I jerked my thumb at the empty place.

"Miss Carver's."

"Where is she?"

"Two days ago . . . she moved out."

"The police see her?"

He nodded, a fast snap of the head. "Maybe that's why she moved out."

"You going to empty this place out?"

"Guess I got to. The lease is up next month, but it was paid in advance. Hope I don't get in trouble renting so soon."

"Who paid it?"

"Torn's name is on the lease." He looked at me pointedly.

"I didn't ask that."

"She handed me the dough." I stared at him hard and he fumbled with his pajamas again. "How many times do I have to tell you guys. I don't know where she got the dough. Far as I know she didn't do any messing around. This place sure wasn't no office or that nosy old lady of mine would've known about it."

"Did she have any men here to see her?"

"Mister," he said, "there's twelve apartments in this rat-trap and I can't keep track of who comes in and who goes out so long as they're paid up. If you ask me right off I'd say she wasn't no tramp. She was a dame splitting her quarters with another dame who paid her dough and didn't make trouble. If a guy was keeping her he sure didn't get his money's worth. If you want to know what I think then I'd say yes, she was being kept. Maybe the both of 'em. The old lady never thought so or she would've given them the boot, that's for sure."

"Okay then," I said, "that's it."

He held the door open for me. "You think anything's going to come of this?"

"Plenty."

The guy was another lip licker. "There won't be . . ."

"Don't worry about it. You know how I can reach the Carver girl?"

The look he gave me was quick and worried. "She didn't leave no address."

I made it sound very flat and businesslike. "You know . . . when you step in front of the law there's charges that can be pressed."

"Aw, look, mister, if I knew . . ." His tongue came out and passed over his mouth again. He thought about it, shrugged then said, "Okay. Just don't let my wife know. She called today. She's expecting some mail from her boyfriend and asked me to send it to her." He pulled in a deep breath and let it out in a sigh. "She don't want anybody to know where she is. Got a pencil?"

I handed him one with the remains of an envelope and he jotted it down.

"Wish I could do something right for a change. The kid sounded pretty worried."

"You don't want to buck the law, do you friend?"

"Guess not."

"Okay, then you did right. Tell you what though . . . don't

bother giving it out to anyone else. I'll see her, but she won't know how I reached her. How's that?"

His face showed some relief. "Swell."

"By the way," I said, "what was she like?"

"Carver?"

"Yeah."

"Kind of a pretty blonde. Hair like snow."

"I'll find her," I said.

The number was on Atlantic Avenue. It was the third floor over a secondhand store and there was nothing to guide you in but the smell. All the doorbells had names that had been there long enough to get dirtied up, but the newest one said TRENTEN when it didn't mean that at all.

I punched the button three times while I stood there in the dark, heard nothing ringing so I eased myself into the smell. It wasn't just an odor. It was something that moved, something warm and fluid that came down the stairs, tumbling over slowly, merging with other smells until it leaked out into the street.

In each flight there were fourteen steps, a landing, a short corridor that took you to the next flight and at the top of the last one, a door. Up there the smell was different. It wasn't any fresher; it just smelled better. A pencil line of light marked the sill and for a change there was no bag of garbage to trip over.

I rapped on the door and waited. I did it again and springs creaked inside. A quiet little voice said, "Yes?"

"Carver?"

Again, "Yes." A bit tired-sounding this time.

"I'd like to speak to you. I'm pushing my card through under the door."

"Never mind. Just come right in."

I felt for the knob, twisted it and pushed the door open.

She was sitting there swallowed up in a big chair facing me, the gun in her hand resting on her knee in a lazy fashion and there wasn't even the slightest bit of doubt that it would start going off the second I breathed too hard.

Carver wasn't pretty. She was small and full bodied, but she wasn't pretty. Maybe no dame can be pretty with a rod in her mitt, even one with bleached white hair and a scarlet mouth. A black velvet robe outlined her against the chair, seeming like the space of nighttime between the white of her hair and that of the fur-lined slippers she wore.

For a minute she looked at me, her eyes wandering over me

slowly. I let her look and pushed the door shut. Maybe she was satisfied by what she saw, maybe not. She didn't say anything, but she didn't put the gun away either. I said, "Expecting someone else?"

What she did with her mouth didn't make up a smile. "I don't know. What have you to say?"

"I'll say what it takes to make you point that heater someplace else."

"You can't talk that loud or that long, friend."

"Do I reach in my pocket for a smoke?"

"There's some on the table beside you. Use those."

I picked one up, almost went for my lighter in my pocket, thought better of it and took the matches that went with the cigarettes. "You're sure not good company, kid." I blew a stream of smoke at the floor and rocked on my toes. That little round hole in the tip of the automatic never came off my stomach.

"The name is Mike Hammer," I told her. "I'm a private investigator. I was with Berga Torn when she got knocked off."

This time the rod moved. I was looking right down the barrel.

"More," her mouth said.

"She was trying to hitch a ride to the city. I picked her up, ran a roadblock that was checking for her, got edged off the road by a car and damn near brained by a pack of hoods who were playing for keeps. I was there with my head dented in when they worked her over and behind the wheel of the car they pushed over the cliff. To them I was a handy, class-A red herring that was supposed to cover the real cause of her death only it didn't quite happen that way."

"How did it happen?"

"I was thrown clear. If you want I'll show you my scars."

"Never mind."

So we stared at each other for a longer minute and I was still looking down the barrel and the hole kept getting bigger and bigger.

"You loaded?"

"The cops lifted my rod and P.I. ticket."

"Why?"

"Because they knew I'd bust into this thing and they wanted to keep me out."

"How did you find me?"

"It's not hard to find people when you know how. Anybody could do it." Her eyes widened momentarily, seemed to deepen, then narrowed sharply.

"Suppose I don't believe you," she said.

I sucked in a lungful of smoke and dropped the butt to the floor. I didn't bother to squash it out. I let it lie there until you could smell the stink of burned wool in the room and felt my face start to tighten around the edges. I said, "Kid, I'm sick of answering questions. I'm sick of having guns pointed at me. You make the second tonight and if you don't stow that thing I'm going to beat the hell out of you. What'll it be?"

I didn't scare her. The gun came down until it rested in her lap and for the first time the stiffness left her face. Carver just looked tired. Tired and resigned. The scarlet slash of her mouth made a wry grimace of sadness. "All right," she said, "sit down."

So I sat down. No matter what else I could have done, nothing would have been more effective. The bewilderment showed on her face, the way her body arched before sinking back again. Her leg moved and the gun dropped to the floor and stayed there.

"Aren't you . . ."

"Who were you expecting, Carver?"

"The name is Lily." Her tongue was a lighter pink against the scarlet as it swept across her lips.

"Who, Lily?"

"Just . . . men." Her eyes were hopeful now. "You . . . told me the truth?"

"I'm not one of them if that's what you mean. Why did they come?"

The hardness left her face. It seemed to melt away like a film that should never have been there and now she was pretty. Her hair was a pile of snow that reflected the loveliness of her face. She breathed heavily, the robe drawing tight at regular intervals.

"They wanted Berga."

"Let's start at the beginning. With you and Berga. How's that?"

Lily paused and stared into the past. "Before the war, that's when we met. We were dance-hall hostesses. It was the first night for the both of us and we both sort of stuck together. A week later we found an apartment and shared it."

"How long?"

"About a year. When the war came I was pretty sick of things and went into a defense plant. Berga quit too . . . but what she did for a living was her business. She was a pretty good kid. When I was sick she moved back in and took care of me. After the war I lost my job when the plant closed down and she got a friend of hers to get me a job in a night club in Jersey."

"Did she work there too?" I asked.

The white hair made a negative. "She was . . . doing a lot of things."

"Anybody special?"

"I don't know. I didn't ask. We went back living in the same apartment for a while, though she was paying most of the bills. She seemed to have a pretty good income."

Lily's eyes came off the wall behind my head and fastened on mine. "That's when I noticed her starting to change."

"How?"

"She was . . . scared."

"Did she say why?"

"No. She laughed it off. Twice she booked passage to Europe, but couldn't get the ship she wanted and didn't go."

"She was that scared."

Lily shrugged, saying nothing, saying much. "It seemed to grow on her. Finally she wouldn't even leave the house at all. She said she didn't feel well, but I knew she was lying."

"When was this?"

"Not so very long ago. I don't remember just when."

"It doesn't matter."

"She went out once in a while after that. Like to the movies or for groceries. Never very far. Then the police came around."

"What did they want?"

"Her."

"Questions or an arrest?"

"Questions, mostly. They asked me some things too. Nothing I knew about. That night I saw someone following me home." Her face had a curious strained look about it. "It's been that way every night since. I don't know if they've found me here yet or not."

"Cops?"

"Not cops." She said it very simply, very calmly, but couldn't quite hide the terror that tried to scream the answer out.

She begged me to say something, but I let her squeeze it out herself. "The police came again, but Berga wouldn't tell them anything." The tongue moistened the lips again. The scarlet was starting to wash away and I could see the natural tones on the wet flesh. "The other men came . . . they were different from the police. Federal men, I think. They took her away. Before she came back . . . *those* men came."

She put something into the last three words that wasn't in the others, some breathless, nameless fear. Her hands were tight balls with the nails biting into the palms. A glassiness had passed over her eyes while she thought about it, then vanished as if afraid it had been seen.

"They said I'd die if I talked to anyone." Her hand moved up and covered her mouth. "I'm tired of being scared," she said. Her head drooped forward, nodding gently to the soft sobs that seemed to stick in her chest.

What's the answer? How do you tell them they won't die when they know you're lying about it because they're marked already?

I got up and walked to her chair, looked at her a second and sat down on the arm of it. I took her hand away from her face, tilted her chin up and ran my fingers through the snow piled on top of her head. It was as soft and as fine as it looked in the light and when my fingers touched her cheek she smiled, dropped her eyes and let that beauty come through all the way, every bit of it that she had kept hidden so long. There was a faint smell of rubbing alcohol about her, a clean, pungent odor that seemed to separate itself from the perfume she wore.

Her eyes were big and dark, soft ovals under the delicate brows, her mouth full and pink, parted in the beginning of a smile. My fingers squeezed her shoulder easily and her head went back, the mouth parting even further and I bent down slowly.

"You won't die," I said.

And it was the wrong thing to say because the mouth that was so close to mine pulled back and everything had changed. I just sat there next to her for a little while until the dry sobs had stopped. There were no tears to be wiped away. Terror doesn't leave any tears. Not that kind of terror.

"What did they want to know about Berga?"

"I don't know," she whispered. "They made me tell everything I knew about her. They made me sit there while they went through her things."

"Did they find anything?"

"No. I . . . I don't think so. They were horribly mad about it."

"Did they hurt you?" I asked.

An almost imperceptible shudder went through her whole body. "I've been hurt worse." Her eyes drifted up to mine. "They were disgusting men. They'll kill me now, won't they?"

"If they do they've had it."

"But it would still be too late for me."

I nodded. It was all I could do. I got up, took the last smoke out of my old pack and tapped the butt against my knuckle. "Can't I take a look at that suitcase of hers?"

"It's in the bedroom." She pushed her hair back with a tired motion. "The closet."

I walked in, snapped on the light and found the closet. The suitcase was there where she said it was, a brown leather Gladstone that had seen a lot of knocking around. I tossed it on the bed, unfastened the straps and opened it up.

But nothing was in there that could kill a person. Not unless a motive for murder was in a couple old picture albums, three yearbooks from high school, a collection of underwear, extra-short bathing suits, a stripper's outfit and a batch of old mail.

I thought maybe the mail would do it, but most of them were trivial answers from some friend to letters she had written and were postmarked from a hick town in Idaho. The rest were steamship folders and a tour guide of southern Europe. I shoved everything back in the suitcase, closed it up and dropped it in the closet.

When I turned around Lily was standing there in the doorway, a fresh cigarette in her mouth, one hand holding the robe closed around her waist, her hair a white cloud that seemed to hover about her. When she spoke the voice didn't sound as though it belonged to her at all.

"What am I to do now?"

I reached out and folded my hand over hers and drew her closer to me. The fingers were cold, her body was a warm thing that wanted to search for something.

"Got any place to go?"

"No," faintly.

"Money?"

"Just a little."

"Get dressed. How long will it take?"

"A . . . a few minutes."

For the briefest interval her face brightened with a new hope, then she smiled and shook her head. "It . . . won't do any good. I've seen men like that before. They're not like other people. They'd find me."

My laugh was short and hard. "We'll make it tough for them just the same. And don't kid yourself about them being too different. They're just like anybody else in most ways. They're afraid of things too. I'm not kidding you or me. You know what the score is so all we can do is give it a try."

I stopped for a second and let a thought run through my head again. I grinned down at her and said, "You know . . . don't be a bit surprised if you live a lot longer than you think you should."

"Why?"

"I have an idea the outfit who worked you over don't really know what they're after and they're not going to kill any leads until they get it."

"But I . . . don't have any idea . . ."

"Let them find that out for themselves," I interrupted. "Let's get you out of here as fast as we can."

I dropped her hand and pushed her into the bedroom. She looked at me, her face happy, then her body went tight and it showed in the way her eyes lit up, that crazy desire to say thanks somehow; but I pulled the door shut before she could do what she wanted to do and went inside opening a fresh deck of Luckies.

The gun was still there on the floor, a metallic glitter asleep on a bed of faded green wool. The safety was off and the hammer was still back. All that time in the beginning I was about a literal ounce away from being nice and dead. Lily Carver hadn't been fooling a bit.

She took almost five minutes. I heard the door open and turned around. It wasn't the same Lily. It was a new woman, a fresh and lovely woman who was a taller, graceful woman. It was one for whom the green gabardine suit had been intended, exquisitely molding every feature of her body. Her legs were silken things, their curves flashing enough to take your eyes away from the luxury of her hair that poked out under the hat.

It wasn't a worried or a scared Lily this time. It was a Lily who took my arm and held it tightly, smiling a smile that was real. "Where are we going, Mike?"

It was the first time she had said my name and I liked the way she said it.

"To my place." I told her.

We went downstairs and out on Atlantic Avenue. We played a game of not being seen in case there were watchers and if there were they weren't good enough to keep up with us. We used the subway to go home and took a cab to the door. When I was sure nobody was in the lobby I took her in.

It was all very simple.

When we got upstairs I told her to hop into the sack and showed her the spare bedroom. She smiled, reached out and patted my cheek and said, "It's been a long time since I met a nice guy, Mike."

That strange excitement seemed to be inside her like a coiled spring. I squeezed her wrist and she knew what I was saying without having to use words and her mouth started to part.

I stopped it there.

Or maybe she stopped it.

The spring wound tighter and tighter, then I let her go and walked away.

Behind me the door closed softly and I thought I heard a whispered "Good night, Mike."

I started it that night. At three-thirty the word went out in the back room of a gin mill off Forty-second and Third. Before morning it would yell and before the night came again it would pay off. One way or another.

Wherever they were, whoever they were, they would hear about it. They'd know me and know what the word meant. They'd sit and think for a little while and if they knew me well enough maybe they'd feel a little bit sweaty and not so sure of themselves any more. They couldn't laugh it off. With anybody else, perhaps, but not with me.

Wise guys. A pack of conniving slobs with the world in their hands and the power and money to buck a government while they sat on their fat tails, yet before morning there wouldn't be one of them who didn't have a funny feeling around his gut.

This time they had to move.

The word was out.

I went back to the apartment and listened at the door of Lily's room. I could hear her regular, heavy breathing. I stood there a minute, took a final drag on the butt, put it out and headed for my sack.

chapter seven ▬▬▬▬▬▬▬▬▬▬▬▬▬

SHE WAS UP when the phone rang in the morning. I heard the dishes rattling and smelt the coffee. She called out, "Any time you're ready, come eat."

I said okay and picked up the phone.

The voice was low and soft, the kind you'd never miss in a million years. It was the best way to wake up and it showed in my voice when I said, "Hi, Velda, what's doing?"

"Plenty is doing, but nothing I want to talk about over the phone."

"Get something?"

"Yes."

"Where are you now?"

"Down at the office. A place you ought to try to get to once a week, at least."

"You know how things are, honey," I said.

Lily looked in the door, waved and pointed toward the kitchen, I nodded, glad that Velda didn't know how things were right then.

"Where were *you* last night? I called until I was too tired to stay awake and tried again this morning."

"I was busy."

"Oh, Pat called." She tried to keep her voice its natural huskiness but it wanted to get away.

"I suppose he said too much."

"He said enough." She stopped and I could hear her breathing into the phone. "Mike, I'm scared."

"Well don't be, kitten. I know what I'm doing. You ought to know that."

"I'm still scared. I think somebody tried to break into my apartment last night."

That one got a low whistle out of me. "What happened?"

"Nothing. I heard a noise in the lock for a while but whoever was trying it gave up. I'm glad I got that special job now. Are you coming over?"

"Not right away."

"You ought to. A lot of mail is piling up. I paid all the bills, but you have a sackful of personal stuff."

"I'll get to it later. Look, did you make out on that info?"

"Somewhat. Do you want it now?"

"*Right* now, kitten. I'll meet you in the Texan Bar in an hour."

"All right, Mike."

"And kitten . . . you got that little heater of yours handy?"

"Well . . ."

"Then keep it handy but don't let it show."

"It's handy."

"Good. Grab a cab and get over there."

"I'll be there in an hour."

I slapped the phone back, hopped up and took a fast shower. Lily had everything on the table when I got there, a hopeful smile on her face. The table was spread with enough for a couple of lumberjacks and I ate until I made a dent in the mess, then went for seconds on the coffee.

Lily handed me a fresh pack of Luckies, held out a match and smiled again when I slumped back in my chair. "Have enough?"

"Are you kidding? I'm a city boy, remember?"

"You don't look like a city boy."

"What do I look like?"

Her eyes did it slow. Up and down twice, then a steady scrutiny of my face. For a minute it was supposed to be funny, but the second time there was no humor in it. The eyes seemed to get bigger and deeper with some faraway hungry quality that was past defining. Then almost as quickly as it had come there was a crazy, fearful expression there in its place that lasted the blink of an eye and she forced a laugh out.

"You look like a nice guy, Mike. I haven't seen many nice guys. I'm afraid they make an impression."

"Don't get the wrong impression, Lily," I told her. "I used to think I wasn't much of a sentimentalist, but sometimes I wonder. Right now you're pretty important to me so I may look like a good egg to you. Just don't go walking off with anything while you're here or I'll look different to you."

Her smile got bigger. "You're not fooling me."

I tossed the butt in my empty cup and it fizzled out. "So I'm getting old. You don't stay young in this racket very long."

"Mike . . ."

I knew what she was going to say before she said it. "I'll be gone for awhile. I don't know how long. The chances are nobody will be up here, but just to keep from sticking our necks out, don't answer that door. If a key goes in the lock it'll be me. Keep the chain on the door until I open it, look for yourself then to make sure and then open up."

"Supposing the phone rings?"

"Let it ring. If I want you I'll call the janitor, have him push the doorbell twice, then I'll call you. Got it?"

"I got it."

"Good. Now take it easy until I get back."

She gave me a slow, friendly wink and a grin, then followed it up with a soft kiss that formed on her lips and crossed the room to me. She was all dressed up with no place to go and didn't care, a beautiful white-headed doll with funny eyes that said she had been around too long and seen too many things. But now she looked happy.

I went downstairs, waited until a cab cruised by and grabbed it. We made the Texan Bar with ten minutes left out of the hour so I loafed around outside until a cab pulled into the curb and Velda got out.

Getting out of a cab is one of the things most women don't do right. But most women aren't Velda. Without half trying she made a production out of it. When you saw her do it you knew she wasn't getting out of a cab so much as making an entrance onto the street. Nothing showed, but there was so much to show that you had to watch to see if it would happen or not and even when it didn't you weren't a bit disappointed.

She turned around, gave me that impish grin and took my arm with a tight squeeze that said she was happy as all get out to see me and the guy with the packages beside me sighed and muttered something about some guys having all the luck.

Inside the Texan we picked a booth as far back as we could get, ordered up lunch for Velda, a beer for me and then she handed me the envelope from her handbag. "As much as I could get. It cost two hundred and a promise of favors to be repaid . . . if necessary."

"By you?"

Her face darkened, then twisted into a smile. "By you."

I slipped my finger under the flap and drew out the sheets. One was a handwritten copy of the sanitarium report with the rest filling in Berga Torn's life history. Velda had carried out instructions. At the bottom of the last page was a list of names.

Evello's was there. So was Congressman Geyfey's. At the tail end was Billy Mist and when I held my finger on it Velda said, "She went out with him periodically. She was seen with him, but whenever it was, the spotlight was on him . . . not her."

"No," I said softly, "the spotlight is always on Billy. The picture's starting to get dirty."

'Mike . . .'" She was tapping her nails against the table. "Who is Billy Mist?"

I grunted, picked up a Lucky and lit it. "It's a picture that goes back pretty far. He used to be known as Billy the Kid and he had as many notches on his rod as the original, if they still notch rods. Just before the war he went legit. At least on the outside he looked clean. He's been tied into a lot of messy stuff but nothing's been proven against him."

"So?"

"He's a known Mafia connection," I said. "He sits pretty high, too."

Velda's face paled a little. "Brother!"

"Why?"

"Eddie Connely gave me the lead this morning in Toscio's Restaurant. He and another reporter seemed to have a pretty good inside track on the Torn gal, both of them being on the police beat. Trouble was, they had to suppress most of it and they were pretty disgusted. Anyway, Eddie mentioned Billy Mist and pointed him out. He was over at the bar and I turned around to look at him. About then he happened to turn around too, caught me watching him and got the wrong slant on things. He left his drink, came over and handed me the slimiest proposition I ever heard right out in the open. What I told him no lady should repeat, but Eddie and his pal got a little green and I thought the Mist character would pop his buttons. Eddie didn't say much after that. He finished his coffee, paid the check and out they went."

I could feel my teeth showing through the grin. My chest was tight and things were happening in my head. Velda said, "Easy, chum."

I spit the cigarette out and didn't say anything for a minute. Billy Mist, the jerk with the duck's-tail haircut held down with a pound of grease. The tough guy who took what he wanted whenever he wanted. The uptown kid with the big money and the heavy connections.

When I got rid of the things in my head I squinted at her across the table. "Kitten, don't ever say I'm the guy who goes looking for trouble."

"Bad, Mike?"

"Bad enough. Mist isn't the type to forget. He can take anything except a slam at his manhood."

"I can take care of myself."

"Honey . . . *no* dame can take care of herself, including you. Be careful, will you?"

She seemed to smile all over. "Worried, Mike?"

"Certainly."

"Love me?"

"Yeah," I said, "I love you, but I go for the way you are and not the way you could look if Mist started working you over." I grinned at her and slapped my hand down over hers. "Okay, I'm not the romantic type this early and in this place."

"I don't care."

She sat there, tall and straight, the black pageboy hair swirling around her shoulders like a waterfall at night with the moon glinting on it. Broad-shouldered, smooth and soft-looking, but firm underneath. She always had that hungry animal quality about her, eyes that drank everything in and when they looked at me seemed to drain me dry. Her mouth was expressive, with full, ripe lips that shone wetly, a crimson blossom that hid even white teeth.

I said it again and this time it sounded different and her fingers curled up over mine and squeezed.

A guy like me doesn't take the kind of look she was giving me very long. I shook my head, got my hand loose and went back to the report she had compiled.

"Let's not get off the track." Her laugh was a silent thing, but I knew she felt the same way I did. "We have three names here. What about the other three?"

Velda leaned across the table to see where I was pointing and I had to keep my eyes down. "Nicholas Raymond was an old flame apparently. She went with him before the war. He was killed in an auto accident."

It wasn't much, but to pick up details like that takes time. "Who said?"

"Pat. The police know that much about her."

"He's really going all out, isn't he?"

"The next one came from him too. Walter McGrath seemed to be another steady she was heavy on. He kept her for about a year during the war. She had an apartment on Riverside Drive then."

"He local?"

"No, from out of state, but he was in the city often."

"Business?"

"Lumber. Gray-market operations on steel too. He has a police record." She saw my eyebrows go up. "One income-tax evasion, two arrests for disorderly conduct, one conviction and suspended sentence for carrying concealed weapons."

"Where is he now?"

"He's been in the city here for about a month taking orders for lumber."

"Nice." She nodded agreement.

"Who's this Leopold Kawolsky?"

Velda frowned, her eyes turning a little darker. "I can't figure that one out. Eddie tapped him for me. Right after the war Berga was doing a number in a nightclub and when the place closed down there was a street brawl that seemed to center around her. This guy knocked off a couple of men giving her a hard time and a photog happened along who grabbed a pic for the front page of his tabloid. It was pure sensationalism, but the picture and the name stuck in Eddie's mind. The same thing happened about a month later and one of those kids who snap photos in the night clubs caught the action and submitted it for the usual pay-on-acceptance deals. That's how Eddie remembered who the girl was so well."

"The guy, honey . . . what about him?"

"I'm coming to him. From the pictures he looked like an ex-fighter. I called the sports editor of a magazine and he picked the name out for me. Kawolsky fought under the name Lee Kawolsky for a year and was looking pretty good until he broke his hand in training. After that he dropped out of the picture. Now, about a month and a half after the last public brawl Lee was hit by a truck and killed. Since there were two deaths by cars in the picture I went into the insurance records and went over them carefully. As far as I could tell, or anybody else for that matter, they were accidents, pure and simple."

"Pure and simple," I repeated. "The way it would have to look."

"I don't think so, Mike."

"Positive."

"Good enough." I ran my eyes over the copy of the medical report, folded it before I finished it and tucked it back into the envelope. "Brief me on this thing," I said.

"There really isn't much. She appeared before Dr. Martin Soberin for an examination, he diagnosed her case as extreme nervousness and suggested a rest cure. They mutually agreed on the sanitarium she was admitted to, an examination there confirmed Dr. Soberin's diagnosis and that was that. She was to stay there approximately four weeks. She paid in advance for her treatment."

If ever there was a mess, this was it. Everything out of place and out of focus. The ends didn't even try to meet. Meet? Hell, they were snarled up so completely nothing made any sense.

"How about this Congressman Geyfey?"

"Nothing special. He was seen with her at a couple of political rallies. The man isn't married so he's clean that way. Frankly, I don't think he knew anything about her."

"This keeps getting worse."

"Don't get impatient. We're only getting started. What did Pat have to say about her?"

"It's all in writing. Probably the best parts they're not telling. Except for her connection with Evello she didn't seem to be out of the ordinary for a kid with her tastes. She was born in Pittsburgh in 1920. Her father was Swedish, her mother Italian. She made two trips to Europe, one when she was eight to Sweden, the next one in 1940 to Italy. The jobs she held didn't pay the kind of money she spent, but that's easy to arrange for a babe like that."

"Then Evello's the connection?"

"Evello's the one," I said. She looked at my face and her breathing seemed to get heavier. "He's here in New York. Pat'll give you the address."

"He's mine then?"

"Until I get around to him."

"What's the angle?"

"An approach. Better arrange for a regular introduction and let him do the rest. Find out who his friends are."

Only her eyes smiled. "Think I can pull it off?"

"You can't miss, baby, you can't miss."

The smile in her eyes got bigger.

"Where are you carrying the heater, kitten?"

The smile faded then. It got a little bit cold and deadly. "The shoulder rig. Left side and low down."

"Nobody'd ever notice, kitten."

"They're not supposed to," she said.

We finished eating and went back into the daylight. I watched her get into the cab the way she had got out and when the hack turned the corner I could feel the skin on my shoulder crawl thinking about where she was going. The next cab that came along I flagged down, gave him a Brooklyn address with instructions to stop by the Atlantic Avenue apartment first. The answer came fast enough when we reached the joint. The name was still on the wall but the neighbors said she had moved out during the night and the apartment was empty. A small truck with the trunks of a new customer started backing into the curb as we drove away.

The second Brooklyn address belonged to a newspaper man who had retired ten years ago. He was forty-nine years old but looked seventy. One side of his face had a scar that ran from the corner of his eye to his ear and down to his mouth. If he took off his shirt he could show you the three dimples in his stomach and the three larger angry pink scars in his back. One arm couldn't move at the elbow. He hadn't retired because he had wanted to. Seems like he had written an exposé about the Mafia one time.

When I came out it was two hours later and I had a folio of stuff under my arm that would have been worth ten grand to any good slick magazine. I got it free. I took another cab back uptown, sat in the back room of a drugstore a buddy of mine ran, went through it twice, then wrapped it and mailed it back to the guy I got it from. I went into a bar and had a beer while the facts settled down in my mind. While I sat there I tried to keep from looking at myself in the mirror behind the back bar but it didn't work. My face wasn't pretty at all. Not at all. So I moved to a booth in the back that had no mirrors.

Evello's name was there. Billy Mist's name was there. In the very beginning. They were punks then but they showed promise. The guy in Brooklyn said you didn't pick up the connections any more because most likely the boys had new assignments. They had been promoted. That was a long time ago so by now they should be kings. There were other names that I didn't know, but before long I'd know. There were empty spaces where names should be but couldn't be supplied and those were in the throne room. Nobody knew who the royalty was. They couldn't even suspect.

Big? Sure, they were big. But then even the big ones would hear the word and their bigness would start to leak out all the holes. I was thinking about it and wondering if they had heard it yet when Mousie Basso came in.

Guys like Mousie you see around when there's not too much light and never see around when the heat's on. Guys like Mousie you see in the papers when the police pull in their dragnet at a time when there were no holes in the walls for them to duck into. In the faces of guys like Mousie you can tell the temperature of the underworld caldron or read your popularity with the wrong people by the way they shy away or hang on to you.

From Mousie's face I knew I was hot.

I knew, too, I wasn't very popular.

Mousie took one look at me sitting there, shot a quick look at the door and would have been out if I hadn't been reaching inside my coat for a smoke at the time. Mousie got white past the point of being pale when he saw where my hand was and when I gave him the nod to come over, he didn't walk, he slunk.

I said, "Hello, Mousie," and the corner of his mouth made a fast, fake smile and he slid into the booth hoping nobody had seen him.

He grabbed a nervous cigarette that didn't do him a bit of good, shook out the match and flicked it under the table. "Look, Mr. Hammer, you and me ain't got a thing to talk about. I . . ."

"Maybe I like your company, Mousie."

His lips got tight and he tried hard to keep from watching my hands. Half under his breath he said, "You ain't good company to be seen with."

"Who says?"

"Lots of people. You're nuts, Mr. Hammer . . ." He waited to see what would happen and when nothing did, said, "you go blowing off your stack like you been doing and you'll be wearing a D.O.A. tag on your toe."

"I thought we were friends, kid." I bit into my sandwich and watched him squirm. Mousie wasn't happy. Not even a little bit.

"Okay, so you did me a favor. That doesn't make us that kind of buddies. If you want trouble you go find it by yourself. Me, I'm a peace-loving guy, I am."

"Yeah."

Mousie's face sagged under the sarcasm. "So I'm a chiseler. So what? I don't want shooting trouble. If I'm small potatoes that's all I want to be. Nobody gets bumped for being small potatoes."

"Unless somebody sees them talking to big potatoes," I grinned at him.

It scared him, right down to his shoes. "Don't . . . don't kid around with me, will you? You don't need me for nothing. Besides which if you do I ain't giving or selling. Lay off."

"What did you hear, Mousie?"

His eyes were quick things that swept the whole room twice before they came back to me. "You know."

"What?"

"You're going to scramble some people."

"What people." I didn't ask him. I told him to say it.

He whispered the word. "Mafia." Then as if it had been a key he swallowed he spilled over with the things he had been holding down while his eyes bulged in his head. His hands grabbed the edge of the table and hung on while the butt he had started to smoke burned through the tablecloth. "You're nuts. You went and got everybody hopped up. Wherever you go you'll be poison. Is it true you got something on the wheels? You better clam if you have. That kind of stuff is sure to lead to trouble. Charlie Max and Sugar . . ." The mouth stopped and stayed open.

"Say it, Mousie."

Maybe he didn't like the way I had edged forward. Maybe he saw the things that should have been written across my face.

The bulging eyes flattened out, sick. "They're spending advance money along the Stem."

"Moving fast?"

I could hardly hear his voice. "Covering the bars and making phone calls."

"Are they in a hurry?"

"Bonus, probably."

Mousie wasn't the same guy who came in. He was the mouse, but a mouse who didn't care any more. He was the mouse who spilled his guts to the cat about where the dog was and if the dog found out, he was dead. He reached for the remains of the cigarette, tried to drag some life into it and couldn't make it. I shook a new one out of my pack and handed it to him. The light I held out was steady, but he couldn't keep the tip of the butt in it. He got it going after a few seconds and stared into the flame of the lighter.

"You ain't scared a bit, are you?" He looked at his own hands, hating himself. "I wish I was that way. What makes a guy like me, Mr. Hammer?"

I could hate myself too. "Guys like me," I said.

The laugh came out his nose like he didn't believe me. "One guy," he said, "just one big guy and everybody gets hopped up. For anybody else, even the mayor, they wouldn't even blink, but for you they get hopped up. You say you're going to scramble and they make like a hillbilly feud. The word goes out and money starts passing hands. Two of the hottest rods in town combing the joints looking for you and you don't even get bothered enough to stop eating. They know you,. Mr. Hammer. Guess maybe everybody knows something about you. That's why Charlie Max and Sugar Smallhouse got the job. They don't know nothing about you. They're Miami boys. You say you're going to do something, you do it and always there's somebody dead and it ain't you. Now the word has it you're going to scramble the top potatoes. Maybe you will and maybe you won't. With anybody else I'd take bets on your side, only this time it's different."

He stopped and waited to see what I'd say. "It's not so different."

"You'll find out."

He saw my teeth through the smile and shuddered. It does funny things to some people. "The word still goes," I said. "From now on to the end they'll have to stay away from windows and doors. They'll never be able to go out alone. Every one of the pack will have to keep a rod in his fist and wait. They'll have to double check everything to make sure I won't find out who they are and no matter how hard they try I'll reach them. Their office boys'll try to check me off but they're like flies on the wall. I'm going to the top. Straight up. I'm finding out who they are and when I do they're dead. I know how they operate . . . they're bad, but they know me and I'm worse. No matter where I find them, or when . . . any time, any place . . . that's it. The top dogs, those are the ones I want. The slime who pull the strings in the Mafia. The kings, you understand? I want them."

My grin got bigger all the time. "They've killed hundreds of people, see, but they finally killed the wrong dame. They tried to kill me and they wrecked my car. That last part I especially didn't like. That car was hand built and could do over a hundred. And for all of that a lot of those top dogs are paying through the kiester starting now. That's the word."

Mousie didn't say anything. He stood up slowly, his teeth holding his bottom lip to keep it up. He jerked his head in what was supposed to be a so-long and slid out from behind the table. I watched him walk to the door, forgetting the sandwich that lay on top of the counter. He opened the door slowly, walked out to the sidewalk and turned east, not looking to either side of himself. When he had gone I got up myself, paid my bill and took the change to a phone booth.

Pat was home and still up. I said, "It's me, pal. Velda told me you heard the news."

He sounded a little far away. "You don't have much sense, do you?"

"They're looking for me. Two boys by the name of Charlie Max and Sugar Smallhouse."

"They have reps."

"So I hear. What kind?"

"Teamwork. Max is the one to watch. They're killers, but Smallhouse likes to do it slow."

"I'll watch Max then. What else?"

"Charlie Max is an ex-cop. He'll probably have a preference for a hip holster."

"Thanks."

"Don't mention it."

I slapped the receiver back on the hook. The dime plinked into the box and the gaping mouth of the thing laughed at me silently. Well, in a way it was a pretty big joke. The army of silent men couldn't stay silent. I didn't know them but they knew me. They were just like the rest; crumbs who knew how to play a one-sided game, but when they were playing somebody who could be twice as silent, twice as dirty and twice as quick they broke in the middle and started begging. Someplace in the city were people with names and some without names. They were organized. They had big money in back of them. They had political connections. They had everything it took to stay where they were except one thing and that was me with my own slab in a morgue. They know what to expect from the cops and what to expect from the vast

machine that squatted on the Potomac but they didn't know what
to expect from me. Already one guy had told them, a punk with
crooked yellow teeth who had had a gun on me and lost it. Then
they'd ask around if they didn't already know and the stories
they'd hear wouldn't be pretty. The fear they handed out so freely
to others they'd taste themselves, knowing that before long, if I
was still alive, they'd have to chew the whole lump and swallow
it.

At the cigarette counter I picked up a fresh deck of Luckies,
went out into the air and headed for the Stem. Out there were
the hunters spending advance money. Cold boys with reps who
didn't know the whole score. They knew the word was out and
wanted to cut it off.

But they didn't hear the whole word. Before the night was over
they'd hear a lot of things that might make them want to change
their minds. One of the things was the rest of the word. They'd
find out the hunters were being hunted.

Just for the fun of it.

chapter eight ████████████████

THE *Globe* gave me the information on Nicholas Raymond. It
was an old clipping that Ray Diker dragged out for me and which
wouldn't have been printed at all if there hadn't been an editorial
tie-up. The press was hot on hit-and-run drivers and used his case
to point up their arguments about certain light conditions along
the bridge approaches.

Nichols Raymond got it as he stepped into the street as the
light changed and his body was flung through a store window.
Nobody saw the accident except a drunk halfway down the block
and the car was never tracked down. The only details about him
were that he was forty-two years old, a small-time importer and
lived in an apartment hotel in the lower Fifties.

I told Ray Diker thanks and used his phone to call Raymond's
old address. The manager told me in a thick accent that yes, he
remembered Mr. Nick-o-las Raymondo, he was the fine man who
always paid his bills and tipped like a gentleman extreme. It was

too bad he should die. I agreed with him, poked around for some personal information and found that he was the kind nothing can be said about. Apparently he was clean.

Finding something on McGrath was easy. The papers carried the same stuff Velda had passed to me without adding anything to it. Ray made a couple of calls downstairs and supplied the rest. Walter McGrath was a pretty frequent visitor to some of the gaudier night clubs around town and generally had a pretty chick in tow. A little persuasion and Ray managed to get his address. A big hotel on Madison Avenue. The guy was really living.

We sat there a few minutes and Ray asked, "Anything else?"

"Lee Kawolsky. Remember him?"

Ray didn't have to go to his files for that. "Good boy, Mike. It was a shame he couldn't follow through. Broke his hand in training and it never healed properly. He could have been a champ."

"What did he do for a living after that?"

"Let's see." Ray's face wrinkled in thought. "Seems like he bartended for Ed Rooney a bit, then he was doing a little training work with some of the other fighters. Wait a sec." He picked up the phone again, called Sports and listened for a minute to the droning voice on the other end. When he hung up he had a question in his eyes.

"What's the pitch, Mike?"

"Like what?"

His eyes sharpened a bit as they watched me. "Lee went to work for a private detective agency that specialized in supplying bodyguards for society brawls and stuff. One of his first assignments was sticking with a kid who was killed across the river a few days ago."

"Interesting," I said.

"Very. How about the story angle?"

"If I knew that I wouldn't be here now. How did he die?"

"It wasn't murder."

"Who says?"

He picked up a pipe, cradled it in his hand and began to scrape the bowl with a penknife. "Killers don't drive the same beer truck for ten years. They aren't married with five kids and don't break down and cry on the street when they've had their first accident."

"You got a good memory, kid."

"I was at the funeral, Mike. I was interested enough to find out what happened."

"Any witnesses?"

"Not a one."

I stood up and slapped my hat on. "Thanks for the stuff, Ray. If I get anything I'll let you know."

"Need any help?"

"Plenty. There's three names you can work on. Dig up anything good and I'll make it worth your while."

"All I want is an exclusive."

"Maybe you'll get one."

He grinned at me and stuck the pipe in his mouth. Ray wasn't much of a guy. He was little and skinny and tight as hell with a buck, but he could get places fast when he wanted to. I grinned back, waved and took the elevator to the street.

Dr. Martin Soberin had his office facing Central Park. It wasn't the world's best location, but it came close. It took in a corner, was blocked in white masonry with venetian shuttered windows and a very discreet sign that announced his residency. The sign said he was in so I pushed the door while the chimes inside toned my arrival.

Inside it was better than I thought it would be. There was a neat, precise air about the place that said here was a prominent medical man suited to the needs of the upper crust, yet certainly within the financial and confidential range of absolutely anybody. Books lined the walls, professional journals were neatly stacked on the table and the furniture had been chosen and arranged to put any patient at ease. I sat down, started to light a cigarette and stopped in the middle of it when the nurse walked in.

Some women are just pretty. Some are just beautiful. Some are just gorgeous. Some are like her. For a minute you think somebody slammed one to your belly then your breath comes back with a rush and you hope she doesn't move out of the light that makes a translucent screen out of the white nylon uniform.

But she does and she says hello and you feel all gone all over. She's got light chestnut hair and her voice is just right. She's got eyes to go with the hair and they sweep over you and laugh because she knows how you feel. And only for a moment do the eyes show disappointment because somehow the cigarette gets lit as if she hadn't been there at all and the smoke from my mouth smooths out any expression I might have let show through.

"The doctor in?"

"Yes, but he's with a patient right now. He'll be finished shortly."

"I'll wait," I said.

"Would you care to step inside while I make out a card for you?"

I took a pull on the Lucky and let it out in a fast, steady stream. I stood up so I could look down at her, grinning a little bit. "Right now that would be the nicest thing I could think of, but I'm not exactly a patient."

She didn't change her expression. Her eyebrows went up slightly and she said, "Oh?"

"Let's say I'll pay the regular rates if it's necessary."

The eyebrows came down again. "I don't think that will be necessary." Her smile was a quick, friendly one. "Is there any way I can help you?"

I grinned bigger and the smile changed to a short laugh.

"Please," she said.

"How long will the doctor be?"

"Another half hour perhaps."

"Okay, then maybe you can do it. I'm an investigator. The name is Michael Hammer, if it means anything to you. Right now I'd like to get some information on a girl named Berga Torn. A short while back Dr. Soberin okayed her for a rest cure at a sanitarium."

"Yes. Yes, I remember her. Perhaps you'd better come inside after all."

Her smile was a challenge no man could put up with. She opened the door, walked into the light again and over to a desk in the corner. She turned around, saw me standing there in the doorway and smoothed out her skirt with a motion of her hands. I could hear the static jump all the way across the room and the fabric clung even closer than it had.

"You'd be surprised how fast a person decides he really isn't sick after all," she said.

"What about the women patients?"

"They get sicker." Her mouth pursed in a repressed laugh. "What are you thinking?"

I walked over to the desk and pulled up the straight-backed chair. "Why a dish like you takes a job like this."

"If you must know, fame and fortune." She pulled out a file case and began to thumb through the cards.

"Try it again," I said.

She looked up quickly. "Truly interested?"

I nodded.

"I studied to be a nurse right after high school. I graduated, and quite unfortunately, won a beauty contest before I could start practicing. A week later I was in Hollywood sitting on my . . . sitting around posing for stills and nothing more. Six months later

I was carhopping at a drive-in diner and it took me another year to get wise. So I came home and became a nurse."

"So you were a lousy actress?"

She smiled and shook her head.

"It couldn't have been that you didn't have a figure after all?"

Her cheeks sucked in poutingly and her eyes looked up at me with a you-should-know-better expression. "Funny enough," she said, "I wasn't photogenic. Imagine that?"

"No, I can't."

She sat up with the three typewritten cards in her hand. "Thank you, Mr. Hammer." Her voice was a song of some hidden forest bird that made you stop whatever you were doing to listen. She laid the cards out in front of her, the smile fading away. "I believe this is what you came for. Now can I see your insurance credentials, and if you have your forms I'll . . ."

"I'm not an insurance investigator."

She gave me a quizzical look and automatically gathered the cards together. "Oh . . . I'm sorry. You know, of course, that this information is always confidential and . . ."

"The girl is dead. She was murdered."

She went to say something and stopped short. Then: "Police?"

I nodded and hoped she didn't say anything more.

"I see." Her teeth pinched her lower lip and she looked sideways at the door to her left. "If I remember I believe the doctor had another policeman in to see him not long ago."

"That's right. I'm following up on the case. I'd like to go over everything personally instead of from reports. If you'd rather wait for the doctor . . ."

"Oh, no, I think it will be all right. Shall I read these off to you?"

"Shoot."

"To be brief, she was in an extremely nervous condition. Over-work, apparently. She was hysterical here in the office and the doctor had to administer a sedative. Complete rest was the answer and the doctor arranged for her to be admitted to the sanitarium." Her eyebrows pulled together slightly. "Frankly, I can't possibly see what there is here to interest the police. There was no physical disorder except symptoms brought on by her mental condition."

"Could I see the cards?"

"Certainly." She handed them to me and leaned forward on the desk, thought better of it when my head turned, smiled and sat back again.

I didn't bother with the card she had read from. The first gave the patient's name, address, previous medical history and down at the bottom along the left side was the notation *RECOM-MENDED BY* and next to it was the name William Wieton. The other card gave the diagnosis, suggested treatment and corroboration from the sanitarium that the diagnosis was correct.

I looked at the cards again, made a face at the complete lack of information they gave me, then handed them back.

"They help any?"

"Oh, you can never tell."

"Would you still like to see the doctor?"

"Not specially. Maybe I'll be back."

Something happened to her face. "Please do."

She didn't get up this time. I walked to the door, looked back and she was sitting there with her chin in her hands watching me. "You ought to give Hollywood another try," I said.

"I meet more interesting people here," she told me. Then added, "Though it's hard to tell on such short acquaintance."

I winked, she winked back and I went out on the street.

Broadway had bloomed again. It was there in all its colorful glory, stretching wide-open arms to the sucker, crying out with a voice that was never still. I walked toward the lights, trying to think, trying to put bits together and add pieces where the holes were.

I found a delicatessen, went in and had a sandwich. I came out and headed up Broadway, making the stops as I came to them. Two hours went by in a hurry and nothing had happened. No, I didn't stay on the Stem because nobody would be looking for me on the Stem. Later maybe, but not now.

So I got off the Stem and went east where the people talked different and dressed different and were my kind of people. They didn't have dough and they didn't have flash, but behind their eyes was the knowledge of the city and the way it thought and ran. They were people who were afraid of the monster that grew up around them and showed it, yet they couldn't help liking it.

I made my stops and worked my way down to the Twenties.

I had caught the looks, seen the nods and heard the whispers.

At any time now I could have picked the boys out of a line-up by sight from the descriptions that came to me in an undertone.

In one place something else was added. There were others to watch for too.

Two-thirty and I had missed them by ten minutes.

The next half hour and they seemed to have lost themselves.

I got back to the Stem before all of the joints started closing down. The cabbie dropped me on a corner and I started the rounds on foot. In two places they were glad to see me and in the third the bartender who had pushed a lot of them my way tried to shut the door in my face, mumbling excuses that he was through for the night. I wedged it open, shoved him back inside and leaned against it until it clicked shut.

"The boys were here, Andy?"

"Mike, I don't like this."

"I don't either. When?"

"About an hour ago."

"You know them?"

His head bobbed and he glanced past me out the side window. "They were pointed out to me."

"Sober?"

"Two drinks. They barely touched 'em." I waited while he looked past me again. "The little guy was nervous. Edgy. He wanted a drink but the other one squashed it."

Andy ran his hands down under his fat waistband to keep them still. "Mike . . . nobody's to say a word to you. This is rough stuff. Do you . . . well, sort of stay clear of here until things blow over."

"Nothing's blowing over, friend. I want you to pass it around where It'll get heard. Tell the boys to stay put. I'll find them. They don't have to go looking for me any more."

"Jeepers, Mike."

"Tell it where it'll get heard."

My fingers found the door and pulled it open. The street outside was empty and a cop was standing on the corner. A squad car went by and he saluted it. Two drunks turned the corner behind his back and mimicked him with thumbs to their noses.

I turned my key in the lock. I knew the chain should be on so I opened the door a couple of inches and said, "It's me, Lily."

There was no sound at first, then only that of a deeply drawn breath being let out slowly. The light from the corner lamp was on, giving the room an empty appearance. She drifted into it silently and the glow from her hair seemed to brighten it a little.

Something was tight and strange in the smile she gave me through the opening in the door. Strange, faraway, curious. Something I couldn't put my finger on. It was there, then it was gone and she had the door unhooked and I stepped inside.

It was my turn to haul in my breath. She stood there almost

breathlessly, looking up at me. Her mouth was partly open and I could see her tongue working behind her teeth. For some reason her eyes seemed to float there, two separate dark wells that could knead your flesh until it crawled.

Then she smiled, and the light that gilded her hair made shadows across the flat of her stomach and I could see the lush contours harden with an eager anticipation that was like her first expression . . . there, then suddenly gone like a frightened bird.

I said, "You didn't have to wait up."

"I . . . couldn't sleep."

"Anybody call?"

"Two. I didn't answer." Her fingers felt for the buttons on the robe, satisfied themselves that they were all there from her chin down to her knees, an unconscious gesture that must have been a habit. "Someone was here." The thought of it widened her eyes.

"Who?"

"They knocked. They tried the door." Her voice was almost a whisper. I could see the tremor in her chin and from someplace in the past I could feel the hate pounding into my head and my fingers wanted to squeeze something bad.

Her eyes drifted away from mine slowly. "How scared can a person get, Mike?" she asked. "How . . . scared?"

I reached out for her, took her face in my hands and tilted it up. Her eyes were warm and misty and her mouth a hungry animal that wanted to bite or be bitten, a questioning thing waiting to be tasted and I wanted to tell her she never had to be scared again. Not ever.

But I couldn't because my own mouth was too close and she pulled away with a short, frenzied jerk that had a touch of horror in it and she was out of reach.

It didn't last long. She smiled and I remembered her telling me I was a nice guy and nice guys have to be careful even when the lady has been around. Especially a lady who has just stepped out of the tub to open the door for you and had nothing to put on but a very sheer silk robe and you know what happens when those things get wet. The smile deepened and sparkled at me, then she drifted to the bedroom and the door closed.

I heard her moving around in there, heard her get into the bed, then I sat down in the chair facing the window and turned out the light. I switched the radio on to a late station, sitting there, seeing nothing at all, my mind miles away up in the mountains. I was coming around a curve and then there was that Viking girl standing there waving at me. She was in the beams of the lights, the tires shrieking to a stop, and she got closer and closer until there was no hope of stopping the car at all. She let out one final scream that had all the terror in the world in it and I could feel the sweat running down the back of my neck. Even when she was dead under the wheels the screaming didn't stop, then my eyes came open and my ears heard again and I picked up the phone and her cry stopped entirely.

I said a short hello into it, said it again and then a voice, a nice gentle voice asked me if this was Mike Hammer.

"That's right," I said. "who's this?"

"It really doesn't matter, Mr. Hammer. I merely wanted to call your attention to the fact that as you go out today please notice the new car in front of your building. It belongs to you. The papers are on the seat and all you have to do is sign them and transfer your plates."

It was a long foul smell that seeped right through the receiver. "What's the rest of it, friend?"

The voice, the nice gentle voice, stopped purring and took on an insidious growl. "The rest of it is that we're sorry about your other car. Very sorry. It was too bad, but since things happened as they did, other things must change."

"Finish it."

"You can have the car, Mr. Hammer. I suggest that if you take it you use it to go on a long vacation. Say about three or four months?"

"If I don't?"

"Then leave it where it is. We'll see that it is returned to the buyer."

I laughed into the phone. I made it a mean, low kind of laugh that didn't need any words to go with it. I said, "Buddy . . . I'll take the car, but I won't take the vacation. Someday I'll take you too."

"However you wish."

I said "That's the way it always is," but I was talking to a dead phone. The guy had hung up.

They were at me from both ends now. The boys walking around the Stem on a commission basis. One eye out for me, the other for the cops that Pat would have scouting. Now they were being generous.

Like Lily had said, how scared could a person get? They didn't like the way it was going at all. I sat there grinning at the darkness outside thinking about the big boys whose faces nobody knew.

Maybe if I had boiled over like the old days they would have had me. The waiting they didn't go for.

I shook a Lucky out of the pack and lit it up. I smoked it down to the end, put it out, then went in and flopped down on the bed. The alarm was set for eight, too early even at that hour, but I set it back to seven and knew I'd be hating myself for it.

The heap was a beauty. It was a maroon Ford convertible with a black top and sat there gleaming in the early morning sunlight like a dewdrop. Bob Gellie walked around it once, grinning into the chrome and came back and stood by me on the sidewalk.

"Some job, Mike. Got twin pipes in back." He wiped his hands on his coveralls and waited to see what came next.

"She's gimmicked. Bob. Think you can reach it?"

"Come again?" He stared at me curiously.

"The job is a gift . . . from somebody who doesn't like me. They're hoping I step into it. Then goes the big boom. They're probably even smart enough to figure I'd put a mechanic on the job to find the gimmick so it'll be well hidden. Go ahead and dig it out."

He wiped the back of his hands across his mouth and shoved the hat back further on his head. "Best thing to do is run it in the river for a couple of hours."

"Hop to it, Bob, I need transportation."

"Look, for a hundred I can do a lot of things, but . . ."

"So I'll double it. Find the gimmick."

The two C's got him. For that many pieces of paper he could take his chances with a gallon of soup. He wiped his mouth clean again and nodded. The sun wasn't up over the apartments yet and it was still cool, but it didn't do much for the beads of sweat that started to shape up along Bob's forehead. I went down to a restaurant, filled up with breakfast, spent an hour looking in store windows and came back.

Bob was sitting behind the wheel looking thoughtful, the hood in front of him raised up like a kid with his thumb to his nose. He got out when he saw me, lit a cigarette and pointed to the engine. "She's hot, Mike. A real conversion."

I could see what he meant. The heads were finned aluminum jobs flanking dual carburetors and the headers that came off the manifold poked back in a graceful sweep.

"Wonder what she's like inside?"

"Probably complete. Think your old heap could take this baby?"

"I haven't even driven this one yet. Find the stuff?"

His mouth tightened and he looked around him once, fast. "Yeah. Six sticks wired to the ignition."

"It stinks."

"That's what I thought too," he told me. "Couldn't find a thing anyplace else though. Checked the whole assembly inside and out and if there's more of it the guy who placed it sure knew his business."

"He does, Bob. He's an expert at it."

I stood there while he finished his butt. He walked around the hood, got down under the car and poked around there, then came back and looked at the engine again.

Then his face changed, went back a half dozen years into the past, got tight, relaxed into a puzzled grin, then he looked at me and snorted. "Bet I got it, Mike."

"How much?"

"Another hundred?"

"You're on."

"I remember a booby trap they set on a Heinie general's car once. A real cutie." He grinned again. "Missed the general but got his driver a couple of days later."

He slid into the car, bent down under the dash and worked at something with his screwdriver. He got out looking satisfied, shoved his tools under the car and crawled in with them. The job took another twenty minutes and when he came out he was moving slowly, balancing something in his hand. It looked like a section of pipe cut lengthwise and from one end protruded a detonation cap.

"There she is," he said. "Nice, huh?"

"Yeah."

"Rigged to the speedometer. A few hundred miles from now a contact would have been made and you'd be dust. Had the thing wrapped around the top section of the muffler. What'll I do with it?"

"Drop it in the river, Bob. Keep the deal to yourself. Drop up to my place tonight and I'll write you a check."

He looked at the thing in his hand, shuddered and held it even tighter. "Er . . . if it doesn't mean anything to you, Mike . . . I'd like to have the dough now."

"I'm good for it. What're you worried . . ."

"I know, I know, but if anybody's after you this bad you might not live to tonight. Understand?"

I understood. I went up and wrote him out a check, gave him an extra buck for the cab fare to the river and got in the car. It wasn't a bad buy at all for three C's. And one buck. Then I started it up, felt good when I heard the low, throaty growl that poured out of the twin pipes and eased the shift into gear for the short haul north.

Pat had been wrong about Carl Evello being in the city. In one week he had gone through two addresses and the last was the best. Carl Evello lived in Yonkers, a very exclusive section of Yonkers.

At first the place seemed modest, then you noticed the meticulous care somebody gave the garden, and saw the Cadillac convertible and new Buick sedan that made love together in a garage that would have looked well as a wing on the Taj Mahal. The house must have gone to twenty rooms at the least and nothing was left out.

I rolled up the hard-topped driveway and stopped. From someplace behind the house I could hear the pleasant laughter of women and the faint strains of a radio. A man laughed and another joined him.

I cut the engine and climbed out, trying to decide whether I should crash the party or go through the regular channels. I started around the car when I heard tires turn into the driveway and while I stood there a light-green Merc drove up behind me, honked a short note of hello, revved up fast and stopped.

Beauty is a funny thing. Like all babies are beautiful no matter how they're shaped. Like how there are times when any woman is beautiful as long as she's the color you want. It's not something that only shows in a picture. It's a composite something that you can't quite describe, but can recognize the second you see it and that's the way this woman was.

Her hair was a pale brown ocean that swirled with motion and threw off the sunlight that bounced into it. She smiled at me, her mouth a gorgeous curve that had a peculiar attraction so that you almost missed the body that bore it. Her mouth was full and wet as if it had just been licked, a lush mouth with a will of its own and always hungry.

She walked up with a long stride, pressing against the breeze, smiling a little. And when she smiled her mouth twisted a bit in the corner with an even hungrier look and she said, "Hi. Going to the social?"

"I wasn't," I said. "Business, now I'm sorry."

Her teeth came out from under the soft curves and the laugh filled her throat. For the barest second she gave me a critical glance, frowned with a mixture of perplexed curiosity and the smile got a shade bigger. "You're a little different, anyway," she said.

I didn't answer and she stuck out her hand. "Michael Friday."

I grinned back and took it. "Mike Hammer."

"Two Mikes."

"Looks like it. You'll have to change your name."

"Uh-uh. You do it."

"You were right the first time . . . I'm different. I tell, not get told."

Her hand squeezed in mine and the laugh blotted out all the sounds that were around us. "Then I'll stay Michael . . . for a time, anyway." I dropped her hand and she said, "Looking for Carl?"

"That's right."

"Well, whatever your business is, maybe I can help you out. The butler will tell you he isn't in so let's not ask him, okay?"

"Okay," I said.

This, I thought, is the way they should be. Friendly and uncomplicated. Let the good breeding show. Let it stick out all over for anybody to see. That was beauty. The kind that took your hand as if you were lovers and had known each other a lifetime, picking up a conversation as if you had merely been interrupted in one already started.

We took the flagstone path that led around the house through the beds of flowers, not hurrying a bit, but taking in the fresh loveliness of the place.

I handed her a cigarette, lit it, then did mine.

As she let the smoke filter through her lips she said, "What *is* your business, by the way? Do I introduce you as a friend or what?"

Her mouth was too close and too hungry looking. It wasn't trying to be that way. It just was, like a steak being grilled over an open fire when you're starved. I took a drag on my own butt and found her eyes. "I don't sell anything, Michael . . . not unless it's trouble. I could be wrong, but I doubt if I'll need much of an introduction to Carl."

"I don't understand."

"Sometime look up my history. Any paper will supply the dope."

I got looked at then like a prize specimen in a cage. "I think I will, Mike," she smiled, "but I don't think anything I find will surprise me." The smile went into that deep laugh again as we turned the corner of the building.

And there was Carl Evello.

He wasn't anything special. You could pass him on the street and figure him for a businessman, but nothing more. He was in his late forties, an average-looking joe starting to come out at the middle a bit but careful enough to dress right so it didn't show. He mixed drinks at a table shaded by a beach umbrella, laughing at the three girls who relaxed in steamer chairs around him.

The two men with him could have been other businessmen if you didn't know that one pulled the strings in a racket along the waterfront that made him a front-page item every few months.

The other one didn't peddle forced labor, hot merchandise or tailor-made misery, but his racket was just as dirty. He had an office in Washington somewhere and peddled influence. He shook hands with presidents and ex-cons alike and got rich on the proceeds of his introductions.

I would have felt better if the conversation had stopped when I walked over. Then I would have known. But nothing stopped. The girls smiled pleasantly and said hello. Carl studied me during the name swapping, his expression one of trying to recall an image of something that should have been familiar.

Then he said, "Hammer, Mike Hammer. Well, of course. Private detective, aren't you?"

"I was."

"Certainly. I've read about you quite often. Leave it to my sister to find someone unusual for an escort." He smiled broadly, his whole face beaming with pleasure. I'd like you to meet Al Affia, Mr. Hammer. Mr. Affia is a business representative of a Brooklyn outfit."

The boy from the waterfront pulled his face into a crooked smile and stuck out his hand. I felt like whacking him in the mouth.

I said, "Hello," instead and laughed into his eyes like he was laughing in mine because we had met a long time ago and both knew it.

Leo Harmody didn't seem to do anything. His hand was sticky with sweat and a little too limp. He repeated my name once, nodded and went back to his girl.

Carl said, "Drink?"

"No thanks. If you got a few minutes I'd like to speak to you."

"Sure, sure."

"This isn't a social visit."

"Hell, hardly anybody comes to see me socially. Don't feel out of place. This a private talk?"

"Yeah."

"Let's go inside." He didn't bother to excuse himself. He picked up a fresh drink, nodded to me and started across the lawn toward the house. The two goons sitting on the steps got up respectfully, held the door open and followed us in.

The house was just what I expected it to be. A million bucks properly framed and hung. A fortune in good taste that didn't come from the mouth of a guy who started life on the outer fringe of a mob. We went through a long hall, stepped into a study dominated by a grand piano at one end and Carl waved me to a chair.

The two goons closed the door and stood with their backs to it. I said, "This is a private talk."

Carl waved unconcernedly. "They don't hear anything," then sipped his drink. Only his eyes showed over the lip of the glass. They were almond-shaped and beady. They were the kind of eyes I had seen too many times before, hard little diamonds nestling in their soft cushions of fat.

I looked at the goons and one grinned, rising on his toes and rocking back and forth. Both of them had a bulge on the right hip that meant just one thing. They were loaded. "They still have ears."

"They still don't hear anything. Only what I want them to hear." His face beamed into a smile. "They're necessary luxuries, you might say. There seem to be people who constantly make demands on me, if you know what I mean."

"I know what you mean." I pulled a cigarette out and tapped thoughtfully against the arm of the chair. Then I let him watch me make a smile, turning a little so the two goons could see it too. "But they're not worth a damn, Carl, not a damn. I could kill you and the both of them before any one of you could get a rod in his fist."

Carl half rose and the big goon stopped rocking. For a second he stood that way and it looked like he'd try it. I let my smile tighten up at the edges and he didn't try it after all. Carl said, "Outside, boys."

They went outside.

"Now we can talk," I said.

"I don't like that kind of stuff, Mr. Hammer."

"Yeah. It spoils 'em. They know they're not the hot rods they're paid off for being. It's kind of funny when you think of it. Put a guy real close to dying and he changes. I mean real close. They're only tough because they're different from ordinary people. They have little consciences and nothing bothers them. They can shoot a guy and laugh because they know they probably won't get shot back at, but like I said, let 'em get real close to dying and they change. They found out something right away. I got a little conscience too."

All the time I was speaking he was half out of his chair. Now he slid back into it again and picked up his drink. "Your business, Mr. Hammer."

"A girl. Her name was Berga Torn."

His nostrils seemed to flare out a little. "I understand she died."

"Was killed."

"And your interest in it?"

"Let's not waste time, you and me," I said. "You can talk to me now or I can do it the hard way. Take your pick."

"Listen, Mr. Hammer . . ."

"Shut up. You listen. I want to hear you tell me about your connection with the dame. Nothing else. No crap. You play games with somebody else, but not me. I'm not the law, but plenty of times there were guys who wished the law was around instead of me."

It was hard to tell what he was thinking. His eyes seemed to harden, then melted into the smile that creased his mouth. "All right, Mr. Hammer, there's no need to get nasty about anything. I've told the police exactly what the score was and it isn't important enough to keep back from you if you're genuinely interested. Berga Torn was a girl I liked. For a while back there I . . . well, kept her, you might say."

"Why?"

"Don't be ridiculous. If you know her then you know why."

"She didn't have much to offer that you couldn't get someplace else."

"She had enough. Now, what else is there?"

"Why did you break it off?."

"Because I felt like it. She was getting in my hair. I thought you had a reputation with women. You should know what it's like."

"I didn't know you checked up on me that close, Carl."

The eyes went hard again. "I thought we weren't playing games now."

I lit the cigarette I was fooling with, taking my time with that first drag. "How do you stand with the Mafia, Carl?"

He played it nice. Nothing showed at all, not even a little bit. "That's going pretty far."

"Yeah, I guess it is." I stuck the cigarette in my mouth and stood up. "But it's not nearly as far as it's going to go." I started for the door.

His glass hit the desk top and he came forward in his seat again. "You sure put up a big stink for a lot of small talk, Mr. Hammer."

I turned around and smiled at him, a nice dead kind of smile that had no laugh behind it and I could see him go tight from where I stood. I said, "I wasn't after talk, Carl. I wanted to see your face. I wanted to know it so I'd never forget it. Someday I'm going to watch it turn blue or maybe bleed to death. Your eyes'll get all wide and sticky and your tongue will hang out and I won't be making any mistake about it being the wrong joe. Think about it Carl, especially when you go to bed at night."

I turned the knob and opened the door.

The two boys were standing there. All they did was look at me and it wasn't with much affection. I was going to have to remember them too.

When I got back outside Michael Friday spotted me and waved. I didn't wave back so she came over, a mock frown across her face. I couldn't get my eyes off her mouth, even when she faked a pout. "Bum steer," she said, "no business?"

She looked like a kid, a very beautiful kid and all grown up where it counted, but with the grin and impishness of a kid nevertheless. And you don't get sore at kids. "I hear you're his sister."

"Not quite. We had the same mother but came from different hatches."

"Oh."

"Going to join the party?"

I looked over at the group still downing the drinks. "No thanks. I don't like the company."

"Neither do I for that matter. Let's both leave."

"Now you got something," I said.

We didn't even bother with good-byes. She just grabbed my arm and steered me around the building, talking a blue streak about nothing at all. We made the front as a car was coming up the driveway and as I was opening the door of my new heap it stopped and a guy got out in a hurry, trotted around the side and opened the door.

I started wondering what the eminent Congressman Geyfey was

doing up this way when he was supposed to be serving on a committee in Washington. Then I stopped wondering when he took the woman's arm and helped her out and Velda smiled politely in our direction a moment before going up the path.

Michael said, "Stunning, isn't she?"

"Very. Who is she?"

She stayed deadpan because she meant it. Her head moved slightly as she said, "I don't know. Most likely one of Bob's protégés. He seems to do very well for himself."

"He doesn't if he overlooked you."

Her laugh was quick and fresh. "Thank you, but he didn't overlook me, I overlooked him."

"Nice for me," I grinned. "What's a congressman doing with Carl? He may be your brother, but his reputation's got spots on it."

Her grin didn't fade a bit. "My brother certainly isn't the most ethical man I've known, but he is big business, and in case you haven't known about it, big business and government go hand in hand sometimes."

"Uh-uh. Not Carl's kind of business."

This time her frown wasn't put on. She studied me while she slid into the car and waited until I was behind the wheel. "Before Bob was elected he was Carl's lawyer. He handled some corporation account Carl had out West." She stopped and looked into my eyes. "It's wrong someplace, isn't it?"

"Frankly, Friday gal, it stinks."

I started the engine, sat and listened to it purr a minute then eased the gearshift in. All that power under the hood was dying to let go and I sat on it. I took the heap down the drive, rolled out to the street and swung toward the center of town. We didn't talk. We sat and rode for a while and watched the houses drift past. The sun was high overhead, a warm ball that smiled at the world, a big warm thing that made everything seem all right when everything was so damned wrong.

Pretty soon it would come. I thought about how she'd put it and how I'd answer it. It could come guarded, veiled or in a roundabout way, but it would come.

When it did come it was right out in the open and she asked, "What did you want with Carl?" Her voice sounded sleepy and relaxed. I glanced at her lying back there so lazily against the cushions, her hair spilling down the back of the seat. Her mouth was still a wet thing, deliciously red, firm, yet ready to vibrate like the strings on a fiddle the moment they were touched.

I answered her the same way she asked it, right out in the open. "He had a girl once. She's dead now and he may be involved in her murder. Your big-business brother may have a Mafia tie-up."

Her head rolled on the seat until she was looking at me. "And you?"

"When I get interested in people like your brother they usually wind up dead."

"Oh." That's all. Just "Oh" and she turned and looked out the window, staring straight ahead.

"You want me to take you back?"

"No."

"Want to talk about it?"

Her hand reached over and took the deck of Luckies from the seat beside me. She lit two at the same time and stuck one in my mouth. It tasted of lipstick, a nice taste. The kind that makes you want to taste it again, this time from the source.

"I'm surprised it took this long," she said. "He used to try to fool me, but now he doesn't bother. I've often wondered when it would happen." She breathed in deeply on the smoke, then watched it whip out the half-opened ventilator. "Do you mind if I cry a little bit?"

"Go ahead."

"Is it serious trouble?"

"You don't get more serious than killing somebody."

"But was it Carl?"

Her eyes were wet when they turned in my direction. "I don't know," I said.

"Then you're not sure?"

"That's right. But then again, I don't have to be sure."

"But . . . you're the police?"

"Nope. Not anybody. Just such an important nobody that a whole lot of people would like to see me knocked off. The only trouble is they can't make the grade."

I pulled the car to the curb, backed it into the slot in front of a gin mill and cut the engine. "You were talking about your brother."

She didn't look at me. She worked the cigarette down to a stub and flipped it into the gutter. "There isn't much to tell, really. I know what he's been and I know the people he's associated with. They aren't what you would call the best people, though he mixes with them too. Generally he has something they want."

"Ever hear of Berga Torn?"

"Yes, I remember her well. I thought Carl had quite a crush on her. He . . . kept her for a long time."

"Why did he dump her?"

"I . . . I don't know." There was a catch in her voice. "She was a peculiar sort of girl. All I remember is that they had an argument one night and Carl never bothered with her much after that. Somebody new came along."

"That all?"

Michael nodded.

"Ever hear of the Mafia?"

She nodded again. "Mike . . . Carl isn't . . . one of those people. I know he isn't."

"You wouldn't know about it if he was."

"And if he is?"

I shrugged. There was only one answer to a question like that.

Her fingers were a little unsteady when they picked up another cigarette. "Mike . . . I'd like to go back now."

I lit the butt for her and kicked the motor over. She sat there, smoked it out and had another. Never talking. Not seeming to do anything at all. Her bottom lip was puffed up from chewing on it and every few minutes her shoulders would twitch as she repressed a sob. I drove up to the gateway of the house, leaned across her and opened the door.

"Friday . . ."

"Yes, Mike?"

"If you think you know an answer to it . . . call me."

"All right, Mike." She started to get out, stopped and turned her head. "You looked like fun, Mike. For both of us, I'm honestly sorry."

Her mouth was too close and too soft to just look at. My fingers seemed to get caught in her hair and suddenly those lovely, wet lips were only inches away, and just as suddenly there was no distance at all.

The bubbling warmth was just what I expected. The fire and the cushiony softness and the vibrancy made a living bed of her mouth. I leaned into it, barely touched it and came away before there was too much hunger. The edges of her teeth showed in a faint smile and she touched my face with the tips of her fingers, then she climbed out of the car.

All the way back to Manhattan I could taste it. The warmth and the wetness and a tantalizing flavor.

The garage was filled so I parked at the curb, gassed up for an excuse to stay there and walked into the office. Bob Gellie was busy putting a distributor together, but he dropped it when I came in.

I said, "How did it go, kid?"

"Hi, Mike. You gave me a job, all right."

"Get it?"

"Yeah, I got it. I checked two dozen outlets before I found where those heads came from. A place out in Queens sold 'em. The rest of the stuff I couldn't get a line on at all. Most of it's done directly from California or Chicago."

"So?"

"They were ordered by phone and picked up and paid for by a messenger."

"Great."

"Want me to keep trying?"

"Never mind. Those boys have their own mechanics. What about the car?"

"Another cutie. It came out of the Bronx. The guy who bought it said it was a surprise for his partner. He paid cash. Like a jerk the dealer let him borrow his plates and it got driven down, the plates were taken off and handed back to the dealer again." He opened the drawer and slid an envelope across to me. "Here's your registration. I don't know how the hell they worked it but they did. Them guys left themselves wide open."

"Who bought the car?"

"Guess."

"Smith, Jones, Robinson. Who?"

"O'Brien. Clancy O'Brien. He was medium. Mr. Average Man. Nobody could describe him worth a hoot. You know the kind?"

"I know the kind. Okay, Bob, call it quits. It isn't worth pushing."

He nodded and squinted up his face at me. "Things pretty bad, Mike?"

"Not so bad they can't get worse."

"Gee."

I left him there fiddling with his distributor. Outside the traffic was thick and fast. Women with bundles were crowding the sidewalks and baby carriages were parked alongside the buildings.

Normal, I thought, a nice normal day. I hauled my heap away from the curb, cut back to Broadway and headed home. It took thirty minutes to get there, another thirty for a quick lunch at the corner and I went into the building fishing my keys out of my pocket.

Any other time I would have seen them. Any other time it would have been dark outside and light inside and my eyes wouldn't have been blanked out. Any other time I would have had a rod on me and it wouldn't have happened so easy. But this was now and not some other time.

They came out of the corners of the lobby, the two of them, each one with a long-nosed revolver in his fist and a yen to use it. They were bright boys who had been around a long time and who knew all the angles. I got in the elevator, leaned against the wall while they patted me down, turned around and faced the door as they pushed the LOBBY button instead of getting off, and walked out in front of them to my car.

Only the short one seemed surprised that I was clean. He didn't like it at all. He felt around the seat while his buddy kept his gun against my neck, then got in beside me.

You don't say much at a time like that. You wait and keep hoping for a break, knowing that if it came at all it would be against you. You keep thinking that they wouldn't pop you out in broad daylight, but you don't move because you know they will. New York. This is New York. Something exciting happening every minute. After a while you get used to it and don't pay any attention to it. A gunshot, a backfire, who can tell the difference or who cares. A drunk and a dead man, they both look the same.

The boy next to me said, "Sit on your hands."

I sat on my hands. He reached over, found my keys in my pocket and started the car. "You're a sucker, mac," he said.

The one in the back said, "Shut up and drive." We pulled out into the street and his voice came again. This time it was closer to my ear. "I don't have to warn you about nothing, do I?"

The muzzle of the gun was a cold circle against my skin. "I know the score," I said.

"You only think you do," he told me.

chapter nine ▰▰▰▰▰▰▰▰▰▰▰▰▰▰▰

I COULD FEEL the sweat starting down the back of my neck. My insides were all bottled up tight. My hands got tired and I tried to slide them out and the side of the gun smashed into my head over my ear and I could feel the blood start its slow trickle downward to join the sweat.

The guy at the wheel threaded through Manhattan traffic, hit the Queens Midtown Tunnel and took the main drag out toward the airport. He did it all nice and easy so there wouldn't be any trouble along the way, deliberately driving slowly until I wanted to tell him to get it rolling and quit fooling around. They must have known how I felt because the guy in the back bored the rod into me every time I tightened up and laughed when he did it.

Overhead an occasional plane droned in for a landing and I thought we were going into the field. Instead he passed right by it, hit a stretch where no cars showed ahead and started to let the Ford out.

I said, "Where we going?"

"You'll find out."

The gun tapped my neck. "Too bad you took the car."

"You had a nice package under the hood for me."

The twitch on the wheel was so slight the car never moved, but I caught the motion. For a second even the pressure against my neck stopped.

"Like it?" the driver asked.

He shouldn't have licked his lips. They should have taught him better.

The pitch was right there in my lap and I swung on it hard. "It stunk. I figured the angle and had a mechanic pull it."

"Yeah?"

"So I punch the starter and blooie. It stunk."

This time his head came around and his eyes were little and black, eyes so packed with a crazy terror that they watered. His foot slammed into the brake and the tires screamed on the pavement.

It wasn't quite the way I wanted it but it was just as good. Buster in the back seat came pitching over my shoulder and I had his throat in my hands before he could do a thing about it. I saw the driver's gun come out as the car careened across the road and when it slapped the curbing the blast caught me in the face.

There wasn't any sense holding the guy's neck any more, not with the hole he had under his chin. I shoved as hard as I could, felt the driver trying to reach around the body to get at me while he spit out a string of curses that blended together in an incoherent babble.

I had to reach across the corpse to grab him and he slid down under the wheel still fighting, the rod in his hand. Then he had it out from the tangle of clothes and was getting up at me.

But by then it was too late. Much too late. I had my hand clamped over his, snapped it back and he screamed the same time the muzzle rocketed a bullet into his eyeball and in the second before he died the other eye that was still there glared at me balefully before it filmed over.

They happened fast, those things. They happen, yet time seems to drag by when there's only a matter of seconds and the first thing you wonder is why nobody has come up to see what was going on, then you look down the road and the car you saw in the distance when it all started still hasn't reached you yet, and although two kids across the street are pointing in your direction, nobody else is.

So I got in the driver's side, sat the two things next to me in an upright position and drove back the way we came. I found a cutoff near the airport, turned into it and followed the road until it became a one-lane drive and when I reached its limit there was a sign that read DEAD END.

I was real cute this time. I sat them both under the sign in a nice, natural position and drove back home. All the way back to the apartment I thought of the slobs who gave me credit for finding both gimmicks in the heap and then suddenly realized I was dumber than they figured and the big one was still there ready to go off any second.

Night had seeped in by the time I reached the apartment. I parked and went up to the apartment, opened the door enough to call in for her to take the chain off, but it wasn't necessary at all.

There was no chain.

There was no Lily either and I could feel that cold feeling crawl up my back again. I walked through the rooms to be sure, hoping I was wrong when I was right. She was gone and everything she owned was gone. There wasn't even a hairpin left to show that she had been there and I was so damned mad my eyes squinted almost shut and I was cursing them, the whole stinking pack of them under my breath, cursing the efficiency of their organization and the power they held in reserve, swearing at the way they were able to do things nobody else could do.

I grabbed the phone and dialed Pat's number. Headquarters told me he had left for the day and I put the call through to his apartment. He said hello and knew something was up the minute he heard my voice. "Lily Carver, Pat, you know her?"

"Carver? Damn, Mike . . ."

"I had her here at the apartment and she's gone."

"Where?"

"How am I supposed to know where! She didn't leave here by herself. Look . . ."

"Wait up, friend. You have some explaining to do. Did you know she had been investigated?"

"I know the whole story, that's why I pulled her out of Brooklyn. She had the city boys, the feds and another outfit on her back. The last bunch pulled a fast one today and got her out of here somehow."

"You stuck your neck out on that one."

"Ah, shut up," I said. "If you have a description, pass it around. She might know what it was the Torn kid was bumped for."

His breathing came in heavy over the receiver. "A pickup went out on her yesterday, Mike. As far as we knew she disappeared completely. I wish to hell you let me in on the deal."

"What have you got on her?" I asked him.

"Nothing. At least not now. A stoolie broke the news that she was to be fingered for a kill."

"Mafia?"

"It checks."

"Damn," I said.

"Yeah, I know how you feel." He paused, then, "I'll keep looking around. There's big trouble winding up, Mike."

"That's right."

"Stuff has been pouring in here."

"Like what?"

"Like more tough guys seen on the prowl. We picked up one on a Sullivan rap already."

I grunted. "That law finally did some good."

"The word is pretty strong. You know what?"

"What?"

"You keep getting mentioned in the wrong places."

"Yeah." I lit up a smoke and pulled in a deep drag. "This rumble strictly on the quiet between you and me?"

"I told you yes once."

"Good. Anybody find a pair of bodies propped up against a sign in Queens?"

He didn't say anything right away. Then he whispered huskily, "I should've figured it. I sure as blazes should've figured it."

"Well, just don't figure me for your boy. I checked my rod in a few days ago."

"How'd it happen?"

"It was real cute," I said. "Remind me to tell you someday."

"No wonder the boys are out for you."

"Yeah," I said, then I laughed and hung up.

Tonight there'd be more. Maybe a whole lot more.

I stood there and listened and outside the window there was another laugh. The city. The monster. It laughed back at me, but it was the kind of a laugh that didn't sound too sure of itself any more.

Then the phone jangled and the laugh became the muted hum once more as I said hello. The voice I half expected wasn't there. This one was low and soft and just a little bit sad. It said, "Mike?"

"Speaking."

"Michael Friday, Mike."

I could visualize her mouth making the words. A ripe, red mouth, moistly bright, close to the phone and close to mine. I didn't know what to answer her with, except, "Hi, where are you?"

"Downtown." She paused for a moment. "Mike . . . I'd like to see you again."

"Really?"

"Really."

"Why?"

"Maybe to talk, Mike. Would you mind?"

"At one time I would. Not any more."

Her smile must have had the same touch of sadness her voice had just then. "Perhaps I'm using that for an excuse."

"I'd like that better," I said.

"Will you see me then?"

"Just say where and when."

"Well . . . one of Carl's friends is giving a party this evening. I'm supposed to be there and if you don't mind . . . could we go together? We don't have to stay very long."

I though about it a minute. I let a lot of things run through my mind, then I said, "Okay, I don't have anything else on the fire. I'll meet you in the Astor lobby at ten. How's that?"

"Fine, Mike. Shall I wear a red carnation or something so you'll know me?"

"No . . . just smile, kid. Your mouth is one thing I'll never forget."

"You've never really got close enough to tell."

"I can remember how I said good-bye the last time."

"That isn't *really* close," she said as she hung up.

I looked at the phone when I put it down. It was black, symmetrical and efficient. Just to talk to somebody put a thousand little things into operation and the final force of it all culminated in a minor miracle. You never knew or thought about how it happened until it was all over. Black, symmetrical, efficient. It could be a picture of a hand outlined in ink. Their organization was the same and you never knew the details until it was too late.

That's when they'd like me to see the picture.

When it was too late.

How many tries were there now? The first one they spilled me over the cliff. Then there was laughing boy who kept his gun in his pocket. And don't forget the dead-end sign. That one really must have scared them.

The jerks.

And someplace in the city were two others. Charlie Max and Sugar Smallhouse. For a couple of grand they'd fill a guy's belly with lead and laugh about it. They'd buck the biggest organization in the country because theirs was even bigger. They wouldn't give a damn where they scrammed to because wherever they went their protection went too. The name of the Mafia was magic. The color of cash was even bigger magic.

My lips peeled back over my teeth when I thought of them. Maybe now that they knew about the dead-end sign they'd do a little drinking to calm themselves down. Maybe they'd be thinking if they really were good enough after all. Then they'd decide that they were and wait around until it happened and if it came out right in a penthouse somewhere, or in a crummy dive someplace else one of the kings would swallow hard and make other plans and begin to get curious about footsteps behind him and the people around him. Curiosity that would put knots in their stomach first, tiny lumps that would harden into balls of terror before too long.

Ten o'clock. It was still a few hours off.

Ten o'clock, an exquisite, desirable mouth. Eyes that tried to eat you. Ten o'clock Michael Friday, but I had another appointment first.

I started in the low Forties and picked the spots. They were short stops because I wasn't after a good time. I could tell when I was getting ripe by the sidewise looks that came my way. In one place they started to move away from me so I knew I was nearing the end. A little pigeon I knew shook his head just enough so I knew they weren't there and when his mouth pulled down in a tight smile I could tell he wasn't giving me much of a chance.

Nine fifteen. I walked into Harvey Pullen's place in the Thirties. Harvey didn't want to serve me but I waited him out. He went for the tap and I shook my head and said, "Coke."

He poured it in a hurry, walked away and left me by the faded redhead to drink it. A plainclothesman I recognized walked in, had a fast beer at the bar, took in the crowd through the back mirror, finished his butt and walked out. In a way I hoped he had spotted me, but if he did he was better at spotting than I was at keeping from being spotted.

She didn't move her mouth at all. Sometimes the things they pick up in stir pay off and this was one of them. She said, "Hammer, ain't 'cha?"

"Uh-huh."

"Long John's place. They're settin' you up."

I sipped my Coke. "Why you?"

"Take a look, buster. Them creeps gimme the business a long time ago. I coulda had a career."

"Who saw them?"

"I just came from there."

"What else?"

"The little guy's a snowbird and he's hopped."

"Coppers?"

"Nobody. Just them. The gang in the dump ain't wise yet."

I laid the Coke down, swirled the ice around in the glass and rubbed out my cigarette. The redhead had a sawbuck on her lap when I left.

Long John's. The name over the door didn't say so, but that's what everybody called it. The bartender had a patch over one eye and a peg leg. No parrot.

A drunk sat on the curb, puking into the gutter between his legs. The door was open and you could smell the beer and hear a pair of shrill voices. Background music supplied by a jukebox. Maybe a dozen were lined up at the bar talking loud and fast. The curses and filth sifted out of the conversation like minor high lights and the women's voices shrilled again.

The boys were pros playing it cute.

Sugar Smallhouse was sitting at the corner of the bar, his back facing the door so anybody coming in wouldn't recognize him.

Charlie Max was in the back corner facing the door so anybody coming in he'd recognize.

They played it cute but they didn't play it right and Charlie Max took time out to bend his head into the match he held up to light his cigarette and that's when I came in and stood behind his partner.

I said, "Hello, Sugar," and thought the glass he held would crumple under his fingers. The little hairs on the back of his neck went up straight like what happens to a dog when he meets another dog, only on this mutt the skin under the hair happened to be a pale, pale yellow.

Sugar had heard the word. He had heard other people talk. He knew about the sign marked DEAD END and about me and how things hadn't happened as they were planned. I could feel the things churning through his head as I reached under his arm for the rod and all the while Sugar never moved a muscle. It was a little rod with a big bore. I flipped the shells out of the cylinder, dropped them in my pocket and put the gun back in its nest. Sugar didn't get it. He sweated until it soaked through the collar of his shirt but he still didn't get it.

Long John came up, saw me half hidden behind Sugar and said, "What'll it be, feller?" Then Sugar got it while Long John's eye got big and round. I had my hands around his middle in just the right spot, jerked hard and fast with my locked thumbs going into flesh under the breastbone like a kid snapping worms. Hard and fast . . . just once, and Sugar Smallhouse was another drunk who was sleeping it off at the bar.

And Charlie Max was a guy suddenly alive and sober coming up out of his chair, trying to clear a gun from a hip holster to collect his bonus. Eternity took place right then in the space of about five seconds of screaming confusion. Somebody saw the gun and the scream triggered the action. Charlie's gun never got quite cleared because the dame beside him pushed too hard getting away and his chair caught him behind the knees. They were all over the joint, cursing, pushing, falling out of the way and fighting to make the door. Then the noise stopped and it was just a tableau of silent panic because the crowd was behind me and there was nothing more to do except stand there with fascinated terror as Charlie Max scrambled for his rod and I closed in with a couple of quick steps.

The gun was there in his fist, coming up and around as I brought my foot up and the things that were in Charlie's face splashed all over the floor. His face looked soft and squashy a second, became something not at all human and he tried once more with the gun.

Nobody heard that kick because his arm made too much noise.

Somehow his eyes were still there, swelling fast, yet still bright.

They were eyes that should have been filled with excruciating pain, but horror pushed it out as he saw what was going to happen to him.

"The job was too big, buddy. Somebody should have told you how many guys I put on their backs with skulls split apart because they were gunning for me." I said it real easy and reached for the gun.

The voice behind me said, "Don't touch it, Hammer."

I looked up at the tall guy in the blue pin-striped suit, straightened and grunted my surprise. His face stayed the way it was. There were two more of them standing in the back of the room. One was trying to wake up Sugar Smallhouse. The other came forward, ran his hands over me, looked at his partner with a startled expression that was almost funny before giving me a stare that you might see coming from a kid watching a ballplayer hit a homer.

There wasn't a damn thing they could do and they knew it, so I turned around, walked back outside and started crosstown to the Astor.

Washington had finally showed up.

She was waiting there in a corner of the lobby. There were others who were waiting too and used the time just to watch her. Some had even taken up positions where they could move in if the one she was waiting for didn't show up. She wasn't wearing a red carnation, but she did smile and I could almost feel that mouth on me across the room.

Her hair was the same swirly mass that was as buoyant as she was. There aren't many words to describe a woman like Michael Friday as she was just then. You have to look at the covers of books and pick out the parts here and there that you like best, then put them all together and you have it. There was nothing slim about her. Maybe a sleekness like a well-fed, muscular cat, an athletic squareness to her shoulders, a sensual curve to her hips, an antagonizing play of motion across her stomach that seemed unconsciously deliberate. She stood there lazily, flexing one smoothly rounded leg that tightened the skirt across her thigh.

I grinned at her and she held out her hand. My own folded around it, stayed there and we walked out together. "Waiting long?" I asked her.

She squeezed my arm under hers. "Longer than I usually wait for anyone. Ten minutes."

"I hope I'm worth it."

"You aren't."

"But you can't help yourself," I finished.

Her elbow poked me. "How did you know?"

"I don't," I said. "I'm just bragging."

There wasn't any smile there now. "Damn you," she whispered. I could feel her go all tight against me, saw her do that trick with her tongue that left her mouth damp and waiting. I pulled my eyes away and opened the door of the cab that sat at the curb, helped her in and climbed in after her.

"Where to?"

She leaned forward, gave an address on Riverside Drive and eased back into the cushions.

It seemed to come slowly, the way sleep does when you're too tired, the gradual coming together of two people. Slow, then faster and all of a sudden her arms were around me and my hands were pressing into her back and my fingers curled in her hair. I looked at that mouth that wasn't just damp now, but wet and she said, "Mike, damn you," softly and I tasted the hunger in her until the fury of it was too much and I let her go.

Some shake and some cry, some even demand right then, but all she did was close her eyes, smile, open them again and relax beside me. I held out a cigarette, lit it for her, did mine and sat there without saying anything until the cab stopped by the building.

When we were in the lobby I said, "What are we supposed to be doing here, gal?"

"It's a party. Out-of-town friends of Carl and his business associates get together."

"I see. Where do you come in?"

"You might call me a greeter. I've always been the go-between for my big brother. You might say . . . he takes advantage of my good looks."

"It's an angle." I stopped her and nodded toward one of the love seats in the corner. She frowned, then went over and sat down. I parked next to her and turned out the light on the table beside me. "You said you wanted to talk. We'll never make it upstairs."

Her fingers made nervous little motions in her lap. "I know," she said softly. "It was about Carl."

"What about him?"

She looked at me appealingly. "Mike . . . I did what you told me to. I . . . found out all about you."

"So?"

"I . . . it's no use trying to be clever or anything. Carl is mixed up in something. I've always known that." She dropped her eyes to her hands, twining her fingers together. "A lot of people are . . . and it didn't seem to matter much, really. He has all sorts of important friends in government and business. They seem to know what he does so I never complained."

"You just took whatever he gave you without asking," I stated.

"That's right. Without asking."

"Sort of what you don't know won't hurt you."

Michael stared blankly at her lap for a few seconds. "Yes."

"Now you're worried."

"Yes."

"Why?"

The worry seemed to film her eyes over. "Because . . . before it was only legal things that gave him trouble. Carl . . . had lawyers for that. Good ones. They always took care of things." She laid her hand over mine. It shook a little. "You're different."

"Say it."

"I . . . can't."

"All right. You're a killer, Mike. You're dirty, nasty and you don't care how you do it as long as you do it. You've killed and you'll keep killing until you get killed yourself."

I said, "Just tell me one thing, kid. Are you afraid for me or Carl?"

"It isn't for you. Nothing will ever touch you." She said it with a touch of bitterness that was soft and sad at the same time.

I looked at her wonderingly. "You're not making sense now."

"Mike . . . look at me closely and you'll see. I . . . love Carl. He's always taken care of me. I love him, don't you see? If he's in trouble . . . there are other ways, but not you, Mike, not you. I . . . wouldn't want that."

I took my hand away gently, lit a cigarette and watched the smoke sift out into the room. Michael smiled crookedly as she watched me. "It happened fast, Mike," she said. "It sounds very bad and very inadequate. I'm a very lovely phony, you're thinking and I can't blame you a bit. No matter what I ever say, you'll never believe me. I could try to prove it but no matter how hard I tried or what I did, it would only make it look worse so I won't try any more at all. I'd just like to say this, Mike. I'm sorry it had to be this way. You . . . hit me awfully hard. It never happened to me before. Shall we go up now?"

I got up, let her take my arm and walked to the elevator. She hit the top button and stood there facing the door without speaking, but when I squeezed her arm her hand closed tighter around mine and she tossed her hair back to start the smile she'd have when we got out.

Carl's two boys were by the door in the foyer. They wore monkey suits and on them the term was absolutely descriptive. They started their smiling when they saw Michael and stopped when they saw me. You could see them exchange looks trying to figure the next move and they weren't up to it. We were through the door and a girl was taking my hat while they stood there watching us foolishly.

The place was packed. It was loud with laughs and conversation to the point where the music from the grand piano in the corner barely penetrated. Quiet little men with trays passed through the huddled groups handing out drinks and as heads turned to take them I could spot faces you see in the paper often. Some you saw in the movies too, and there were a few you heard making political speeches over the air.

Important people. So damn important you wondered about the company they kept because in each group were one or two not so important unless you looked at police records or knew what they did for a living.

There were hellos from a dozen different directions. Michael smiled, waved back and started to steer me toward the closest group. Leo Harmody was there in all of his self-assuming importance, ready to introduce her to the others. I took my arm away and said, "You go to it, baby. I'll find the bar and get a drink."

She nodded, a trace of a frown shadowing the corner of her mouth.

So I went to the bar.

Where Affia was holding Velda's hand and Billy Mist was giving her a snow job while Carl Evello watched cheerfully.

Velda was good. She showed pleasant curiosity and smiled. Carl wasn't so good. He got a little white.

Billy Mist was even worse. He got color in his greasy face but most of it was deep red and his lips tightened so much his teeth showed. I said, "If you're wondering, Carl, your little sister invited me along."

"Oh?"

"Charming girl," I said. "You'd never know she was your sister."

Then I looked at Billy. I was hating his guts inside and out so hard I could hardly stand still. I looked him over real slow like I was trying to find a spot in the garbage pail for the latest load and said, "Hello, stupid."

They can't take it. You can tear their heart out with one word and they can't take it. Billy's face was something ready to blow up like a landmine and he wasn't even thinking of the consequences. He was all alone in the room with me for that brief second and his hand tightened, got ready to grab something under his coat and right at the top of everything he felt I just stood there lazy-like and said, "Go ahead."

And he thought and thought about the dead men and watched his bubble bust wide open because his mind was telling him he'd never make it while he faced me and he got like Carl. White.

But I wasn't watching Billy Mist any more. I was watching Al Affia, plodding Al Affia who had the waterfront sewed up. Ignorant, thickheaded, slow Al who kept stroking Velda's hand all the while and who didn't turn color or go tight or do anything at all except say, "What's the matter with you guys?"

Velda repeated it. "What *is* the matter? After all . . ."

"Forget it, honey," Billy told her. "Just kidding around. You know how it is."

"Sure you know how it is," Al said.

I looked at the Brooklyn boy and watched him carve his face into a grin, muscle by muscle. Somebody should have mentioned Al's eyes to the boys. They weren't a bit stupid. They were small and close together, but they were bright with a lot of things nobody ever knew about. Someday they'd know.

"Nobody introduced me to the lady," I said.

Carl put his drink down on the bar, afraid to let go of it. "Hammer, I believe it is." He looked at me questioningly and I grinned. "Yes, Mike Hammer. This is Miss Lewis. Candy Lewis."

"Hello, Candy," I said.

"Hello, Mike."

"Neat. Very neat. Model?"

"I do fashions for newspaper advertising."

Good mind, that secretary of mine. Nice and easy to explain to Billy how come she was shooting it with a couple of newshawks. I wondered how she had smoothed out his feelings.

She knew what I was thinking and went me one better. "What do you do, Mr. Hammer?"

They were watching me now. I said, "I hunt."

"Big game?"

"People," I said, and grinned at Billy Mist.

His nostrils seemed to flare out a little. "Interesting."

"You'll never know, chum. It gets to be real sport after a while."

His mouth pressed together, a nasty smirk starting. "Like tonight. I got me two more. You ever hunt?"

His face wasn't red any more. It was calm and deadly. "Yeah, I hunt."

"We ought to try it together sometime. I'll show you a few tricks."

A low rumble came from Al's chest. "I'd like to see that," he laughed. "I sure would."

"Some people haven't got the guts for it," I told him. "It looks easy when you're always on the right side of a gun." I took them all in with one sweep of my eyes. "When you're on the wrong end it gives you the squirms. You know what I mean?"

Carl was on the verge of saying something. I would like to have heard it, but Leo Harmody came up, bowed himself into our little clique with a deep laugh and spoke to Velda. "Could I borrow you long enough to meet a friend of mine, my dear?"

"No, certainly not. You don't care, do you, Billy?"

"Go ahead. Bring her back," he told Leo. "We was talking."

She smiled at the four of us, got down off the stool and walked away. Billy wasn't looking at me when he said, "You better stay home nights from now on, wise guy."

I didn't look at him either. I kept watching Velda passing through the crowd. I said, "Any time, any place," and left them there together. A waiter came by with a tray, offered me a drink and I picked one up. It was a lousy drink but I threw it down anyway.

People kept saying hello just to be polite and I said hello back. I picked Michael out of the crowd and saw that she was looking around for me too. Just as I started toward her I heard a whispered, "Mike!"

I stood there, took another drink from a passing waiter and sipped it. Velda said, "Meet me on the corner in an hour. The drugstore."

It was enough. I walked off, waved to Michael and waited while she made excuses to her friends.

Her smile looked tired, her face worried, but she swung across the room and held her hands out to me. "Enjoying yourself?"

"Oh, somewhat."

"I saw you talking to my brother."

"And friends. He sure has great friends."

"Is everything . . . all right?"

"For now."

She sucked her lip between her teeth and frowned. "Take me home, Mike."

"Not tonight, kid." Her face came up, hurt. "I've been read off," I said. "I'm unhealthier than ever to be seen with. When it happens I don't want you around."

"Carl?"

"He's part of it."

"And you think I am too."

"Michael, you're a nice kid. You're lovely as hell and you have everything to go with it. If you're trying to get something across to me I don't get it. Even if I did I wouldn't trust you a bit. I could go crazy nuts about you but I still wouldn't trust you. I told you a word the last time I saw you. It was Mafia. It's a word you don't speak right out because it means trouble. It's a word that has all the conniving and murder in the world behind it and as long as it touches you I'm not trusting you."

"You . . . didn't feel that way . . . when you kissed me."

There was no answer to it. I ran my hand along her cheek and squeezed her ear while I grinned at her. "A lot of things don't make much sense. They just happen."

"Will I see you again?"

"Maybe."

She walked to the door with me, said good-bye and let her tongue run over her mouth slowly like she was enjoying the taste of something. I grabbed my hat and got out of there fast before she talked me into something I wasn't going to get talked into.

The two goons were still outside. There was something set in their faces and they didn't move when I went past them. When the elevator came up I stepped in, hit the button marked B and had a smoke on the way down. The door opened, I hit the main-floor buzzer as I got out and the elevator went back up a floor.

It wasn't hard to get out of there the back way. I went past the furnaces, angled around closed storerooms and found the door. There was a concrete yard in back bordered by a fence with a door that swung into the same arrangement on the other side. This time I met a young kid firing one of the furnaces, held out a bill as I went by and said, "Dames. You know how it is." He nodded wisely, speared the bill and went back to his work whistling.

I found the drugstore and went in for a soda. They sold magazines up front so I brought one back with me while I waited. It was five minutes past the hour when Velda came in, saw me and slipped into the booth.

"You get around, Mike."

"I was thinking of saying the same to you. How come you tangled with Mist?"

"Later. Now listen, I haven't too much time. Earlier this evening two names came up. One of Carl's men turned in a report and I was close enough to hear it. The report was that somebody had double-checked on Nicholas Raymond and Walter McGrath. Carl got all excited about it.

"At the time I was talking to Al and Billy and had my back to Carl. He sent the guy off, called Billy off and I could tell from Billy's face that he passed the news on to him. He looked like a dead fish when he came back to the bar with us. He was so mad his hands were shaking."

I said, "Did Affia get the news?"

"Most likely. I excused myself for a few minutes to give him a chance to pass it politely."

"I wonder about something, Kitten."

"What?"

"I made a few phone calls."

"It sounded more important than that."

"Maybe Washington is getting hot."

"They'll have to get hotter," Velda grinned. "Billy said he had to talk a little business tonight." She reached in her handbag and brought out something. "He gave me a key to his apartment and told me to go ahead up and wait for him there."

I whistled between my teeth and picked the key out of her fingers. "Let's go then. This is hot."

"Not me, Mike. You go." There was a deadly seriousness about her face.

"What's the rest of it, Velda?"

"This is a duplicate key I dragged Carlo Barnes out of bed to make up for me. It took some fast and fancy working to get it so quickly."

"Yeah."

"Al Affia caught the pitch and invited me up to his place for awhile *before* I went to Billy's," Velda said softly.

"The lousy little . . ."

"Don't worry about it, Mike."

"I'm not. I'm just going to smash his face in for him, that's all." I sat there with my hands making fists and the hate pumping through my veins so hard it hurt.

Velda squeezed my hand and dumped a small aspirin bottle out of her bag and showed it to me. There weren't any pills in it, only a white powder. "Chloral," she said. "Don't worry."

I didn't like it. I knew what she figured to do and I didn't go for the play. "He's no tourist. They guy's been around."

"He's still a man."

My mouth felt dry. "He's a cagey guy."

Her elbow nudged her side meaningly. "I still have that, Mike."

You have to do things you don't want to do sometimes. You hate yourself for it but you still have to do it. I nodded, said, "Where's his place?"

"Not Brooklyn. He has a special little apartment under the name of Tony Todd on Forty-seventh between Eighth and Ninth Avenues." She pulled a note pad out, jotted down the number with the phone to go with it and handed it over. "Just in case, Mike."

I looked at it, memorized every detail there, then let the flame of my lighter wipe it out of existence. My beautiful, sleek animal was smiling at me, her eyes full of excitement and when you looked hard you could see the same thing there that you could see in mine. She stood up, winked and said, "Good hunting, Mike."

Then she was gone.

I gave her five minutes. I followed the shadows further uptown along the Drive to the building Billy Mist owned.

For the first time I was glad he was such a big man. He was so damn big he didn't have to stake anybody out around his place. He could relax in the luxury of security, knowing that just one word could bring in an army if anybody tried to take the first step across the line.

It was another one of those things that came easy. You go in like you belonged there. You get on the elevator and nobody notices. You get off and go down the hall, then stick the key in the lock and the door opens. You get treated to the best that money can buy even if the taste is crummy.

There were eight rooms in all. They were spotlessly clean and treated with all the care a well-paid maid could give them. I took forty-five minutes going through seven of them without finding one thing worth looking at until I came to the eighth.

It was a little room off the living room. At one time it must have been intended for a storeroom, but now it had a TV set, a tilt-back chair with an ottoman in place facing it, a desk and a bookcase loaded with pulps. Out of eight rooms here was the place where Billy Mist spent his solo time.

The desk was locked, but it didn't take more than a minute to get it open. Right in the middle section was a dimestore scrapbook fat with clippings and photos and he was in all of them. My greasy little friend was one hell of an egotist from the looks of the thumbmarks on the pages.

Another ten minutes went by going through the book and then I came to Berga's picture. There was no caption. It was just a rotogravure cutout and Billy was grinning at the camera. Berga was supposed to be background but she outsmiled Billy. Two pages later she came up again only this time she was with Carl Evello and it was Billy who was in the background talking to somebody hidden by Carl's back. I found two more like that, first with Billy, then with Carl, and topping it all was a close-up glossy of Berga at her best with *"love to my Handsome Man"* penned in white across the bottom.

Nothing else unless you wanted to count the medicine bottles in the pigeonholes. It looked like the cabinet in the bathroom. Billy must have had a pretty nervous stomach.

I closed the desk, locked it and wiped it clean. I went back to the living room, checked my watch and knew the time was getting close. I picked up the phone and dialed Pat's home number. Nobody answered so I called headquarters and that's where he was. It was a tired, disgusted Pat that said hello.

"Busy, Pat?"

"Yeah, up to my ears. Where have you been? I've been calling between your office and your house all night."

"If I told you you'd never believe it. What's up?"

"Plenty. Sugar Smallhouse talked."

I could feel the chills crawl up my legs until the hairs on the backs of my hands stood straight out.

"Give, Pat. What's the score?"

He lowered his voice deliberately and didn't sound like himself at all. "Sugar was on the deal when Berga got bumped. Charlie Max was called in on the job but didn't make it."

"Come on, come on. Who did he finger?"

"He didn't. The other faces were all new to him."

"Damn it," I exploded, "can't you get something out of him?"

"Not any more, pal. Nobody can. They were taking the two downtown to the D.A.'s and somebody chopped them."

"What're you talking about?"

"Sugar and Charlie are dead. One federal man and one city cop are shot up pretty bad. They were sprayed by a tommy gun from the back seat of a passing car."

"Capone stuff. Hell, this isn't prohibition. For Pete's sake. Pat, how big are these guys? How far can they go?"

"Pretty far, it looks like. Sugar gave us one hot lead to a person with a Miami residence. He's big, too."

I could taste something sour in my mouth. "Yeah," I said, "so now he'll be asked polite questions and whatever answers he gives will satisfy them. I'd like to talk to the guy. Just him and me and a leather-covered sap. I'd love to hear his answers."

"It doesn't work that way, Mike."

"For me it does. Any trace of the car?"

"Sure, we found it." He sounded very tired. "A stolen job and the gun was still in it. We traced it to a group heisted from an armory in Illinois. No prints. Nothing. The lab is working on other things."

"Great. A year from now we'll get the report. I'd like to do it my way."

"That's why I was calling you."

"Now what."

"That screwball play of yours with Sugar and Max. The feds are pretty sore about it."

"You know what to tell them," I said.

"I did. They don't want to waste time pulling you out of jams."

"Why, those apple heads! Who are they supposed to be kidding? They must have had a tail on me all night to run me down in that joint and they sure waited until it was finished before they came in to get their suits dirty."

"Mike . . ."

"Nuts to them, brother. They can stick their heads . . ."

"Shut up for a minute, will you!" Pat's voice was a low growl. "You didn't have a tail . . . those two hoods did. They lost the boys and didn't get picked up again until they reached Long John's."

"So what?"

"So they needed a charge to drag them in on. The boys caught the tail, ditched their rods someplace and when one of our plain-clothesmen braced them they were clean. They had a second tail and didn't know it, but they didn't take any chances and pulled some pretty fancy footwork just in case. If they could have been pulled in on a Sullivan rap we would have squeezed something out of them. You didn't leave them in condition to talk."

"Tell 'em thanks," I grunted. "I don't like to be gunned for. I'll try not to break up their next play."

"Yeah," Pat said sourly.

"Anything on Carver yet?" I asked him.

"Not a thing. We have two freshly killed blondes, more or less.

One's been in the river at least three days and the other was shot by an irate lover just tonight. They interest you?"

"Quit being funny." I looked at my watch. Time was getting too damn short. I said, "I'll buzz you if anything turns up, otherwise I'll see you in the morning."

"Okay. Where are you now?"

"In the apartment of a guy named Billy Mist and he's due in any second."

His breath made a sharp hissing sound over the phone as I hung up.

I had almost timed it too close. The elevator marker was climbing toward the floor when I reached it and just in case I stepped around the corner of the stairs, went up to the first landing and waited.

Billy Mist and a heavyset muscleman came off the elevator, opened the apartment door and went in. There wasn't anything I wanted to talk to him about so I took the stairs back down instead of the elevator and got out the front door in one piece.

I got halfway down the block when some elusive little thing flashed across my mind and my eyes twisted into a squint as I tried to catch it. Something little. Something trivial. Something in the apartment I should have noticed and didn't. Something that screamed out to be seen and I had passed it by. I tried to bring it into focus and it wouldn't come and after a minute or so it passed out of sight altogether.

I stood there on the corner waiting for the light and a taxi swung by. I had the briefest glimpse inside the back and I saw Velda sitting there with somebody else. I couldn't stop it and I couldn't chase it. I had to stand there and think about it until I was all mixed up and I wasn't going to feel right until I knew the score. An empty cab came along and I told him to take me down to Forty-seventh Street.

The house was in the middle of the block. It was a beat-up affair fifty years old bearing the scars only a neighborhood like that can give it. The doorbell position said Todd lived on the ground floor in back. I didn't have to do any ringing because the front door was open. The hall was littered with junk I had to push aside until I came to the door that had *Todd* written on the card in the square metal holder.

I didn't have to ring any bells here either. This door was open too. I shoved it open and the light streamed out around me, light that glistened off the fetid pools of vomit on the floor, shining even more ominously from the drops of blood between the pools.

The blood was in the hall too, and the light picked it up. It made sticky sounds on the soles of my shoes.

With a rod in my hand I would have felt better. It's company that can do your talking for you and a voice they listen to. I missed the rod, but I went in anyway but on my toes ready to move if I had to.

Nothing happened.

But I saw what had happened.

The glasses were there on the table with a half-empty bottle of mixer and an almost empty fifth of whisky. Ice had melted in the bowl with a few small pieces floating on top of the water.

On the floor was the remains of a milk bottle and there was blood all over one piece. Velda had given him the chloral treatment and he went out, but somehow he had spilled it out of his system and made a play for her. He would have killed her if he could have but she got him with the milk bottle.

Then it hit me all at once and I felt like adding to the pools on the floor. She had gone about in her search, left for Billy's and Al snapped out of it. He didn't stay cold as she had expected him to and Al would have got the news to him by now.

I made a grab for the phone in the corner, spun the dial to Pat's number again and sweated until he answered. I said, "Listen fast, Pat and no questions. They got Velda. She went up to Billy Mist's place and walked into a trap. Get a squad car up there as fast as you can. Got that? Get her the hell out of there no matter what happens and be damn fast about it because they may be working her over." I shot my number to him and told him to call back as soon as word came through.

When I hung up I was cold with sweat and tasting the cotton in my mouth. I closed the door and hoped Al would come back so I could do things to him myself. I didn't move out of the room until I got impatient waiting for the phone to ring, then I prowled through the place.

There was a full cabinet of liquor I was going to try but the smell of it sickened me when I got the bottle near my mouth so I shoved it back again. *Damn it, I thought, why doesn't he call!*

I started a butt going, spit it out after a second drag and went around the place some more. To keep my mind still and the buzzing out of my ears I used my eyes and saw why Al kept the place at all. For what he wanted it was a pretty good base of operation. There were souvenirs all over the place. It was a sloppy hovel, but sloppiness was part of the setup and probably nobody complained.

Al must have even done a little work there when he was finished with his parties. There were work sheets and union reports spread out on the table and a batch of company check stubs in the drawer held together by a rubber band. Like a sap he left a pair of empty checkbooks in the same drawer and the hundred and fifty he made a week from the company wouldn't have backed up the withdrawals shown in the books.

So he had a sideline. He cheated the government most likely. Try to find whose name the checking account was in and there'd be fun.

The phone still didn't ring so I rolled a stack of blueprints that showed dock layouts. At least two of them did. Nine of the others were ships, plans that were blown up in detail until they centered around one mass of lines I couldn't make out. I threw them all back on the table and started to walk away as the phone rang.

I caught it before the ring was finished and Pat said, "You Mike?"

"Speaking."

"What're you pulling, kid?"

"Cut the funny stuff, Pat, what happened?"

"Nothing, except a pair of my men are highly squiffed off. Mist was in bed alone. He let the cops in, let them look around, then chewed the hell out of them for pulling a search. He made one phone call and I've been catching it ever since."

I wasn't hearing him. I laid the phone back on its rack and stared at it dumbly. It started to ring again. It went through the motions four times, then stopped.

Outside it had started to rain. It tapped the windows in the back of the room, cutting streaks through the dust. When I looked again the dust was gone completely and the window seemed to have a live wavy motion about it. I pulled the Luckies out of my pocket, lit one and watched the smoke. It floated lazily in the dead air, then slowly followed a draft that crossed the room.

I was thinking things that scared me.

My watch counted off the seconds and each tick was louder and more demanding, screaming not to be wasted.

I went back to the table, unfolded the blueprints, pushed the first two aside and looked at the legend on the bottom of the nine others.

The ship's name was there. Same ship. The name was *Cedric*.

It was starting to hang together now. When it was too late it was starting to hang together.

They wouldn't kill her yet, I thought. They'd do a lot of things, but they wouldn't kill her until they were sure. They couldn't afford the chance.

Then when they were sure they'd kill her.

chapter ten ███████████████████████

I SLEPT HARD. The rain on the windows kept me asleep and I went through the morning and the rest of the day with all the things I pictured going through my mind and when they came together in one final, horrible ending I woke up. It was nearly six in the evening but I felt better. Time was too important to waste but I couldn't afford to let it pass while I was half out on my feet.

There was a box of frozen shrimp in the refrigerator. I put on the fire and while it cooked up I put through a call. It took two more to locate Ray Diker and his voice sounded as sharp and pinched as his face. He said, "Glad you called, Mike. I was going to buzz you."

"Got something?"

"Maybe. I followed up on Kawolsky. The office he worked for pulled out the records and I got the details. He was hired to cover the Torn kid. She complained that someone was following her and she was a pretty scared baby. She paid the fee in cash and they put Lee on permanent duty. He picked her up in the morning and took her home at night."

"You told me that already, Ray."

"I know, but here's the good part. Lee Kawolsky quit reporting to the office in person after a week of it. He started checking in by phone. The office got ideas about it and put another man outside the apartment and found out Lee was pulling a voluntary twenty-four-hour duty. He was staying with the dame all the time."

"The office complain?"

"What for? It was his business and if she wanted it that way why sound off on it. Her checks still rolled in."

"Did they leave it that way?"

"There wasn't much they could do. The report the other investigator sent in said Lee was doing a fairly serious job of bodyguarding. He had already got into a couple of scrapes over her and she seemed to like it."

It was another thread being woven into place. The rope was getting longer and stronger.

Ray said, "You still there?"

"I'm still here."

"What did you call me for then?"

"The driver of the truck who killed Lee. Got that too?"

"Sure. Harvey Wallace. He lives upstairs over Pascale's saloon on Canal Street. You know where the place is."

"I know," I said.

"Might have something here on Nick Raymond."

"What?"

"He retailed imported tobacco through a concern in Italy. He had his name changed from Raymondo to Raymond before the war. Made a few trips back and forth every year. One of his old customers I ran down said he didn't look like much, but he spent the winters in Miami and dropped a wad of cabbage at the tables there. He was quite a ladies' man too."

"Okay, Ray. Thanks a lot."

"Got a story yet?"

"Not yet. I'll tell you when."

I hung up and turned the shrimp over in the pan. When they were done I ate, finished my coffee and got dressed.

Just as I was going out, the front-door buzzer went off and when I opened it the super was standing there with his face twisted up into one big worry and he said, "You better come downstairs, Mr. Hammer."

Whatever it was he didn't want to speak about in the hall and I didn't ask him. I followed him down, got into his apartment and he motioned with his thumb and said, "In there."

She was sitting on the couch with the super's wife wiping the tears away from her face, filthy dirty and her clothes torn and dust streaked.

I said, "Lily!" and she looked up. Here eyes were red things that stared back at me like a rabbit cornered in its hole.

"You know her, Mr. Hammer?"

"Hell yes, I know her." I sat on the couch beside her and felt her hair. It was greasy with dirt, its luster completely gone. "What happened, kid?"

The eyes filled with tears again and her breath came in short, jerky sobs.

"Let her alone a little bit, Mr. Hammer. She'll be all right."

"Where'd you find her?"

"In the cellar. She was holed up in one of the bins. I never would've seen her if I didn't see the milk bottles. First-floor tenants were squawking about somebody stealing their milk. I seen those two bottles and looked inside the bin and there she was. She said to call you."

I took her hand and squeezed it in mine. "You all right? You hurt or anything?"

She licked her lips, sobbed again and shook her head slowly.

The super's wife said, "She's just scared. Supposing I get her cleaned up and into some fresh clothes. She had a bag with her."

White outlined the red of Lily's eyes. She pulled back, her face tight. "No . . . I . . . I'm all right. Let me alone, please let me alone!" Then there was something fierce about the way she looked at me and bit out, "Mike . . . take me with you. Please. Take me with you!"

"She in trouble, Mr. Hammer?"

I looked at him steadily. "Not the kind of trouble you know about."

He saw what I meant, spoke rapidly to his wife in that language of his and her wise little eyes agreed.

"Help me get her upstairs."

The super took her bag, hooked one arm under hers and she came up from the couch. We used the service elevator in the rear, made my floor without meeting anybody and got her inside the apartment.

He said, "Anything I can do to help, just let me know."

"Right. Clam up about this. Tell your wife the same."

"Sure, Mr. Hammer."

"One other thing. Get me a damn big barrel bolt and slap it on my door."

"First thing tomorrow." He closed the door and I locked it after him.

She sat there in the chair like a kid waiting to be slapped. Her face was drawn and the eyes in it were as big as saucers. I fixed her a drink, made her take it all and filled it up again.

"Feel better?"

"A . . . little."

"Want to talk?"

Her teeth were a startling contrast to her skin when she bit her lip and nodded.

"From the beginning," I said.

"They came back," she said. Her voice was so low I could barely hear it. "They tried the door and one of them did something with the lock. It . . . opened. I sat there and I couldn't even scream. I couldn't move. The . . . the chain on the door stopped them." A shudder went through her whole body.

"They were arguing in whispers outside about the chain, then they closed the door and went away. One of them said they'd need a saw. I . . . couldn't stay here, Mike. I was terrified. I threw my clothes in the bag and ran out but when I got to the street I was afraid they might still be watching and I went down the cellar! Mike . . . I'm . . . I'm sorry."

"That's all right, Lily. I know how it is. Did you see them?"

"No. No, Mike?"

The shudder racked her body again and she bit into her finger.

"When . . . that man found me . . . I thought he was . . . one of them."

"You don't have to worry any more, Lily. I'm not going to leave you here alone again. Look, go in and clean up. Take a nice hot bath and fix your hair. Then get something in your stomach."

"Mike . . . are you . . . going out?"

"For a little while. I'll have the super's wife stay with you until I get back. Would you mind that?"

"You'll hurry back?"

I nodded that I would and picked up the phone. The super's wife said she'd be more than glad to help out and would come right up.

From in back of me Lily said, "I'm so dirty. Ask her to bring some rubbing alcohol, Mike."

She said she'd do that too and hung up. Lily had finished her drink and lay with her head against the back of the chair watching me sleepily. The tautness had left her cheeks and color had come back to her mouth. She looked like a dog who had just been lost in the swamp then suddenly found his way home.

I started the water in the tub, filled it and lifted her out of the chair. She was light in my arms, completely relaxed, her breathing soft against my face. There was something too big in her eyes while she was so close to me and the strain of it showed in the corner of her mouth. She dug her fingers into my arms with a repressed hunger of a sort, sucked in her breath in a series of almost soundless staccato jerks and before I could kiss her she twisted her head and buried it against my shoulder.

The super's wife came in while she was still splashing around in the tub. She made clucking noises like a mother hen and wanted to go right to her, but the door was locked so she started scrounging some chow up in the kitchen. The bottle of alcohol was on the table and before I left I knocked on the door.

"You want a rub-down, Lily?"

The water stopped splashing.

"Glad to give you a hand if you want," I said.

She laughed from inside and I felt better. I left the bottle by the door, told the mother hen I was leaving and got.

Seven thirty-two. The gray overcast brought a premature dusk to the city, a gloomy wet shroud that came down and poured itself inside your clothes. It was the kind of night that made the city withdraw into itself, leaving the sidewalks empty and people inside the glass-fronted stores staring aimlessly into the wet.

I left my car where it was and hopped a cab down to Canal. He let me out at Pascale's and I went in the door on the right of the place. Here the hall was clean, clear and well lit. You could hear the hum of voices from the gin mill through the walls, but it diminished as I went up the stairs.

She was a short woman, her hair neatly in place with a ready smile that said hello.

"Mrs. Wallace?"

"Yes."

"My name is Hammer. I'd like to talk to your husband if he's home."

"Certainly. Won't you come in?"

She stepped aside, closed the door and called out, "Harv, there's a gentleman here to see you."

From inside a paper rustled and kids' voices piped up. He said something to them and they quieted down. He came out to the kitchen with that expression one stranger has for another stranger, nodded to his wife, then to me and stuck out his hand.

"Mr. Hammer," his wife said and smiled again. "I'll go in with the children if you'll excuse me."

"Sit down, Mr. Hammer." He pulled a chair out by the table, waved me into it and took one himself. He was one of those big guys with beefy shoulders and thinning hair. There was Irish in his face and a trace of Scandinavian.

"This'll be quick," I told him. "I'm an investigator. I'm not digging up anything unpleasant just for the fun of it and what you say won't go any further."

His tongue rolled around his cheek and he nodded.

"Sometime ago you drove the truck that killed a man named Lee Kawolsky."

The side of his face moved.

"I explained . . ."

"You don't get the angle yet," I said. "Wait. As far as you were concerned it was an out-and-out accident. Your first. It was one of those things that couldn't be helped so you weren't touched for it."

"That's right."

"Okay. Like I said, it's been a long time since it happened. Nobody else but you saw it. Tell me, have you ever gone over the thing in your mind since?"

Harvey said very quietly, "Mr. Hammer . . . there are some nights when I never get to sleep at all."

"You could see the thing happen. Sometimes the details would be sharp, then they'd fade?"

He squinted his eyes at me. "Something like that."

"What are you uncertain about?"

"You know something, Mr. Hammer?"

"Maybe."

This time he leaned forward, his face set in a puzzled grimace. "It's not clear. I see the guy coming out from behind the L pillar and I'm yelling at him while I slam on the brakes. The load in the truck lets go and rams the wall back of the cab and I can feel the wheels . . ." He stopped and looked down at his hands. "He came out too fast. He didn't come out walking."

Harvey looked at me, his eyes beseeching. "You know what I mean? I'm not making up excuses."

"I know," I said.

"I came out of the cab fast and he was under the axle. I know I yelled for somebody to help me. Sometimes . . . I think I remember a guy running. Away, though. Sometimes I think I remember that and I can't be sure."

I stood up and put my hat on. "You can stop worrying then. It wasn't an accident." His eyes came wide open. "It was murder. Kawolsky was pushed. You were the sucker."

I opened a door, waved a finger at him. "Thanks for the help."

"Thank . . . you, Mr. Hammer."

"It's over with so there's no use fooling with the report," I said.

"No . . . but it's good to know. I won't be waking up in the middle of the night any more now."

Ten minutes after nine. In the lobby of the hotel a row of empty telephone booths gaped at me. Two people were sitting in the far corner holding hands. One other, not looking as though he belonged there, was reading the paper and dripping water all over the floor.

The girl at the magazine counter changed a buck into dimes for me and I took the end booth on the row.

Thirty cents got me my party. His voice was deep and fat and it never sounded right coming out of the skinny little neck. He'd need a shave and his suit pressed but he didn't give a damn for either. He was strictly a nobody up until the squash was put on bookie operations then all of a sudden he was a somebody. He had a mind like a recording machine and was making hay in the new deal of black-market betting operations.

I said, "Dave?"

"Right here."

"Mike Hammer."

The voice got closer to the phone and almost too casual. I could see him with his hand cupped around the mouthpiece and his eyes watching everybody in the place. "Sure, boy, what'cha doin?"

"They're saying things along the row, Dave?"

"Piling up, big boy. Everybody got it."

"How do you feel about it?"

"Come on, mister, you know better'n that." The meaning sifted out of his words and I grinned. There was no humor in the grin.

I said, "I got what they want, kid. You tell it in the right places."

"You're killing me. Try again."

"So you saw me. I was in the bag and let it slip."

His voice dropped an octave. "Look, I'll do a lot of things, but you don't mess with them monkeys. They make a guy talk. Me, I got a big mouth when I get hurt up."

"It'll set, Dave. This is a big one. If it was a little one I'd ask somebody else. They got Velda. Understand that?"

He said three sharp, nasty curses at the same time. "You're trading."

"I'm willing. If it don't come off I'll blow the thing apart."

"Okay, Mike. I'll spin it. Don't bother calling me again, okay?"

"Okay," I said and hung up.

I walked over to the desk and the clerk smiled. "Room, sir?"

"Not now, thanks. I'd like to see the manager."

"I'm afraid you can't. He's gone for the evening. You see . . ."

"He live here?"

"Why, er . . . why, yes, but . . . "

I let a bill do the talking. The guy was well-dressed but underpaid and the ten looked big. "No trouble. I have to speak to him. He won't know."

The bill left my fingers magically. "Suite 101." He pointed a long forefinger across the room. "Take the stairs past the mezzanine. It's quicker."

There was a buzzer beside the door. I leaned on it until I heard the knob turn and a middle-aged, sensitive Latin face was peering out at me. The professional smile creased his lower jaw, pulling the thin mustache tighter and he cocked his head in an attentive attitude ready to hear my complaint. His eyes were telling me that he trusted it would be a good one because Mr. Carmen Trivago was preparing to leave in a moment for a very important engagement.

I gave him a shove that wiped the smile clean off his face and he stumbled back inside while I closed the door. There was an instantaneous flash of mingled terror and hatred in his expression that dissolved into indignation as he drew himself up stiffly and said, "What is the meaning of this?"

"Get back inside."

"I . . . "

My hand cracked him across the mouth so hard he hit the wall, flattened against it, making unintelligible noises in his throat. He wasn't so stiff when I gave him a shove into the living room. He was all loose and jelly-like as if his bolts were ready to come apart.

I said, "Turn around and look at me." He did. "I'm going to ask you things and you answer them right. If you think you'd do better by lying look at my face and you won't lie. Let me catch you in one and I'll mangle you so damn bad you won't even crawl out of this dump for a month. Just for the hell of it I ought to do something to you now so you know I'm not kidding about it."

Carmen Trivago couldn't stand up any more. His knees went as watery as his eyes and he slumped crookedly on the edge of a chair.

"No . . . don't . . . "

"His right name was Nicholas Raymondo. With an 'O.' You were the only one who knew that. I thought it was your accent, but you knew his name, didn't you?"

His mouth opened to speak but the words wouldn't come out. He nodded dumbly.

"Where'd he get his dough?"

The spread of his hands said he didn't know and before he could shake his head to go with it I rocked him with another open-handed slap that left the prints of my fingers across his jaw.

He couldn't take anything at all and tried to burrow into the chair while he moaned, "Please. No . . . I tell you . . . anything. Please."

"When, then?"

"He had . . . the business. From abroad he . . . "

"I know about that. Business didn't give him the kind of money he spent."

"Yes, yes. It is true. But he never said. He spoke of big things but he never said . . . "

"He liked dames."

Carmen's eyes told me he didn't get what I was driving at.

I said slowly, "So do you. Two of a kind, you guys. Lady killers. You knew his right name. Those things only come when you know a person. You know that much and you know a lot more. Think about it. I'll give you a minute. Just one."

His neck seemed to stretch out of shape as he held his head up. The longer he looked at me the more he curled up inside and his mouth started to move. "It is true . . . he had the money. It was enough. He was . . . satisfied to spend it all on much foolishness. There would be more soon, he told me, much more. At first . . . I thought he was making a boast. But no. He was serious. Never would he tell me more than that."

I took a slow step a little closer to him.

His hands went up to hold me off. "It is true, I swear it! This other money . . . several times when he was feeling, how you say it, high? he would ask me how I would like to have two million dollars. It was always the same. Two million dollars. I would ask how to get it and would smile. Raymondo . . . he had it, I know he had it. I tell you, this money was no good. I knew it would happen someday. I knew . . . "

"How?"

This time his eyes made passes around me, looking for something that wasn't there yet. "Before he . . . died . . . there were men. I knew of these men."

"Say the word."

It almost stuck in his throat, but he managed it. "Mafia," he said hoarsely.

"Did Raymondo know he was being followed?"

"I do not think so."

"You didn't tell him?"

He looked at me as if I was crazy.

"You never thought he was killed accidentally either, did you?" The fear showed in his face so plain it was a voice by itself. "You knew the score right along," I said.

"Please . . ."

"You're a crummy little bastard, Trivago. There's a lot of dead people lying around because you made them that way."

"No, I . . ."

"Shut up. You could have sounded off."

"No!" He stood up, his hands claws that dangled at his sides. "I know them! From Europe I know them and who am I to speak against them. You do not understand what they do to people. You . . ."

My knuckles cracked across his jaw so hard he went back over the arm of the chair and spilled in a heap on the floor. He lay there with his eyes wide open and the spit dribbling out of his open mouth started to turn pink. He was the bug caught in the web trying to hide from the spider and he backed into the hornet's next.

Carmen Trivago would never be the same again.

I used the phone in the lobby again. I buzzed my apartment and the super's wife answered it. I hadn't told her not to do so, she was doing me a favor. I told her it was me, asked if everything was okay and she said it was. Lily was asleep with the door locked but she could hear her breathing and talking in there. Her husband was making doubly sure things stayed quiet by pretending to do some work in the hall outside.

There were three other phone calls. A Captain Chambers had called and wanted to see me right away. I thanked her and hung up.

I turned up the collar of my trench coat and stepped out into the rain. The wind was lashing it up the street in waves now, pounding it against the buildings, and as the cars went by you had a quick look at the drivers as the wipers ripped it aside before the faces muddled into a liquid haze.

The cab didn't wait to be called. He pulled into the curb and I hopped in, gave him the address and stuck a smoke in my mouth.

Someplace Velda was looking at the rain. It wouldn't be a pleasant sound, not this time. She'd be crazy with fear, scared so hard she wouldn't be able to think. They weren't the kind you could stall. She could only wait. And hope.

And someplace the people who had her were thinking too. They were thinking of a long string of kills and two fresh ones propped up against a dead-end sign. They were thinking of the word that went out and before they'd do anything at all they'd think harder still and it wouldn't be until I was dead that they'd feel right to do what they wanted to her.

I wasn't the cops and I wasn't the feds. I was one guy by himself but I was one who could add to the score without giving a damn at all. I was the one guy they were afraid of because the trail of dead men hadn't stopped yet. It was a trail that had to be walked and they were afraid of stepping on it.

Pat was in his office. You had to look twice to make sure he wasn't asleep, then you saw the light glinting off his almost-closed eyes and saw the movement of his mouth as he sucked on the dry pipe.

I threw my hat on the desk and sat down. He didn't say anything. I got out my next-to-last Lucky, held a light to it and let the smoke go. He still didn't say anything. I didn't have the time to trade thoughts. "Okay, chum, what is it?"

The pipe came out of his mouth slowly. "You conned me, Mike."

I started to get warm all over, an angry flush that burned into my chest. "Great. Just like that I gave you the business! You don't say anything . . . you sit there like a dummy then pull the cork. Say what's eating you or I'll get the hell out of here."

What distrust was in his face turned uncertain. "Mike, this thing is a bombshell. The biggest staff that ever operated on one case is out there working. They're going night and day looking for the answer, then you come up with it ready to trade off for something."

I sat back in the chair. I took a deep, relieved pull on the smoke and grinned. "Thanks for the compliment. I didn't know it would get back so fast. Where'd you pick it up?"

"Every stoolie we know has his ears open. What are you trading for?"

My grin pulled tight at the edges, flattened across my teeth and stayed that way. "Velda. The bastards have Velda. She suckered Al Affia into a trap that didn't work and got caught in one herself. She played it too smart and now they have her."

It was quiet in the room. The clock on the wall hummed over the drone of the rain outside, but that was all.

"You don't look too worked up about it," Pat said. Then he saw my eyes and took it back without saying so out loud.

"They'll want to be sure. They'll want to know if I have it or not before they cut loose on her. They'll have to be sure. Right in the beginning they thought Berga Torn passed it on to me, went through my apartment. If it was anybody else they could have taken it easy, but not with me. They knew what was going to happen."

"Let's have it, Mike."

"The answer?" I said. I shook my head. "I don't have it. Not where I can reach out and touch it yet. I need more details."

"So do we. I thought we were sharing this thing."

"I didn't forget. What have you got?"

Pat stared at me a long time, reached out and fanned a few papers across his desk. "Berga didn't escape from the sanitarium. She had it planned for her. She had a guest early that evening, a woman. The name and address were phony and we got no description except that she had brown hair. An attendant stated that she was pretty nervous after the guest left."

I cut in with, "How come you're just finding this stuff out?"

"It's a private sanitarium and they were afraid of ruining their reputation. They held off until we scared them. Anyway, we checked everybody in the place that night and came up with a spot from a couple of female visitors in the next room.

"When the closing bell rang they stood outside in the hall a few minutes talking. They were close to Berga's door and overheard a voice saying . . . " He glanced down at the sheet and read from it ". . . 'they're after you. They were at the house today.' " The rest of it we had to put together and when we had it the dame was telling her something about the main gate, to be as casual as possible, and there would be a car waiting for her at the northwest corner."

Pat stopped and tapped the sheet. He tapped the stem of the pipe against his teeth and said, "On that corner was an F.B.I. wagon so whoever was waiting had to take up another spot. She got scared out of the deal and started hitchhiking when she didn't see the person she was expecting."

I said, "She saw the person, all right. He was in another car. She knew damn well she was being followed."

"There's something wrong," Pat said.

"Yeah. Like murders on the books as accidents."

Pat's jaw worked. "Proof?"

"No, but that's the way it happened." I couldn't see his face, but I knew what he was thinking. In his own way he had covered every detail I had. "The first one was Nicholas Raymond. That's where the answer is, Pat."

His eyes peered out at me. "Nicholas Raymond was a Mafia agent. He ran an import business as an excuse to make frequent overseas trips."

I didn't answer so he said, ". . . he was the guy who ran the stuff into this country that was turned into cash for Mafia operations."

He was watching me so closely that you couldn't see anything but the black pupils of his eyes. His face was all screwed up with the intensity of watching me and it was all I could do to hold still in the chair. I covered by dragging in another lungful of smoke and letting it go toward the ceiling so I could do something with my mouth except feel it try to stretch out of shape.

The picture was perfect now. It was the most beautiful piece of art work I had ever seen. The only trouble was I couldn't make out what it was all about nor who drew it.

I said, "How much would two million in narcotics before the war be worth now, Pat?"

"About double."

I got up and put on my hat. "That's what you're looking for, friend. A couple of shoe boxes that big. If I find them I'll tell you about it."

"Do *you* know where it is?"

"No. I have a great big fat idea, but if it's stayed buried this long it won't hurt anybody staying buried a while longer. All I want is the person who is after it because that person has Velda. If I have to I'll dig it up and trade for her."

"Where are going now?"

"I think I'm going out and kill somebody, Pat," I said.

chapter eleven ▰▰▰▰▰▰▰▰▰

THE COP AT the switchboard told me to go ahead and use the phone. He plugged in an outside line and I dialed the number that got me Michael Friday. I said, "Your line clear? This is Mike."

"Mike! Yes . . . There's no one here."

"Good. Now listen. There's a place called the Texan Bar on

Fifty-sixth Street. Get down there as fast as you can. I'll be waiting. You got that?"

"Yes, but . . . ."

I hung up on her. It was the best thing you could do with a woman when you wanted her to move fast. She'd be a good hour getting there which was just what I needed.

They were changing shifts outside the building and the flow of cops was getting thicker. I stepped outside, flagged down a cab and gave him the address of Al Affia's place. The rain had thinned traffic down to a minimum and he didn't take long getting there.

Nothing had changed. The blood was still there on the floor, dried into a crusty maroon. Close to the door the air was a little foul and inside it was worse. I shoved the door open, snapped on the light and there was Al grinning at me from the corner of the room, but it was a horrible kind of grin because somebody had broken him into pieces with the whiskey bottle. He wasn't killed plain. He was killed fancy as a person could be killed. He was killed so that he couldn't make any sound as he died and whoever did it must have had a great time laughing because Al died slow.

What I came for was gone. There were still two of the blueprints on the table but they showed the layout of the docks. The rest were missing. I picked the phone up, dialed the operator and said very quietly, "Operator . . . get me the local office of the F.B.I."

Somebody said briskly, "Federal Bureau of Investigation, Moffat speaking."

"You better get down here, Moffat," I said. I laid the phone down gently alongside the base and walked out.

They'd know. They were lads you never noticed in the crowd, but they were all eyes and ears and brains. They worked quietly and you never read about them in the papers, but they got things done and they'd know. Maybe they knew a lot more than I thought they'd know.

She was waiting for me at the bar. She was a lusty, beautiful woman with a mouth that made you hungry when she smiled at you as you came in. There was humor in her eyes, but the wonder and curiosity showed below in the little lines that radiated from the corners of her lips.

There was nothing in mine. I could feel them flat and dull in their sockets. I nudged my chin to the booths in the back and she followed me. We sat down and she waited for me to say something and all I could think of was the last time I had sat here it was with Velda and now time was getting short.

I took the cigarette she held out from the case, lit it and leaned on the table. "How much do you love your brother, kid?"

"Mike . . . "

"I'm asking the questions."

"He's my brother."

"Partially."

"That's doesn't matter."

"He's mixed up in one of the dirtiest rackets you'll ever find. He has a part in it someplace and is paid off in the blood and terror you'll find wherever you find the Mafia operating. He's part of a chain of killers and thieves, yet you like what his money can buy. Your love doesn't stop anyplace, does it?"

She sat away from me as if I held a snake out at her.

"Stop, Mike, please stop!"

"You can stay on his side or mine, kid. The choice is up to you."

The hysteria was caught in her chest. Her mouth wasn't pretty any more. One little sob got loose and that was all. "Al Affia is dead. So far he's the latest. He isn't the last. Where do you stand?"

It came out slowly. She fought it all the way and won it. "With you, Mike."

"I need some information. About Berga Torn." She dropped her head and toyed with the ashtray. "Your brother played around with her some time ago. Why?"

"He . . . hated that woman. She was a tramp. He hated tramps."

"Did she know it?"

Michael shook her head. "In public he seemed fond of her. When we were alone . . . he said awful things about her."

"How far did he go?"

She looked up helplessly. "He kept her. I don't know why he did it . . . he didn't like her at all. The woman he did care for at the time left him because he spent all his time . . . nights . . . with Berga. Carl . . . was upset about it. One night he had an argument with someone about her in his study. He was so mad afterward he went out and got drunk, but he never saw Berga after that. He had an argument with her, too."

"You know about Carl's testifying before a congressional committee?"

"Yes. It . . . didn't seem to bother him. Not until . . . he heard that . . . she was going to speak against him."

"That was never made public."

"Carl has friends in Washington," she said simply.

"Yet he never worried about it?"

"No."

"Let's go back further, sugar. Let's go back before the war. Was there any time you can remember when something bothered Carl so much it damn near drove him nuts?"

The shadows around her eyes deepened, her hands pressed together tightly and she said, "How did you know? Yes, there was . . . a time."

"Now go over it slowly. Think about it. What did he do?"

Something panicky crossed her face. "I . . . nothing. He was hardly ever home. He wouldn't let me talk to him at all. When he was at home all he did was make long-distance calls. I remember because the phone bill was almost a thousand dollars for the month."

My breath was coming in hot. It hissed in between my teeth with a whisper and burned into my lungs. I said, "Can you get that bill? Can you get the itemized list that went with it?"

"I . . . might. Carl keeps everything . . . in the safe at home. Once I saw the combination on the back of the desk blotter."

I wrote down an address. Pat's. But all I gave her was the address and the apartment number. "Find it. When you do, bring it here." I folded the paper into her hand and she dropped it into her bag after looking at it long enough to etch it into her memory.

He'd get it. He'd pass it on and the boys in the blue suits would tie into it. They had the men and the time and the means. They'd do in a day what it would take me a year to do.

I snubbed out my butt, pulled the belt tight on the trench coat and stood up. "You'll spend the rest of your life hating yourself for doing this. Hating me too. If it gets too much I'll take you around and show you a lot of dirty little kids who are orphans and some widows your own age. I can show you pictures of bodies so cut up you'll get sick. I'll show you reports of kids who have killed and are condemned to death because they were sky-high on dope when they decided to see what it was like to burn a man down. You won't be stopping it all. You'll slow it down a little, maybe, but a few people who would have died will go on living because of you."

For a few seconds she seemed completely empty. If there was any emotion in her it had drained out and all she was left with were her thoughts. They showed on her face, every one of them. They showed when she looked back into the past and brought to life what she had known all along but had refused to acknowledge. They showed when the life came back to her eyes and her mouth. She tilted one eyebrow at me, did something to her head that shook her hair loose down her back.

"I won't hate you, Mike? Myself, perhaps, but not you."

I think she knew it then. The thought of it hung in the air like a charged cloud. Michael said, "They'll finally kill me, won't they, Mike." It wasn't a question.

"What's left of them . . . if they ever find out . . . would like to think they will. They'd like to kill me too. You can always remember one thing because they'll be remembering it too. They're not as big as they think they are."

She smiled, a wan, drawn smile. "Mike . . ."

I took the hand she held out to me.

"Kiss me again. Just in case."

The wetness glistened on her lips. They were firm lips, large, ripe, parted slightly over the even lines of her teeth. There was fire there that grew hotter as I came closer. I could see her mouth open even more, the tip of her tongue impatiently waiting, then the impatience broke and it met me before lips did.

I held her face in my hands, heard the soft moan she made, felt her nails biting into my arms through the coat, then I let her go. She trembled so violently she had to press her hands against the booth and the fiery liquid of her mouth passed on into her eyes.

"Please go, Mike," she said.

And I went. The rain took me back again, put its arms around me and held tight. I became part of the night, part of the wet, part of the noise and life that was the city. I could hear it laughing at me, a low, dull rumble with a sneer in it.

I walked down the side streets, crossed the avenues and got back to my kind of people again. I drifted through the night while my mind was days away and I was saying it off to myself and wondering how many other people were doing the same things. I was looking at a picture through the rain, knowing what was going on and not being able to make out the details.

It was a picture of a grim organization that stretched out its tentacles all over the world with the tips reaching into the highest places possible. It was an organization fed on the money of destruction and one tentacle was starving. The two million that was sent to feed it never arrived. No, that was wrong. It did arrive, but someplace it sat and was still there. In its sitting it had doubled its worth and the tentacle wanted it bad. It had to feast now to live. It was after the food with all the fury of its hunger, ready to do anything in the final, convulsive gesture of survival.

You could say it started with Berga. She wasn't the girl in the headlights any longer. She was younger now, a tall luscious Viking with eyes that could draw a man. She was a blonde snare with a body full of playful curves that held out triple challenges, a body full of dares waiting to be taken up. She was coming home from a visit to Italy and in the hidden hours on board that ship she had found a person who was ready to call the dare. He wasn't a special kind of a man. He was a guy with a small export business who could pass unnoticed in the crowd. He was a guy with a legitimate excuse to travel at certain times. He was a guy who was part of a great plan, a guy named Nicholas Raymond who really wasn't anything at all and because of it was the one they used as a messenger to bring in the vital food for the tentacle over here.

But he had a fault and because of it a lot of people died and the tentacle was starving. He liked the women. And Berga was special. He liked her so much he never followed the plan of delivery through and made plans to use the stuff himself. He and Berga. Two million bucks after conversion. Tax free. Someplace the stuff was still there. Maybe it took them a long time to find him again, or maybe they wanted the stuff first and were afraid the secret would die with him. However it was it took him a while to die. Maybe they thought Berga had it then. And she died. That put it on me.

I was thinking of something then. Horror, terror, fear . . . all of it that was there in her face for a little while, a confusion of emotions that stopped too suddenly.

I cursed to myself as the minute details started to fall into place, spun around and yelled at a cab. He jammed on the brakes, swerved slightly and was hardly stopped before I had the door opened. I told him where to take me and sat on the edge of the seat until we got there.

The elevator took me up to my office. I got out jangling my keys from my hand, stuck one in the lock and turned it. The outer office was empty, her typewriter a forlorn thing under its cover. Velda's desk was covered with mail separated into classified piles of bills, personals and miscellaneous. I went through them twice, didn't find what I was looking for, then spotted the pile that had come through the door slot I had pushed aside when I came in. There wasn't anything there, either. I went back to the desk, the curse still in my mouth when I saw it. The sheet lay under the stapler with the top under the flap of the envelope. I turned it over and saw the trade name of a gasoline company.

It was a simple statement. One line. *"The way to a man's heart—"* and under it the initials, *"B.T."* Velda would have known, but Velda never saw it. Berga must have scribbled it at the service station after lifting the address from the registration tacked to the steering post of my heap, but it was the old address. The new one was on the back out of sight and she hadn't seen the lines drawn through the words that voided it.

I looked at it, remembered her face again and knew what she was thinking when she wrote it. I felt the thing crumple in my hand as I squashed it in my fingers and never heard the door open behind me.

He stood in the doorway of my inner office and said, "I trust you can make something out of it. We couldn't."

I knew he had a gun without looking. I knew there were more of them without seeing them and I didn't give a damn in the world because I knew the voice. *I knew the voice and it was the one I said I'd never forget!* The last time it spoke I was supposed to die and before it could speak again I let out a crazy sound of hate that filled the room and was at them in a crouch with the bullets spitting over my head. I had the guy in my hands feeling my fingers tear his eyes loose while he screamed his lungs out and even the gun butt pounding on the back of my skull didn't stop me. I had enough left to lash out with my foot and hear it bite into flesh and bone and enough left to do something to one of them that turned his stomach inside out in my face. The horrible, choked scream of anguish one was letting out on the floor diminished to a whimper before disappearing altogether in the blackness that was closing in around me. Far in the distance I thought I heard sharp, flat sounds and a voice swearing hoarsely. Then I heard nothing at all.

It was a room. It had one window high off the floor and you could see the pinpoints that were stars through the film of dirt on the glass. I was spread-eagled on the bed with my hands and legs pulled tight to the frame and when I tried to twist, the ropes bit into my skin and burned like acid. The muscles in my side had knotted in pain over ribs that were torturous hands gripping my chest.

There was a taste of blood in my mouth and as I came awake my stomach turned over and dragged long, agonized retches up my throat. I tried to breathe as deeply as I could, draw the air down to stop the retching. It seemed to take a long time before it stopped. I lifted my head and felt my hair stick to the bed. The back of it throbbed and felt like it was coming off so I let it ease back until the giddiness passed.

The room took shape, a square empty thing with a musty odor

of disuse filling it. I could see the single chair in one corner, the door in the wall and the foot of the bed. I tried to move, but there wasn't an inch of play in the ropes and the knots that tied them only seemed to get tighter.

I wondered how long I had been there. I listened for sounds I could place but all I got was the steady drip of water outside the window. It was still raining. I listened even more intently, straining my ears into the silence and then I knew about how long I had been there.

My watch had stopped. I could see the luminous hands and number so it hadn't broken . . . it just stopped. This wasn't the same night it had happened. Everything I felt seemed to pour out of my mouth and I fought those damned ropes with every ounce of strength in me. They bit in, cut deeper and held like they were meant to and when I knew it wasn't any use fighting them I slumped back cursing myself for being so jackassed stupid as to walk into the deal without a rod and let them take me. I cursed myself for letting Velda do what she wanted to and cursed myself for not playing it right with Pat. No, I had to be a damned hero. I had to make it by myself. I had to take on the whole organization at once knowing what they were like and how they operated. I passed out advice all around then forgot to give some of it to myself.

There were footsteps in the other room that padded up to the door. It opened into an oblong of yellow light framing the man and the one behind him who stood there. They were opaque forms without faces but it didn't matter any more. One said, "He awake?"

"Yeah, he's out of it."

They came in and stood over me. Two of them and I could see the billies in their hands.

"Tough guy. You were hard to take, mister. You know what you did? You pulled the eyes right out of Foreman. He screamed so loud my friend here had to tap him one and he tapped too hard and now Foreman's lying in a Jersey swamp dead. They don't come like Foreman any more. You know something else? You ruptured Duke, you bastard. You fixed him good, you did."

"Go to hell," I said.

"Still tough. Sure, you got to keep up the act. You know it won't do any good even if you got down on your knees and begged." He grunted out a laugh. "Pretty soon the boss is coming in here. He's going to ask you some questions and to make sure

you answer we're going to soften you up a little bit. Not much
. . . just a little bit."

The billy went up slowly. I couldn't keep my eyes off it. The
thing reached his shoulder then snapped down with a blur of
motion and smashed into my ribs. They both did it then, a pair
of sadistic bastards trying to kill me by inches, then one made
the mistake of cutting for my neck and got the side of my head
instead and that wonderful, sweet darkness came back again where
there was no more pain or sound and I tumbled headlong into
the pool.

But the same incredible pain that had brought the sleep brought
the awakening. It was a pain that turned my whole body into a
mass of broken nerve ends that shrieked their messages to my
brain. I lay there with my mouth open sucking in air, wishing I
could die, but knowing at the same time I couldn't yet.

*The body doesn't stand for that kind of torture very long. It
shocks itself into forgetting it and soon the pain goes away. It isn't
gone for good, but the temporary relief is a kiss of love. It lies
there in that state of extreme emergency, caring for its own, and
when the realization of another emergency penetrates it readies
itself to act again.*

I had to think. There had to be gimmick somewhere and I had
to find it. I could see the outlines of the bed and feel the ropes
that tied me to the steel frame. It was one of those fold-away
things with a heavy innerspring mattress and I was laced down
so tightly my hands dented the rolled edges of it. I looked down
at my toes, over my head at my hands and took the only way
out.

There was noise to it, time involved, and pressures that started
the blood flowing down my wrists again. I rocked the bed sideways
until it teetered on edge, then held my breath as it tipped. I hit
the floor and the thing came halfway over on top of me before
it slithered back on its side. The mattress had pulled out from
under my feet and when I kicked around I got the lower half
entirely free of the springs. I had to stop and get my breath, then
when I tried the second time it came away from under my hands
too and I had the play in the ropes that I needed. They were wet
and slippery with my own blood. My fingernails broke tugging at
them, but it was the blood that did it. I felt one come free, the
next one and my hand was loose. It only took a few minutes
longer to get the other one off and my feet off the end of the
bed and I was standing up with my heart trying to pound the
shock away and the pain back in place.

I didn't let it get that far. I was half drugged with exertion but I knew what I had to do. I put the bed back on its legs, spread the mattress out and got back the way I had been. I was able to dummy the ropes around both feet and one hand and hoped they wouldn't see the one I couldn't get to.

Time. Now I could use a little time. Every second of it put strength back in my body. I lay there completely relaxed, my eyes closed. I tried to bring the picture back in focus and got part of it. I got Berga and Nicholas Raymond and a guy pushing him into the path of a truck. I was thinking that if they had pulled an autopsy on the body they would have found a jugful of stuff in his veins that made him a walking automaton.

The picture got just a little bit clearer and I could see the work they did on Berga. Oh, it had to be easy. With two million bucks in the bag you don't barge around until you're sure what you're doing. First they tried to scare her, then came the big con job. Carl Evello, the man-about-town putting on the heavy rush act, trying to get close enough to the babe to see what she knew.

I thought about it while I lay there, trying to figure the mind of one little guy who thought he could beat the Mafia out of a fortune and pretty soon I was reading his thoughts as if they were my own. Raymond had planned pretty well. In some way he had planted the secret of his cache with Berga so that she'd have to do some tall thinking to get to it. It had taken her a long time, but she had finally caught on and the Mafia knew when she did. She had hired a bodyguard that didn't work but she still wouldn't let go of what she knew because as soon as she did she'd take the long road too. Maybe she saw her way out of it when Uncle Sam put the squeeze on Evello. Maybe she thought with him away she'd have a chance. If she did she thought wrong. They still got to her.

My eyes opened and squinted at the ceiling. A couple more details were looking for a place to crawl into and I was just about to shove them there when I heard the voices outside.

They didn't try to be quiet. Two of them were bragging that I'd be ready to spill my guts and the other one said I had better be. It was a quiet voice that wasn't a bit new to me. It said, "Wait here and I'll see."

"You want us to come in, boss? He might need more softening."

"I'll call you if he does."

"Okay, boss."

Chairs rasped against the floor as the door opened. I could see the two of them there starting to open a bottle on the table, then the door closed and he was feeling for a light switch. He swore at the blackness, struck a match and held it out in front of him. There was no light, but a candle in a bottle was on the chair and he lit it. He put the bottle down beside me, drew up the chair and lit a cigarette.

The smoke tasted sweet in my nostrils. I licked my lips as I watched the butt glow a deep red and he grinned as he blew the cloud across my face.

I said, "Hello, Carl." I made it good and snotty, but he didn't lose the grin.

"The infamous Mike Hammer. I hope the boys did a good job. They can do a better one if I let them."

"They did a good job."

I rolled my head and took a good look at him. "So, you're . . . the boss."

The grin changed shape this time. One side of it dropped caustically. "Not quite . . . yet." The evil in his eyes danced in the candlelight. "Perhaps by tomorrow I will be. I'm only the boss locally . . . now."

"You louse," I said. The words seemed to have an effort to them. My breathing was labored, coming through my teeth. I closed my eyes, stiffened and heard him laugh.

"You did a lot of legwork for us. I hear you blundered right on what we have been looking for."

I didn't say anything.

"You wanted to trade. Where is it?"

I let my eyes come open. "Let her go first."

He gave me that twisted grin again. "I'm not trading for her. Funny enough, I don't even know where she is. You see, she wasn't part of my department."

It took everything I could do to hold still. I could feel the nervous tremors creeping up my arms and I made fists of my hands to keep from shaking.

"It's you I'm trading for. You can tell me or I can walk out of here and say something to the boys. You'll want to talk then."

"The hell with you."

He leaned a little closer. "One of the boys is a knife man. He likes to do things with a knife. Maybe you can remember what he did to Berga Torn." I could see the smile on his face get ugly. "That isn't even a little bit what he'll do to you."

The side of his hand traced horrible gestures across my body, meaningful, cutting gestures with the nastiest implications imaginable in them. Then the gestures ended as the side of his palm sliced into my groin for emphasis and the yell that started in my throat choked off in a welter of pain and I mumbled something Carl seemed to want to hear and he bent forward saying, "What? What?"

And that repeated question was the last Carl Evello ever spoke again because he got too close and there were my hands around his throat squeezing so hard his flesh buried my fingers while his eyes were hard little marbles trying to roll out of their sockets. I squeezed and pushed him on his knees and there wasn't even any sound at all. His fingernails bit into my wrists with an insane fury that lived only a few seconds, then relaxed as his head went back with his tongue swelling in the gaping opening that was his mouth. Things in his throat stretched and popped and when I let go there was only the slightest wheeze of air that trickled back into lungs that were almost at the bursting point.

I got him on the bed. I spread him out the way I had been and let him lie there. The joke was too good to pass up so Carl lived a minute longer than he should have. I tried to make my voice as close to his as I could and I called to the door, "He talked. Now put him away."

Outside a chair scraped back. There was a single spoken word, silence, and the slow shuffle of footsteps coming toward the door. He didn't even look at me. He walked up to the bed and I could hear the *snick* as the knife opened. The boy was good. He didn't drive it in. He put it in position and pushed. Carl's body arched, trembled and as I stepped away from the candle the boy saw the mistake and knew he had made the last one. I put everything I could find into the swing that caught the side of his neck and mashed his vertebrae into his spinal cord and he was dead before I eased him to the floor.

Cute. Getting cuter all the time.

I came out of the door with a yell I couldn't keep inside me and dived at the guy at the table. His frenzied stare of hesitation cost him the second he needed to clear his rod and while he was still digging for it my fingers were ripping into his face and my body smashed him right out of the chair. The gun hit the floor and bounced across the room.

My knees slammed into him, brought a scream bubbling out of his mouth that snapped off when my fist twisted his jaw out of shape. He didn't try for the gun any more. He just reached for his face and tried to cover it but I didn't let him have the pleasure out of not seeing what was happening. His eyes had to watch everything I did to him until they filmed over and blanked out when the back of his head cracked against the floor. The blood trickled out his nose and ears when I stood over him, a bright red that seemed to match the fire burning in my lungs. I pulled him inside to the other two, tangled his arms around the boy who still held the knife and left them that way.

Then I left. I got out on the street and let the rain wash me clean. I breathed the air until the fire went out, until some of the life I had left back inside crawled into my system again.

The guy sitting in the doorway ten feet away heard me laugh. His head jerked up out of the drunken stupor and he looked at me. Maybe he could see the way my face was and understand what was behind the laugh. The eyes bleary with cheap whiskey lost their glassiness and he trembled a little bit, trying to draw back into his doorway. My laugh got louder and he couldn't stand it, so he stood up and lurched away, looking back twice to make sure I was still there.

I knew where I was. Once you put in time on Second Avenue you never forget it. The storefront I came out of was dirty and deserted. At one time it had been a lunch counter, but now all that was left was the grease stains and the FOR RENT sign in the window. The gin mill on the corner was just closing up, the last of the human rubble that inhabited the place drifting across the street until he dissolved into the mist.

I walked slow and easy, another one of the dozens you could see sprawled out away from the rain. Another joe looking for a place to park, another joe who couldn't find one. I made the police call box on the second corner down, got it open and said hello when I heard the voice answer. I didn't have to try hard to put a rasp into my voice, I said, "Copper, you better get somebody down this way fast. Somebody screaming his head off in that empty dog wagon two blocks south."

Two minutes were all they took. The siren whined through the rain and the squad car passed me with its tires spitting spray. They'd find a nice little mess, all right. The one guy left could talk his head off, but he was still going to cook in the hot squat up the river.

I pulled my wallet out and went through it. Everything was there except money. Even my change was gone. I needed a dime like I never needed one before and there wasn't even a character around to bum one from. Down the street, lights of a diner threw a yellow blob on the sidewalks. I walked toward it, stood outside the door a second looking at the two drunks and the guy with the trombone case perched on the stools.

There wasn't any more I could lose so I walked in, called the counterman over and tossed my watch on the counter. "I need a dime. You can hold my watch."

"For a dime? Mac, you nuts? Look, if you need some coffee say so."

"I don't need coffee. I want to make a phone call."

His eyes went up and down me and his mouth rounded into a silent "oh." "You been rolled, huh?" He fished in his pocket, tossed a dime on the counter and pushed my watch back to me. "Go ahead, mac, I know how it is."

Pat wasn't at home. My dime clinked back and I tried his office. I asked for Captain Chambers and he wasn't there either. The cop on the board wanted to take a message and the captain would take care of it when he came in. I said, "Pal, this kind of message won't wait. It's something he's been working on and if I can't get word to him right away he's going to hit the roof."

The phone dimmed out as the operator spoke away from it. I could hear the hurried exchange of murmurs, then: "We'll try to contact the captain by radio. Can you leave your phone number?"

I read it off the dial, told him I'd wait and hung up. The counterman was still watching me. There was a steaming hot cup of coffee by an empty stool with a half pack of butts lying alongside it. The guy grinned, nodded to the coffee and made himself a friend. Coffee was about all my stomach would hold, but it sat there inside me like a million bucks in my hand. It took the shakes out of my legs and the ache from my body.

I lit a smoke, relaxed and watched the window. The wind in the street whipped the rain against the plate glass until it rattled. The door opened, a damp blast momentarily freshening the air. Another musician with a fiddle case under his coat sat down tiredly and ordered coffee. Someplace off in the distance a siren moaned, and a minute later another crossed its fading echo. Two more came on top of it, not close, but distant voices racing to a sore spot in the great sprawling sick body of the city.

Corpuscles, I thought. That's what they were like. White corpuscles getting to the site of the infection. They'd close in and wipe out the parasites and if they were too late they'd call for the carpenter corpuscles to come and rebuild broken tissue around the wound.

I was thinking about it when Pat walked in, tired lines around his eyes, his face set in a frozen expression. There was a twitch in the corner of his mouth he tried to wipe away with the back of his hand.

He came over and sat down. "Who kicked the crap out of you, Mike?"

"I look that bad?"

"You're a mess."

I could grin then. Tomorrow, the next day, the day after, maybe, I'd be too sore to move, but right then I could grin. "They reached me but they didn't hold on to me, chum."

His eyes got narrow and very, very bright. "There was a dirty little mess not too far from here. That wouldn't be it, would it?"

"How good is it like it stands?"

Pat's lips came apart over his teeth. "The one guy left is wanted for three different kills. This one finishes him."

"The coroner say that?"

"Yeah, the coroner says that. I say that. We have two experts on the spot who say that too but the guy doesn't say that. The guy doesn't know what to say. He's still half out and he says things about a girl named Berga Torn he worked over and when he knew what he did it woke him up and now he won't say anything. He's the scaredest clam you ever saw in your life."

"So it stands?"

"Nobody'll break it. Now what do you say about it?"

I took a big pull on the butt and stamped it out in the ashtray. "It's a detail. Right now it doesn't mean a damn one way or other to you or me. Someday over a beer I'll make it into a good story."

"It better be good," Pat said. "I have all hell breaking loose around my ears. Evello's sister came to us with a list of phone calls yesterday and we tracked down the names into the damnedest places you ever saw. We have some of the wheels in the Mafia dangling by their you-know-whats and they're scramming for cover. They're going nuts down in Florida and on the Coast the police have pulled in people big enough to make your hair stand on end. Some of 'em are talking and the thing's opening wider."

He passed his hand over his eyes and drew it away slowly. "Damn it, we're up as far as Washington itself. It makes me sick."

The shake was back in my legs again. "Talk names, Pat."

"Names you don't know and some you do. We have the connections down pat but the ones up top are sitting tight. The Miami police pulled a quick raid on a local big shot and turned up a filing case of information that gives us a line into half the narcotics outlets in the States. Right now the federal boys have assigned extra men to pick up the stuff and they're coming home loaded."

"How about Billy Mist?" I asked him.

"Nothing doing. Not a word on him so far. He can't be located, anyway."

"Leo Harmody?"

"You got another case? He's howling police persecution and threatening to take things up with Congress. He can yell because there's nothing we can slap him with."

"And Al Affia's dead," I said.

Pat's head turned toward me, his eyes a sleepy gray. "You wouldn't know anything about that, would you?"

"It couldn't've happened to a better guy."

"He was chopped up good. Somebody had a little fun."

I looked at him, lit another smoke and flipped the match in the ashtray where it turned into a charred arc. "How far did you get with him?"

"Not a thing. There wasn't a recognizable print on that bottle."

"What's the word on it, Pat?"

His eyes got sleepier. "His waterfront racket is going skyhigh. There's been two killings down there already. The king is dead, but somebody is ready to take his place."

The rain had the sound of a rolling snare drum. It was working up in tempo, backed by the duller, more resonant peals of thunder that cracked the sky open. The three drunks stared at the window miserably, hugging their cups as an anchor to keep from drifting out into the night. The fiddle player shrugged, paid his bill and tucked the case back under his coat and left. At least he was lucky enough to grab an empty cab going by.

I said, "Do you have the picture yet, Pat?"

"Yeah, I have a picture," he said. "It's the biggest one I ever saw."

"You're lost, kid."

The sleepiness left his eyes. His fingers turned the ashtray around slowly, then he gave me that wry grin of his. "Play it out, Mike."

I shrugged. "Everything's coming your way. Now you're having fun. What started it?"

"Okay, so it began with Berga."

"Let's not forget it. Let's tie it all up together so when you're out there having fun you'll know why. I'll make it short and sweet and you can check on it. Ten, twelve, maybe fifteen years ago a guy was bringing a package of dope into the country for delivery to the Mafia. He tangled with a dame on board and fell for her. That's where Berga came into it. Instead of handing over the package he decided to keep it for his sweetie and himself even though he ran the risk of being knocked off."

"Nicholas Raymond," Pat said.

I knew the surprise showed on my face when I nodded. "Nicholas had them on the spot. They couldn't bump him until they located the stuff and he wasn't stupid enough to lead them to it. There was two million bucks' worth in that consignment and they needed it badly. So Nick goes on living with this gal and one day he dies accidentally. It's a tricky pitch but it isn't a hard one. They figured that by this time he would have passed the secret along to her or she would have found out herself somehow.

"But it didn't happen that way. Nick was trickier than they thought. He got the word to her in case something happened to him, but even she didn't know where it was or what it was that keyed it. I guess they must have tried to scare it out of her for a while because she hired herself a bodyguard. He played it too good and moved in. The Mafia didn't like that. If he came across the stuff they'd be out of luck, so he went too."

Pat was watching me closely. There was an expression on his face like I wasn't telling him anything new, but he wasn't saying a word.

"Now we come to Evello. He gets a proper knockdown to her somehow and off he goes on the big pitch. He gave her the whole treatment and probably winds it up with a proposal of marriage to make it sound good. Maybe he over-played his hand. Maybe he just wasn't smart enough to fool her. Something slipped and Berga got wise that he was one of the mob. But she got wise to something else too. *About then she suddenly discovered what it was they were all after and when she had the chance to get Evello creamed before that Congressional committee she put in her bid, figuring to get the stuff on her own hook later.*"

Now Pat's face was showing that he didn't know it all. There were sharp lines streaking out from the corners of his eyes and he waited, his tongue wetting down his lips from time to time.

I said, "She pulled out all the stops and so did they. The boys with the black hands get around. They scared her silly and by that time it didn't take much. She went to pieces and tried to fight it out in that sanitarium."

"That was her biggest mistake," Pat said.

"You mentioned a woman who came to see her."

He gave a slow nod, his hands opening and closing slowly. "We still can't make her."

"Could it have been a man dressed like a dame?"

"It could have been anything. There was no accurate description and no record of it."

"It was somebody she knew."

"Great."

"Now the stuff is still missing."

"I know where it is."

Pat's head came around faster this time.

"The two million turned into four by just sitting there," I said. "Inflation."

"Damn it, Mike, where?" His voice was all tight.

"On the good ship *Cedric*. Our friend Al Affia was working on the deal. He had given all the plans to her in his dive back there and whoever killed him walked off with them."

"Now you tell me," he said hoarsely. "Now you spill it when somebody has had time to dig it loose."

I took a deep breath, grunted when the sting of pain stabbed across my chest and shook my head. "It's not that easy, Pat. Al had those plans a long time. I'm even beginning to think I know why he was bumped."

Pat waited me out.

"He tried to sucker Velda into his dump for a fast play at her. She slipped him a dose of chloral and while he was out started turning the place upside down. Al didn't stay out very long. He got sick, his stomach dumped the stuff overboard and he saw what she was doing. Velda used the bottle on him then."

His eyes snapped wide open. "Velda."

"She didn't kill him. She bopped him one and it cut his head open. He staggered out after her and got word to somebody. That somebody caught the deal in a hurry and someplace she's still sweating." All at once every bit of pain in my body flooded back and trapped me in its agony before fading away. I finished with, "I hope."

"Okay, Mike, let it looose! Damn it, what else have you got? So the kid's sweating, you hope . . . and I hope too. You know them well enough to realize what's liable to happen to her now."

"She was on her way to see Billy Mist." My grin turned sour and my teeth came out from under my lips again. "The cops didn't find her."

"Supposing she never reached there?"

"It's a possibility I've been considering, friend. I saw her pass in a cab and she wasn't alone."

I was going warm again. The coffee didn't sit so well in my gut any more. I thought about it as long as I could, then shut out the picture when I buried my face in my hands.

Pat kept saying. "The bastards, the bastards!" His nails made a tattoo of sound on the counter and his breathing was almost as hard as mine was. "It's breaking fast, but it's not wide open yet, Mike. We'll get to Billy. One way or another."

I felt a little better. I took my hands away and reached for the last butt in the pack. "It won't break until you get the stuff. You and the whole staff up in Washington can work from now until ten years later and you won't make a hole in the organization big enough to stop it. You'll knock it kicking but you won't kill it. Slowing it down a little is all we can hope for. They're going to hang on to Velda until somebody has that four million bucks lined up."

"I'm the target, chum. Me personally. I've scared the crap out of those guys as individuals . . . not as an organization. They know I don't give a damn what happens to the outfit, the dough or anything that goes with it. All I want is a raft of hides nailed to the barn door. That's where I come in. I'm the little guy with a grudge. I'm the guy so damn burned up he's after a man, not an organization. I'm the guy who wants to stand there and see him die and he knows it. He wants that consignment of narcotics in the worst way but before it does him any good I have to die first.

"So they're holding Velda. She's the bait and she's something else besides. I've been getting closer to this than anybody else and they've known something I never got wise to. Berga passed the clue to me before she died and I've been sitting on it all this time. For a little while they had it, but they couldn't make it out. They expect me to. When I do I'll have to use it to ransom Velda with it."

"They're not that dumb, Mike," Pat told me.

"Neither am I. Someplace the answer slapped me in the teeth and I was in such a hurry I missed it. I can feel the damn thing crawling around in my head and can't lay my finger on it. The damn arrogant bastards . . . "

Pat said, "The head is pretty far from the body."

"What?"

He looked out the window and watched the rain. "They can afford to be arrogant. The entire structure of the Mafia is built on arrogance. They flaunt the laws of every country in the world, they violate the integrity of the individual, they're a power in themselves backed by ruthlessness, violence and some of the shrewdest brains in existence."

"About the head and the body, I mean."

"We can smash the body of this thing, Mike, but in this country the head and the body aren't connected except by the very thin thread of a neck. The top man, men, or group is a separate caste. The organization is built so that the head can function without the body if it comes to it. The body parts can be assembled any time, but it's an assembly for the benefit of the head, never forget that. It's a government. The little people in it don't count. It's the rulers who are important and the government is run solely for their benefit and to satisfy their appetites. They're never known and they're not going to be known."

"Unless they make one stinking little mistake," I said.

Pat stopped looking at the rain.

I rubbed the ache out of my side. "The stuff is on the *Cedric*. All you have to do is find the ship. The records will carry the stateroom Raymond used. When you find it call Ray Diker at the *Globe* and give him first crack at the details of the yarn. Tell him to hold the story until I call you. By then I'll have Velda."

"Where are you going?"

"The last time you asked that I said I was going out to kill somebody." I held out my hand. "Gimme a fin."

He looked puzzled, scowled, then pulled five ones out of his pocket. I laid two of them on the counter and nodded to the counterman to come get it. He was all smiles.

"Where's Michael Friday?"

"She said she was going to your place to see you."

"I wasn't home."

"Well, she's not reporting to me on the hour."

"No police guard?"

His frown got bigger this time. "I tried to but she said no. One of the feds pulled out after her anyway. He lost her when she got in a cab."

"Sloppy."

"Lay off. Everybody's up to their ears in this thing."

"Yeah. You going to trace the *Cedric?*"

"What do you think. Where are you going?"

I let a laugh out that sounded hollow as hell. "I'm going out in the rain and think some more. Then maybe I'll go kill somebody else."

I could see Pat remembering the other years. Younger years when the dirt seemed to be only on the surface. When being a cop looked good and the law was for protection and guidance.

When there weren't so many strings and sticky red tape and corruption in high places.

His hand went into his pocket and brought out the blued .38. He handed it to me under the shelf of the hanger. "Here, use this for a change."

And I remembered what Velda had said and I shook my head. "Some other time. I like it better this way."

I went out and walked down the street and let the rain hit me in the face. Someplace there was a gimmick and that was what I had to find. I reached the subway kiosk, bought a pack of Luckies and dropped them in my pocket. I waited for the uptown local and got aboard when it came in.

With every jolt the train took I could feel the shock wear off a little bit more. It got worse and when it was too bad I stood up and leaned against the door, watching the walls of the tunnel go by in a dirty blur.

A gimmick. One lousy little gimmick and I could have it. It was there trying to come out and whenever I thought I had it my stomach would retch and I'd lose it.

The train pulled into the station, opened its multitude of mouths but I was the only one who stepped out. I had the platform all to myself then, so I let go and the coffee came up.

There weren't any cabs outside. I didn't waste time waiting for one. I walked toward my apartment not conscious of the rain any more, hardly conscious of the protest my body was setting up. I felt my legs starting to go when I reached the door and the super and his wife took a startled look at me and helped me inside.

Lily Carver came up out of the chair, holding back the sharp intake of her breath with the back of her hand. Her eyes went soft, reflected the hurt mine were showing, then she had my hand and helped me into the bedroom.

I flopped on the bed and closed my eyes. Hands loosened my collar and pulled at my shoes. I could hear the super telling his wife to stay out, and hear her frightened sobs. I could hear Lily and feel her hands on my forehead. For a second I glimpsed the white halo of her hair and saw the sensuous curves of her body in hazy detail hovering over me.

The super said, "You want me to call a doctor, Mr. Hammer?"

I shook my head.

"I'll call a cop. Maybe . . ."

I shook my head again. "I'll be okay."

"You feel good enough to talk a minute?"

"What?" I could feel the sleep closing in as I said it.

"A woman was here. Friday, her name was. She left you a note in an envelope and said it was pretty important. She wanted you to see it as soon as you came in."

"What was in it?"

"I didn't look. Should I open it?"

"Go ahead."

The bed jounced as he got up. It left me rocking gently, a soothing motion of pure comfort and there was a heaviness under my closed eyes too great to fight. Then the bed jounced again as he sat down and I heard the tearing of paper.

"Here it is." His voice paused. "Not much in it though."

"Read it," I said.

"Sure. *'Dear Mike . . . I found the list. Your friend has it. I found something much more important too and must see you at once. Call me. Please call me at once. Love Michael.'* That's all there is to it, Mr. Hammer."

"Thanks," I said, "thanks a lot."

From the other room his wife set up a nervous twittering. His fingers touched me. "Think it'll be all right if I go back?"

Before I could nod Lily said, "Go ahead. I'll take care of him. Thank you so much for everything."

"Well . . . if you need me, just call down."

"I'll do that."

I got my eyes open one last time. I saw the smooth beauty of her face unmarred by anything now. She was smiling, her hands doing things to my clothes. The strange softness was back in her eyes and she whispered, "Darling, darling . . . "

The sleep came. There was a face in it. The face had a rich, wet mouth, full and soft. It kept coming closer, opening slowly. It was Michael and in my dream I grinned at her, fascinated by her lips.

chapter twelve ▰▰▰▰▰▰▰▰▰▰▰

YOU HURT TOO much to sleep. You wake up and it hurts more so you try to go back to sleep. There's a physical ache, a gnawing your body tries vainly to beat down and might have if the pain in your mind wasn't even worse. Processions of thoughts hammer at you, gouge and scrape until the brain is a wild thing seeking some kind of release. But there isn't any release. There's fire all around you, the tongues of it licking closer, needling the skin. The brain screams for you to awaken, but if you do you know the other things . . . the thoughts, will be more searing pain so you fight and fight until the mind conquers and you feel the awakening coming on.

I thought I heard voices and one was Velda's. She kept calling to me and I couldn't answer back. Somebody was hurting her and I mouthed silent curses while I fought invisible bonds that held me tied to the ground. She was screaming, her voice tortured, screaming for me and I couldn't help her. I strained and kicked and fought but the ropes held until I was breathless and I had to lie there and listen to her die.

I opened my eyes and looked into the darkness, knowing it was only a dream but going nuts because I knew it could be real. My breathing was harsh, laboring, drying my mouth into leathery tissue.

The covers were pulled up to my neck, but under them there was nothing. The skin over my bruised muscles felt cool and pliable, then I found the answer with the tips of my fingers as they slid along flesh that had been gently oiled with some aromatic unguent. From somewhere the faint clean odor of rubbing alcohol crossed my nostrils, disturbing because of its unusual pungent purity. It was the raw smell of fine chemistry, the sharp, natural smell you might expect, but don't find in fresh, virgin forests.

Slowly, waiting for the ache to begin, I pulled my arm free, laid it across the bed, felt the warmth of a body under the back of my hand, then jerked it away as she almost screamed and pulled out of reach to sit there bolt upright with eyes still dumb with sleep reflecting some emotion nobody in the world would be able to put his finger on.

"Easy, Lily . . . It's only me."

She let her breath out with more of a gasp than a sigh, trying to wipe the sleep from her eyes. "You . . . scared me, Mike. I'm sorry." She smiled, sat on the edge of the bed and put her shoes on.

Her dreams must have been pretty rough too. She had taken care of me, lay there while I slept until her eyes closed too. She was a good kid who had been through the mill and was scared to death of a return trip. She wasn't going to get it from me.

I said, "What time is it?"

Lily checked her watch. "A little after nine. Can I get you something to eat?"

"What happened to the day?"

"You slept through. You groaned and talked . . . I didn't want to wake you up, Mike. Can I get you some coffee?"

"I can eat. I need something in my gut."

"All right. I'll call you." Her mouth creased in a smile, one corner of it pulling up with an odd motion. I let my eyes drift over her slowly. As they moved her hands tightened at her throat and the strangeness came back in her face. The smile disappeared into a tight grimace and she twisted around to go out the door.

Some of them are funny, I thought. Beautiful kids who would do anything one minute and scared stiff of doing it the next.

I heard her in the kitchen, got up, showered, managed to get the brush off my face and climbed into some clean clothes. I could hear things frying when I got on the phone and dialed Michael Friday's number.

The voice that answered was deep and guarded. It said, "Mr. Evello's residence," but the touch of Brooklyn in the tone was a plain as the badge it wore.

"Mike Hammer. I'm looking for Michael Friday, Carl's sister. She there?"

"I'm afraid . . ."

"Is Captain Chambers there?"

It caught the voice off base a second. "Who'd you say this was?"

"Hammer. Mike Hammer."

There was a muffled consultation, then: "This is the police, Hammer, what did you want?"

"I told you. I want Friday."

"So do we. She isn't around."

"Damn!" It exploded out of me. "You staked out there?"

"That's right. We're covering the place. You know where the girl is?"

"All I know is that she wants to see me bad, feller. How can I reach Chambers?"

"Wait a minute." The phone blanked out again and there was more talk behind a palm stretched over the mouthpiece. "You gonna be where you are a while?"

"I'll be here."

"Okay, the sergeant here says he'll try to get him for you. What's your number?"

"He knows it. Tell him to call me at home."

"Yeah. You get anything on that Friday dame, you pass it this way."

"No leads?"

"No nothing. She disappeared. She came back here after she left headquarters the other day, stayed a couple of hours and grabbed a cab into Manhattan."

"She was coming to see me," I said.

"She was what!"

"I was out. She left a note and took off again. That's why I called her place."

"I'll be damned. We checked all over the city to find out where she went to."

"If she's using cabs maybe you can pick her up from when she left here."

"Sure, sure. I'll pass it along."

The phone went dead and I socked it back in its hanger. Lily called me from the kitchen and I went out and sat down. She had it ready on the table, that same spread like she thought I was two more guys and instead of it looking good my stomach tried to sour at the sight of it. All I could think of was another one gone. Another kid cut down by a pack of scrimy hoods who wanted that two million bucks' worth of hell so bad they'd kill and kill and kill until they had every bit of it.

I smashed my fist into the table, saying the same dirty words over and over until Lily's face went a pasty white and she backed against the wall. I was staring into space, but she was occupying the space ahead of me and whatever she saw going across my face made her shrink back even further.

How stupid were they? How far did they have to go? Wasn't their organization big enough to know every damn detail inside and out? They wouldn't be reaching the stuff now, not with the cops going over every inch of the *Cedric*. The whole shebang was coming apart at the edges and instead of piling up the counts against them they ought to be on the run.

Lily slid out of sight. She came up against me and reached out her hand until it was on my shoulder. "Mike . . ."

I looked at her without seeing her.

"What is it, Mike?"

The words started out of me. They came slow at first, then turned into a boiling current that was taking in the whole picture. I was almost finished with it when I could feel the sharp points of the gimmicks sticking out and ran my mind back to pick them up. Then I sat and cursed myself because I wasn't fast enough. They weren't there any more.

There was just one minor little detail. Just a little one I should have thought of long ago. I said to Lily, "Did you go to see Berga Torn in the sanitarium at all?"

Her eyebrows knit, puzzled. "No, I didn't." She pinched her lower lip between her teeth. "I called her twice and the second time she mentioned that someone had been to see her."

I was half out of my chair. "Who? Did she say who?"

She tried hard for it, reaching back through the days. "I think she did. I honestly didn't pay any attention at the time. I was so worried about what was happening it didn't register."

I had her by the shoulders, squeezing my fingers into her skin. "The name's important, kid. That somebody tipped the whole thing. Right then was the beginning of murder that hasn't ended yet. As long as you got that name in your head a killer is going to be prowling around loose and if he ever knows you might have it you're going the same way Berga did."

"Mike."

"Don't worry about it. I'm not letting you out of my sight for a minute any more. Damn it, you got to dig that name out. You understand that?"

"I . . . think I do. Mike, please . . . you're hurting me."

I took my hands down and she rubbed the places where they had bitten in. There were tears in the corners of her eyes, little drops of crystal that swelled and I took a step closer to her. I reached out again, more gently this time, close enough for a second to taste the faint crispness of rubbing alcohol.

Lily smiled again. It was like the first time. The kind of smile you see on the face of a person waiting for death and ready to receive him almost gratefully. "Please eat something, Mike," she whispered.

"I can't, kid. Not now."

"You have to have something in your stomach."

Her words sent something racing up my back. It was a feeling you get when you know you have something and you can't wait to get it out of you. You stand there and wait for the final answer, waiting, waiting, waiting.

It was there in my hand when the phone set up a jangling that wouldn't stop. I grabbed the extension and Pat barked a short hello. I asked him, "Did you find Friday?"

He held his voice down. He sat on it all the way but the roughness showed through anyway. "We didn't find a damn thing. Nothing, got that? No Friday, no jug of hop, no nothing. This town's a madhouse. The feds are cutting a swath through the racket a mile wide and we still haven't come up with the stuff. Mike, if that stuff sits there . . ."

"I know what it means."

"Okay then, are you holding anything back?"

"You know better."

"Then what about Friday? If she was up there . . ."

"She wanted to see me. That's all I know."

"You know what I think?"

"I know what you think," I repeated softly. "Billy Mist . . . where's he?"

"You'd never guess."

"Tell me."

"Right now he's having supper at the Terrace. He's got an alibi for everything we can throw at him and nobody's going to break it for a damn long while. He's got people in Washington batting for him and boys with influence pulling strings so hard they're knocking us silly . . . Mike . . ."

"Yeah?"

"Find Velda?"

"Not yet, Pat. Soon."

"You're not saying it right, friend."

"I know."

"In case it makes you feel better, I put men on it."

"Thanks."

"Figured it might not be holing out like you expected."

"Yeah."

"Something else you better know. Your joint's been covered. Three guys were stationed around waiting for you. The feds picked them up. One of the muscle lads is in the morgue."

"So?"

"There may be more. Keep your eyes open. You may have a tail or two if you leave. At least one'll be our man."

"They're sticking close to me." I said the words through my teeth.

"You're primed for the kill, Mike. You know why? I'll tell you. News has it you were part of the thing from the beginning. You've been fooling me and everybody else, but they got the pitch. Tell me one thing . . . *have* you been shoving it in me?"

"No."

"Good enough. We'll keep playing it this way then."

"What about the *Cedric*?"

He cursed under his breath. "It's screwballed, Mike. It's the whole, lousy, stinking reason behind all this. The ship is in a Jersey port right now undergoing repairs. She was a small liner before the war and was revamped to carry troops. All the staterooms were torn out of her and junked to make it over into a transport. The stuff might have been there once, but it's been gone a long time now. None of this should've happened at all."

I let a few seconds pass before I spoke. I was feeling cold and dead all over. "You got a lot of people you've been wanting to get."

"Yeah, a lot of them." His voice was caustic. "A lot of punks. A lot of middle-sized boys. A few big ones. Medusa even lost a few of her heads." He laughed sarcastically. "But Medusa is still alive, buddy. She's one big head who doesn't care how many of her little heads she loses. We can chop all the little ones off and in a few months or years she'll grow a whole new crop as vicious as ever. Yeah, we're doing fine. I thought we did good when I had a look at the shiv hole in Carl. I felt great when I saw Affia's face. They were nothing, Mike. You know how I feel now?"

I didn't answer him. I put the phone back while he was still talking. I was thinking of Michael Friday's wet, wet mouth and the way Al Affia *had* looked and what Carl Evello had told me. I was thinking of undercurrents that could even work through an organization like the Mafia and I knew why Michael Friday had tried to see me.

Lily was a drawn figure slumped in the chair. Her fingers kept pushing the silken strands away from her eyes while she watched me. I said, "Get your coat."

"They'll be waiting for us outside?"

"That's right, they'll be waiting."

Even the last shred of hope she had nursed so long left her face. There was a dullness in her eyes and in the way she walked.

"We'll let them wait," I said, and she turned around and grinned with some of the life back in her.

While I waited for her I turned out the light and stood in front of the window watching the city. The monster squirmed, its bright-colored lights marking the threshing of its limbs, a sprawling octopus whose mouth was hidden under a horribly carved beak. The mouth was open, the beak ready to rip and tear anything that stood in its way. It made sounds out there, incomprehensible sounds that were the muted whinings of deadly terror. There were no spoken words, but the sounds were enough. The meaning was clear.

"I'm ready, Mike."

She had on the green suit again, trimly beautiful, her hair gone now under a pert little hat with a feather in it. The expression on her face said that if she must die it would be quick and clean. And dressed. She was ready. We both were ready. Two very marked people stepping out to look for the mouth of the octopus.

We didn't go down the stairs. We went up to the roof and crossed the abutments between the apartments. We found the door we wanted through the roof of a building a hundred yards down and used that. We took the elevator to the basement and went out through the back. The yard there was an empty place, too steeped in darkness to reflect any of the window lights above. The wall was head-high brick, easy to get over. I pushed Lily up, got over myself and helped her down. We felt our way around the wall until we reached the other basement door but the luck we had had bent a little around a lock under the knob.

I was ready to start working on it when I heard the muffled talk inside and the luck unbent a little bit. I whispered to Lily to keep quiet and pushed her against the side of the building. The talk got louder, the lock clicked and somebody shoved the door open.

The stream of light that flooded the yard didn't catch us. We stayed behind the door and waited. The kid with the wispy mustache backed out swearing under his breath while he tugged at a leash and for a second I was ready to jump him before the racket started. Lily saw it too and grabbed my hand so hard her nails punched holes into my skin. Then the kid was out and walking toward the wall in back with so much to say about people who have cats taken for a walk on a leash that he never saw us go through the door at all.

We got out the other end of the building and circled around the block to the garage. Sammy was just coming on duty and waved my way when he saw us. It was a funny kind of a wave with a motion of the other hand under it. I pushed Lily in ahead of me and closed the door.

Sammy didn't know whether to laugh or not. He decided not

to, wrinkled up his face in a serious expression and said, "You hot, Mike?"

"In a way I'm boiling. Why?"

"People been around asking about your new heap. One of the boys tipped me that there's eyes watching for it."

"I heard the story."

"Hear what happened to Bob Gellie?" His face grew pretty serious.

"No."

"He got worked over. Something to do with you."

"Bad?"

"He's in the hospital. Whatever it was he wouldn't talk."

The bastards knew everything. What they didn't know they could find out and when they did the blood ran. The organization. The syndicate. The Mafia. It was filthy, rotten right through but the iron glove it wore was so heavy and so sharp it could work with incredible, terrible efficiency. You worked as they'd tell you to work or draw the penalty. There was no in-between. There was only one penalty. It could be slow or fast, but the result was the same. You died. Until they died, until every damn one of them was nothing but decaying flesh in a pile on the ground the killings would go on and on.

"I'll take care of him. You tell him that for me. How is he?"

"Bob'll come through it. He won't ever look the same, but he'll be okay."

"How do you feel, Sammy?"

"Lousy, if you gotta know. I got me a .32 in the drawer there that's gonna stay right handy all night and maybe afterward."

"Can you get me a car?"

"Take mine. I figured you'd be asking so I have it by the door nosing out. It's a good load and I like it, so bring it back in one piece."

He waved to the door, pulled down the blind over the window and followed us into the garage. He hauled the door up, grinned unhappily when we pulled out and let it slam back in place. I told Lily to get down until I was sure we were clear, made a few turns around one-way streets, parked for a few minutes watching for lights, then pulled out again and cut into traffic.

Lily said, "Where are we going, Mike?"

"You'll see."

"Mike . . . please. I'm awfully scared."

Her lower lip matched the flutter of her voice. She sat there pinching her hands together, her arms making jerky movements against her sides to control the shudder that was trying to take over her body.

"Sorry, kid," I told her. "You're as much a part of this as I am. You ought to know about it. We're going to see what made a woman want to see me pretty badly. We're going to find out what she knew that put her on the missing list. There isn't much you can do except sit tight, but while you're sitting there's plenty you can do. Remember that name. Dig up every detail of that talk you had with Berga and bring that name out."

She looked straight ahead, her face set, and nodded. "All right, Mike. I'll . . . try." Then her head came around and I could feel the challenge of her stare but couldn't match it while I was weaving through the traffic. "I'd do *anything* for you, Mike," she finished softly. There was a newness in her voice I'd never heard before. A controlled excitement that made me remember how I had awakened and what she was thinking of. Before I could answer she turned her head with the same suddenness and stared straight ahead again, but this time with an excited expression of anticipation.

There were only two men assigned to the place when we got there. One sat in the car and the other was parked in a chair by the door looking like he wanted a cigarette pretty bad. He gave me that frozen look all cops keep in reserve and waited for me to speak my piece.

"I'm Mike Hammer. I've been cooperating with Captain Chambers on the deal here and would like to take a look around. Who do I see?"

The freeze melted loose and he nodded. "The boys were talking about you before. The captain say it's okay?"

"Not yet. He will if you want to go get a call in to him."

"Ah, guess it's okay. Don't touch anything, that's all."

"Anybody around inside?"

"Nope. Joint's empty. The butler took an inventory of liquor before he left though."

"Careful guy. I'll be right out."

"Take your time."

So I went in and stood in the long hallway. I held a light up to the Lucky between my lips and blew a thin overcast into the air. There were lights on along the walls, dim things that gave the place the atmosphere of a funeral parlor and hardly any light.

In the back of my mind I had an idea but I didn't know how to start it going. You don't walk in and pick up important things after the cops have been through a place. Not unless they don't want what you're looking for.

I made the rounds of the rooms downstairs, finished the butt and snubbed it, then tried upstairs. The layout was equally as elaborate, as well appointed as the other rooms, a chain of bedrooms, a study, a small music room and a miniature hobby shop on the south side. There was one room that smelled of life and living. It had that woman smell I couldn't miss. It had the jaunty, carefree quality that was Michael Friday and when I snapped the lights on I saw I was right.

There was an orderly disarray of things scattered around that said the woman who belonged to the room would be back. The creams, the perfumes, the open box of pins on the dresser. The bed was large with a fluffy-haired poodle doll propped against the pillows. There were pictures of men on the dresser and a couple of enlarged snapshots of Michael in a sailboat with a batch of college boys in attendance.

Scattered, but neat.

Other signs too, professional signs. A cigar ash in the tray. Indentations in the rolled stockings in the box where a thumb had squeezed them. I sat on the edge of the bed and smoked another cigarette. When I had it halfway down I reached over to the night table for an ashtray and laid it on the cover beside me. The tray made an oval in the center of the square there, a boxy outline in dust. I picked it up, looked at the smudge on the cover and wiped at it with my fingertip.

The other details were there too, the thin line of grit and tiny edges of brownish paper that marked the lip of a box somebody had spilled out in emptying it on the bed. With my fingers held together the flat of my hand filled the width of the square and two hands made the length. I finished the butt, put it out and went back downstairs.

The cop on the porch said, "Make out?"

"Nothing special. You find any safes around?"

"Three of 'em. One upstairs, two downstairs. Nothing there we could use. Maybe a few hundred in bills. Take a look yourself. There's a pair in his study."

They were a pair, all right. One was built into the wall behind a framed old map of New York harbor, but the other was a trick job in the window sill. Carl was kicking his psychology around when he had them built. Two safes in a house a person could expect, but rarely two in the same room. Anyone poking around couldn't miss the one behind the map, but it would take some inside dope to find the other. The dial was pretty badly beaten up and there were fresh scratches in the wood around the thing. I swung the door open, held my lighter in front of it and squinted around. The dust marked the outline of the box that had been there.

The cop had moved to the steps this time. He grinned and jerked his head at the house. "Not much to see."

"Who opened the safes?"

"The city boys brought Delaney in. He's the factory representative of the outfit who makes the safes. Good man. He could make a living working lofts."

"He's doing all right now," I said. I told him so-long and went back to the car. Lily was waiting, her face a pale glow behind the window.

I slid under the wheel, sat there fiddling with the gearshift, letting the thought I had jell. Lily put her hand on my arm, held it still and waited. "I wonder if Pat found it," I muttered.

"What?"

"Michael Friday stooled on her brother. She went back home and found something else but this time she was afraid to give it to the police."

"Mike . . ."

"Let me talk, kid. You don't have to listen. I'm just getting it in order. There was trouble in the outfit. Carl was expecting to take over somehow. In that outfit you don't work your way up. Carl was expecting to move up a slot so somebody else had to go. That boy knew what he was doing. He spent some time getting something on the one he was after and was going to smear him with it."

I put it through my mind again, nodded, and said, "Carl was close enough to start the thing going so the other one knew about it. He went after what Carl had and found it gone. By that time the cops were having a field day with the labor department of the organization so he had a good idea who was responsible. He must have tailed her. He knew she had it and what she was going to do with it so he nailed her."

"But . . . who, Mike? Who?"

My teeth came apart in the kind of a smile nobody seemed to like. I was feeling good all over because I had my finger on it now and I wasn't letting go. "Friend Billy," I said. "Billy Mist. Now he sits quiet and enjoys his supper. Someplace he's got a dame on the hook and enjoying life because whatever it was Carl had isn't any more. Billy's free as a bird but he hasn't got two million in the bush to play with. He's got an ace in the hole with Velda in case the two million shows up and a deuce he can discard anytime if it doesn't. The greasy little punk is sitting pretty where he can't be touched."

The laugh started out of my chest and ripped through my throat. It was the biggest joke I ever laughed at because the whole play was made to block me out and I wasn't being mousetrapped. I was going back a couple of hours to the kitchen and what Lily had said and back even further to a note left in my office. Then, so I wouldn't forget how I felt right there at the beginning when I wanted to kill something with my hands, I went back to Berga and the way she had looked coming out of that gas station.

I kicked the engine over, pulled around the squad car and pointed the hood toward the bright eyes of Manhattan. I stayed with the lights, watching the streets click by, cut over a few blocks to the building with the efficient look and antiseptic smell and pulled in behind the city hearse unloading a double cargo.

It was a little after one but you could still find dead people around.

The attendant in the morgue called me into his office and wanted to know if I wanted coffee. I shook my head. "It takes the smell away," he said. "What can I do for you?"

"You had a body here. Girl named Berga Torn."

"Still have it."

"Slated for autopsy?"

"Nope. At least I haven't heard about it. They don't usually in those cases."

"There will be one in this case. Can I use the phone?"

"Go ahead."

I picked it up and dialed headquarters. Pat wasn't around so I tried his apartment. He wasn't there, either. I buzzed a few of the places he spent time in but they hadn't seen him. I looked at my watch and the hand had spun another quarter. I swore at the phone and at myself and double cursed the red tape if I had to go through channels. I was thinking so hard I wasn't really thinking at all and while I was in the middle of it the door of the office opened and the little guy with the potbelly came in, dropped his bag on the floor and said, "Damn it, Charlie, why can't people wait until morning to die?"

I said, "Hi, doc," and the coroner gave me a surprised glance that wasn't any too pleased.

"Hello, Hammer, what are you doing here? Should I add 'again'?"

"Yeah, add it, doc. I always seem to come home, don't I?"

"I'd like it better if you stayed out of my sight."

He went to go past me. I grabbed his arm, turned him around and looked at a guy with a safe but disgusting job. He went up on his toes, tried to pull his arm away, but I held on. "Listen, doc. You and I can play games some other time. Right now I need you for a job that can't wait. I have to chop corners and it has to be quick."

"Let go of me!"

I let go of him. "Maybe you like to see those bodies stretched out in the gutter."

He turned around slowly. "What are you talking about?"

"Suppose you had a chance to do something except listen for a heartbeat that isn't there for a change. Supposing you had it in your hand to kick a few killers right into the chair. Supposing you're the guy who stands between a few more people living or dying in the next few hours . . . how would you pitch it, doc?"

The puzzle twisted his nose into a ridge of wrinkles. "See here . . . you're talking like . . ."

"I'm talking plain. I've been trying to get some official backing for what I have in mind but nobody's home. Even then it might take up time we can't spare. That chance I was talking about is in your hand, doc."

"But . . ."

"I need a stomach autopsy on a corpse. Now. Can do?"

"I think you're serious," he said in a flat tone.

"You'll never know how serious. There may be trouble later. Trouble isn't as bad as somebody having to die."

I could see the protest coming out of the attendant. It started but never got there. The coroner squared his shoulders, let a little of the excitement that was in my voice trickle into his eyes and he nodded.

"Berga Torn," I told the attendant. "Let's go see her."

He did it the fast, easy way you do when you cut corners. He did it right there in the carrier she lay on and the light overhead winked on the steel in his hand. I didn't get past the first glimpse because fire does horrible things to a person and it was nicer to remember Berga in the headlights of the car.

I could hear him, though.

I could even tell when he found it.

He did me the favor of cleaning it before he handed it to me and I stood there looking at the dull glitter of the brass key wondering where the lock to it was. The coroner said, "Well?"

"Thanks."

"I don't mean that."

"I know . . . only where it goes nobody knows. I thought it would be something else."

He sensed the disappointment and held out his hand. I dropped the key in it and he held it up to the light, turning it over to see both sides. For a minute he concentrated on one side, held it closer to the bulb, then nodded for me to follow him across the room. From a closet he pulled out a bottle of some acrid liquid, poured it into a shallow glass container, then dropped the key in. He let it stay there about twenty seconds before dipping it out with a glass rod. This time the dullness was gone. It was a gleaming thing with a new look and no coating to dull the details. This time when he held it in the light you could see *City Athletic Club, 529* scratched into the surface and I squeezed his arm so hard he winced through his grin.

I said, "Listen, get on the phone out there and find Captain Chambers. Tell him I found what we were looking for and I'm going after it. I'm not going to take any chances on this getting away so he can hop up to my office for a print of this thing."

"He doesn't know?"

"Uh-uh. I'm afraid somebody else might find out the same way I did. I'll call you back to see how you made out. If there's any trouble about . . . back there . . . Chambers'll clear things. Someday I'll let you know just how much of a boost up you gave the department."

The excitement in his eyes sparkled brighter and he was holding his jaw like a guy who's just done the impossible. The morgue attendant was on his way over for an explanation and apparently he wanted it in writing. He tried to stop me for some talk on the way out but I was in too much of a rush.

Lily knew I had it when I came bouncing down the stairs, opened the door for me and said, "Mike?"

"I know almost all the answers now, chicken." I held up the key. "Here's the big baby. Look at it, a chunk of metal people have died for and all this time it was in the stomach of a girl who was ready to do anything to beat them out of it. The key to the deal. For the first time in my life a real one. I know who had it and what's behind the door it opens."

As if the words I had said were a formula that split open Valhalla to let a pack of vicious, false gods spill through, a jagged streak of lightning cut across the sky with the thunder rolling in its wake. The first crashing wave of it was so sudden Lily tightened against it, her eyes closed tight.

I said, "Relax."

"I . . . can't, Mike. I hate thunderstorms."

You could feel the dampness in the air, the fresh coolness of the new wind. She shuddered again and turned up the little collar of her jacket around her neck. "Close the window, Mike."

I rolled it up, got the heap going and turned into traffic heading east. The voice of the city was starting to go quiet now. The last few figures on the streets were starting to run for cover and the cabs picked up their aimless cruising.

The first big drops of rain splattered on the hood and brought the scum flooding down the winshield. I started the wipers, but still had to hunch forward over the wheel to see where I was going. I could feel time going by. The race of the minutes. They never went any faster or any slower, but they always beat you. I turned south on Ninth Avenue, staying in tempo with the lights until I reached the gray-brick building with the small neon sign that read CITY ATHLETIC CLUB.

I cut the engine in front of the door and went to get out. Lily said, "Mike, will you be long?"

"Couple of minutes." Her face seemed to be all pinched up.

"What's the matter, kid?"

"Cold, I guess."

I pulled the blanket from the seat in the back and draped it over her shoulders. "You're catching something sure as hell. Keep it around you. I'll be right back."

She shivered and nodded, holding the edges of the blanket together under her chin.

The guy at the reception desk was a sleepy-eyed tall guy who sat there hating everybody who bothered him. He watched me cross the hall and didn't make any polite sounds until I got to him.

He asked one question. "You a member?"

"No, but . . ."

"Then the place is closed. Scram."

I pulled a fin out of my wallet and laid it on the desk.

He said, "Scram."

I took it back, stuffed it away and leaned across the chair and belted him right on his back. I picked him up by his skinny arms and popped him a little one in the gut before I threw him back in his chair again. "The next time be nice," I said. I held out the key and he looked at it with eyes that were wide awake now.

"You bastard."

"Shut up. What's the key for?"

"Locker room."

"See who has 529."

He curled his lip at me, ran his hand across his stomach under his belt and pulled a ledger out of the desk drawer. "Raymond. Ten-year membership."

"Let's go."

"You're nuts. I can't leave the desk. I . . ."

"Let's go."

"Lousy coppers," I heard him say. I grinned behind his back and followed him down the stairs. There was a sticky dampness in the air, an acrid smell of disinfectant. We passed a steam room and the entrance to the pool, then turned into the alcove that held the lockers.

They were tall affairs with hasps that allowed you to install your own lock. Raymondo had slapped on a beauty. It was an oversized brass padlock with a snap so big it barely passed through the hasp. I stuck the key in, turned it and the lock came apart.

Death, crime and corruption was lying on the floor in two metal containers the size of lunch pails. The seams were welded shut and the units painted a deep green. Attached to each was the cutest little rig you ever saw, a small CO_2 bottle with a heavy rubber ball attached to the nozzle. The rubber was rotted in the folds and the hose connection had cracked dry, but it didn't spoil the picture any. All you had to do was toss the unit out of a porthole, the bottle stopper opened after a time interval and the stuff floated to the top where the rubber ball buoyed it until it was picked up.

The answer to the *Cedric* was there too, a short story composed of sales slips stapled together, a yarn that said Raymondo had taken good care of his investment and was on hand to pick up the junk when they stripped the ship. There was one special item marked *"wall ventilators—12.50 ea. 25.00."*

I squatted down to pull them out and the guy down the end came away from the wall, showing too much curiosity. The stuff had to be dumped someplace but I couldn't be carrying it to the dumping ground. Pat had to see it, the Washington boys would want a look at it. I couldn't take any kind of a chance at all on losing it. Not now.

So I shut the door and closed the lock through the hasp. It had been there a lot of years . . . a few more hours wouldn't hurt it any. But now I had something I could talk a trade with. I could describe the stuff so they'd be sure and it would be my way all the way.

The guy followed me back upstairs and got behind his desk again. He was snottier looking than ever but when I stood close the artificial toughness faded into blankness and he had to lick his lips.

I said, "Remember my face, buddy. Take a good look and keep it in your mind. If anybody who isn't a cop comes in here wanting to know about that locker and you kick through with the information I'm going to break your face into a dozen pieces. No matter what they do I'll do worse, so keep your trap shut." I turned to go, stopped a second and looked back over my shoulder. "The next time be polite. You could have made dough on the deal."

My watch read five minutes to three. Time, time, time. The rain was a solid sheet blasting the sidewalks and spraying back into the air again. I yelled for Lily to open the door, made a dash for it and slid aboard. She trembled under the gust of cold air that got in with me, her face set tighter than it was before.

I reached over and put my arm around her shoulders.

She was pulled tight as a drumhead, a muscular stiffness that made her whole body almost immobile. "Cripes, Lily, I got to get you to a doctor."

"No . . . just get me where it's warm, Mike."

"I haven't got much sense."

She forced a smile. "I . . . really don't mind . . . as long as you . . ."

"No more chasing around, kid. I found it. I can take you back now."

There was a catch in the sob that came out of her. Her eyes glistened and the smile didn't have to be forced.

I sat there looking into the rain, pulling on a Lucky while I figured it out. I said, "You'll go back to my apartment, kid. Dry off and sit tight."

"Alone?"

"Don't worry about it. There are cops stationed around the building. I'll tip them to keep the place well covered. We have to move fast now and I can't waste time. I have a key to a couple of million bucks in my pocket and I can't put all my eggs in one basket. I'm getting a duplicate of that key made and you're hanging on to it until Captain Chambers picks it up. I don't want you to move out of that place until I get back and don't pull a stunt like you did before. Let's go, I still have a fast stop to make that won't take more than five minutes."

That was all it did take. My friend turned out the key while he swore at the world for getting him out of bed so I left him to buy a good night in a gin mill for his trouble.

We reached my block at a quarter to four with the rain still lashing at the car in frenzied bursts. There was a patrol wagon at each end and two plainclothesmen were standing in the doorway. When they saw us they looked so mad they could bust and one spit disgustedly and shook his head.

I didn't give them a chance to ask questions. "Sorry you were standing guard over a hole, friend. One of these things. We got this business breaking over our heads and I can't go explaining every move I make. I've been putting in calls all over the lot for Pat Chambers and if one of you guys feels like expediting things you'll get on the line too."

I pointed to Lily. "This is Lily Carver. They're after her as bad as they are me. She's got a message for Pat that can't wait and if anything happens to her between now and when he sees her he'll have your hides. One of you better take her up and stick outside in the hall."

"Johnston'll go."

"Good. You'll call around for Pat."

"We'll locate the captain somehow."

I got Lily inside, saw her through the front door with the cop beside her and felt the load go lighter.

"You got something, Hammer?" The cop was watching me closely.

"Yeah. It's almost over."

His grunt was a sarcastic denial. "You know better, buddy. It never ends. This thing is stretched all over the states. Wait till you see the morning papers."

"Good?"

"Lovely. The voters'll go nuts when they see the score. This town is going to see a reform cleanup like it never happened before. We had to book four of our own boys this evening." His hand turned into a fist. "They were playing along with them."

"The little guys," I said. "They pay through the nose. The wheels keep rolling right along. They string the dead out and walk over them. The little guy pays the price."

"We got wheels too. Evello's dead."

"Yeah." I said.

"How far did they get with his stepsister?"

"As far as here, buddy. People are thinking about that."

I looked across the lobby at him. "They would. They'll try to put the finger anyplace."

Michael Friday and her wet, lovely mouth. The mouth that never did get close enough, really close. Michael Friday with the ready smile and the laugh in her walk, Michael Friday who got tired of the dirt herself and put herself on my side of the fence. Coming to me with the thing I wanted even more than the stuff in the locker. She should have known. Damn it, those things had been happening under her nose. She should have known the kind of people she was messing around with. They're fast and smart and know the angles and they're ready to follow through. She should have thought it out and got herself a cordon of cops instead of cutting loose herself to get the stuff to me. Maybe she knew they'd be after her. Maybe she thought she was as smart as they were. Berga thought those things too.

Lovely Michael Friday. She steps outside and they have her. She could have been standing right where I was that minute. The door behind her locks shut. There's only one person outside and that's the one she's afraid of. Maybe she knew she only had a minute more to live and her insides must have been tumbling around loose.

Like Berga. But Berga did something in that minute.

I got that creepy feeling again, an indescribably tingling sensation that burned up my spine and touched my brain with thoughts that seemed improbable. I looked down at my feet, my teeth shut tight, squinting at the floor. The cop's breathing seemed the loudest thing in the room, even drowning out the thunder and the rain outside. I walked to the mailbox and opened it with my key.

Michael had thought too. She had left an empty envelope in there telling me exactly what she meant. It didn't have my name on it, but I read the message. It said, "William Mist," but it was enough.

It was a more than enough. It was something else. The gimmick I was looking for, the one I knew I had come across someplace else but I couldn't put my finger on. But for a little while it was enough.

I crumpled the thing up into a little ball and dropped it. I could feel the hate welling up in me until I couldn't stand it any more. My head was filled with a crazy overture of sound that beat and beat and beat.

I ran out of the place. I left the cop standing there and ran out. I forgot everything I was doing except for one thing when I got in the car. Light, traffic? Hell, nothing mattered. There was only one thing. I was going to see that greaseball die between my fingers and he was going to talk before he did. The car screamed at the corners, the tail end whipping around violently. I could smell the rubber and brake lining and hear the whining protest of the engine and occasionally the hoarse curses that followed my path. The stops were all out this time and nothing else counted.

When I reached the apartment building I didn't push any bells to be let in. I kicked out a pane of glass on the inside door, reached through the hole and turned the knob. I went up the stairs to the same spot I had been before and this time I did hit the bell.

Billy Mist was expecting somebody, all right, but it wasn't me. He was all dressed except for his jacket and he had a gun slung in a harness under his shoulder. I rammed the door so hard it kicked him back in the room and while he was reaching for his rod I smashed his nose into a mess of bloody tissue. He made a second try while he was on the floor and this time I kicked the gun out of his hand under the table and picked him up to go over good. I held him out where I wanted him and put one into his ribs that brought a scream choking up his throat and had the next one ready when Billy Mist died.

I didn't want to believe it. I wanted him alive so bad I shook him like a rag doll and when the mouth lolled open under those blank eyes I threw him away from me into the door and his head and shoulders slammed it shut. His broken face leered at me from the carpet, the eyes seeing nothing. They were filmy already. I let it go then. I let that raspy yell out of me and began to break things until I was out of breath.

But Billy still leered.

Billy Mist, who knew where Velda was. Billy Mist who was going to talk before he died. Billy Mist who was going to give me the pleasure of killing him slowly.

It was thinking of Velda that smoothed it. My hands stopped shaking and my mind started thinking again. I looked around the mess I had made of the place, avoiding the eyes on the floor.

Billy had been packing. He had been five minutes away from being killed and he was taking a quick-acting powder. The one suitcase had a week's supply of clothes in it but he could afford to buy more when he got there because the rest of the space was taken up by packets of new bills.

I was picking the stuff apart when I heard them at the door. They weren't cops. Not these boys. They wanted in because I was there and nothing was stopping them.

How long ago was it that I asked Berga how stupid could she get?

Now I was the one. Sammy had told me. They were waiting for me. Not in squad cars on the corner of my block. Not for the Ford because by now they'd have figured the switch. So I go busting loose with the pack on my back and now I was up the tree.

Shoulders slammed into the door and a vertical crack showed in it. I walked to the overturned chair, picked up Billy's rod and kicked the safety off. They were a little stupid, too. They knew I was traveling clean but forgot Billy would be loaded. I pumped five fast ones through the wood belly-high and the screams outside made a deafening cacophony that brought more screams from others in the building.

The curses and screams didn't stop the others. The door cracked again, started to buckle and I turned and ran into the bathroom. There was a barrel bolt on the door made for decency purposes only and wouldn't hold anything longer than a minute or two. I slid it in place, took my time about opening the bathroom window and sighting along the ledge outside.

I got my feet on the sill, started to go through when my arm swept the bottles from the shelf. Dozens of bottles. A sick man's paradise and Billy had been a very sick man after all. There was one left my arm didn't touch and I picked it up. I stared at it, swore lightly and dropped it in my pocket.

The door inside let loose. There was more letting loose too. Shots and shrieks that didn't belong there and I crawled through the window before I could find out why. I felt along the ledge with my toes, leaning forward at an angle with my hands resting on the building on the other side of the airway. I made the end where the building joined, found handholds on the other sills and went up.

For a change I was glad of the rain. It covered the noises I made, washed clean places for my fingers and toes and when I reached the roof bathed me in its coolness. I lay there on the graveled top, breathing the fire out of my lungs, barely conscious of the fury going on in the streets. When I could make it, I got across the building, got on the fire escape and crawled down.

Somebody in a dark window was screaming her lungs out telling the world where I was. Shouts answered her from someplace else and two shots whined off into the night.

They never found me. I hit the yard and got out of there. Sirens were converging on the place and a hundred yards off the rapid belch of a tommy gun spit a skinful of sudden destruction into the airway.

I laughed my fool head off while I stood there on the sidewalk and felt good about it. In a way it paid to be stupid as long as you overdid it. I was too stupid to figure the boys planted around my apartment would follow me and too stupid to remember there were the Washington boys who would run behind them. It must have made a pretty picture when they joined forces. It was something that had to come. The Mafia wasn't a gang, it was a government. And governments have armies and armies fight.

The trouble was that while the war raged the leader got away and had time to cover his tracks. I pulled the bottle out of my pocket, looked at it and threw it away.

Not this leader. He wasn't going anywhere except a hole in the ground.

chapter thirteen ▰▰▰▰▰▰▰▰▰▰

THE OFFICE WAS dark. Water leaked through the hole I had made in the glass and the pieces winked back at me. Nobody at the desk. No beautiful smile, challenging eyes. I knew where to look and pulled the file out. I held a match to it and the pieces clicked in place. I put the card back and went through the rooms.

Off the inner office a door led to stairs that ran up, thickly carpeted stairs that didn't betray the passage of a person. There was another door at the top and an apartment off it. I kicked my shoes off, laid the change in my pocket on the floor and walked away from the one that showed the light.

There was only one room that was locked, but those kind of locks never gave me any trouble at all. I stepped inside, eased the door shut and flicked my lighter.

She was laced into an easy chair with a strait jacket, her legs tied down. A strip of adhesive tape across her mouth and around it were red marks where other tapes had been ripped off to feed her or hear what she had to say. There was a sallowness about her face, a fearful, shrunken look, but the eyes were alive. They couldn't see me behind the lighter, but they cursed me just the same.

I said, "Hello, Velda," and the cursing stopped. The eyes didn't believe until I moved the lighter and the tears wiped out her vision. I took the ropes off, unlaced the jacket and lifted her up easily. The hurt sounds she wanted to make but couldn't came out in the convulsions of her body. She pressed against me, the tears wetting my face. I squeezed her, ran my hands across her back while I whispered things to her and told her not to be afraid any more. I found her mouth and tasted her, deeply, loving the way she held me and the things she said without really saying anything.

When I could I said, "You all right?"

"I was going to die tonight."

"Somebody'll take your place."

"Now?"

"You won't be here to see it." I found the key in my pocket and pressed it in her hand. I gave her my wallet to go with it and pulled her to the door. "Take a cab and find yourself a cop. Find Pat if you can. There's an address on that key. Go hold what's in the locker it opens. Can you do that much?"

"Can't I . . ."

"I said get a cop. The bastards know everything there is to know. We can't lose any time at all . . . and most of all I can't lose you at all. Tomorrow we'll talk."

"Tomorrow, Mike."

"It's crazy this way. Everything's crazy. I find you and I'm sending you off again. Damn it, move before I don't let you go."

"Tomorrow, Mike," she said and reached for me again. She wasn't tired now, she was brand-new again. She was a woman I was never going to let go again ever. She didn't know it yet, but tomorrow there would be more than talk. I wanted her since I had first seen her. Tomorrow I'd get her. The way she wanted it. Tomorrow she was going to belong to me all the way.

"Say it, Mike."

"I love you, kitten. I love you more than I've ever thought I could love anything."

"I love you too, Mike." I could feel her grin. "Tomorrow."

I nodded and opened the door. I waited until she had gone down the steps and this time walked the other way. To where the light showed.

I pushed it open, leaned against the sill and when the gray-haired man writing at the table across the room spun around I said, "Doctor Soberin, I presume."

It caught him so far off base I had time to get halfway across to him before he dipped his hand in the drawer and I had his wrist before he could get the thing leveled. I let him keep the gun in his hand so I could bend it back and hear his fingers break and when he tried to yell I bottled the sound up by smashing my elbow into his mouth. The shattered teeth tore my arm and his mouth became a great hole welling blood. His fingers were broken stubs sticking at odd angles. I shoved him away from me, slashed the butt end of the rod across the side of his head and watched him drop into his chair.

"I got me a wheel," I said. "The boy at the top."

Dr. Soberin opened his mouth to speak and I shook my head.

"You're dead, mister. Starting from now you're dead. It took me a long time. It didn't really have to." I let out a dry laugh at myself. "I'm getting too old for the game. I'm not as fast as I used to be. One time I would have had it made as soon as I rolled it around a little bit.

"The gimmick, doc, there's always that damned gimmick. The kind you can't kick out of sight. This time the gimmick was on the bottom of that card your secretary made out on Berga Torn. She asked who sent her and she said William Mist. She signed the card, too. You pulled a cutie on that one. You couldn't afford to let a respectable dame know your business, and you knew she wouldn't put her name on a switch. You knew there might be an investigation and didn't want any suspicious erasures on the card so you simply dug up a name that you could type over Mist to make the letters fit. Wieton comes out pretty well. Unless you looked hard you'd never pick it up."

He had gone a deathly pale. His hand was up to his mouth trying to stop the blood. It was sickening him and he retched. All that came up was more blood. The hand with the broken fingers looked unreal on the end of his arm. Unreal and painful.

"You took a lot of trouble to get the information Berga had under her hat. A lot of clever thinking went into that deal at the sanitarium. You had it rigged pretty nicely, even to a spot where she could be worked over without anybody getting wise. Sorry I spoiled your plans. You shouldn't have wrecked my heap."

Something childish crept into his face. "You . . . got . . . another one."

"I'll keep it too. I didn't go for the booby trap, doc. That was kid stuff."

If his face screwed up any tighter he was going to cry. He sat there moaning softly, the complete uncertainty of it all making him rock in his chair.

I said, "This time I do it your way. I was the only one you were ever afraid of because I was like the men you give orders to. I'm not going to talk to you. Later I'll go over the details. Later I'll give my explanations and excuses to the police. Later I'll get raked over the coals for what I'm going to do now, but what the hell, doc. Like I said, I'm getting old in the game. I don't care any more."

He was quiet in his chair. The quiet that terror brings and for once he was knowing the hand of terror himself.

I said, "Doc . . ." and he looked at me. No, not me, the gun. The big hole in the end of the gun.

And while he was looking I let him see what came out of the gun.

Doctor Soberin only had one eye left.

I stepped across the body and picked up the phone. I called headquarters and tried to get Pat. He was still out. I had the call transferred to another department and the man I wanted said hello. I asked him for the identification on a dead blonde and he told me to wait.

A minute later he picked up the phone. "Think I got it. Death by drowning. Age, about . . ."

"Skip the details. Just the name."

"Sure, Lily Carver. Prints just came in from Washington. She had 'em taken while she worked at a war plant."

I said thanks, held the button down on the phone, let it go and when I heard the dial tone started working on my home number.

She said, "Don't bother, Mike. I'm right here."

And she was.

Beautiful Lily with hair as white as snow. Her mouth a scarlet curve that smiled. Differently, now, but still smiling. Her body a tight bundle of lush curves that swelled and moved under a light white terrycloth robe. Lovely Lily who brought the sharpness of an alcohol bath in with her so that it wet her robe until there was nothing there, no hill or valley, no shadow that didn't come out.

Gorgeous Lily with my .45 in her hand from where she had found it on the dresser.

"You forgot about me, Mike."

"I almost did, didn't I."

There was cold hate coming into her eyes now. Hate that grew as she looked again at the one eye in the body beside the table. "You shouldn't have done that, Mike."

"No?"

"He was the only one who knew about me." The smile left her mouth. "I loved him. He knew about me and didn't care. I loved him, you crumb you!" The words hissed out of her teeth.

I looked at her the way I did when she first held a gun on me. "Sure. You loved him so much you killed Lily Carver and took her place. You loved him so much you made sure there were no slips in his plan. You loved him so much you set Berga Torn up for the kill and damn near made sure Velda died. You loved him so much you never saw that all he loved was power and money and you were only something he could use.

"You fitted right into the racket. You were lucky once and smart the rest of the time. You reached Al after Velda left but you had time to catch up with her. By the way, did you ever find out why Al died? He was giving friend Billy Mist the needle. Billy knew what had happened when you called him down to tell him his girlfriend wasn't what she was cracked up to be. With Billy that didn't go and he carved up his playmate. Nice people to have around."

"Shut up."

"Shut up hell. You stuck with me all the way. You ducked out because you thought the boys had me once, then came back when you found out I propped them up against a dead-end sign. You passed the word right under my nose and had Billy packing to blow town. What a deal that was. I even showed you how to get out of my apartment without a tail picking you up. That's why you're here now. So what was supposed to happen? You go back to your real identity? Nuts. You're part of it and you'll die with it. You played me for a sucker up and down Broadway but it's over. This isn't the first time you've pointed a rod at me, sugar. The last time was a game, but I didn't know it. I'm still going to take it away from you. What kind of a guy do you think I am anyway?"

Her face changed as if I had slapped her. For an instant the strangeness was back again. "You're a deadly man, Mike."

Then I saw it in her face and she was faster than I was. The rod belched flame and the slug tore into my side and spun me around. There was a crazy spinning sensation, a feeling of tumbling end over end through space, an urge to vomit, but no strength left to vomit with.

My eyes cleared and I pushed myself up on an elbow. There was a loose, empty feeling in my joints. The end was right there ahead of me and nothing I could do about it.

Lily smiled again, the end of the .45 drifting down to my stomach. She laughed at me, knowing I could raise myself to reach for it. My mouth was dry. I wanted a cigarette. It was all I could think about. It was something a guy about to die always got. My fingers found the deck of Luckies, fumbled one loose and got it into my mouth. I could barely feel it lying there on my lips.

"You shouldn't have killed him," Lily said again.

I reached for the lighter. It wasn't going to be long now. I could feel things start to loosen up. My mind was having trouble hearing her. One more shot. It would be quick.

"Mike . . ."

I got my eyes open. She was a strong, pungent smell. Very strong. Still lovely though.

"I thought I almost loved you once. More than . . . him. But I didn't, Mike. He would take me like I was. He was the one who gave me life, at least, after . . . it happened. He was the doctor. I was the patient. I loved him. You would have been disgusted with me. I can see your eyes now, Mike. They would have been revolted.

"He was deadly too, Mike . . . but not like you. You're even worse. You're the deadly one, but you would have been revolted. Look at me, Mike. How would you like to kiss me now? You wanted to before. Would you like to now? I wanted you to . . . you know that, don't you? I was afraid to even let you touch me. You wanted to kiss me . . . so kiss me."

Her fingers slipped through the belt of the robe, opened it. Her hands parted it slowly . . . until I could see what she was really like. I wanted to vomit worse than before. I wanted to let my guts come up and felt my belly retching.

She was a horrible caricature of a human! There was no skin, just a disgusting mass of twisted, puckered flesh from her knees to her neck making a picture of gruesome freakishness that made you want to shut your eyes against it.

The cigarette almost fell out of my mouth. The lighter shook in my hand, but I got it open.

"Fire did it, Mike. Do you think I'm pretty now?"

She laughed and I heard the insanity in it. The gun pressed into my belt as she kneeled forward, bringing the revulsion with her. "You're going to die now . . . but first you can do it. Deadly . . . deadly . . . kiss me."

The smile never left her mouth and before it was on me I thumbed the lighter and in the moment of time before the scream blossoms into the wild cry of terror she was a mass of flame tumbling on the floor with the blue flames of alcohol turning the white of her hair into black char and her body convulsing under the agony of it. The flames were teeth that ate, ripping and tearing into scars of other flames and her voice the shrill sound of death on the loose.

I looked, looked away. The door was closed and maybe I had enough left to make it.